The World's
Greatest Conspiracies

The World's Greatest Conspiracies

History's Biggest Mysteries,
Cover-Ups, and Cabals

EXPANDED AND UPDATED

Jonathan Vankin
&
John Whalen

CITADEL PRESS
Kensington Publishing Corp.
www.kensingtonbooks.com

CITADEL PRESS BOOKS are published by

Kensington Publishing Corp.
119 West 40th Street
New York, NY 10018

First Printing (Newly Expanded Edition): July 2010

10 9 8 7 6 5 4 3 2 1

Printed in the United States of America

Library of Congress Control Number: 2003106188

ISBN-13: 978-0-8065-2878-6
ISBN-10: 0-8065-2878-8

To our parents

The idea of the paranoid style would have very little contemporary relevance or historical value if it were applied only to people with profoundly disturbed minds. It is the use of paranoid modes of expression by more or less normal people that makes the phenomenon significant.

—Richard Hofstadter

We ought not to be too paranoid about paranoia, ought not to be too afraid of ambiguity and irreducible doubt, too afraid of confronting worst-case scenarios and outer-limits possibilities on the grounds merely that they disarm, dishumanize, and defeat us.

—Carl Oglesby

Perhaps if we clearly defined this thing we call paranoia it would not cause us to behave so foolishly. Genuine paranoia actually contains at least three ingredients—fear, suspicion, and mystification. Technically, it is heightened awareness, but not yet perfect awareness.

—Kerry W. Thronley

Contents

Part XII: Madness for a New Millennium

Part XIII: Disinformation, Please

Conspiracy, N'est-ce pas?

There really are, as one of our favorite writers, Jim Hougan says, two kinds of history, the safe, sanitized "'Disney version,' so widely available as to be unavoidable . . . and a second one that remains secret, buried, and unnamed."

This book is not a Disney production.

But we differ with Hougan (investigative author of *Spooks* and *Secret Agenda*, two classic exposés of clandestine politics), on one minor point. The "second" version of history does have a name: "conspiracy theory."

The label itself is a reason why the secret history remains buried—if it is mere "theory" then it can't really be "history," correct?

Not in our view. In even the driest recounting of historical "fact" there is much theory—and in conspiracy theory there is much fact. This is not to say that we should all throw up our hands and admit that everything's subjective and that no one can ever figure out what's true or false. Quite the opposite. We hope that this book will help broaden the definition of what *could* be true because that definition is so narrow right now.

The success of this book—it has had a half-dozen printings, two major updates, been translated into several languages, spawned a Web site, and had a guest appearance on *The X-Files*—is testimony to the fact that we succeeded: The definition of what could be true has indeed expanded in recent years.

Of course, we don't presume to take exclusive credit for the fermenting of conspiracy theory in the public imagination during the 1990s. For that, we must credit a confluence of social phenomena—a conspiracy of trends, if you will. Those trends include the explosive growth of the populist communication venues like the Internet and talk radio, the ongoing erosion of public faith in political institutions and traditional journalism, and, of course, Hollywood's eagerness to capitalize on the prevailing *Zeitgeist* of suspicion.

On the other hand, we have discussed our subject matter with a great many people—and have found that they still don't know the details of very many conspiracy theories. Even in the era of *The X-Files* and countless Web sites devoted to the subject of conspiracies, there are still relatively few reliable outlets for exploring the secret history.

The "Disney" version of history could just as easily be called the "*New York Times* version" or the "TV news version" or the "college textbook version." The main resistance to conspiracy theories comes not from people on the street, but from the media, academia, and government—people who manage the national and global economy of information.

There is certainly a lot of resistance there and the reasons why are multifarious, complex, and probably deserve a book of their own. A few of the main ones (vastly oversimplified) are:

- *Vested interests.* Conspiracy theories, by their nature, attack established authority. People in positions of authority fight back as you'd expect they would.
- *Laziness.* A good conspiracy is tough to crack. It's easier to rewrite a press release and then act 100 percent certain that

you know what you're talking about when someone calls you on it later.

- *Armchair psychoanalysis*. Pundits and pontificators tend to deal with conspiracy theories not on their merits, but as symptoms of the mental problems afflicting those who advocate them. Unfortunately, many of the most vocal conspiracy theorists do little to dispel this stereotype. However, the armchair Freudians rarely admit that their own views also have deep-seated psychological motivations. It is unsettling to face the possibility that, to quote the Firesign Theater, "everything you know is wrong."
- *Peer pressure*. Because most reporters, political scientists, and politicians shy away from conspiracy theories, few are willing to stick their necks out and risk being laughed at by their buddies.
- *Bad associations*. For years "conspiracy theory" was almost synonymous with "Jewish conspiracy." Sadly, the anti-Semitic "theory" (if it can be called that) has been around for thousands of years and won't go away, lately finding unfortunate expression in the rantings of Malaysian prime minister Mathair Mohamad, eager to lay blame on the Jews for the collapse of the Asian economies in the 1990s.

In earlier editions of the book, we avoided examining the so-called Jewish conspiracy. Even though this book evaluates all theories, we felt uneasy including the Jewish conspiracy. We'd seen too many instances of hate mongers using debunked information out of context to further the dangerous myth. Finally, however, we decided to include a chapter on the origins of the spurious theory. Why? Because so many latter-day conspiracy theories revolve around the fraudulent tale of the Jewish conspiracy.

Its existence tends to unfairly discredit other conspiratorial interpretations of events that have nothing to do with making scapegoats of any ethnic or religious group.

- *Faith in democracy*. We'd like to believe our system of government protects us from the sort of things that go on in more "backward" countries.
- *Denial*. Many conspiracy theories deal with the darker side of human nature and the capacity of "respectable" people to do some very nasty things. It feels better to pretend that if I'm OK, you're OK.
- *Conspiracy*! Let's face it, these things happen. And when they do, the conspirators are not likely to fess up at the first hint that they've been smoked out.

None of those reasons says anything about whether any particular conspiracy theory is true or false, worth considering or dismissing.

So that makes the following *The World's Greatest Conspiracies*? We confess, our criteria were rather flexible. Many were included for a combination of their importance and the availability of checkable facts to back them up. We chose others, frankly, for their entertainment value. If there's one problem we've found with conspiracy theories that bugs us more than any other, it's the determination of conspiracy theorists to take their subject matter *so* seriously that Gerald "Case Closed" Posner (see pages 549–51) looks like David Letterman by comparison.

What we're mainly exploring here is a different way of seeing the world. Just as Henry Kissinger cracks us up every time he intones his shoot-from-the-hip opinions as if he's reading from a stone tablet, we also see a good deal of unintentional humor in the dissenting conspiratorial worldview.

One thing we do not want to do here is talk down to you or insult your intelligence. We'll let the George Wills and Ted Koppels of the world instruct you in what you're *supposed* to believe. All we ask from the reader is an open mind and a little intellectual courage. Even Walt Disney gave us nightmares sometimes.

Acknowledgments

This is a book that almost didn't happen. But it did, thanks to two people. First, our agent and friend, Ken Swezey, who stuck with the project for fifteen months before a contract was finally signed. And equally important is our editor, Kevin McDonough, who believed in the project and saw its potential. Our lasting thanks to them both.

This topic is deceptively difficult to write about. We're deeply indebted for research assistance to Ron Bonds of IllumiNet Press, one of the most daring small publishers in the country; to Kenn Thomas, editor of *Steamshovel Press*, one of the best in a strangely growing field of conspiracy-oriented publications; and to Jim Martin, editor of *Flatland*, part book catalog, part magazine, all quite fascinating (and a great place to start your conspiracy/alternative-politics-and-literature library). For readers who want to pursue this topic further, we recommend contacting IllumiNet at Box 2808, Lilburn, GA 30226; *Steamshovel* at Box 23715, St. Louis, MO 63121; and *Flatland* at Box 2420, Fort Bragg, CA 95437.

We also acknowledge the support of our former employer, Metro Newspapers, and particularly, Bob Hansen, Sharan Street, David Cohen, and Dan Pulcrano.

JONATHAN VANKIN'S PERSONAL ACKNOWLEDGMENTS:
The circumstance under which I wrote my portion of this book were far from ideal, making the moral, emotional, and

practical support of a great many people more valuable than ever. Three people deserve spots at the top of that list. First, my parents, Jean and Larry Vankin, who in addition to providing all the essentials of parenthood (love, inspiration, money, etc.), served as my personal research assistants—a task far exceeding the call of parental duty. My love and thanks always.

My most special thanks to Debbie Picker. She did so much for me that a mere thank-you for her love, understanding, and patience seems far from adequate. She was my partner through this rather memorable experience, and will be through many more, I hope.

Heartfelt gratitude—for a wide variety of personal reasons—goes to: my sister, Laura Vankin; Dan Reichert and Andrea Marcovicci (double to Dan, my closest friend over many years and miles); the Shimogaito family, Teruko, Yoshiko, and Takehiro; Al Edmonds; Hal March (still the world's coolest . . .); Gary Sherman; Louis Theroux; Eric London; Holli Richards; Brent Filson (still my mentor); Trevor Loring; Judge Sande Mazer Moss and Bill Deane; three generations of Pickers, Si and Lorraine, Ben and David; Coleen Curran (for everything); Lisa Stone-Norman; Ichiro Taniguchi; Ryuji Nakazono; Ann Walker, Matt Maranz; Jamesfinkle@twics.com; Jay Whearley; and I'm sure a large number of people I'll think of once the book has gone to press and kick myself.

Equally important, my thanks to the many people who have given me their time, inspired me, or in some other tangible way helped me along with what has now become a two-book project.

Clark Coolidge merits a special mention for, perhaps unwittingly, getting me started on this particular track. Mark Stewart should be mentioned in the same light. And thanks to: Evelyn Fazio; Kurt Anderson; Congressman Don Edwards (retired); Robert Anton Wilson; E.J. McCarthy; John Strausbaugh; Emily Reichert; Tom Snyder; Kerry Thornley; G. Gordon Liddy; Adam Parfrey; Paul Theroux; Jim Martin; Anthony Summers; Jason Neely; Jim Keith; Mickey Z.; R. U. Sirius and Queen Mu; Suzanne Guyette; Mike Litchfield; Dave

Emory; Greg Krupey; K-Talk radio, Salt Lake City; John Judge; Trowbridge Ford; William Bramley; Don Kennison; Al Kunzer; Jim and Ken Collier; Laura Lindgren; Don Oldenburg; Loompanics; Stuart Swezey and Brian King; Jo Glorie; Nancy Sayles; Dennis Hayes; Sally Robinson, and anybody else I've inadvertently, and with sincere apologies, omitted.

Finally, but perhaps most important for this book, my deepest gratitude to John Whalen, my collaborator (no "co-conspirator" jokes, please).

JOHN WHALEN'S PERSONAL ACKNOWLEDGMENTS:
It seems that everybody has a favorite conspiracy. My thanks to the many folks who shared their pet cabals, news clippings, suppressed files, hunches, ah-ha's, and other smoking guns.

Of course, a special thanks goes to my parents, Patricia and Frank Whalen, who took me to see *All the President's Men* at an impressionable age.

Ann Walker also deserves top billing. Her generosity, encouragement, and patience know no bounds, at least none that I've been able to rest, and that's saying a lot.

Others who helped guide me through the dizzying labyrinths of conspiracy research deserve a nod of appreciation (although some of them may take umbrage at the loaded term, *conspiracy*). They include, in no particular order, Jim Hougan; Robert Gettlin; John Stockwell; Stephen Pizzo; Norman Solomon; Henry Lincoln; Peter Dale Scott; Joel Bleifuss; Robert Parry; Ben Bagdikian; Ed Connolly; Dave Emory; Pete Brewton; Al Kunzer; Ralph McGehee (for his indispensable computer database, CIABASE, order it ASAP: Box 5022, Herndon, VA 22070); Marc Cooper; and Ellen Ray.

And, of course, a special thank-you goes to Jonathan Vankin, an excellent writing partner without whom this book would have been half as long.

I

Your Tax Dollars at Work

1

CIAcid Trip

LSD was invented in Switzerland by Albert Hofmann, a researcher for Sandoz pharmaceuticals. It did not spontaneously appear among the youth of the Western world as a gift from the God of Gettin' High. The CIA was on to acid long before the flower children.

So, for that matter, were upstanding citizens like Time-Life magnate Henry Luce and his wife, Clare Boothe Luce, who openly sang the praises of their magical mystery tours during the early sixties. Henry, a staunch conservative with close connections to the CIA, once dropped acid on the golf course and then claimed he had enjoyed a little chat with God.

While the cognoscenti had the benefit of tuned-in physicians, other psychedelic pioneers took their first trips as part of CIA-controlled research studies.

At least one person committed suicide after becoming an unwitting subject of a CIA LSD test, crashing through a high-story plate-glass window in a New York hotel as his Agency guardian watched. (Or perhaps the guardian did more than watch. In June 1994 the victim's family had his thirty-year-old

3

corpse exhumed to check for signs that he may have been thrown out that window.) Numerous others lost their grip on reality.

MK-ULTRA was the code name the CIA used for its program directed at gaining control over human behavior through "covert use of chemical and biological materials," as proposed by Richard Helms. The name itself was a variation on ULTRA, the U.S. intelligence program behind Nazi lines in World War II, of which the CIA's veteran spies were justly proud.

Helms later became CIA director and gained a measure of notoriety for his Watergate "lying to Congress" conviction and a touch of immortality in Thomas Powers's aptly named biography, *The Man Who Kept the Secrets*. Helms founded the MK-ULTRA program and justified its notably unethical aspects with the rationale, "We are not Boy Scouts."

At the time, the spook scientists suspected that LSD had the potential to reprogram the human personality. In retrospect, they were probably right—Timothy Leary spoke in similar terms, though he saw unlimited potential for self-improvement in this "reprogramming." The CIA and the military simply couldn't figure out how to harness the drug's power. Thank goodness. Their idea was not to open "the doors of perception" but to convert otherwise free human beings into automatons.

"We must remember to thank the CIA and the army for LSD," spoke no less an authority figure on matters psychedelic than John Lennon. "They invented LSD to control people and what it did was give us freedom."

Or did it? The acid-tripping intersection between the CIA and the counterculture is one of the areas where the on-the-record facts about MK-ULTRA meld into the foggy region of conspiracy theory. It has been suggested, even by prominent participants in the counterculture, that with LSD the CIA found the ultimate weapon against the youth movement.

Officially, the MK-ULTRA program ran from 1953 to 1964, at which time it was renamed MK-SEARCH and continued until 1973. However, U.S. intelligence and military operations with the same purpose had been ongoing at least since World War II and likely chugged ahead for many years after MK-ULTRA's publicly stated conclusion. MK-ULTRA encompassed an undetermined number of bizarre and often grotesque experiments. In one, psychiatrist Ewen Cameron received CIA funding to test a procedure he called "depatterning." This technique, Cameron explained when he applied for his CIA grant (through a front group called the Society for the Investigation of Human Ecology), involved the "breaking down of ongoing patterns of the patient's behavior by means of particularly intensive electroshocks," in addition to LSD. Some of his subjects suffered brain damage and other debilitations. One sued the government and won an out-of-court settlement in 1988.

Then there was operation "Midnight Climax," in which prostitutes lured unsuspecting johns to a CIA bordello in San Francisco. There they slipped their clients an LSD mickey while Agency researchers savored the "scientific" action from behind a two-way mirror, a pitcher of martinis at the ready.

Author John Marks, whose *The Search for the Manchurian Candidate* is one of the most thoroughgoing volumes yet assembled on U.S. government mind-control research, readily admits that all of his source material comprised but ten boxes of documents—but those took him a year to comprehend despite the aid of a research staff.

Marks writes that he sought access to records of a branch of the CIA's Directorate of Science and Technology, the Office of Research and Development (ORD), which took over behavioral (i.e., mind control) research after MK-ULTRA's staff dispersed.

Marks was told that ORD's files contained 130 boxes of documents relating to behavioral research. Even if they were all released, their sheer bulk is sufficient to fend off even the most dedicated—or obsessed—investigator. To generate such an intimidating volume of paper must have taken considerable time and effort. Yet curiously, the CIA has always claimed that its attempts to create real-life incarnations of Richard Condon's unfortunate protagonist Raymond Shaw—the hypnotically programmed assassin of *The Manchurian Candidate*—were a complete bust.

If their demurrals are to be trusted, then this particular program constitutes one of the least cost-effective deployments of taxpayer dollars in the history of the U.S. government, which is rife with non-cost-effective dollar deployments.

The CIA's most effective line of defense against exposure of their mind-control operations (or any of their operations, for that matter) has always been self-effacement. The agency portrays its agents as incompetent stooges, encouraging the public to laugh at their wacky attempts to formulate cancer potions and knock off foreign leaders.

Under this cover story, MK-ULTRA's research team was nothing but a bunch of ineffectual eccentrics. "We are sufficiently ineffective so our findings can be published," quipped one MK-ULTRA consultant.

Despite the findings of a Senate committee headed by Ted Kennedy that U.S. mind-control research was a big silly failure, and even though Marks—whose approach is fairly conservative—acknowledges that he found no record to prove it, the project may have indeed succeeded.

"I cannot be positive that they never found a technique to control people," Marks writes, "despite my definite bias in favor of the idea that the human spirit defeated the manipulators."

A sunny view of human nature, that. And indeed a consoling one. But the human spirit, history sadly proves, is far from indomitable. The clandestine researchers explored every possible means of manipulating the human mind. The CIA's experiments with LSD are the most famous MK-ULTRA undertakings, but acid was not even the most potent drug investigated by intelligence and military agencies. Nor did they limit their inquiries to drugs. Hypnosis, electronic brain implants, microwave transmissions, and parapsychology also received intense scrutiny. Marks, Kennedy, and many others apparently believe that the U.S. government failed where all-too-many far less sophisticated operations—from the Moonies to Scientology to EST—have scored resounding triumphs. Brainwashing is commonplace among "cults," but not with the multimillion-dollar resources of the United States government's military and intelligence operations?

For that matter, the (supposed) impetus for the program was the reported success of communist countries in "brainwashing." The word itself originally applied to several soldiers who'd fought in the Korean War who exhibited strange behavior and had large blank spots in their memories—particularly when it came to their travels through regions of Manchuria. Those incidents were the inspiration for Condon's novel, in which a group of American soldiers are hypnotically brainwashed by the Korean and Chinese communists and one is programmed to kill a presidential candidate.

Interestingly, the belief that one's psyche is being invaded by radio transmissions or electrical implants is considered a symptom of paranoid schizophrenia. But there is no doubt that the CIA contemplated using those methods and carried out such experiments on animals, and the way these things go it would require the willful naïveté of, say, a Senate subcommittee to maintain that they stopped there. Even Marks, who exercises the journalistic wisdom to stick only to what he can back up with hard documentation, readily acknowledges that the clandestine researchers "probably" planted electrodes in the brains of men. Marks points out that the electrode experiments "went far beyond giving monkeys orgasms," one of the researchers' early achievements.

The ultimate goal of mind control would have been to produce a Manchurian Candidate assassin, an agent who didn't know he (or she) was an agent—brainwashed and programmed to carry out that most sensitive of missions. Whether the program's accomplishments reached that peak will probably never be public knowledge. So we are left to guess whether certain humans have been "programmed to kill." In 1967, Luis

Castillo, a Puerto Rican arrested in the Philippines for planning to bump off Ferdinand Marcos, claimed (while in a hypnotic trance) that he had been implanted with a posthypnotic suggestion to carry out the assassination. Sirhan Sirhan, convicted as the assassin of Robert F. Kennedy, showed unmistakable symptoms of hypnosis. A psychiatrist testifying in Sirhan's defense said that the accused assassin was in a trance when he shot Kennedy, albeit a self-induced one. Author Robert Kaiser echoed that doctor's conclusions in his book *RFK Must Die!* Others, of course, have offered darker conjectures regarding the origins of Sirhan's symptoms.

James Earl Ray, the convicted assassin of Martin Luther King, also had a known fascination with hypnosis, and, more recently, British lawyer Fenton Bressler has assembled circumstantial evidence to support a theory that Mark David Chapman, slayer of John Lennon, was subject to CIA mind control. Way back in 1967, a book titled *Were We Controlled?*, whose unknown author used the pseudonym Lincoln Lawrence, stated that both Lee Harvey Oswald and Jack Ruby were under mind control of some kind. The book may have had at least a trace of validity: Something in the book convinced Oswald's mother that the author was personally acquainted with her son.

Did MK-ULTRA spin off a wave of history-altering assassinations—did it whelp a brood of hypnoprogrammed killers? The definitive answer to that question will certainly never reach the public. We are left, with John Marks, to hope on faith alone that it did not, but always with the uneasy knowledge that it could have.

Perhaps not through assassinations, and perhaps not even intentionally, MK-ULTRA definitely altered a generation. John Lennon was far from the only sixties acid-hero to make the connection between the mood of the streets and the secret CIA labs. "A surprising number of counterculture veterans endorsed the notion that the CIA disseminated street acid en masse to deflate the political potency of the youth rebellion," write Martin Lee and Bruce Shlain in *Acid Dreams*, their chronicle of both the clandestine and countercultural sides of the LSD revolution.

"By magnifying the impulse toward revolutionism out of context, acid sped up the process by which the Movement became unglued," the authors continue. "The use of LSD among young people in the U.S. reached a peak in the late 1960s, shortly after the CIA initiated a series of covert operations designed to disrupt, discredit, and neutralize the New Left. Was this merely a historical coincidence, or did the Agency actually take steps to promote the illicit acid trade?"

The tale of Ronald Stark, told by Lee and Shlain, may provide the connection between the CIA and the Left. Stark was a leading distributor of LSD in the late 1960s—the same time acid use was at its heaviest—and apparently a CIA operative. The Agency has never admitted this, but an Italian judge deciding in 1979 whether to try Stark for "armed banditry" in relation to Stark's many contacts with terrorists (among other things, Stark accurately predicted the assassination of Aldo Moro) released the drug dealer after finding "an impressive series of scrupulously enumerated proofs" that Stark had worked for the CIA "from 1960 onward."

"It could have been," mused Tim Scully, the chief of Stark's major LSD-brewing outfit (a group of idealistic radicals called the Brotherhood who grew to feel exploited by Stark), "that he was employed by an American intelligence agency that wanted to see more psychedelic drugs on the street." But Lee and Shlain leave open the possibility that Stark may have been simply one of the world's most ingenious con artists—a possibility acknowledged by most everyone to come in contact with Stark.

The CIA's original "acid dream" was that LSD would open the mind to suggestion, but they found the drug too potent to manage. Sometime around 1973, right before MK-ULTRA founder and, by then, CIA director Richard Helms hung up his trenchcoat and stepped down from the CIA's top post, he ordered the majority of secret MK-ULTRA documents destroyed due to "a burgeoning paper problem." Among the eradicated material, Lee and Shlain report, were "all existing copies of a classified CIA manual titled *LSD: Some Un-Psychedelic Implications*.

There exists today no on-paper evidence (that anyone has yet uncovered) that MK-ULTRA was the progenitor of either a conspiracy to unleash remote-controlled lethal human robots or to emasculate an entire generation by oversaturating it with a mind-frying drug. But MK-ULTRA was very real and the danger of a secret government program to control the thoughts of its citizens, even just a few of them at a time, needs no elaboration.

MAJOR SOURCES

Budiansky, Stephen, Erica E. Goode, and Ted Gest. "The Cold War Experiments." *U.S. News & World Report*. 24 January 1994.

Lee, Martin, and Bruce Shlain. *Acid Dreams*. New York: Grove Press, 1985.

Marks, John. *The Search for the Manchurian Candidate*. New York: Dell, 1979.

2

Get Castro!

If the Cold War incubated a kind of national hysteria, nowhere was the delirium more frenzied than in Florida of the early 1960s. Clandestine plots to topple Fidel Castro bred like mosquitoes in the Everglades. The U.S.-backed Bay of Pigs invasion, which ended in disaster, only compounded the tropical madness. As Cold War fever rose, the CIA launched one of its most scandalous episodes, a series of surreal attempts to assassinate Castro employing Florida's Cuban exiles and the nation's top Mafiosi.

As President Johnson later put it, "We were running a damn Murder, Incorporated in the Caribbean." Although three presidents had at least some knowledge of the CIA plots, in several cases the Agency appears to have operated autonomously—and against presidential authority.

In 1975, Senate hearings held in the wake of Watergate's revelations exposed the CIA's so-called "executive action" programs. The Senate Select Intelligence Committee, chaired by Frank Church, uncovered eight failed attempts to ice Castro and a handful of murder plots aimed at other heads of state.

11

Quite conservatively, the committee decided to dub its findings "alleged assassination plots." Moreover, according to the testimony of CIA Brahmins, all of the murder plots misfired. Notwithstanding these claims, there is reason to believe the hearings rooted up only a sampling of the Agency's political hits.

As good a place as any to begin the tale is with that elemental spook E. Howard Hunt, the CIA propagandist whose name became synonymous with Watergate, Bay of Pigs, and a scorecard of subterfuge that defined a quarter century. Returning from Cuba, the CIA officer drew up a list of strategic recommendations. At the top of the list: Whack Castro. The agency apparently took Hunt's advice, for in 1960 the CIA brain trust began plotting the Cuban leader's permanent "elimination."

To get the ball rolling, in August of that year the CIA's Office of Medical Services sprinkled a box of Castro's favorite Cuban cigars with a virulent toxin. The resulting stogie was so lethal that merely sucking on it would "terminate" the hardiest dictator within moments. Castro was to visit the United Nations in New York, and it is possible that the tainted cigars were to be proffered there. What happened next isn't clear. According to one report, the New York Police Department was informed by CIA officers of aborted plans to kill Castro with a box of *exploding* cigars, Three Stooges-style.

Other unrealized plans—including several intended to assassinate the man's character, if not the man himself—managed to be even less practical than the gag stogies.

- One early brainstorm involved spraying Castro's broadcasting studio in Havana with "super acid," a concentrated form of LSD, which, it was hoped, would cause Fidel to tune in, turn on, and go nuts during a public speech. A variation on that theme would have had the CIA's Technical Services Division lacing those all-purpose cigars with LSD, thereby dispatching the unflappable Marxist on a prover-bial bad trip.

- Another scheme proposed sprinkling Castro's shoes with thallium salts, a potent depilatory that would cause his beard, eyebrows, and pubic hair to fall out. His cherished Latin machismo called into question, Castro would the-oretically whither in stature and self-respect, like a fol-lically deprived Samson.

- As for the more lethal plots, one idea called for Castro, an avid scuba diver, to be presented with a wet suit by an American lawyer then negotiating for the release of Bay of Pigs prisoners. The Technical Services Division went so far as to purchase a scuba suit and contaminate the respirator with tuberculosis bacilli. Nothing if not scrupulous, they also treated the suit itself with fungus spores that would cause the rare skin disease, madura foot. Alas, the shuttle diplomat took the initiative and gave Castro an uncontami-nated suit, thereby defusing a plan that, if successful, would hardly have fallen under the category of "covert operation."

- Another Ian Fleming-esque scheme called for an exploding conch shell to be placed on the sea floor in an area where Castro often went diving. Ultimately, this plan was scrapped as impractical.

- In his autobiography, CIA operative Felix Rodriguez—a close confidant of George Bush—says he tried three times to enter Cuba on kill-Castro missions. The missions were his idea and at the time he didn't know that the CIA was his silent patron. In 1987, asked by the Iran-Contra committee whether he took part in the CIA's attempt to poison Castro's favorite smokes, Rodriguez replied indignantly, "No sir, I did not. But I did volunteer to kill that son of a bitch in 1961 with a telescopic rifle."

- Perhaps the most visionary proposal came from the fertile mind of General Edward Lansdale, who supervised the Kennedy administration's covert war on Castro. The gen-

eral hoped to spark a counterrevolution by spreading the
word to devout Cuban Catholics that the Second Coming
was imminent and that Castro was none other than the
anti-Christ. At the appointed hour, Christ, Himself, would
surface off the shores of Cuba aboard an American submarine as star shell flares illuminated the heavens. In a
pique of Cold War rapture, it was hoped, the Cubans would
rise up and spontaneously overthrow their satanic leader.

In light of these fantasies, it might be tempting to conclude
that the CIA couldn't hit the broad side of a barn with a deluxe
sniper scope. As in many an airing of the CIA's dirty linen, low
comedy tended to soften public outrage, a circumstance in
which Agency crypt keepers may have taken comfort.

However, the Agency's assassination program was anything
but frivolously pursued. Concurrent with the earliest Castro
plots of 1960, the CIA's deputy director, Richard Bissell, asked
his science advisor, Sidney Gottlieb, to research assassination
techniques. The fruit of Gottlieb's labor was a portable murder
kit, complete with a lethal biological agent, hypodermic needles, and rubber gloves.

Gottlieb hand-delivered the kit to Africa, where the CIA
station chief had been ordered to assassinate Congolese dictator
Patrice Lumumba. Apparently, attempts to poison Lumumba
failed. In 1975, the Senate Intelligence Committee found that
the CIA had sponsored a separate hit on Lumumba using
European mercenary assassins. That plan fell apart when the hit
man turned out to be as out of control as "an unguided missile,"
in the words of the Agency's Congo station chief. According to
the official story, Lumumba's own countrymen saved the CIA
from having to do the dirty work, taking the initiative and
murdering their leader in January 1961.

But doubts linger about the CIA's supposed hands-off role. In
his book, *In Search of Enemies*, Agency veteran John Stockwell
writes that one CIA officer boasted to him about driving
around with Lumumba's body in the trunk of his car.

A few months after Lumumba's timely demise, Dominican Republic autocrat Rafael Trujillo was assassinated. Although the CIA had generously donated guns to dissidents who made it clear they intended to off Trujillo, it was, the CIA swore, local boys who lethally perforated their leader. Of course, it is quite possible they did it with the CIA-provided arms.

Author Dick Russell relates another possibility in his book about the JFK assassination, *The Man Who Knew Too Much*. Russell tracked down and interviewed a retired army colonel named Bill Bishop after hearing him described as "some kind of contract killer for the CIA." When Russell met him, Bishop blithely announced, "I made the hit on Trujillo....That's one mission I'm kinda proud of, because a lot of my associates said it couldn't be done."

If fortuitously timed assassinations bore few CIA fingerprints, plots in which the Agency took the initiative always seemed to go unconsummated, if we're to believe CIA luminaries like former director Richard Helms. For instance, in February 1960 Helms endorsed a plan to see that Iraqi junta chief Abdul Karim Kassem be "incapacitated" with a poisoned handkerchief. Although the whiz kids in the Technical Services Division whipped up a toxic hankie and forwarded it to Kassem, the general evidently never got a runny nose.

Considering the capriciousness of murder by sniffles, perhaps it's understandable that the CIA turned to the Mafia, old pros in the liquidation racket. In the case of Castro, it was a match made in, well, heaven; for the Mafia also had its heart set on killing the Cuban. Mob boss Meyer Lansky had already put a million-dollar bounty on Castro's head. Castro's rise to power in Cuba following the 1959 revolution didn't sit well with the mob, to put it mildly. The Cuban leader had confiscated the Mafia's lucrative casino operations in Havana, which were even more profitable than the syndicate's holdings in Las Vegas.

Of course, recruiting the mob was nothing new: during World War II, the Office of Naval Intelligence had used Mafiosi to guard the New York waterfronts against saboteurs and to assist in the Allied invasion of Sicily. (For his trouble, mob boss Lucky Luciano won an early prison release, and the American and Sicilian Mafias got a new lease on life.) But to sic the goodfellas on Castro must have seemed like the ultimate neat idea. And as far as Cosa Nostra bosses were concerned, putting a powerful government agency in the Mafia's debt had obvious appeal.

So with the imprimatur of Agency director Allen Dulles, and using "dirty tricks" freelancer Robert Maheu as a go-between, the CIA made the mob an offer it couldn't refuse: a $150,000 reward for anyone "tough enough" to bump off Castro—but, more importantly, government sanction to do the job. On loan from Howard Hughes, Maheu had handled a number of "sensitive" projects for the CIA. These included a bogus porno film production starring a doppelgänger of Indonesian President Sukarno and a Richard Nixon–spearheaded propaganda war on Greek shipping magnate Aristotle Onassis. (According to Maheu, a hard-boiled Nixon, swept away by the intrigue, barked: "If it turns out we have to kill the bastard, just don't do it on American soil.")

In the autumn of 1960, two months before John F. Kennedy's narrow electoral victory, Maheu introduced his pal, Vegas don John Roselli, to the CIA's Jim O'Connell. In Miami, Roselli introduced the two spooks to Chicago Godfather Sam "Momo" Giancana and Florida's powerful mob boss Santos Trafficante. Both Giancana and Trafficante had seen their interests in Cuba fizzle when Castro shuttered the drug and gambling rackets. Trafficante was especially peeved; he had controlled Cuba's rackets before Castro locked him up in the aftermath of the 1959 revolution. So as not to blow their cover, the mobsters adopted suitably innocuous code names: Roselli was "John Rawlston" and Giancana was introduced as "Sam Gold." The redoubtable Trafficante retained a measure of his ethnicity, becoming "Joe Pecora."

The industrious Technical Services Division set about producing a batch of botulinum toxin pills that would dissolve in

soup, coffee, or cocktails. After a few refinements and successful tests on monkeys, the CIA passed the pills on to Roselli in
February 1961. The plan was to have one of Trafficante's well-
placed Cuban contacts slip Castro the lethal Mickey. The first
attempt went awry when the designated poisoner, a member of
Castro's inner circle, lost his job. A second attempt in April
failed as well, reportedly because Castro suddenly stopped
frequenting his favorite restaurant.

After the Bay of Pigs rout in April 1961, the mob plot went
dormant for nearly a year. When it was reactivated, Maheu and
Momo were judged to be security risks and were left out.
(Momo's boasting about knocking off Castro had reached J.
Edgar Hoover's twitching ears, jeopardizing the CIA's deniability.) Helms assigned a new Agency coordinator to the
project, the hard-drinking, tough-talking William Harvey.
Harvey formalized the Agency's "assassination bureau" under
the code name ZR/RIFLE and on the Cuban front he now
headed Task Force W, the CIA's anti-Castro mission. Phase two
featured more poison pills, rifles, and explosives over the course
of eleven more months—but all these plots failed as well.
Castro kept on breathing. In February 1963, Harvey released
Agent Roselli from his tour of duty. Neither Harvey nor Helms
had informed CIA director McCone of Mafia phase two.

So what did the Kennedy brothers know and when did they
know it? That became a subtle but emphatic theme in the
testimony of Agency regulars before the Senate's Church committee. Though CIA honchos tried to show that they were just
following Kennedy directives, the committee never reached a
definitive conclusion. In his biography of Richard Helms, *The
Man Who Kept the Secrets*, Thomas Powers called these murky
waters "the deepest secret of all—who gave the orders?"

We know that the mob plots began before the JFK's election,
under the Eisenhower administration. More than a year after
the first CIA-Mafia collaboration, Attorney General Robert
Kennedy was briefed on the operation. Lawrence Houston, the
CIA's house lawyer of the time, testified that the younger

Kennedy was "mad as hell" because his prosecutions of Gian-cana and other mobsters had been jeopardized. Houston testi-fied that RFK declared, "I trust that if you ever try to do business with organized crime again—with gangsters—you will let the attorney general know." At that very moment, however, Harvey, Helms, and Roselli were thick as thieves.

But there's also reason to believe that early in his administra-tion Jack Kennedy knew about the Mafia operation. According to JFK's sometime mistress, Judith Campbell Exner, who was also Giancana's moll, the president conferred with Giancana early on. Those contacts, Campbell said, "had to do with the elimination of Castro."

But there is evidence that the Kennedy brothers, though supportive of early assassination plotting, later took a dim view of the killing spree. Robert Kennedy reportedly told two aides that upon learning of the first Mafia plot, he "turned it off." He was mistaken. In late 1961, the president was clearly pondering the policy of murder when he asked journalist Tad Szulc, "What would you think if I ordered Castro to be assassinated?" When Szulc expressed his dismay, Kennedy agreed and said his advisors had been pressuring him to have Castro killed. Accord-ing to Senator George Smathers, himself a fierce Castro oppo-nent, JFK was "horrified" at the prospect of a Castro assassination and "complained that the CIA was almost autonomous."

Apparently the Kennedy brothers weren't informed of yet *another* series of CIA attempts to plug Castro beginning in the autumn of 1963. Harvey's replacement, Desmond FitzGerald (the idea man behind the poison wet suit and explosive conch shell), began cultivating an agent ideally placed to knock off the Cuban leader.

Rolando Cubela, a major in the Cuban army, was not only an intimate of Castro's, but a disgruntled one, unhappy with the growing Soviet influence in Cuba. In a deception remarkable for its audacity, FitzGerald (with Helms's approval) met with

Cubela in Paris, posing as Robert Kennedy's personal representative, without RFK's knowledge. (Cubela later told journalist
Anthony Summers that FitzGerald also claimed to be a U.S.
senator.) FitzGerald, without any authority to do so, promised
Cubela that the U.S. government would fully back a coup
against Castro. FitzGerald subsequently arranged for Cubela to
receive a "pen" that could inject a poison (Blackleaf 40) into a
certain blustering autocrat.

But while the CIA was talking termination with Cubela,
Kennedy had already softened his formerly hawkish Cuban
policy. To be sure, Robert Kennedy was still approving
"pinprick" assaults on Cuba, but the administration seems to
have changed its tack. In early 1963, with the U.S.-Soviet
nuclear test ban treaty under negotiation, the Kennedy administration began cracking down on "unauthorized" raids against
Cuba (and on Soviet ships anchored there) by the revanchist
exiles. CIA contact agents were among the anti-Castro Cubans
detained and prosecuted.

And, as Anthony Summers reported in his JFK assassination
study, *Conspiracy*, during the final months of his life, Kennedy
sent diplomatic feelers out to Castro. Through an American
advisor to the United Nations, Kennedy had begun to make
secret overtures to Castro—at precisely the same moment
FitzGerald was assuring Cubela that the Kennedys would back
an anti-Castro coup. Although stealth diplomacy didn't get very
far (Kennedy was assassinated two months later), the president's
former special advisor, historian Arthur Schlesinger, found the
CIA's timing peculiar.

As he told Summers: "The whole Cubela thing raises even
deeper questions. The CIA was reviving the assassination plots
at the very time President Kennedy was considering the possibility of normalization of relations with Cuba—an extraordinary action. If it was not incompetence—which in the case of
the CIA cannot be excluded—it was a studied attempt to
subvert national policy."

MAJOR SOURCES

Hinckle, Warren, and William Turner. *Deadly Secrets*. New York: Thunder's Mouth Press, 1992.

Hougan, Jim. *Spooks: The Haunting of America—The Private Use of Secret Agents*. New York: William Morrow and Company, 1978.

Powers, Thomas. *The Man Who Kept the Secrets: Richard Helms and the CIA*. New York: Pocket Books, 1979.

Rodriguez, Felix I., and John Weisman. *Shadow Warrior*. New York: Simon & Schuster, 1989.

Russell, Dick. *The Man Who Knew Too Much*. New York: Carroll and Graf, 1992.

Senate Select Committee on Government Operations with Respect to Intelligence Activities. *Alleged Assassination Plots Involving Foreign Leaders*. Washington: U.S. Government Printing Office, 1975.

3

Breeding Better People

The following two statements were authored in the same year, 1925, by two public figures generally supposed to have not much in common:

"Those who are physically and mentally unhealthy and unfit must not perpetuate their sufferings in the bodies of their children. Through educational means the state must teach individuals that illness is not a disgrace but a misfortune for which people are to be pitied, yet at the same time it is a crime and a disgrace to make this affliction the worse by passing it on to innocent creatures out of a merely egotistic yearning."

"It is better for all the world, if instead of waiting to execute degenerate offspring for crime or to let them starve for their imbecility, society can prevent those who are manifestly unfit from continuing their kind."

The latter opinion comes from Justice Oliver Wendell Holmes of the U.S. Supreme Court, writing for the majority in the case of *Buck v. Bell*. The former statement appeared in *Mein Kampf* by Adolf Hitler. Eugenics wasn't just for Nazis.

The "racial hygiene" programs of Nazi Germany were by far

21

the most catastrophic application of eugenic "theory," but they were neither the first nor last. In the early twentieth century, fourteen countries, including the United States, approved some type of eugenic legislation. In the first thirty years of this century, thirty of these United States passed sterilization laws. By one estimate, as many as sixty thousand people were "legally" sterilized. The true number can never be known because many operations in penal and mental institutions went unreported.

The United States of America, in fact, was the first industrialized nation to enact racial purification laws. In the late nineteenth century the states of Michigan and Massachusetts castrated numerous mental patients and young boys exhibiting such genetic imperfections as "persistent epilepsy," "imbecility," and "masturbation with weakness of mind."

Castration evidently hit a little too close to home for the average member of the public to stomach, so vasectomy became the preferred method for sterilizing males, and its equivalent, salpingectomy, became the preferred sterilization method for women.

Justice Holmes to the contrary, courts were not generally favorable toward sterilization laws. As early as 1912, the New Jersey Supreme Court struck down a law allowing for the sterilization of "feeble minded" people, including, according to the law's wording, "idiots, imbeciles, and morons."

"Imbeciles" and "idiots" were a virtual obsession for eugenics-happy legislators. Indiana's law was designed to "prevent procreation of confirmed criminals, idiots, imbeciles, and rapists." California's statute (California sterilized far more people than any other state) allowed, with a note from a doctor, the "asexualization" of "any idiot" as well as any prison inmate who had shown evidence that he was "a moral or sexual degenerate." An Iowa law targeted people "who would produce children with tendency to disease, deformity, crime, insanity, feeble-mindedness, idiocy, imbecility, epilepsy, or alcoholism."

Though courts often ruled against the eugenics laws, sterilization programs continued unabated, and most of the state laws stayed on the books well into the 1970s and 1980s, though they haven't been applied since the early part of the century when California, for example, sterilized 6,200 "feeble minded" people.

The status of "feeble mindedness" was determined largely by the then recent invention of the IQ test, as well as by scientists' rather arbitrary judgments of what counted as appropriate behavior.

By these standards not only "idiots, imbeciles, and morons" but entire ethnic groups were deemed "inferior." Interestingly, there is no available record of a scientist judging his or her own group "inferior."

Zany racial theorizing with a "scientific" foundation has gone on at least since the industrial revolution. With industrialization, the world's prosperity ballooned and it looked like there would at last be more than enough wealth to go around. At the same time, it created the need for a permanent class of unfortunates to operate the heavy equipment.

Consequently, the owners had to come up with some halfway respectable explanation of why they deserved Newport mansions and everyone else merited nineteen-hour days in the mill struggling to keep their digits out of the the widget-making machines. The answer was Social Darwinism, the pseudo-biological notion that certain types of people are born to breathe asbestos dust for six bucks an hour while others have "cellular phones and Malibu beach houses" somehow inscribed in their genetic code.

From the start, the most enthusiastic eugenics advocates emerged from society's upper strata. David Starr Jordan, president of Stanford University, also headed Cold Spring Harbor, the nation's first biolab devoted to building a better human. Mrs. E. H. Harriman endowed the Eugenics Records Office (ERO)—the eugenicists' think tank—with a $15,000 grant and reached into her own pocketbook to cover staff salaries.

John D. Rockefeller, whose progeny personified the American ruling class, was the ERO's number-two cash cow. The first "Race Betterment Conference" took place in Battle Creek, Michigan, at the initiative of Dr. John Harvey Kellogg, whose family business still leads the Western world in Froot Loops production (a contribution to the betterment of the species if ever there was one).

The plutocrats were in league with scientists, many with formidable reputations. These scientists expended immeasurable energy trying to "prove" that blacks were stupid, Jews were greedy, Mexicans were lazy, women were nutty and so on—as well as the corollary; rich, white people with good table manners and glowing report cards were genetically superior. This massive waste of time began when Victorian Englishman Sir Francis Galton published his observations that the most "eminent" members of British society, by and large, had very eminent parents. That might not seem like much of a revelation today, but apparently it was so mindblowing to Galton that he could think of no other causal factor than pure heredity. Charles Darwin himself paid homage to Galton's "admirable labors" in establishing that "genius...tends to be inherited."

Galton came up with the term *eugenics* to advocate breeding better humans. Like so many theoreticians of his day, he asserted, among other things, that blacks lagged behind whites on the evolutionary scale. This ugly bit of quackery, like a wart, won't seem to go away.

As recently as the 1960s, Columbia University psychologist Henry Garrett maintained that people of African lineage are in fact 200,000 years behind those of fairer complexion. In the midst of the civil rights movement he condemned desegregation, with its presumably inevitable sexual mingling of blacks and whites, as "breeding down."

The attempt to codify existing class structure in some kind of biological schemata drags on. And it is worth noting that the endeavor is *not* limited to Klansmen or fringey crypto-fascists (as is, for example, the bogus-scholarly project to establish that the Holocaust never happened). The elite media's warm reaction to such questionable outpourings as Harvard ant expert Edward O. Wilson's 1975 manifesto, *Sociobiology: The New Synthesis* and its 1978 follow-up *On Human Nature*—e.g., a fawning *Time* magazine cover story, and a Pulitzer Prize for Wilson—reveals an unsettling eagerness on the part of powers-that-be to embrace the idea that some people are inherently better than others.

The issue is hardly passé. The Pioneer Fund, established in 1937 to finance "study into the problems of human race betterment," according to its charter (and that's a *revised* charter), was still handing out grants in 1989. University of Delaware researcher Linda Gottfredson got $174,000 to study the supposed relation between race and job performance.

The Pioneer Fund is not racist, said its president, New York lawyer Harry Weyher. It is merely concerned about "problems of heredity in the human race."

From the conviction that some members of the human race have hereditary "problems" it is but a short leap to advocacy of eugenic action. William Shockley, the Nobel Prize–winning electronics pioneer, advanced a proposal in total seriousness to pay persons—black persons—with low IQ scores a cash incentive of $1,000 per point below 100 to have themselves sterilized.

But nowhere is the urge of the "establishment" to justify its existence in scientific terms embodied better than in the person of Konrad Lorenz. A trailblazer in the field of ethology, the study of how behavior patterns are supposedly fixed by genetics, and a source for some of Wilson's key points, the Austrian-born Lorenz was accepted as a member of Germany's Nazi Party on June 28, 1938. In 1942, Lorenz wrote a paper employing principles of ethology and calling for a "self-conscious, scientifically based race policy" administered by "our best individuals" with the aim of inducing "a more severe elimination of morally inferior human beings."

Sadly enough, exactly that program was already well under way at the time, under the guidance of the same "best individuals" who accepted Lorenz into their political party.

Lorenz's bestseller *On Aggression* contained most of the same ideas, albeit stated in more politically palatable language. *On Aggression*, Lorenz's popularized explication of his life's work in ethology, was described by one journalist as appearing "to confirm the prejudices of an authoritarian Right."

In 1973, amid protests from scholars worldwide who knew of his past affiliations and understood his enduring ideological affinity for those prejudices, Konrad Lorenz traveled to Stockholm, Sweden, to accept his Nobel Prize.

MAJOR SOURCES

Chorover, Stephan L. *From Genesis to Genocide: The Meaning of Human Nature and the Power of Behavior Control*. Cambridge, Mass.: MIT Press, 1983.

Parfrey, Adam. "Eugenics: The Orphaned Science" In *Apocalypse Culture*, edited by Adam Parfrey. Los Angeles: Feral House, 1990.

Reilly, Philip R. *The Surgical Solution: A History of Involuntary Sterilization in the United States*. Baltimore: Johns Hopkins University Press, 1991.

Much of this chapter was based on research compiled by G. Lawrence Vankin.

4

The Disaster Agency

The plague of hurricanes, earthquakes, and other natural disasters that beset America during the late 1980s seemed to mystify the Federal Emergency Management Agency (FEMA). While victims pleaded for attention, the bureaucracy charged with handling disaster relief fumbled and stalled. Alas, if only catastrophe had taken a more familiar form—say, nuclear war, border-storming "aliens," or rampaging radicals— FEMA would have known *precisely* what to do: Slam subversives into national detention centers, declare martial law, suspend the U.S. Constitution, and govern from underground bunkers until the apocalypse is contained and mopped up.

Most Americans had never even heard of this obscure government agency before syndicated columnist Jack Anderson reported in October 1984 that FEMA had prepared bizarre "standby legislation" that would, in the event of a national crisis, "suspend the Constitution and the Bill of Rights, effectively eliminate private property, abolish free enterprise, and generally clamp Americans in a totalitarian vise." In any self-respecting banana republic, such a document might be called a

27

blueprint for a coup d'état. FEMA called it "national security" planning.

Cold War delirium only partly explains FEMA's preoccupation with junta-minded plotting during the Reagan era. To understand how a disaster relief agency came to think of itself as a "junior CIA or FBI," as one critic put it, it's helpful to consider the mind-set that launched the Reagan Revolution. In 1981, Ronald Reagan and his arch-conservative troops marched into Washington determined to extinguish a conflagration that had, in fact, long since burned itself out. In the eyes of the president's aging posse, however, the flaming hippies, militant minorities, and draft-dodging radicals of the sixties and early seventies continued to pose a clear and present danger.

Thus was born FEMA. Or, more accurately, thus was it born again. Jimmy Carter had established the agency as a catchall for natural-disaster relief and civil defense planning. But under Reagan, FEMA immediately went off the deep end, eyeing peaceful demonstrators as potential bomb-throwing terrorists.

To head the agency, Reagan and presidential counsel Edwin Meese III (later U.S. attorney general) tapped their old friend "General" Louis O. Giuffrida, a stealth-obsessed ex-California National Guard officer who preferred to be addressed according to his former rank in that organization. Giuffrida was eminently qualified for what Reagan and Meese had in mind. Prepared for all contingencies, he had himself deputized so he could pack a sidearm at the office.

During the late sixties and early seventies, Giuffrida had served as Governor Reagan's terrorism advisor and at Reagan's request founded the California Specialized Training Institute (CSTI), a school for police and military commandos. To quote an early CSTI instruction manual: "Legitimate violence is integral to our form of government, for it is from this source that we can continue to purge our weaknesses."

Giuffrida and Meese (then Governor Reagan's chief assistant) helped develop a plan to purge California of its militant *and* peaceful protesters. Operation Cable Splicer, a variation of the army Garden Plot, a "domestic counterinsurgency" scheme, spied on suspected radicals and marshaled maximum force to squash riots and legitimate demonstrations alike.

But if the early seventies were heady days for military and civil defense planners, the budding 1980s turned out to be a veritable renaissance for cold warriors. As Reagan warned complacent Americans about the Evil Empire and the communist horde (which was bivouacked just south of Texas, the Gipper claimed), the Pentagon prepared plans for World War IV—mere World War III preparations being hazardously short-sighted. Giuffrida, meanwhile, battened the hatches at FEMA. Signs were posted warning employees that SECURITY IS EVERYBODY'S BUSINESS. A new phone system was installed to record each number dialed, and memos were circulated reminding staffers that personal phone calls were *verboten*: "Calling to say you will be home late could result in a fine or separation from the job," advised one memorandum.

FEMA-sponsored conferences obsessed over the possibility of "radical environmentalists" teaming up with terrorists and doing unkind things to nuclear power plants. In fact, FEMA's R & D work made the CIA's LSD dabbling look like a 4H project. According to Donald Goldberg, who helped research Jack Anderson's column, government scientists advised FEMA on mob control techniques such as "injecting terrorists with stimulants and tranquilizers to manipulate their actions in times of crisis, or zapping them with microwaves to alter their perceptions."

Given the dense trench-coat atmospherics, it was probably inevitable that one Lieutenant Colonel Oliver North would find a home away from home in Giuffrida's FEMA. As White House National Security Council liaison to FEMA, the Iran-Contra point man reportedly collaborated with Giuffrida in drawing up secret wartime contingency plans, possibly including the scheme to commandeer the Bill of Rights. Although North denied helping draft such a plan, Congressional Iran-Contra investigators never adequately grilled him on the matter. When

Texas representative Jack Brooks asked North about his work for FEMA, Senate panel chairman Daniel Inouye gavelled Brooks to silence, insisting that the question dealt with classified matters. Such was the persuasiveness of FEMA's national security stamp.

FEMA's wartime crisis strategy was tested in a series of simulated war games conducted in conjunction with Pentagon maneuvers. In early 1984, FEMA, military, and other government officials met in portentous secrecy to plan a "readiness exercise" code-named Rex-84.

FEMA coordinated Rex-84 with the military's Night Train 84 operations, which deployed thousands of troops in Honduras near Contra supply bases in April 1984. The FEMA portion of the simulation involved an international crisis, presumably a U.S. invasion of Nicaragua, which supposedly would set off "uncontrolled population movements" (as one declassified FEMA memo described it), with hordes of "refugees" swarming over the Mexican border into the United States.

According to an August 1985 article in *Penthouse* magazine co-authored by Goldberg, during the exercise FEMA would round up some 400,000 fictional "aliens" in a six-hour period and detain them (or, rather, *simulate* rounding up and detaining them) in military camps throughout the United States. FEMA apparently justified the concentration camps by presuming that terrorist moles would be peppered among the refugees.

But as Goldberg noted, the Mexican border's daunting terrain made an influx of gate crashers on the order of hundreds of thousands highly unlikely. In fact, more than one critic has suggested that Rex-84 was really a drill to practice rounding up crowds of *American* citizens. It would have been a game plan not unlike Cable Splicer or Garden Plot, designed to quash public protests in the event of a controversial government deed—an invasion of Central America, for example.

Indeed, Giuffrida had once considered tossing Americans into concentration camps. In a 1970 paper written as an army student, Giuffrida devised a hypothetical plan for incarcerating black radicals, describing how to build and run detention camps.

That Rex-84 dealt with more than merely apprehending illegal immigrants is certain. A heavily censored FEMA memo obtained by the *Miami Herald* described the Alpha Two phase of the exercise, as a test of "emergency legislation, assumption of emergency powers...etc." In other words: martial law.

The joint FEMA-military martial law plan was more than a simulation. Shortly before the Rex-84 drill, the Pentagon Joint Chiefs of Staff had prepared an internal document itemizing the military's purported authority to proclaim martial law in times of crisis, take over local policing, and even run the courts. It was a dubious claim at best. The Posse Comitatus Act forbids the military from operating in the United States, a prohibition backed by Supreme Court precedent.

But Giuffrida was already on record as a martial law booster. In a 1972 CSTI course manual on civil disorder, Giuffrida described martial law as "the legal means available to control people during a civil disorder," including "the replacement of all civil government by the military."

The "standby" emergency legislation that columnist Anderson exposed prescribed nothing less than an American police state. Called the Defense Resources Act, the draft plan would presumably gather dust on the shelf until a time of crisis, when it would be presented to a preoccupied Congress for speedy approval. In fact, the benevolently titled legislation granted the president near-dictatorial powers, including the authority to censor communications, ban antigovernment strikes, nationalize industry, seize private property for "the national defense," and authorize loyalty oaths to the state.

To augment the Defense Resources Act, FEMA prepared a draft presidential executive order to be invoked by the commander in chief during an "emergency." The order would put FEMA in charge of all government agencies. According to the *Miami Herald*, the executive order activated the aforementioned

legislation, thereby removing Congress and constitutional democracy from the equation entirely.

Alas, FEMA's ambitious plans were truncated shortly after
the Rex-84 games, when Attorney General William French
Smith complained about the agency's attempted power grab. In
a letter addressed to North's boss (and fellow Iran-Contra
player), Robert McFarlane, Smith warned that FEMA was
trying to anoint itself "emergency czar." And, as Smith demurred, FEMA's generous definition of crisis encompassed
"'routine' domestic law emergencies." Smith's objections apparently killed the draft executive order.

Though the full scope of the Rex-84 games remains obscure,
the Ollie North connection is particularly interesting, given
that North was simultaneously working with the Pentagon and
the CIA on plans for combat forces in Central America. Was
FEMA plugged into the Iran-Contra scandal coordinated by
North? Because Congress chose not to pursue that avenue of
Contragate, we don't know for certain. However, allegations
have been made. Daniel Sheehan, crusading (perhaps recklessly
so) attorney with the Christic Institute law firm, suspected that
Rex-84 served as cover for illegal arms shipments to the
Nicaraguan Contras. Citing unnamed sources (including one
described as a member of FEMA's legal division), Sheehan
claimed that FEMA distributed "hundreds of tons of small arms
and ammunition" to civilian militiamen in "state defense
forces" in the United States.

From the early days of the Reagan administration, FEMA
had prodded state legislatures to form state defense forces,
which would act as paramilitary police in the event of a
national crisis. Militia in several states were recruited by placing
ads in *Soldier of Fortune*–style magazines. In several instances
state defense forces subsequently had to be purged of neo-Nazis,
white supremacists, and other unsavory characters.

According to Sheehan, FEMA's plan was to distribute the
guns and ammo to state defense forces as part of the Rex-84 war
games. The militiamen would return only half of the artillery

and would smuggle the remainder to the Contras, thereby circumventing the congressional ban on lethal aid to the Nicaraguan guerrillas.

Though the scheme certainly sounds like a "neat idea" worthy of the North brain trust, it's hard to imagine how even FEMA could justify parceling out guns and ammo for the sake of a war *simulation*. Because Sheehan never got a chance to argue his case in court (a judge threw out the Christics' sweeping lawsuit, calling it "frivolous"), his theory has to be filed under the category of "interesting speculation."

Other speculation about FEMA having its fingers in the Iran-Contra cookie jar revolves around a tip to Senate investigators in 1983 that C-130 and C-141 cargo planes were bound for Texas. Because the planes were rigged with troop seats, Senate staffers suspected that they were secretly ferrying troops to Central America. FEMA insisted the flights were part of its supersecret "continuity of government" (COG) program, and utterly refused to discuss the matter further.

FEMA made COG another of its obsessions. Under COG, FEMA has the last word in national eschatology. While mundane natural disaster plans gathered dust during the 1980s, FEMA beefed up its rather fanciful strategies for surviving a nuclear war, with emphasis on survival of the federal government. And the rest of us? Well, as Reagan's deputy undersecretary of defense put it: "Dig a hole, cover it with a couple of doors, and then throw three feet of dirt on top.... If there are enough shovels to go around, everyone is going to make it."

Under the aegis of FEMA, top government brass have the benefit of rather more lavish excavations, with the crown jewel being a top-secret underground fortress built during the early 1950s (and predating the elaborate James Bond movie sets) at a cost of more than $1 billion. The Facility, as it is known, is a sort of nuclear winter White House situated beneath the solid granite of Mount Weather in Bluemont, Virginia, forty-five miles west of Washington. It has been described as an "underground city," complete with roads and a battery-powered subway. It boasts office buildings and hospitals, private apartments and dormitories, and a power plant and artificial lake illuminated by fluorescent light. Rounding out the science fiction furnishings are a color video phone system and one of the world's most powerful supercomputers.

In the event of a major nuclear or other catastrophe, surviving feds would run the country from The Facility as well as from FEMA's underground command center in Olney, Maryland, and up to fifty regional bunkers salted throughout the nation. There's even an underground Pentagon more than six hundred feet below solid granite just north of Camp David.

Unfortunately, during a national catastrophe the feds administering the former United States might not be familiar names to you. FEMA's COG scheme involves about three thousand unelected, unaccountable people recruited and trained by FEMA "to serve in executive positions in the federal government in time of national security emergency."

FEMA under Giuffrida never had a chance to retreat to its mole-man cities, govern by remote control, or even demonstrate the uses of "legitimate violence." Giuffrida resigned in 1985, reportedly under pressure from Pentagon and FBI officials who saw in the ambitious "general" a more imminent emergency: their endangered fiefdoms.

MAJOR SOURCES

Chardy, Alfonso. "North Helped Revise Wartime Plans." *Miami Herald*, 9 July 1987.

Emerson, Steven. "America's Doomsday Project," *U.S. News & World Report*, 7 August 1989.

Goldberg, Donald, and Indy Badhwar. *Penthouse*, August 1985.

Peck, Keenen. "The Take-Charge Gang." *The Progressive*, May 1985.

Poundstone, William. *Bigger Secrets*. Boston: Houghton Mifflin Company, 1986.

Sheehan, Daniel P. *Affidavit of Daniel P. Sheehan*. 12 December 1986.

5

The Sickening Secret

No one can be certain what genius first realized that disease could be turned from an uncontrollable killer into a weapon. Maybe some fourteenth-century Tartar. Perhaps the same one who got the bright idea, as he watched his comrades dropping from plague during their three-year siege of the Genoan-occupied Black Sea town of Caffa, to catapult cadavers over the city walls.

Nice move, if a little shortsighted. The Genoans fled the city all right. Then they dispersed, bacillus-ridden, throughout Europe.

Or perhaps it was whichever German surmised that anthrax might do quite nicely in cutting down Europe's livestock supply during World War I. It really doesn't matter who thought of it first, the fact is, biowar got its biggest boost from exactly the effort designed to curtail it: the 1925 Geneva Convention. On June 17, 1925, most of the global powers at the convention affixed their stamps to a protocol banning the use of biological weapons.

There were two important abstainees. The United States

didn't sign, which was slightly curious because at that point, America showed little interest in developing germ weapons. The other no-show was a different story. With the impetus of an ambitious and, in a twisted way, visionary young military doctor named Shiro Ishii, Japan had become infatuated with dreams of infecting its enemies. A decade later Japan occupied Manchuria and Ishii commanded his very own biowar empire, replete with the emperor's seal.

The sprawling operation was centered in a remote Manchurian town called Pingfan and was euphemistically named the Anti-Epidemic Water Supply Unit, Unit 731, now better known as the Ishii Corps.

Unit 731's research methods were scientifically sloppy and ethically, well, not quite right. Their test subjects were humans: Koreans, Chinese, and Russians at first. Then, after Japan went to war with the West, American, British, and Australian prisoners found themselves marched, shipped, and hauled to an encampment near the faraway Manchurian city of Mukden. There they were met by a masked welcoming committee of medical personnel who greeted them by spraying some indeterminate liquid in their faces, ramming glass probes in their rectums, and injecting them with mysterious serum.

Many of the soldiers, unsurprisingly, died. But their bodies were not disposed of according to orthodox disease-control techniques. To say the least. The creepy team of scientists came back and dissected the corpses.

These practices were a matter of routine for Ishii's Unit 731, whose vast kingdom of disease is thought to have traversed much of eastern Asia. The lab at Pingfan, alone, held germ factories that bred eight tons of toxins per month. It also contained an impressive flea farm useful in vectoring Ishii's personal favorite malady, bubonic plague. Ishii's unit pelted several Chinese cities with "flea bombs," igniting outbursts of plague.

Unit 731 infected thousands of human beings, American and British POWs among them, with plague, tetanus, anthrax, botulism, meningitis, tuberculosis, and a potpourri of similar noxious concoctions. Ishii's team of medical experts coolly charted their subjects' illnesses from infection to death. Prisoners who complained of crippling diarrhea were "tested" by being compelled to run laps around the camp until they dropped from exhaustion. Some were made to stand naked in 40-below weather until their limbs froze, ostensibly to study the effects of disease in cold climates. The details aren't really important.

At least not to the United States War Department and General Douglas MacArthur. In Ishii and his files, the military brass realized, they had a motherlode of data that the United States could never develop on its own due to—as two American biowarfare researchers eloquently put it upon returning from interviews with Ishii and his underlings in Tokyo—"scruples attached to human experimentation."

Taking a unique approach to supporting our boys in the field, MacArthur suggested a deal that would allow Ishii and the rest of Unit 731's mad scientists immunity from war-crimes prosecution if they would just share their test results with American researchers, an arrangement that suited Ishii just fine. Only the state department objected, on grounds that later revelation of the deal might "seriously embarrass" the U.S. government.

Ishii slipped into reclusive retirement, devoted, according to his daughter, to religious study—though rumors ran rampant that he made repeated visits to Korea helping the United States mount a biowarfare campaign there. Dr. Murray Sanders, the military physician who finally blew the whistle on the secret deal, believed that Ishii gave lectures at Fort Detrick, Maryland, where American scientists immersed themselves in a supersecret germ weapons project after the war.

Many of Ishii's top associates went on to illustrious and rewarding careers with Japanese universities, corporations, and the government. The doctor who oversaw the cold-weather experiments struck lucrative deals with commercial fisheries as a "freezing specialist." His contribution to the frozen fish industry can only be guessed at.

The extensive unpleasantness that was Unit 731 remains one of World War II's more obscure large-scale crimes against humanity, thanks to both a U.S. government coverup reflex and Japan's always intriguing compulsion to transform, ignore, or reinvent its own history.

Indeed, if a Tokyo graduate student in the early eighties hadn't stumbled across a shred of Ishii's scant remaining paper trail, the Japanese public might never have known about its existence.

But it seems Ishii's empire extended into Tokyo, where things become a little tougher to conceal, seeing as how there are fifteen million people there. In 1989, a construction crew hit on a chock-full stash of human remains beneath the pavement of Shinjuku, Tokyo's futuristic redevelopment zone. "The remains were found just steps from the site of the wartime laboratory of Lt. Gen. Shiro Ishii," reported the *Asahi Evening News*, which noted the belief of Kanagawa University Professor Keiichi Tsuneishi—Japan's leading 731 authority—that Ishii's unit had transported the bodies of its victims to Tokyo for further "study."

In August of 1993, several Chinese families, who think that bones of family members may be among the ghoulish heap, began demanding that Japan identify the skeletons. So far the government's approach to the unusual archaeological find has been ho-hum, declining to investigate where the bones came from or run any tests.

Not that the United States always provides a better example of openness, at least on the topic of biowarfare. For some reason, a chapter of Peter Williams and David Wallace's book *Unit 731: The Japanese Army's Secret of Secrets*, was omitted from the American edition. It appeared in England, Australia, Canada, and New Zealand.

The chapter was titled "Korean War" and it explored the still controversial evidence that the United States military employed Ishii's techniques against China and North Korea. The charges had been around since the fifties, and were either hushed up or brushed off as commie propaganda (REDS' PHOTOGRAPHS ON GERM WARFARE EXPOSED AS FAKES—EVIDENCE IS CONCLUSIVE, hollered a March 15, 1952, *New York Times* headline). Williams and Wallace base their account largely on the findings of the International Scientific Commission for the Facts Concerning Bacterial Warfare in Korea and China (ISC), the one source "generally accepted today as being of high quality," the authors say.

The ISC found that numerous Chinese and Korean sites suffered unexplained outbreaks of bubonic plague and other diseases that coincided with the appearance of nonindigenous or out-of-season insects in those areas. A Chinese plague expert who examined the Korean outbreak told the ISC that his results "explain the reasons why the Americans deliberately protected the Japanese bacteriological war criminals." The United States used Ishii's "flea bomb" method to spread the plagues, ISC evidence indicated.

Nor were fleas the only weapon deployed by American biowarriors. On an April night in 1952 an American F-82 fighter was spotted flying over a Chinese village near the Inner Mongolian border. With the break of day, residents were greeted by an infestation of more than seven hundred voles. Of the voles who survived both the night cold and ravaging cats, many "were sluggish or had fractured legs."

A test on one dead vole showed that it was infected with plague. At first, "the Commission was puzzled how the voles had been dropped from the air," write Williams and Wallace. "But Unit 731 had devised such methods."

In North Korea, the ISC learned of a bizarre clam bombing. In what the ISC determined was a failed attempt to contaminate a local water supply, American planes unloaded cholera-infested clams on a hillside near a water purification plant.

"Japanese research had shown that marine lamelli-branch mollusks were well suited as media for the growth of cholera vibrio," Williams and Wallace report.

Such were the rewards of MacArthur's secret deal. Several

Mukden survivors—who years later still suffered from unexplained outbreaks of fever and illness—tried to pry the truth from their own recalcitrant governments. As late as 1987, British and American Mukden vets were told "no evidence" existed that Allied prisoners were victimized by Ishii's brand of scientific inquiry. In fact, such evidence had existed for more than forty years, and was known to MacArthur when he conceived the secret deal.

It was through this covert pact, and the subsequent conspiracy to cover it up within the U.S. and British governments, that Shiro Ishii became the father of modern biological weapons. The U.S. biowarfare program was lackadaisical until 1942, when Chiang Kai-shek wrote a letter to Winston Churchill filling him in on Ishii's machinations. The British had their own, quite minor research effort going, and the United States joined in. A year later, the Americans got their own project off the ground at a place called Camp—later Fort—Detrick in Maryland.

The quest for the "biological bomb" was conducted under the same air of paranoid self-importance as was its atomic counterpart. But unlike the Manhattan Project, which drew leading physicists of the day, biowarfare research repulsed the nation's top biologists who recoiled from the endeavor. Those darn scruples again.

The government announced the biowarfare project in 1946, but the public's horrified response prompted the army's chief of staff, Dwight Eisenhower, to slap a three-year gag order on the project—broken only by Defense Secretary James Forrestal's 1949 debunking of public concerns as "unduly spectacular."

In the meantime, Fort Detrick, now largely an outpost of the CIA, plugged away at such unspectacular enterprises as the search for toxins that could disguise assassinations as natural deaths and other spooky schemes that have since became the stuff of spy-buff legend.

U.S. researchers did test toxins on humans, albeit volunteers. Prison inmates and, weirdly, Seventh Day Adventists lined up to get shot up with psittacosis, equine encephalitis, and tularemia.

But it still wasn't enough. One of the biggest problems in deploying biological weapons is somehow ensuring that— oops!—the germs don't blow back in your own army's face. To check how germ clouds drifted under actual weather conditions, the military started dousing American cities with bacteria.

A 1950 "attack" on San Francisco, in which a navy minesweeper spewed rare serratia bacteria all over the City by the Bay, sent eleven people to the hospital. One person died. Researchers also unleashed toxins into the Pentagon air conditioning system and the New York subways.

A lawsuit against the government by the San Francisco victim's family revealed three hundred "open air" germ tests between 1950 and 1969. In 1972 the U.S. government officially renounced the development and use of biological weapons.

Even so, secret germ tests continue, though often under the aegis of universities and private research institutes. Today's experiments have an ominous twist—genetic engineering. In 1986 the Wistar Institute, a venerable research facility in Philadelphia, infected Argentinian cattle with genetically altered rabies virus, catching Argentinian cattle ranchers completely by surprise.

The University of Oregon embarked on similar experiments in New Zealand.

The military found the biology business a hard habit to break. Despite the 1972 ban, the Defense Department was allowed to clone a Shiga toxin gene. Shiga toxin causes dysentery. The military, public spirited as ever, asserted that it merely sought a vaccine against the terminally runny affliction. But if the history of germ warfare research proves anything, it's that in the wacky world of infectious disease, defense and offense are often interchangeable.

The foreboding epilogue, or perhaps epitaph, to this unfortunate account is spelled A-I-D-S. The thesis that this fin de siècle epidemic sprang from biowarfare genetic experiments, perhaps on purpose, is common currency among conspiracy traffickers. Needless to add, there's nothing on the record to confirm it.

But then, there was "no evidence" that American prisoners were subjects of Ishii's human experiments either.

MAJOR SOURCES

Harris, Robert, and Jeremy Paxman. *A Higher Form of Killing: The Secret Story of Chemical and Biological Warfare*. New York: Hill and Wang, 1982.

McDermott, Jeanne. *The Killing Winds: The Menace of Biological Warfare*. New York: Arbor House, 1987.

Piller, Charles, and Keith Yamamoto. *Gene Wars: Military Control Over the New Genetic Technologies*. New York: Beech Tree Books, 1988.

Williams, Peter, and David Wallace. *Unit 731: The Japanese Army's Secret of Secrets*. London: Hodder and Stoughton, 1989.

6

A Lovely Little War

Looking back on it, the Gulf War—if America's massive assault on Iraq with minimal resistance can really be called a "war"—seems like surreal theater. Few events have so keenly delineated the distance between reality and spectacle. Even more alarming, the war left little question which domain we inhabit. Other than the obvious—yes, Saddam Hussein did invade Kuwait and, yes, that was really, really bad—very little in the predominant government-media view of the situation intersected with anything verifiable.

The U.S. government's actions leading up to, during, and after the war suggest that the inaugural battle of the New World Order was some kind of a manufactured crisis with a hidden agenda.

"The shallow, Nintendo view of the war on TV was false," former Pentagon defense expert Pierre Sprey testified to Congress. "It was created by hand-picked videotapes and shamelessly doctored statistics." "Surgical" air strikes? "About as surgical as operating on a cornea with machetes," as one *Washington Post* columnist wrote just a month into the bombardment.

"Kuwait will once again be free," predicted George Bush,

43

announcing the start of bombing. "Long martial law hinted by Kuwait," noted a *New York Times* headline as the war wound down.

George Bush said that Saddam Hussein was in some ways worse than Hitler. His point is arguable, but the fact is that the very same George Bush signed a National Security Directive in 1989 ordering closer ties with Iraq and clearing the way for $500 million in credits to Mr. "Worse-than-Hitler." This is not surprising. Bush had spent nearly a decade in an administration weirdly enamored with Iraq, despite occasional public denunciations of Saddam Hussein's police-state governance.

"Saddam's military machine is partly a creation of the Western powers," reported investigative journalist Murray Waas. Throughout Iraq's eight-year war of attrition with Iran, the governments of France, Britain, and Germany sold the Iraqi strongman everything from fighter planes and Exocet missiles to ingredients for brewing nerve gas. The United States—technically—maintained an embargo on arms sales to Iraq, but the Reagan administration let it be circumvented by encouraging third-party munitions sales as well as through direct sales of "dual use" technology: computers, even helicopters, which the Iraqis pledged to use only for "education" or "recreation." Nudge, nudge, wink, wink. According to Waas, when Bush took office as president, dual-use sales "shifted into a far more alarming area—the prerequisites of weapons of mass destruction."

After the brief Gulf War, inquiries into these arms transactions erupted into a short-lived scandal dubbed Iraqgate. At the center of the storm was a seemingly insignificant Atlanta branch of a multinational Italian bank, Banca Nazionale del Lavoro (BNL), which somehow spirited $5 billion to Iraq over two years until raided by the FBI on August 4, 1989. Yet under the Bush administration, the accused bank managers were not indicted for more than a year. And then, by some coincidence, the indictment was returned one day after Bush declared a cease fire in the Gulf War.

Officials of the tiny BNL branch were portrayed as "rogue operators" by government prosecutors who didn't find it worth their time to ask how $5 billion (yes billion) could find its way from one bank to a "worse-than-Hitler" dictator without the knowledge of government officials or at least the bank's higher-ups in Italy.

The Reagan and Bush administrations shared not only money and matériel but also intelligence information with Saddam as Iraq battled the forces of the evil Ayatollah in Iran.

"In other words," said former Reagan National Security Council staffer Howard Teicher, "we advised the Iraqis on how to prepare for war with the United States."

Leading up to the invasion of Kuwait, the United States sent Saddam Hussein not only aid but also comfort. Just a week before the August 2, 1990, invasion, Saddam sat down with U.S. ambassador April Glaspie—the now-infamous "green light" meeting. Glaspie was unnervingly blasé given the impending crisis. She even made a point of noting that the United States had "no opinion on the Arab-Arab conflicts, like your border disagreement with Kuwait." She also told Saddam that none other than Secretary of State James Baker had passed on word that "the issue was not associated with America."

Saddam apparently took Glaspie's remarks as carte blanche, and maybe they were intended that way. Hard to believe, given the administration's later public position, but this laissez-faire attitude was wholly consistent with Bush administration policy. A few days after the Glaspie-Hussein confab, and just three days before the invasion, John Kelly, the assistant secretary of state in charge of the Middle East, testified before Congress, where he was asked if in the event of an Iraqi military action, "is it correct to say that we have no treaty, no commitment, which would oblige us to use American forces?"

"That's exactly right," Kelly replied. Another shining green light.

No one promised the United States would *not* use force. But if the Bush administration's aim was to prevent war, it was

picking an odd way to go about it. If anything, Bush and his
buddies were egging the Iraqis on.

The Kuwaiti al-Sabah monarchy, which stood to suffer the
most, also exhibited bizarre behavioral symptoms. In a preinvasion summit Iraq demanded $10 billion from Kuwait as com-
pensation for singlehandedly fending off the forces of Islamic
fundamentalism for eight years by engaging Iran in a disastrous
stalemate war. The demand was not altogether unreasonable,
and, in fact, Kuwait agreed to pay. But the al-Sabahs offered
only $9 billion—a deliberate slap in the face. Later, after other
agreements were reached, Kuwait would alter their terms. At
the time, Saddam's troops were massing on the Kuwaiti border.
Courage on the al-Sabah's part? Not likely, since they were the
first ones out of the country when the tanks rumbled south.
They chilled out in a five-star Saudi hotel while Bush's "coalition" fought their battle.

"If Saddam comes across the border, let him come," said
Kuwait's foreign minister, Sheikh Sabbah, to Jordan's King
Hussein in the midst of the preinvasion non-negotiations. "The
Americans will get him out."

He had reason for confidence. When Iraqi troops ransacked
the Kuwaiti Foreign Ministry they found a November 22, 1989,
memo recording the results of a meeting between Kuwaiti
officials and officials of the CIA.

"We agreed with the American side that it was important to
take advantage of the deteriorating economic situation in Iraq
in order to put pressure on that country's government to
delineate our common border. The Central Intelligence Agency
gave us its view of appropriate means of pressure...."

The CIA denounced the document as bogus—but admitted
that the meeting took place.

There was another interesting, if somewhat less sinister
meeting—this one on April 12, 1990—with five U.S. senators
powwowing with the "Butcher of Bagdhad." Republican Alan
Simpson sucked up to ol' Butch, telling him that his problems
"lie with the Western media and not with the U.S. govern-

ment....And it is a haughty and pampered press; they all consider themselves political geniuses."

This sentiment was echoed later by Glaspie, who shared with Saddam her opinion that "if the American president had control of the media his job would be much easier."

Ah, but during the Gulf War the American president did have control of the media. As did the military. Herding reporters into "press pools" proved effective—helped along by the journalists' acquiescence.

"If you look at it from the outset, the press was reflecting the views of the government," said *Los Angeles Times* Washington Bureau chief Jack Nelson, "and it never really changed."

Robert Fisk, Middle East correspondent for the British *Independent* was one of the few reporters to ignore the pools. When he showed up at one scene where the pool reporters had clustered awaiting the official military handouts, he was met by an NBC reporter who greeted him by saying, "You asshole. You'll prevent us from working. You're not allowed here. Get out."

The vituperative press pooler was Brad Willis, whose version of the incident, as recounted in *Harper's* publisher, John MacArthur's, book about the Gulf War press, included an extra detail. Fisk, Willis claimed, *posed* as a pool member and Willis, displaced by Fisk, was then bounced from the scene as a result. If Fisk's gambit succeeded, not only Willis but the whole pool would have been deprived of coverage because the nature of pool reporting was not to compete for the best story but to share the military's prescrubbed version of the story.

"It was a textbook example of the probably deliberate divide-and-conquer strategy of the U.S. military," wrote MacArthur. "Fisk, of course, wanted an uncensored exclusive and would do whatever it took to get it; he didn't want to share. Willis, playing by the Pentagon rules, was angry at the prospect of getting beaten by another reporter who was breaking the rules."

Consequently, with Fisk one of the rare exceptions, war

reporting took on a quasi-Orwellian demeanor. The press-promulgated paradigm of the conflict was Yellow Ribbonsville, U.S.A. versus Satanic Saddam. American reporters, almost to the one, referred to the U.S. military as "we," obviating any remaining distinction between journalist and subject and casting time-honored "objectivity" to the desert winds. Iraqi Scud missiles became "terrorist weapons" and "horrifying machines of death," while U.S. bombs were "smart." When *Newsweek* put the Stealth bomber on its cover it asked, "How many lives can it save?"

"That was the spin," marvel media critics Martin Lee and Norman Solomon in their book, *Unreliable Sources*. "American weapons don't destroy lives; they save them!" After all, dead Iraqis did not count as "casualties." They were merely "collateral damage," which in *Time* magazine's definition meant "dead or wounded civilians who should have picked a safer neighborhood."

"Denial was the key to the psychological and political structures supporting the war," Lee and Solomon wrote.

As for the war's motives, the interests of Western-based multinational oil companies and perhaps more important, the Western banks where Kuwaiti and Saudi oil Sheiks stowed their profits were treated with silence.

While Bush administration propaganda was treated as fact, the U.S. media was quick to denounce Iraqi "propaganda," even when it wasn't propaganda—as in the infamous case of the Baby Milk Bombing. A week into the war, CNN's Peter Arnett, the only Western reporter in Bagdhad, drew global condemnation for reporting that an allied bombing raid had destroyed Iraq's only infant-formula factory, leaving the nation's newborns hungry.

The U.S. military pooh-poohed the Iraqi claim. "It was a biological weapons facility, of that we are sure," said Joint Chiefs chairman Colin Powell. But the French contractors who built the plant and the New Zealand dairy technicians who visited it regularly swore it was exactly what the Iraqis said it was.

The *MacNeil/Lehrer News Hour* showed a short clip of wounded Iraqi civilians—with the commentary that the scenes were subject to "heavy-handed manipulation" by the Iraqi government. As Lee and Solomon point out, the barely subliminal message was that anyone concerned about Iraqi suffering was a Saddam Hussein dupe.

Late in 1991, former Bob Woodward collaborator Scott Armstrong reported another unstated motivation for the war—though his story in the left-wing *Mother Jones* magazine met with major media indifference. Armstrong wrote that the previous decade, and at an astronomical cost of $200 billion, the United States and Saudi Arabia had assembled a massive infrastructure of "superbases" in the desert. This was all done without public, or even congressional knowledge. The war protected those bases, and the bases were instrumental in fighting the war.

Bush's star burned bright in the Gulf War glow, but somehow he managed to fritter away his political capital and lose his reelection attempt. But even in defeat, Bush, or at least his kids and pals, got a boon from the Gulf War. According to reporter Seymour Hersh, Neil and Marvin Bush; family friend and Bush's secretary of state, James Baker; and once high-flying chief of staff John Sununu (among others) have all worked hard to strike war-spoils deals with the Kuwaiti government.

Baker represented Enron, America's biggest builder of natural gas pipelines. The Enron exec who dispatched Baker to Kuwait wondered aloud to Hersh: "Is there any reason American companies shouldn't profit from the war in Kuwait?"

American politicians continue to profit. Bush's successor, Bill Clinton, enjoyed a healthy boost in his then-pallid polls when on June 26, 1993—two and a half years after the Gulf War ended—he ordered another bombing raid on Bagdhad.

Why? The given rationale was that the Iraqis had attempted

to assassinate Bush when the ex-president had visited Kuwait a few months earlier. Kuwait arrested seventeen supposed low-level conspirators in the plot, but as Hersh reported, "The American government's case against Iraq—as it has been outlined in public, anyway—is seriously flawed."

The dread Iraqi terrorists hand-picked for the Bush job included a coffee shop owner and a male nurse—the latter was the only source of information about the supposed plot. Most of the aspiring assassins were whiskey smugglers. The Kuwaitis have been known to exaggerate, especially about Iraqi violations of their sovereignty. When a group of Iraqi fishermen unwisely landed on the Kuwaiti island of Bubiyan, the Kuwaiti press release said that an Iraqi naval force had attempted to invade the island only to be defeated by crack Kuwaiti troops.

None of the male nurse's evidence has proved conclusive, or even close. The most solid bit of evidence is the "signature" of an electronic remote control detonator found in the bomb allegedly sent to blow up Bush. But Hersh reports that the piece was a common scrap of circuit board whose signature was anything but distinctive.

It is doubtful whether the "real" reason why the United States went to war in the Persian Gulf will ever emerge—and even more doubtful whether there was a single, identifiable motive. Unlike in Vietnam, where the ambiguous outcome elicited natural suspicions, in the Gulf the decisiveness of victory has buried the reality deeper than any Iraqi or American soldier who went to a sandy grave.

MAJOR SOURCES

Armstrong, Scott. "Eye of the Storm." *Mother Jones*, November-December 1991.
Hersh, Seymour M. "A Case Not Closed." *New Yorker*, 1 November 1993.
———. "The Spoils of the Gulf War." *New Yorker*, 6 September 1993.

Kamen, Al. "Was It a Milk Factory or a Weapons Plant?" *Washington Post* (in *San Jose Mercury News*), 8 February 1991.

Lee, Martin A., and Norman Solomon. *Unreliable Sources: A Guide to Detecting Bias in News Media*. New York: Lyle Stuart, 1991.

MacArthur, John R. *Second Front: Censorship and Propaganda in the Gulf War*. New York: Hill and Wang, 1992.

Royce, Knut. "A Trail of Distortion Against Iraq." *Newsday*, 21 January 1991.

Salinger, Pierre, and Eric Laurent. *Secret Dossier: The Hidden Agenda Behind the Gulf War*. New York: Penguin Books, 1991.

Sifry, Micah, and Christopher Cerf, eds. *The Gulf War Reader*. New York: Random House, 1991.

7

The Adventures of the Keystone Kommandos

The assault on an apocalyptic religious sect calling themselves the Branch Davidians, in the tumbleweed flatlands of Waco, Texas, on April 19, 1993, followed in the grand tradition of American law enforcement mayhem.

This proud heritage includes such landmarks as the incineration of the Symbionese Liberation Army house in Los Angeles; the aerial firebombing of the black-separatist MOVE organization's communal apartment complex in Philadelphia—still the only American city ever to have been bombed from the air; and the Chicago police's 4 A.M. assault on Fred Hampton, riddling the Black Panther boss with bullets while he was sleeping in his own bed.

The Waco massacre that claimed the lives of eighty-six sect members (and a handful of federal agents) at the Branch Davidians' compound was more than a tad paramilitary. But the incident may have had much in common with the slaughter

52

at Jonestown, Guyana, fifteen years earlier. Either it was a mass suicide—or mass murder by the government, which then tried to blame the victims for their own deaths.

In the six-week staredown before the Bureau of Alcohol, Tobacco, and Firearms (ATF) and the FBI went gonzo on the "cultists," the media flooded the nation with imprecations, encouraged by the authorities, that the Branch Davidians—led by the "Wacko from Waco" David Koresh (née Vernon Howell)—were likely to commit mass suicide at any time, just like those Jonestown nuts. Of course, given the feds' aural assault on the Davidians, the Kool-Aid solution may have appeared a not unwelcome option. Replicating a technique used four years earlier to flush Manuel Noriega from his sanctuary, the feds blared an earsplitting mishmash of noise that included the sound of rabbits being slaughtered, chanting Tibetan monks, roaring jet engines, and the Nancy Sinatra hit, "These Boots Were Made For Walking."

As if that wasn't torture enough, floodlights blazed all night long into the two-story ranch house where Koresh's followers struggled to catch a little shut-eye while the fed/press mob swelled and swarmed outside. But worst of all, the agents cut off all utilities and food supplies to the commune, an embargo enforced even when Koresh pleaded for replenishment of the group's baby milk supply almost six weeks into the standoff.

The siege began February 28 when the ATF embarked on a "surprise" attack against the Mount Carmel commune. The operation was so surprising that three local TV crews were on hand to capture it on videotape and two reporters stationed themselves in a nearby tree to get a fifty-yard-line view of the excitement. The attack produced a stalemate, with the ATF force incurring a 20 percent casualty rate (four dead, sixteen wounded).

At least some, if not all of the fallen feds were victims of the ATF commandos' own gunfire. According to communications specialist Ken Fawcett, who authored an affidavit based on his analysis of unedited video of the initial raid, the first shot was accidental. An agent's assault rifle somehow discharged and killed another ATF agent, Stephen Willis.

The full-scale battle began when an agent accidentally shot himself in the leg. Thinking they were under attack, the rest of the ATF platoon unleashed a fusillade of machine-gun shells.

In a network TV interview, ATF director Stephen Higgins tried to pin the lost "element of surprise" on leaks by a person or persons unknown. When several ATF agents later sued a Waco newspaper, the public learned that the ATF itself leaked the raid. Testifying before the Senate Judiciary Committee, Higgins was prudent enough not to repeat his lie. But even if no one had been tipped, an ATF chopper buzzed the compound before the commandos attacked. Being not complete idiots, the sect members probably surmised that something was up.

On April 19, the feds—with the FBI now leading the charge ahead of a chastened ATF—attacked in earnest, replete with armored vehicle assaults and an eight-hour barrage of CS, an especially noxious and flammable tear gas, usually fortified with kerosene. The compound burst into flames, the conflagration helped along by shock waves from M-60 tanks bashing the house. The surviving Davidians claimed, not implausibly, that the tanks actually started the fire by knocking over kerosene lamps that the electricity-denied sect was using to light the place. The tanks punched holes in the compound walls. The ventilation may have contributed in accelerating the blaze.

Koresh perished along with most of his followers, including many children.

The FBI immediately announced that two survivors of the cremated cult had confessed to sparking the fires. The bureau later pulled back a bit, noting that the cult members had not actually confessed—but they might as well have, because FBI sharpshooters personally witnessed them "cupping their hands."

An "independent" investigation later incriminated the Davidians, apparently confirming the Jonestownesque mass-suicide tale. But the truth about the Waco fire remains murky. It is worth noting that the fire investigator was a former ATF agent. The fellow's wife still worked in the ATF's Houston office, which was directed by senior agent Phil Chojnacki. It was Chojnacki who reportedly hovered over the compound in a helicopter before the ATF's February "surprise" raid.

Another lingering mystery is why the feds carried out their dime-store Green Beret operation at all. Conspiracy theories abound. One lawyer who claimed to represent some Branch Davidian members and their families, warned that over the weeks of the standoff there were troop movements across the nation and trainloads of U.N. tanks sighted in Portland, Oregon. As Peter Jennings said on a special report in the aftermath of the Branch Davidian's destruction, "this is a warning of things to come."

A writer for the magazine *Soldier of Fortune* suggested that the ATF was motivated by nothing more than petty vindictiveness. On February 21 Koresh was interviewed by an ATF agent and, in an apparent fit of hubris, screened a pro-gun group's anti-ATF video for his interrogator's benefit. On February 25 the ATF applied for the search warrant that resulted in the crisis.

Speculation aside, the only on-the-record purpose for the initial attack was to serve that search warrant. There is no evidence that the ATF informed the Branch Davidians of their intent to serve the warrant (though an ATF agent is said to have shouted something about it as the assault got underway), or that the Davidians refused them entry. Under the law, both must take place before law enforcement may use force to serve a warrant. The ATF could have asked for a special "no knock" warrant, but did not.

In a taped phone call after the initial raid, a puzzled Koresh told an ATF negotiator, "It would've been better if you just called me up or talked to me. Then you all could have come in and done your work."

There are even doubts over whether the Branch Davidians

were engaged in anything illegal at all. It is true that they were well stocked with arms and explosives—but popular assumptions to the contrary, there is nothing against the law about either, as long as all the paperwork is in order. At least some of the explosives had been purchased to excavate a ditch for a swimming pool. The pool was still under construction when the commune found itself at war.

Midway through the stalemate, the ATF suddenly announced that the Branch Davidians were manufacturing methamphetamines in a secret commune laboratory. No one bothered to ask, first of all, where this information came from, and second, what it had to do with anything. The ATF has no jurisdiction to enforce laws against drugs. Nor does the ATF have any authority to nab child molesters, another charge that helped demonize Koresh in the national media.

It is likely the drug-lab story was concocted to explain the Big Brotherish black National Guard helicopters circling over the site in violation of a Texas law that forbids use of state helicopters by federal authorities except in drug cases.

The methamphetamine allegation, significantly, never appeared in any legal document. As one skeptical reporter noted, it's not a crime to lie to the press, but fudging before a judge carries a few consequences.

On the other hand, the ATF affidavit filed in applying for the February 28 search warrant was not a model of accuracy. In it, ATF agent Davy Aguilera claims—in what later served as evidence of Koresh's fanaticism—that on April 6, 1992, Koresh warned a Texas Human Services official that he was a "messenger from God" and that when he revealed his true nature, "the riots in Los Angeles would pale in comparison to what was going to happen in Waco, Texas."

Scary stuff, except that when Koresh issued this alleged threat the L.A. riots were still three weeks away.

The ATF also claimed that they had to bust up the Davidians because Koresh, Hitler-style, had been bunkered up in there for weeks. In fact, he ventured into town at least once a week. He had sauntered out to a Waco night spot just two nights before the February attack.

The ATF never officially charged Koresh et al. with anything worse than illegal weapons possession. Five years before, Koresh and six associates were arrested by local police on attempted murder charges. Yet they cooperated fully (and were later acquitted). And how did the Waco sheriffs manage to avert the bloodletting that the federal authorities found ineluctable?

"We treated them like human beings," said Waco D.A. Vic Feazell, "rather than storm-trooping the place."

MAJOR SOURCES

Dingell, John D., III. "Licensed to Slaughter." *Incite Information*, July-August 1993.

Fawcett, Ken. "Why Waco?" In *Secret and Suppressed*, edited by Jim Keith. Portland, OR: Feral House Press, 1993.

Pate, James L. "Waco's Defective Warrants: No Probable Cause for Raid on Ranch Apocalypse." *Soldier of Fortune*, August 1993.

Report of Linda Thompson, American Justice Federation. Published electronically. Copy in authors' possession.

This chapter owes a debt to research compiled by Kenn Thomas.

8

The Conspiracy Queen and the G-Men

On April 23, 1981, agents of the Federal Bureau of Investigation arrived at Mae Brussell's home in the rustic, seaside burg of Carmel, California, to find out what she knew about a conspiracy to assassinate President Ronald Reagan.

It was the first and only face-to-face encounter between Brussell and the FBI, which at that time had kept a file on her for more than thirteen years.

Mae Brussell died of cancer seven years later at the age of sixty-six, closing a seventeen-year career of discursive radio broadcasts—based out of Bay Area nonprofit stations—that all but invented an entire genre of political research that has yet to find a place in the mainstream even today.

Brussell did not invent conspiracy theory. That human obsession had been around for a long time. But she pioneered the theory that a fascist cabal—directly traceable to the Third Reich itself—was the ultimate source of power in the United States and the world. What made her both more fascinating and

58

more threatening (depending on your point of view) than the garden-variety conspiracy buff was the fact that her ideas were not spun from the fabric of her imagination, but from her reading list. In 1964, while still a mild-mannered suburban housewife, she purchased, read, and—over the next several years—indexed and cross-referenced all twenty-six volumes of the Warren Commission's evidence in its investigation of President Kennedy's assassination.

By the time of her death, her home library alone held about six thousand books and twenty years' worth of newspaper clippings (she read seven papers a day) and magazine articles. In her lifetime, she generated hundreds of tape-recorded broadcasts and several published articles on topics as diverse as the CIA's connection to the kidnapping of Patricia Hearst, the Jonestown massacre, Watergate, satanism, and so on.

She had also accrued a worldwide following which, when she died, became certain that "the intelligence community" was responsible for the death of their spiritual leader.

The legends of Mae Brussell's conflict with the heat are legion. But the paper trail is not plentiful. The Secret Service kept a file on her, but it was generated mainly because Brussell was not content merely to spout her opinions over the air.

"More than half of the file's [144 pages] would not exist," wrote one researcher who read the file, "if she had simply refrained from sending letters to presidents, calling up various police agencies, or visiting Maureen Reagan." Much of the remainder of the Secret Service file arose from the fact that Brussell's father, Rabbi-to-the-Stars Edgar Magnin, was a personal friend of Richard Nixon, whom Brussell expended no small amount of energy excoriating.

But if a hint exists anywhere that "the man" treated Mae Brussell as someone worth snuffing (or at least worth having her privacy invaded), we figured it would come from that most paranoid of domestic police forces, J. Edgar Hoover's FBI.

The 1981 interview is the first Brussell-FBI meeting recorded in the thirty-eight pages of her file released under the Freedom of Information Act (FOIA). If there were others, perhaps on a less formal basis, they are not mentioned. The Bureau does note that sixteen pages of the file, comprising four documents, have been withheld because "the vast majority of information in these four documents pertains to other individuals."

The "other individuals" in Mae Brussell's life were a vast and varied lot. They ranged from her father, a leader of L.A.'s Jewish community, to Bruce Roberts, purported author of the Gemstone File (see chapter 40). One can only speculate on what those confidential pages contain. Maybe nothing.

The public pages mention a few references to "pretext inquiries" about Brussell. That's when an agent or informer gathers information by pretending to be someone else. Sneaky, sure, but they did it to Brussell—or, more accurately, to her father—as early as 1966, five years before she went on the air with her weekly all-conspiracy radio program.

An apparently apropos-of-nothing teletype memo tagged, "Assassination of President John Fitzgerald Kennedy. Miscellaneous Information," is dated September 17, 1967, even though it refers to incidents from the first two months of the previous year. The memo originated in the FBI's San Francisco bureau, and is directed to the director (Hoover) and the New Orleans and Dallas offices.

"San Francisco files reveal that on 1/20/66 [blacked out] private investigator, Carmel, Calif., reported that a client advised that May [sic] Magnin Brussell had expressed great alarm over fact that U.S. is becoming fascist and a fascist coup would occur within two years. Advised she is daughter of Rabbi Edgar F. Magnin, Wilshire Temple, Los Angeles. [Blacked out] advised she recently moved to Carmel Valley with several small children and it was rumored she has 'left wing' leanings and is not in good favor with her father."

The Teletype goes on to mention the "pretext inquiry" at Rabbi Magnin's residence, a check of Brussell's credit records (which seem to reveal nothing except the name and occupation of her husband), and a review of Monterey County sheriff's records on Brussell that proved "negative." The memo notes a letter to the editor Mae penned and an op-ed piece in which she "takes the view Lee Harvey Oswald was not a communist."

The Teletype's conclusion: "no further action being taken by SF."

Needless to say, The Teletype was, in fact, apropos of something, and the next document in the file, a memo from "Director, FBI" to Dallas sheds a little light on what prompted the sudden interest in the then-unknown Mrs. Brussell.

"Due to the fact that Mrs. Brussell has been in contact with James [sic] Garrison at New Orleans and has made public comments concerning the investigation, Dallas and San Francisco are to immediately incorporate the information received concerning her into an appropriate letterhead memoranda suitable for dissemination....This matter is to be handled immediately."

The FBI's more-than-idle curiosity about New Orleans district attorney Garrison's JFK assassination probe has been documented widely and well. By powwowing with Garrison, Mae got swept up in the Bureau's net. But there was more to it than that, though from the released documents it's hard to tell exactly what.

A note attached to the "director's" reply states without further elaboration that a September 17, 1967, Delta Airlines flight from Dallas to San Francisco received a bomb threat and that "Mrs. May [sic] Magnin Brussell who was boarding this flight for San Francisco made comments at Love Field, Dallas, she had conducted research on the Kennedy assassination and had been in conference with D.A. Jim Garrison, New Orleans, for three days."

The implication seems to be that Mae claimed she was the target of the bomb threat. The FBI's late-1967 interest in Brussell must have been prompted by the Delta Airlines incident, spurred on when the Bureau realized that she'd been hanging out with Garrison.

Nothing further appears in the thirty-eight pages regarding

the Delta bomb threat or Mae's possible relation to it. By the time of the next entry in the file, Mae Brussell had embarked on her public career as an innovator of American conspiracy theories. She was planning to edit a publication called *Conspiracy Newsletter*. A single-page memorandum on U.S. Government letterhead (at the bottom of which appears a picture of a Minuteman and the slogan "Buy U.S. Savings Bonds Regularly on the Payroll Savings Plan") shows that the FBI was up to its tricks again.

"On 12/19/72," says the memo from the San Francisco office, "a pretext call was placed to [blacked out] by SA [blacked out] under guise of a student desiring a copy of his new publication. [blacked out] advised that publication of the *Conspiracy Newsletter* has been delayed indefinitely. He advised that both he and *MAE BRUSSELL*, who would be editor of the publication, currently do not have time to work on it.

"In view of the above, this matter is being closed; however, San Francisco will remain alert for possible future publication of *Conspiracy Newsletter*."

It is indeed comforting to know that the nation's top law enforcement personnel remained "alert" against such threats to public safety as "publication of *Conspiracy Newsletter*." But again, there seems to be a piece missing from the FOIA file's picture.

The single page in the file is headed "Re Bureau letter to San Francisco, 8/25/72." Where's the letter? Not in the file. The innocent explanation would be that Mae Brussell was not mentioned by name in the letter, which given the extreme literal-mindedness of the FBI's FOIA staff, of course, rules out including the letter in her file.

The first three paragraphs of the "Re Bureau letter" memo are blacked out, the largest single deletion in the released pages of Mae Brussell's FBI file. Along with the absence of the earlier letter, the blackout leaves the origin of the FBI's interest in *Conspiracy Newsletter* a mystery.

The next document, dated November 6, 1975, is equally

intriguing, though for different reasons. By this time Mae was well known as, shall we say, an "alternative" radio personality. Week after week she took to the public-access airwaves to unleash almost incomprehensibly complicated monologues of conspiracy.

Mae notified an assistant U.S. attorney—who then passed on the info to the FBI—that she had received the following correspondence (the letter appeared to have been signed, but the name is blacked out):

"Mae, you are thinking yourself in a circle of madness. Charles Manson has been 28 years in prison and all that B.S. you are running is only a reflection of what the news and books have programmed your soul's mind brain to.

"You are looking for attention. It seems as if you are looking for your death wish in the Family."

An unrelated document dated five years later refers back to this incident and states flat out that "during October and November of 1975 she received threatening letters from [blacked out] member of the Manson family."

Now, true, the Mansonites dispensed death threats at about the same rate that meter maids hand out parking tickets. But they made good on plenty. If any organization deserves credibility when threatening to off someone, it's Charlie's kids. Yet according to the FBI document "Assistant U.S. Attorney F. Steele Langford stated that the contents of the extortion letter did not amount to a threat."

Pursuant to that sage assessment, the FBI ordered "no additional investigation." In a bold and decisive step, however, the FBI advised Mae to "change her telephone number to an unlisted number and to immediately contact the FBI upon receipt of any additional such communications."

Maybe they were too busy awaiting publication of *Conspiracy Newsletter* to worry about death threats from the Manson family, but the FBI's inaction must have seemed eerie when Mae died in 1988, just a few months after canceling her radio show—after almost two decades—in response to a death threat. (Though her terminal cancer was described as unremarkable by her doctor, Mae's followers have speculated vigorously that her enemies had the technology and motivation to deliberately transmit the dread disease.) Her topic of concern at the time was satanic cults in the military. She also held the view, oft-mentioned in the FBI documents, that the Manson gang was connected to a U.S. intelligence or military operation.

The file next compiles Mae's 1976 correspondence with the FBI's director Clarence Kelley regarding her insistence that the body buried in Howard Hughes's grave is not Howard Hughes ("Remember, you were appointed by Richard Nixon, who played around with the law in his own hands. Did he put you there to hide, à la Watergate, or are you going to name those agents, your employees, who MADE THE POSITIVE IDENTIFICATION?"). Then the final fourteen pages deal exclusively with Mae's claim, made in April of 1981, that John Hinckley had placed her house under surveillance, the claim that prompted FBI agents to drop in on her in person.

Coming less than a month after the assassination attempt on President Reagan, Mae's claim, which she duly reported to the authorities, that Hinckley paid her a visit in January of that year attracted understandable interest. The episode began when Rudy Giuliani, then a U.S. attorney, now mayor of New York City, brought Mae's call to the FBI's attention. On April 23 the FBI interviewed her at her home.

She told them how, on January 13, she noticed a white sedan parked across the street from her house. She immediately assumed that the occupants of the vehicle were spying on her. A man and a woman sat in the car and Mae confronted them. The man remained silent, for the most part. When Reagan was shot, Mae recognized photographs of the accused assailant as the same quiet young man she had seen parked in front of her home.

After Mae's death, many of her friends and followers soared to incredible levels of paranoia, stashing her voluminous clip files where the heat couldn't reach them, but when she had FBI agents in her living room, Mae practically begged them to explore her private library.

She went so far as to request that the FBI set up a "task force" solely to wade through the "thousands of newspaper clippings and hundreds of books she has collected," according to a May 4, 1981, FBI report of the visit.

"The Bureau should be advised that any further contact with Mrs. Brussell regarding her theories would not be considered a wise expenditure of investigative effort," concludes the un-characteristically wry report.

Another memo about the Hinckley incident and Mae's excit-ing FBI houseguests contains the agents' assessment that "Mrs. Brussell is well known to be mentally unstable and is not taken seriously by the local community concerning her conspiracy theories."

Interestingly, the Secret Service file on the Hinckley incident, while ultimately dismissing Mae's report, notes that "the sub-ject, Brussell, appears legitimate."

Mae Brussell's FBI encounter ends with the alleged Hinckley-sighting and subsequent agent interview, though Mae remained at large for seven more years. Did the FBI completely lose interest in her after fourteen years, finally writing her off as a harmless nut? Did she give up on contacting them, and consequently, on getting her name placed in FBI records? Or is there something else in the file's unreleased pages.

The file ends with the FBI's brief summary of its contact over the years with Mae Brussell. The final incident it describes, that last official mention of Mae in FBI records, comes from a phone call she placed to the Monterey Resident Agency in 1977. The story is a poignant one, in a bizarre way.

"She advised that she was concerned over a situation regard-ing one of her daughters. She noted that a young man who was appearing in a play with her daughter had shown a romantic interest in her. This individual appeared to have plenty of money although he had no visible means of support. Brussell thought this individual might be an 'agent provocateur' directed against her by the FBI via her daughter."

MAJOR SOURCES

Beebe, Greg. "Conspiracy Theorists Ponder the Mae Brussell Question." *Santa Cruz Sentinel*, 28 February 1992.

Despot, X. Sharks. "Mae Brussell: Secret Service Files on the Queen of Conspiracy Theorists." *Steamshovel Press*, no. 8 (Summer 1993).

Vankin, Jonathan. *Conspiracies, Cover-Ups, and Crimes*. New York: Dell, 1992.

Whalen, John. "All Things Conspired." San Jose *Metro*, 17 November 1988.

Mae Brussell's FBI file, in authors' possession.

9

Microfilm at 11

In 1977, Carl Bernstein—of Woodward/Bernstein fame—reported that "more than four hundred American journalists... in the past twenty-five years have secretly carried out assignments" for the CIA. The *New York Times*—one of the CIA's most valuable media collaborators, according to Bernstein's sources—subsequently spread the blame a bit by putting the figure at "more than eight hundred news and public information organizations and individuals."

It was an astonishing revelation. For more than two decades, scores of distinguished reporters had let the CIA peek at their notes. They had assisted in the recruitment of foreign spies. They acted as Agency messengers abroad. Some of them even drew a paycheck courtesy of a trench-coated Uncle Sam.

If the prospect of the fourth estate shilling for intelligence agencies wasn't troubling enough, many of the CIA's journalist-spooks had knowingly spread propaganda abroad. And more than a few times, disinformation sown overseas filtered back home, the "blowback" or "domestic fallout" roosting in American newspapers as the gospel truth. It is also clear that CIA "black," or unattributed, propaganda has at times been aimed squarely—and illegally—at Americans.

The Agency also managed to place its own operatives inside some of the most prestigious American news organizations. As *New York Times* and *Time* magazine "employees," CIA spies enjoyed the perfect cover. Masquerading as inquisitive reporters, Agency operatives could turn up anywhere and ask probing questions without arousing suspicion.

"One journalist is worth twenty agents," a high-level CIA official told Bernstein. The CIA's faux newsmen even underwent training to learn to act and talk like reporters. Meanwhile, bona fide reporters were schooled in the elite art of spycraft: secret writing, surveillance techniques, and other skills.

The CIA's media manipulation organ came to be known in Agency parlance as the Propaganda Assets Inventory. Frank G. Wisner, the Agency's first chief of covert action, immodestly called it Wisner's Wurlitzer, a way of orchestrating public opinion anywhere in the world. Though Wisner committed suicide in 1961, his tune carried on for several more decades. In addition to its journalist assets and agents, the CIA has subsidized or owned as many as fifty newspapers, news services, radio stations, and magazines—mostly abroad but also at home. For instance, the Agency operated proprietary papers like the *Rome Daily American*, the *Manila Times*, and the *Bangkok Post*.

We may never know the full scope of the CIA's media manipulations, thanks to the deft maneuvers of former Agency directors William Colby and George Bush, who managed to curtail a Senate probe into the matter. Stonewalled at every turn and cowed by warnings that it was embarking on a latter-day "witch-hunt," the Senate Select Intelligence Committee chaired by Frank Church "deliberately buried" the results of its inquiry into the CIA-journalist connection, wrote Bernstein.

But we do know that top news executives gave their blessing to the rental of reporters as spies, informants, and propagandists. As former CIA director William Colby put it, "Let's not pick on some poor reporters. Let's go to the managements. They were witting." In their quest to combat "global communism," Bernstein wrote, "America's leading publishers allowed themselves and their news services to become handmaidens to the intelligence services."

The list of print and broadcast news executives who collaborated with the CIA was a rarefied one, including former *New York Times* publisher Arthur Hayes Sulzberger, Columbia Broadcasting System president William Paley, *Time* and *Life* magazine founder Henry Luce, and James Copley of Copley News Service (which happily turned over information on antiwar and black protesters, published CIA-produced editorials, and loaned at least twenty-three employees to the Agency). Other media mastodons who lent themselves to the CIA included ABC TV (a well-known, unnamed correspondent was said to be a CIA asset), NBC, the Associated Press, United Press International, Reuters, *Newsweek* magazine, Scripps-Howard, Hearst Newspapers, and the *Miami Herald*.

According to Bernstein's CIA and Senate sources, the two most important Agency assets, by virtue of their vast foreign reporting resources, were the *New York Times* and CBS. At the *Times*, the late Arthur Hayes Sulzberger approved cover arrangements for more than a half dozen CIA employees posing as *Times* staffers in foreign bureaus. Even though Sulzberger was close to then-Agency director Allen Dulles, he agreed to sign a secrecy agreement, as did his nephew, C. L. Sulzberger. According to several CIA sources, C.L. Sulzberger, the *Times*'s late foreign affairs columnist, once slapped his byline on a CIA briefing paper and published it verbatim. (Sulzberger called this charge "a lot of baloney.") The *Times* submitted stories to Dulles and later to his replacement, John McCone, for vetting and approval. More than once, McCone "edited" out certain bits of information from the stories, in effect deciding for the *Times* which news was "fit to print."

Like CBS's Paley and the elder Sulzberger, *Time* and *Life* magazine founder Henry Luce was a close chum of Dulles, who often enlisted the aid of his arch-conservative publishing pal. Luce allowed staff members to work for the CIA and offered jobs and credentials to CIA officers. He even appointed a personal representative to deal with the CIA, *Life* magazine publisher C. D. Jackson, who cut his teeth as the CIA's "special consultant to the president for psychological warfare." (Given Jackson's prominence as an American media czar, one has to ask, *psychological war against whom*? Conspiracy researchers certainly see *Life*'s glomming onto the Zapruder film footage of the JFK assassination as suspicious. Not only did Jackson's magazine buy up the rights to the film and keep it vaulted for years, it published frames from the famous home movie footage out of sequence, giving the incorrect impression that Kennedy's head snapped forward, as the Warren Commission wrongly concluded in its efforts to convince the public that a lone assassin fired from behind.)

Henry Luce's wife, Clare Boothe Luce, reportedly also knew of some of the CIA's undercover employees. A right-wing socialite who traveled in spooky circles, Madame Luce sponsored anti-Castro activities based in Florida and later became a founding director of an organization with the evocative title, Association of Former Intelligence Officers.

Although information swapping with intelligence operatives was once considered part of the give and take between reporters and their sources, some of the CIA-media alliances went well beyond the pale. Noted columnist Stewart Alsop, who wrote for the *New York Herald Tribune*, the *Saturday Evening Post*, and *Newsweek*, "was a CIA agent," according to a high-ranking Agency official quoted by Bernstein. Alsop helped plant disinformation in foreign media and evaluate potential CIA assets abroad. Alsop's brother, Joseph, pooh-poohed the charge, but one-upped his sibling by telling Bernstein that he, *himself*, was closer to the CIA than brother Stew.

The distinction between reporting and propagandizing for the CIA grew hazier still in the case of Hal Hendrix, one of the Agency's most valuable assets during the 1960s. As the *Miami*

News's Latin America correspondent, Hendrix was at ground zero in the Agency's covert action hotbed. According to Bernstein, Agency files contain lengthy reports of Hendrix's activities on behalf of the CIA. Though Hendrix has denied having anything but a "normal journalistic relationship" with the CIA, his coworkers referred to him as "The Spook."

Hendrix later ditched his reporting job and went to work for the International Telephone and Telegraph Corporation (ITT) in Chile. He perjured himself before a Senate committee probing CIA and ITT involvement in the covert campaign to thwart the election in 1970 of leftist leader Salvador Allende. Asked about the provenance of a cable he sent to inform an ITT vice president that the Nixon administration had approved plans "to keep Allende from taking power," Hendrix claimed the source of his information had been a Chilean friend. Whoops. A CIA cable subsequently turned up disclosing that Hendrix's real source was an Agency officer.

According to Bernstein, journalists were used extensively in the CIA's attempts to undermine Allende. Reporters disbursed funds to Allende's foes. They wrote anti-Allende propaganda for CIA-controlled publications. When some of this propaganda burrowed its way into the American media, it was hardly accidental. A 1970 CIA assessment spoke of "continued replay of Chile theme materials" in the American press, including the *New York Times* and *Washington Post*. "Propaganda activities," the report went on, "continue to generate good coverage of Chile developments along our theme guidance."

After the revelations of the late 1970s, how many journalists continued to shill for the CIA is anyone's guess. Although the *New York Times* reported that the CIA had terminated its relationship with journalists, in fact, the Agency under George Bush had only banned *paid*, full-time relationships, while Bush left the door open to pro-bono and part-time collaboration. In 1980, a *Los Angeles Times* headline announced CIA 'MIGHTY WURLITZER' IS NOW SILENT.

End of story? Maybe not. Even though the rationale for the

earlier media-CIA partnership—Cold War–era "national security"—is presumably dead and buried, a classified CIA report that surfaced in 1992 would suggest that the affair continues. The report on CIA "openness" stated that the Agency's public affairs office "now has relationships with reporters from every major wire service, newspaper, news weekly, and television network in the nation." Apparently these relationships have been fruitful for the CIA, because they have "helped us turn some 'intelligence failure' stories into 'intelligence success' stories...." In many cases, the report continued, "we have persuaded reporters to postpone, change, hold, or even scrap stories that could have adversely affected national security interests."

It sounds as if the Mighty Wurlitzer plays on.

MAJOR SOURCES

Bernstein, Carl. "The CIA and the Media." *Rolling Stone*, 20 October 1977.

Crewdson, John M., and Joseph B. Treaster. "CIA: Secret Shaper of Public Opinion." *New York Times*, 25–27 December 1977.

Lee, Martin A., and Norman Solomon. *Unreliable Sources: A Guide to Detecting Bias in News Media*. New York: Lyle Stuart, 1991.

10

Playing Those Mind Games

Make all the Dionne Warwick jokes you like. The U.S. government takes this psychic stuff seriously, and as late as June 1995 was lavishing your tax dollars—almost $21 million of them—on those nutty 900 numbers.

Well, not *literally* on 900-number psychic hot lines. But it's the same idea. According to a Reuter's report on November 30, 1995, "for at least twenty-three years...U.S. spy agencies funded people supposedly capable of 'remote viewing' to visualize hidden or distant objects without actually seeing them." The Skeptics Society must have had seizures.

The skeptics' unease was presumably allayed by the media's chuckling in reporting the story—which started in a Jack Anderson column on October 29. Anderson had first reported the existence of the program in 1984—it was run for a while out of the Stanford Research Institute. But when the rest of the media picked up the revelations after Anderson's 1995 follow-up, the approach was one of general amusement mingled with the usual pontificating about the government's predilection to toss money down the drain.

Ted Koppel featured the psychic spook research on the November 28, 1995 edition of *Nightline*. While one guest—a CIA technical adviser—revealed that some of the research yielded "eight martini" results (in other words, results so startling that it took the researchers eight martinis to regain their composure or, perhaps, to cast themselves into paroxysms of vomiting), in general Koppel and his guests scoffed at the research. Most panelists stuck to the official figure of a "15 percent" success rate in the psychic experiments. One assumes that ratio could be achieved by luck alone.

According to journalist Daniel Brandt, however, "not for the first time, there's more to this story than Ted Koppel acknowledges." Brandt cites the colorfully named Ingo Swann, who worked on the ESP project at Stanford and says that the government (the military and intelligence agencies) actually hit its target of not 15 but 65 percent success.

The point of the story is not to vouch for the reality of psychic powers—though if Swann's claim is correct, the secret scientists may have been on to something—but to show that the U.S. intelligence community is open to almost anything when it comes to the battlefield of the mind. The CIA's MK-ULTRA program, with its efforts to use LSD and other drugs to create the perfect mind-controlled agent, are well documented (see chapter 1). Did the effort end with the publicly funded trip-fest?

Oklahoma bombing suspect Timothy McVeigh was subject to much derision for supposedly claiming that he returned from his military service with a microchip implanted in his butt. But McVeigh was only the most-publicized self-proclaimed implant victim. Dozens of "support groups" exist for people claiming to be subjects of microchip mind control and for "wavies," those who believe that their thoughts are being tampered with via microwave transmissions from some mysterious source.

Hearing voices in one's head is, of course, a prominent symptom of certain kinds of mental illness. Aha! What better cover for covert mind-control experiments! It's certainly easy to ridicule the wavies and their ilk. It should, however, be noted that "respectable" researchers have dabbled in this area. Sometimes more than dabbled.

The most famous of those was Dr. Jose Delgado, inventor of the "stimoceiver" implant and author of the 1969 book (from mainstream publisher Harper & Row) *Physical Control of the Mind: Toward a Psychocivilized Society*. In this watershed work, Delgado—who once stopped a charging bull in its tracks in a daring demonstration of his wacky gadget—advocates using technology to keep the dangerous, antisocial impulses of the public-at-large under control. "The technology for nonsensory communication between brain and computers through the intact skin is already at our fingertips," he wrote. Delgado admitted, however, that with present knowledge "it is highly improbable that electrical correlates of thoughts or emotions could be picked up."

Of course, Delgado was writing almost three decades ago, and, as he noted then, "we are advancing rapidly in the pattern recognition of electrical correlates of behavior." The technology was not without its encumbrances, however.

"One of the limiting factors in these studies was the existence of wires leading from the brain to the stimoceiver outside of the scalp," wrote Delgado. "The wires represented possible portal of entry for infection and could be a hindrance to hair grooming."

It would hardly be worth creating a society of perfectly behaved citizens if they weren't well groomed. To solve this problem, Delgado developed "a small three-channel stimulator which can be placed subcutaneously...The instrument is solid state, has no batteries and can work indefinitely." In other words, a brain implant.

Psychosurgery and brain manipulation—whether by lobotomy, electroshock, or drugs—has long been an accepted way to control behavior. The stimoceiver is really just a high-tech twist on the old theme. The difference is, Delgado lobbied for its use as a means of social management, not merely individual therapy.

Has Dr. Delgado's wondrous creation and its descendants (if, in fact, any such devices exist) found an array of unwilling customers? Ed Light hosts a site on the Internet called "Mind Control Forum" in which he chronicles dozens of cases of people who claim to be victims of remote control. Light also claims to be a victim himself, which probably wouldn't do much for his credibility with Ted Koppel.

Others, however, are at least open-minded. Tom Porter, a software engineer who runs a Web site devoted to research into government mind-control experiments (and who does not claim victimization), says he has spoken to "several purported survivors of trauma-based mind-control who had significant, although not conclusive corroborating evidence," and that "I am inclined to give these people the benefit of the doubt."

Light's Internet site contains a section devoted to Brian Bard, who not only says that he has been the subject of implant mind-control experiments but also posts MRI scans of his head on the site. According to his own readings of these pictures, they show a couple of tiny devices in his skull, one shaped like a tuning fork.

To accept the stories of the self-proclaimed "victims" requires accepting not only an incredible level of ruthlessness on the part of the controllers but also perhaps more of a leap of faith, that the technology could actually work. As the closest thing to a smoking gun in that area, Light offers a 1961 article by Cornell University researcher Allen Frey titled "Human Auditory Response to Modulated Electromagnetic Energy" from the *Journal of Applied Psychology* (vol. 17, no. 4, pp. 689–692).

The thesis of this highly technical article was that "using extremely low average power densities of electromagnetic energy, the perception of sounds was induced in normal and deaf humans."

There is a long way between "the perception of sounds" and controllable, intrusive voices. Julianne McKinney of the Association of National Security Alumni (a group that opposes covert operations) wrote a controversial 1992 article in the Association journal *Unclassified*. In that piece, she said, "typically, persons who complain of being 'zapped by radio waves' and of 'hearing voices' are stigmatized as psychotic, delusional, or schizophrenic....Based on our preliminary investigation, including interviews with the affected individuals, we conclude that the matter is serious and should be pursued further."

The paper was entitled "Microwave Harassment and Mind-Control Experimentation," which pretty much summed it up. However, in a supplement to the piece, McKinney noted that one major objection to her thesis was that "no substantive proof has been furnished in this document which confirms that directed-energy technologies exist."

She goes on to note that "in these past ten months, directed-energy-based surveillance and anti-personnel systems suddenly leaped off of physicists' drawing boards into the world of reality, thus obviating the criticism...."

McKinney's "project" catalogs complaints from "experimentees," which skyrocketed, predictably, after she published her paper. The complaints came in from people saying that they were survivors of Satanic cults (supposedly connected to the military), "programmed assassins" from the Vietnam war, and UFO abductees, among others.

"It has been suggested that the long-term objective of all this experimentation," McKinney wrote, "is to develop a system by which all (surviving) citizens of this country can be monitored and tracked by a sophisticated, perhaps satellite-based cybernetics system."

In his booklet "The Controllers," circulated widely on the Internet, writer Martin Cannon argues that the UFO abductee phenomenon is a massive cover for a massive mind-control project. Through hypnosis, Cannon argues, mind-control guinea pigs are persuaded that their very-human captors and tormentors hail not from Washington but from Sirius. Or somewhere out there. Cannon points to a Delgado-style implant as the possible (heavy emphasis on "possible") means by which the UFO hallucinations are induced.

"Once an abductee has been implanted—and if we are to trust hypnotic regression accounts of abductees at all, the first implanting session may occur in childhood—the chip-in-the-brain would act as in intensifier of the signal. Such an individual could have any number of 'UFO' experiences while his or her bed partner dozes comfortably."

The UFO abduction scenario would indeed provide perfect cover, because not only would it hide the true source of the victim's trauma, it also discredits the victim's story.

As Cannon points out, when it comes to mind-control experiments, "victims elicit sympathy only insofar as they remain anonymous. Intellectually, we realize that MK-ULTRA and its allied projects must have affected hundreds, probably thousands of individuals. Yet we react with deep suspicion whenever one of these individuals steps forward and identifies himself, or whenever an independent investigator argues that mind control has directed some newsworthy person's otherwise inexplicable actions."

The situation is, as Cannon says, a catch-22. "If you say that you are a manufactured madman, you were probably mad to begin with." As crazy as all of these claims sound, however, it's worth keeping an open mind—so to speak.

"A mind is a terrible thing to waste," quips Cannon, "and a worse thing to commandeer."

MAJOR SOURCES

Brandt, Daniel. "Mind Control and the Secret State." NameBase Newsline. January–March 1996.

Cannon, Martin. "The Controllers: A New Hypothesis of Alien Abduction." Unpublished manuscript, 1990.

McKinney, Julianne. "Microwave Harassment and Mind-Control Experimentation." Silver Spring, MD: Association of National Security Alumni, 1992 (Supplement 1993).

Reuter News Service. "U.S. Fielded Psychics as Part of its Arsenal." November 30, 1995.

11

'Scuse the Pentagon While They Cook the Sky

In an Arctic compound 200 miles east of Anchorage, Alaska, the Pentagon has erected a powerful transmitter designed to beam more than a gigawatt of energy into the upper reaches of the atmosphere. Known as Project HAARP (High-frequency Active Auroral Research Program), the $30 million experiment involves the world's largest "ionospheric heater," a prototype device designed to zap the skies hundreds of miles above the earth with high-frequency radio waves. Why irradiate the charged particles of the ionosphere (which when energized by natural processes make up the lovely and famous phenomenon known as the Northern Lights)? According to the U.S. Navy and Air Force, co-sponsors of the project, "to observe the complex natural variations of Alaska's ionosphere." That, says the Pentagon, and also to develop new forms of communications and surveillance technologies that will enable the military to send signals to nuclear submarines and to peer deep underground.

Opponents of HAARP—a coalition of environmentalists, Native Americans, Alaskan citizens, and, of course, conspiracy trackers—believe that the military has even more Strangelovian plans for this unusual hardware, applications ranging from Star Wars missile-defense schemes to weather modification plots and perhaps even mind-control experiments.

The HAARP complex is situated within a 23-acre lot in a relatively isolated region near the town of Gakona. When the final phase of the project is completed in 1997, the military will have erected 180 towers, 72 feet in height, forming a "high-power, high-frequency phased array radio transmitter" capable of beaming in the 2.5-to-10-megahertz frequency range, at more than 3 gigawatts of power (3 billion watts). According to the navy and air force, HAARP "will be used to introduce a small, known amount of energy into a specific ionospheric layer" anywhere from several miles to several tens of miles in radius. Not surprisingly, navy and air force PR (posted on the official HAARP World Wide Web Internet site, an effort to combat the bad press the project has generated), downplays both the environmental impacts of the project and purported offensive uses of the technology.

However, a series of patents owned by the defense contractor managing the HAARP project suggests that the Pentagon might indeed have more ambitious designs. In fact, one of those patents was classified by the navy for several years during the 1980s. The key document in the bunch is U.S. patent number 4,686,605, considered by HAARP critics to be the "smoking raygun," so to speak. Held by ARCO Power Technologies, Inc. (APTI), the ARCO subsidiary contracted to build HAARP, this patent describes an ionospheric heater very similar to the HAARP heater. In the APTI patent—subsequently published on the Internet by foes of HAARP—Texas physicist Bernard J. Eastlund describes a fantastic offensive and defensive weapon that would do any megalomaniacal James Bond supervillain proud. According to the patent, Eastlund's invention would heat plumes of charged particles in the ionosphere, making it possible to, for starters, selectively "disrupt microwave transmissions of satellites" and "cause interference with or even total disruption of communications over a large portion of the earth." But like his hopped-up ions, Eastlund was just warming up. Per the patent text, the physicist's "method and apparatus for altering a region in the earth's atmosphere" would also:

- "cause confusion of or interference with or even complete disruption of guidance systems employed by even the most sophisticated of airplanes and missiles";
- "not only...interfere with third-party communications, but [also] take advantage of one or more such beams to carry out a communications network at the same time. Put another way, what is used to disrupt another's communications can be employed by one knowledgeable of this invention as a communications network at the same time";
- "pick up communication signals of others for intelligence purposes";
- facilitate "missile or aircraft destruction, deflection, or confusion" by lifting large regions of the atmosphere "to an unexpectedly high altitude so that missiles encounter unexpected and unplanned drag forces with resultant destruction or deflection of same."

If Eastlund's brainchild sounds like a recipe for that onetime cold war panacea, the Strategic Defense Initiative (AKA Star Wars), it's probably no coincidence. The APTI/Eastlund patent was filed during the final days of the Reagan administration, when plans for high-tech missile defense systems were still all the rage. But Eastlund's blue-sky vision went far beyond the usual Star Wars prescriptions of the day and suggested even more unusual uses for his patented ionospheric heater.

"Weather modification," the patent states, "is possible by...altering upper atmospheric wind patterns or altering solar absorption patterns by constructing one or more plumes of particles which will act as a lens or focusing device." As a result, an artificially heated ionosphere could focus a "vast amount of sunlight on selected portions of the earth."

HAARP officials deny any link to Eastlund's patents or plans. But several key details suggest otherwise. For starters, APTI, holder of the Eastlund patents, continues to manage the HAARP project. During the summer of 1994, ARCO sold APTI to E-Systems, a defense contractor known for counter-surveillance projects. E-Systems, in turn, is currently owned by Raytheon, one of the world's largest defense contractors and maker of the SCUD-busting Patriot missile. All of which suggests that more than just simple atmospheric science is going on in the HAARP compound.

What's more, one of the APTI/Eastlund patents singles out Alaska as the ideal site for a high-frequency ionospheric heater because "magnetic field lines...which extend to desirable altitudes for this invention, intersect the earth in Alaska." APTI also rates Alaska as an ideal location given its close proximity to an ample source of fuel to power the project: the vast reserves of natural gas in the North Slope region—reserves owned by APTI parent company ARCO.

Eastlund also contradicts the official military line. He told National Public Radio that a secret military project to develop his work was launched during the late 1980s. And in the May/June 1994 issue of Microwave News, Eastlund suggested that "The HAARP project obviously looks a lot like the first step" toward the designs outlined in his patents.

Is HAARP capable of anything on Eastlund's wish list? The military says no, pointing out that the power levels used in the Alaskan transmitter are too low to achieve Eastlund's goals. That may well be true—Eastlund's designs call for more powerful bursts of high-frequency radio waves than the HAARP prototype will be able to muster. However, the project's own environmental impact reports warn that the HAARP transmissions could pose a danger to airplanes up to four miles away. And according to Gar Smith, editor of the environmental magazine, *Earth Watch Journal*, the energy that drives HAARP could be a thousand times more powerful than the military's most powerful PAVE PAWS over-the-horizon radars, which emit "incidental" sidelobe radiation that can disrupt cardiac pacemakers up to seven miles away and cause the "inadvertent detonation" of bombs and flares in passing aircraft. The official HAARP "fact sheet" reassures jittery paranoiacs that the effects of ionospheric heating will always dissipate in a matter of minutes. Yet good soldier Eastlund boasts in his patent that the radiation "can also be prolonged for substantial time periods so that it would not be a mere transient effect that could be waited out by an opposing force.

"Thus," he continues, "this invention provides the ability to put unprecedented amounts of power in the earth's atmosphere at strategic locations and to maintain the power injection level...in a manner more precise and better controlled than heretofore accomplished by the prior art...the detonation of nuclear devices of various yields at various altitudes."

Eastlund's patent really trips into conspiratorial territory in its References Cited section. Two of the sources documented by Eastlund are *New York Times* articles from 1915 and 1940 profiling none other than Nikola Tesla, a giant in the annals of conspiratorial history. Tesla, a brilliant inventor and contemporary of Edison, developed hundreds of patents during his lifetime and is often credited with inventing radio before Marconi, among a host of other firsts. Of course, mainstream science has never fully acknowledged Tesla's contributions, and his later pronouncements (he vowed that he had developed a technology that could split the earth asunder) have left him straddling that familiar historical territory where genius meets crackpot. Not surprisingly, fringe science and conspiracy theory have made Tesla something of a patron saint. Whenever talk radio buzz or Internet discussion turns to alleged government experiments to cause earthquakes or modify weather, references to government-suppressed "Tesla Technology" are sure to follow.

Judging from the APTI patent, Tesla was a major inspiration for the Eastlund ionospheric heater. The first *New York Times* article, dated September 22, 1940, reports that Tesla, then eighty-four years old, "stands ready to divulge to the United States Government the secret of his 'teleforce,' with which, he said, airplane motors would be melted at a distance of 250 miles, so that an invisible Chinese Wall of Defense would be built around the country." Quoting Tesla, the *Times* story continues: " 'This new type of force,' " Mr. Tesla said, would operate through a beam one hundred-millionth of a square centimeter in diameter, and could be generated from a special plant that would cost no more than $2,000,000 and would take only about three months to construct.' " The second *New York Times* story, dated December 8, 1915, describes one of Tesla's more well-known patents, a transmitter that would "project electrical energy in any amount to any distance and apply it for innumerable purposes, both in war and peace." The similarity of Tesla's ideas to Eastlund's invention are remarkable, and by extension the overlap between Tesla and HAARP technology is downright intriguing.

Apparently, APTI and the Pentagon are taking Eastlund's— and by extension, Tesla's—ideas seriously. As authors Nicholas J. Begich and Jeane Manning point out in the 1996 book, *Angels Don't Play This HAARP*, another of the Eastlund/APTI patents outlines a technology for transmitting electrical energy à la Tesla's war-and-peace project.

On the conspiracy circuit, any nexus between Tesla and Tesla-like military plans is likely to be as explosive as a warhead passing through one of Eastlund's ion plumes. From here the speculation about HAARP tends to rocket into somewhat thinner air. In *Angels Don't Play This HAARP*, which is subtitled, "Advances in Tesla Technology," authors Begich and Manning suggest that in addition to modifying the weather, the military's Tesla-HAARP technology might be used as a form of mass mind-control.

"The impact of RF [radio-frequency transmissions] on human physiology," they write, "is well known to the air force and has been described in publications dating back to 1986." If Begich and Manning don't conclusively prove a connection between HAARP and government schemes to "disrupt mental processes" via pulsed radio-frequency transmissions, they do dig up a motherlode of elitist pontification by cold warriors obsessed with controlling the American hoi polloi. Zbigniew Brzezinski—former National Security Advisor to President Carter—puffed in 1970 that a "more controlled and directed society" would evolve, one in which the "elite would not hesitate to achieve its political ends by using the latest modern techniques for influencing public behavior and keeping society under close surveillance and control." Infuriating and outrageous, yes. But it doesn't actually prove anything about the goals of HAARP.

Even more interesting, but still not the smoking gun that some HAARP critics believe it to be, are the forecasts of geophysicist Gordon J. F. McDonald, a vintage cold war strategist who comes off sounding like Dr. Strangelove on speed. Begich and Manning quote a McDonald précis calling for electronic pulses aimed at broad geographic regions. "In this way," McDonald explains, "one could develop a system that would seriously impair the brain performance of a very large populations in selected regions over an extended period.... No matter how deeply disturbing the thought of using the environment to manipulate behavior for national advantages, to some, the technology permitting such use will very probably develop within the next few decades." (Never a lover of subtlety, McDonald titled a chapter on weather modification in one of his books, "How to Wreck the Environment.") Clearly, mind control has been the holy grail of anal-retentive national security obsessors since the days of the CIA's MK-ULTRA program. And it certainly wouldn't be surprising to find the Pentagon toying with that notion in Alaska, although the evidence for it hasn't surfaced (yet).

On the farthest fringes of speculation, HAARP has attained

that ultimate status of conspiracy theory template, onto which any ideology, philosophy, or pathology can attach its own interpretation and customized "facts." It comes as no shock to find UFOs circling these outer limits of HAARPology: the HAARP frequencies are the same radio frequencies associated with UFO appearances and abductions, say some theorists, suggesting either than alien UFOs use a similar technology or that UFOs are a government hoax implemented with HAARP-like hardware, or both). Beyond UFOs, other theorists claim that HAARP is a "death ray" with northern exposure, is responsible for various recent earthquakes and power outages in the Western United States, is a plot to implement a "genetic reprogramming" of the human race, or ultimately represents a battle between earthly villains and New Age "ascended masters" from dimensions beyond.

Back on earth, the fact remains that HAARP certainly isn't the simple science fair project described by its Pentagon handlers. To quote HAARP's godfather, Bernard Eastlund, "HAARP is the perfect first step toward a plan like mine.... The government will say it isn't so, but if it quacks like a duck and it looks like a duck, there's a good chance it is a duck."

MAJOR SOURCES

Begich, Nicholas J., and Jeane Manning. *Angels Don't Play This HAARP: Advances in Tesla Technology*. Anchorage, Alaska: Earth Pulse Press, 1996.

"HAARP Fact Sheet." Published by U.S. Department of the Navy, on the Internet.

United States Patent Number 4,686,605. Inventor: Bernard J. Eastlund. Assignee: APTI, Inc. August 11, 1987. (Republished on the Internet.)

Zickuhr, and Gar Smith. "Project HAARP: The Military's Plan to Alter the Ionosphere." Earth Island Journal, Fall 1994.

12

Big Lies

"Every government is run by liars, and nothing they say should be believed," remarked journalist-gadfly I. F. Stone at the height of the Cold War. While some might quibble with the sweep of the statement, during the last half century national-security obsessions indeed often put the truth into cryonic suspension.

When the Reagan administration got caught scaremongering lies about Libya, Secretary of State George Shultz felt obliged to quote Winston L. S. Churchill: "In time of war," he said, "the truth is so precious it must be attended by a bodyguard of lies." Of course, the United States wasn't *actually* at war with Libya, but it was, Shultz helpfully offered, "pretty darn close." In fact, Shultz had his sequence of events a bit confused. It was the bodyguard of lies that actually helped get us "pretty darn close" to war in the first place—not exactly what Churchill had in mind.

It's no secret that all governments sow scurrilous disinformation about their foes. Soviet commissars convinced their subjects that all of America was a war zone of rampaging, psychopathic criminals. During the 1980s, Soviet propagandists latched on to the theory that AIDS was a biological weapon perfected in U.S. military labs (see chapter 53) and persuaded much of the third world that such was the case.

Soviet disinformationists also spread the rumor in Latin America that minions of the United States were abducting children in an evil scheme to steal human organs. This black pearl of calumny is still reverberating: In the past several years, several unfortunate (and innocent) American tourists visiting Guatemala have been killed or seriously injured by mobs of angry locals convinced that they were meting out justice to evil child abductors.

An oft-used CIA technique for "disinforming" Americans without breaking the letter of the law involved planting unattributed, or "black," propaganda in the foreign press in hopes that the American media would pick up the bogus story. According to a 1977 *New York Times* report, former CIA officers "spoke of unmistakable attempts to propagandize the American public indirectly through 'replay' from the foreign press," particularly during the Vietnam War. A 1970 CIA assessment spoke of "continued replay of Chile theme materials" in the American press, including the *New York Times* and *Washington Post*. "Propaganda activities," the report went on, "continue to generate good coverage of Chile developments along our theme guidance."

John Stockwell, head of the CIA's Angola Task Force during the 1970s, has described planting a phony story in the African press about Cuban soldiers raping Angolan women. Days later, the story made headlines in the American press, as expected.

In wartime (or pretty darn close to it) that celebrated bodyguard of lies has often been mustered, usually to stir up popular support for military adventures. President Johnson used the infamous Gulf of Tonkin incident, in which American destroyers were supposedly attacked off the coast of North Vietnam but really weren't, as a pretext to escalate the war. In the months leading up to Operation Desert Storm, the Bush administration endorsed, but didn't concoct, the lie that Iraqi soldiers ripped babies from incubators in a Kuwaiti hospital. Later, the Pentagon's claims about the celebrated Patriot missile were exposed as being, shall we say, somewhat phantasmal. In fact, according to several independent analysts, the defense missile missed most of its targets—incoming Iraqi Scud missiles—and exacted a not inconsiderable amount of damage on the cities they were supposed to be defending.

West European intelligence officers were convinced that the Soviets were also adept at transforming the worldwide popularity of UFO speculation into their own crafty intelligence tool. The UMMO UFO cult of Spain—its adherents are convinced that they are in contact with extraterrestrial aliens from a cosmic government called UMMO—may have begun as a mischievous hoax. However, according to UFO researcher Jacques Vallee, the French government came to suspect that the Soviet Union had infiltrated the cult for obscure purposes that might have involved manipulation of religious belief systems. Vallee points out that many of the pseudoscientific "revelations" channeled to earthlings from the UMMO entitites contained "very advanced" theories about cosmology. "Very advanced cosmology about twin universes," Vallee explains, "involving some data that had to have come straight out of the unpublished notes of Andre Sakharov." Only the KGB would have had access to those notes, French intelligence officials decided.

But why would the Soviets go to the trouble to manipulate an obscure New Age cult? Per Vallee, there are at least a couple of reasons: Cults are an ideal way to incubate ideas—and irrational belief systems—that might later prove destabilizing to enemy governments. Moreover, a cult might provide cover for foreign spies doing technical assessment; after all, the UMMO "channelings" were distributed to noted Western scientists, who were encouraged to correspond with UMMOs representatives on earth.

When it comes to the black art of espionage, we've come to expect the most devious means and the worst intentions. But there's something especially rankling when the U.S. government purposely deceives the American public.

Not surprisingly, the CIA, ever on the sociotechnological cutting edge, pioneered propaganda as a form of "mind control" to help mold public opinion during the heyday of the cold war. Once-secret CIA documents from the early 1950s describe "broad" mind-control operations both overseas and domestically (in violation of the Agency's charter) and high-level meetings convened to discuss "the broader aspects of psychology as it pertains to the control of groups or masses...." Drawing on the lingo of Madison Avenue, agency officials pondered "means for combating communism and 'selling' democracy."

Consumers of this psychological bill of goods were often American citizens. Ironically, part of the propaganda operation was an effort to convince the public that it was the Soviets (and certainly not the CIA) who had unilaterally launched a "sinister...battle for men's minds" involving "brain perversion techniques...so subtle and so abhorrent to our way of life that we have recoiled from facing up to them," as agency director Allen Dulles intoned in a foreboding speech. Edward Hunter, a CIA propagandist turned "journalist," coined the lurid term "brainwashing," and the official government line charged the Chinese and Soviets with bleaching the patriotic brain cells of American soldiers, transforming them into robotic "Manchurian Candidates."

In reality, though, then-secret CIA memos maintained that there was "no indication of Red use of chemicals" and that the Soviets had no interest in controlling minds via "narcotics, hypnosis, or special mechanical devices." The CIA, on the other hand, did take great interest in brainwashing foreigners and Americans through its notorious MK-ULTRA program launched three days after Dulles's scarifying speech. As authors Martin Lee and Norman Solomon wrote in their book *Unreliable Sources*, "It appears that the communist brainwashing scare was a propaganda ploy, a kind of 'brainwashing' or mind control in its own right designed to dupe the American people."

But when it comes to disinformation in a wide-screen, Cinemascope format, the former thespian Ronald Reagan deserves top billing. Assisted by a gullible press corps, the Reagan administration fobbed off sundry falsehoods on an unsuspecting public.

Early in the Reagan epoch, the State Department reawakened cold-war angst when it released a white paper purporting to have exposed a global Communist conspiracy to arm El Salvador's leftist rebels. The Commie brouhaha was later debunked as a hoax.

Soon after the El Salvador scare, Secretary of State Alexander Haig warned the world that the Soviets were spraying innocents in Laos, Cambodia, and Afghanistan with a deadly chemical weapon. The poison, dubbed "Yellow Rain," supposedly fell from the sky with devastating results. The hideous weapon turned out to be the natural drizzle of bee feces. State Department documents eventually emerged indicating that U.S. cold warriors pushed the false story despite warnings by various government analysts that there was no evidence to back it up.

Then there was the aforementioned disinformation campaign against Libyan leader Mu'ammar al-Qaddafi, who was fingered as the hub of an international terrorist network, the mastermind behind a plot to assassinate Reagan. The goofiest result of this campaign of canards was a *New York Post* headline that read: "MADMAN MOAMAR NOW A DRUGGIE DRAG QUEEN"! Alas, it was too good to be true. A memo from Iran-Contra fall-guy John Poindexter to Reagan later surfaced, describing a disinformation program to destabilize the Libyan government.

The Reagan administration took its propaganda efforts seriously enough to establish a de facto bureau of domestic disinformation, dubbed euphemistically the Office of Public Diplomacy (OPD). Described by a high-ranking U.S. official as a "vast psychological warfare operation" aimed at the American public, the OPD was run by a CIA propagandist whom Director William Casey had transferred to the National Security Council in an effort to sidestep the ban on CIA meddling in domestic affairs. The OPD enlisted army psywar experts in the campaign to win American hearts and minds over to Reagan's foreign policy.

The OPD focused on Reagan's Nicaragua obsession, especially "gluing black hats" on the leftist Sandinista government and "white hats" on the Contras, as a 1986 memo put it. In addition to producing slick flyers and lobbying Congress, the OPD slipped "scoops" to credulous reporters, including the canard that the Soviets planned to ship MIG fighter planes to Nicaragua.

In 1987 a General Accounting Office probe of the OPD concluded that the Reaganites had operated "prohibited, covert propaganda activities" at the expense of the American public. Jack Brooks, the congressman from Texas, called the OPD's work an "illegal operation" intended "to manipulate public opinion and congressional action." The OPD officially shut down soon after the Iran-Contra scandal began to make headlines.

And last, but hardly least, are more recent revelations that during the Reagan era the Pentagon doctored the results of "Star Wars" weapons testing. When criticized for concealing the less-than-stellar performance of the high-tech, multibillion-dollar boondoggle, military brass invoked that old Cold War rationale: We couldn't afford to let the Russkies know we had a space-age lemon on our hands. Of course, fooling the Soviets necessarily meant pulling the wool over Congress and the American public, too. Which certainly didn't hurt when it came time to ask for more astronomical funding.

MAJOR SOURCES

Crewdson, John M., and Joseph B. Treaster. "CIA: Secret Shaper of Public Opinion." *New York Times*, 25–27 December 1977.
Lee, Martin A, and Norman Solomon. *Unreliable Sources: A Guide to Detecting Bias in News Media*. New York: Lyle Stuart, 1991.
Vallee, Jacques. *Messengers of Deception: UFO Contacts and Cults*. Berkeley, CA: And/Or Press, 1979.

II

From Beyond

13

Classified Secrets of the Sky

What crashed in Roswell, New Mexico?

Something large and silvery wobbled through the air and plowed into the desert dirt with a tremendous ka-boom. That much, generally speaking, goes without dispute. The date was July 2, 1947.

It is also a fact-on-record that the government took an immediate interest in...well, whatever it was. The air force dispatched a team to scoop up the wreckage—one metallic chunk was about four feet long—and flew some back to Wright-Patterson Air Force Base in Dayton, Ohio, for scrutiny. General Roger Ramey, the officer in charge, ordered his men not to talk to the press. But before Ramey could clamp a lid on the affair, the base's public information officer issued a press release announcing government acquisition of a "flying disc." An Albuquerque radio station picked up a leak of the story. As it broadcast a report, a wire came through from the FBI.

"Attention Albuquerque: cease transmission. Repeat. Cease transmission. National security item. Do not transmit. Stand by..."

A day later, the air force held a press conference and announced that what crashed at Roswell was a balloon.

The UFO saga actually began a few days earlier when businessman and avocational aviator Kenneth Arnold chased a squadron of nine "bobbing and weaving" objects as he flew in his private plane. He described the objects as "saucer shaped." Some pithy wag at an AP bureau dropped the phrase "flying saucers" into a wire dispatch and, forever, into the English language. The air force said that Arnold had pursued "a mirage."

There have been innumerable UFO reports since 1947. Some have been captured on film, still and moving (the UFOs and the film). They pop up all over the world, even in outer space. NASA astronauts have reported seeing weird objects, and UFO scribe Sean Morton, coauthor of *The Millennium Factor*, says that NASA photos of the so-called "dark side" of the moon remain, for some reason, classified.

The myth that UFOs only reveal themselves to corn huskers and residents of trailer parks is easily dispelled. A quick scan of UFO history books shows the air corps of one nation or another pursuing unidentifiable "blips" on a regular basis.

On November 23, 1953, an F-89 interceptor was chasing a UFO over Lake Superior when, according to radar operators, the two blips on the screen seemed to merge into one which then blinked off the screen. The jet and its pilot, Lieutenant Felix Moncla, were gone without a trace. For some reason, the air force file on the vanishing contains just two pages. One of them is a page from a book debunking UFO theories.

Nevertheless, Roswell (which among the UFO-intrigued has achieved one-word status) remains the most important landmark in the UFO coverup because, apparently, it has actually been covered up. There is no mention of the crash in the air force's Project Blue Book files. Blue Book recorded all UFO reports that crossed an air force desk along with their various "scientific" explanations. Generally considered the Warren Report of the UFO phenomenon—a coverup posing as an investigation—Blue Book gives Roswell increased prominence by its omission.

Some might write the whole incident off as unlikely, noting that a spacecraft capable of navigating the firmament and engineered to endure the rigors of interstellar travel is unlikely to crash like so many Cessnas. But then there is Majestic 12 (MJ-12). Among many UFOlogists, there is strong belief in the existence of MJ-12.

A committee of twelve eminent military, intelligence, and academic personages, the group was allegedly chartered to manage and conceal the most important event in world history—contact with aliens. Albeit dead ones.

According to the MJ-12 "eyes only" briefing paper prepared for Dwight Eisenhower when he was still president-elect, four "Extraterrestrial biological entities," or EBEs, turned up two miles from the crash site. According to some accounts, two of the aliens were still alive at the time and one put up a struggle. The EBE carcasses are now allegedly kept on ice in Los Alamos, New Mexico.

The problem with the Majestic 12 document—the only hard evidence that MJ-12 ever took a meeting—is that it may well be a hoax. No one in a position to do so has ever authenticated it.

There is only one mention of MJ-12 in any other official paper, a November 1980 air force analysis of a UFO film that outlines in minute detail how the government is "still interested" in UFO sightings, which it investigates through "covert cover."

That document, like the original MJ-12 paper, somehow seems too good to be true—the smoking gun that every good conspiracy theory needs and lacks. It would be as if some researcher combing through CIA JFK files suddenly produced a memo reading, "Assassination of president scheduled for 11/22/63, Dallas. After consultation with FBI, director recom-

mends triangulation of crossfire be utilized." It would kind of
make you wonder.

Real or not, MJ-12 has spawned no shortage of legends and
speculation, primarily that it still exists and is still administering the UFO coverup, coping with each alien abduction and
saucer crash as it comes up. "Suicided" journalist Danny
Casolaro included MJ-12 as a tentacle in his postulated secret
government "Octopus." (See chapter 24.) In some versions of
the tale, MJ-12 is in charge of cooperation and negotiation with
the alien race among us.

Or should that be "races"? John Lear, a self-described former
intelligence agent who is now one of the leading voices on the
UFO circuit, charges that the government is aware of a veritable
Rainbow Coalition of EBEs.

These range from three types of insecto-humanoid Grays,
skinny and eggheaded enemies of all mankind, to the friendly
Blonds, who look more like humans but who, despite their
general good nature refuse to break the Star Trekkish "universal
law of noninterference" to save us from the evil Grays. Also on
the roster are the Hairy Dwarves (self-explanatory), the Very
Tall Race (also self-explanatory), and the mysterious Men in
Black.

The existence of the Robertson Panel, unlike that of MJ-12, is
not dubious. Convened by the Central Intelligence Agency in
January 1953, this board of scientists issued a report that was
not fully declassified until 1975.

Chaired by one Dr. H. P. Robertson, the panel met secretly in
the Pentagon for five days. They looked at the UFO cases that
appeared to be the most credible—and dismissed every single
one of them.

Merely denying the existence of unexplainable or extraterrestrial UFOs, as the Roberston panel did, hardly constitutes a
coverup, except under the most circular logic. The panel,
however, moved considerably beyond debunking. It recommended that the government take pains to squelch UFO reports,

to the point of promulgating an anti-UFO "education" campaign.

"This education could be accomplished by mass media such as television, motion pictures, popular articles," the CIA panel's report said. It went on to suggest using "psychologists familiar with mass psychology" to help assemble the program and even wondered if Walt Disney Studios might be interested in producing anti-UFO cartoons.

The report went on to recommend that UFO enthusiast groups should be placed under surveillance due to "the possible use of such groups for subversive purposes."

None of the Robertson Panel's rather conspiratorial musings prove that the government really has something to hide; deep-frozen aliens, for example. On the other hand, they do give a depressing clue as to how institutions respond to ideas that they deem, in the words of the panel report, "a threat to the orderly functioning of the protective organs of the body politic."

MAJOR SOURCES

Andrews, George C. *Extra-Terrestrial Friends and Foes*. Lilburn, GA: IllumiNet Press, 1993.

Good, Timothy. *Above Top Secret: The Worldwide UFO Cover-up*. New York: Quill William Morrow, 1988.

Good, Timothy. *Alien Contact: Top Secret UFO Files Revealed*. New York: William Morrow, 1993.

Randle, Capt. Kevin D. *The UFO Casebook*. New York: Warner Books, 1989.

14

Apolloscam

On July 20, 1969, Neil Armstrong planted his left foot in the lunar dust and became the first human to walk on the moon. Unfortunately, that stellar moment in history may have been marred by one not-insignificant detail: If inquiring author Bill Kaysing has it right, Armstrong made his giant leap for mankind not 240,000 miles above Earth in the barren Sea of Tranquillity, but a mere 90 miles north of lusty Las Vegas on a top-secret movie soundstage. Yes, as Kaysing tells it, the nation was gulled into believing that Armstrong and Edwin E. "Buzz" Aldrin, Jr., were gamboling through a bona fide lunar landscape, when in fact the two "actors" were hamming it up in a sinister government production that qualifies as the greatest hoax of all time.

Sheer lunacy, you say? Not according to the millions of skeptics who watched the spectacle of men walking on the moon in disbelief. And not according to Kaysing, who outlined his highly evolved theory in a self-published exposé, *We Never Went to the Moon*. A former technical writer for Rockwell International (which contributed to the alleged "moon missions"),

Kaysing claims no direct knowledge of NASA's shenanigans. Rather, his certainty derives from the epistemological alignment of a "hunch," photographic "proof," and a gnawing feeling that "the government is a specialist in hoaxing the public."

If his thesis is, well, somewhat weightless in the hard evidence department, Kaysing more than compensates with copious enthusiasm. "America's 30 Billion Dollar Swindle!" he declares, played itself out over the course of five more sham moon landings and involved "well-faked photographs," phony moon rocks, and "programmed astronauts"—not to mention "the help of father-figure [Walter] Cronkite as the journalistic goat."

First and foremost, Kaysing has questions—questions that NASA and the former astronauts evade like a grifter dodges the "heat":

- In photographs of the lunar sky, why are no stars visible, and why are the astronauts "extremely evasive regarding stars"? With no blocking atmosphere, the celestial tableau would have been "the most magnificent available to mortal man," Kaysing writes. The answer, he posits, is that NASA's set decorators knew they couldn't dupe professional astronomers with an ersatz starry backdrop.
- If the moon's surface was powdery enough for deep footprints, why didn't the lunar lander's rocket thruster dig a gaping crater? And why in photographs is there no moon dust on the lander's legs?
- If the moon was proven to be "sterile" after the first Apollo mission, why were astronauts in later missions held in quarantine so long? Kaysing submits that they needed quality time in an airstream trailer to "1) eliminate guilt feelings; 2) study and memorize moon data; and 3) practice responding to questions."
- "Why did so many astronauts end up as executives in very large corporations?"

Kaysing provides answers to most of the questions, including the most obvious—why would NASA go to the trouble of faking the Apollo moon shots? It seems the space agency launched its elaborate ruse when, after years of technological screwups and bureaucratic snafus, NASA realized it would never put a man on the moon by the close of the 1960s.

To avoid international embarrassment, NASA and the military's stealth apparatus, the Defense Intelligence Agency (DIA), established a top-secret operation that Kaysing calls the Apollo Simulation Project (ASP). For their secret base of operations, the cold-blooded ASP team chose a site in Nevada adjacent to land used by the Atomic Energy Commission in nuclear bomb testing—the perfect deterrent to the overly curious. Of course, ASP's secret base also had the advantage of being less than an hour's drive from "a twenty-four-hour-a-day, seven-days-a-week, anything-goes resort boasting more than thirty large casinos." According to Kaysing, who presents his case in semiomniscient fashion, ASP quite naturally hooked up with the Vegas "Cosa Nostra," which patriotically provided the space program with expert "services," apparently in the lethal splashdown department, so to speak.

In its desert redoubt, ASP excavated an underground cavern and installed "a complete set of the moon." (Some word-of-mouth versions of the moonscam theory place the phony set in Arizona or New Mexico.) In fact—and in the absence of traditional journalistic sourcing, we must take Kaysing at his word on most "facts"—none other than film director Stanley Kubrick assisted in the plot, generously using his *2001: A Space Odyssey* to develop the Hollywood special effects required to foist the NASA hoax on an unsuspecting public. (It makes you wonder what *The Shining* was all about.)

According to Kaysing, ASP's modus operandi went something like this:

- An *empty* Saturn V rocket lifts off in Florida—in full public view, thereby lending the Apollo con a patina of authenticity. However, once out sight, the ghost rocket ditches into the South Polar Sea.

- The "astronauts" are jetted to ASP's Nevada complex where they enjoy "every conceivable luxury, including a few of the shapeliest showgirls from Las Vegas, cleared for secret, of course." When Armstrong and his fellow playboy thespians aren't earning membership in the 240,000 Mile High Club, so to speak, they "are free to wander about and play the slots" and "sample the twenty-four-hour buffet from the Dunes" hotel. (In this moral vacuum, the well-informed Kaysing reports, one of the astronauts may have "socked an ASP official in a dispute over a showgirl named Peachy Keen.")
- When the curtain finally rises, the special-effects team, TV cameramen, and "ASP moon walk director" create a near-seamless piece of performance art, as Armstrong recites his scripted "one-small-step" line. Every aspect of the phony video feed is "meticulously" choreographed, down to the "boo-boos," jokes, "and seeming improvisations of the astronauts." Meanwhile, NASA cooks up counterfeit "moon rocks," the purported hard evidence of the journey, in a high-tech ceramics kiln.
- In time for their triumphal return to Earth, the astronauts are coaxed away from the Vegas vixens and whisked to a hidden air base south of the Hawaiian Islands (the "Tauramoto Archipelago," Kaysing obligingly specifies). There they are sealed inside a dummy space capsule and dropped from a C5-A transport plane into the roiling seas.

If the plot sounds a lot like the 1979 film *Capricorn One*, which dramatized a similar cabal involving a bogus mission to Mars, it is because, according to Kaysing, Hollywood borrowed the idea from the first edition of his book.

Like the O. J. Simpson-Telly Savalas film (or any conspiracy hypothesis worth its salt), Kaysing's theory has its martyrs, a whole cemetery full. There's Tom Baron, the aerospace technician who complained to Congress about dangerous corner-cutting in the Apollo program—and died in a train accident "just *four days* after he testified." There are also the three astronauts—including Gus "the Right Stuff" Grissom—who died on the launchpad in a 1967 "mishap" when fire swept through their capsule. Grissom had groused publicly about Apollo's safety troubles, leading Kaysing to postulate that perhaps the DIA arranged a little "accident" to silence the whistle-blower and impress other loud-mouth fly-boys.

And, as in many a postulated conspiracy, this one involves brainwashing. Kaysing suggests that the astronauts might have been subjected to state-of-the-art mind-control techniques and turned into "Manchurian Candidates," thus ensuring their obedient participation in the hoax. This, he postulates, might explain their subsequent reclusiveness and, in some cases, "severe mental problems."

What are they trying to hide, anyway? Kaysing wonders. Neil Armstrong "will not speak on the phone to me," our author complains in his book. Buzz Aldrin apparently won't appear on talk shows alongside Apollo's intractable critic. Despite their seeming aloofness, however, the space jockeys may in fact be *very* interested in the California researcher's doings: Kaysing intimates darkly that agents of Armstrong keep close tabs on his ongoing quest to defrock Apolloscam.

Alas, NASA's secrets remain as impenetrable as any Vegas vault. Barring unforeseen revelations, hectoring ex-astronauts may be the only way for Kaysing to get to the bottom of the conundrum. Like David flinging tiny Earth rocks at a space-suited Goliath, the intrepid investigator has issued a standing challenge: "I am willing," Kaysing pledges, "to debate any or all of the astronauts at any time on live TV or in person anywhere."

So far the Manchurian Spacemen have declined to take that one small step.

MAJOR SOURCE

Kaysing, Bill. *We Never Went to the Moon: America's Thirty Billion Dollar Swindle!* Soquel, CA: Holy Terra Books, 1991.

15

Saucer Blitz!

Sure, they lost World War II, but never underestimate the stick-to-itiveness of the Nazis. Second to none in sinister invention, the Third Reich's mad scientists were capable of attempting practically anything—so long as the project was ethically dubious or ambitiously screwy, on a Wagnerian scale. No wonder, then, that when it comes to the origin of flying saucers, some consider the Nazis at least as suspect as space-warping ETs.

There is at least a theoretical cornerstone for such speculation. During the war, Hitler's Dr. Strangeloves apparently dabbled with designs for flying disks. Whether they were successful isn't quite so indisputable, but in late 1944, Reuters news agency reported that the Germans had a "secret" air defense weapon that resembled "the glass balls that adorn Christmas trees. They have been seen hanging in the air over German territory, sometimes singly, sometimes in clusters. They are colored silver and are apparently transparent."

Allied pilots reported numerous sightings of these so-called Foo Fighters (from the French *feu*, for fire), which they encountered throughout Europe and even in Japan and Turkey. According to pilots' reports, the mysterious objects had the disquieting habit of pursuing squadrons, occasionally outrunning the speediest conventional aircraft. Allied intelligence agencies scrambled to get the goods on a possible Nazi secret weapon, thought to be something along the lines of "high altitude, high-velocity balloons." After the war, investigators sifted through German records, but ultimately ruled out the possibility of Jerry-built flying disks, fire balls, or swift, maneuverable balloons. In short order, the strange, unexplained phenomenon was all but forgotten.

All *but*, for theoreticians in the Nazi-centric wing of UFO-logy have exposed the sweeping (and highly speculative) post-war history of German achievement in saucer science. If you buy this premise, Foo Fighters were mere Model Ts in the march of German saucerology. In his magnum opus on world conquest by Nazi-connected bluebloods, *Casebook on Alternative 3*, conspiracy pathfinder Jim Keith relates the findings of one Renato Vesco. According to Vesco, author of a tome called *Intercept—But Don't Shoot*, Foo Fighters were forerunners of something called Kugelblitz, the Ball Lightning Fighter. Keith reports that the massive Kugelblitz conformed to "popular concepts of 'flying saucers.'" Though it seems unlikely that these giant craft advanced beyond the blueprint stage, if they got even that far, Keith relays various accounts of saucers launching from construction sites in Prague, Czechoslovakia, and Breslau, Germany, in early 1945.

Then there is the "confidential Italian document," supposedly liberated by an informant, which, according to Keith, described a rather one-sided dogfight between Allied planes and a mysterious vehicle: "A strange flying machine, hemispherical, or at any rate circular, in shape, attacked them at a fantastic speed, destroying them in a few seconds without using any guns." Of course, the problem with stunning and anonymous documents is that they also tend to be apocryphal.

But not even the formidable Kugelblitz could reverse the course of war for the doomed Third Reich. Did Nazi saucerology hunker down and die with the suicidal Führer, then, or did it merely latch on to a new sponsor, as did so many German rocket scientists and superspies? There's actually evidence to suggest the latter. According to a 1955 CIA memorandum dredged up by UFO researcher Timothy Good, aerospace engineer John Frost, who designed a disk-shaped aircraft for the U.S. military, "is reported to have obtained his original idea for the flying machine from a group of Germans just after World War II."

Good's well-documented reporting jibes with more speculative claims that German saucer scientists took their ambitious blueprints to the Soviet Union and to the United States. According to Keith, German scientist Rudolph Schriever maintained "that the various UFO reports since the end of the war showed that his Kugelblitz designs had been discovered and put into production."

Keith also submits that the German saucer scientist named Miethe moved to the United States after the war and worked on John Frost's experimental saucer, the famous "Avro flying disk." Manufactured by A. V. Roe Ltd. of Canada, and funded jointly by the U.S. Army and Air Force during the 1950s, the Avro VZ-9 was an operative flying saucer powered by a jet engine turbine and an array of exhaust nozzles that could propel the craft in any direction—except, unfortunately, up. Although Pentagon self-congratulation was typically over the top, film footage of test flights showed the Avro disk teetering awkwardly a few pathetic inches above the icy airport tarmac. In 1954 the Canadian Defense Ministry dropped the project altogether, reporting that "it served no purpose."

Was the U.S. saucer program a bust? Not according to witnesses who described glimpsing disks similar to the Avro prototype in hangers at military bases in California and Ohio during the 1960s. If we're to believe the anonymous testimony of "eyewitnesses," these late-model "zip craft" were capable of reaching supersonic speeds and lofty altitudes—a far cry from the wobbly Avro contraption.

In 1950, *U.S. News and World Report* jumped on the government UFO bandwagon and told its readers to sober up in an article titled, "Flying Saucers—The Real Story: U.S. Built First One in 1942." Calling the new aircraft a "revolutionary" hybrid of helicopter and jet plane, *U.S. News* knowingly informed its readers that "space ships" and "Martians" had nothing to do with the mysterious sightings. Anyone encountering a UFO was actually witnessing a secret military test flight.

If *U.S. News* aspired to be a voice of sobersided authority during the UFO craze of the 1950s, the government itself may have been spiking the celestial punch, according to some theorists. They maintain that for decades the government has discreetly encouraged speculation about extraterrestrial UFOs and little gray men as a cover for its ongoing development of very terrestrial saucer technology.

Other UFOlogists prefer to turn that theory on its head. They suggest that far from baiting the public with myths about extraterrestrial aliens, the government encourages articles like the *U.S. News* piece to direct attention away from the *real* source of saucer technology: actual extraterrestrial aliens.

Ideal's UFO Magazine exposed the *real* story when it quoted a "Lieutenant Colonel George Edwards (USAF-retired)," who purportedly worked on the Avro VZ-9 project: "Although we weren't cut in on it, we knew that the air force was secretly test-flying a real alien spacecraft. The VZ-9 was to be a 'cover,' so the Pentagon would have an explanation whenever people reported seeing a saucer in flight."

The theory goes that the U.S. government had come into possession of several alien-built saucers, beginning with the alleged 1947 crash in the desert outside of Roswell, New Mexico. By the late 1980s, "extraterrestrial biological entities" (EBEs) had recklessly ditched (or generously donated) as many as nine saucers, which were now in the clutches of the coverup-inclined U.S. government. Despite attempts by the best and brightest American scientists to "reverse engineer" the other-worldly craft, all efforts thus far have failed to recreate the eerily advanced alien technology. (Some enterprising researchers, however, theorize that the government did unlock the secrets of the saucers and used futuristic alien technology to send Americans to the moon—in the 1950s!)

The current hotbed of government UFO testing is supposedly a mysterious military enclosure in the desert north of Las Vegas known variously as Dreamland, Area 51, and S-4. By day, experimental stealth planes take wing in the base's restricted airspace, but at night the pulsing saucers are said to hover and zag in veritable celestial gridlock, as hotshot (earthling) test pilots give warp drive a go, or maneuver with genuine alien saucernauts.

Theories about alien saucers at Dreamland got their big break in 1989 when an engineer named Bob Lazar stepped forward to tell the world (or at least viewers of Vegas station KLAS-TV) that as a government employee at S-4, he had inspected a bona fide alien saucer. Lazar claimed that the craft, which he called the "sport model," was propelled by "gravity amplifiers" and powered by an "antimatter reactor"—incidentally, the state of the art in speculative UFO physics since the 1950s. Unfortunately, Lazar's story has remained controversial, not least because thus far no one has managed to unearth proof of his claimed MIT and Cal-Tech credentials (although his junior college attendance records are beyond dispute).

If other researchers are to be believed, the aliens at Dreamland have got nothing on the Aryans at the South Pole. UFOlogist Vladimir Terziski is partial to the theory that during the final days of World War II, a tattered Third Reich repaired to Antarctica aboard flying saucers and U-boats (perhaps with Wagner's *Ride of the Valkyries* thundering the background). Not surprisingly, some theorists place the Führer, himself, on board a sub or saucer high-tailing it to the South Polar cap.

Terziski reports that he has come into possession of a startling video documentary "by the secret German society" known as the Thule Gesellschaft, the occult Thule Society, which, before the appearance of Hitler, concocted much of the twisted ideology later adopted by the Nazis. If Terziski's updated information on the Thule Society is to be taken seriously, the Germans built "ten-meter diameter" saucers of the Vril series and giant dreadnought discs "for antishipping warfare." They also outfitted their interplanetary saucers—yes, you read right—with "electro-magneto-gravitic" drives (mass- produced like Volkswagens, no less) and colonized the moon as early as 1942! Lunar *lebensraum* was only the beginning. That same year, according to the Terziski, the Nazis speared the Antarctic ice with swastika flags and renamed the continent Neu-Schwabenland. Then they burrowed underground (an echo of Nazi hollow Earth theories?) and established the subterranean capital of New Berlin, which today sports a population of two million *sieg heilers*, terrorizes surface dwellers with fascist saucers, and, of course, secretly enjoys most-favored nation trading status with the U.S. government.

One final note on goose-stepping Saucer-Waffen: An interesting factoid overlooked by most Nazi-centric UFOlogists is the famous abduction story of Barney and Betty Hill. Betty, we should remember, described the offending saucer jockeys as wearing uniforms "similar to air force" and speaking with a "foreign" accent. Barney got right to the point, initially describing their leader as looking "like a German Nazi. He's a Nazi...."! Achtung! Today Poland, tomorrow the Milky Way!

MAJOR SOURCES

"Flying Saucers—The Real Story: U.S. Built First One in 1942." *U.S. News & World Report*, 7 April 1950.

Good, Timothy. *Alien Contact: Top Secret UFO Files Revealed*. New York: William Morrow and Company, 1993.

Keith, Jim. *Casebook on Alternative 3: UFOs, Secret Societies and World Control*. Lilburn, GA: IllumiNet Press, 1994.

Terziski, Vladimir. "Secret Research on Antigravity and Space Flight Organized by the German Secret Societies During World War II." *Steamshovel Press*, no. 9 (Fall 1993).

Vallee, Jacques and Janine. *Challenge to Science: The UFO: Enigma*. New York: Ballantine, 1975.

16

Saucer Therapy

Most debate between UFO believers and skeptics hovers around whether the phenomenon originates in outer space or with some explainable "scientific" source. But there is a third option. What if UFOs are some form of mysterious technology serving the purpose of mass psychological manipulation?

Could UFOs be the first step in a plan to establish a totalitarian government masquerading as a "star child" religion? Do those lights in the sky herald the coming of New Age Nazis from beyond? Perhaps Arthur C. Clarke's all-powerful *2001* monolith has already arrived—except this time it's pissed off!

"The main effect of UFOs on their witnesses is a conditioning process," says Jacques Vallee, a French astronomer whose renown has come primarily from his writings on UFOs. "Through exposure to its powerful imagery, man appears to be acquiring new forms of behavior and new models of his relationship to the world of nature."

Vallee quickly points out that "to conclude that UFOs are

111

nothing more than secret devices deployed by some intelligence agency would be wrong and simplistic." But he nonetheless asserts that there is some sort of genuine technology behind UFOs, and if that technology is not the product of human ingenuity (a possibility Vallee entertains) it is being manipulated by ingenious humans toward some cryptic end.

Jay Katz (a pseudonym for prolific conspiracist Jim Keith) notes numerous instances of verified spookery within the contactee community in his spiral-bound tract *Saucers of the Illuminati*. He points the finger at such suspicious characters as CIA psychological warfare specialist Nicholas de Rochefort and other named CIA "assets" who infiltrated and undermined the National Investigations Committee on Aerial Phenomena, an early civilian UFO group. He reserves particular scorn for John Lear, a former CIA pilot "who has done more than anyone... to convince the public that aliens are among us, living in huge underground bases and collaborating with the government to put us all in the vat-prepared soup." Then there is self-admitted government informer William Moore who helped publicize the famous MJ-12 documents.

"For the general public, I suspect the possibility that UFOs are controlled in some fashion by humans for some secret, conspiratorial purpose is almost unthinkable," writes Katz. "There is an almost total media blackout about the possibility that UFOs are anything other than an extraterrestrial phenomenon."

John Keel is another UFO researcher who dismisses the ET and "scientific" explanations as equally loony, choosing instead to log the "medical and psychological effects" of UFO contact on its victims. He sees UFOs as a "Trojan horse," infiltrating human society to deliver a probably unwelcome payload that has yet to be revealed. As for the human spirit's ability to overcome the sinister designs of the mind-controllers, Keel is not overly sanguine. "We are biochemical robots helplessly controlled by forces that can scramble our brains, destroy our memories, and use us in any way they see fit," he says.

Just as Keel has noted that "men in neat coveralls were seen monkeying with telephone and power lines" in the vicinity of a strange series of UFO incidents in Virginia, *Saucers of the Illuminati* questions the meaning of reports of "aliens" driving off from UFO landings in ordinary, motorized vans. Katz takes note of crowds that gather for "UFO watching parties" outside the army's "top secret" Area 51 in Nevada and remarks wryly, "the relatively common occurrence of garden variety humans being seen in the vicinity of, entering and leaving, and sometimes piloting UFOs may be a significant clue as to the meaning and origin of these craft."

While Keel has studied primarily the experiences of individuals, Vallee is concerned with contactee cults. These groups of hardcore UFO believers always center on some figure who claims direct relations with alien visitors. And in these groups that now exist on the fringes of society and politics Vallee sees the germ of a new "high demand" religion and political philosophy.

The idea seems absurd at first. But almost any idea powerful enough to win the slavish devotion of millions of humans must originate in the alleged contact between humans and a superior intelligence: numerous Olympian gods descending to meddle in the affairs of everyday Greeks; Moses and the burning bush; Jesus appearing to Paul on the road to Damascus.

Or more recently, the Mormon Church. Its founder, Joseph Smith, was visited by an "angel" who told him where to find the long-buried tablets inscribed with *The Book of Mormon*. In twentieth-century parlance, Smith had a "close encounter of the third kind."

On the more cynical end of the spectrum, note the Church of Scientology, created by pulp science fiction scribe L. Ron Hubbard, whose quasi-religious and very expensive techniques to recover the "Thetan" inside us all woos Tom Cruises and John Travoltas from far and wide.

There's a whole subgenre of UFO literature devoted to the notion that mankind's most significant religious experiences may be misread incidents of extraterrestrial contact. The above-noted *2001* utilizes that theme. Erik Von Daniken's *Chariots of the Gods*—which unlike the Kubrick film, purported to be nonfiction—caused an early seventies sensation with its claims that various ancient wonders (the pyramids, the planes of Nazca) were constructed in tribute to, if not actually by, extraterrestrials.

But Vallee's hypothesis cuts the other way: "Close encounters" could just be misinterpretations of the religious experience.

Are "miracles," visions, angelic visitations, and UFO contacts all the same natural phenomenon whose explanation falls outside traditional concepts of nature and physics? This question takes Vallee into a digression about the nature of not merely UFOs but reality itself. To make his lengthy and not-entirely-comprehensible argument as concise as possible, Vallee feels that our modern understanding of the universe is based on a mistake. We assume "linear" causality: one thing leads to another. I punch you in the nose, you fall down. I explain Vallee's theories of reality, you become hopelessly confused.

Instead, Vallee postulates that we inhabit an "associative" universe where conventional "if A then B" logic does not apply. Rather, the logic of coincidence prevails.

His analogy is a computer database. Computers store information randomly and retrieve it using commands. When we enter keywords in a computer databank, we are attempting to produce coincidences. Where, in our conspiracy theory database, do the words "assassination" and "cancer" coincide? Just punch in the magic words and from the chaos of randomized digits come five articles about Mae Brussell.

The universe in which we live, breathe, and perceive, Vallee says, is in fact nothing more than a "process by which informational associations are retrieved and traversed."

In a universe of coincidence, weird phenomena would be "expected, even common," writes Vallee, "and UFOs would lose much of their alien quality." Anyone who understood even a little of this abstruse concept could figure out a way to manipulate those phenomena for their own presumably nefarious purposes. Vallee, like Katz, finds most contactee and UFO study groups rife with spies from the government and other quarters more difficult to discern. Their purpose is beyond investigation, almost as much so as that of the UFOs themselves.

"Contactee systems often include belief in higher races and in totalitarian systems that would eliminate democracy," Vallee notes. The cults he investigated are prone to theories of their own racial superiority based on presumed descent from the "star children." The social consequences of those beliefs are not cheerful to contemplate.

Katz concludes that the teleology of the UFO phenomenon could be the inauguration of a global monarchy. Vallee is less specific. "If the Manipulators do exist, I certainly salute their tenacity, but I am curious about their goals," he says. "One would like to know more, then, about the image of humanity such manipulators harbor in their own minds—and in their hearts. Assuming, of course, that they do have hearts."

MAJOR SOURCES

Katz, Jay. *Saucers of the Illuminati*. Lilburn, GA: IllumiNet Press, 1993.
Keel, John. *Disneyland of the Gods*. New York: Amok Press, 1988.
Vallee, Jacques. *Messengers of Deception*. New York: Bantam Books, 1980.

17

Alien Autopsy

For more than four decades, UFO pupils and proselytes have been waiting for a single piece of unambiguous, irrefutable evidence to materialize. It could come at any time, dropping from the skies like a biblical rain, humbling the most strident skeptics. It might be a scrap of exotic metal forged not on this earth; a devastatingly clear photograph (one that's actually in focus); or, in the best-case scenario, that holiest of extraterrestrial grails: the empirical flesh and, well, *whatever* of an alien being, dead or alive.

In early 1995 it became clear that something big—on the order of the Second Coming or the UFOlogical equivalent thereof—was in the offing. A story alighted on a British television talk show, and from there the Internet and all points of the globe: A smalltime video distributor in London would soon make public U.S. government film footage documenting the forensic autopsy of an extraterrestrial humanoid—a real, *dead* E.T. And not just any alien stiff, but a casualty of the famous Roswell incident, that 1947 crash of a flying disk—

116

perhaps two—in the New Mexican desert. Or so *that* story, detailed in chapter 10, goes.

Flanked by the kind of fanfare normally reserved for a major Hollywood summer release, the now-infamous "Roswell Autopsy" footage did indeed materialize in August 1995—on the Fox network (home if *The X-Files*) in the United States and similarly sensationalized TV broadcasts in more than thirty countries worldwide. The Fox special attracted 10 million viewers in its first airing, picking up millions more in subsequent airings (which threaten to continue into 1996 and beyond).

The footage itself consists of twenty minutes of black-and-white film showing two surgeons dissecting a bipedal figure that matches, more or less, today's popular description of that "breed" of E.T. commonly designated as "grays." Short, bulbous of head, hairless, with sloe eyes and slender limbs, the creature is endowed with all the features that a generation of earthlubbers weaned on films like *Close Encounters of the Third Kind* and books like Whitley Strieber's *Communion* might expect of a bona fide space alien.

However, at least from the standpoint of today's E.T.-savvy dilettantes, this cosmic John Doe also has an almost too-humanlike quality that doesn't quite jibe with the typically reported earless, nostril-impaired, slit-mouthed creatures who terrorize the bucolic homesteaders of middle America.

The 16mm film has a cinema-verité quality that certainly lends an air of authenticity to the eerie medical procedure: Grainy, sometimes poorly exposed and often out-of-focus, the handheld camera jostles like the footage you might see on the six-o'clock news—a subtle psychological nudge that, intentional or not, encourages viewers to suspend disbelief.

But is the footage authentic? Or is it yet another hoax of the variety that have been foisted on the public from time to time since the first saucer crazes of the late 1940s? Although in the months leading up to the world television premiere several prominent UFOlogists endorsed the film as being possibly genuine, the community of UFO researchers, in the main, has subsequently denounced the film as a hoax—and a poorly executed one at that.

So far, no one has stepped forward to confess to fraud. Frankly, though, when it comes to the autopsy film, we're convinced that it is phony. The few journalists who have bothered to investigate the entrepreneurs behind the release of the film have uncovered a slew of suspicious circumstances and contradictions. Beyond that, the footage itself raises far too many doubts and fails too many critical tests to be considered a genuine *anything*, other than a *genuine fake*, that is.

Having tipped our hand, it's time to collect our rhetorical scalpel and scissors—holding the latter properly between our thumb and middle finger, *unlike* the "surgeons" in the autopsy film—in an effort to dissect the footage and its problematic origins.

As the Curies were to radium and Schliemann was to Troy, Ray Santilli is to the first-ever international television broadcast of an alien postmortem. According to Santilli, who owns a small video distribution company in London, he "discovered" the autopsy film in either the summer of 1992 or the summer of 1993 (he's changed his story on that count) while purchasing rare film clips of Elvis Presley (you just *knew* Elvis had to figure into this story) from a retired American cameraman named "Jack Barnett." As Santilli tells it, during that transaction, the cameraman mentioned, "By the way, I have something else to show you." As Santilli explained on the Fox-TV special, "We looked at it. It was just the most incredible piece of film, and obviously my first impression is this can't be real."

Be that as it may, Santilli managed to put such doubts to rest and, after returning to England, raised an undisclosed sum of money to purchase twenty-two reels of film (or fifteen reels, according to Santilli's earliest claims) documenting the autopsy and "debris and recovery footage." According to Santilli, the cameraman—who wished to remain anonymous—had worked for the "Army Air Force and special forces" during the 1940s and 1950s. In addition to witnessing the most famous alien event in modern history (the autopsy), he had the Forrest Gump—like fortune to film early secret atomic tests conducted under the auspices of the Manhattan Project.

Per Santilli, on June 2, 1947, the cameraman was summoned from Washington, D.C., to Roswell, New Mexico. He was told to film "everything he could" at a desert site where, he had been led to believe, a secret spy plane had crashed. A month later he was dispatched to Fort Worth Air Station in Texas to film the dissection of one of the aliens. Somehow, the cameraman managed to withhold from his superiors more than 100 minutes of crucial footage documenting those historic events, footage that gathered dust in his attic for more than four decades, a rather dubious claim on the face of it no matter how low your opinion of competence levels in the U.S. armed forces.

The rest of the story is, well, history of sorts. Eight months after the autopsy tale's first mention on a British "chat show," Fox's "entertainment division" aired the footage in an ominously toned pseudo-documentary, garnering impressive ratings in the process. Santilli (and presumably his mysterious financial backer, whom he has referred to as a "film collector" who wishes to remain anonymous) parlayed his otherworldly find into earthly lucre by retailing the television and video rights to production companies worldwide.

The film itself—now available at your local video store—is a mixed bag as far as credibility goes. From certain angles, the big-headed "humanoid" looks like an organic creature, maybe even one that habitually stalked late-night motorists. Yet from other vantage points it resembles a rather unconvincing Hollywood prop. The "doctors" who conduct the morbid operation—veiled from head to toe in white hazardous materials suits—go through the motions of a real autopsy and actually cut the lifeless E.T. open. But they also seem to handle the body far too gingerly, as if ministering to a fragile and expensive latex dummy.

The expert opinions marshaled against the autopsy footage

itself are fairly devastating, despite the misleading and selective quoting of forensic surgeons and Hollywood special effects artists in the Fox special.

Surgeons and clinical pathologists have noted assorted implausibilities in the operation, which was "performed with far less diligence and skill than a routine [earthly] autopsy," according to Dr. Joseph A. Bauer, M.D., a surgeon who critiqued the film for *The Skeptic* magazine. The slap-dash opening of body cavities and the skull, the surgeon's improper grip on his cutting tool and the utter lack of effort made to analyze, document, or measure the extracted body organs all add up to bad drama "contrived by low-budgeted, poorly advised nonprofessionals," writes Bauer.

The filming of the operation is another dead giveaway: The camera work is much too melodramatic for a military documentary. For starters, the photographer used a jerky hand-held camera rather than a steadying tripod, which was standard issue at the time. Moreover, as military cameramen of the same era have noted, standard procedure at the time would have involved the use of color film (medical procedures were usually filmed on color stock), a still photographer, and a ceiling-mounted camera. You might imagine even more due diligence would be afforded at the autopsy of an exotic extraterrestrial species previously unknown to humankind.

Even more suspicious is the cameraman's tendency to move the camera too close to the subject during key scenes, throwing the image conveniently out of focus. Almost teasingly, he also tends to focus on the doctors' backs during critical moments, as if he can't find a clear vantage point in an operating room occupied by only two other living people. Amateurish work like that certainly wouldn't have earned the photographer important assignments for long. As Joe Longo, the president of the International Combat Camera Association, an organization of former combat cameramen, put it after seeing the autopsy footage, "If anybody in my unit shot film in that manner, he'd be back scrubbing pots in the kitchen."

You might also expect to see a horde of military personnel supervising such a sensitive operation—but the only people visible in the film are the two "surgeons" and a third man standing behind a glass partition (and wearing a surgical mask that conveniently obscures his identity).

Perhaps the most interesting and persuasive debunking of the footage has come from Hollywood special effects experts. A survey by Trey Stokes (an effects artist who worked on films such as *The Abyss, Batman Returns* and *Robocop*) of Hollywood special-effects professionals elicited a unanimous response: The autopsy film is almost certainly a fake. "Whether you believe something weird happened at Roswell, New Mexico, or not," Stokes writes in an article published on the Internet, "the 'alien' in this film sure as heck looks like a competently-made (but far from perfect) dummy."

On its exhaustively documented Internet site, Stoke's firm, the Truly Dangerous Company (TDC), offers its special-effects recipe for how the alien might have been constructed and itemizes the autopsy "bleeps and blunders":

- The rolls of fat and muscle of the creature don't sag as you would expect from a supine cadaver. Instead, the tissue on the thighs, chin and armpits "all seem to indicate gravity pulling toward the toes....All of which suggests this body was created from the body cast of a standing person." Just like they do it in Hollywood.
- The cameraman must be psychic: he always knows in advance where to point the camera in order to record interesting things happening—before they happen! "As the doctor moves the scalpel along the neck and across to the chest, the camera doesn't move on," TDC explains. "Instead, it remains focused on the side of the neck for several seconds—until blood begins to drip from the wound." According to TDC, the dripping blood was likely piped into the incision point via tubes hidden inside the dummy, a Hollywood technique known in the trade as "blood gag."

• The cameraman just as often stops filming when crucial details are about to be revealed. After the examiner cuts open the chest of the creature, for example, the cameraman apparently decides to take a coffee break, thus failing to film the sternum removal, an inexcusable omission. Was it too hard to fake the chest bone structure? ask the professionals at TDC.

TDC offers its own speculation on how the dummy might have been fabricated without busting any budgets, using state-of-the-art silicone gel casting techniques (and using a short person as a "model"). And on its Internet site, TDC presents an "alien face-off" comparing the Santilli alien to special-effects pro Steve Johnson's alien dummy built for Showtime's *Roswell* TV movie. (Their verdict: Johnson's little gray man is much more convincing.)

Even more damaging evidence against the autopsy film has come from Santilli himself, if inadvertently, in his constantly fluctuating, often contradictory claims about the origins of the film.

In a "detailed statement" from the cameraman (whom Santilli initially had declined to name) posted on Santilli's Internet site, the elderly lensman described an astounding scene in which he filmed soldiers approaching the crash site amid the "screams of the freak creatures that were lying by the vehicle." In other words, most-see TV. Unfortunately, however, this portion of the footage has yet to turn up on the Fox network or in any other venue outside of the descriptive prose marshaled by Ray Santilli. Ratcheting the credibility of "The Cameraman's Story" down a few more generous notches is the fact that since the initial airing of the autopsy footage, this document has disappeared from Santilli's Internet World Wide Web site.

That wasn't the only astonishing claim that would later evaporate. In his initial descriptions of the autopsy footage, Santilli claimed that President Truman could be seen watching the operation from behind a glass window. This, Santilli told crop circle researcher and author Colin Andrews in the winter 1995 issue of *Circle Phenomenon Research International Newsletter*, erased any lingering suspicion about the authenticity of the footage: "I had no doubts when I saw President Truman," Santilli was quoted as saying. According to Philip Mantle, research director for the British UFO Research Association (BUFORA), Santilli remarked to him that "if it wasn't Truman, it was as damned good actor."

Well, if it was an actor, he apparently walked off the set before filming could be completed, because the vaunted Truman footage is nowhere to be seen in any of the autopsy footage released thus far. As Roswell researcher Kent Jeffrey put it in his comprehensive deconstruction of "Santilli's Controversial Autopsy Movie (SCAM)," "Because such scenes as that of President Truman and the debris site would be extremely difficult and expensive to hoax, there seemed at first to be a real possibility that the footage might be genuine. Unfortunately, the spectacular claims about these scenes have turned out to be false, apparently blatant lies."

Santilli offered a different explanation: Unfortunately, the Truman footage was lost during development of the film, "which was too badly damaged to retrieve an image." Darn the luck.

There is also the analysis of the film, a matter on which Santilli has issued several misleading statements. Santilli did submit film samples for authentication, including a fragment to the Eastman Kodak Company, maker of the purported stock used by the cameraman; Kodak was able to confirm that the identification code on the edge of the film indicated stock produced in either 1927, 1947, or 1967. However, the film samples that Santilli has given up for analysis have been either blank leader or an ambiguous image of a doorway. No one has been able to examine a piece of film containing the image of the ostensible alien, so the photographic verifications of the film that Santilli has referred to are utterly meaningless. Santilli claimed on the Seattle television program, "Town Meeting," that he had supplied English and French broadcasters with "film with image," which the broadcasters had turned over to Kodak. But according to Jeffrey, "Extensive checking has revealed that no broadcaster... or the Eastman Kodak Company has ever been given a single frame 'with image' of the alleged alien autopsy footage."

When asked by British UFO researcher Philip Mantle why he hadn't released a segment of film featuring an image of the alien, Santilli replied: "Plenty of film has been released with a variety of images, including the images of the autopsy room. Giving away film with the creature would be a last resort as the frames are far too valuable. I think it is also unnecessary as it is part of the same material already released."

The most devastating blow against the case for the film's authenticity is that, as Jeffrey puts it, "there is no cameraman, and there is no film." Santilli's elderly cameraman, the linchpin of the autopsy tale, is apparently a fictional contrivance.

Santilli, who insists that the cameraman is a real, living personage, has identified the chap as one "Jack Barnett" and even arranged for Barnett to place a phone call to Philip Mantle. However, the French television network TF1 discovered during a critical investigation of the autopsy film that contrary to his claims, Santilli purchased the rare Elvis footage not from military cameraman "Jack Barnett," but from Cleveland, Ohio, disc jockey Bill Randle. The photographer who filmed the Elvis performance? *Jack Barnett*. When confronted with this discovery on French television, Santilli backpedaled and admitted that, yes, he had purchased the Elvis footage from Randle, but then later had met the military cameraman. Trouble was, the real Jack Barnett—at least the one who shot footage of the future King of Rock in 1955, had never exposed a millimeter of film for the U.S. military. And even less helpful to Santilli's version of events was that the real Jack Barnett had died in 1967, at age sixty-one.

To be sure, after TF1's revelation of Barnett's nonstarter status, so to speak, Santilli offered a new explanation for this discrepancy in his story: "Jack Barnett," he explained in an interview with Philip Mantle, "is not the real name of the cameraman; if I had given the real name the world would be on his doorstep by now. Jack Barnett is a name that we (including the cameraman) adopted because it was a safe way of handling the problem."

When it comes to rearranging the facts of his story to meet the challenges of his legion of critics, it seems that Santilli, like Elvis, the muse that led him to the autopsy footage, is everywhere. He's hard to pin down. "Do you know that the film is genuine 1947 stock," asks Mantle, "but that it does not depict an alien and in turn has nothing to do with UFOs?"

Santilli is ready for that one, too. "The film is 1947 stock," he answers, "however I do not know what the creature is."

MAJOR SOURCES

Alien Autopsy, the Fox Network TV special, 1995.
"Alien Autopsy Goofs," from the Truly Dangerous Company World Wide Web Internet page.
Jeffrey, Kent. "Santilli's Controversial Autopsy Movie (SCAM)," published on the Internet.
Mantle, Susan and Philip. "Ray Santilli: Questions and Answers," from *UFO Times*, published on the Internet.
Roswell Centre. Ray Santilli's World Wide Web Internet page.

18

The Moon-Mars Coverup

While chapter 14 explains a possible NASA conspiracy to hoax the moon landing, another strain of space-age skepticism holds that NASA did in fact send men to the moon but inevitably hushed up the astronauts' stunning discoveries of alien intelligence. This school of conspiratorial thinking has even spawned a new (speculative) scientific discipline, "exoarchaeology," the study of purported alien ruins on other planets in our solar system.

In the summer of 1996, NASA gave these rubblerousers a motivational boost when the space agency announced it had discovered a meteorite containing microscopic formulations that resemble fossilized single-cell organisms. And the meteorite, discovered years ago in Antarctica, was probably from Mars. Of course, ancient Martian germs are a far cry from a Red Parthenon, but space-archaeologists took the news as a sign that they were on the right track.

Without the advantages of direct access to the big alien

artifacts that NASA so jealously hoards (if you buy this premise), earthbound exoarchaeologists are forced to extract their astounding discoveries from fuzzy, pixilated photographs taken by astronauts and unmanned space probes. Despite the obvious handicaps inherent in this approach to science, a dedicated community of researchers, scholars, conspiracy path-finders, and not a few tabloid journalists have constructed an epic scenario: Not only was the moon once teeming with alien architects and construction workers, but so was Mars.

For more than a decade, the most visible and vocal proponent of the Martian and lunar lost city theories has been Richard C. Hoagland, a lucid science writer and adviser to CBS News during the Apollo lunar missions. (In another of his many achievements, Hoagland was instrumental in organizing the letter-writing campaign that persuaded President Ford to chris-ten the first space shuttle, *Enterprise*, in honor of the old *Star Trek* TV show.) In the mid-1980s, Hoagland convened a team of scientists to analyze an enigmatic sphinxlike object captured in several NASA photographs of Mars.

The "Mars face," as it is known, officially joined the annals of conspiratorial history in the summer of 1976, when the *Viking 1* orbiter swooped around the red planet for its thirty-fifth orbit. Soaring 1,000 miles over the Martian surface, snapping pictures of the desert region known as "Cydonia," *Viking 1* captured a most unusual image: a mile-wide geograph-ical feature that resembles the front view of a human face or, at least, a humanoid face (MONKEY FACE ON MARS screamed one tabloid headline). In the two fuzzy images, which have since become well known, the "face" does indeed appear to have eyes, a nose, and a mouth.

Although NASA dismissed the picture as a trick of light on a natural geological formation, two computer scientists unaffili-ated with the space agency, Vincent DiPeitro and Gregory Molenaar, digitally enhanced the images using a computer technique they had devised. And they found even more stunning details: The eyes in the face appeared to have pupils; the strange visage sported a mouthful of teeth and even a hairline.

Enter Hoagland, lifelong science fiction buff and unabashed envelope pusher. After examining prints of DiPietro and Molenaar's digitally enhanced photos, Hoagland quickly put his own imprimatur on the discovery. A face on Mars—well, that's pretty astounding—but Hoagland one-upped his colleagues by discerning much, much more in the photos: Several miles southwest of the face Hoagland claimed to see the remains of a city, surrounded by mile-long pyramids, bordered by a fortresslike formation featuring an exposed "honeycomb" of floors (was this a skyscraping alien condo?), bisected by a "main avenue" and huddled around a "town square."

"An entire city laid out—on Mars!—with the precision of a Master Architect," Hoagland expounded in his book, *The Monuments of Mars*, striking a tone worthy of Schliemann, discoverer of ancient Troy. "I had indeed discovered some kind of artificially constructed Martian 'complex.'"

But Hoagland, not one to rest on the laurels he bestowed himself, was just warming up. Each of his subsequent discoveries would dwarf the previous one. Taking compass and calculator to the small 5-inch-by-5-inch print of the digitally enhanced photo, Hoagland discerned a series of mathematical relationships and proportions between the features on the face, the nearby "city," and a third object, a five-sided pyramidal structure. Announced Hoagland: All of the key angles in the city and the five-sided object pointed to the face. The alignment of other landmarks seemed to be related to the rising sun on Mars during summer and winter solstice.

By the mid-1990s, Hoagland was still improving on his previous discoveries. He claimed that his latest exacting measurements of the Cydonia photos revealed a complex series of geometric patterns "whose purpose seems to introduce us to a set of equations opening up a whole new window on physics." This new paradigm-shattering science Hoagland called Hyperdimensional Physics, which, he explained to *OMNI* magazine, "provides a fundamental connection between the four forces of nature" and also might make it possible for us to do cool things like tapping into energy from another dimension.

Not surprisingly, mainstream scientists and NASA officials are inclined to scoff at Hoagland's theories, although a number of researchers with an interest in frontier science have taken up the question of the Mars Face. Critics have complained that Hoagland's theories are far too speculative, given the available data—a few equivocal photos. And they have a point. Reading Hoagland's book on Cydonia, you're left with the feeling that he's looking at different photos than the ones included in his paperback, which seem far too ambiguous to support the superstructure of Hoagland's industrious theories.

By the end of the book, Hoagland has exhumed passages from Sumerian mythology and drawn links between the "pyramids" of Mars and those of Egypt to make his case or the ultimate purpose behind the Mars Face. Might the massive sculpture be a celestial billboard designed to inform us that ancient alien astronauts (1) set up a base on Mars, (2) abducted our evolutionary ancestors to the red planet, (3) created a race of highly intelligent alien-human hybrids, (4) shuttled them back to earth, (5) tutored them in the finer points of civilization, and (6) left a picture of us behind in Cydonia so that we (Hoagland first and then the rest of us) might one day rediscover our roots? As Hoagland—clearly proud of his possible heritage as the progeny of those transplanted hybrids—succinctly puts it, "*We* might ultimately be the 'Martians.'"

If that sounds like a plot from a science fiction novel, well, it is. In his book Hoagland frequently pays homage to Arthur C. Clarke, who first offered this scenario as the plot of *2001: A Space Odyssey*, in which big brothers from beyond leave spacefaring earthlings an archaeological beacon (on the moon) that directs them to their mysterious origins.

Also true to the plot of *2001* are the sundry conspiracy theories that have become a part and parcel of the Cydonia phenom (which includes a cottage industry of books, T-shirts, Mars Face sculptures, and Internet sites). In *2001*, the government covers up its stunning discovery of an alien obelisk on the moon. In the culture of Cydonia speculation, the prevailing plot has NASA frantically trying to paper over the truth about the lost city of Mars, misfiling key photos and even sabotaging its own missions. The failure of the *Mars Observer* probe—which was scheduled to shoot high-resolution pictures of Cydonia—in August 1992 is considered by many to be NASA's lowest moment. Just before it entered orbit around the red planet, *Mars Observer* suddenly stopped transmitting its signal home. After unsuccessful efforts to resuscitate the suspiciously mute probe, NASA wrote off the mission, blaming the failure on a fuel leak. Of course, face watchers believed otherwise: NASA had to destroy *Mars Observer*, in order to keep the secrets of Cydonia buried. Or was it some other force, from an unearthly source, maybe Mars, that felt compelled to destroy the robot spacecraft?

Which brings us to the conspiratorial rumors surrounding the many failed Russian expeditions to Mars. Despite a history of mysterious mechanical failures on all but one of its unmanned missions to the red planet, the former Soviets tried again in the late 1980s. Two unmanned spacecraft, Phobos 1 and 2, were launched with the intention of photographing the surface of the red planet and one of its moons, Phobos. Phobos 1 suffered a mechanical failure en route to Mars. In 1989 Phobos 2 arrived at its destination and took extensive photographs of the Martian surface before its rendezvous with Phobos. Then it too suddenly "expired," as the Russians put it. In one of the pictures beamed back to earth before the demise of Phobos 2 a cigar-shaped shadow can be seen looming on the surface of Mars. Some conspiracy searchers claim that the shadow was cast by an alien spacecraft just before it blew the Russian probe to smithereens. A spacecraft perhaps piloted by the media-shy "Cydonians," themselves.

To be sure, planetary scientists have a much more dull, albeit plausible, explanation: The shadow on Mars was cast by the Martian moon Phobos, an irregularly shaped *natural* satellite.

The NASA cover-up theory, if we're to entertain it with any degree of seriousness, requires a motive. Reenter Hoagland, Cydonia's busiest press agent, and lately expanding his research into new planetary venues.

In early 1996, at a press conference in Washington, D.C., Hoagland unveiled his most recent astounding discoveries. As his press release teased, Hoagland promised to uncork THIRTY-YEAR-OLD SUPPRESSED EVIDENCE REVEALING ANCIENT ARTIFICIAL STRUCTURES ON MOON.... PHOTOS SHOW ASTRONAUTS WALKING AMID APPARENT LUNAR RUINS, ON "LEAKED" NASA AND SOVIET SPACE PHOTOGRAPHS. Hoagland clearly aimed to turn the consensus history of NASA, and indeed the entire history of mankind, on its ear.

The "press conference of the millennium," as Hoagland had touted it, predictably had little effect on the status quo. Trouble was, the supposedly uncanny evidence amounted to a series of computer-enhanced—and, once again, extremely blurry—photographs that didn't look remotely like "alien artifacts" to the "untrained eye." In fact, to the untrained eye Hoagland's geodesic domes and crystal castles dangling from lunar guy wires resembled, more than anything else, mundane photographic distortions magnified by amateurish computer enhancement.

However, Hoagland did manage to deliver some interesting documents that had been fermenting for thirty-plus years. The first was a 1960 NASA–commissioned report by the Brookings Institution recommending that any future discoveries of alien life be hushed up so as not to upset twentieth-century earth civilization. The second was a peculiar rider in NASA's charter establishing the space agency as a branch of the military. Admittedly, those two documents are intriguing, and they're sure to fuel conspiratorial speculation for years to come. But Hoagland pushed the envelope of credibility by claiming that they served to bolster a "deliberate thirty-year-old superpower coverup" to keep earthlings in the dark vis-à-vis amazing discoveries on Mars and our own moon.

No doubt about it, the Mars Face is genuinely peculiar. And it's certainly worth another visit. But the interplanetary space opera Hoagland has built around that genuine anomaly is far less structurally sound than the alien buttresses and crystal domes he envisions. The latest chapter in Hoagland's ever-developing saga is about as sweeping as the *Dune* trilogy: Perhaps our ancient astronaut cousins, Hoagland speculates, having blown up their home world into tiny little pieces (giving us the asteroid belt between Mars and Jupiter) migrated to Mars, where they built the city of Cydonia. At some point in our prehistory, they artificially relocated the moon into earth's orbit, thereby influencing the origin of life here.

To quote from his favorite TV show, where Hoagland had arrived by 1996 was hardly a place No Man had gone before. William L. Brian II, Oregon-based author of the 1982 book *Moongate: Suppressed Findings of the U.S. Space Program*, sketched out a similar planet-shaking, NASA-scamming history of the solar system.

Brian set out to build a case (complete with algebraic proofs—and more caution-to-the-wind speculation than Hoagland has ever mustered) for NASA's "monstrous suppression" of the facts about alien intelligence on the moon.

The basis of Brian's cosmic thesis is his belief that NASA is lying when it says the moon's gravity is one-sixth that of the earth (Hoagland disagrees with this assumption). Using calculations too complex to go into here—they're helpfully assembled in appendix B of his book—Brian purports to prove that NASA learned during the 1960s that the moon's gravitational field was actually a whopping 64 percent as strong as the earth's.

The implications of this discovery are staggering, per Brian, staggering enough to warrant one of NASA's patented cover-up jobs. For if the moon's gravity is close to that of the earth, Brian explains, Newton's Law of Universal Gravitation is all wrong and conventional physics is teetering on a "shaky foundation." Furthermore, strong lunar gravity also means that the moon might be able to sustain an atmosphere, and where there's air, there just might be life. And where there's life, it follows that there might also be futuristic sci-fi monorails, OK?

But we're getting ahead of Brian's proofs of the conspiracy:

- He has scrutinized films and photographs of Apollo astronauts puttering around the moon and is unimpressed by the so-called athletic feats promised by NASA. If you accept NASA's claims, astronauts on the moon would barely nudge the scales at one-sixth of their earth weight. According to Brian's calculations (appendix F of his book), a 185-pound man wearing a space suit of equal weight should have been able to jump six feet off the ground. Yet apparently white astronauts can't jump, for they never cleared more than a pathetic eighteen inches. Brian suggests that NASA used the bulky space suits in an unconvincing attempt to explain away this "anemic jumping." (Critics of Brian have offered a less exotic explanation: Pressurized space suits make it difficult to bend the knees.) To give the illusion of low-gravity frolicking, Brian continues, NASA probably used "semi-slow-motion" photography.
- The lunar landscape turned out not to be filled with craggy peaks as expected but was gently rounded, as if eroded by wind and water. Gorges looked for all the world like dry river channels, Brian reports.
- Certain NASA photos of the moon exhibit signs of atmospheric diffusion, according to Brian's analysis. Did NASA retouch its moon photos to blot out blue sky and replace it with inky black?
- Then there is the peculiar *Apollo 10* photo of the moon from space showing a band of blue haze wrapped around the rocky orb. It does look remarkably like pictures of the earth's atmosphere taken from space. Moreover, Neil Armstrong, upon seeing the moon from this same angle is said to have commented, "I can see the sky all around the moon." Hmm.

Brian wagers that the moon's atmosphere might be as dense

as the earth's and perhaps even as breathable. "It follows that the [space] suits were probably only used during filming to propagate the cover-up," he submits. Oh yeah? Then what of *Apollo 15*'s recreation of Galileo's famous experiment in which a hammer and feather, dropped on the supposedly airless moon, fell at the same rate? (Hoagland, in a bit of weird synchronicity, is the one who came up with the idea for this experiment.) Brian is, of course, undaunted by NASA's trickery: "The feather probably concealed a rather heavy object."

Brian also draws on sources of information somewhat less exacting than his pocket calculator to outline a plot somewhat more conjectural than your average 1950s invaders-from-Mars movie. That is, your average 1950s invaders-from-Mars movie with a cold war conscience.

For like the space traveler Klaatu in the 1950s sci-fi classic, *The Day the Earth Stood Still*, and like Hoagland, Brian issues a stern warning to NASA, its military puppet masters and all others who flaunt a "mega-death type of mentality." Submits Brian: "If advanced intelligences exist in the universe which are superior to Earth men, the militarists will eventually meet their match in outer space."

Indeed, the astronauts might already have met their alien match, under blue lunar skies. Dutifully noting the "questionable" provenance of the information (the *National Enquirer*), Brian proceeds to report that after Armstrong and Edwin E. "Buzz" Aldrin Jr. landed on the moon, "immense UFOs lined up on the far side of the crater and monitored the astronauts." This story is a standard in UFO lore, and various accounts have Armstrong admitting, off the record, of course, that the place was crawling with alien goons.

It seems that UFOs have kept close tabs on NASA's manned space program from the get-go. There are the famous sightings of unidentified bogies, including John Glenn's "fireflies," the luminous particles seen on many a space flight but typically dismissed by wet-blanket NASA cover-up artistes as "chipped paint" and not UFO exhaust. There are also the possibly apocryphal, yet always descriptive, sightings by rocket jockeys of "disc-shaped" objects hovering near and/or following NASA space capsules, usually in concert with mysterious equipment failures ("electronic glitches" in NASA's argot of misdirection).

Extrapolating from the, well, ambitious claims of 1950s-era UFO contactees George Adamski (author of *Flying Saucers Have Landed*) and Howard Menger (*From Outer Space to You*), Brian suggests a not-so-original motive behind the alien stalking of NASA: Nervous about Earth's entry into the nuclear sweepstakes, UFOs were monitoring terrestrial war-making technology. NASA's missions, because they were "decoys" for military research, according to Brian, became a prime target of UFO surveillance. "Human beings...have an extremely bad reputation for being killers," Brian editorializes. "How could UFO occupants trust Earth nations to be benevolent when these nations have such war-filled histories and are developing weapons which are more and more powerful?"

Adamski (a prolific UFO abductee who fraternized with very Nordic-looking Venusians and Saturnians) and Menger both reported being taken to dome-shaped UFO bases on the moon. (Shades of Hoagland.) Brian takes their tales as corroboration of his own notions: Hardly the lunar wasteland of NASA propaganda, the moon is actually rather pleasant, with a "saffron-colored sky;" vegetation and animal life in certain temperate zones; snowcapped mountains covered with timber, lakes, rivers; alien "communities of varying sizes;" and, natch, an antigravity monorail.

As for the cratering of the moon, Brian pulls a theory apparently out of the heavenly firmament, explaining that those familiar features are in fact the handiwork of "sophisticated weapons" used in "a terrible war involving the moon," which took place "less than 30,000 years ago." Apparently taking a cue from filmmaker George Lucas, Brian describes a Star wars–like scenario in which a hollow planet between Mars and Jupiter was obliterated by high-tech particle beams, leaving behind our latter-day asteroid belt. That asteroid belt planet ("hereafter referred to as Maldek," he writes, somewhat inexplicably) had a moon, which, thanks to "great levitating or gravity-inducing beams" was transported into the orbit of its new host: planet Earth. (Again, shades of Hoagland.)

These are the only few of the interplanetary secrets guarded by NASA, which might also know that the Earth and moon, like woebegone Maldek, are hollow—and therefore prone to destruction by cosmic super weapons. (Which would constitute an injustice to the inhabitants who dwell inside our hollow Earth, another classic conspiracy theory abducted by Brian.) Likewise, NASA has yet to come clean on UFO antigravity propulsion. Perhaps, Brian meditates aloud, NASA itself has mastered such science fiction technology for use in its own moon vehicles; this might also explain the government's official silence on the subject of UFOs.

NASA might also know that a number of moons and planets in the solar system are inhabited by people with superior technologies, not unlike Adamski's bottle-job Venusians, Saturnians, and Martians (who spoke perfect unaccented American English, fortuitously enough). "We can hope," Brian concludes with a note of cold war foreboding, "that these people will keep the superpowers in check, since the use of space for military purposes could eventually lead to our destruction."

Brian's theories echo another wing of aerospace conspiracy conjecture, the insanely sweeping "Alternative 3" plot. Alternative 3 began as a hoax, a fictional parody of the conspiracy mindset aired as a "mockumentary" on British television in 1977. But the sinister (and satirical) allegations soon developed a cult following among literal-minded conspiratologists.

As "exposed" by a gaggle of whistleblowers (like alcoholic former astronaut "Bob Grodin") on Britain's Anglia TV, Alternative 3 was a plot hatched by a global klatch of blue bloods to abandon the polluted, overpopulated planet Earth to the stinking masses. Alternatives 1 and 2, scrapped as impractical by NASA and its international overlords, would have involved exploding nuclear bombs in the sky to burn off atmospheric pollution and building vast subterranean cities, respectively. The more pragmatic Alternative 3, however, was a plan to spirit Earthling elitists and unsuspecting "batch consignments"— hapless rubes abducted by terrestrial UFOs and enslaved via mind control—to domed cities on the moon and Mars.

As an American plotter puts it in a transcript uncloaked by Anglia TV's journalistic stalwarts: "Ethics! What the hell do some of these guys think we're all at! Jesus! We're smack in the middle of the most vital exercise ever mounted...with the survival of the whole human race swinging on it...and they bleat about ethics."

Despite that Alternative 3 was more wicked satire than evil master plan, some conspiracy trackers remain suspicious. In his recent volume, *Casebook on Alternative 3*, conspiracy sentry Jim Keith expertly debunks the "poorly done, science fictional hoax" and then proceeds to demonstrate over the course of 159 pages that the British production was actually "fiction based on fact." Alternative 3 "is right about one thing," Keith muses apocalyptically. "Smart money is on the end of the world."

Well, come to think of it, Biosphere 2, that very real quasi-scientific experiment in the Arizona desert in which seven men and women donned Star Trekkish jumpsuits and sealed themselves inside a domed ecocosm, is an eerie parallel to the Alternative 3 plot. In fact, the Biospherans' authoritarian leader was a Southwestern cultist who initially described the experiment as the next phase in human evolution, a preparation for humankind's inevitable migration to Mars. Next stop: Cydonia!

MAJOR SOURCES

Brian, William L. *Moongate: Suppressed Findings of the U.S. Space Program and the NASA-Military Cover-Up*. Portland, OR: Future Science Research Publishing, 1982.

Hoagland, Richard C. *The Monuments of Mars: A City on the Edge of Forever*. Berkeley, CA: North Atlantic Books, 1987.

Keith, Jim. *Casebook on Alternative 3: UFOs, Secret Societies and World Control*. Lilburn, GA: IllumiNet Press, 1994.

19

The X-Files *Conspiracies*

When the original edition of the book you are now holding first hit bookstores in 1995, a television series about a couple of FBI agents who investigate paranormal activity and government conspiracies was beginning to build a cult following. Since then, *The X-Files* has shed its cult status and become a global phenomenon, drawing a huge audience in America and worldwide.

A major factor behind the success of the series (and the big-budget movie it spawned) is its canny ability to tap into the paranoid *Zeitgeist*. Conspiracy theories have become a sort of latter-day mythology, an alternative explanation of how things *really* work. And *The X-Files* mines that psycho-terrain every week. In fact, there's a fair amount of real-world conspiracy speculation woven into the dramatic matrix of *The X-Files*. (We were more than pleased when the first edition of this book turned up as a prop in one of the best episodes of *The X-Files*—the second-season finale, "Anasazi.")

To quote the show's knowing epigram, "The truth is out there." How out there? Well, not as as far as you might think.

The pilot episode established the show's central mystery—that the government is somehow involved in a cover-up of evidence of alien visitation. The mythology of UFO cover-up is probably the most powerful conspiracy theory of the twentieth century, and it's at the core of *The X-Files*. Staples of UFO lore that would appear again and again in the show include references to alien abduction (Mulder believes that his sister was abducted by aliens); references to the alleged 1947 crash of a flying saucer in Roswell, New Mexico; and the notion that the government has entered into some kind of nefarious pact with extraterrestrials.

The suppression of conspiratorial evidence would also become an ongoing theme of *The X-Files*. Just as real-world tales of Roswell and other UFO events repeatedly feature government efforts to bury the evidence, so, too, did the pilot introduce that theme, giving us fleeting glimpses of the first in a series of exhumed alien corpses (which would always vanish by the end of the episode). In the pilot's epilogue, an alien artifact retrieved by Mulder's partner, Special Agent Dana Scully, is secreted in a Penatgon basement alongside a cornucopia of similarly buried evidence. The agent of the cover-up is also introduced; known to fans as "the Cigarette-Smoking Man," he's the enigmatic government bureaucrat with no name but with apparently unrestricted authority and a serious nicotine addiction (a habit personifying evil on television of the 1990s).

The second episode, "Deep Throat," reinforced the series' conspiratorial framework by introducing a character modeled on that most famous of mysterious government informants, Watergate's Deep Throat. His motives were never clear, nor were his affiliations (at least not until later seasons had filled in some of the saga's backstory). But he would direct Mulder—and often misdirect him—deeper into the mystery of the alien-government confab.

The "Deep Throat" episode also found Mulder and Scully, investigating a secret military base modeled on Area 51, the real-world Nevada site where the government is rumored to be flying experimental aircraft based on alien technology (see chapter 15). At the climax of that episode, having glimpsed such a top-secret craft, Mulder has his memory of the incident erased by government agents dressed in black—a visual reference to the legendary Men in Black of UFO lore (see chapter 20).

At the close of the first season, Mulder and Scully learn that the alien cover-up involves government experiments with extraterrestrial DNA. In the first-season finale, "The Erlenmeyer Flask," Mulder and Scully discover that for some undisclosed purpose human guinea pigs were being mutated with extraterrestrial DNA. The manufacture of alien-human hybrids is, of course, an staple theme of UFO conspiracy theory. "The Erlenmeyer Flask" also featured one of the mutants spewing toxic gases (and green fluid) from a wound—a riff on the bizarre, real-life case of a Southern California woman who emitted toxic fumes in a hospital.

The second season featured even more references to extant conspiracy theories, both in the ongoing saga of the alien cover-up and in stand-alone episodes. The CIA's real-world MK-ULTRA mind-control experiments informed "Blood," in which unknown agents use hallucinogenic drugs and electronic stimuli to drive residents in a small town to commit violent murders. Naturally, when Mulder figures out what's really going on, all traces of the experiment disappear. And the military's real tests of amphetamines and other stimulants on soldiers on the battlefield inspired "Sleepless," an episode about a Vietnam vet subjected to sleep-deprivation experiments; his decades-long bout with insomnia drives him into a state of homicidal dementia.

In the sly episode "José Chung's 'From Outer Space,'" the show delved into the labyrinthine and surreal myths of the Men in Black (see chapter 20), and the conspiracy theory that the government itself conducts UFO hoaxes as a kind of psychological warfare (see chapters 15 and 16).

Other references to popular conspiracy tales were included in episodes about the Chupacabra, the mysterious crash of commercial jet à la TWA 800, the infamous (and probably hoaxed) video of an alien autopsy, and a UFO cult that meets a tragic demise, not unlike the Heaven's Gate group.

The X-Files also pays homage to the archetypal conspiracy theorist in the form of "The Lone Gunmen," three recurring characters who publish *The Magic Bullet* newsletter and deliver expository dialogue to Mulder whenever he's stumped. And the figure of the archconspirator was satirized in an episode filling in background details fo the Cigarette-Smoking Man, who proves to be a ubiquitous plotter, even squeezing the trigger in the JFK assassination!

Meanwhile, the UFO cover-up subplot thickened over the course of several episodes. In a two-part episode, Scully is abducted, apparently by government agents (as opposed to aliens), who perform a medical procedure on her. In subsequent episodes, we learn that Scully has received a tiny microchip implant in the back of her neck—another familiar theme in UFO lore.

As the series progressed, viewers were introduced to the cabal behind Scully's abduction and the ongoing government cover-up, never named but known to fans as "the Syndicate." The group—a kind of gentlemen's club of middle-aged white guys with an aversion to brightly lit rooms—employs the Cigarette-Smoking Man as capo and fixer. They exert a sweeping influence over the U.S. government, as well as other governments worldwide. Clearly interational consortium is inspired by conspiracy theories of the New World Order, that secret international klatch of business aristocrats who control world affairs (see chapter 47).

Although their raison d'être has remained murky (and subject to the ongoing creative revisions of the series' writers and producers), ultimately it is revealed that the Syndicate has entered into a pact with extraterrestrial invaders ("colonizers," in the show's parlance). The secret work of the Syndicate involves cloning experiments to create a race of alien-human hybrids (who have the toxic green fluid coursing through their veins). The plot dates back to 1948 and involves former Nazi scientists whose eugenics work was part of Hitler's final solution. This, of course, is a reference to the very real Operation Paperclip, a secret American intelligence operation that imported German scientists, many of whom were guilty of war crimes, into the United States after the war and granted them immunity in return for scientific knowledge (see chapter 59). In a bit of conspiratorial cross-pollination, *The X-Files* grafts this theory onto popular speculation about alien-human hybrid experiments.

In third-season episodes "Nisei" and "731," we learn that the secret hybrid project also involved Japanese scientists imported to the United States after the war; the latter episode includes references to the actual Unit 731, which conducted brutal experiments on American and Chinese prisoners of war (see chapter 5).

Naturally, as the series' ongoing references to the overarching conspiracy accumulated like gelatinous alien secretion, confusion reigned. In as effort to reduce viewer mystification before the release of *The X-Files* feature film (and undoubtedly to reassure fans that there was, in fact, a method behind the madness), series creator Chris Carter divulged a few salient plot details in a hidden (of course) track on the movie-soundtrack CD.

Per Carter, the Syndicate is a shadow government of collaborationists (like the Nazi-friendly Vichy government of France during World War II) who have been granted "immunity or asylum" by the alien invaders. In return, the Syndicate has agreed to pave the way for colonization by developing a hybrid spieces "cloned from human ova and alien biomaterial." The title of the cloning project: "Purity Control." The Syndicate is also charged with covering up that fifty-year-long operation. (And they would've gotten away with it if it weren't for those meddling kids Mulder and Scully.

Of course, the plot gets even denser, not like the "black oil" goo that is the interim state of the colonizing aliens, before they infect their human hosts. According to Carter, the Syndicate has been secretly rebelling against its master race by developing a vaccine that kills the alien colonizers after they virally possess humans.

Enter *The X-Files* feature film—subtitled *Fight the Future*—in which Carter and company further thickened the plot with real-life conspiracy theories. The alien colonists, it turns out, have been on earth since prehistoric times—which, of course, echoes the ancient astronauts' branch of UFOlogy.

Meanwhile, the Syndicate has enlisted the Federal Emergency Management Agency (FEMA), to shepherd the invasion plans in the United States. At that time, FEMA is to round up dissidents, declare martial law, and take over all government functions. That, minus the alien overlay, is the gist of real-life conspiracy theories revolving around FEMA, a disaster-relief agency that actually did develop contingency plans during the Reagan administration to suspend the Constitution, declare martial law, and lock up dissidents in concentration camps (see chapter 4).

Also featured in the movie is a government-ordered bombing of a building in Dallas (forever conspiratorially significant after the JFK assassination), a plot device taking its cue from conspiracy theories about the terrorist bombing of the federal building in Oklahoma City (see chapter 54). And rounding out the paranoid verisimilitude is an underground UFO base at the South Pole, a staple in both hollow-earth speculation and Nazicentric UFO theories (see chapter 15).

Although the feature film promised to clarify the saga's intricate mystery to longtime viewers, the fictional conspiracy remained every bit as murky as its real-life counterparts. Which is, of course, the nature of conspiracy theories. Every new revelation is always merely the tip of another iceberg. The mystery's the thing.

As a matter of fact, Mulder's trademark axiom in the series, which neatly sums up the impulse of paranoid savants, serves as a good rule of thumb for fans expecting definitive, clear-cut plot resolutions from creators of lucrative entertainment franchises: "Trust no one."

20

The Real *Men in Black*

Hollywood's version of the Men in Black (MIB)—
from the blockbuster movie of the same name—bears little
resemblance to the actual legend of the MIB. In the film,
Tommy Lee Jones and Will Smith are badass galactic cops
sporting Armani suits and wraparound Ray-Bans. (Though
they're rule-busting mavericks, they nonetheless obligingly
comply with a corporate dress code, thereby realizing every
young film exec's fantasy image of himself.) To quote the film's
promotional tag line, the cinematic MIB are "protecting the
Earth from the scum of the universe."

In the much more interesting real-world myth, the MIB
usually *are* the scum of the universe. That is, they're the bad
guys, menacing heavies from another world or shifty fixers
dispatched by the cover-up-obsessed government.

(It's interesting—and a bit unsettling—that in Hollywood's
riff on the myth, the MIB become "good guys" to root for, even
though they're members of an elite and xenophobic secret-
police organization not unlike the Nazi SS. Apparently in
Hollywood of the nineties, it's politically correct to round up

144

degenerate foreigners as long as they drool copious amounts of outer-space endoplasm.)

In modern accounts, the MIB are usually connected in some way to UFO activity. The most common scenario has them appearing on the scene after a UFO encounter to intimidate witnesses with extremely peculiar and often threatening behavior. Dressed in ill-fitting or out-of-style black suits, the classic MIB tend to travel in twos or threes (but also often singly). Their modes of transport vary. They seem to prefer to cruise the paranormal backstreets in black limousines, but they've also have been known to pilot the occasional van and, in a few recent accounts, have traded up to that all-purpose conspiracy vehicle, the black helicopter. Yet despite their outré mien, the MIB most often seem to "buy American," usually vintage 1950s Cadillacs that, eerily enough, often smell brand-new.

Witnesses who report MIB sightings often describe "foreign-looking" men with exotic features; it's as if they're "from elsewhere." They look "Oriental" or "Indian" and have "deeply tanned" skin, although sometimes their complexions are extremely pale. The eyes of the MIB are usually described as slanted or "bulging," as if from a thyroid condition. Their noses and chins are often "pointy," and their cheekbones are set high on their faces. Though some are tall and thin, with preternaturally long fingers, others are short or stout. They may or may not have fingernails.

Stranger still is their reputed behavior, which tends to be disturbingly erratic or downright goofy: In one account a MIB who seems to be suffering overexposure to West Virginia's oxygen-rich atmosphere is offered some Jell-O, which he attempts to drink like a beverage. Another MIB is initially perplexed when shown the strange terrestrial implement we know as the ballpoint pen, but then becomes gleefully spastic as he absconds into the street with the prize.

MIBs frequently speak tortured English with outlandish accents; in some accounts they don't move their lips when they communicate, suggesting a knack for telepathy, while in other encounters they speak like "machines." When it comes to the MIB, the subtext is always "We're not from around here."

Separating the truly inexplicable MIB encounters from the sundry hoaxes and hearsay is no mean feat. So many of the MIB tales, which first arose during the UFO flaps of the 1950s, apparently began as pranks or visits by officious government agents investigating the hullabaloo over "flying saucers."

The book that introduced the world to the modern MIB was a lively little tome with the best title ever: *They Knew Too Much About Flying Saucers*. Penned in 1957 by theatrical booking agent and saucer buff Gray Barker, the book was a minor masterpiece in the basement-hobbyist genre of UFOlogy. Barker, a kind of do-it-yourself Fox Mulder, had been investigating reports of flying saucers and backwoods monsters in his home state of West Virginia when he met Albert K. Bender, a somewhat eccentric Connecticut man who had recently formed a group ambitiously called the International Flying Saucer Bureau (IFSB). Bender asked Barker to organize a West Virginia chapter and act as the IFSB's "chief investigator."

But Bender's initial enthusiasm for investigating flying saucers quickly chilled after he was paid a visit by three "men in black suits." At first, Bender hinted that the men were government agents who had threatened him because "I had stumbled upon something that I was not supposed to know."

Later, Bender began to insinuate that the men might have been extraterrestrial in origin. Chronicler Barker, who knew how to promote the hell out of the horror flicks he booked in local bijous, escalated the suspense like voltage darting up a Jacob's ladder. The balance of *They Knew Too Much About Flying Saucers* was devoted to speculating on the sinister, yet all-too-opaque, provenance of these dark-suited enforcers.

According to Barker, UFO investigators in Australia and New Zealand had been similarly "shushed up" by intimidating visitors in black suits. One researcher claimed to have received a call from a machinelike voice that stated, "I warn you to stop interfering in matters that do not concern you," and then, apparently to make sure the other party had not missed the significance of the robotic elocution, signed off with "I am...from another planet." According to Barker, the strange phenomena down under soon escalated to include poltergeist activity and visitations from "invisible entities" lounging in very visible moccasin slippers.

As Barker was quick to note, Bender and his Commonwealth counterparts hadn't been the first to encounter UFO-connected MIBs. In 1947 a harbor patrolman named Harold A. Dahl had reported one of the earliest modern saucer sightings, near Maury Island, Washington. Dahl and his fifteen-year-old son saw six doughnut-shaped, metallic objects a hundred feet in diameter hovering over Puget Sound. One of the objects, which seemed to be experiencing mechanical difficulty, discharged a load of liquid, metallic slag. The hot debris fell toward Dahl's boat, injuring his son and killing his dog, after which the objects flew away.

The aftermath of the "Maury Island Affair," as it came to be known, is what interested Barker. According to Dahl, the next morning, a man in a black suit confronted him at a local restaurant, offering an exact account of the previous day's incident. Then the man threatened Dahl, telling him that harm would befall him and his family if he told anyone about the incident. But Dahl was undeterred, and his story got out. From there, the case becomes even murkier, with Dahl later confessing that the whole scenario had been a hoax and then, naturally, recanting that *mea culpa,* generally escalating the confusion.

Regardless of what really happened off Maury Island, the MIB were now a very real part of UFO lore, thanks in no small way to Barker's bestseller. And the mysterious men of what was now being called the "Silence Group" quickly became an obsession of saucer chasers.

Eventually, Barker persuaded Bender to go public with the full story of his "shushing." The result was a 1962 book, *Flying Saucers and the Three Men,* ostensibly authored by Bender but heavily edited by Barker. Unfortunately, after the giddy buildup of Barker's prequel, Bender's tell-all came as a major letdown. Reading more like fan-boy sci-fi than the interplanetary exposé it purported to be, *Flying Saucers and the Three Men* was brimming with all the pulpy clichés of the day, from teleportation to underground saucer bases to mid-atlantic alien dialogue like "Please be advised to discontinue delving into the mysteries of the universe."

After contacting the saucer men telepathically from his bedroom (by mentally projecting a message of "utmost friendship" into the cosmos), Bender eventually meets three MIBs face-to-face. They are "dressed in black clothes...like clergymen" but wearing "hats similar to Homburg style." Per Bender, "The eyes of all three figures suddenly lit up like flashlight bulbs....They seemed to burn into my very soul." To make a long story short, the MIBs announce that they are visitors from the planet "Kazik" on a secret mission to steal earth seawater. With what can only be the deadpan irony of an advanced extraterrestrial race, they explain that they will confide in Bender because "one day you will write about this, and we are certain nobody will believe you, but you will be much wiser than anyone else on your planet."

It is, of course, possible that a kernel of truth lies at the heart of Bender's fantastic tale: As head of the impressive-sounding International Flying Saucer Bureau, Bender may indeed have been paid a visit by government types curious about then-ubiquitous reports of flying saucers; and from there the impressionable Bender may have let his imagination run wild. Barker would eventually suggest as much.

But the real trouble with the MIB legend is that Barker himself is so acutely tangled in its origins. Barker died in 1985, but in recent years his friends have confirmed that he was an inveterate hoaxer.

Indeed, he may turn out to be one of the great pranksters of the twentieth century: According to his friend and fellow MIB chronicler John Keel (more on Keel in a moment), Barker "left behind a rich heritage of practical jokes and UFO hoaxes which...are now an integral part of flying saucer literature. He paved the way for the myriad of hoaxes of the 1980s."

In the afterward of his book *The Mothman Prophesies,* Keel claims that it was Barker who invented the tale of Hanger 18, the supposedly top-secret air-force repository of crashed alien saucers and ET corpses at Wright-Patterson Field in Ohio. And Keel maintains that Barker also fabricated the "Edwards Air Force Base fairy tale (in which he names several of his personal friends as witnesses, along with President Eisenhower)." Both of those whoppers (according to Keel) "served as the framework for the MJ-12 and Roswell, New Mexico, 'crashed saucer' hoaxes that absorbed the attention of many UFO buffs throughout the 1980s." (And well into the 1990s, we might add. And if Keel *is* correct, latter-day UFOlogists, many of whom accept the MJ-12 and Roswell stories as bedrock truth, are perched on a rather unstable fault line.)

Another former Barker confederate, Lonzo Dove, told conspiracy chronicler Jim Keith that Bender's three mysterious men were none other than Barker and two pals in disguise. According to Dove, it was all a "cruel joke" at Bender's expense.

Another friend of Barker's, UFO researcher Jim Moseley, told Keith that Barker "did take Bender seriously, at the beginning. Then, when he realized that Bender was either not sane or not truthful...when he lost faith in Bender, which was within the first couple of years, in '55 or '56, after that [Barker] was just enjoying himself and making money."

Which brings us to the next major wave in MIB encounters. Over the course of a year in 1966 and 1967, the town of Point Pleasant, West Virginia, was plagued by a series of extremely bizarre paranormal events centering around sightings of a humanoid, winged creature that came to be known as "the Mothman." Interestingly, West Virginian Gray Barker would surface more than once on the periphery of events in Point Pleasant that year, which gives us ample reason to suspect the hand of a merry hoaxer at work. But the sheer scope of the weirdness suggests the involvement of other agencies as well, paranormal or otherwise.

John Keel chronicles that hysteria in his classic book *The Mothman Prophesies*. Hapless citizens who came face-to-face with the red-eyed birdman or who chanced upon the glowing aerial lights that haunted Point Pleasant that year were often paid visits by the MIB.

In November 1966, not far from where the Mothman would soon make its first appearances, appliance salesman Woodrow Derenberger encountered a UFO "shaped like an old-fashioned kerosene lamp chimney, flaring at both ends." The unlikely craft landed on the highway in front of Derenberger, forcing him to hit the brakes. A five-foot-ten-inch-tall man with dark skin exited the strange vehicle and approached Derenberger's car. Grinning, the visitor addressed Derenberger without moving his lips, ostensibly through telepathy. His name was "Indrid Cold," and he said he hailed from "a country much less powerful" than the United States.

After a brief exchange, Cold returned to his craft, which took off into the night sky. Soon Derenberger began receiving threatening phone calls, warning him to keep quiet about the encounter, plus calls featuring spooky electronic whoops and lulus (another staple of MIB harassment). According to Derenberger, the spaceman continued to contact him telepathically and in person. Cold came from the planet Lanulos "in the galaxy of Ganymede." Derenberger became a bit of a local celebrity, and his story fleshed itself out as time went on: The appliance salesman was eventually whisked to Brazil and then to planet Lanulos.

At about the same time, Derenberger was having his first confabs with Indrid Cold and others in the Point Pleasant region were running into mysterious, foreign men in suits. There were MIBs and black sedans around every corner, it seemed:

- After witnessing a UFO fly over her backyard, Mary Hyre, a newspaper reporter in Point Pleasant, had a succession of oddball visitors in thick-soled shoes. A large black car often followed her, peeling away when she noticed it and once screeching to a halt and disgorging a man with a flash camera.
- At one point, two short men wearing black overcoats called on Hyre at the newspaper office. According to Hyre, they looked almost like twins, with dark complexions and "Oriental" features. One of them inquired about the rash of flying-saucer reports and then blurted out, "What would you do if someone did order you to stop writing about flying saucers?" Later that same day, another small, Asian-looking man in black visited her office. He had abnormally long fingers and an unfamiliar accent. He introduced himself as "Jack Brown," a UFO researcher, and then stuttered, "What—would—what would you do—if someone ordered—ordered you to stop? To stop printing UFO stories." He denied knowing the other two men but claimed to be a friend of Gray Barker's.
- Apparently, it was the same Jack Brown who visited several other Point Pleasant residents that day, including a woman who had seen the Mothman. Again, he mentioned Gray Barker and added that he also was a friend of Mary Hyre and John Keel. He fumbled with a large reel-to-reel tape recorder that he apparently did not know how to operate.
- After observing a spherical UFO with four landing gears and a bottom-mounted propeller, Tad Jones reported the incident to the police. The next morning, someone had slipped a note, hand-printed in block letters, under his door. It read: "We know what you have seen, and we know that you have talked. You'd better keep your mouth shut." Several days later, a second note arrived via the same means. It was printed on a piece of cardboard that had been singed around the edges, and read: "...there want [sic] be another warning."
- A week later, Jones saw a man standing at the site of the

earlier UFO encounter. "He was very tanned," Jones said, "or his face was very flushed. He looked normal and was wearing a blue coat and a blue cap with a visor...something like a uniform, I guess. I noted he was holding a box in his hand. Some kind of instrument. It had a large dial on it, like a clock, and a wire ran from it to his other hand."

- Other UFO and Mothman witnesses received the peculiar phone calls with either electronic noises on the other end or voices described as "metallic" or "machinelike," often speaking in a foreign language.
- The MIB began harassing eightteen-year-old Connie Carpenter soon after she crossed paths with the Mothman when she was driving home from church. "Jack Brown" showed up at her house, doing his usual shtick, including the Gray Barker and Mary Hyre references. While Connie was walking to school, a black 1949 Buick sidled up alongside her. The driver, a young, well-dressed man in his twenties reached out and grabbed her, trying to pull her into the car. Connie escaped, but the next morning someone slipped a penciled note under her door: "Be careful girl," it read. "I can get you yet."

A disastrous coda to the Point Pleasant hauntings was soon to come. In *The Mothman Prophesies,* Keel writes that a Long Island woman named "Jane" received from the MIBs a forewarning of that disaster. After a close encounter with a piercing beam of light during a drive through the woods, Jane received a phone call from a machinelike voice that instructed her to locate a specific book at the local library. As Keel tells it, Jane found the book and read page 42, as instructed. As she looked at the page, "the print became smaller and smaller, then larger and larger." Then it "changed into a message" informing her she would be given a series of predictions.

The forecasts were delivered in the person of a grinning "Hawaiian" with Asian eyes who wore a gray suit and rode in the passenger section of a shiny new black Cadillac. He called himself Apol. Keel, whom Jane had contacted, was kept informed about each new prediction. Per Keel, many of Apol's predictions of plane crashes took place on schedule. But Apol's augury that "the Pope would be knifed to death in a bloody manner" and that "the Antichrist will rise up out of Israel" were among the misses. When Keel hypnotized Jane, she allegedly remembered several more boffo predictions that Apol had made, including Robert F. Kennedy's assassination and a December 15 disaster in Point Pleasant. On that day, the town's seven-hundred-foot Silver Bridge collapsed, killing forty-six people.

Whatever was really going on in Point Pleasant, it sure made for a damn good read. (A major Hollywood studio currently has plans to adapt the story into a feature film.) That Gray Barker was on the scene, ostensibly chronicling the events but perhaps tweaking them along, is the kind of thing that sets our paranoid antennae twitching.

In an interview with Jim Keith, Keel admitted that Barker was behind some of the Point Pleasant hijinks: "He did a lot of the phone nonsense, and I tracked him down on it." Keith points out: "Was it simply an accident that the Mothman encounters, the most incredible of paranoid flaps, took place in Gray Barker's home state of West Virginia?"

It's possible that Barker had confreres who helped him pull off at least some of the paranormal special effects that plagued Point Pleasant. But the sheer scope of the supernatural shenanigans suggests that there were other agendas at play. In his thoroughgoing volume *Casebook on the Men in Black,* author Jim Keith hypothesizes that Point Pleasant may have been a testing ground for a government experiment in mass hysteria. After all, the CIA illegally conducted mind-control tests on unsuspecting U.S. citizens as part of its notorious MK-ULTRA project, and thanks to the Agency's subsequent disposal of most MK-ULTRA records, we'll never know the full scope of those *official* pranks. Perhaps the government did use Point Pleasant residents as guinea pigs in a psychological-warfare experiment.

But just as it's impossible to dismiss all of the Mothman happenings as practical jokes or psywar operations, so, too, is it

impossible to dismiss all MIB accounts as hoaxes. The UFO
literature is rife with inexplicable encounters with MIBs. In
fact, UFOlogists have found similar accounts of preternatural,
prankish, and often menacing beings in black throughout the
annals of folklore. Jacques Vallee and others have painstakingly
cataloged the cosmology of fairies, sprites, elves, and demons in
mythology that behave uncannily like modern UFO pilots.
Whether those MIB motifs are merely images stored in humankind's collective unconscious or evidence of something more
literal is open to debate.

On the extreme vanguard of literal patrol, conspiracy author
William Bramley posits in his book *The Gods of Eden* that
extraterrestrial MIBs were behind the plague. He cites a summary written in 1682: "In Brandenburg there appeared in 1559
horrible men, of whom at first fifteen and later on twelve were
seen. The foremost had beside their posteriors little heads, the
others fearful faces and long scythes, with which they cut at the
oats, so that the swish could be heard at a great distance...."
Immediately after this MIBish visit to the oat fields, the plague
broke out in Brandenburg, leading Bramley to wonder: "What
were the long scythe-like instruments they held that emitted a
loud swishing sound? It appears that the 'scythes' may have been
long instruments designed to spray poison or germ-laden gas."

Or maybe not.

MAJOR SOURCES

Barker, Gray. *They Knew Too Much About Flying Saucers*. Lilburn,
GA: IllumiNet Press, 1997.
Bender, Albert K. *Flying Saucers and the Three Men*. Clarksburg, WV:
Saucerian Books, 1962.
Bramley, William. *The Gods of Eden*. New York: Avon Books, 1990.
Keel, John A. *The Mothman Prophesies*. Lilburn, GA: IllumiNet Press,
1991.
Keel, John A. *Operation Trojan Horse*. Lilburn, GA: IllumiNet Press,
1996.
Keith, Jim. *Casebook on the Men in Black*. Lilburn, GA: IllumiNet
Press, 1997.

III

They Died Alone

21

The Sex Goddess Who Knew Too Much

The main question that comes out of the case history of Marilyn Monroe's death is not whether she was murdered or even by whom, but how the men who ran this country in 1962 ever found time to do their jobs. They were all too busy with Marilyn Monroe.

The Kennedy brothers, Jack and Bobby, president and attorney general respectively, were either in bed with her for hours at a time or talking dirty to her on the phone for even longer. Sam "Momo" Giancana—the Chicago/Vegas mob boss who, some say, *really* ran the country—was preoccupied with the sex icon to end all sex icons, and wiretapped her—as did Teamster leader and Kennedy-hater Jimmy Hoffa. Giancana saw her as a means to gain power over the Kennedys. He bedded her too. At one point Momo boasted to another gangster that he had one up on the Kennedys because he was the last to have sex with Marilyn before her death.

And, unsurprisingly, J. Edgar Hoover spent his time listening to recordings taken from bugs in every room in her house—or anyone else's house or hotel where she stayed.

The Marilyn tapes, according to Hollywood private eye Fred Otash, who recorded and retained many of them, are "probably the most interesting tapes ever made—with the exception of Watergate."

Come on. What's on the Watergate tapes but a bunch of old lawyers cussing, smoking cigarettes, and grumbling about politics? The Marilyn tapes are said to contain lengthy recordings of America's most glamorous movie star doing the nasty with America's most glamorous president. And other intriguing episodes. Private investigator Milo Speriglio, who had spent thirty years on the Monroe case, says that the tape recorders were rolling right through Marilyn's murder.

Among researchers, writers, and sleuths who claim either to have heard some of these tapes or know what's on them—or to have just done a lot of legwork—there is a dazzling spectrum of opinions on how the former Norma Jean Baker met her demise at age thirty-six, on August 4, 1962. And at whose hands. Most of the hypotheses involve the Kennedy brothers and Giancana, with Hoover in the wings, as always, watching.

Speriglio names none other than Jack Kennedy himself, in collusion with his morally bankrupt father Joe (by that time incapacitated by a stroke that diminished his physical and mental faculties but apparently left his capacity for evil unscathed), as ordering the hit. Marilyn had become too pesky. Her constant calls to the White House and the Justice Department had become a hot gossip item for Washington insiders. And there was the omnipresent threat of a press conference at which Marilyn would blow the lid off her relationship with the Kennedy brothers, an option Marilyn was apparently considering. Not only did she jeopardize the Kennedy dynasty, but national security. In some kind of weird attempt to impress his extramarital flame, Bobby blabbed secret info about the CIA-Mafia kill-Castro plots to Marilyn Monroe, of all people. Or so the story goes. The official version is that Marilyn committed suicide by barbiturate overdose.

But even *Goddess* author Anthony Summers, who believes that Marilyn did not intentionally kill herself and goes no further than to "leave open" the possibility of murder, seems in his book to have been persuaded that Bobby Kennedy was at Marilyn's bungalow the night of her death. The attorney general may have visited her on a humane "mission of mercy," that night, Summers, perhaps wishfully, speculates.

Marilyn was extremely distraught that day, attempting to call everyone she knew in a fit of despair over her broken relationships with the Kennedy brothers. Career minded as always, they rather cruelly led her on then cut her off. In most versions of the story, Bobby initiated his relationship with Marilyn mainly to protect the president. Jack saw Marilyn as a fling. She saw him as marrying material. She harbored delusions of First Ladydom and when Jack grew bored of her, she wouldn't let him go. In stepped Bobby, who made the tragic error of falling in love with her.

Some biographers have written that Marilyn Monroe carried a Kennedy child in 1962, though whether it was supposed to be Jack's or Bobby's is not clear.

According to Summers's recreation of events, Bobby Kennedy would have arrived to find Monroe already in the throes of overdose, but alive. He, or an aide, called an ambulance, which was to take Marilyn to the hospital, but she died en route. When the younger Kennedy brother saw that his paramour had passed, he switched immediately into coverup mode. No matter how she died, it would not look good for the aspiring next president to show up at a hospital towing the corpse of America's favorite sex symbol.

The ambulance, according to Summers, turned around and returned to the bungalow. The body that wet dreams were made of was laid out on the bed, the room straightened, and a call placed to Marilyn's confidant and psychiatrist Robert Green-

son. It was Greenson who, officially, discovered the deceased
Marilyn Monroe. By this time Bobby was safely out of L.A.
Maybe. A police officer named Lynn Franklin tells of pulling
over a car driven by Peter Lawford sometime after midnight—
hours after Marilyn died. Bobby Kennedy was in the backseat.

Unlike some other writers on the topic, Summers admits that
his scenario might be "wrong in certain details, but it is a fair
construction from the information now available." He also says
that, probably, "no serious crime was committed that night."
But the death of Marilyn Monroe was, in Summers's view,
Bobby Kennedy's Chappaquidick—a case of being in the wrong
place at the wrong time with the wrong dead woman. But
Bobby got away where his younger brother Ted got caught.

In the updated edition of his book, Summers interviews an
unnamed source who claims to have heard tapes of Marilyn's
final night. The tapes appear to have been edited. Bobby
Kennedy, Peter Lawford, and Marilyn Monroe are on the
tapes—the two ex-lovers screaming at each other while Lawford tries to calm them down. At one point, according to
Summers's informant, there are sounds of a struggle. Bobby may
have pushed Marilyn onto the bed.

The tapes leave the impression, according to Summers, that
Marilyn was dead when Bobby left the house after his second
visit of the evening and that later there was a phone call placed
to Marilyn Monroe's home. On the tapes, someone picks up the
phone, but says nothing. When Marilyn's body was found, she
clutched a phone in her hand. The implication, according to
Summers, is that it was placed there—the call was intended to
establish a phone record that Marilyn was alive and answering
the phone at a time when she was, in fact, far too dead to chat.

Conspiracy theorists and medical examiners alike have long
been bothered by the absence of pill residue in Marilyn's
stomach and the lack of any glass of water in her apartment
with which she could have swallowed the massive overdose
required to kill her. And medical examiners never found any
signs of injected drugs either. Summers was the first to publicly

postulate the one method of ingestion that would leave no trace, unless checked for. It wasn't.

Peter Lawford, the debauched actor and Kennedy in-law who arranged Jack's West Coast trysts, knew something about Marilyn's death, but took his secrets to his drug-and-booze induced grave. When one of his former wives asked him if he knew how Marilyn died, he made an odd remark.

"Marilyn took her last big enema."

The starlet "complained of chronic constipation," Summers wrote. "Enemas relieve that complaint. Their use was also a common fad, particularly among show business people in those days, as an aid to instant weight loss." Marilyn Monroe had been taking enemas for years.

The rectal ingestion theory is now a common one. *Double Cross,* written by the late Sam Giancana's godson also named Sam Giancana, and his brother, Chuck, says that Marilyn's killers listened to Giancana's wiretaps as they lurked near her home, waiting for the opportune moment to strike. They overheard Bobby Kennedy and another man in the house irate at Marilyn. Finally, Bobby ordered Marilyn sedated and left. The hit men sneaked in and, as Marilyn lay in a drugged stupor, admistered a lethal "suppository."

The latest Marilyn book at the time of this writing, Speriglio's *Crypt 33* (titled for the compartment where Monroe's body was stored at the L.A. County morgue), describes how gangland superstar Johnny Roselli—a Giancana associate who is better known for his involvment in the CIA-Mafia plots to kill Castro and, by some accounts, JFK—showed up at Marilyn's house to distract her (they knew each other; Roselli traveled in show biz circles) while two hit men sneaked in the back. One knocked her out with a chloroform-soaked cloth, then the other administered the killer enema. It is unclear from the rather choppily written *Crypt 33* whether Speriglio bases his scenario on evidence from the actual Marilyn tapes, though he seems to imply that he does.

Crypt 33 includes Speriglio's assertion that Joe and Jack

Kennedy beseeched Giancana to rub Marilyn out and that the gangster, always looking for leverage with the Kennedys, happily obliged. The book revises Speriglio's earlier theory, spelled out in *The Marilyn Conspiracy*. Namely, that Giancana and Hoffa, under pressure from Bobby Kennedy and aware, through wiretaps, of his affair with Monroe, set him up for scandal. Slaying his sex-queen-on-the-side was part of the plot. But the Kennedy coverup worked. Neither Bobby nor Jack suffered destruction. Until later. And then by somewhat different methods.

The coverup continues. On that point all the Marilyn writers concur. Whether she was murdered, committed suicide, or died by accidentally misjudging her capacity to tolerate downers (Summers's preferred hypothesis), there is no question that the Kennedy brothers got involved with her in some way that grew too dangerous. In 1985, possibly for this reason, ABC killed a story on its *20/20* news magazine that independently corroborated the information in Summers's book *Goddess*. The half-hour segment included information about several of Jack Kennedy's other affairs, including liaisons with mob moll Judith Campbell Exner and suspected Nazi spy Inga Arvad.

ABC's higher-ups were skittish and ordered the segement trimmed. Finally it was down to thirteen minutes when ABC News president Roone Arledge, a close friend of Robert Kennedy's wife Ethel, killed it altogether. He denied that his friendship had any bearing on his decision, condemning his own reporters' story as "sleazy." According to Hugh Downs, one of the network's more staid on-air personalities, the "sleazy piece" was "more carefully documented than anything any network did during Watergate."

One biography recounts that more than a decade after Marilyn Monroe's death, a TV actress named Veronica Hamel, later well-known on the show *Hill Street Blues*, purchased the house where Marilyn lived and died. During redecorating, she discovered a thicket of aged wires sticking out of the roof. The actress hired a private contractor to destroy the cables that had transmitted the sounds of Marilyn Monroe's anguished life and eerie death to a place in history where they have never been found.

MAJOR SOURCES

Brown, Peter Harry, and Patte B. Barham. *Marilyn: The Last Take.* New York: Signet Books, 1993.

Gregory, Adela, and Milo Speriglio. *Crypt 33, the Saga of Marilyn Monroe: The Final Word.* New York: Birch Lane Press, 1993.

Speriglio, Milo. *The Marilyn Conspiracy.* New York: Pocket Books, 1986.

Summers, Anthony. *Goddess: The Secret Lives of Marilyn Monroe.* New York: Onyx Books, 1986.

22

Lizard King Lives!

In all likelihood, rock and roll legend Jim Morrison is buried in Paris's Père-Lachaise cemetery. That fact, of course, hasn't inhibited numerous "sightings" of the Doors' lead singer since his would-be death in 1971. Chalk it up, if you will, to the rock icon's prodigious mythology—like Dead Elvis's perpetual loitering or the Virgin Mary's fondness for making cameo appearances on tortillas.

Still, the circumstances of Morrison's death were quite mysterious and confusing. It's not surprising that a crop of postmortem rumors sprang up insinuating that by the good graces of assorted conspiracies—from the political to the supernatural—the Lizard King lives. Indeed, the official version of Morrison's death is in some respects even less believable than the surreal myths.

Officially, Morrison died at about 5 A.M. on July 3, 1971, of a heart attack, a rather improbable fate for a twenty-seven-year-old man—although somewhat less so for a rock star prematurely weathered by a decade of gut-flushing bacchanalia. As his longtime girlfriend, Pamela Courson, told the story, Morrison decided to take a bath in their Parisian flat one evening. Courson went to bed and the next morning discovered Morrison's corpse in the tub.

Bizarre rumors began to surface almost immediately, undoubtedly nursed along by Courson's puzzling attempts to screw a lid on the news. Courson initially told reporters that Morrison was "not dead but very tired and resting in a hospital." Nonetheless, word began to wend through Paris that Morrison had died of a heroin overdose in the sleazy underground nightclub, Rock 'n' Roll Circus. (Another popular rumor had it that Morrison OD'd on cocaine, a drug that he was known to binge on.) Rumor had it that Morrison was hustled home and deposited in the bathtub in an attempted revival. Of course, there were no witnesses.

Although Courson was claiming that Morrison was still alive days after his demise, in fact, a Parisian doctor had already signed the death certificate, listing the deceased as "James Morrison, Poet." The coffin was sealed before either the American Embassy or Morrison's family had been notified. No autopsy was performed. Only a full six days later, after Morrison's quiet burial at Père-Lachaise, did Doors manager Bill Siddons hold a press conference announcing the news that the "Young Lion" had died of a heart attack brought on by a blood clot and possibly a lung infection.

The *Los Angeles Times* stirred doubts when it headlined a story, WHY MORRISON DEATH NEWS DELAY? Inevitably, there was talk of a coverup. After all, only Courson, a couple of French medical examiners, and unknown police officers had actually *seen* Morrison's corpse. Not even Siddons (who jetted to Paris after Courson denied Morrison's death over the phone and then broke down crying) thought to open the casket when he arrived at the flat.

There were other improbable details in the official scenario, which subsequently fueled bizarre lore: How had an American rock star like Morrison finagled his way into Père-Lachaise, the historic French cemetery where luminaries like Balzac, Chopin,

Molière, and Oscar Wilde are entombed? For some unex-plained—ergo, suspicious—reason, the headstone didn't ap-pear for several months, and the grave remained unmarked. When Doors drummer John Densmore later visited the ceme-tery, he announced, "...the grave is too short!"

In addition to the unsubstantiated theory of the nightclub heroin OD, which was favored by Parisians, an assortment of alternate scenarios began to circulate.

One political conspiracy theory had it that Morrison was assassinated in a plot masterminded by those crew-cut reaction-aries at the FBI. In a scheme to snuff the radical New Left and hippie movements, J. Edgar Hoover's boys had iced not only Morrison, whose popularity, antiauthoritarian bent, and native smarts made him a threat to the American Way, but Janis Joplin and Jimi Hendrix, who had "allegedly" died of drug ODs earlier. (The theory was docu-dramatized in the low-rent film, *Down on Us*, later retitled *Beyond the Doors*.)

It wasn't as farfetched a scenario as it now seems, given the government's very real plots to undermine the New Left and the FBI's attempts to discredit Martin Luther King, Jr. (not to mention troubling government links to King's assassination). And after Morrison's infamous Miami arrest (for allegedly waving his wand onstage) the FBI did launch an investigation into his past. Of course, aside from a total lack of evidence, the theory just doesn't gel because Morrison refused to rent himself to any political causes. So why would "the man" hassle with a political hit?

The occult theories about Morrison's death sprout from his well-known dabbling in the esoteric arts (he was "married" in a Wiccan ceremony and believed that an Indian spirit inhabited his body). One had it that he died when someone plucked his eyes out with a knife to "free his soul." Another supernatural theory proposed that a jilted mistress in New York killed Morrison via transatlantic witchcraft. Some chose to think that Jim's spirit had sloughed off its mortal coil (as Courson claimed he had often done during trances), but this time canceled the return trip.

The most popular theories have it that Morrison, the martyred artist in a *Jesus Christ, Superstar* sense, somehow defied death, either metaphysically or literally. Morrison gets out alive!

As James Riordan and Jerry Prochnicky wrote in their Morrison biography, *Break On Through*, his "bizarre lifestyle inspired such thinking." Morrison's notorious disappearances had sparked death rumors before, and the confusion surrounding his apparently authentic death only egged on speculation. He had often talked about scrapping the burdens of super-celebrity by faking his own death and vanishing into the heart of Africa or some other suitably mysterious place. He told intimates that he would use the nom de guerre Mr. Mojo Risin' (the famous anagram of *Jim Morrison* in the song, "L.A. Woman") to contact them after he had "split to Africa." And Morrison was fascinated with conspiratorial scenarios that had the Disciples stealing the body of Christ from the crypt in what he jokingly called "the Easter heist."

Not surprisingly, then, the sightings began soon after his "death," at first in Paris, and then in Los Angeles, where a black-leather-bedecked Morrison reportedly hung out in underground gay nightclubs. A Bank of America employee in San Francisco claimed to be handling the account of someone calling himself and resembling Jim Morrison, although the clerk, later contacted by journalists, admitted he wasn't certain it was the Doors singer. In 1974, the rumor mill shifted into overdrive when Capitol Records released an album called *Phantom's Divine Comedy*, with a band identified as drummer X, bassist Y, and keyboardist Z—and with a lead singer who sounded eerily like Morrison. (A recent account has it that the Morrison sound-alike was actually proto-punk rocker Iggy Pop.)

One legend, described in *Break on Through*, had it that "at an obscure radio station in the Midwest Jim supposedly showed up in the dead of night and did a lengthy interview that explained it all." Of course, after the interview the mystery dude vanished again, and "no recordings of the interview exist."

Other rumors placed Morrison in Louisiana, where he was said to be living a secret life. In what looks like a connection to the Bank of America sightings, the incognito Morrison purportedly wrote and published a 1975 book called *The Bank of America of Louisiana*, under the auspices of the Zeppelin Publishing Company. The book's disclaimer, which states that names in this fiction "based on fact" had to be changed or "I would find myself back in the courts," is signed "Jim Morrison." The final line in the book is cryptically hoaky, just as we'd expect from an immortal sixties rocker: "B of A & Company, USA...where monkey business is big business."

But these sorts of rumors were inspiring, at least to a group of fans who, armed with Morrison's dental records, attempted to exhume the peregrinating corpse's casket—without success. Eventually, though, even Doors keyboardist Ray Manzarek was moved to remark, "If there's one guy who would have been capable of staging his own death—getting a phony death certificate or paying off some French doctor... and putting a hundred and fifty pounds of sand into a coffin and splitting to some point on this planet—Africa, who knows where—Jim Morrison would have been the guy to pull it off."

The speculation only gets funkier and, of course, foggier.

Thanks to the fact that Morrison's father, Steven Morrison, had been an admiral in the U.S. Navy, and was therefore "privy to intelligence and counterintelligence information," theories of an espionage role in Jim's death inevitably sprouted. According to conspiratologist Thomas Lyttle, a Scandinavian magazine published an article "detailing French intelligence efforts to assassinate Jim Morrison in Paris."

In his mondo Morrison essay in the anthology, *Secret and Suppressed*, not only does Lyttle fuse the espionage and spooky mystical theories, he mounts that double-header to the Louisiana doppelgänger, breeding a full-tilt conspiracy Cerberus.

Lyttle begins with the theory that crass commercial interests intervened in Morrison's spiritual transmigration (just as record execs compromised his earthly artistry). How Lyttle gets from A to B to C is a bit confusing, but boiled down to basics: he contends that Morrison dabbled in voodoo/voudon mysticism, which holds that the soul or aura needs a few months' quality time in which to successfully split to the beyond. Voodoo high priests, according to this tradition, have been known to intercept astral-bound souls, collecting their prize in a clay jar called a *canari*. This raises the question: Was Morrison's aura "bought and sold and then collected on that fateful day in Paris when he 'died'?"

According to Lyttle, the *canari* that captured Morrison's elemental identity was none other than Zeppelin Publishing Company, the same Louisiana outfit behind the aforementioned Jim Morrison/B of A book. (Lyttle states, but doesn't exactly prove, that the original Jim Morrison founded the Zeppelin organization himself, which seems to suggest that Morrison 1 approved the sale of his soul.) And the "high priest"? Again, according to Lyttle it was the mysterious proprietor of "B of A Company," who "owns an active passport and IDs under the name of James Douglas Morrison and claims to actually be the not-so-dead rock star!"

What this means is that the soul of Morrison 1 possesses the physical body of the mysterious Morrison 2, to whom Lyttle assigns the shorthand, JM2. And apparently JM2 was into more than just sex, drugs, and morose poetry. According to Lyttle, JM2 "claimed to be operating as an intelligence agent for a number of domestic and international groups including the CIA, NSA, Interpol, Swedish Intelligence, and others." Lyttle reports that he has seen documents, presumably provided by JM2, purporting to chronicle JM2's CIA work and "rogue financial activities with the Bank of America" on behalf of intelligence agencies, including "experiments to destabilize foreign currencies." Lyttle warns that he can't authenticate these papers, "but everything looked extremely official and very elaborate," he reassures.

Appropriately so, for JM2's plot is wonderfully elaborate. As Lyttle reports, JM2 has claimed publicly that there are "numerous" Morrison doubles doing yeoman's work in an obscure espionage cabal involving CIA sociological experiments. What's more, all the James Douglas Morrisons "knew one another and met from time to time to work it all out."

Whew. It makes you wonder whether that "Paul McCartney is Dead" hoax was in fact orchestrated by James Bond's archnemesis, Ernst Stavro Blofeld.

JM2's astral projections notwithstanding, a more mundane explanation for the suspicious secrecy surrounding the original Morrison's death emerged in the 1991 biography, *Break on Through*. Although Pamela Courson took her secret to the grave in 1974 after overdosing on heroin, authors Riordan and Prochnicky interviewed close friends to whom she had confided.

They reported that a despondent Morrison found Courson's heroin stash and overdosed—perhaps snorting it, for he was afraid of needles—in the Parisian flat. The next morning Courson discovered the corpse, and with the help of a close friend, attempted to prevent the sort of media circus that paraded around the drug-related deaths of Hendrix and Joplin. Somehow, Courson and company managed to persuade a French doctor to certify the death as a heart attack, thereby precluding an official autopsy. Meanwhile, they inveigled permission to lay Morrison to rest quietly in Père-Lachaise, days before informing the world, hardly knowing that they'd also laid the foundation for Morrison's mythological resurrection.

MAJOR SOURCES

Hopkins, Jerry, and Danny Sugerman. *No One Here Gets Out Alive*. New York: Warner Books, 1980.

Lyttle, Thomas. "Rumors, Myths and Urban Legends Surrounding the Death of Jim Morrison." In *Secret and Suppressed*, edited by Jim Keith. Portland, OR: Feral House, 1993.

Riordan, James, and Jerry Prochnicky. *Break on Through: The Life and Death of Jim Morrison*. New York: William Morrow and Company, 1991.

23

The Godfather Part III: The Real Story

As spiritual leader to the world's 800-million-strong Catholic population, the Pope is hardly an isolated figure. But Alberto Luciani, Pope John Paul I, who led those 800 million for just thirty-three days, died all alone one autumn night in 1978.

David Yallop, an English investigative journalist, has made the best case that the pope was poisoned. His book *In God's Name* argues that despite the brevity of his papacy, Luciani was bent on reform. Highest on Luciani's list of things that needed setting right: the Vatican Bank and related church financial institutions—the real Roman Empire.

By Luciani's time, following the reign of Giovanni Montini, Pope Paul VI, the Vatican Bank had mutated into a multinational high-finance hydra, diversified into regions not likely to have been frequented by the Holy Spirit. The transformation had begun five decades earlier when the Vatican struck a lucrative deal with Benito Mussolini's fascist government and followed up by inking a similar pact with Hitler.

Luciani desired nothing less than to undo the previous 50 years of history. Speaking to the Vatican diplomatic corps, his first official words as pope—prior even to his inaugural Mass— were: "We have no temporal goods to offer, no economic interests to discuss."

Quite a statement for the inheritor of a banking and real estate conglomerate with combined assets topping $3 billion; a force so unstoppable that a decade earlier it nearly demolished the Italian economy. When the Italian government displayed the gall to request a few taxes be paid on the Vatican's corpulent stock portfolio, the Holy See threatened to dump all of its holdings onto the Italian stock exchange, an exercise that would have strangled Italy's economy. Vatican Inc. remained tax exempt.

Perhaps the nastiest of the Vatican Bank's unsavory affiliations tied it to the penumbral P2, a mysterious Masonic-lodge-cum-criminal-syndicate with members in the highest reaches of government, the Mafia, and the Vatican itself.

Not incidentally, P2 was also a neo-fascist political cadre (at least Vatican financiers have kept consistent company over the years) responsible for assorted terrorist actions including a disastrous train station bombing in Bologna.

For P2 founder Licio Gelli—business partner of Klaus Barbie, financial backer of Juan Peron, paid CIA contact, and honored guest at Ronald Reagan's 1980 inauguration—finance and fascism are symbiotic. One Gellian aphorism holds, "the doors to all bank vaults open to the right."

The Vatican Bank was operated by an American bishop named Paul Marcinkus, who, for reasons never explained, was strolling through the Vatican village at dawn the very morning the Pope was discovered deceased. Marcinkus, not previously known for 6 A.M. power walks, had entered into numerous agreements on the bank's behalf with P2 members Michele Sindona and Roberto Calvi.

Sindona, now in prison, was an international speculator and mafioso who engineered frauds that led to the largest bank failures in American and Italian history. Marcinkus alternately claimed an ongoing business partnership with Sindona and denied ever meeting him.

Of the other P2 financier, Marcinkus once said, "Calvi merits our trust. This I have no reason to doubt."

"His comments are particularly illuminating," notes Yallop with a certain dry bemusement, "coming as they did just eight months after Calvi had been fined $13.7 million and sentenced to four years imprisonment, and only seven months after the Vatican and Marcinkus discovered (if we believe the Vatican version) that Calvi had stolen over $1 billion and left the Vatican to pay the bill."

Roberto Calvi was corrupt beyond comprehension, an Italian banker who pilfered millions upon millions in his career of white-collar crime. He liked to instruct his buddies to read Mario Puzo's novel, *The Godfather*, a copy of which was always on or near his person. "Then you will understand the ways of the world," advised this deeply immoral man.

How amusingly ironic, then, that Calvi's own death and the Byzantine scandals leading up to it formed the basis for *The Godfather Part III*, the second sequel to the film version of Puzo's gangster epic.

Calvi met his timely demise at the end of a noose affixed to the underside of London's Blackfriar's Bridge. Tough luck for Calvi, who though his hanging was ruled suicide by a coroner, seems certain to have met his picturesque doom courtesy of his P2 comrades. He must have been feeling acrobatic to scale the underside of the bridge and string himself up from beneath, rather than over the side the quick and easy way. For that matter, he could have just jumped, which would have been far more convenient considering his pockets were loaded with bricks.

Four hours before Calvi's death, his secretary fatally defenestrated in Italy.

Under the direction of Marcinkus, the Vatican Bank fronted for Calvi's complex and illegal stock deals. The Vatican Bank nominally owned numerous companies controlled in reality by Calvi. The setup scratched both backs. The Vatican and Calvi each raked in millions. Calvi was also P2's financial manager. Whenever P2 "puppetmaster" Gelli phoned the banker, he used the code name *Luciani*.

The uncommonly principled papacy of Alberto Luciani placed this gnarly net in grave jeopardy. Luciani intended nothing less than divesting the Vatican of both its vast wealth—the church, like Jesus, should be poor, the new pope believed—and of Bishop Paul Marcinkus.

If indeed Luciani died on September 28, 1978, of "natural causes," it was a phenomenal break for Gelli, Calvi, Sindona, and Marcinkus, as well as for the Mafia and P2. The first three men on that list had already demonstrated more than the mere capacity to plot and order murders. In addition to rival crooks, they'd killed various investigators for seeking a peek inside their dirty deals.

Marcinkus may not have had a history of murder but his motive for doing away with Pope John Paul I was no less powerful than that of his colleagues in chicanery. If Gelli, Sindona, or Calvi—most likely all three in concert—overlooked the opportunity to arrange for the pope's death they must have been careless crooks, and, after the pontiff keeled over, the luckiest men then alive.

Pope John Paul I, the world's most powerful and influential religious leader, conducted his daily business under security about as tight as that provided for the guy who delivered his morning papers. That is to say, none.

Not only was Luciani unguarded and unattended the eve he expired, but some sources say that when his fatal distress set in, whatever and whenever it was, he pushed a special bedside alarm button. The flashing alarm light went ignored and the guard in charge of what passed for the night's security detail was in bed. No one asked why the light in the papal apartment, clearly visible from outside, burned throughout the night though the pope stuck to a regular regimen of 9:30 bedtimes.

No autopsy was performed on Pope John Paul I, to the great consternation of Italian journalists, who—understandably, given Italian political history—are much quicker to suspect conspiracy than their American counterparts. The Vatican tried to pacify the protesting press, falsely stating that church law prohibited autopsies on popes (there was never any such edict).

The death was ruled the result of acute myocardial infarction, though no death certificate was issued to that, or any other effect.

According to Yallop, in the absence of an autopsy, a fatal dose of the drug digitalis would be indistinguishable from a heart attack. The same could be said for a multitude of other toxins. But Yallop focuses on digitalis because Gelli instructed all P2 members to commit suicide with a dose of that drug, provided by their benevolent lodge, if pressured to reveal secrets of the quasi-Masonic crypto-fascist group.

Yallop's sources tell him that when the pope was found, his stiffening fingers were clutching a set of notes detailing many of the changes he proposed in Vatican operations. The Vatican announced that he held a copy of *The Imitation of Christ*. The first reporters who heard that claim broke out in guffaws.

"It's difficult to believe that the death was natural," said a top aide to the French archbishop Marcel Lefebvre, "considering all the creatures of the devil who inhabit the Vatican."

When Karol Wojtyla, John Paul II, won election as Luciani's successor he received an immediate briefing on the radical plans of Pope John Paul I. He implemented not a single one.

MAJOR SOURCE

Yallop, David. *In God's Name*. New York: Bantam Books, 1984.

24

The Man Who Got Too Close

Just after 12:30 in the afternoon on August 10, 1991, chambermaids at the Sheraton Inn in Martinsburg, West Virginia, stumbled upon a grisly sight. In room 517, a nude man lay in the bathtub, his white knees protruding from a pool of bloody water. Blood was everywhere, spattered on the wall above the tub and smeared on the bathroom's tile floor.

The dead man was Danny Casolaro, a forty-four-year-old freelance journalist and would-be novelist from Fairfax, Virginia. His wrists were deeply slashed in twelve places. Under the body, paramedics found a straight-edge razor blade, an empty beer can, a paper coaster and two white plastic garbage bags. Nearby was a scrawled note that read in part, "Please forgive me for the worst possible thing I could have done."

It certainly looked like a garden-variety suicide. Which, apparently, is why the county coroner decided against an autopsy and released the body to a local mortician. The undertaker embalmed the corpse that same evening, before next of kin had been notified, a move that was not only hasty, but also illegal.

Had Martinsburg's finest immediately contacted Casolaro's family, they might have handled the case a bit more gingerly. For when notified of his brother's death two days after the fact, Anthony Casolaro, a physician, instantly recalled Danny's warning to him the previous week: "I have been getting some very threatening phone calls. If anything happens to me, don't believe it was accidental." On top of that, the day before and on the day of his death, someone had made a series of threatening phone calls to Casolaro's home. And according to Danny's housekeeper, who picked up the phone, the threats were hardly subtle. "You son of bitch," went one. "You're dead."

An ardent if somewhat unseasoned journalist, Danny Casolaro had claimed to family and friends that he was on the verge of exposing a tangled cabal he called "the Octopus," a sprawling conspiracy theory. Casolaro believed that an international klatch of seven or eight men had masterminded a host of scandals with tentacles extending to the controversial October Surprise, the alleged 1980 deal between the Reagan-Bush campaign and Iran to keep U.S. hostages on ice; the Inslaw affair, which revolves around charges that the Reagan Department of Justice stole computer software from a private firm; Iran-Contra; and the BCCI banking scandal, believed by Casolaro to be the funding arm (or tentacle) of many a national security conspiracy. In a book proposal, Casolaro had described, in his typically enthusiastic prose style, a "web of thugs and thieves who roam the earth with their weapons and their murders, trading dope and dirty money for the secrets of the temple."

The fatal trip to Martinsburg seemed extremely significant to Casolaro's family and friends because, as Casolaro had boasted to just about everyone he bumped into, there he planned to rendezvous with a supersource who would lock the final pieces of the Octopus puzzle into place.

Chagrined by national media coverage of their negligence

(and improbable rumors that the town was in cahoots with the Octopus combine), Martinsburg authorities quickly opened a belated investigation, including a full-blown autopsy by the state medical examiner. Although the chain of evidence had been broken, and rather drastically at that, local and state officials came back with findings that vindicated the original conclusion: Casolaro had killed himself, they confidently stated. There was supposedly no evidence of a struggle, and the wounds appeared to be self-inflicted, according to the local authorities. There was also the straightforward suicide note— in Casolaro's own handwriting.

Nonetheless, critics argued, the local police overlooked or underplayed other evidence that at least *suggested* more sinister possibilities:

- Before the emergency crews had arrived on the scene, Barbara Bittinger, the assistant head housekeeper at the Sheraton, saw two bloody towels under the sink. As she later told investigative journalist John Connolly, "It looked like someone threw the towels on the floor"—and it wasn't the maids—"and tried to wipe the blood up with their foot, but they didn't get the blood, they just smeared the floor." The police only briefly questioned Bittinger. Yet her account of the towels was corroborated by the professional cleaner who later scoured the room—and threw the towels away.

- According to a George Washington University physician who reviewed the autopsy, Casolaro's deep wrist gashes didn't have the usual "hesitation marks" of the aspiring suicide who tests his pain threshold. In Casolaro's case, this apparent gusto was all the more peculiar, for, according to friends and family, he was exceedingly squeamish. FBI special agent Thomas Gates, whom Casolaro had used as a sounding board for his theories, later told a congressional committee that Martinsburg police described the wounds to him as "hacking" lacerations, which sounds much more violent than the official "no struggle" line.

- Local police were unable to account for Casolaro's missing notes, which he reportedly trundled to Martinsburg in a briefcase. Both notes and briefcase had vanished without a trace.
- A waitress in the Sheraton cocktail lounge recalled that Casolaro had entered the bar with a man she described as "maybe Arab or Iranian." Police were never able to locate that man.
- And Casolaro's family and many friends found it hard to believe that he had taken his own life. Described as outgoing, upbeat, and boyishly exuberant, Casolaro seemed an unlikely candidate for suicide.

Danny Casolaro, without a doubt, had mixed with a cast of strange and possibly dangerous characters. Like many a conspiracy researcher who bites into that rotten apple, Casolaro found himself in a beguiling world of intrigue where the right knowledge, if you can only amass enough of it, promises to unlock America's encrypted history. Unfortunately, the spooks, thugs, and con artists who populate that David Lynchian landscape often embroider fact with outright fantasy—for reasons that remain, to say the least, obscure.

The character who nudged Casolaro into the conspiracy abyss was an oddball genius named Michael Riconosciuto. Described as a "mad scientist" and a "pathological liar" who expertly weaves fact and fantasy, Riconosciuto claims involvement in just about every national security scandal of the last decade.

In notes and conversation Casolaro dubbed his mad scientist source "Danger Man." Riconosciuto vaulted into Casolaro's universe during the spring of 1990. The introduction was made by a mutual acquaintance, Bill Hamiltion, who was mired in his own private conspiracy, the notorious Inslaw scandal.

Riconosciuto had been feeding information to Hamilton, the proprietor of Inslaw, Inc., about the alleged theft of Hamilton's proprietary computer software by officials in the Reagan administration's Department of Justice. Hamilton had won some early battles in his pitched war with cronies of Attorney General Edwin Meese III. The bone of contention, Hamilton's PROMIS software, was a powerful and potentially Orwellian computer program designed to integrate law enforcement databases nationwide, enabling government authorities to keep tabs on court cases, defendants, criminals, attorneys, cops, judges, and just about anyone else who appears on the radar screens of the criminal justice system.

Hamilton and his high-profile lawyer, former U.S. attorney general Elliot Richardson, charged that Meese's crew had violated a contractual agreement to use a more primitive version of PROMIS and had plundered an advanced, proprietary version of the computer program. Two federal judges sided with Hamilton, ruling that the Meese Department of Justice "took, converted, and stole" Hamilton's PROMIS "by trickery, fraud, and deceit."

Typically, after the scenery-chewing Riconosciuto made his grand entrance, the Inslaw affair got even weirder, bouncing to distant points on the globe like an overheated spy novel. Casolaro found himself in a seductive world of intrigue.

Riconosciuto told Hamilton and Casolaro that he had modified the PROMIS software for sale to foreign countries. The man fencing the stolen computer program, according to Riconosciuto, was an Ed Meese pal named Dr. Earl Brian. It got even better: Riconosciuto claimed that profits from the stolen merchandise were Brian's reward for helping to broker the October Surprise deal for the 1980 Reagan-Bush campaign. As Danger Man told it, he and Brian had personally delivered a $40 million payoff to the Iranians at an alleged October 1980 rendezvous in Paris, purportedly attended by Iranian mullahs, George Bush, and future CIA Director Bill Casey. Brian, of course, has denied any association with Riconosciuto, the Inslaw affair, or the October Surprise.

It might have been easy to dismiss Riconosciuto as a complete crank, except that certain aspects of his story checked out. Hamilton *had* discovered that the Canadian Mounties were using the stolen PROMIS software. Witnesses claimed to have seen Riconosciuto and Brian together on the Cabazon Indian reservation in Indio, California, where Riconosciuto said he had modified PROMIS and developed high-tech weapons for the Nicaraguan Contras. Other sources acknowledged that Riconosciuto and Brian were indeed involved in a joint venture between the Cabazon Indians and the Wackenhut Corporation, a private security firm known as the CIA's favorite dirty job contractor. The venture used the Cabazon tribe's quasi-sovereign status to skirt restrictions on manufacturing and selling arms. According to a report by the Riverside County district attorney, local cops hired for security at the reservation referred to Brian as "being with the CIA."

And the Machiavellian purpose of Riconosciuto's software modifications? To turn PROMIS into a tool of international espionage, a high-tech bugging device that would be distributed to "scores" of foreign intelligence and police agencies. Unbeknownst to the hapless foreigners, CIA computer hackers would then have an electronic "trap door" giving them secret access to foreign intelligence data.

After Hamilton introduced Casolaro to Danger Man, Riconosciuto proceeded to drop additional bombshells. He claimed to have sabotaged the CIA-connected, money-laundering Nugan Hand Bank; to have designed "fuel-air explosives" for the Contras; and to have helped develop the cannon-like Super Gun produced for Iraq by Gerald Bull, who was murdered in Brussels. Each of these angles Casolaro dutifully recorded in his book proposal. According to Casolaro's notes, Riconosciuto also ushered the journalist into the outer limits of conspiratorial UFOlogy, claiming knowledge of the government's secret dealings in the Nevada desert with space aliens.

Like many a semiomniscient Deep Throat, though, Riconosciuto promised but never delivered evidence buttressing his loftiest claims, including tape recordings that were to have proved he had hobnobbed with Reagan's CIA director, Bill Casey.

But Riconosciuto did direct Casolaro to some very dangerous characters, indeed. Shortly before his death, Casolaro made plans to visit Riconosciuto's old stomping ground, the Cabazon reservation—hardly hospitable territory for whistle-blowers. During the early 1980s one tribe member's attempts to oust the reservation's white administrator, John Philip Nichols, came to a dramatic halt when someone fired a bullet into the malcontent's forehead, execution style. A former bodyguard of Nichols claimed, before emigrating hastily to South America, that his boss had hired the killers and ordered him to pay them off.

Nichols, a globetrotting "social worker," liked to brag about having worked on CIA plots to assassinate Fidel Castro and overthrow Chilean President Salvador Allende (who was eventually assassinated). During the mid-1980s, Nichols was convicted for soliciting the murder of five people. He got a generously light sentence and was back on the reservation eighteen months later.

Casolaro also became chummy with an entrepreneur whom he would have been wise to christen *Extreme* Danger Man. Apparently Robert Booth Nichols (no family relation to John Philip Nichols) had worked on the Cabazon-Wackenhut joint venture. He soon replaced Riconosciuto as Casolaro's most important contact in the conspiratorial funhouse. At first Casolaro was drawn to this suave figure, who has been described as "Clark Gable without the ears." Later Casolaro would refer to him as "a thug who acted like a gentleman."

Casolaro eventually learned that the FBI had identified Robert Booth Nichols as a drug trafficker and money launderer with ties to the Gambino organized crime family and the Japanese mob, the Yakuza. (Nichols unsuccessfully sued the government for slander.) Three days before his death, Casolaro told a special agent of the FBI that Nichols had warned him, "If you continue this investigation, you will die." Casolaro wasn't sure if it was a threat or a show of concern.

Investigative journalist John Connolly has suggested that while it might not have been the Octopus that killed Casolaro, perhaps he was done in by some rogue element encountered during his investigation. In a well-researched *SPY* magazine article, Connolly wrote that Casolaro had discovered from a former special prosecutor in the Department of Justice that Nichols had once offered to become a mob informant—a snitch. That knowledge, Connolly speculated, might have placed Casolaro in extreme danger. As Connolly put it, "If John Gotti, for example, had ever found out what Danny Casolaro had found out, Nichols would be a dead man."

To be fair, though, Nichols had quite an alibi. The day before Casolaro's death, Nichols told Bill Hamilton that he was leaving for Europe that same evening. Days later, when he called Casolaro's brother to offer his condolences, Nichols mentioned that he had just returned from London.

Other journalists have guessed at alternatives to foul play, including the possibility that Casolaro grew suicidally despondent over his inability to get published or his failure to get to the bottom of the Octopus cabal. The fact that the autopsy revealed trace amounts of an antidepressent drug helped fuel such speculation. The autopsy also revealed that Casolaro had early symptoms of multiple sclerosis, and suicide theorists have suggested that he took his life rather than develop full-fledged MS. Of course, these are all just guesses.

Just as Casolaro's surviving notes shed little light on his demise, they are equally vague about the precise shape of the conspiracy he claimed to be on the verge of exposing. We know that he planned to interview "renegade" CIA agent Edwin Wilson, then languishing in a federal prison on charges of supplying explosives to Libyan leader Mu'ammar Qaddafi. Along with a number of other veteran CIA operatives, Wilson figures in the Christic Institute's theory of the "secret team" (see chapter 60) a coven of spooks purportedly responsible for two decades' worth of national security scandals, from the JFK hit to drug trafficking in Southeast Asia to Iran-Contra and beyond. Although the Christic theory has been widely ridiculed (and its related civil suit tossed out of court), the fingerprints of

Wilson and other CIA operatives have indeed turned up in a number of "off-the-books" operations.

While the Octopus as unified-field conspiracy theory may sound a bit farfetched, Casolaro certainly was loping through some very ominous terrain. A House committee looking into the Inslaw affair thought as much and recommended that Casolaro's death be investigated further.

In early 1994, the Clinton Department of Justice decided to open a nationwide probe into the Casolaro case. As Casolaro's phone pal, FBI special agent Gates, told the House committee: "There is cause for suspicions."

MAJOR SOURCES

Casolaro, Danny. "Behold, a Pale Horse: A True Crime Narrative." In *Secret and Suppressed.* Portland, OR: Feral House, 1993.

Connolly, John. "Dead Right." *SPY,* January 1993.

Connolly, John. "Inside the Shadow CIA." *SPY,* September 1992.

Connolly, John, and Eric Reguly. "Badlands." *SPY,* April 1992.

Corn, David. "The Dark World of Danny Casolaro." *The Nation,* 28 October 1991.

Fricker, Richard L. "The Inslaw Octopus." *Wired,* 1.1 (1993).

"The Inslaw Affair: Investigative Report by the Committee on the Judiciary." Washington: U.S. Government Printing Office, 1992.

Ridgeway, James, and Doug Vaughan. "The Last Days of Danny Casolaro." *Village Voice,* 15 October 1991.

25

The Cloud Buster

Like his famous "cloud-buster," an exotic contraption of metal pipes and snaking tubes designed to make rain *and* disperse clouds, Wilhelm Reich provoked extreme reactions. To devoted Reichians, he was and is a martyred genius, a man whose revolutionary scientific discoveries drove his spiteful enemies—the government, the medical establishment, the communists—to destroy him.

But to his detractors, Reich was various other things, few of them flattering. Take your pick: mad scientist, medical "quack," eccentric sexologist, paranoid schizophrenic, haywire conspiracy theorist. Sure, he had once been a pioneering psychoanalyst and a student of Freud, a genius even, but somewhere along the line he went off the deep end.

The truth, of course, may fall short of both extremes. But there's no doubt that Wilhelm Reich, who died in prison in 1957, *was* a latter-day heretic. His spectacular, far-ranging theories about orgastic inhibition, cancer, nuclear radiation, weather modification, cosmic "orgone" energy, and UFOs (to name only a few) were, shall we say, radical departures from the orthodoxy of his day—or any day, for that matter.

Even if Reich was delusional when he claimed to be the victim of an overt conspiracy by "HIGs" (hoodlums in government) and "Red Fascists"—as he named his tormentors in later years—there's also no doubt that he was plagued by a far subtler kind of "conspiracy." As a stubborn, unrelenting iconoclast, Reich was fated to butt heads with the scientific establishment and the political order. For their part, disdainful of what could only be way-out pseudoscience, the orthodoxies did what orthodoxies do when faced with the radically unconventional: They marginalized the oddball by rejection, ridicule, innuendo, and, ultimately, legal action.

Given that level of hostility to his work, it's easy to see how Reich eventually grew into the role of "conspiracy theorist." And also why many Reichians continue to believe he was deliberately murdered.

But we're way ahead of the story.

It begins in the Vienna of Sigmund Freud, where young Willy Reich embarks on a life-long quest for what would become his Holy Grail (and ultimately his undoing): the "life-fulfilling" energy of sexual potency. As a rising star in the psychoanalysis movement, Reich refashioned Freud's early libido theory into what he now called his theory of "orgastic potency." Where Freud hypothesized that unconscious sexual repression led to neurosis, Reich took the theory to its logical, literal extreme, asserting that all neurosis is caused by blocked up orgastic energy. In other words, she's gotta have it, and so does he.

Needless to say, Reich's ideas about sexual healing didn't thaw frigid Austria of the 1920s. Reich was just too radical for Vienna and too much the renegade even for psychoanalysis. Once referred to as "Freud's pet," Reich increasingly found himself in the doghouse. For one thing, Reich was bedding some of his fraulein patients and prescribing masturbation to others—not exactly what Freud had in mind when he institutionalized the couch. But it was Freud's decision to scrap the libido theory altogether (partly in response to this young wild man who had taken Freud's sexual metaphor to literal extremes) that finally put Reich on frosty terms with psychoanalysis.

By the mid-1930s, after an equally parabolic career in the Communist Party of Berlin (they loved his critique of Hitler's "sex-politics," but sex education for *der jugend*, ages eight to twelve? *Nein!*), Reich had moved to Scandinavia, on the outs with sexually hung-up Marxists and one step ahead of the sado-masochistic Nazis. In Norway, Reich made the first of his unrelenting scientific discoveries vindicating his theory of orgastic energy: the "bions."

Reich found that rotting matter—even when sterilized—broke down into microscopic blue "vesicles" that were in some sense "alive." Reich dubbed these particles "bions" and believed them to be quasi-life forms somewhere between inanimate and animate matter. Some bions pulsed with a kind of radioactive energy that caused Reich's skin to welt when he placed them on a slide over his hand.

Reich decided that this radiation, which fueled the bions, was the "life force" energy he would later christen "orgone," so-named because it was, he said, identical to the sexual energy of orgasm. As far as Reich was concerned, he had bridged the gap between psychology and biology, isolating the energy that charges both mind and body.

Of course, the scientific establishment had another opinion: Reich was an unhinged dilettante whose hat was obviously too tight. Though Reich never claimed to have "created" life (he had merely tapped its source, he said), the Dr. Frankenstein label stuck, encouraged no doubt by the Austrian's peculiar experiments measuring the bioelectrical orgastic energy of kissing couples.

As the skeptical biologists saw it, Reich's throbbing bion vesicles were garden-variety microbes, or else he was misinterpreting some other mundane phenomenon. But Reich's careful replications of the experiment, taking into account those criticisms, always produced the same results. And though mainstream science has yet to systematically recreate the experiment, various modern researchers claim to have reproduced Reich's uncanny, hard-to-explain micro-critters.

Whatever the significance of his discovery, Reich's unconventionality proved to be of far greater interest to Norway's popular press: Who was this foreign shrink seeing patients in their underwear, advising them to touch themselves, conducting bioelectrical smooching experiments, and now causing vesicles to *throb*, for God sakes? Provincial Oslo was scandalized, and as the 1930s drew to a close, Reich, cursing his professional and political enemies, packed his bags for the seemingly hospitable climes of America.

Reich's research took off in New York and at Orgonon, as he dubbed his summer home in Rangeley, Maine, after the orgone energy. (Reich loved inventing technical neologisms, which lent an aura of authority to his unaccepted theories. The science of orgone energy? Orgonomy. Radium enriched with concentrated orgone? Orur.)

In 1940, Reich formulated his orgone energy theory, announcing that the cosmic life force not only streamed through the sexually healthy individual and between the pulsing bions, indeed it was "everywhere." (In sexually repressed people, however, orgone energy was stopped up, creating emotional and physical tension, or "armoring.") Reich believed he could see the bluish orgone charge crackling between the stars in the night sky and in a darkened room.

He managed to contain the orgone field emitted from bions in a specially built box lined on the inside with sheet metal and insulated on the outside by wood and other organic materials. Reich believed that the metal reflected the radiation inward. This unlikely invention Reich dubbed the "orgone energy accumulator." It would later bring the wrath of the Food and Drug Administration (FDA), the American Medical Association, and the psychiatric establishment down upon him.

The accumulator seemed to amplify the bion radiation, and

looking through the contraption's porthole, Reich got an eyeful of some sci-fi special effects: bluish vapors and flickering yellow lines and dots. But even when there were no bions in the box, Reich saw the same effect, albeit in a diminished form. As Reich explained it, the omnipresent atmospheric orgone was passing through the box and accumulating inside.

Reich racked up some interesting results with his orgone accumulators. When he put his hand inside an empty accumulator, he reported a warm tingling sensation. When he measured the temperature inside the box, it was on average a half degree warmer than room temperature, apparently evidence of the energy accumulation.

To establish his amazing find, Reich wasted little time arranging "a meeting of minds," as he described it, with Albert Einstein. Cordially, Einstein agreed to see him. Reich spent five hours in the famous physicist's Princeton home explaining his theories and urging Einstein to look through a hollow tube to view the orgone energy in the darkened room. We can only guess what Einstein really thought, but he graciously listened. Reich later delivered an accumulator, and Einstein conducted the temperature experiment, but concluded that the phenomenon was probably due to convection currents cooling the room.

Einstein's biographer, Ronald Clark, depicted the physicist as humoring the misguided psychoanalyst, "this eccentric, distraught figure [who] seems already to have slipped down the slope toward charlatanry or madness."

But Reich biographer Myron Sharaf reports that there have been at least twenty "positive replications" of Reich's temperature experiment since the 1950s, some with precise controls to eliminate the "convection" effect.

The Einsteinian rebuff didn't discourage the indomitable Reich from making further discoveries. "We're not playing for peanuts, here," he liked to say in stentorian Austrian tones.

Reich branched out into cancer research. He discovered

another kind of microscopic bion that grew from decaying matter: a black, rod-like organism that could immobilize the bluish, amoeba-like bion. He called these new organisms T-bacilli. When he injected mice with T-bacilli, the rodents died, many of them after developing cancer. Reich learned that he could cultivate many T-bacilli from the blood of cancer patients, but few from the blood of healthy persons. Were the bions a key to understanding cancer?

Reich found that cancerous mice "treated" in the orgone accumulator lived on average seven weeks longer than the sick rodents deprived of such therapy. Not surprisingly, Reich and his colleagues soon began building phone-booth-size accumulators for themselves—and for cancer patients.

Of the fifteen terminal cancer patients Reich saw in the early 1940s, six lived five to twelve months longer than expected, but then died. Six others were still alive when Reich published his findings two years later. Reich maintained that the orgone treatment reduced their pain and the size of their tumors. But he never claimed, as the FDA would later erroneously charge, that the accumulators could cure cancer. In fact, Reich believed that the accumulator alone couldn't treat the underlying cause of cancer: that clogged up libido, again. (Reich's emphasis on holistic health and the connection between mental and physical well-being was far ahead of its time.)

Then there was the orgone-powered engine, which has given Reich's numerous critics something to nosh on. It certainly *sounds* like that quintessential American swindle, the perpetual motion machine. Actually, according to Sharaf, who was a student and colleague of Reich's, the motor ran on a combination of orgone energy, concentrated in an attached accumulator, and electricity, but in "an amount insufficient to rotate the wheel without the accumulator."

When the student who built the motor deserted Orgonon—with the device—an increasingly paranoid Reich suspected that his engineering whiz kid was being coerced by the Atomic

Energy Commission, the communists, or some other malefactor. (Reich never published details about the contraption, giving rise to more doubts about its authenticity.)

As Sharaf reports about Reich's conspiratorial thinking, "He had always been capable of such erroneous pattern-finding, but this tendency increased sharply in his last years." If Reich's preferred villains seem a tad grandiose, we should remember that in the double-barreled tunnel of the nuclear age and the Cold War, paranoia was a bumper American crop.

In 1950, with the Korean War stoking up fears of global nuclear scrimmage, Reich hoped that his orgone accumulator might help treat radiation sickness. Thus began the dramatic Oranur Experiment, which many Reichians cite as a watershed—for science *and* conspiracy.

The orgone hit the fan, so to speak, when Reich placed one milligram of radium inside a series of nested accumulators. Almost immediately, Geiger counters went haywire, off the scale. Laboratory workers became dizzy and nauseated. The atmosphere was described as "oppressive" and "charged." But when removed from the room and tested outside, the radium registered normal Geiger counter readings.

Nonetheless the radiation in the room wouldn't dissipate. Reich, who had awakened the next day with a full-body tan, continued the experiment anyway. When he returned the radium to the accumulator, a bluish cloud could be seen through the windows of the room. People as far as ninety feet away from the building claimed to feel the sickening effects, which lasted for weeks. Later, when Reich's grown daughter, Eva, placed her head inside the empty accumulator, she lapsed into a near-comatose state and only revived several hours later.

So what was the Oranur Effect (Reichspeak for "orgone antinuclear") all about? Reich concluded that nuclear radiation had transformed the atmospheric orgone energy into a malignant force, just as healthy bions could decay into T-bacilli. Reich called this negatively amplified energy Deadly Orgone Radiation, or DOR. Backing up Reich's belief that orgone had "run amok" was an article in the *New York Times* of February 3, 1951—three weeks after the experiment. The *Times* reported that unusually potent levels of radioactivity had been detected in a three hundred- to six hundred-mile radius, centered near... Rangeley, Maine!

Conspiracy researcher Jim Martin believes that Reich's subsequent legal traumas were linked to his accidental discovery of the Oranur Effect. "Wilhelm Reich was imprisoned," writes Martin, "because he stumbled onto frightening facts about nuclear radiation during the early 1950s, a critical point in that newly developed industry." The dirty secret uncovered by Reich? "That there is *no shielding possible* against the biological effects of nuclear radiation," says Martin.

Nuclear goons not withstanding, at the time of Oranur, Reich was already in hot water with HIGs from the Food and Drug Administration. The FDA's antennae began twitching after two negative magazine articles about Reich appeared in *Harper's* and *New Republic*. Written by a freelance journalist named Mildred Brady, who privately called Reich's cancer theories "crackpot," the articles drew sly comparisons between sexologist Reich and the bohemian sex scene. Brady also drew subtle parallels between Reich and that always-alarming American phenomenon, the cult prophet. Brady's prophetic inference was clear: "the growing Reich cult," if not regulated, might wind up "disciplined by the state." Most damaging, however, Brady gave the erroneous impression that Reich claimed his accumulators would give patients "orgastic potency" and would cure cancer.

Once again, Reich found himself in need of a good press agent. Other journals picked up the scent and amplified Brady's distortions, as in *Collier's* claim that "the accumulator can lick everything from the common cold to cancer, according to Dr. Reich." *True* magazine just called it "the Marvelous Sex Box," which makes Reich's low-tech accumulator sound like Woody Allen's "orgasmatron" from the movie *Sleeper*. The message was clear: Reich was a dangerous quack. And maybe even some kinda *prevert*. Spurious rumors began to circulate that

Orgonon was a sex racket or "nudist camp" that was "fed" children from a nearby summer camp. In between "orgies," female patients were said to have been…"masturbated" on the premises.

Reich, the one-time-communist-turned-Republican was convinced that his old foes, the Stalinists (Red Fascists), were behind the *New Republic* assault: After all, as every right-winger in the nation knew, the magazine's managing editor, Henry A. Wallace, was indeed connected to American communists, via his 1948 run for the presidency on the Progressive Party ticket.

Reichian writer Jim Martin also suspects a Stalinist connection. Martin points out that *New Republic* owner, Oxford wag Michael Straight, had not only jump-started Wallace's presidential campaign, he was a confessed (but reluctant) Soviet spy. More than that, *New Republic* was connected to Wall Street billionaires linked to the Rockefellers and British internationalists. Quoting from that group's sympathetic chronicler, the late Professor Carroll Quigley: *New Republic*'s "original purpose," as envisioned by Wall Street bankers, "was to provide an outlet for the progressive left and guide it quietly in an Anglophile direction." Given the fact that many right-wingers saw the Brit-inflected Wall Streeters as pawns of the Soviets, maybe Reich had a point when he later blurted to prison psychologists that the Rockefeller Foundation "made me a tool of its socioeconomic interpersonal relations." Or maybe not.

Reich hit upon a less complicated explanation when he formulated his somewhat self-serving, albeit perceptive, concept of the "emotional plague." Basically, what Reich meant by the phrase was the kind of intolerance that drives certain people to "persecute" those they deem "immoral" or otherwise unconventional. In other words, a witch-hunt, or at least the kind of superior ridicule that banishes unusual thinkers to the fringes.

There's no doubt that Brady's negative press helped set the stage for the FDA campaign against Reich, which was egged on by the American Medical Association and the psychiatric establishment. The investigation dogged Reich for years, as the FDA attempted without success to find a dissatisfied accumulator owner—for Reich had been shipping the "devices" (as the FDA always called them) to eager customers throughout the East Coast. All the while, the quack-baiting continued.

Shaken but not stirred, Reich continued his research into the Deadly Orgon Radiation (DOR), which he now saw as a global threat in the age of nuclear testing. After the Oranur Experiment, he had noticed "black" smog-like clouds hovering oppressively over the landscape. Convinced that these were DOR vapors, Reich invented his cloud-buster, which acted like a lightening rod, draining the DOR from the sky. Reich also used the machine—the hardware had a futuristic low-tech look, like something out of the movie, *Mad Max*—to make rain. At any rate, he convinced local farmers that he could modify the weather. They paid him to successfully reverse a drought. Later, Reich mounted the cloud-buster on the back of a truck and took it into the Arizona desert, looking like the Road Warrior, himself. He was convinced that DOR was causing the deserts to expand, and he set out to see if he could reverse the trend.

In the meantime, the FDA threw down the gauntlet. In 1954, at the FDA's request, Maine's attorney general filed a complaint against Reich, asking for an injunction. The complaint suggested that Reich was a charlatan, and it shamelessly distorted many of Reich's careful disclaimers about the accumulators. Reich stubbornly refused to appear in court, perhaps not fully understanding the American legal system, perhaps starting to buckle under the pressure. The FDA won its injunction, which was frightfully sweeping: Reich was ordered to destroy not only his accumulators, but also all literature "promoting" both the accumulators *and* his theories about orgone energy. That covered just about everything he had ever written, and Reich was one prolific author.

Furious, Reich shot off a telegram to the offending HIGs, threatening a deluge courtesy of his cloud-buster: "We are flooding the East as you are drying out the Southwest. You do not play with serious natural-scientific research." As biographer Sharaf writes, "Snow in Rangeley and rain along the New England coast came after Reich's weather operations; it had not been predicted." Thrilled, Reich slam-dunked a telegram to J. Edgar Hoover, trumpeting his ominous achievement.

By now Reich was convinced that President Eisenhower was secretly watching over him, grateful for Reich's anti-UFO "space gun." Whenever air force jets zoomed overhead, Reich took it as the presidential equivalent of a wink.

For Reich had taken up a lonely battle. In his book, *Contact With Space*, he speculated that the drivers of UFOs—"CORE men" (Cosmic ORgone Energy)—possibly had malevolent designs on the planet. "There was no escape from the fact that we were at war with a power unknown to man," he wrote. UFOs were causing the desertification of the earth, their "slag" exhaust spreading oppressive DOR through the atmosphere. Reich tied this theory to his idea of the "emotional plague": Man's "emotional desert" was abetting the UFOs in their scheme to smother the planet with DOR.

Back on Earth, the FDA and the state "Red Fascist HIGs, under Moskau [sic]" initiated contempt of court proceedings after one of Reich's colleagues shipped orgone accumulators across state lines. Reich represented himself at the trial and tried to make the case for conspiracy, but the judge rightly pointed out that the place for that had been the first trial. Still, Reich aroused the judge's interest when he pointed out that the chief prosecutor had been a former colleague at Orgonon, which raised all sorts of unsavory possibilities, from conflict of interest to entrapment.

But it was water over the dam. Reich was convicted on May 7, 1956, and sentenced to two years in prison, an especially harsh sentence for an ailing fifty-nine-year-old. That summer, FDA agents supervised the destruction of fifty-three accumulators. After an unsuccessful eleventh-hour intervention by the ACLU, the FDA oversaw the burning of more than six tons of books and other publications, including Reich's classics, *The Sexual*

Revolution and *The Mass Psychology of Fascism*, which were written long before he built his first accumulator. Despite the ugly specter of a bonfire of books—which Reich had seen before in Germany—the popular press made not a peep.

Reich died in prison, of "heart complications," on November 3, 1957, just two months before his parole.

Reichians see several details about his death as being suspicious: A manuscript he claimed to be writing never turned up. Reich had mentioned to his wife that when he asked for aspirin, he had gotten two pink pills instead; when she sent a letter requesting to see the hospital dispensary record, the warden penciled in its margin, "NO." And according to Jim Martin, Reich's daughter, Eva, now suspects foul play.

But a deus ex machina isn't really necessary to explain Reich's end. The doctor's radical ideas, his brilliant but often flawed pattern-finding, and his domineering will always brought the "emotional plague" crashing down on top of him. It still hangs like a DOR cloud, obscuring Reich's numerous contributions to psychology and therapy, sociology, child-rearing, and, who knows?—maybe even to biology and physics.

MAJOR SOURCES

Martin, Jim. "Who Killed Wilhelm Reich?" In *Apocalypse Culture* (expanded and revised edition), edited by Adam Parfrey. Los Angeles: Feral House, 1990.

Martin, Jim. "Quigley, Clinton, Straight, and Reich." *Steamshovel Press*, no. 8 (Summer 1993).

Sharaf, Myron. *Fury on Earth: A Biography of Wilhelm Reich*. New York: St. Martin's Press, 1983.

Wilson, Colin. *The Quest for Wilhelm Reich*. Garden City, NY: Anchor Press/Doubleday, 1981.

Thanks to Jim Martin of *Flatland* for compiling research used in this chapter.

26

The Hermit Billionaire

As fantastically wealthy manipulators go, Howard R. Hughes was king. The billionaire's Midas touch had less to do with his fabled technical and financial genius than with endless secret deals and covert political bribes. "I can but any man in the world," Hughes liked to boast. Indeed, Hughes's conspiratorial authority stemmed from his ability—and eager inclination—to purchase loyalty from anyone, including the president of the United States, in a position to advance his, well, idiosyncratic designs.

Everything about Hughes was larger than life, including his paradoxical legend. Heir to a Houston fortune based on a drill bit patent that revolutionized oil mining, the dashing young Hughes captured the American imagination during the Great Depression years. Cowboy aviator, Hollywood playboy, patriotic military contractor, maverick financier, Hughes was like a comic book hero whose can-do exploits knew no limits. Later in life, as his eccentricities metastasized into madness, the darker portrait emerged: the stringy-haired old man, a ranting lunatic with a mortal fear of germs holed up in a penthouse hermitage.

Throughout his life, Hughes's obsession with control expressed itself in a mania for espionage and spookery, especially as it applied to nurturing his substantial neuroses. However, despite his seeming omnipresence in the eye of many a stormy conspiracy, Hughes was just as manipulated by others. Known to spooks as the "Stockholder," Hughes fronted for CIA covert operations, sometimes unknowingly; Hughes, the demented shut-in, saw his empire manipulated by remote control.

We join the Hughes saga during the late 1950s, with the arrival of the shadowy and somewhat sleazy Robert Maheu, fountainhead of many real and imagined Hughes conspiracies. In the late fifties, Hughes hired Maheu to intimidate would-be blackmailers and spy on dozens of Hollywood starlets toward whom Hughes felt possessive. Maheu was a former FBI man whose private security firm fronted for the CIA on ultra-sensitive (read: illegal) missions.

By the time he became Hughes's private spook, Maheu already had impressive credentials, supervising contract kidnappings for the CIA and acting as the Agency's literal pimp, hiring prostitutes to service foreign dignitaries and their peculiar sexual appetites. Maheu's most notorious CIA job was as a go-between in a failed 1960 plot to assassinate Fidel Castro, which recruited the Mafia to do the "hit." Friendly with the darndest folks, Maheu enlisted the aide of Vegas mobster John Roselli ("Uncle Johnny" to Maheu's children), Chicago godfather Sam "Momo" Giancana, and powerful Florida mob boss Santos Trafficante (see chapter 2).

Apparently, Hughes had no involvement in Maheu's freelance CIA work but delighted in the spook's exploits and connections, which only enhanced the billionaire's reputation and influence. (According to journalist Jim Hougan, Maheu informed Hughes of his efforts on behalf of the CIA to off Castro.) By some accounts, however, the Stockholder was the Agency's single largest contractor. In dedicating his resources to the CIA, though, Hughes wasn't guided entirely by selfless motives. During the late sixties, he asked Maheu to offer his empire to the Agency as a CIA front. At the time the Hughes fortune was threatened by major legal troubles; the beleaguered billionaire hoped to deflect the nettlesome litigation with a "national security" shield.

One of Maheu's extracurricular assignments that Hughes did support was a successful effort to foil a "Dump Nixon" movement threatening the unlikable vice president's place on the 1956 Eisenhower ticket. As Maheu fell into Nixon's orbit, Nixon in turn felt the pull of Hughes's considerable gravitational field.

Hughes thought of the Red-baiting Nixon as his man, and the billionaire's audacious patronage suited Nixon's political ambitions. Unfortunately for Nixon, Hughes cash would always be something of a liability. During the 1960 presidential race, the press reported that the Hughes Tool Company had loaned $205,000 to Nixon's hapless brother, Donald (who was attempting to revive his failing Nixonburger restaurants). Disclosure of the Hughes loan, which was never repaid, damaged Nixon in the final days of the campaign, giving Jack Kennedy a much-needed boost. Typically, Hughes fared better on his end of the apparent quid pro quo. Less than a month after his loan to the vice president's brother, the IRS reversed a previous decision and granted tax-exempt status to the Howard Hughes Medical Institute, an obvious tax shelter of dubious charitable merit.

Of course, the arch-conservative Hughes could be bipartisan when it came to greasing presidential wheels. He ordered Maheu to offer both Presidents Johnson and Nixon a million-dollar bribe to stop nuclear bomb tests in Nevada. In the mid-sixties, Hughes had holed up in a Las Vegas penthouse, and he considered the nuclear testing to be a personal threat to his health. Maheu claims to have disregarded both orders.

The next bomb to explode in the Nixon-Hughes orbit was a metaphorical one that would prove politically fatal to Nixon. Because the shadow of Howard Hughes hung over Watergate, staff investigators of the Senate Watergate Committee were convinced that the phantom billionaire was the key to understanding the scandal. But under pressure from senators, investigators deleted from their final report forty-six pages that concluded Hughes had indirectly triggered the break-in. Some have suggested that committee chairman Sam Ervin and his Senate colleagues, many of whom were recipients of Hughes money, staved off personal embarrassment by burying the Hughes connection.

But what role, if any, did Hughes play in Watergate? Always tangled in power politics, the billionaire seems to have been a motivating, albeit peripheral, presence in the scandal. Hughes's former Washington lobbyist, Lawrence O'Brien, was chairman of the Democratic National Committee (DNC) during the Watergate era. O'Brien had joined the Hughes payroll in 1968 when "the Old Man," exercising his option to purchase the powerful and well connected, ordered Maheu to hire Bobby Kennedy's key men in the aftermath of the senator's assassination. And as the self-absorbed Hughes saw it, "aftermath" meant before the blood had dried, on the night of the assassination.

O'Brien drove Nixon to paroxysms of rage. Not only was he a former major domo of the Kennedy clan and the Democratic party's top apparatchik, O'Brien was now plugged in to the Hughes empire, and theoretically privy to the billionaire's many deals with the president. At first, Nixon ordered his staff to delve into the O'Brien-Hughes connection with an eye toward collecting dirt on the DNC chairman. Later, White House aides worried that O'Brien might have damaging information on Nixon-Hughes dealings. One of those affairs involved an unreported $100,000 cash contribution to Nixon from the billionaire. Nixon's banker and bagman, Bebe Rebozo, stashed the cash in Florida. It's possible that this secret and illegal money fix became part of the notorious White House slush fund that subsidized dirty tricks and, later, bought the silence of the Watergate burglars.

There were other quid pro quos. Hughes's generous support

of the Nixon regime coincided with exceedingly favorable treatment (some would say exceedingly illegal treatment) on antitrust issues, aiding his efforts to corner the market on Las Vegas hotel-casinos.

According to the traditional view of the scandal, O'Brien's office was the primary target of both break-ins at the Watergate office complex. However, a persuasive revisionist theory suggests that O'Brien wasn't the burglars' primary target. Indeed, this view doesn't necessarily contradict that the Nixon White House was obsessed with the O'Brien-Hughes connection. It seems likely that some of the White House cohorts in crime, including "plumber" G. Gordon Liddy, were misled to believe they were bugging O'Brien's phone "to find out what O'Brien had of a derogatory nature about us," as Liddy put it in his 1980 book, *Will.*

Nixon, then, possibly fearful of losing another election thanks to Hughes, may have set the Watergate machinery in motion, without specifically knowing what Liddy et al. were doing. As H. R. Halderman, Nixon's chief of staff, later wrote: "On matters pertaining to Hughes, Nixon sometimes seemed to lose touch with reality. His indirect association with this mystery man may have caused him, in his view, to lose two elections."

Of course, it's clear that Hughes, himself, was in the dark about Watergate, just as he was literally in the dark in "malodorous" hotel rooms worldwide, shooting up codeine and gobbling down Valium "blue bombers." By the early seventies, Hughes was a withered bundle of neuroses who handled all objects with Kleenex "insulation" as a prophylactic against germs. His decaying teeth; corkscrewing toenails; greasy, shoulder-length hair; and Rip Van Winkle beard seemed to mock his dapper appearance of the thirties and forties. His human contact was limited to his Mormon nursemaids.

Hughes seems to have lost control of his empire a year and a half before the Watergate break-ins. During the so-called Thanksgiving coup of 1970, a struggle within the Hughes organization for control of the Old Man and his assets came to a head. The heavy-handed conspirator was oblivious to the deft conspiracy carried out by his top staff. Hughes executives, led by Bill Gay, the Mormon administrator who had shrewdly handpicked the billionaire's attendants, spirited Hughes on a stretcher from his ninth-floor penthouse in Las Vegas's Desert Inn Hotel, down the fire escape and into an awaiting jet, which whisked him away to the Bahamas.

The cognizant loser was super spook Robert Maheu, whose controversial rise within the Hughes apparat came to abrupt halt. Gay and company resented Maheu's unsubtle power grabs, luxuriant salary and perks, questionable business decisions, and penchant for promoting himself as the Old Man's "alter ego." Maheu, in turn, accused his rivals of kidnapping Hughes against his will.

The Thanksgiving coup spawned other conspiracy theories. One IRS agent reported to his superiors that he believed Hughes died in Las Vegas in 1970 and that "key officials in charge of running his empire concealed this fact at the time in order to prevent a catastrophic dissolution of his holdings." According to the IRS conspiracy theorist, a double "schooled in Hughes's speech, mannerisms, and eccentricities" had been deployed. (In fact, Hughes did employ doubles during the sixties to distract press hordes while the rich and famous invalid made his stretcher-bound escapes.)

But Hughes was still alive—and apparently a willing denizen of the Bahamas, as he subsequently informed the world in a rare telephonic press conference. In the same interview, Hughes took the opportunity to denounce Maheu as a "no-good, dishonest son of a bitch" who "stole me blind."

With Gay's control over Hughes's nursemaids, it was easy for Maheu's rivals to monopolize the Old Man's ear even before the exodus from Vegas. Spiriting Hughes to the Bahamas enabled Gay and company to cut off Maheu from his power base and to insulate Hughes from having to testify if any of the ongoing legal actions against corruption in his empire; this was crucial, for if Hughes were to appear publicly, it might have become obvious that the emperor wore no clothes and had no sanity—rendering him incapable of managing his affairs.

Considering the testy Old Man's decline and his pathological fear of facing human beings, then, it's a bit surprising that he managed to make several personal appearances before small audiences. During a short stay in Managua he met face to face with Nicaraguan dictator Generalissimo Anastasio Somoza and a U.S. ambassador and later, to his custodian's alarm, demanded to pilot airplanes as he had in his prime. Considering this sudden coming out after years in phobic seclusion, perhaps the doppelgänger theory isn't so outlandish after all, though accounts of Hughes stripping to the buff at the controls and demanding to fly in a blinding rainstorm sound like the real McCoy. Regardless, Hughes's brief forays outside of his musty hotel cloister would soon come to an end, following a bathroom fall that broke his hip. Thereafter, Hughes would remain bedridden until his death two and a half years later.

It's not clear how much the Stockholder knew about his minders' agreement to act as cover for a CIA project to raise a sunken Soviet submarine northwest of Hawaii. The top secret "Project Jennifer" involved the *Glomar Explorer*, a massive ship supposedly owned by Hughes's Summa Corporation. Ostensibly Hughes's latest oversize business venture, the *Glomar Explorer* was to test pioneering techniques of mining the ocean floor. That, anyway, was the CIA's cover story. In reality, the ship was designed to plunge a prehensile steel claw on a three-mile tether to the ocean floor in an effort to retrieve a Soviet submarine that contained valuable code books.

When word of the real doings in the Pacific eventually leaked to the press, Hughes was hailed once again as a figure larger than life. In fact, by then the six-foot-three maverick financier was an emaciated 90-pound husk more concerned with enemas than spy craft. Finally, on April 5, 1976, a jet ambulance ferrying Hughes's cadaver from Acapulco touched down in Houston. Such was the reclusive millionaire's enigma that his fingerprints were taken and sent to the FBI for verification. It was Howard R. Hughes, all right. The IRS agent had been wrong.

His overall condition suggested abject neglect. X rays revealed broken hypodermic needles lodged in his arms. He was malnourished and dehydrated. Why hadn't his doctors checked him into a hospital long ago, regardless of his protests? In Acapulco, Hughes had lain in a coma for three days before his personal doctors summoned a Mexican physician, who was "aghast" at the patient's condition. The Mexican police suspected foul play.

Even Maheu has modified his original kidnapping theory— but was Hughes in some sense the willing captive of his staff? Clearly, his own mental and physical decline had rendered him incapable of managing his affairs long before his death. Early on, his withdrawal into seclusion enabled his staff to control his interaction with the outside world. Later he was, for all intents and purposes, preserved in a state of suspended animation, his drug-glazed eyes fixed on a third or fourth showing of ironically titled B-movies like *The Brain That Wouldn't Die* while his employees conducted the Hughes interests. In a sense it's a tribute to Hughes's conspiring mind that the Stockholder continued to front for the CIA long after he was little more than an extremely wealthy vegetable.

MAJOR SOURCES

Barlett, Donald L., and James B. Steele. *Empire: The Life, Legend, and Madness of Howard Hughes.* New York: Norton, 1979.

Colodny, Len, and Robert Gettlin. *Silent Coup: The Removal of a President.* New York: St. Martin's Press, 1991.

Drosnin, Michael. *Citizen Hughes.* New York: Holt, Rinehart and Winston, 1985.

Hougan, Jim. *Spooks: The Haunting of America—The Private Use of Secret Agents.* New York: William Morrow, 1978.

Maheu, Robert, and Richard Hack. *Next to Hughes.* New York: HarperCollins, 1992.

IV

Mondo Politics

27

Votescam

No political act requires quite the same leap of faith as voting. Sure, the average citizen's one chance to participate in democracy comes at the ballot box. But what happens to your vote once you've pulled the lever, punched the computer card, or placed an X through the appropriate box?

Ken and Jim Collier "discovered" that at least on national election nights—the only time the ballot count really counts—the votes are all processed through a central corporation. A private corporation. The owners of this entity are the same media that report the results of the elections. When the News Election Service (NES) was incorporated back in 1964 by ABC, CBS, NBC, the Associated Press, and United Press International, it either put the vote count under the aegis of a responsible media organization concerned about reporting accurate and timely election returns, or in the clutches of a power-mad cabal.

The Colliers elect to see it as the latter, which is not surprising, because, as the authors of the book *Votescam*, the Collier brothers are the nation's self-styled leading advocates of the theory that all national elections, presidential and congressional, are rigged.

The News Election Service provides an ideal mechanism for chicanery—especially in the cyber-epoch of computerized voting. A little monkey-wrenching with a single, central, and private vote-tabulating computer—well, it's much cleaner than taking reams of paper ballots out into the West Texas outback and incinerating them as Lyndon Johnson did in an early congressional race. And it's more civilized than digging up the dead, or at least their voter registration cards.

The Collier hypothesis is as follows: The major media corporations use their direct and discreet access to NES to fix election results in advance. This not only enables them to make incredibly accurate projections, but, more significantly, to pick the president and the Congress. Not surprisingly, these politicians turn out to be slaves to corporate interests.

The actual vote totals are verified by county registrars—the only public officials responsible for counting votes. But that process doesn't wind up until months later. By that time everyone's lost interest, the media doesn't report those official results anyway, and if they did, there is ample time to tamper with those counts as well.

The media companies whelped NES when they realized that their prior practice of assembling returns individually led to occasionally embarrassing discrepancies in their reporting. These days, however, the actual returns have become irrelevant. Media election reporting derives almost exclusively from exit polls, in which a representative from a polling group hired by an individual media company asks voters leaving the polls a simple question: "Who'dja vote fer?"

Exit polling has been widely (and rightly) criticized for removing the electoral process from the hands of voters and transferring it to the statisticians. But at least it represented a small step toward decentralized election reporting. News organizations were, once again, actually competing—thus mitigating the chance of the next chief exec being selected by a coffee klatch somewhere in the bowels of Rockefeller Plaza.

In 1990, that hope withered.

"The three major television networks and Cable News Network," reported the *New York Times* on February 26, 1990, "have agreed to create a single election day exit poll of voters that would provide the same information at the same time to each organization."

The new unified group has operated since the 1990 congressional elections. Votescam becomes Pollscam.

Vote fraud in America is as old as American democracy. The Colliers simply posit its existence on a rather more expansive scale than the seemingly infinite number of well-documented local riggings. Computer technology only makes altering vote totals easier. The most popular election software, EL-80, has been found by independent computer experts to have switched the names of candidates, failed to record some votes, and failed to print out error reports. El-80 is also easily accessible to anyone with a basic knowledge of computer language. It is written in COBOL, and anyone who knows that language— and by the early eighties any college student who wanted to could learn it—can break into the program.

Taken together, say the Colliers, centralization of election reporting, vulnerability of high-tech voting, and corporate power adds up to one grim finality:

"It is the prescription for the covert stealing of America."

MAJOR SOURCE

Collier, James M. *Votescam: The Stealing of America*. New York: Victoria House, 1993.

28

The Mother of All "Gates"

Watergate, the mother of all scandals branded something *gate*, may be America's most famous conspiracy. Most of us are familiar with at least the outlines of the scandal: a "third-rate burglary"; Richard Nixon's attempts to cover up that crime and countless others; the eighteen-and-a-half-minute gap in the White House tapes; Nixon's manipulation of the CIA and FBI in the furtherance of said coverup; "I am not a crook," yet, inexorably, Nixon's near-impeachment and resignation.

But stop and think for a moment about how little we actually know about the specific conspiracy that got the whole dirty snowball rolling. For starters, who ordered the break-ins at the Democratic National Committee (DNC) headquarters in the Watergate office complex, and why? Just whose phone was bugged? And when the coverup began, exactly who was covering up for whom?

Ah, into that yawning gap of knowledge leap the Watergate revisionists. Armed to the teeth with explosive counter-theories

212

and ostensible smoking guns, some are diehard soldiers in the struggle to rehabilitate Richard Nixon. Others really have unearthed compelling evidence that casts doubt on conventional assumptions about the scandal.

Regardless of the angle, all interpretations of the Watergate saga inevitably begin during the shifty hours of June 17, 1972. Responding to an early-morning call by a Watergate complex security guard, plainclothes cops stumbled upon five overdressed burglars cowering behind furniture in the Democratic National Committee's sixth-floor offices. The second-story men included CIA-trained Cuban exiles and "ex"-CIA wire man James McCord. They were carrying cameras, bugging devices, and lock-picking tools. Running the "black-bag" job from a nearby hotel room were "former" CIA operative E. Howard Hunt and White House "Plumber" G. Gordon Liddy. Hunt had recruited the anti-Castro Cubans, loyal to the super-spook since their nostalgic Bay of Pigs days. Hunt, Liddy, and McCord were the hands-on henchmen in Nixon's dirty tricks squad.

As conventional history tells it, the burglars were either attempting to plant an electronic bug in a telephone belonging to the liberal Democrats, or they were trying to remove/replace a malfunctioning bug positioned during an earlier break-in.

Yet there have always been problems with this theory—and despite its popularity, it remains just that: an unproven "theory." For starters, the burglars have told conflicting stories about what they were after: Was it dirt that DNC Chairman Larry O'Brien kept on Nixon, as Liddy earnestly suggested, or was it intelligence from another area of the office, as Hunt and two of the Cubans later claimed? If so, why risk so much for apparently so little? As Nixon's director of congressional relations later noted, "You take some damn chances if they're worthwhile, but that was crap."

Not surprisingly, the "unindicted co-conspirator" himself wholeheartedly agreed: "The whole thing was so senseless and bungled that it almost looked like some kind of a setup," Nixon announced in his memoir, typically giving himself the benefit of the doubt and flipping the story upside down to cast himself as the victim. The actual culprits? His supernumerary enemies, of course. Shortly before he was crowbarred from office, Nixon discovered "new information that the Democrats had prior knowledge and that the [Howard] Hughes organization might be involved.... And there were stories of strange alliances."

Which brings us to the Democratic Trap theory, popular among diehard Nixon loyalists. Trap-gate has a factual anchor in seven volumes of executive-session testimony taken during the Senate Watergate investigation. The Senate testimony reveals that in April 1972, a New York private eye named A. J. Woolsten-Smith tipped off Larry O'Brien's deputy and also journalist Jack Anderson to a brewing spy operation against the DNC. Woolsten-Smith described the inchoate operation in some detail, from the Watergate office target to the Cuban personnel on the GOP team.

Armed with this information, Nixon-friendly theorists use twisted Nixonian logic to deflect blame for the resulting scandal: The donkey party *knew* the Republican burglars were going to break into the Watergate building, *so the Dems set us up!*

Theorists as disparate as the late H. R. Haldeman (Nixon's chief of staff) and left-wing critic Carl Oglesby have endorsed another version of the Trap theory. They suggest that Carl Shoffler, the police officer who made the Watergate arrests, was tipped off to the burglary in advance—either by the Democrats or by one of the burglars.

The evidence aligned "against" Shoffler? He had already finished his shift, but signed up for an additional eight hours of late-night work—on his birthday. When the call from the dispatcher came, Shoffler and his fellow officers were only a few blocks away from the Watergate, as if "awaiting the dispatcher's summons." And not least, an acquaintance of Shoffler, Edmund Chung, testified that in a subsequent dinner conversation, he got the "impression that Shoffler had advance knowledge of the break-in."

Shoffler denied making that statement and claimed that Chung had attempted to "bribe" him with a $50,000 "loan" if only Shoffler would "confess" to prior knowledge. Shoffler also suggested to the Senate that maybe Chung was a CIA agent, although that was never proven, nor did it even seem likely. Shoffler denied having any foreknowledge of the break-in and said of his decision to work overtime, "I just felt like it." And there the Cop Trap theory dead-ends.

Other entrapment theories posit a constellation of alternative villains, including those ubiquitous Howard Hughes operatives, Jack Anderson, and the CIA. The late Gary Allen, the cabal-sniffing John Birch Society author, titled a chapter in his book on the Rockefellers, "Was Nixon Watergated?" After all, Allen noted, the rise of Gerald Ford also brought zillionaire Nelson Rockefeller a proverbial heartbeat away from his much-coveted Oval Office.

The strongest revisionist theories arrived relatively late in the post-Watergate era, to a hissy fit of media disapproval. Finally, a critical mass of new evidence had coalesced to challenge the official story, the tale that had lionized a generation of aging journalists.

Secret Agenda, by Jim Hougan, and *Silent Coup*, by Len Colodny and Robert Gettlin, make a compelling case for the theory that Watergate didn't necessarily proceed from the top of the organization chart down.

According to *Silent Coup*, the key to the Watergate mystery was presidential counsel John Dean, a sort of conspiracy of one. This is a controversial recasting of Dean, whom history records as a peripheral player who turned whistle-blower and fingered the ostensible ringmasters in the scandal: ex-attorney general John Mitchell, chief of staff H. R. Haldeman, domestic affairs adviser John Erlichman and, of course, Nixon.

So what was Dean's agenda? Nothing so dull as tapping phones or scouring files for political dirt. For, according to *Silent Coup* and *Secret Agenda*, the Holy Grail of Watergate was sex! In *Secret Agenda*, Hougan suggests that the real target of the break-ins was a secret file featuring names, phone numbers, and perhaps even glossy pictures of prostitutes. At the time of the break-ins, a high-priced call-girl ring had been operating out of the posh Columbia Plaza apartment building a few blocks away from the Watergate complex.

According to Phillip Bailley, a young lawyer-pimp connected to that prostitution ring, a staffer at DNC headquarters had been arranging liaisons between the prostitutes and Democratic bigwigs. Apparently, at the DNC offices there was a file containing pictures and vital stats of the prostitutes, for marketing purposes.

It may have been Bailley's arrest for sexual pandering that triggered the fateful second Watergate break-in. As Colodny and Gettlin reveal, John Dean took a special interest in Bailley's well-publicized arrest. In a highly irregular and apparently unauthorized move, the presidential counsel took it upon himself to summon the federal prosecutor on the Bailley case to his office for a personal debriefing. It was then that Dean got a peek at important evidence: Bailley's address books.

According to Colodny and Gettlin, who build on Hougan's case, Dean's then-fiancée, Maureen Biner, was a friend and roommate of the prostitution ring's madam. What's more, Colodny and Gettlin confirmed that Maureen "Mo" Biner's name, phone number, and nickname, "Clout" (after all, she was about to marry the president's counsel), appeared in Bailley's confiscated address books. But Bailley's little black books also listed the girls from the Columbia Plaza ring.

Silent Coup's hypothesis? That with the press and FBI sniffing at the exposed call-girl ring, Dean had his own embarrassing, albeit tangential, connection to the D.C. strumpets. Consequently, he took it upon himself to dispatch the burglars to the Watergate on a fishing expedition. (*Silent Coup* is oddly silent on whether or not the DNC kept a dossier on "Clout.")

According to Colodny and Gettlin, then, the *real* motive behind the Watergate break-ins was considerably less conspiratorial (but a lot more steamy) than presidentially authorized blackmail or political counterintelligence. Dean wanted to know what was in the DNC's secret hooker files.

In detail too complicated to go into here, *Silent Coup* presents compelling evidence to suggest that Dean micromanaged a coverup immediately following the Watergate arrests—not to shield Nixon, but to cover his own exposed posterior. In this theory, Nixon really is a bit of a dupe, certainly responsible for many other high crimes and misdemeanors, but genuinely bewildered by news of the "third-rate burglary" (yet, being Nixon, reflexively jumping in to cover up a specific crime he knew next to nothing about).

But Dean's agenda (or Nixon's, if you prefer the traditional top-down theory) may not have been the only one operating in the murky waters of Watergate.

As investigative author Jim Hougan proferred on the twentieth anniversary of the break-in, "If one tries to understand Watergate in terms of a single monolithic operation conducted by a team of spooks with a unified goal, it will defy understanding."

Secret Agenda lays out fascinating evidence that suggests the burglars, themselves, may have had competing motives. Hougan singles out Bible-thumping wireman James McCord, an "ex"-CIA officer who ran Nixon's campaign security and joined Liddy's team of White House Plumbers. McCord's activities during the two break-ins were peculiar, to say the least, and perhaps even counterproductive.

An early attempt to penetrate the Watergate building was scuttled when McCord informed his fellow burglars that an alarm system prevented entry—an alarm that, Hougan discovered, didn't exist. Moreover, McCord made himself scarce at key moments during the break-ins and handled the job so sloppily that he must have been the most incompetent CIA officer since the guy who dreamed up the plot to make Castro's hair fall out. Unless, that is, McCord had designs of his own.

Was McCord trying to sabotage the operation? Hougan

theorizes that McCord was keeping tabs on the White House operation for his erstwhile employer, the CIA. Perhaps, Hougan suggests, McCord was protecting a CIA operation that snooping White House operatives were about to expose: DNC Chairman O'Brien, a Howard Hughes asset, may have had knowledge of the Agency's top-secret joint venture with the Hughes organization to raise a sunken Soviet submarine in the Pacific. Or, speculates Hougan, perhaps the call-girl ring was part or parcel of an illegal CIA operation. The Agency's illegal experimentation with mind control and drugs often involved prostitutes. Another possibility is that the CIA was spying on the prostitutes' clients—Democratic apparatchicks—for sexual blackmail purposes.

Which brings us, in a roundabout way, to Deep Throat. If McCord was under deep cover, and Dean was in deep doodoo, who was Deep Throat, the mysterious government source who fed *Washington Post* scribe Bob Woodward a steady stream of Watergate information?

In the Deep Throat wing of Watergate theory, there are enough candidates to fill an underground parking garage. High on the list is Robert Bennett, who was Howard Hughes's public relations flack and E. Howard Hunt's boss at a D.C. public relations firm that routinely provided cover for CIA operatives. (Bennett is currently a U.S. senator from Utah.) What really set alarms off about Bennett was that, per Hougan, he bragged about being a key source to Woodward and said that Woodward was "suitably grateful."

Other suspects on the Throat short list include Mark Felt, then-deputy FBI director; Ken Clawson, onetime-*Post*-reporter-turned-White-House-aide (author Ron Rosenbaum's fave candidate); David Gergen (John Dean's onetime choice, and now doing quite nicely as an aide to President Bill Clinton); and in Hougan's book, Admiral Bobby Ray Inman, the intelligence veteran and multidiscipline conspiracist (UFOlogists claim he's confessed to government knowledge of alien saucers, and Inman—himself no slouch as a conspiracy theorist—recently denounced a supposed cabal involving *New York Times* columnist Bill Safire, Senator Bob Dole, and the Israel lobby, which was out to submarine his short-lived nomination as Bill Clinton's defense secretary).

Silent Coup's nominee for Deep Throat is the most popular choice of all, however: General Alexander Haig. It was Hougan who first uncovered Bob Woodward's little-known connections to the Pentagon and, yes, to Al Haig. Before becoming a reporter, Hougan revealed, Woodward was a naval officer with a high-level assignment as military briefer to the chairman of the Joint Chiefs of Staff, Admiral Thomas H. Moorer. Moorer and other military sources have acknowledged that Woodward regularly briefed Henry Kissinger aide Al Haig in the White House basement.

Woodward admitted to Hougan that he had, in fact, been a military briefer, but denied having briefed Haig. However, several years later, when Colodny and Gettlin followed up on Hougan's reporting, Woodward denied that he had *ever* been a military briefer—*period*. As Colodny and Gettlin see it, Woodward has sought to obscure his naval career in an effort to cover his relationship with Deep Throat/Al Haig.

According to *Silent Coup*, Haig had his own secret agenda— and again the hapless Nixon comes off as a victim of his underlings' perfidy. Colodny and Gettlin allege that Haig fed Woodward a stream of self-serving information and *dis*information, in an effort to keep the Watergate spotlight on Nixon.

Why? According to *Silent Coup*, the Watergate scandal threatened to expose skeletons in Haig's own closet: In the early days of Nixon's administration, before the Watergate burglaries, write Colodny and Gettlin, Haig had been involved in a Pentagon spy ring that purloined secret foreign policy documents from National Security Adviser Henry Kissinger. Hardliners at the Pentagon, including Admiral Moorer, had worried that Nixon was too dovish on Vietnam and Communist China. According to *Silent Coup*, Haig was a ringer for the hawks.

The ambitious Haig had managed to cover his own tracks in

that affair, allege Colodny and Gettlin. That is, until Watergate began to expose other crimes and misdemeanors revolving around the Nixon administration. It was then, argue Colodny and Gettlin, that the president's new chief of staff began to manipulate the Watergate coverup in an effort to keep investigators from learning about the Pentagon spy ring. Consequently, Haig made Nixon look even more guilty—perhaps intentionally forcing the purported peacenick out of office. Hence the "silent coup."

Obviously Watergate is the conspiracy that keeps on giving. In fact, that scandal and the JFK assassination comprise the two foci in modern American conspiracy theory. There were even connections made between the Dallas hit and Watergate, an apparent nexus that opened the eyes of many budding conspiratologists to the possiblity that a black web of corruption lay just beneath the glossy surface of American politics. For starters, CIA-trained Watergate burglar Frank Sturgis had played a suspicious role as disinformationist in the wake of the Kennedy slaying, in an effort to pin the blame on Fidel Castro. Hunt and the Cubans had also been key players in the CIA's anti-Castro operations of the early 1960s, a touchstone of Cuban enmity for JFK. And according to some conspiracy theorists, Hunt and Sturgis bear an uncanny resemblance to two of the well-groomed "three tramps" arrested in Dealey Plaza and later released.

Nixon, himself, the man who gained so much from the death of his rival, just happened to be in Dallas on the day of the assassination, as a lawyer working for Pepsi. Much later when he began to flounder in the currents of Watergate, Nixon would issue bizarre, frantic warnings to CIA director Richard Helms that if the Agency didn't hop on the coverup bandwagon, Watergate would expose "the whole Bay of Pigs thing." This prompted H. R. Haldeman to write in his book, *The Ends of Power*, "It seems that in all of those Nixon references to the Bay of Pigs, he was actually referring to the Kennedy assassination....In a chilling parallel to their coverup at Watergate, the

CIA literally erased any connection between Kennedy's assassination and the CIA."

An entire tributary in Watergate speculation sluices around Haldeman's vague, evocative comment. Was *Bay of Pigs* Nixon's code phrase for a CIA role in the Kennedy assassination, and was he attempting to blackmail Helms into cooperating? Or was Nixon referring to the CIA's then-unexposed plots to bump off Castro—using Cubans trained by the CIA at the time of the Bay of Pigs invasion, Cubans who later resurfaced as Watergate burglars?

Helms, "the man who kept the secrets," isn't talking. And Nixon, publicly rehabilitated in his death, took the secret to his grave, where "strange alliances" of enemies will have a difficult time setting him up to spill the beans.

MAJOR SOURCES

Colodny, Len, and Robert Gettlin. *Silent Coup: The Removal of a President*. New York: St. Martin's Press, 1991.

Haldeman, H. R. *The Ends of Power*. New York: Times Books, 1978.

Hougan, Jim. *Secret Agenda: Watergate, Deep Throat and the CIA*. New York: Random House, 1984.

Rosenbaum, Ron. *Travels With Dr. Death and Other Unusual Investigations*. New York: Penguin Books, 1991.

29

Libido-gate

Judging from Washington's perennial sex scandals, power truly is the ultimate aphrodisiac—to paraphrase that seventies-epoch Casanova, Henry Kissinger, in a slightly different context. For young wonks and old goats alike, political prowess tends to breed hubris and hormones.

Not surprisingly, then, in the nation's pulsing capital, the fine art of sexual blackmail has what you might call "a history."

The pioneering figure of Washington "sexmail" was that creepiest of peeping G-men, J. Edgar Hoover. Thanks to his infamous sex files, which contained dirt on just about everyone in Washington short of his shoeshine boy, Hoover managed to dominate the capital (and eight presidents) for nearly half a century.

Not surprisingly, Hoover's busiest period came while John F. Kennedy occupied the White House and its many bedrooms. By several accounts, when rumors were rampant that Kennedy was going to pinkslip the aging, annoying FBI chief, Hoover put his plenary Kennedy files to work, thereby saving his own hide. With an obsession more than verging on the pathological,

222

Hoover had bugged JFK's legion love nests and tapped the princess phones of assorted Kennedy playmates, including mob moll Judith Campbell Exner and superstarlet Marilyn Monroe—whose bedroom was purportedly heavily trafficked by both Kennedy brothers.

The bug-eyed Hoover also glommed onto in-flight tapes of Jack and actress Angie Dickinson summiting in the boudoir of a chartered aircraft. Typically playing both sides against the middle, Hoover leaked info to the tabloid press about an old Kennedy affair with a senate secretary and about Kennedy's rumored former marriage, and then "put Kennedy in his debt by supplying background for the *Newsweek* rebuttal," according to journalist Anthony Summers.

When it came to recording Jack's and Bobby's compromising positions, Hoover had company. The Mafia and Jimmy Hoffa also managed to plant electronic bedroom ears in Marilyn Monroe's inner sanctum, especially at roué actor and Kennedy in-law Peter Lawford's beach house.

Hoover used the same tactics in his vendetta against Martin Luther King, Jr., bugging the civil rights leader's tryst spots with assorted paramours, spreading untrue gossip that King was a "switch-hitter," even marshaling surveillance photographs of King in the same room as a known—gasp—homosexual. Transcripts were leaked to the press, but the media didn't bite.

Hoover even had a bimbo file on Richard Nixon, of all the unlikely party animals. As Anthony Summers reports in his revisionist Hoover biography, *Official and Confidential*, while Nixon was vice president, he met a young Hong Kong travel guide named Marianna Liu. Convinced that Liu was a spy for communist China (a "Chicom"), the CIA had British intelligence train its infrared camera lenses on Nixon's bedroom window during his visits to Hong Kong. Liu and Nixon swore to Summers that there was never any sex, but Hoover was described as reading the Nixon-Chicom file "gleefully" and showing it to Dick before he became president.

Never one to let "evidence" get in the way of salacious

innuendo, Hoover later came up with a report claiming that future Watergate boys H. R. Haldeman, John Ehrlichman, and Dwight Chapin were homosexual lovers. This was in 1969, before Watergate, and Hoover's source, an unidentified bartender, was claiming that the three were whooping it up at homosexual parties in the Watergate hotel. Of course, it wasn't true, and as Ehrlichman told Summers, "I came to think that Hoover did this to show his claws, or ingratiate himself to Nixon—probably both."

In Washington, what goes around comes around, and Hoover's actual homosexuality was hardly a well-kept secret among his numerous enemies. Mob boss Meyer Lansky liked to boast that he "fixed that son of a bitch" Hoover, purportedly by acquiring graphic photos of Hoover fellating his lifelong companion, Clyde Tolson. According to Summers, by the late 1940s there were also pictures of Hoover vamping as a closet drag queen. Even that quintessential CIA garbologist, counterspy catcher James Jesus Angleton was in on the act, purportedly having his mits on incriminating Hoover sex pics.

Blackmail or not, the mob's sway over Hoover *was* enormous: Publicly, the all-American, morally unimpeachable lingerie-wearing FBI director refused to admit that the Mafia even existed.

Hoover went to his grave more than two decades ago, taking his voluminous "personal and confidential" sex files with him. Of course they mysteriously vanished, giving rise to assorted conspiracy theories, including the possibility that Hoover loyalists destroyed them, that the CIA snatched them up, and even that Nixon's Watergate Plumbers made a bungled attempt to get their hot little mits on the explosive cache.

So, with Hoover out of the picture, is sexual extortion in Washington merely a historical idiosyncrasy, like Hoover, and the Kennedys, the product of a more reckless era?

Well, sexual blackmail may have a more enduring place in Washington politics than we tend to suspect. More than one vice investigator in Washington believes that mob-controlled call girls, intelligence operatives, and even Washington lobbyists have long run an underground racket aimed at sexually compromising Congress and the administration.

Conspiracy researcher Peter Dale Scott calls it "an ongoing, highly organized, and protected operation." Scott, a former Canadian diplomat and professor of English at the University of California, Berkeley, goes so far as to suggest that Washington's sex syndicate, exploited by intelligence spooks and the mob, has "driven the major scandals of Washington since at least the beginning of the Cold War."

Apparently, behind every good political scandal is a prostitute. Scott isn't alone in this thinking. According to Scott, "a retired Washington detective, one who played a small but important role in Watergate," believes that mob pimps and bigwig lobbyists use pricey call girls to put the squeeze on key officials. This is apparently a reference to Carl Shoffler, incidentally the arresting police officer who slapped cuffs on the Watergate burglars.

During a 1982 investigation into the use of "drugs and sexual activity to lobby congressmen," Shoffler did indeed advise congressional investigators to look into a male prostitution ring that serviced Capitol Hill. The veteran police detective believed that the sex ring might be linked to a high-flying Washington lobbyist, Robert Keith Gray, who had more than a few connections to CIA folk. According to Peter Dale Scott, some Washington investigators also suspected that the gay sex ring was connected to D.C. crime boss Joe "the Possum" Nesline.

Unfortunately, the congressional probe petered out before it got anywhere. Summing up the untested Libido-gate hypothesis, however, one of the congressional investigators put it this way to author Susan Trento: "If a lobbyist wants to use hookers to influence legislation, there's a pool of talent he draws from. There are certain madams in town that they make connections with. By simple logic, if you're in the business of influencing people with male prostitutes or kids, there has to be that supply chain.... [If] we start to identify some of the clients, it's possible we could find the suppliers for intelligence, organized crime, and lobbyists." In other words, follow the honey.

Former (and fugitive) CIA officer Frank Terpil had no compunction about identifying one such client, his former employer. Terpil told investigative author Jim Hougan that CIA-run sexual blackmail setups were common in Washington during the Watergate years. Terpil fingered his former partner, Ed Wilson, as the facilitator of one such CIA operation. Terpil claimed that Wilson ran the CIA mantrap from Korean agent Tong Sun Park's George Town Club, the Korean intelligence front that figured in the 1970s Koreagate scandal.

"Historically," Terpil explained, "one of Wilson's agency jobs was to subvert members of both houses [of Congress] by any means necessary....Certain people could be easily coerced by living out their sexual fantasy in the flesh....A remembrance of these occasions [was] permanently recorded via selected cameras."

Of course, we should note that Terpil hasn't offered any proof to back up that claim, and ex-CIA officers—not least of all, ones who have been convicted in absentia for terrorist activities—aren't celebrated for their candor. On the other hand, sexual blackmail was indeed a favorite CIA method of "turning" foreign agents or otherwise compromising them to do Uncle Sam's bidding. Considering all of the Agency's illegal doings on domestic soil during the last four decades, Terpil's story certainly seems plausible.

Interestingly, Robert Keith Gray, the omnipresent superlobbyist whose name came up during the 1982 gay sex ring investigation, also pops into the George Town Club-Terpil milieu. Gray, who (coincidentally or not) gravitates toward spy nests, was the club's first overseer and also a director at Terpil's firm, Consultants International, a notorious CIA proprietary front.

And speaking of strange coincidences, it might be nothing more than evidence that networking is key in D.C., but Terpil's and Korean lobbyist Park's names turned up a few years earlier in the trick book of a cathouse madam linked to yet another famous scandal, the biggest scandal of all: Watergate.

The theory that the Watergate affair sprang, unintentionally, from the bosom of a political sex ring was first proposed by journalist Jim Hougan in his fascinating book, *Secret Agenda*.

The madam, Heidi Rikan, worked out of Washington's posh Columbia Plaza apartment building, located across the street from the Watergate office complex. Hougan suggests that Rikan's call-girl ring may have been "either a CIA operation or the target of a CIA operation."

Briefly, Hougan's hypothesis is this: The Columbia Plaza girls were servicing a very interesting political clientele: Democratic muckamucks who placed their orders for companionship from a phone inside the Democratic National Committee headquarters in the Watergate building. Discovering this fruitful setup, Nixon's henchmen decided to target the Democratic fornicators. But in doing so, they stood a good chance of exposing the heavy breather already bugging the phone lines: the CIA. Ergo, the CIA's moles in the White House (allegedly superpatriotic conspirators James McCord and E. Howard Hunt) were forced to sabotage the Watergate break-ins in order to protect the CIA's highly illegal sex sting from Nixon's overeager burglars.

An illegal CIA sexpionage gambit unintentionally triggering the downfall of Richard Nixon? Say it ain't so!

Does the sexpionage industry go back even further in history than the babes of Watergate? Conspiracy theorist-emeritus Peter Dale Scott is game enough to hazard an affirmative. Employing the semiotics of conspiracy research—wherein names connect to other names, dates, and misdeeds, creating a tableau of suspicion that is usually intriguing, if not always conclusive—Scott has connected the dots.

Most interestingly, the Watergate madam, Heidi Rikan, was a girlfriend of mobster Joe "the Possum" Nesline, whose alleged connection to the Capitol Hill gay sex scandal a decade later aroused the suspicions of Washington detectives.

Assorted boyfriends and former husbands of both Rikan and her sometime roommate, Mo Biner (who married key Watergate figure John Dean, which makes Mo a pivotal character, according to scandal revisionists), were associated with the Quorum, an early 1960s "swingles" club run by Bobby Baker, a former aide to Lyndon Johnson. Scott surmises that all roads led to Baker's club for a reason: the Quorum functioned a lot like the mob-and-intelligence-infested sex traps of the 1970s.

It was Bobby Baker who introduced President Kennedy to an East German bombshell named Ellen Rometsch, whom JFK, true to form, promptly bedded. Scott speculates that J. Edgar Hoover leaked word of this international indiscretion to the press. Whether or not Hoover was behind the leaks, they nearly ignited a global scandal. That's because JFK's nubile Valkyrie also happened to be sleeping with a Soviet diplomat, a coincidence that, if revealed, wouldn't have served Kennedy well at the height of the Cold War. The threat of a "bimbo eruption" with international implications forced Bobby Kennedy into scandal-kibosh mode.

Scott notes that the JFK-Rometsch peccadillo paralleled the scandalous 1962 affair that toppled British war minister John Profumo. Profumo publicly confessed to romping with Christine Keeler, a party doll/prostitute working for sexual procurer Stephen Ward. That scandal proved doubly damaging to Profumo because Keeler was simultaneously servicing, yes, a Soviet diplomat. And more recent revelations have disclosed that the British intelligence agency MI5 "had been using the Stephen Ward sex ring for some time to compromise the Soviet agent." Scott wonders, Did MI5 set out to compromise Profumo as well? Did the hyperlibidinous JFK blunder into a similar sex trap?

Interestingly, there is a more direct connection between JFK's peccadilloes and the MI5-manipulated Profumo affair. During the summer of 1963, Hoover's porous sex files began leaking again, resulting in press reports that a high U.S. official had slept with two members of Britain's Ward-Keeler sex ring, the very ring that toppled Profumo. That high U.S. official, no surprise, was the prodigious JFK. Scott observes that "MI5, as Britain's counterintelligence agency, maintained direct relations with both Hoover in the FBI" and the CIA. Did the Brits help Hoover set up Kennedy for a fall?

Bobby Baker, catalyst of the JFK-Rometsch affair, later boasted that he had in his possession letters from the East German woman that could prove embarrassing to the Kennedys, which per Scott, "strengthens the impression of an ongoing, sophisticated blackmail operation" in this nation's carnal capital.

Perhaps. Or maybe it just proves that in Washington eventually everyone gets screwed.

MAJOR SOURCES

Hougan, Jim. *Secret Agenda: Watergate, Deep Throat, and the CIA.* New York: Random House, 1984.

Scott, Peter Dale. *Deep Politics and the Death of JFK.* Berkeley, CA: University of California Press, 1993.

Summers, Anthony. *Official and Confidential: The Secret Life of J. Edgar Hoover.* New York: Pocket Books, 1994.

Trento, Susan B. *The Power House: Robert Keith Gray and the Selling of Access and Influence in Washington.* New York: St. Martin's Press, 1992.

30

October Surprise

Few conspiracy theories have galled Washington more than the so-called October Surprise. Little wonder. Controversial speculation that the 1980 Reagan-Bush presidential campaign cut a treasonous deal with Iran to forestall the release of American hostages indicts not only a political party and two presidents, it also tends to confirm our worst suspicions about cynical political manipulation, casting doubt on the validity of the democratic process itself.

As far as official Washington is concerned, however, the October Surprise is pure bunkum. During the final days of the Bush administration, two congressional probes jettisoned the charges as a historical canard. As they say in the conspiracy-debunking business, case closed!

Or is it? Like the official investigations into the assassination of President Kennedy, the October Surprise probes raised almost as many questions as they purported to answer. We'll return to those questions presently.

First, the case for conspiracy.

High noon, January 20, 1980. In his inaugural address

President Ronald Reagan stares down the camera and promises Americans "an era of national renewal." Like slick crosscutting in a Hollywood thriller, his timing is impeccable: Twenty minutes later, as if by the force of his words alone, fifty-two American hostages are suddenly liberated after more than a year of humiliating captivity in Iranian clutches. As Reagan rides tall in the saddle and a diminished Jimmy Carter shuffles back to Georgia, few comment on the curious timing.

Two months earlier, however, Reagan had crowed about a "secret plan" involving the hostages. "My ideas require quiet diplomacy," he had boasted, "where you don't have to say what it is you're thinking of doing." Campaign bluster or a revealing admission?

An agglomeration of fact, rumor, and, curiously, elements of misdirection began to grow. Yet it wasn't until 1988, during Vice President George Bush's own bid for the presidency, that the October Surprise theory had its public coming out. The theory's proponents accused the Reagan-Bush campaign of plotting to steal the 1980 election by striking a deal with the Ayatollah Khomeini to keep the American hostages on ice until after the November elections. By sabotaging the legitimate U.S. government's attempts to free the hostages, the theory went, the Republicans would prevent a Carter-engineered "October Surprise" that might give the flagging Democrat an eleventh-hour political boost.

Certain facts were suggestive: A 1981 congressional probe into the Reagan campaign's theft of White House briefing books on the eve of a presidential debate disclosed that the Republicans had set up an espionage network that gathered intelligence on the Carter campaign and the president's efforts to liberate the hostages.

Reagan campaign manager William Casey, who would later become CIA chief, was receiving highly classified reports on closely held Carter administration secrets. A pedigreed spook who delighted in cloak and dagger work, Casey had served as a spy master in the OSS, the CIA's World War II precursor. But he remained an intelligence zealot even after his official break with spy central; as a Wall Street lawyer, he offered tax consulting to CIA front companies. Even his mumbling inflection, which sounded like he carried a mouth full of pebbles, suggested a propensity for the sub rosa.

But did Casey's machinations go further than campaign espionage? Did he conduct secret negotiations with Iranian hostage takers—and perhaps even strike a pact to keep the Americans captive in Iran? In short, did the Republicans pull their own October Surprise?

In this swampy terrain, the evidence grows murkier. In 1988, former Iranian president Abolhassan Bani-Sadr claimed to have secondhand knowledge that such a deal had occurred. Then living in exile outside Paris, Bani-Sadr claimed his sources in Iran informed him that George Bush had flown to meetings in Paris to seal the deal in mid-October 1980.

Soon a motley collection of arms dealers, convicts, con men, and errant spooks chimed in, signing onto the growing October Surprise witness list. Several claimed to have seen Bush glad-handing Iranian mullahs at a Paris hotel or flapping across French airport tarmac on or about the weekend of October 18. Most of the "witnesses" reported Casey sightings at the Paris tryst as well. Soon the list of attendees was bulging, like the roster at a Shriners' convention. Everyone and his CIA handler had been at the Paris rendezvous, it seemed. Most claimed that French and Israeli intelligence operatives were also on hand to shepherd the clandestine deal and presumably enjoy a buffet-style luncheon.

According to several other sources, Casey also attended a series of earlier meetings with a Khomeini emissary in Spain. According to Iranian arms dealer Jamshid Hashemi, he and his late brother, Cyrus, brought Casey and Iranian mullah Mehdi Karrubi together at Madrid's Ritz Hotel for two sets of meetings, in July and August 1980. As Hashemi told it, Casey proposed a quid pro quo: If Iran would hold the hostages until after the election, the incoming Reagan administration (which had yet to go through the formality of getting elected) would release Iranian funds and assets that had been frozen after Khomeini toppled the Shah of Iran and seized the American Embassy. The Reaganites would also emancipate $150 million in military hardware that the shah had already purchased—equipment desperately needed as Iran's war with Iraq heated up. At the second Madrid meeting, Karrubi returned to announce that Khomeini had approved the deal.

According to Jamshid Hashemi, the Republicans managed to slip the ol' payola to Iran even before the election—thanks to the connivance of Israel, which donated the necessary military hardware. If the October Surprise scenario was accurate, then it seems the secret arms-for-hostages deals later exposed during the Iran-Contra scandal could be backdated to 1980.

Although Casey had died of a brain tumor in 1987 and wasn't available to mumble a response, Bush and his campaign operatives denied the charges.

Unfortunately, the more loquacious sources claiming involvement in the secret deal were, by and large, denizens of the shady international arms bazaar. Some seemed to mingle verifiable fact with seedy fantasy. Chief among the semi-omniscient sources in this category was Ari Ben-Menashe, an ex-Israeli intelligence officer who claimed to have seen Bush at the Paris meetings. Ben-Menashe also claimed to know of the earlier Madrid meetings. As a military intelligence liaison with Iran in 1979 and 1980, Ben-Menashe helped broker the Reagan-Iran deals, he claimed. He also reported that Israel made shipments of light artillery and military hardware to Iran in 1980, in defiance of President Carter's arms embargo, to grease the October Surprise deal.

But journalists caught Ben-Menashe gilding his story, and Israeli officials claimed he wasn't who he said he was. On this latter point, though, Israel's intelligence honchos were even less reliable than Ben-Menashe. At first, they denied he had worked for them. But when Ben-Menashe produced letters of reference from Israeli intelligence brass, they changed their story, insisting now that he had merely been a peon translator—and an unreliable, exaggerating, damnable peon at that.

Yet other Israeli officials acknowledged Ben-Menashe's access to the top echelons of military intelligence; one called him "our Ollie North." Ben-Menashe clearly had access to very inside information. It was he who exposed the Reagan administration's arms-for-hostages schemes of the mid-1980s, tipping off the Lebanese newspaper that broke the story (only after *Time* magazine rebuffed his overtures).

If Ben-Menashe was maddeningly evasive, several sources, including Richard Brenneke, turned out to be unconditional frauds. A self-professed arms dealer from Portland, Oregon, the nerdy, cigar-sucking Brenneke had gained currency as a central October Surprise figure after he beat a perjury rap in federal court. Justice Department prosecutors failed to persuade a jury that Brenneke had lied when he testified in court that he had seen Bush and former Bush aide Donald Gregg at the Paris parley. (Brenneke, grandiloquent in the manner of Churchill's butler, also claimed to have ordered refreshments for the event.) Brenneke later went on to feather his nest in the conspiracy theory, making the absurd claim that he had also attended the Madrid meetings.

But Brenneke's tales imploded—rather suspiciously—when he hired a ghost writer to help him craft a memoir of his October Surprise peregrinations. When his coauthor/sometime paramour Peggy Robohm stumbled upon the obvious inconsistencies in Brenneke's tales, he invited her to check his story against his voluminous files, which contained personal desk calendars, credit card receipts, and other arcana from 1980. What Robohm found was irrefutable evidence showing that Brenneke had gone nowhere near Europe in the fall of 1980, but, rather, had left a paper trail placing him in greasy spoon cafes and cheesy motels in the Pacific Northwest.

His book deal blown, his budding celebrity crushed, his credibility zilch, how naive was this man who, in the paper-shredding age, did essentially the opposite, offering up his own impeachment papers? His timing was certainly interesting. Brenneke unraveled his own credibility as pressure was mounting for a congressional investigation into the October Surprise. Was Brenneke a disinformation time bomb awaiting an opportune moment to explode the October Surprise charges? Lending credence to such a possibility was another false prophet in the October Surprise rogue's gallery.

Soon after Brenneke injected himself into the October Surprise affair, a source calling himself "Razine" began calling journalists and making similar boasts. Speaking in a bogus southern drawl, Razine described himself as a retired CIA officer who had read a report at spook HQ in Langley, Virginia, placing Bush at the Paris meetings. Razine confirmed that Brenneke had also attended the meetings. But Razine was eventually unmasked as a one-time literature professor named Oswald LeWinter, who had once been convicted on drug smuggling charges.

When confronted by journalists, LeWinter claimed: "I was asked by some people to mount a disinformation campaign." He was paid $100,000, he submitted, by employers connected with U.S. intelligence, to make "sure that the media lost interest, that the story was discredited."

Brenneke and LeWinter had exchanged phone calls during their fifteen minutes of media fame, raising the possibility of a coordinated effort.

But LeWinter subsequently undercut his confession with the *new* claim that he had actually been dispatched to Paris in October 1980 to help expunge evidence of the clandestine assignation. Later, under oath to the House of Representatives' October Surprise task force, he doubled back *yet again*, this time declaring that he had fabricated all previous claims about the October Surprise as revenge against Uncle Sam for his drug bust. (LeWinter told the House task force that he improvised the alias *Razine* when a conspiracy tracker called him "just after he had finished eating a bowl of raisin bran.")

However pathological his lying, LeWinter was on the mark

when he gloated to journalists from PBS's *Frontline* program that "the October Surprise story did not break before the [1988] election, and, to my knowledge, it hasn't broken yet. The promised critical mass never came to be."

Debunkers in the media and Congress zeroed in on the errant sources, bagging them all with the likes of Brenneke and LeWinter. Yet the debunkers spun an equally improbable counterconspiracy tale in which a cabal of international grifters concocted the entire October Surprise opera, exchanging notes and embellishing their stories along the way. Why? The motive, according to the debunkers, had something to do with a vendetta by arms dealers against Reagan-Bushies following a U.S. sting operation that netted a gaggle of these "merchants of death." No matter how you look at it, the October Surprise orbits a bizarro world of conspiracy.

While Senate investigators concluded that there probably wasn't a secret deal between Reaganites and Iranian mullahs, they conceded that Casey was "fishing in troubled waters," having "conducted informal, clandestine, and potentially dangerous efforts on behalf of the Reagan campaign to gather intelligence" on Carter's hostage negotiations with Iran. The House task force, however, utterly dismissed both possibilities.

But several key findings of the House task force—dominated by Republican investigators hostile to the October Surprise charges—were either demonstrably false or inconclusive.

Casey's supposedly bulletproof alibi exonerating him from charges that he attended the Madrid meetings was actually full of holes. All agreed that Casey had been in London for several days following the date of the alleged Madrid meeting. Yet his whereabouts on the two days in question were unaccounted for, giving him ample time to have attended a covert colloquy in Madrid. But a former Reagan campaign staffer emerged to claim that Casey couldn't have been in Madrid before he jetted to London, because on those disputed dates, Casey had been his guest at the elite, male-only Bohemian Grove retreat in Northern California. Others recalled seeing Casey at the Grove, but couldn't pin down which weekend. In endorsing this alibi, the task force chose to ignore or downplay receipts, the diary entry of another Bohemian Grove camper, Casey's own desk calendar, and other solid evidence that made a more persuasive argument for Casey hunkering down at the Grove on the weekend *following* his European junket.

When Casey's family finally produced documents from the old spook's files, passports and calendar pages from the disputed dates were curiously missing and unaccounted for.

There were other flaws in the congressional probes, including the casual dismissal of sources unfairly lumped in with the likes of Brenneke and LeWinter. In addition to former President Bani-Sadr, there were two other Iranian officials who claimed to have had heard of the Republican-Iranian contacts of 1980: foreign minister Sadegh Ghotbzadeh, who told the French press in September 1980 that the Republicans were "trying to block a solution" to the hostage crisis, and former defense minister Ahmad Madani, who reported that Cyrus Hashemi had informed him in 1980 of Casey's efforts to negotiate covertly with Iran.

Perhaps the most reliable sources to surface were Claude Angeli, chief editor for *Le Canard Enchaine*, a French newspaper, and David Andelman, a former *New York Times* and CBS News reporter. Angeli told the task force that French intelligence officials, who refused to go on the record, claimed that their organization provided "cover" for meetings between the Reagan camp and Iranian officials on October 18 and 19, 1980. Andelman, who ghost wrote the autobiography of Alexandre de Marenches, the former head of French intelligence, testified that "de Marenches acknowledged setting up a meeting in Paris between Casey and some Iranians in late October 1980." By the time Andelman dropped his bombshell, the House task force had already interviewed de Marenches, who denied any knowledge of such meetings. Unable to reach de

Marenches for further questioning after Andelman made his
claim, the task force decided to take the French clandestine
services veteran at his previous word.

Granted, the congressional probes did dispel a number of
rumors and false leads. But they also left too many key
questions dangling, like those mentioned above, for their
reports to constitute the final word on the theory.

One last remark, from the inimitable figure in whose name
the October Surprise deal—if it isn't a fantastic hoax—was
carried out. In 1991, while playing golf with George Bush in
Palm Springs, Ronald Reagan gave reporters a sound bite. In
1980, he had "tried some things the other way," that is, to *free*
the hostages. What things? He refused to say, because "some of
these things are still classified." Classified? How did an unelected political campaign manage to classify *anything*? Later,
in a letter responding to congressional inquiries about the
comment, Reagan had a *partial* memory recovery. On the golf
course, he had been referring to his public support of "things"
President Carter had been doing. As for what he meant by
"classified" information, well, memory lane was not a through
street. "I cannot recall what I may have had in mind when I
made that statement."

MAJOR SOURCES

"Joint Report of the Task Force to Investigate Certain Allegations
    Concerning the Holding of American Hostages by Iran in 1980."
    Washington: U.S. House of Representatives, 3 January 1993.
"The 'October Surprise' Allegations and the Circumstances Surround-
    ing the Release of the Hostages Held in Iran: Report of the Special
    Counsel." Washington: U. S. Senate, 19 November 1992.
Parry, Robert. *Trick or Treason: The October Surprise Mystery*. New
    York: Sheridan Square Press, 1993.
Sick, Gary. *October Surprise: America's Hostages in Iran and the
    Election of Ronald Reagan*. New York: Times Books, 1991.
Snepp, Frank. "October Surmise." *Village Voice*, 25 February 1992.

31

The Trouble With Vince

The dark trail that led Vincent Foster to his final repose, splayed under a tree in Virginia's Ft. Marcy Park, hole in his head and gun by his side, may well have been pebbled with nothing but his own melancholy.

No doubt Foster, the number-two legal adviser to President Bill Clinton and a member of Clinton's Arkansas inner circle, was troubled. He never adjusted to Washington's backstab-at-will social climate, came under heavy fire for a relatively minor scandal involving the White House travel office, and was the subject, at least tangentially, of a scathing string of *Wall Street Journal* editorials. On top of all that, his marriage was shaky, and his long-standing friendship with the president's high-profile wife, Hillary, was icing over.

Enough to drive a fellow to bid this cruel world goodbye? In a legal-pad scribbling that could have been either his intended final farewell or just notes for a resignation letter, Foster lamented, perspicaciously, that in Washington, "ruining people is considered sport." Perhaps shaken that their little game went a bit too far, numerous pundits pondered the meaning of

Foster's death. The conclusion: We didn't kill him! The forces that compel a man to suicide will always be mysterious.

If it was suicide.

Foster was last seen alive on the afternoon of July 20, 1993. He had just finished munching down his lunch while reading a newspaper at his desk. At around 1:00 P.M., after downing the sandwich and a handful of M&M's he picked up his suit jacket and told his assistant to dig into the rest of the melt-in-your-mouth candy-coated chocolate treats. He'd be back later. Sometime between then and 7:00 P.M., Foster was killed by a gunshot wound to the head.

Shortly before his death, forty-eight-year-old Vince Foster asked his Arkansas doctor to phone a Washington pharmacy and prescribe an antidepressant medication. His appearance, once ruggedly debonair, had withered. And he wrote that note. When a guy with Foster's history is found lying under a tree with a .38 on the ground next to him, suicide seems the logical assumption.

There has been, however, very little that's logical in the aftermath of Foster's death. Almost every fact has been disputed in a blizzard of conspiracy theorizing and, it should be added, some credible investigative reporting. Not surprisingly, the bulk of the indictments come from Bill Clinton's adversaries on the right, who take a macabre delight in the very thinly veiled implication that the president somehow arranged the assassination of his own close friend.

Presumably the motive would be that Foster knew too much about the president's involvement in the interminable Whitewater scandal. But there are even wilder theories (and theories about those theories). In those scenarios, the overly earnest lawyer from Little Rock—the lonely good man driven to despair by the amoral Washington power game—turns into an international spy and financial sophisticate moving millions in tainted cash through secret Swiss accounts. And, perhaps, trafficking in the ultimate lethal contraband: nuclear launch codes.

The conspiracy theories, or at least the theorists, got a morale boost when Whitewater Special Prosecutor Kenneth Starr hired forensic expert Henry C. Lee to chew up and spit out the evidence surrounding Foster's death. According to Britain's *Daily Telegraph*, one of the few nonnutty media outlets on either shore of the pond doing much investigation into Foster's demise, "Lee is a household name in the U.S."

Not in our household. But we'll take his bona fides for granted and concur with occasionally overzealous *Telegraph* man-in-Washington Ambrose Evans-Pritchard, who suggested that "the first thing he may want to look into is whether or not the autopsy report by the Virginia medical examiner's office was fabricated."

That would be a good place to start if one were so inclined. And many are. But you don't have to be a right-wing kook, conspiracy buff, or foamy-mouthed Clinton hater to admit that there's much about Foster's final curtain that just ain't kosher.

For starters, as Evans-Pritchard eagerly notes, for a guy who supposedly blew his own brains out right there under the elms, Foster was rather stingy with his bleeding. Fairfax County EMT's who picked up Foster's cadaver noted no significant amount of blood at the scene and got none on their outfits, despite "cradling the victim's head." This despite the fact that poor Vince supposedly blew an inch-and-a-half-wide gap in the back of his skull.

But did Foster even have an exit wound in the back of his head? Shades of JFK! Evans-Pritchard suggests that the head was more or less intact. The doctor who certified Foster's death told the *Telegraph* snoop that he never saw a wound in the back of Foster's head. Of course, the doctor admitted that he "didn't spend much time looking back there." One suspects, however, that a wound the size of Foster's supposed perforation wouldn't take much poking around to uncover.

The British reporter quotes several other doctors who examined the autopsy records who also failed to find the exit wound. Foster's X rays, Evans-Pritchard asserts, have either disappeared or were never taken in the first place. Reports are muddled on that account.

Citing anonymous sources, Evans-Pritchard reported that the special prosecutor was mulling the possibility that Foster's fatal wound was inflicted with a more-discreet .22 and that the .38 six-shooter found next to the body was, in fact, planted there by person or persons unknown.

And why the confusion over when the Clinton administration actually learned of Foster's death? Arkansas state trooper Roger Perry, back in Little Rock, said he got a call from one Helen Dickey, a minor White House aide, sometime between 5:51 P.M. and 6:15 P.M. The White House didn't hear of the death until 8:30, but Dickey was on the phone "kind of hysterical, crying, real upset," the trooper recounted in the *Telegraph*. "She told me that Vince got off work, went out to his car in the parking lot and shot himself in the head."

The initial Secret Service report was that Foster was found in his car, which may have been an error because the body was "officially" found lying on the ground in the park. For that matter, the person who discovered the body remains a mystery as well, identified only as a "confidential witness."

The anomalies go on and on. Chris Ruddy of the *Pittsburgh Tribune-Review* was Evans-Pritchard's American counterpart in raising the doubts in the mainstream press. He reported that Polaroids taken of Foster's body show a "wound, puncture or other trauma" on the right side of Foster's neck—and that one of the EMTs (the same ones, presumably, who were not covered with Foster's blood) noted "a small caliber bullet hole" in that same spot. Another paramedic said that he saw a hole in Foster's forehead. Foster, it appears, was veritably riddled with bullets.

Investigator Robert Fiske, who prepared the initial reports on Foster's death, said the wounds did not exist. But Ruddy retorts that Fiske never looked at the original Polaroids. Just third-generation low-quality copies.

Even the alleged suicide note, torn to bits and discovered six days later by Foster's boss when the shreds fell out of Foster's briefcase, may not be authentic. In October 1995 three forensic handwriting analysts, one of them from Oxford, declared the note a forgery. They compared the note to twelve other samples of Foster's writing. The note didn't match up.

There are dozens of such "discrepancies" in the Foster case. But if indeed Foster was murdered, what's the motive? On May 22, 1995, Evans-Pritchard wrote a story uncovering an odd fact that could prove important to untangling the Foster death conundrum. For two years before his death Foster had been making flights to Switzerland, sometimes staying less than a single day. He'd brought a ticket to Geneva three weeks before his death but never used it and got a refund.

Records uncovered by the British journalist show Foster buying a ticket to Switzerland on November 1, 1991, with his return trip on November 3—a quick trip for the $1,490 it cost him. A year later he made another whirlwind Swiss jaunt, heading out on December 17, 1992, and coming back on December 19. And those flights weren't the first for the not-so-accidental tourist. He flew to Turkish Kurdistan in December 1988 and had logged over 500,000 frequent flier miles by the time he died.

According to Evans-Pritchard, Foster rolled up 197,853 miles on Delta Airlines alone, buying many of his tickets at an "executive fare" discount, available only to government officials—at a time well before Foster was a government official.

Says Evans-Pritchard: "This raises the question: was Foster a U.S. agent at a time when he was ostensibly in private practice as a Little Rock lawyer?"

James R. Norman certainly believed so. Norman was, of all things, a senior editor at *Forbes* magazine. And he came up with the most elaborate conspiracy theory yet to explain the Foster death. He wrote it as an article for *Forbes*. Which promptly rejected it.

No big surprise there, really. But the rejection itself only furthered the conspiracy theory. On top of that, Norman's theory itself became the subject of a conspiracy theory.

Norman's article was eventually published in the August 1995 issue of *Media Bypass*, a right-wing magazine full of conspiracy stuff and so named because it *bypasses* the mainstream *media*. Get it? Later, Norman wrote another article and began propagating his theories on the Internet, where he was joined by economist and software entrepreneur J. Orlin Grabbe. The hypotheses they came up with came to be identified as the Norman-Grabbe theory, and, in essence, here's what it said:

Foster was indeed despondent, but not because of any editorials in the *Wall Street Journal*. His "deep funk" was induced when Foster learned that the CIA was investigating him for espionage. He was laundering money for Israel and, possibly, selling nuclear secrets to the same country; the nuclear launch codes that the president must use to identify himself before he gives the push-the-button order.

The story goes back to the infamous PROMIS software case, in which the U.S. Justice Department stole a valuable piece of criminal records tracking software from a small company called Inslaw (see chapter 17). The software, it is said, could be modified to track most anything and to include a secret "back door" to give knowing intelligence agents undetectable access to records kept by PROMIS.

The back door in PROMIS gave the National Security Agency the ability to eavesdrop on bank transactions the world over. But first it had to be installed the world over. And that's where Foster's links to the intelligence community originate, according to Norman-Grabbe. Foster, who worked for Little Rock's prestigious Rose Law Firm, was a secret liaison between the NSA and CIA and a Little Rock bank data processing company called Systematics. According to Norman, Systematics's real business was moving around billions of dollars in "black" money for illegal arms sales, CIA drug running, and various other nasty operations.

Systematics's accounts really flourished when Bill Clinton came into office. But sometime shortly thereafter, a group of "hackers" inside the CIA found Foster's secret bank account when they came across his name in a Mossad database. They took it upon themselves—without CIA authorization—to yank $2.73 million out of it and return the money to the U.S. Treasury. This same merry band of computer spooks then packed their Cray supercomputer in some kind of a high-tech van and bopped around the country siphoning money from the illegal accounts of various bigwigs.

One of those bigwigs was former secretary of defense Caspar Weinberger, at that time the publisher of *Forbes* magazine. It's all coming together now....

An amazing story, but is it true? Much of Norman's original article is based on anonymous sources—and the sources who are named are questionable. They include Michael Riconosciuto, the self-proclaimed former intelligence operative doing time on a drug charge and who has become something of a supersource from his jail cell, attaching himself to most every conspiracy to come along since 1980. They also include Ari Ben-Menashe, the alleged onetime Israeli intelligence officer who, while not in jail, has functioned as a similar supersource. And as his key source Norman claims a colorful character named Charles S. Hayes, until recently "one of the CIA's most dangerous, unpredictable—and most effective—contract operatives."

Journalist Daniel Brandt, who specializes in covering this sort of thing (his NameBase database is a treasure trove of research on covert operations and other conspiracies), has a conspiracy theory of the conspiracy theory. He suspects that the Norman-Grabbe hypothesis "has all the earmarks of disinformation."

Brandt notes a number of logical inconsistencies and improbabilities in the N-G conspiracy theory. For one thing, "a group of low-level CIA hackers would not be likely to take unauthorized action of this magnitude." Sure, Foster couldn't exactly go to the cops to complain about having his covert cash nicked out of his account, but if he was really such a major player, wouldn't he have the type of heavy connections to seek a more personal form of justice? And wouldn't this occur to the CIA whiz kids, who ought to be just a wee bit trepidatious?

Even if the hackers did go around breaking into foreign computers, the likelihood that the Mossad (or any intelligence agency) keeps the names of its agents on a networked computer seems rather low. Finally, the story that Foster was handing over secret nuclear launch codes to the Israelis seems most preposterous of all. The Israelis would know that such codes were worthless—and Foster would know that they knew—because if the Pentagon had even the slightest suspicion that those most sensitive of codes could be compromised, "they'd unplug the entire system immediately and rebuild it from scratch," says Brandt.

The irony in Brandt's conspiracy theory is that Brandt does not discount the possibility that Foster was murdered. In fact, he says, there's a "50–50 chance" of it. But Brandt worries that the Norman-Grabbe scenario is a hodgepodge of fact and falsehood designed to throw legitimate investigators off the track, and, ultimately, discredit the whole murder case by association. (Brandt does not believe that Norman and Grabbe themselves are in on this plot; they are "merely guilty of excessive enthusiasm," presumably duped by their sources.)

If the N-G story is *itself* the result of some kind of covert operation, that suggests that someone somewhere wants investigators thrown off the trail of Foster's death. If Norman and Grabbe's theory is a fabrication, it actually lends *more* credence to the possibility that Foster was done in.

Bill Clinton's tormentors are game to blame him for Foster's death, but here's one last conspiracy theory: Norman's sources are all in the intelligence community in one way or another. In other words, they're in the same genus of people who were involved in the various Reaganite covert ops in the 1980s. If they are the ones producing the disinformation, then they must also be the ones with something to hide in the death of Vince Foster. Look at it that way and the murder, if murder it was, of Clinton's friend appears more like a conspiracy *against* the president than one masterminded by him. Could the death of Vince Foster have been part of some devious master plan to

bring down Bill Clinton, more effectively than any series of
Wall Street Journal editorials?

Or was Vince Foster simply the victim of ultracynical Washington, more tragic than sinister, on the losing end of a sport
where reputations are the stakes and lives sometimes the price
of defeat?

MAJOR SOURCES

Brandt, Daniel. "The Norman-Grabbe Theory Regarding Vince Foster: Why We Should Be Careful." *NameBase,* 19 September 1995.

Evans-Pritchard, Ambrose. "A Death That Won't Die." *The American
Spectator,* November 1995.

————. "Secret Swiss Link to White House Death." *Daily Telegraph,*
22 May 1995.

Fineman, Howard, and Bob Cohen. "The Mystery of the White House
Suicide." *Newsweek,* 2 August 1993.

Jaynes, Gregory. "The Death of Hope." *Esquire,* November 1993.

Norman, James R. "Fostergate." *Media Bypass,* August 1995.

Ruddy, Chris. "Foster Death Discrepancies are Abundant: Did His
Neck Suffer Trauma?" *Pittsburgh Tribune-Review,* 16 June, 1995.

Stewart, James B. "The Last Days of Vince Foster." *Newsweek,* 18
March 1996.

Deborah Picker assisted with research for this chapter.

32

The Vast Right-Wing Conspiracy

Amid the *fin-de-siècle* lunacy of the anti-Clinton crusades, it seems like a miracle when anyone actually exercises plain common sense or accomplishes the obvious. But that's exactly what happened on April 1, 1998, when a Republican, George Bush–appointed judge consigned Paula Jones's spurious sex-harassment lawsuit against Clinton to the dustbin of history.

Of course, the Clinton story continued even as we were furiously scribbling these words. Who knows what leaks, lies, and surreptitiously recorded audio tapes will turn up in the future? But as of this moment in conspiracy theory, this chapter contains the facts as we know them.

For the benefit of our readers born after 1994, Jones is a former Arkansas state employee who claimed that Bill Clinton (while he was running for president in 1992) invited her up to his hotel room, where he dropped his pants and showed her his, uh, campaign staff. He then, allegedly, asked Jones if she wished to "kiss it."

Grungy behavior on Clinton's part if Jones's story is true (and it morphed many times along the way). But actionable? Jones thought so, perhaps egged on by well-heeled Clinton haters. After waiting around for a couple of years, she fired off a lawsuit at Clinton, who had since become president of the United States.

The lawsuit dragged on for years, literally, and Clinton's conservative opponents squeezed it for every drop of political mileage they could get out of it, even leaking Jones's alleged observation that the presidential penis bore a distinct left-angled bend.

For some bizarre reason understood only by themselves, the justices of the U.S. Supreme Court ruled that Jones's lawsuit should be heard during Clinton's presidential term. That cleared the way for more distractions. Foremost among them was the allegation that Clinton had received oral sex from a buxom ex-intern named Monica Lewinsky. Clinton denied this charge in a sworn deposition.

Asked about the allegations in a network television interview, Bill's wife, Hillary, responded with preternatural calm. Not only did she stand by her hubby, she asserted that these charges—and most of the other allegations leveled against Clinton (see chapters 31 and 61 for further examples)—stemmed from what she now famously dubbed "the vast right-wing conspiracy" against President Clinton.

And there is where our story begins.

The story should have ended when Jones's lawsuit got tossed out in its entirety by Judge Susan Webber-Wright. Needless to say, the decision has produced much weeping and wailing and gnashing of teeth on the part of the pathological Clinton haters and vast right-wing conspirators. In an atypical moment of clarity, even Rush Limbaugh noted, in the wake of the dismissal, that too many Clinton haters "have their lives wrapped up" in

Clinton's fate. But all the bluster can no longer obscure the crystal-clear fact that Jones simply had no case!

The unequivocal dismissal, then, left no doubt that the Jones case was nothing but a political hit all along. How else could such a flimsy claim have wreaked so much havoc for so long? The judge saw what anyone not blinded by the stage fog pumped out by the big media windbags had seen all along.

(Okay, here's the obligatory disclaimer: we're not making any judgment on whether or not alleged hotel-room weenie waggler Clinton actually did what Jones accused him of or not. The point is, as a legal case, there never was anything there.)

The end of the Jones suit didn't put an end to the under-reported but nevertheless compelling revelations of right-wing machinations. While most of the corporate media (TV networks, major urban dailies, *Time, Newsweek,* CNN etc.) chased the latest charges that, for example, Lewinsky had preserved a dress stained with the president's semen in an unwashed state, the on-line news-and-arts magazine *Salon* dispatched reporter Murray Waas to find out what was really behind this alleged Vast Right-Wing Conspiracy (which by then had assumed capitalized status).

As *Salon* reported, Attorney General Janet Reno, at the behest of the FBI, pondered her own investigation into the anti-Clinton dirty-tricks campaign. Specifically, she was intrigued by chief Whitewater witness David Hale, the source of some of the most damaging charges against Clinton in that two-decade-old real-estate debacle (again, see chapter 61). Hale, according to *CNN Online,* is alleged to have taken cash payoffs from (indirectly) Clinton bête noir Richard Mellon Scaife.

Scaife, for his part, is the intensely private and intensely rightist heir to Pittsburgh's Mellon-family banking fortune who apparently has financed much of the anti-Clinton crusade. It helps that he owns the *Pittsburgh Tribune-Review,* in which reporter Christopher Ruddy tracked the "murders" of Clinton aide Vince Foster and Commerce Secretary Ron Brown.

The big media gang picked up on pieces of the *Salon*

coverage. On April 8, 1998, CNN tracked down Caryn Mann, former girlfriend of Hale's alleged paymaster. She publicly confirmed *Salon*'s reports that Hale took payments that were ultimately channeled down from Scaife.

Scaife, a right-of-Atilla zillionaire, has served as the Ernst Stavro Blofeld behind the bulk of Clinton bashing, doling out cash to, it seems, virtually anyone willing to publicly accuse Clinton of crimes and misdemeanors ranging from horndog hanky-panky to multiple murder.

Waas, previously best known for his money-trailing Iraqgate exposés after the Gulf War, even detected the hairy, hidden hand of the Mellon Man behind one of the oldest, darkest Clinton conspiracy theories: Mena!

As explained in chapter 61, Mena was the location of an airport in Arkansas from which clandestine flights carried, according to investigators, guns to the Contras and cocaine back into the United States. Clinton allegedly turned a blind eye to the illegal, CIA-linked operation.

According to the anti-Clinton conspiracy theories, Clinton himself profited from the drug operation at Mena. Another variation on the theory has it that Wild Bill's supposed wink-and-nod to the Mena smugglers proves that Clinton, like Bush before him, is nothing more than a pawn of the intelligence community.

Mena conspiracy theories have not emanated exclusively from the Jerry Falwell faction, though Mena did figure heavily in the Falwell-hawked attack video, *The Clinton Chronicles*. Conspiracy researchers of every stripe bought into the Mena scenario. Perhaps there's something to it, perhaps not. We're still waiting for any evidence that rises above the level of innuendo to establish a definitive Clinton-Mena link. So far, we haven't seen any. (And not for lack of looking; check out the right-wing "Washington Weekly" Mena scandal web site; and from a different side of the con coin, our buds at Steamshovel Press have been Mena-minded for years.)

Waas reported that Scaife shelled out a quarter of a million bucks to spread the Mena story and apparently suckered much of the conspiracy "community" in the process.

Scaife, according to Waas's research, hired private dick Rex Armistead to probe Clinton's alleged Mena connection. Scaife even paid for Armistead to fly to far-flung locations—Europe and Belize, to name two—in search of Clinton coke-ring dirt.

When confronted by a reporter about his Scaife connection, Waas reports in *Salon,* Armistead responded, "You better be careful what you write or I'm going to put a lawsuit on you," and, "Are you a Jew?" He denied taking payments from Scaife, but Waas nailed down the paper trail, clever though Blofeld may be!

Armistead fed his "findings" to journalists—particularly at the anti-Clinton scandal rag the *American Spectator*—as well as to congressional investigators and the Drug Enforcement Administration (DEA).

Another note: Scaife isn't the only source of cash for the anti-Clinton coup plotters. On March 31 the *Chicago Sun-Times* got Windy City investment banker Peter W. Smith to fess up to his role in the attempted coup. He has poured about eighty-thousand dollars into an effort to spread dish on the president's shagadelic personal life. Smith's efforts included paying money to the two state troopers who acted as sources for David Brock's now-notorious *American Spectator* article in which the name "Paula" first came up. We all know what that article spawned: the insane juggernaut finally halted on April Fool's Day by Judge Susan Webber-Wright.

However, during all of these rather interesting revelations of a concerted attempt to unseat an elected president, the media remained fixated on l'Affaire Monica. When you sit back and think about it, in the months of relentless reportage that followed the initial Lewinsky scandal, there was very little of substance actually reported. Airtime and column inches were clogged by "leaks," unsubstantiated factoids whispered off the record to reporters by their pals in the office of Independent Counsel Kenneth Starr, the chief Clinton inquisitor.

At the same time, that same media suffers from no lack of navel-gazing commentators pointing out that the Clinton-Lewinsky Affair (the whole thing has that *Man From U.N.C.L.E.* ring to it) has hardly been modern journalism's finest hour. But in all the hand-wringing about the ethics and propriety of "leaks" and how to report them (consensus wisdom: gotta do it, baby!), none have dared utter the dreaded term *disinformation*.

The term "leak" is misleading. It sounds ethically neutral and leaves the door open for the "they all do it" excuse. The self-justifying media and the anti-Clinton pundits fall back on that one a lot: "Starr leaks! Clinton leaks! It's a War of the Leaks!" One, we're supposed to believe, is as bad as the other.

But when a leak is deliberately false, it is no longer a leak. It's a lie, one offered anonymously as fact and reported as such. If that's not the definition of *disinformation,* we don't know what is.

Forgive us for sounding paranoid, but when leak after leak turns up false, is it off-the-wall to think that there's an organized campaign of disinformation? The presumably intended effect of this campaign is: to damage Bill Clinton's reputation and hobble his presidential effectiveness, or worse. Fortunately for Clinton, his overall popularity held; the guy plays hardball with the best of them and is as shrewd a politician as the late twentieth century has seen. A lesser political operator would have been out of there or at least politically crippled. Given the incessant history of anonymously reported lies, we couldn't help but get our conspiracy antennae up at every new "revelation."

The Vast Right-Wing Conspiracy was nothing short of a coup attempt, and everyone willing to look got the rare privilege of watching the coup unfold.

One or two false leaks and we wouldn't bat an eye. The numbers, however, added up faster than the notches on Monica Lewinsky's kneepads. We saw:

- The eyewitness account of the president's steward who supposedly removed from the Oval Office, following a visit by Lewinsky, Kleenex stained with lipstick and "other substances." The ickiness meter went off the chart, but that leak turned out to be a phony, too. As with most of these leaks, no one fessed up to it.
- The Secret Service agent who supposedly witnessed Clinton and Monica in an "ambiguous" position. It was first reported as a "compromising" position before the paper that broke the story, the *Dallas Morning News,* backtracked. Then the whole story turned out to be false, anyway. There was no such witness. No one fessed up to the fib.
- Clinton's Gennifer Flowers testimony. Practically since the scandal broke, it has been widely reported and consequently taken as an article of faith that Clinton, while under oath in his Paula Jones deposition, admitted to a twelve-year-affair with Flowers. Because in a now-historic *60 Minutes* interview during the 1992 presidential campaign Clinton admitted causing "pain" in his marriage but denied the alleged twelve-year-affair, his supposed oathbound confession proves his capacity for lying. However, Clinton admitted to having sex with Gennifer Flowers just once in 1977. That admission would be consistent with his 1992 interview.

There are dark explanations as to why Clinton might have chosen to admit to a one-night stand with Flowers in a sworn deposition twenty-one years after the fact. Maybe he feared that Flowers had kept a semen-stained dress, cunningly anticipating the advent of DNA testing. Or maybe he thought that a not-so-damaging confession of a long-ago indiscretion would make subsequent lies regarding, say, Monica Lewinsky, seem more credible. But the simplest explanation that fits the available facts is that Clinton's testimony is far closer to the truth than Gennifer Flowers', and that Flowers was merely the opening act in a long

running "dirty tricks" campaign to destroy his presidency.
- It's worth noting, also that, back in 1992, Flowers herself adamantly denied the "twelve-year-affair" until the *Star* supermarket tabloid paid her $140,000 to "reveal" it. Heck, for that kind of money, *we* would admit to blowing Bill Clinton. Flowers then turned her story into a *Penthouse* spread replete with naked pix for which she was presumably paid an even larger sum of dough. Heck, for that kind of money, we would—well, never mind. In 1995, Flowers published a book about the "affair." She published another one in 1996. With the emergence of the Lewinsky affair, Flowers received another round of attention and went on a singing tour.
- Then there was "Curriegate." Clinton's personal secretary, the hapless Betty Currie, told the grand jury, operated by grand inquisitor Kenneth Starr, that Clinton had told her to fudge her testimony about whether he and Lewinsky had ever been alone together. Or so it was leaked. The story was flatly denied by Currie's lawyer. Somebody's lying, and given the circumstances, it's probably the anonymous source of the leak rather than Currie's very nonanonymous attorney, who would have much more to lose. (If the leak were substantially accurate, we would expect a more ambiguously worded denial from the lawyer.)
- The retired Secret Service agent who, according to the *Washington Post,* has come forward to say that, back in 1995, he personally let Lewinsky into the Oval Office, where she was alone with the president for a full forty minutes. (If she was doing what everyone assumes she was doing, we have to admit that we admire the president's stamina.) Even other Secret Service agents immediately cast doubt on the account, given by retired Secret Serviceman Lewis C. Fox. Fox, they said, was a uniformed officer, not one of those sunglasses and earpiece guys. Uniformed officers, they say, guard the Oval Office only when the president is not there and the office is vacant. Which really

makes us wonder what Monica was doing in there, but that's another story.

Perhaps the most damaging and, if it really is a fraud, blatant piece of disinformation could turn out to be the infamous talking-points memo.

This weird tidbit of "evidence" was one sheet allegedly passed from Lewinsky to her mother confessor Linda Tripp (the same lady who later turned rat fink on little Lewinsky). The memo gave explicit instructions on how to cover up the Oval Office dalliances. Its very existence seemed improbable. The press puzzled over this supposed smoking gun, but they'd have been better served by trying to track down its real author. Tripp later denied having anything to do with the talking points memo.

We won't even get into the source of the repeated leaks conventional wisdom has it that they came from Starr and/or his operatives. This is one case in which conventional wisdom appears to be on the mark.

The ever-staid *New York Times*—the paper which first got the dubious Betty Currie story—scrambling to cover its grey-lady butt, treated the public to the bizarre spectacle of an editorial in which it chided the Clintonites for their inability to "prove" that the Currie leak came from Starr's forces. Of course, there's almost nowhere else it could have logically come from. (Currie's lawyers? Yeah, sure.) So Clinton's people were quite justified in the public accusations they leveled at Starr.

But the *Times* knows damn well where that leak came from. It was the *Times*'s own story, fercripesake! So the paper prints leaked and probably deceptive information from (in all likelihood) Starr, then sticks out its tongue at the president for his inability to "prove" where the *Times* got its story. What manner of madness is this?

During Watergate, when Bob Woodward and Carl Bernstein incorrectly reported the leaked grand-jury testimony of White House aide Hugh Sloan, a crisis developed inside the *Washington Post*, and the two reporters offered to resign.

Fast-forward twenty-five years to Fellate gate, where that sort of journalistic screwup is happening day after day. And no one seems the least bit red-faced. We could critique Woodward and Bernstein all night long—and wouldn't that be a gas—but at least we can say they had some sense of shame, a quality strangely lacking in today's noninvestigative press corps.

MAJOR SOURCES

Frieden, Terry, and Pierre Thomas. "Hale Accused of Selling Information to Groups." *CNN Online*, 8 April 1998.

Isikoff, Michael, and Evan Thomas. "Clinton and the Intern." *Newsweek*, 2 February 1998.

————. "The Secret Sex Wars." *Newsweek*, 9 February 1998.

Lyons, Gene. "The Roots of the Clinton Smear." *Salon*, 5 February 1998.

Shepard, Scott. "The Dress Rumor: A Stain on Reputable Journalism?" *Atlanta Journal and Constitution*, 31 January 1998.

Solomon, Norman. "Our Man at *The Post*." *EXTRA!*, Jan.–Feb., 1998.

Sweet, Lynn. "Chicago Man Paid Clinton Troopers." *Chicago Sun-Times*, 31 March 1998.

Waas, Murray. "Behind the Clinton Cocaine Smear." *Salon*, 26 March 1998.

Weiner, Tim, and Jill Abramson. "Clinton Foes Have Ties But Deny They Are in Concert." *New York Times*, 28 January 1998.

Weisberg, Jacob. "Leak Soup: The New Absurdity of Anonymous Sources." *Slate*, 12 February 1998.

V
Blood 'n' Guts

33

The Royal Ripper

The definitive Jack the Ripper conspiracy theory became a major motion picture in the apocryphal Sherlock Holmes flick *Murder by Decree*, but it originated in a book called *Jack the Ripper: The Final Solution* by a British journalist, Stephen Knight, who postulated a cabal of Freemasons extending into the highest reaches of British government as the entity responsible for the Whitechapel murders. Knight harbored a particular fixation on Freemasons. He authored another, more general exposé titled *The Brotherhood* and was working on a sequel when he, abruptly, died.

Not even the monarchy came off clean in Knight's ripping yarn, which unfolded thusly:

Amidst an atmosphere of political upheaval and working-class resentment toward the aristocracy in general and the royal family in particular—with seven assassination attempts against Queen Victoria—one wayward but highly placed royal committed a slight indiscretion. He married a commoner. Secretly. And to make matters worse, he got her pregnant first. And, in the crowning gross-out to Victorian sensibilities, she was a Catholic.

The offender was Eddy, the sensitive and bisexual duke of Clarence, second in line to the throne. And considering that his father, the Prince of Wales, was endlessly enmeshed in scandals created by his own ribaldry, to the extent that his ascension to the throne seemed less than a sure thing, Eddy's gaffe posed a palpable threat to the monarchy itself. It was ripe for exploitation by republican rabble rousers, if ever the marriage became public knowledge.

Lord Robert Salisbury, England's prime minister and one of the country's highest-ranking Freemasons, resolved that it would not.

Salisbury acted not simply from patriotism, although he surely adored the British royal tradition, but from self-preservation. He owed his existence, or at least his importance (same thing) to Masonry. And in Britain, Masonry was inextricable from the crown, with none other than the blackguard Prince of Wales sitting as Most Worshipful Grand Master of England. Indeed, the Freemasons were the "power behind the scenes" that an earlier prime minister, Benjamin Disraeli warned about. Freemasonry and the crown could not endure without each other.

Salisbury entrusted the job to one of his dearest Masonic brethren, the royal family's physician and abortionist, Sir William Gull.

With the background set, the specifics of Knight's scenario—with the exception, as it turned out, of one important detail—germinated in a tale spun by Walter Sickert, a British impressionist painter and bohemian about town who moved with ease among East End unfortunates.

But Sickert also, according to his own account, befriended the duke of Clarence. In fact the Heir Presumptive passed as Sickert's fictional brother to facilitate frequent sojourns to the forbidden side of town where he led a parallel life.

While gallivanting in the guise of his alter ego, according to Sickert, Eddy fell in love with, sired a daughter by, and covertly wed a shop clerk named Annie Elizabeth Crook. Eddy's royal relatives would have none of it, of course. They swiftly grounded the young duke and, at the good doctor Gull's directive, shipped his unauthorized bride to an asylum. Or more likely, Knight found, to a "workhouse," i.e., something like a halfway house, but much more lax in recording the comings and goings of inmates.

There were two witnesses to the extraroyal nuptials: Sickert and a gal who worked in the same shop as Annie named Marie Kelly. Once Eddy's elders busted up the unlikely couple, Kelly fled in fear to her Irish home, where by her silence she ensured her safety.

A few years later Kelly returned to the East End, predictably down on her luck. With her only source of income concealed within her knickers, Marie found herself falling in with the wrong crowd.

In no time at all, a few of her comrades-in-harlotry to whom she had unwisely divulged her history—with visions of pound signs dancing in their not-entirely-sober heads—devised and enacted a thoroughly half-assed blackmail scheme, thus committing suicide.

After all, let's not forget the high stakes that Freemasons play for. As one excitable conspiratorialist, extrapolating from Knight's evidence, phrased it, "little did they know that their scheme was standing in the way of World Domination!!!"

Be that as it may, Salisbury certainly felt his Freemasonic job security was again in question and again he delegated authority for continuing the coverup to Gull. The physician carried out the killings in his carriage, driven by one John Netley, who had previously chauffeured Eddy to the East End during those halcyon days of pre-Ripperdom. A third accomplice, identified by Sickert as assistant police commissioner Sir Robert Anderson (another Masonic bigwig), helped lure the victims into the death buggy.

All this according to the painter Walter Sickert, whose son

Joseph relayed the knowledge to Knight. Joseph himself is progeny of the duke—his mother was Annie Crook's daughter Alice, who grew up to become the elder Sickert's paramour.

As for the finer details of the crimes and their coverup, Knight does an admirable job of tracking down and verifying, or at least corroborating, Sickert's scenario. This would mean that the Jack the Ripper murders were no more than routine government skullduggery—no different than silencing witnesses to the JFK assassination (you know, routine stuff). That is, if it were not for the elaborate Masonic symbolism and concordance with Masonic rite under which the slashings were carried out.

While peppering his explication with disclaimers to the effect that most ordinary Masons have no idea what the brethren at the pinnacle of their order are up to, Knight goes to great lengths detailing how the Masonic doctrine binding high-level initiates permits and even encourages them to perform acts of unadulterated evil. While on the one hand he indicts those Masons prone to act upon such doctrine as a "lunatic fringe," he names Gull, Anderson, and even Salisbury as adherents. Very elite lunatics.

The wall-scrawl at one crime scene blaming "Juwes" for the murders—improperly erased by police commissioner (and, of course, Freemason) Sir Charles Warren who claimed to fear an outbreak of anti-Semitic violence—referred not to Jews, Knight says, but to the three Juwes—motley hit men named Jubela, Jubelo, and Jubelum—who snuffed Solomonic architect Hiram Abiff, the prime martyr of Masonic myth. Similarly, the way the killers draped number four victim Catherine Eddowes's displaced digestive tract over her shoulder recalled Hiram's grotesque injuries. Eddowes's body was dumped in Mitre Square, which Knight calls "the most Masonic of all places in London," not least of all because the mitre and the square are basic Masonic implements. Mitre Square was, to boot, the location of several Masonic meeting halls, including Mitre Tavern where Gull's enclave sometimes gathered.

Gull for some reason mistook Eddowes for Kelly and that's why her murder bore the heaviest Masonic symbolism. It was supposed to be the capper. The one that says, "We're the Freemasons and you're not." When they realized they'd hacked up the wrong gal, the killers waited thirty-nine days—that's the Masonic "perfect" number, three times the "favorite" number thirteen, Knight points out—to do the Kelly hit.

The lavish mutilations to Kelly's person apparently conform to same arcane Masonic prescription for how to mutilate people. One supposes that the very presence of guidelines for such activity indicates something amiss in Mason-land. But most important, the murders themselves, their shock value and the panic that erupted during the ten-week reign of Jack the Ripper (be he one or three) represented a reassertion of Masonic supremacy then threatened by working-class unrest.

The principles of advanced Freemasonry, in fact, require such terrorism to counter challenges to the brotherhood's authority, Knight reports. In Sickert's story, Lord Salisbury himself, while somewhat disquieted by the murders, is "pleased" by their public display of Masonic dominance.

Perhaps questionably, Knight relies on *The Protocols of the Elders of Zion* as his source for Masonry's secret agenda, offering but a brief caveat that "the *Protocols* have been the subject of debate since they first appeared in print." He states that their use by anti-Semites twists their true significance and that "they had been in existence for a long time before they were finally published." As such, Knight asserts, "it seems inescapable that they exerted an influence." In particular, he writes, without offering any verification beyond the "it sure looks that way" mode of argument, the *Protocols* exerted an influence on the "fanatical mind" of Sir William Gull.

While Knight's research is persuasive, sometimes ground breaking, he has a tendency to rely on the "what else could it be?" substitute for actual evidence beloved of so many harder-core conspiracy theorists. His assumption that Gull put the *Protocols* into effect is one example. But granting the assumption—not a wholly implausible one—Knight is correct to point out that it doesn't matter whether the *Protocols* are authentic or not. All that's important is what Gull read them to mean.

There is one final twist to Knight's hypothesis. While Knight believes that Anderson, as a good Freemasonic fanatic, was complicitous in covering up the true, composite identity of Jack the Ripper, he finds too many inconsistencies that preclude Anderson from taking part in the killings. The "third man" could only have been, Knight concludes, Walter Sickert.

Sickert's detailed knowledge of the Ripper killings could have derived only from on-site experience. Sickert's own motive can be nothing but survival and protection of the infant who was Eddy's illegitimate offspring and would years later mother Sickert's own son. The Masons must have coerced him with threats, Knight reasons.

Other than Knight's, the favored Ripper conspiracy theory has a syphilitic Prince Eddy himself as the Ripper, his already muddled thinking further warped by disease. A version synthesizing the two hypotheses puts Sickert at the scene of the crimes, but as a babysitter for Eddy, who is under some kind of Masonic mind control. Thus Sickert's guilt is doubled: He is complicitous not only in the killings but in the degradation of his former disciple.

Sickert's aching conscience led him not only to unburden himself to his son (with Anderson in his role) but to plant clues at the crime scenes—the Juwes message among them—to implicate Freemasonry in general and Gull in particular. All of these clues were eliminated or obscured by law-enforcement Masons purporting to investigate the murders. Frustrated, Sickert went on to paint clues into a number of his later works. He often said that certain paintings were inspired by the Ripper murders, or by his old friend Marie Kelly.

"He was a strange man," says Sickert's son Joseph at the conclusion of Knight's book. "He would start weeping for no reason sometimes, terribly moved by something long ago."

MAJOR SOURCES

Knight, Stephen. *Jack the Ripper: The Final Solution.* London: Granada Publishing, 1977.
Rumbelow, Donald. *The Complete Jack the Ripper.* Boston: New York Graphic Society, 1975.

34

Death Squad From the Desert

Nowadays, after a decades-long bombardment of Bundys and Dahmers and Sons of Sam, Night Stalkers, McDonald's massacres, and headless bodies found in topless bars—a world-without-end of pointless gore rushing forth from our TV screens—the impact of Charles Manson's crimes is hard to fathom. They sound almost routine by 1990s standards: five people killed one night, two the next. Stabbed and shot. Blood-writing smeared on walls. Maybe even a little blood drinking, just for good measure. Change the channel, honey, I think the Knicks are on.

On August 9, 1969, a group of Manson's cult followers crept into a house at 10050 Cielo Drive in the Benedict Canyon section of Beverly Hills. The home was rented by film director Roman Polanski and his gorgeous, pregnant bride, actress Sharon Tate. The intruders didn't leave until they'd slaughtered all five humans present (Polanski was out of the country at the time).

America wasn't ready for it. The Manson gang hacked up

supermarket magnate Leno LaBianca and his wife the next eve in similar fashion and from then on there has always been a touch of fear on the land. Even on the coziest, calmest American summer nights, there is indeed something very evil out there. And maybe, just maybe, it is coming for you.

Why did this happen?

Vincent Bugliosi, the prosecutor who put Manson and his (mostly female) killers away for life established a motive and wrote a book about it: *Helter Skelter*. This phrase, scrawled in victims' hemoglobin at the carnage scenes, was, in addition to being the title of a Beatles' song, Manson's term for race war. He hoped the murders would be blamed on black militants, thus sparking an apocalyptic conflict.

In Charlie's ultraracist view the physically superior but mentally inferior blacks would win the war, but then find themselves incapable of governing the wasteland. Thus Charlie and his "Family" cult would emerge from their desert hiding cave and assume control.

Charlie bought this cartoony-bigoted scenario, no doubt. But even the Wizard (as one-time Manson patron Dennis Wilson of the Beach Boys called Manson) acknowledged that "Helter Skelter" was not the true motive for the massacres. Bugliosi said he relied on Helter Skelter because the L.A. police failed to turn up anything else. It never made much sense anyway. If Manson wanted to start a race war, why give up after two nights of bloodshed?

As one female disciple noted, Manson had a selfish motive for everything. Indeed, the other murders he is known to have committed or ordered each had tangible motives involving either drug deals or silencing potential snitches.

Bugliosi sent Manson et al. to the slams with the Helter Skelter case, but he suspected there was more to the story. In the epilogue to his bestseller he notes that Manson appeared to have had some connection to the Process Church of the Final Judgment, the satanic cult whose leader, Robert Moore (aka DeGrimston) spouted rhetoric all-too-Mansonesque.

When Bugliosi asked Manson if he'd ever heard of Moore, Manson snapped. "You're looking at him. Moore and I are one and the same."

Perhaps concerned about its image, the Process Church dispatched two representatives from its Cambridge, Massachusetts, outpost to Bugliosi's office in Los Angeles. They had a nice, civil chat with the young prosecutor, but Bugliosi later found their names registered on the list of Manson's jailhouse visitors for that same day. Bugliosi never found out what kind of a chat they had with Manson, but whenever he tried to probe about the Process Church thereafter, Manson clammed up.

Bugliosi's inquiries were confined by the constrictions of a prosecutorial case, but underground journalist Ed Sanders and investigative reporter Maury Terry traced the "Family" tree with wider-ranging investigations. Sanders authored *The Family*, the most comprehensive treatise on Manson. Terry—a decade or so later—came out with *The Ultimate Evil*, in which he connected Manson (albeit tangentially) to the Son of Sam murders in New York.

Both reporters believe that a soured drug deal was the real motive for the Tate murders. Possibly the LaBianca killings as well. They agree that Manson was subcontracting his homicidal cult to some higher authority. The true target of the Tate murders was probably Vojtek Frykowski, a playboy and LSD dealer who had gotten in over his head. Frykowski, along with his girlfriend Abigail Folger (of the Folger coffee empire), and Hollywood hairstylist-to-the-stars Jay Sebring, were murdered along with Tate.

There are some indications that Rosemary LaBianca was involved in the LSD market too. Her husband, the supermarket mogul, also owed substantial gambling debts.

"Don't you think those people deserved to die?" Manson blurted to an interviewer who caught up with him years after the fact, as he mellowed into middle age. "They were involved in kiddie porn."

Outré porn reels are a potentially lucrative operation, and

kiddie or not, the Tate crowd could very likely have been up to something cinematic. The problem is, no such films have ever turned up.

Some sources in a position to know have gone on record stating that the house at 10050 Cielo Drive was something of a porno soundstage. Terry Melcher, who used to live in the house, was aspiring folkie Manson's major music biz contact. He was also the son of Doris Day, and he said in his mom's autobiography that he knew of at least one "orgy" that was filmed in his old haunt. Sharon Tate was among the ensemble cast. Reportedly other very recognizable Hollywood faces appeared in Cielo Drive epics, many of which had a bondage and pain theme.

Films of nonsimulated raunch and gore seem a popular entertainment (and revenue source, perhaps) for certain types of offbeat groups. One of Sanders's informants claims to have viewed a loop of some Family members dancing on a beach around a beheaded corpse. Films of scantily clad Manson girls ingesting blood and sacrificing animals have also been rumored.

Maury Terry believes that one of the Son of Sam murders was videotaped and that a cameraman was snuffed when the Sam cult came to recover the reel. Terry believes that another cinephile for that shooting of a shooting was the occult hit man dubbed Manson II, later identified as convicted murderer William Mentzer, who moved through the same late-sixties L.A. sex-drugs-porno scene as Manson and knew Abigail Folger.

Terry offers a secondhand quote from "someone in the intelligence community" who says of Mentzer, "We have it that he did a hit in Son of Sam."

The intelligence community?

But it seems the intelligence community may have taken an interest in Manson, as well as in Manson II. Two days after the Tate murders Charlie Manson was spotted driving a spiffy black Mercedes belonging to a big-shot LSD dealer whose boss—the LSD industry's Mr. Big—was, in Terry's description, "said to have been a former Israeli who had strong links to the intelligence community."

If one is truly conspiracy-minded, the name Ronald Stark comes to mind—the international LSD entrepreneur of the late 1960s. While not quite "a former Israeli," Stark was multilingually fluent and often passed for nationalities other than American. His ties to the CIA were apparently so evident that an Italian judge once dismissed a major case against him on grounds that Stark appeared to be working for that U.S. spook hive. And around the time Manson was prowling the West Coast, Stark was preeminent in the acid trade there.

The Los Angeles Police Department was far from the only agency investigating the Tate murders. Seems every law enforcement arm from the FBI on down took an interest. Israeli intelligence also, according to Terry.

Dazzled by the official interest, Sanders once wondered "if the Process was a front for some intelligence operation."

Such musings are, of course, pure speculation, and in the absence of definitive investigations, other intriguing speculations have also been offered regarding the Manson case. The former D.A. of California's Inyo County, Frank Fowles, not only probed Manson's links to the Process—Manson probably intersected with the cult in San Francisco, and according to some accounts, he did join—but also to the Bay Area's Zodiac killer. With an indeterminate number of victims, the Zodiac was never apprehended. He, or they, sent a number of taunting letters to the police chock full of occult cryptography and rambling. A few years later, Son of Sam would exhibit some of the same behavior.

Whoever ultimately ordered the Manson murders can take credit for one sorry accomplishment.

"Manson's Family seemed to wound the best qualities of a generation," wrote Ed Sanders. "Its sharing and self-reliance, its music and wild colors, its love of the outdoors and the natural beauty of America, its search for higher standards, its early sense of the need to protect the environment. Could it be that this one group would put a grotesque and hideous capstone upon a decade that had such a powerful and beautiful promise?"

Richard Nixon and J. Edgar Hoover in cahoots with the CIA could not have done a better job of that.

MAJOR SOURCES

Bugliosi, Vincent. *Helter Skelter*. New York: Bantam Books, 1973.

Newton, Michael. *Raising Hell: An Encyclopedia of Devil Worship and Satanic Crime*. New York: Avon Books, 1993.

Sanders, Ed. *The Family*. New York: Signet Books, 1989.

Schreck, Nicholas, ed. *The Manson File*. New York: Amok Press, 1987.

Terry, Maury. *The Ultimate Evil*. Garden City, NY: Dolphin Books, 1987.

35

"Hello From the Gutters"

The string of .44 caliber shootings that panicked the Big Apple in 1976 and 1977 were plenty horrifying. But if the murders were not the work of a single, deranged gunman now idling in prison, if they were instead rituals of a nationwide drugs-and-death cult—that's scarier still. Turns out, reports journalist Maury Terry, that the Son of Sam killing spree marks the concentric point in a sphere of unsettling satanic conspiracies.

Because, of course, all serial killers without exception are either paranoid schizophrenics or sexually frustrated misfits incapable of involvement in any form of organized conspiracy whatsoever, when police zeroed in on a security guard and former serviceman named David Berkowitz (who had dutifully paid a ticket he'd been issued for illegally parking his car near one of the murder sites) the Son of Sam case was quite comfortably solved.

The alleged lone gunman claimed that he received orders to kill from a neighbor's dog, thus satisfying the "by gosh, there's just no explainin' it" prerequisite. As if it wasn't enough to be just plain bonkers, the overweight, baby-faced Berkowitz matched the other pop-prototype of a mass killer: loner, nerd, a bust with the babes (he was said to be a virgin). Supposedly he had botched two knife attacks on women the previous year.

As so often happens, the official explanation proved inadequate when confronted by actual evidence.

Terry broke the conspiracy story in a 1981 article that ran in the Gannett newspaper *Today*. Berkowitz, the story said, may have participated in just two of the seven attacks. The remainder were planned and executed by other members of the cult. Terry fleshed out the theme in his 1987 tome, *The Ultimate Evil*.

The composite culprit, according to Terry (who's now built a career on his Samophilia), was a satanic cult called The Children that held campy if gruesome rituals (lots of drugs and dog-killings) in Yonkers' Untermeyer Park.

Berkowitz himself first revealed the cult connections in correspondence from prison and chats with cellmates. His reluctance to go into more than sketchy detail and refusal to use the cult angle as a defense argues against the possibility that Berkowitz concocted the tale self-servingly. He appeared comfortable enough to be characterized as a "homicidal exhbitionist" and cooperated on a book with the psychiatrist who diagnosed him as such.

But in late October 1978, David Berkowitz revealed knowledge about a murder that had happened three years before the Son of Sam spree and three thousand miles away.

North Dakota police received an anonymous package containing a book on witchcraft with the words "Arliss Perry, Hunted Stalked and Slain. Followed to Calif. Stanford University" in Berkowitz's handwriting. The book also contained references to the Process Church of the Final Judgment, one of those countercultural mutations that slithered from the dour side of sixties San Francisco. The Process Church's leader, ex-Scientologist Robert DeGrimston (né Moore) was an acknowledged influence on Charles Manson.

Around the same time, the convicted Son of Sam penned a couple of letters from prison going into greater detail about the 1974 murder of Perry, a newlywed devout Christian from North Dakota, whose body was found systematically and symbolically mutilated in a Stanford University campus chapel on October 12, 1974. That date, perhaps coincidentally, was the birthday of occult legend Aleister Crowley—*and* of John Carr, Berkowitz's buddy and a known satanist, who died in 1979 of a shotgun blast to the head on an air force base in North Dakota.

Carr's death was ruled a suicide, though someone had scratched the numbers 666 into the dried blood on his hand and smeared NY SS in his blood on the wall near where the body was discovered. NY SS appears an obvious reference to the Son of Sam slayings in New York and Carr was indeed a real son of Sam. His father was Sam Carr, owner of the dog from which Berkowitz claimed to have received his kill-commands.

Carr also matched eyewitness descriptions of the gunman in one of the Sam slayings, and in one of the Son of Sam letters, Berkowitz (or whoever wrote it) included a reference to "John Wheaties, rapist and suffocator of young girls." Carr had a sister named Wheat and for some reason, John Carr himself went by the nickname Wheaties.

With clues like that it's amazing that police ever had a suspect other than Carr.

There were other should-be suspects. Witnesses at the scene of the Perry murder described a sandy-haired young man skulking around the Stanford chapel shortly after Perry was seen entering it the night of her death. Their descriptions were close to those of the shooter in the second Sam slaying. Berkowitz confirmed that the two descriptions were indeed of the same individual, whom he identified only as Manson II.

According to Berkowitz's intimations, this dangerous fellow was an "occult superstar," an associate of the original Manson who now belonged to a team of satanic contract killers that carried out ritual murders coast to coast—knocking off renegade cultists, potential witnesses, outside meddlers, or just about anyone the cultists deemed worthy of execution. Perry's killing, under this hypothesis, stemmed from her missionary-like attempts to convert a coven of devil worshippers in her native North Dakota.

In 1988 Los Angeles police arrested William Mentzer, a cultist, drug dealer, and one-time bodyguard for paralyzed pornographer Larry Flint. Mentzer was charged with murdering Long Island sleaze impresario Roy Radin who, when he was killed in 1983, was engaged in trying to raise financing for the movie *The Cotton Club*. Radin was also tied up in various cocaine deals with a Miami drug runner named Karen Greenberger who also did business with Mentzer. Terry had long suspected that Radin—whose orgies at his Long Island mansion were known to include videotaped gang rapes, including one starring actress Melanie Hallor from the sitcom *Welcome Back, Kotter*—was the Mr. Big referred to by Berkowitz as the godfather of the Son of Sam cult. This Mr. Big, according to Terry's sources, commissioned the videotaping of one of the Sam murders for his collection of snuff flicks, and even more significantly, for sale throughout a national network of financially well-endowed weirdos and creeps.

In other words, Son of Sam was big business.

Tipped off that some sort of occult clue would be found near the scene of Radin's murder, Terry journeyed to California and examined the site. He discovered a Bible opened to a passage reading "Let us eat and drink, for tomorrow we shall die."

Mentzer, Radin's killer, turned out to be an associate of Charles Manson (in Manson's L.A. social scene; he was not part of the Family) and of Abigail Folger, the coffee heiress killed by Manson's followers at the Sharon Tate house. He was also reportedly in the Bay Area at the time of the Arlis Perry killing.

Berkowitz's inside knowledge of the Perry job came from Manson II himself, who regaled the Yonkers cultists with details of his grisly handiwork when he visited them in New York. The Los Angeles cops openly acknowledged Mentzer's membership in "some kind of hit squad."

Terry's prison source also said that Berkowitz conveyed information that Manson himself was acting on orders when he commanded his Family to slaughter the Tate party and the LaBianca couple. Cultists make spiffy assassins.

If Mentzer is indeed Manson II, and Berkowitz wasn't making the whole thing up, then his very existence links the Son of Sam murders to the Manson massacres eight years earlier— an occult conspiracy cutting through space and time. But how far back?

The Son of Sam correspondence was inscribed with an occult symbol drawn up by nineteenth-century black magic practitioner Eliphas Levi. "I believe somebody put it in my mind to write that," Berkowitz later explained. One of the shootings happened outside a disco called Elephas. And in one of the Sam letters the writer referred to himself as "the chubby behemoth." An elephant?

"Could the Black Magic adept Eliphas Levi have programmed or shaped the Son of Sam happenings from the nineteenth century," wonders hyper-imaginative conspirophile Michael Hoffman II in a 1984 *Conspiracy Tracker* article.

Hoffman connects Son of Sam not only to Manson but, straining credulity rather a bit, to the 1921 rape-slaying of Virginia Rappe by "chubby behemoth" silent movie comic Roscoe "Fatty" Arbuckle. Hoffman pegs that definitive Hollywood Babylon-ish incident as a black magic rite invoking the "elephant force." Arbuckle (who was acquitted of the crime) is said to have violated the unfortunately named Miss Rappe (Virginia Rappe = Virgin Rape) with a wine bottle, a procedure that, according to Hoffman, is a traditional magickal method of simulating the "must" of the elephant, whatever that means.

In any event, the Arbuckle elephantine "ritual" took place at the St. Francis Hotel in "California's mystical city named after St. Francis." (Um, that would be San Francisco?) St. Francis has special significance to occultists, particularly Mason, Hoffman reports.

About forty years later, San Francisco became home to the Process Church.

Hoffman's analysis deserves some sort of praise for its, shall we say, inventiveness. But his comment about the "programmed" Son of Sam may be worth a second glance. Bearing in mind Berkowitz's own comment that "someone put it in my mind" to scribble Eliphas Levi's symbol on his letters (and for that matter, his cover story about receiving orders to kill by remote control—albeit from a dog), Son of Sam may fall into the category of Manchurian Candidate assassins.

California conspiracy-radio-host Dave Emory in a multipart "documentary" copping the title *The Ultimate Evil*, embellished Terry's thesis to bring the "national security establishment" in on the plot.

Berkowitz experimented with LSD while stationed with the military in Korea. To suppose that he took part—wittingly or not—in an MK-ULTRA-style mind-control project is not terribly far-fetched. Nor does it transcend plausibility to postulate that satanic cults provide a perfect vector for nefarious national security types to breed their automaton assassins.

Does *everything* connect through the Son of Sam interface? Recall that in 1974 one of Manson's least repentant disciples, Lynette "Squeaky" Fromme tried to do away with President Gerald Ford. If she'd pulled it off, the presidency would have fallen to none other than Nelson Rockefeller, *appointed* vice-president by Ford—and whose name is synonymous with the Insider multinational corporate capitalist communist Illuminati occult conspiracy. And Ford himself is a Freemason who sat on the Warren Commission, which covered up the death of one president. Had Ford received his possibly poetic justice, Rockefeller would have ascended to ultimate power thanks to a member of the occultist Nazi-satan-worshipping Manson Family, which sprung from the same Process Church that produced the Son of Sam cult and whose offshoots act as killers-for-hire.

MAJOR SOURCES

Newton, Michael. *Raising Hell: An Encyclopedia of Devil Worship and Satanic Crime*. New York: Avon Books, 1993.
Terry, Maury. *The Ultimate Evil*. Garden City, NY: Dolphin Books, 1987.

VI

Unified Field Theories

36

The Enlightened Ones

When it comes to the Illuminati, the line between history and hysteria gets fuzzy.

To place them in their context employing some semblance of rationality, the Bavarian Illuminati, the most renowned of all groups to adopt that appellation, were one of many manifestations of the enlightened (illuminated?) spirit sweeping Europe in the eighteenth century, which saw no higher purpose than to eradicate the centuries-old monarchical/feudal domination that had trapped mankind in the dark ages. The Illuminati were as much products of their age as shapers of it.

On the other hand...

The society's founder, Adam Weishaupt, was a hotheaded, prodigious Ingolstadt University law professor—barely post-adolescent at twenty-six—when he joined the Freemasons in 1774 and shortly set to work blueprinting a utopian schemata to move human civilization into a universal state of nature unshackled by authoritarian strictures. While not lacking in ambition, Weishaupt also possessed enough realism to understand that he required a dedicated bevy of accomplices to pull off this caper.

With a restless mind that rejected all normative systems of belief, young Adam grew into an occultist of sorts, with an enthusiasm for Greek mystery religions. While no one's 100 percent sure what went on inside these cults—they were, after all, mysterious—Weishaupt sussed out enough to pattern his own secret society on their structure. Recruiting five members from a prestigious Masonic lodge over which he'd gained a measure of control, on May 1, 1776 (a retroactively suspicious date, if ever there was one), Weishaupt inaugurated the Order of Perfectibilists, better known as the Bavarian Illuminati.

While Weishaupt himself may have talked a good game, he wasn't much of a "player" in the Masonic politico scene. Again, he shrewdly compensated for his own shortcomings. He executed a recruiting coup, signing up one Adolf Francis, known as Baron Knigge, who by 1780 was already one of the Continent's leading Masons. The baron had attempted for years to unite all the European lodges into one giant, spidery entity of subterfuge. With Knigge's talent for organization, Illuminati rolls quickly swelled to over three thousand—each name plucked from the cream of the Masonic crop—in what amounted to a bloodless coup of the European Freemasonic upper echelon.

On the Continent, Freemasonry was traditionally a refuge for radical intellectuals, politicians, and those who wanted to rub shoulders with them. The Illuminati selected the most dedicated and powerful of these and filtered them through initiation rites more grueling and esoteric than Freemasonry's own. The practice was designed largely to ensure allegiance to Weishaupt and the other chief executives of the order. The Illuminati, thusly, became a secret revolutionary cell whose influence far outstripped its numbers.

Alas, like so many secret organizations, it had a hard time keeping itself secret. After a few defectors spilled some of Weishaupt's classified info in the early to mid-1780s, the Illuminati was specifically decreed to be an outlaw organization and the Bavarian heat came down hard. Weishaupt and a few other leaders fled to neighboring provinces. Or somewhere.

Adam Weishaupt's trail appears to peter out at this point. New Age literary prankster-laureate Robert Anton Wilson has (spuriously) suggested that he escaped to America and knocked off and then impersonated our hemp-smokin', avidly Masonic founding president. Maybe Washington's idiosyncrasies were really Weishaupt's. That speculation is as good as any, because stories about the Illuminati refuse to go away. Almost instantly upon their forced dissolution, rumors began making the rounds that Weishaupt's subversive elitists were still up to their devious schemes. According to the classic exposé *Proofs of a Conspiracy*, published fourteen years after the Illuminati breathed their apparent last, the Illuminati metamorphosed into the German Union and had played a role in—if not caused—the French Revolution, an uprising whose motto, "Liberty, Equality, Fraternity" was explicitly Masonic.

In his wonderful, divagating history of the topic, *The Illuminoids*, Neil Wilgus reports that George Washington, whoever he was, read *Proofs* and felt that its charges deserved wider play. Though, of course, he added, American Masonic lodges engaged in none of the chicanery of their European counterparts. Thomas Jefferson, another Mason (as were most of the founding fathers) had a passing familiarity with Weishaupt's writings. He admired them, saying that he could understand the German radical's penchant for secrecy given the despotism that held dominion over Europe. But if Weishaupt had been in America, said the author of the Declaration of Independence, he "would not have thought of any secret machinery" to propagate his freethinking ideology.

Weishaupt's Illuminati have become the all-purpose conspiracy; the theory that explains everything and always applies. Various versions of the tale list Franklin Delano Roosevelt as an initiated Illuminatus. After all, it was under Roosevelt that the Masonic eye in the pyramid first appeared on U.S. currency.

One anecdote, which likely falls into the category of "urban legend," tells how Charles Manson was identified as a card-carrying member of the Illuminati—on the Oprah Winfrey Show.

One can't help but wonder, however, whether the entire Illuminati story is fabricated. Is it possible that an "Adam Weishaupt" ever existed? His very name smacks of hoaxery— Adam, the first man; Weishaupt, which translates "wise head." Nice moniker for the purported instigator of a world revolution.

While general consensus does seem to hold that such an individual did, at one point, stalk the Earth (though living perhaps not quite as spectacular a life as is often described), Weishaupt is a mythic character like any historical figure: JFK, John Dillinger, Hitler, Casanova, Babe Ruth. A living metaphor. For... what?

Wilgus took the most accurate approach, chronicling not the history of Illuminati but "illuminoids," a neologism defined as "like the Illuminati." Throughout history "enlightenment" or "illumination" has been one of humanity's greatest obsessions. Weishaupt's Bavarian Illuminati, though they receive the widest publicity, were a rather minor exponent of a tradition that probably dates back to the days of prehistory, when some cave shaman first freaked out his flock by sparking fire with flint and sticks. He or she quite literally saw the light. The quest for illumination can be simultaneously baleful and benign. The Force always has its Dark Side. To hear the right-wingers tell it, history has played host to a veritable army of Darth Vaders. Peering through the prism from a different angle, we can see the illuminoids as segments of humanity dissatisfied with our everyday lot on this mudball, reaching above, within, and elsewhere for a better way.

Early mystery sects of the type that inspired Weishaupt may have been among the first manifestations of organized illumination. Jewish cabalism, Christian gnosticism, and Islamic sufism followed, as did a liberal peppering of cults and secret societies from the fearsome Hashishim (assassins) and the ill-fated Knights Templar to smaller occult groups, some (as in Spain and France) actually calling themselves "Illuminati."

Weishaupt's organization fits snugly onto this continuum.

Since the Bavarian Illuminati's ostensible demise, the flame has burned brilliantly. Occult groups from Aleister Crowley's Ordo Templis Orientis to Anton LaVey's Church of Satan occupy one end of the spectrum, feeding the paranoia of that particular strain of Christian who exhausts a reservoir's worth of energy fretting about "satanism." Then who's to say they're so crazy? Who is satan but Lucifer, the fallen "Angel of Light"? The first Illuminatus.

On the more respectable side of things, we spot traces of Illumination in, first of all, the very existence of an "establishment," a ruling class that considers itself possessed of some special knowledge needed to lead, and even more so in establishment institutions: the Council on Foreign Relations, the Trilateral Commission (with its ominous triangular logo), the Bilderberg Group. All are private bodies composed of business, political, and academic "leading lights," so to speak, which, despite the contrary protestations of their members, do in fact wield considerable influence over how geopolitics shape up. The Council on Foreign Relations (CFR) was born as an American offshoot of Cecil Rhodes's British Round Table. Its roster has included most of the presidents and secretaries of state for the last six decades. Henry Kissinger was inducted as a young academic and the CFR published his breakthrough book, *Nuclear Weapons and Foreign Policy*, in which Kissinger originated the idea of "winnable" nuclear war.

When the CIA was founded in 1947, its "old boy network" also connected to the CFR. CIA officials still deliver off-the-record briefings to CFR meetings. The Trilateral Commission, founded by multinational banking demigod David Rockefeller, is an offshoot of the CFR, but with Japan included. Membership in the two groups overlaps considerably. Jimmy Carter was a Trilateral "commissioner," and when he became president, conspiracy theorists were greatly alarmed.

The Netherlands-based Bilderberg Group is more shadowy, but it's the same idea with many of the same members—only with a European accent.

The aim of these elite groups, according to anti-Illuminist lore, is to consolidate control through some form of "one-world government." That is, to set up a "new world order." Oddly, the "meditation room" in the United Nations building is decked out in eye-in-the-pyramid decor. A clue dropped to taunt those of us still in the dark? Not unlike George Bush's repeated public expressions of enthusiasm for creating a new world order. A photograph of Bush in his hospital bed, surrounded by little kids with a pyramid in his lap (can anyone say "fertility rite"?), is said to be the Skull and Bones president's favorite. If that's just a legend, the snapshot is certainly the conspiracy theorists' favorite. This is the same president whose initiation into his alma mater's premier secret society required that he lie naked in a coffin—masturbating.

The Illuminati are everywhere, in one guise or another. All it takes is the will to recognize them. In their Masonic persona, mad genius conspiracy researcher James Shelby Downard has identified their handiwork in the Kennedy assassination.

A writer named Jay Katz (né Jim Keith) in an intriguing monograph titled *Saucers of the Illuminati*, posits the enlightened ones as the all-too-human force behind the UFO phenomenon, while William Bramley in his book *Gods of Eden* makes an unsettlingly cogent case that the Illuminati overlords are in fact aliens—an argument put forth far more loosely by a wide variety of true believers from ultraconspiratorialist Bill Cooper to heavily armed cult priestess Elizabeth Clare Prophet, the millennialist leader of the Church Universal and Triumphant in Montana.

Adam Weishaupt and his cadre of bookworm revolutionaries come off as nickel-and-dimers compared to that lot.

MAJOR SOURCES

Robison, John. *Proofs of a Conspiracy*. Boston: Western Islands Press, 1967.

Wilgus, Neil. *The Illuminoids: Secret Societies and Political Paranoia*. Santa Fe, NM: Sun Books, 1978.

37

The Sorcerers

Some conspiracy theorists question not "the facts" so much as reason itself. James Shelby Downard is one of those mad geniuses with a talent for making the most improbable, impossible, ludicrous, and laughable speculations appear almost plausible. A self-described student of the "science of symbolism," Downard peels away the rational veneer of history and exposes an abyss of logic-defying synchronicities.

Downard dwells upon a confluence of the familiar and the esoteric that, to him, forms a portrait of political conspiracy the purpose of which is not power or money, but alchemy—the mystical science of transformation. By breaking apart and rejoining elements, it was long ago supposed, alchemy could effect most any miracle (for example, changing base metal into gold).

From ancient times through the Enlightenment, science and magic were one and the same. As far as Downard's concerned, the era when science was indistinguishable from sorcery never ended. The Age of Reason and its industrial, postmodern antecedents are facades obscuring the dream world of primeval urges that surfaces only in sleep.

Per Downard, the plotters are Freemasonic alchemists scheming for sovereignty over the realm of uncontrollable impulse. The relatively tame domains of politics, economics, and ideology are mere means to that end.

"Do not be lulled into believing," warns Downard, "that just because the deadening American city of dreadful night is so utterly devoid of mystery, so thoroughly flat-footed, sterile, and infantile, so burdened with the illusory gloss of baseball-hot dogs-apple-pie-and-Chevrolet, that it exists outside the psychosexual domain. The eternal pagan psychodrama is escalated under these modern conditions precisely because sorcery is not what 'twentieth-century man' can accept as real."

Drawing up a brief primer of Downardism seems an impossible task, though not quite as daunting as reading Downard's own essays, which have been set forth for public consumption largely through the good offices of publisher Adam Parfrey, whose small, outré firm, Feral House, has anthologized Downard's essays in a few collections of conspiratorial material. We can do no more than scratch the surface in this forum.

"The United States, which has long been called a melting pot, should more descriptively be called a witches' cauldron wherein the 'Hierarchy of the Grand Architect of the Universe' arranges for ritualistic crimes and psychopolitical psychodramas to be performed in accordance with a Master plan," Downard explains.

That Master plan necessitates execution of three alchemical rites: the creation and destruction of primordial matter; the killing of the king; and the "making manifest of all that is hidden."

Shakespeare's Macbeth is a "killing of the king" drama. MacBeth, who killed his king in accordance with a witches' (alchemists') plot and was himself later killed, is part of the same schemata.

The latter-day reenactment of the MacBeth ritual, says

Downard, was the assassination of JFK in Dealey Plaza, site of the first Masonic temple in Dallas and a spot loaded with "trinity" symbolism. *Three* is, for those not versed in such matters, the most magic of all magic numbers. Downard's observations include:

- Dallas is located just south of the 33 degree of latitude. The 33rd degree is Freemasonry's highest rank.
- Kennedy's motorcade was rolling toward the "Triple Underpass" when he was slain by, according to some analysts, three gunmen. Three tramps were arrested right after the murder. Hiram Abiff, architect of Solomon's Temple and mythic progenitor of Freemasonry was murdered according. to Masonic legend by three "unworthy craftsmen."
- The MacBeth clan of Scotland had many variations of the family name. One was MacBaine, or Baines. Kennedy's successor was Lyndon Baines Johnson, a Freemason.
- *Dea* in Latin means goddess. *Ley* in Spanish can refer to law or rule. Dealey Plaza was "goddess-rule" plaza.
- Blamed for the assassination was a man named Oz, (Oswald) explained by Downard as "a Hebrew term denoting strength." Divine strength is integral to the king-killing rite.
- Oz was killed by Ruby, just as the ruby slippers freed Dorothy from the land of Oz in *The Wizard of Oz*, which writes Downard, "one may deride as a fairy tale but which nevertheless symbolizes the immense power of 'ruby light,' otherwise known as the laser."
- Dealey Plaza is near the Trinity River, which, before the introduction of flood control measures, submerged the place regularly. Dealey Plaza therefore symbolizes both the trident and its bearer, the water-god Neptune.
- "To this trident-Neptune site," writes Downard, "came the 'Queen of Love and Beauty' and her spouse, the scapegoat, in the Killing of the King rite, the 'Ceannaideach' (Gaelic word for Ugly Head or Wounded Head). In Scotland, the Kennedy coat of arms and iconography is full of folklore.

Their plant badge is an oak and their crest has a dolphin on it. Now what could be more coincidental than for JFK to get shot in the head near the oak tree at Dealey Plaza. Do you call that a coincidence?" (For those in our audience still too puzzled by the whole *Wizard of Oz* thing to get that last bit: the "Queen" is Jackie and "Ceannaideach" is the Gaelic form of Kennedy.)

- An earlier "trinity site," in New Mexico, was the location of the first atomic bomb explosion. Chaos and synergy—breaking apart and joining together—are the first principles of alchemy. The atomic bomb broke apart the positive and negative (male and female) elements that compose primordial matter. Physicists refer to this fiendish trickery as "nuclear fission."
- The New Mexico "Trinity" sits on the 33rd degree latitude line.
- The Kennedy assassination's true significance was concealed by the Warren Commission headed by Freemason Earl Warren with Freemason Gerald Ford as its public spokesman. The commission drew its information from the FBI, headed by Freemason J. Edgar Hoover, and the CIA, which transmitted information through its former director, Freemason Allen Dulles, who sat on the commission.
- A decade later, Ford, when president himself, was the target of an attempted assassination in front of the St. Francis Hotel, located opposite Mason Street in the City of St. Francis, San Francisco. Members of the Freemasonic "Hell Fire Club," eighteenth-century London site of many a sex orgy involving such luminaries as Freemason Benjamin Franklin, called themselves "Friars of St. Francis."
- The St. Francis Hotel was also the site of sex orgies. On its premises occurred the rape-murder of Virginia Rappe by silent film comic Roscoe "Fatty" Arbuckle. Virginia Rappe's name is a variation on "virgin rape." The rape of a virgin is an important alchemical sex-magic rite.
- The serpent is a Masonic symbol of king-killing. The

Symbionese Liberation Army, which kidnapped San Francisco newspaper heiress Patricia Hearst, pictured a serpent
on its emblem.
- The name Symbionese means "joined together."
- Patricia Hearst's grandfather, newspaper magnate William
  Randolph Hearst, built a vast estate called San Simeon (St.
  Simon) on La Cuest Encandata, The Enchanted Hill. On the
  estate is a "pool of Neptune" with a statue of Venus, the
  "queen of love and beauty." The Hearst family joined
  together the *San Francisco Chronicle* and *Examiner*.

As mentioned previously, we are able only to touch the most
superficial aspects of the alchemical conspiracy made manifest
in the message of James Shelby Downard. We have ignored his
hint that Marilyn Monroe's death was Freemasonically inspired, in part because "when she was mortal she was subjected
to sexual debauchery, as the innocent are in sorcery rites."

Nor have we covered Downard's argument that the advertising war "between Avis and Hertz car rental corporations
involves fertility symbolism."

Avis and Hertz? For God's sake, let us hope he's misguided.

MAJOR SOURCES

Downard, James Shelby. "The Call to Chaos." In *Apocalypse Culture*,
    expanded and revised, edited by Adam Parfrey. Los Angeles: Feral
    House, 1990.
_____. "King Kill 33 degrees." In *Apocalypse Culture*, edited by
    Adam Parfrey. New York: Amok Press, 1987.
_____. "Sorcery, Sex, Assassination." In *Secret and Suppressed*,
    edited by Jim Keith. Portland, OR: Feral House, 1993.
_____. "Witches' Plot," photocopied manuscript in authors'
    possession.

38

Anglophobia

These days they seem a benign and rather comical lot, those British royals. Face it—when a guy is caught confiding to his mistress his fond wish to take the place of her tampon, as Prince Charles did to Camilla Parker-Bowles, it's hard to take him seriously as the next chief executive of a vast and malignant global conspiracy. But that is just the position to which Prince Charles ascends when he assumes the throne, according to the strain of conspiratorial theorizing that places "the British" at the center of its Copernican universe.

Lyndon LaRouche ranks as the most illustrious of this school of thinkers, such as they are. LaRouche has endured considerable, and perhaps not entirely unjustified, derision for his allegation, "The Queen of England pushes drugs."

But LaRouche is only the most seasoned self-publicizer among British conspiracy theorists. The crowd includes, for example, Lloyd Miller, the entrepreneur behind A-Albionic Research, which fashions itself as a news service à la the Kiplinger *Washington Letter*—only instead of recording the relatively quotidian gossip of Capitol Hill, Miller tracks the

battle for world domination between the British Royal Family
and the Vatican.

At least Miller places another party in the picture. For
LaRouche, the Brits are all. In the definitive statement of
LaRouchism, *Dope Inc.: Britain's Opium War Against the U.S.*
(credited to "a U.S. Labor Party Investigating Team"), the
LaRouche approach to the book's topic, and by extension to
world history, is spelled out in bold type: "the entire world's
drug traffic has been run by a single family since its inception."

And which family might that be?

But the LaRouchies in their somewhat overstated fashion
have a point. Remember that we are dealing with a country that
until relatively recently was the greatest colonizer of other
countries the world had ever seen, with no particular reserva-
tions about taking over the world by any means necessary,
covert or overt, forcing their cricket, crumpets, and marmalade
down the throats of any sub-Saharan tribesman too slow to
dodge a musket ball.

Indeed, state the *Dope Inc.* authors, "To call this a 'conspiracy' would be to abuse the meaning of the term...the British
oligarchy is so much a part of the bedrock of events that it does
not need to act in conspiratorial fashion: by its own description
it merely is and always has been."

Their conspiratorial teleology, according to LaRouche and
those like-minded, is a "New Dark Ages," (NDA for short) with
a world population cropped to its bare minimum by AIDS,
famine, and the occasional nuclear holocaust—until there is
just enough soylent green remaining to feed the profligate
indulgences of those ravenous, sex-crazed, slurping, sucking,
yet fiendishly intelligent oligarchs.

But even the British aristocracy can't go it alone. They've
formed a whole universe of secret societies, private policy
groups, and connected intelligence agencies—involving not
only Brits but Anglophiles from the United States and Europe—
to implement the NDA agenda. These include not only the
usual suspects—Bilderbergers, the Trilateral Commission, and

the Royal Institute for International Affairs—but also some lesser-known entities. Chief among the latter is the Club of Rome (CoR) a Bilderbergerish body comprised of the political, financial, and intellectual aristocracy. The innocuously christened Club has spewed forth a generation of think-tanks, corporations, and other respectable entities working tirelessly to soften up the mass mind with their New Age claptrap, rock music, sex, and dope, at least according to the Anglophobic weltanschauung.

LaRouche, for example, pegs the Grateful Dead as a "British intelligence operation," spawned from the CIA's LSD trials at Stanford University and similar far-out Bay Area institutions of higher education. "That was an Allen Dulles-period operation which was run together with the Occult Bureau types in British intelligence, such as Aldous Huxley," LaRouche states dryly.

"This is part of this satanism business. Call it the counterculture. Call it the Dionysus model of the counterculture."

Okay, it's the Dionysus model of the counterculture.

"Rock is essentially a revival of the ancient Dionysiac, Bacchic ritual," LaRouche continues. "It does have a relationship to the alpha rhythms of the brain. If combined with a little alcohol and more, shall we say, mood-shaping substances, with youth, with funny sex, this does produce a personality change of a countercultural type."

Funny sex?

Dr. John Coleman, a self-described former British intelligence agent who has taken many of LaRouche's notions one better (if that's possible), though from a more "Christian" angle, goes into greater detail.

The Grateful Dead are small game. Coleman goes straight for the biggest prize around. The Beatles, he claims, are nothing more than a Club of Rome experiment cooked up by two famous and widely influential think-tanks: the CoR-managed British research organization known as the Tavistock Institute for Human Relations and its American sibling, the Stanford Research Institute (SRI).

"When Tavistock brought the Beatles to the United States nobody could have imagined the cultural disaster that would follow in their wake," writes Coleman. "The phenomenon of the Beatles was not a spontaneous rebellion by youth against the old social system. Instead it was a carefully crafted plot to introduce by a conspiratorial body which could not be identified, a highly destructive and divisive element into a large population group targeted for change against its will."

To provide tactical support for the Beatles, says Dr. John, Tavistock also "prepared" a new lexicon of "code words signifying the acceptance of drugs" which it deployed the Fab Four to disseminate. This new vocabulary included such words as *teenager, cool, pop music*, and *discovered*.

"Incidentally," Coleman notes, "the word *teenagers* was never used until just before the Beatles arrived on the scene, courtesy of the Tavistock Institute for Human Relations."

While Coleman proves himself no authority on etymology, he displays an affection for rock 'n' roll that makes Albert Goldman look like Lester Bangs. He hesitates to use such "beautiful words" as *music* and *lyrics* in reference to the Beatles because, "it reminds me of how wrongly the word *lover* is used when referring to the filthy interaction between two homosexuals writhing in pigswill."

The Brits have agents everywhere. What would the Beatles have ever amounted to without the assistance of "the scurrilous Ed Sullivan"? asks Coleman.

Now, lest one fall into the trap of supposing that this exercise in mass manipulation ended with the release of Paul McCartney's first solo album, Coleman assures us that through its intelligence agencies, "new sexually degenerate cults are even now being set up by the British Crown. As we already know, all cults operating in the world today are the product of British intelligence acting for the oligarchical rulers."

Coleman is not content to tab the British royals alone as those "rulers."

"That single entity," he writes, "the conspirators' hierarchy, is called THE COMMITTEE OF 300." (As much as Coleman hates rock music, he loves the Shift/Lock key.) "The Committee of 300 is the ultimate secret society made up of an untouchable ruling class," he writes in his book titled, predictably, *Conspirators' Hierarchy: The Story of the Committee of 300.*

"Note how the queen, Elizabeth II, performs the ceremonial opening of the British Parliament?" Coleman observes darkly. "There, in full view, is the head of the Committee of 300."

MAJOR SOURCES

Coleman, Dr. John. *Conspirators' Hierarchy: The Story of the Committee of 300.* Carson City, Nev.: America West Publishing, 1992.
U.S. Labor Party Investigating Team. *Dope, Inc.: Britain's Opium War Against the U.S.* New York: New Benjamin Franklin House, 1978.
Vankin, Jonathan. *Conspiracies, Coverups, and Crimes.* New York: Dell Publishing, 1992.

39

Those Christ Kids

The mysterious French organization known as the Priory of Zion may be a nine-hundred-year-old secret society possessing proof that Jesus Christ survived the crucifixion. What's more, it may also be the repository of Europe's secret history, and indeed the underground annals of all Christendom. Then again, maybe it's just an extremely elaborate hoax. Whichever, it launched a best-selling book, 1982's *Holy Blood, Holy Grail,* by BBC documentary filmmaker Henry Lincoln and historians Michael Baigent and Richard Leigh.

Lincoln and company set out to write about one of France's most enduring riddles, the legend of Rennes-le-Château, an antique village ensconced in the Pyrenees mountains. Legend has it that somewhere beneath its cobblestone streets, Rennes-le-Château harbors a fabulous treasure. Locals are partial to the theory that the stash belonged to the Cathars, Christian heretics stamped out by the Catholic church in the thirteenth century. New Age pilgrims and occultists trek there to partake of the town's supposed spiritual energy; treasure hunters prowl its windswept perimeters in search of more worldly goods; others tie the source of the town's mystical fascination to UFOs.

Whatever the theory, Rennes-le-Château owes its renaissance as a mystical landmark to a nineteenth-century cleric named Bérenger Saunière, and that is where Lincoln, Baigent, and Leigh began their quest.

The story opens in 1885, when the Catholic church assigned Saunière, thirty-three years old, handsome, well-educated—if provincial—to the parish at Rennes-le-Château. Saunière set about restoring the town's tiny church, which sat atop a sacred site dating back to the sixth-century Visigoths. Under the altar stone, inside a hollow Visigothic pillar, the young curé discovered a series of parchments. There were two genealogies dating from 1244 A.D. and 1644 A.D., as well as more recent documents created by a former parish priest during the 1780s. According to Lincoln and his coauthors, these more recent papers contained a series of ciphers and codes, some of them "fantastically complex, defying even a computer" to unlock their secrets.

Saunière took his discovery to the bishop in nearby Carcassonne, who dispatched the priest to Paris, where clerical scholars studied the parchments. One of the simpler ciphers, when translated, read: TO DAGOBERT II KING AND TO SION BELONGS THIS TREASURE AND HE IS THERE DEAD.

Whatever it all meant, apparently it became Saunière's entrée into a new world, with the accent on *worldly*. For during his short stay in Paris, Saunière began to mix with the city's cultural elite, many of whom dabbled in the occult arts. Contemporary gossip had it that the country priest had an affair with Emma Calvé, the famous opera diva who was also a high priestess of the Parisian esoteric underground. She would later visit him frequently in Rennes-le-Château.

When Saunière returned to his parish, he resumed restoration of the church and discovered an underground crypt, supposedly containing skeletons. At this point, his taste in interior design seems to have taken a turn for the, well, peculiar; among the eccentric fixtures he installed were a holy water basin sur-

mounted by a statue of a sneering red demon and an equally
garish wall relief depicting Jesus atop a hill at the base of which
is an object resembling a sack of money. The stations of the
cross had their oddities too: One, set at night, depicted Jesus
being carried into the tomb—or smuggled out of it? Saunière
also installed a series of cipher messages in the fixtures of the
church. He spent a fortune refurbishing the town and developed
extravagant tastes for rare china, antiques, and other pricey
artifacts. Yet how Saunière acquired this apparent windfall
remained a mystery—he stubbornly refused to explain the
secret of his success to the church authorities. When he died in
1917, he was supposedly penniless, yet his former housekeeper
later spoke of a "secret" that would make its owner not only
rich but also "powerful." Unfortunately, she never spilled the
beans.

Lincoln and his coauthors found no treasure, though they
speculated that Saunière might have exhumed *somebody's* loot:
Maybe it was the legendary Cathar hoard, or the nest egg of the
Visigoths, or perhaps the treasure of the Merovingian kings
who ruled the region between the fifth and eighth centuries—
the Dagobert II mentioned in the coded parchment was one of
them. Maybe it was a combination of all three treasures. Or, if
not treasure in the conventional sense, then perhaps Saunière
had discovered some form of forbidden knowledge and had
used it to blackmail someone, say, for instance, the church.

At any rate, during their investigation into the legend of
Saunière, what Lincoln and company *did* discover was less
cashable, yet just as mysterious: an unseen hand "discreetly,
tantalizingly" directing a low-key publicity effort on behalf of
the legend.

At the center of the underground PR campaign they found an
enigmatic and very real figure named Pierre Plantard de Saint-
Clair, apparently the source behind much of the recent literature devoted to the hilltown and its enigmatic priest. Shep-
herded to Paris's Bibliothèque Nationale, our trio of historical
investigators discovered there a provocative genealogy purport-

ing to link Pierre Plantard to King Dagobert II and the Merovingian dynasty. Hardly your run-of-the-mill blue blood, that Monsieur Plantard, for the Merovingians were considered in their day to be quasi-mystical warrior-kings vested with supernatural powers. Ah, but that was only one item on Plantard's impressive family résumé. More on that in a moment.

Throughout these *dossiers secrets* at Paris's national library were tantalizing historical references to a mysterious and ancient secret society called Prieuré de Sion, or Priory of Zion. The word *Zion*, of course, appeared in various ciphers connected with Rennes-le-Château. It also seemed to refer to Mount Zion in Jerusalem, site of the ancient Temple of Solomon.

According to the secret dossiers, the spectral Priory was linked to the famous Knights Templar, an order of warrior monks who defended the European occupation of the Holy Land during the twelfth century. The Templars took their name from the source of their authority and the site of their quarters, built on the ruins of the Temple of Solomon. Of course, this wasn't the first conspiracy theory to cast the Templars as cabalistic bugaboos, yet their supposed connection to the (possibly fictional) Priory of Zion was a new one. Taking a cue from the dossiers, Lincoln and company speculated that the clandestine Priory had hidden behind the Knights Templar, which served as the Priory's armed entourage and public face.

And if these secret dossiers were to be believed, the Priory of Zion was a covert force to be reckoned with. References to well-known historical events suggested that the Priory had been a secret power in Europe ever since the Crusades, a gray eminence manipulating kings and popes in the furtherance of some obscure mission.

According to the musty pamphlets and microfiche in France's national library, through the ages the Priory's leaders had included such luminaries as Leonardo da Vinci, Sir Isaac Newton, Charles Radclyffe, Victor Hugo, and the most recent entry on the list, Jean Cocteau, the twentieth-century artist and author. In all, the list named twenty-six such "grand masters" spanning some seven hundred years!

Could the group have survived into the late twentieth century? Lincoln and company checked with the French authorities and discovered that there was indeed a contemporary organization calling itself Priory of Zion. And who do you think was registered as the group's secretary-general but Pierre Plantard.

When Lincoln finally tracked him down, Plantard turned out to be a wily old aristocrat who had played a small part in the French Resistance. But his deliberate obfuscation seemed intended as much to conceal something as to lure the authors further into the mystery.

Just what was Plantard trying to hide—or *reveal* in his consciously eliptical way? What was the possibly sinister purpose behind the Priory of Zion?

The authors of *Holy Blood, Holy Grail* proposed a theory, as tangled and complicated as the *dossier secrets*, yet entertainingly mounted and surprisingly well argued. Was there a connection, they wondered, between the heretical Cathars of thirteenth-century France, Saunière's Rennes-le-Château, the Templars, and the omnipresent Priory of Zion?

But of course, they ventured. Lincoln and company hypothesized that the fabled Cathar treasure at Renne-le-Château was one in the same with the Merovingian cache *and* the Templars' treasure of King Solomon. At some point, according to Lincoln et al., the treasure had passed from the Merovingians to the Priory of Zion, whose Templar operatives later hustled the precious hoard from the Holy Land to the French Cathars, who, on the eve of their destruction by the church, squirreled the lucre away in the Pyrenees.

But what if the "treasure" was something other than gold? After all, legend had it that the Cathar heretics possessed a valuable, even sacred relic, "which according to a number of legends, was the Holy Grail," itself. During World War II, the Nazis supposedly excavated various sites in the vicinity of

Rennes-le-Château in their futile search for the Grail (which was dramatized in the movie *Indiana Jones and the Last Crusade*).

Was the lost Cathar/Templar/Merovingian/Saunière treasure, then, the fabled Holy Grail, itself? By suggesting that it was, our trailblazing authors were not suggesting that the ominous Priory revolved around a mere religious relic—and a rusty old goblet at that. Lincoln and company had something more ambitious in mind. Boldly reinterpreting centuries of folklore, they proposed that the Grail of medieval romance might have been a coded reference to something much more controversial: the literal bloodline of Christ.

Here's where Lincoln and company shifted into conspiratorial overdrive. Borrowing the thesis of Hugh J. Schonfield's book, *The Passover Plot*, and grafting it onto the enigmatic Plantard clues, Lincoln and his coauthors fashioned a, well, daring theory. Stripped of syllogistic elegance, it goes something like this: Christ survived the crucifixion by "faking" his death or otherwise being "fruitful" before Good Friday, either way leaving behind the wife and kids. The "Christs" subsequently legged it to the south of France where they intermarried with the royal Franks to found what eventually became the mystical Merovingian Dynasty. Ergo, the *real* mission of the Templars and Priory of Zion: to safeguard not just the treasure of the Crusades, but to preserve the Grail, which appeared in medieval texts as "Sangraal" or "Sangreal," and which Lincoln et al. translated to mean *sang réal*, or "royal blood." In other words: the dynastic legacy of Christ, literally.

This, then, might be the stunning secret—and the secret society that evolved through the ages to protect it—that Abbé Saunière stumbled upon in Rennes-le-Château: TO DAGOBERT II KING AND TO SION BELONGS THIS TREASURE AND *HE IS THERE DEAD*. Who He? J.C.

Suddenly, the meandering history of Europe develops a dramatic, cohesive plot line: The persecution of the Cathars by the church, the collusion of Rome in the assassination of King

Dagobert, the successful conspiracy of the Pope Clement V and Phillipe IV of France to suppress the powerful Templars—all were efforts to "eradicate it, Jesus' bloodline." For "it" constituted nothing less than a rival church with a more direct link to J.C.'s legacy than the Vatican could ever claim.

Whew. Fast forward to the twentieth century, and Plantard's Merovingian pedigree has obvious implications.

Of course, Plantard's response to all this virtuoso theorizing was that enigmatic Mona Lisa smile of his. He wasn't about to walk on water, at least not at the behest of three future best-selling authors.

Curiously, in their followup book, *The Messianic Legacy*, Lincoln, Baigent, and Leigh sounded at times almost as if they were proselytizing. Advocating the concept of the lost "priest-king," they argued that a dose of spiritual leadership might not necessarily be a bad thing for rudderless Europe, especially since the historically bickering nations were attempting to unify as an Economic Community anyway. A "theocratic United States of Europe" might be just what the doctor ordered, Lincoln and his associates suggested.

Yet their sequel ended on a decidedly down note, for their subsequent research raised doubts about the true nature of the Priory.

In piercing the confounding veil surrounding Plantard and his mysterious organization, Lincoln and company opened a sordid vault of modern conspiracies. Key Priory documents purporting to trace the royal lineage back to J.C., Himself, were said to have been smuggled out of France by British intelligence agents, possibly at the behest of American spooks. Why were these venal forces sullying the uplifting vision of the Lost King? There were other troubling elements lurking in the background, including Italy's crypto-fascist P2 Masonic lodge, which during the 1980s seemed to have reserved seating at every major conspiracy event.

Could Lincoln, Baigent, and Leigh have stumbled upon an

elaborate, tangled ruse set up for some abstruse objective of spycraft, or perhaps in the service of right-wing European politics? Was Plantard just a clever self-promoter with too much ancien régime leisure time on his hands? Or, if it wasn't a hoax from the get-go, did the Priory of Zion's ancient charter devolve at some point into a club for tweedy intelligence operatives? Was the Grail just a dirty cup filled with slippery spy dust?

During the 1980s, the books struck a ringing chord just about everywhere. The American clergy went ballistic at the suggestion that centuries of Christian dogma amounted to centuries of *false* dogma. Despite the fact that *Holy Blood, Holy Grail* restored the underappreciated French to the center of the cosmos (after all, the Messiah doesn't have an English or American accent, does He?), modern Gallic folk tend to be unimpressed with the trio's revisionist scholarship. And some even resent having their cherished national mysteries paraded on the international marketplace, by profiteering foreigners, no less. Of course, American and British book buyers have been much more generous.

By the 1990s, though, even Lincoln had soured on speculating about the Priory of Zion and its maddeningly hermetic chief executive, Pierre Plantard. "In my old age, I've decided to stick to that which can be verified," Lincoln groused when asked for an update on the secret society.

Though disillusioned, he hadn't finished with the mysterious hill town that launched his modern quest for the Holy Grail—not to mention his book-writing career. In his solo 1991 coffee-table book, *The Holy Place,* Lincoln announced that whatever else it may or may not be, the town called Rennes-le-Château is most certainly the "Eighth Wonder of the Ancient World," an "immense geometric temple, stretching for miles across the landscape." But sounding like the reformed heretic stung once too often by the critical flail, Lincoln offered a rather modest closing caveat: "This book does not claim to have solved the riddle."

Major Sources

Baigent, Michael; Richard Leigh, and Henry Lincoln. *Holy Blood, Holy Grail*. New York: Dell Publishing, 1983.
Baigent, Michael; Richard Leigh, and Henry Lincoln. *The Messianic Legacy*. New York: Dell Publishing, 1986.
Lincoln, Henry. *The Holy Place: Discovering the Eighth Wonder of the World*. New York: Arcade Publishing, 1991.

40

The Gemstone File

The Skeleton Key to the Gemstone File, a twenty-three-page digest of an original sheaf of letters supposedly a thousand pages thick, was authored in 1975 by Stephanie Caruana, then a freelance journalist affiliated with that staid forum for elegant reportage, *Playgirl* magazine. The original Gemstone letters were penned by a mysterious and now long-deceased fellow named Bruce Roberts who was—well, no one's completely sure *who* he was.

Caruana's *Key* has been photocopied thousands of times. The exact number, like much of the information in the *Gemstone File* itself, is beyond verification. The contents are classic conspiracy theory: fact mixed with conjecture, blended with error, and expressed with certitude. Yet the document is so gripping and at the same time so obscure, always looking like a twentieth-generation Xerox, it begs credulity, even investigation.

Fade in.

1932.

Aristotle Onassis, the central figure in this epic—best known as the shipping magnate who married President Kennedy's widow, but described in the *Key's* opening lines as "a Greek drug pusher...who made his first million selling 'Turkish tobacco' (opium) in Argentina"—strikes a deal with bootleggers Meyer Lansky, Eugene Meyer, and Joseph Kennedy to ship illegal hooch into Boston. "Also involved," states *Gemstone*, "was a heroin deal with Franklin and Elliot Roosevelt." (Hmm.)

The chronology crackles through forty-three years of American cloak-and-dagger, fading out in April, 1975, at which time, to quote Caruana's typically delicate phraseology, "Ford, Kissinger, and Rockefeller squat like toads on the corpse of America."

Presumably, that date roughly coincides with the period when Roberts, bedridden by an undoubtedly suspicious ailment, ceased scribbling his original letters and unceremoniously passed away.

Along the way, the *Gemstone File* drops some tantalizing, sometimes puzzling tidbits and makes some outlandish, albeit intriguing assertions. The *File's* plotline concerns the malignant codependency between the U.S. government and the Mafia—a plausible enough hypothesis. But wait. This Mafia has more in common with James Bond's arch-nemesis SPECTRE than with the Sicilian secret society of *Godfather* lore.

And the "crowned head of the Mafia" is Ari O, himself. In fact, conspiracy researcher John Judge has speculated that Ian Fleming based his ubervillain Ernst Stavro Blofeld on Onassis, which would gibe with the *Gemstone File*, for if Bruce Roberts has the story straight Onassis was an evil mastermind and overlord who puppeteered presidents, gangsters, and popes.

Following the critical 1932 deal with Kennedy et al., there came two more watershed triumphs in Onassis's career-according-to-*Gemstone*. In 1957, he ordered Howard Hughes kidnapped and, later, doped to death, which accounts for the eccentric billionaire's storied reclusiveness. This caper gave Onassis control of Hughes's expansive fiscal shogunate, on top of his own already impressive domain.

Then, in 1963, Onassis seized ultimate power. John F. Kennedy, formerly under Onassis's control due to Daddy Joe's debt to the "Big O," unwisely wagged his presidential scepter by backing off on the Bay of Pigs raid, a Mafia (i.e., Onassis) operation to reclaim the Cuban cash cow. JFK "welshed" on the deal so Onassis ordered the president "hit" in Mafia style. Onassis, says *Gemstone*, lived up to "an old Mafia rule: if someone welshes on a deal, kill him, take his gun and his girl: in this case, Jackie and the Pentagon."

Some of the *Gemstone File*'s other provocative "revelations":

- Onassis immediately asserted control over Lyndon Johnson, relaying a message to him on Air Force One en route from Dallas: "There was *no conspiracy*. Oswald was a *lone nut assassin*. Get it Lyndon? Otherwise, Air Force One might have an unfortunate accident on flight back to Washington."
- J. Edgar Hoover possessed the *Gemstone File* and threatened to use it to expose what really happened in Dallas, but he was poisoned first. Someone slipped "sodium morphate" (whatever that is) in his apple pie; a gesture, it may be worth noting, rich in symbolism.
- Katherine Graham, the publisher of the *Washington Post* and daughter of Onassis comrade Eugene Meyer, was Bob Woodward and Carl Bernstein's Deep Throat.
- San Francisco's infamous series of Zebra killings— seemingly random shootings of whites purportedly perpetrated by black militant extremists—were really pulled off by Onassis/Mafia to deep-six a potentially dangerous witness, then distract attention from the murder's true motive, at the same time giving authorities an excuse to crank up the heat on "black terrorists."
- Richard Nixon, a Hughes pawn who became an Onassis vassal after Ari did the number on Howard, was forced to resign when Roberts started squawking. Mafia bosses worried Nixon'd blab about Big O. The eighteen minutes of "accidentally" erased Watergate tapes include Nixon ranting about "that asshole Roberts."

- Nixon made a deal with Gerald Ford, allowing Nixon to "murder anyone he needed to" to cover up Watergate/*Gemstone* (pretty much the same, in this universe).
- The pope was in on this whole thing too.

So who was Bruce Roberts and why was he saying all those terrible things about the good Mr. Onassis? Seems he was a genius of sorts who concocted a process for fabricating artificial gemstones. He tried to sell the invention to Howard Hughes's company only to see the multinational conglomerate rip him off. Righteously steamed, Roberts started digging—discovering that "Hughes" was not Hughes at all but in reality the sinister Onassis. That, anyway, is how Caruana tells the tale.

The two people who claim to have come into closest contact with the penumbral Roberts are Caruana and the ubiquitous Mae Brussell. Brussell said in a 1978 radio show that Roberts sought her out and passed her the file after reading her article "Why Was Martha Mitchell Kidnapped?" in the *Realist*. Caruana met Roberts through Brussell.

Brussell, of course, has been deceased for several years, but Caruana is still kicking. Interviewed by Jim Keith, editor of the definitive work on this topic (cited below), Caruana described Roberts as a real-life James Bond, whereas Brussell had dubbed him "Casper Milquetoast."

His letters, it seems, are widely discussed, but no one save Brussell and Caruana ever got a glance at them. For that matter, at this point, Bruce Roberts's former existence as an actual human being is mostly a matter of Brussell's and Caruana's say-so.

None of which is meant to imply that *Gemstone* is a ruse, or that Roberts is Stephanie Caruana's imaginary friend. If Caruana is a prankster, she is a peculiarly recalcitrant and testy one who engineered her fraud in such a way as to preclude any significant public impact or personal profit. And Brussell, while perhaps known to indulge in the occasional leap of logic, was anything but a hoax artist. Finally, if Roberts, or whoever presented himself as Roberts, was a disinformation artist, he must have specialized in low-impact disinformation.

If not a hoax, it's still tempting to dismiss the *Gemstone File* as the rantings of an admirably dedicated crank. But perhaps it would be kinder, and more accurate, to call the *Gemstone File* history by poetic license, the legacy of a man who was, if only in a peripheral way, history's victim.

MAJOR SOURCES

Caruana, Stephanie. *The Skeleton Key to the Gemstone File*: several photostatic versions in authors' files.
Keith, Jim, ed. *The Gemstone File*. Atlanta: IllumiNet Press, 1992.

41

Apocalypse at a Glance

The end may be near, but exactly how near is the sticky question. As millennium fever sweeps the globe, party planners and doomsayers alike have become fixated on the year 2000. Meanwhile, Judgment Day sticklers have been obssesing over the fact that there never was a "year zero," and therefore A.D. 1 plus two millennia equals *2001*. But pinpointing Armageddon isn't quite that simple. When it comes to end times, there are as many proposed dates as there are fates (Rapture or tribulation? Fire or flood? Demons or Pleiadeans?).

However, in the wake of past doomsday embarrassments (the world didn't end in the year 1000, and the hoopla over the 1987 Harmonic Convergence turned out be the spiritual equivalent of 8-track tape), few latter-day prophets are willing to stick their necks out and name a drop deadline. "What the prophets try to do is make predictions and leave the fulfillment vague," explains Stephen D. O'Leary, a millennial scholar at the University of Southern California. The most successful millennial prophets remain "strategically ambiguous," he says. "The prophets who do get specific tend to be the more marginal ones."

It's no surprise that the Internet, a haven for marginal oracles of all stripes, is home to millenarians who are bold enough to set a date. In fact, the Internet has assumed an important role on the end-times stage. "The Internet will be to the twenty-first century what the printing press was to the sixteenth," says medieval historian Richard Landes of Boston University, who, with O'Leary, cofounded the Center for Millennial Studies. Just as the printing press made apocalyptic tracts available to the public five hundred years ago, the Internet disgorges a vast literature of alternative doomsday scenarios.

"The Internet has increased the amount and the kind of information people have at their disposal to construct millennial scenarios," says O'Leary. "It also gives people a chance to try out different interpretations and prophecies in electronic discussion groups." In effect, he says, "the Internet provides a kind of social reinforcement," a public-address system for "people who might otherwise be relegated to the fringes as crackpots."

Well, in the lottery of multiple Armageddons, today's crackpot may turn out to be tomorrow's messianic seer. So how can the rest of us plan for the ultimate end and/or final beginning? This handy guide to doomsday chronologies is a good place to start:

- July 1999 (Nostradamus): This end date arrives in the summer of 1999 (just in time for that Prince song). Everybody's favorite sixteenth-century doomsayer was uncharacteristically specific when he prophesied that "in the year 1999 and seven months will come a great king of terror from the skies...."Rather than interpreting that to mean Stephen King skydiving, latter-day pessimists are thinking nuclear missile strike. And the pessimists' tent is big enough for everyone: Everyone banking on the end of the world wants a piece of nuclear Nostradamus—New Agers, psychics, fundamentalist Christians, and Tom Clancy fans alike.

- August 18, 1999 (Criswell): Ed Wood's favorite phony TV psychic was brazen enough to narrow down Armageddon to the precise day: "If you and I meet each other on the street that fateful day, August 18, 1999, and we chat about what we will do on the morrow, we will open our mouths to speak, and no words will come out, for we have no future.... You and I will suddenly run out of time!" Of course, Criswell never explained exactly how the world would end, only that future generations will wonder "what on earth was meant by the words 'Henry Ford' or 'Holly-wood.'" But how accurate was Criswell? Well, his record speaks for itself: "Meteor destroys London [in] 1988"; "I predict embalming by radar, where the body is turned to indestructable stone"; "I predict that by 1980 you will be able to lift your own face in your own home for only $5.00."
- 1999 (Edgar Cayce): The "sleeping prophet" pinpointed 1999 as the year of Armageddon, to be followed by the New Age and the Second Coming of Christ. In between, we can expect a number of Hollywood comet/meteor movie-style special effects: A shift in the earth's axis leading to melting polar caps and the sinking of England and Japan. Also, the destruction of San Francisco, Los Angeles, and New York by earthquakes and floods, making it difficult for big-city swells to continue to sneer at small-town America; on the plus side, Atlantis will rise up from the depths of the ocean, opening an entirely new real estate market; and as if that weren't enough, Christ will initiate a "New Age of Peace." Of course, Cayce's loose time line will allow Armageddon to slip until 2001 or 2002, if absolutely necessary.
- 2000ish (Jack Van Impe): The perpetually grinning tele-vangelist is, well, impish when it comes to naming dates: He won't do it. He does, however, offer an "Overview of Major Future Events" somewhat more convoluted than a Thomas Pynchon novel: The Antichrist takes center stage during the

seven-year tribulation, followed by sundry judgments, "War in Heaven," and the "Battle of Armageddon" (neatly illustrated on Van Impe's Internet web site as a horde of marauding Huns), the Second Coming, more judgments, and a thousand years of peace with "Satan Bound," a period that closes with "Satan Loosed," again, kind of like the surprise return of Freddy Kruger at the very end of those slasher movies, after you think he's already been killed. It's all very confusing (did I enter the millennium in a mortal body, or do I need to trade up for resurrection?), which undoubtedly helps Van Impe sell those twenty dollar explanatory videos.

- May 5, 2000 (Richard W. Noone): The author of the book *5/5/2000: Ice—The Ultimate Disaster*, is refreshingly specific: "On May 5 of the year 2000, Mercury, Venus, Mars, Jupiter and Saturn will be aligned with the earth for the first time in 6,000 years. On that day the ice buildup at the South Pole will upset the earth's axis, sending trillions of tons of ice in the water sweeping over the surface of our planet." Though the book jacket claims that "astonishing evidence points to worldwide disaster in our lifetime," said evidence turns out to be culled mostly from the works of fringe scientists such as Emanuel Velikofsky, making it likely that 5/5/2000's major event will be El Torrito's Cinco de Mayo happy hour.

- 2000 or 2007 or 2048 (Hal Lindsey): The bestselling author of our day (more sales than Stephen King) is bearish when it comes to setting the big date. In his earlier books (including *The Late, Great Planet Earth*), however, the modern bard of Christian Apocalypse did let a few numbers loose: Armageddon in the year 2000 and the Second Coming of Christ in 2007 (forty years after the reunification of Jerusalem). However, Lindsey has also cited 2048 (see Bede below) as a possible drop deadline.

- 2001 (Unarius Society): Per interstellar thought messages

received by Southern California UFO disciples, a "Pleiadean starship will land on a rising portion of Atlantis in the area of the Bermuda Triangle...in the year 2001!" At that point, Earth will become the final world to join "an alignment of 33 planets," forming an "Interplanetary Confederation for the Spiritual Renaissance of Humankind on Earth!" Though our Pleiadean "Space Brothers" are wise to tie their arrival to the classic Stanley Kubrick film, the previous E.T.A. for ET of 1985 (when neither starships nor star children showed up) proved that Unarians aren't averse to issuing a cosmic raincheck.

- 2003 (Kalki Avatar): According to the Hindu calendar, the Sree Vishiva Karma Veera Narayana Murthy, avatar of Krishna, will arrive in 2003 to establish the reign of dharma (righteousness). "He will rule over the universe for a period of 108 years, and return to His abode, Vaikunta. Preceding that, the world will be full of calamities and situations will be changing every instant." For example, from 1999 to 2003, we can expect a "rain of blood in towns, villages and forests. Poor quality coins will be used as currencies. The males of goat and ox will sport mammary organs, and will be milked. Blood will flow from the limbs of elephants and horses....Many incurable diseases will be present. A man will have ten women after him, which will result in extreme behaviour in human beings."

- December 21, 2012 (Mayan Calendar): Turns out the "Harmonic Convergence" of 1987 wasn't a bust, after all; it opened a transitional period of cosmic change that will culminate on the day of the winter solstice in the year 2012. So forecasts José Arguelles, the New Age visionary who organized the harmonic festivities of a decade ago. Arguelles is not alone in pinpointing 2012 as the date of the looming endtime. A convergence of New Age thinkers has arrived at the same fateful date, based on the Mayan "Long Count" calendar, a kind of mystical Daytimer which measures a "Great Cycle" of 5,125 years and which runs out of refill pages on—mark your calendar—December 21, 2012. Most Mayan calendar counters expect major "earth changes" of the cataclysmic, rising-Atlantis, sinking–Los Angeles variety. Because the Mayans synchronized their calendar to the skies, spectacular astrological alignments are expected in 2012. Per Arguelles, the year 2012 will transport humankind from the "third dimension" to the "fourth dimension," a new galactic state of consciousness. Other Mayan calendar countdowns peg the New Age apocalypse to December 22, 2012.

- 2058 (Bede the Venerable): The eighth-century theologian calculated that Jesus was born 3,942 years after the creation of the world, which means that the six thousand-year millennial week will end in 2058. So far no one has decided to champion Bede. Alas, latter-day millenarians seem uninterested in his old-school dating.
- 2076 (Year of the Haj): 2076 is the year 1500, according to the Muslim calendar, which has led several Sufi sects to declare 2076 as the end day. Our prediction: American tricentennial hype will probably overshadow the Muslim eschaton.
- 2240 (Jewish Calendar): The year 2240 is the year 6000, according to the Jews. If by then the other doomsday scenarios haven't swept us into either the dustbin of history or a state of cosmological harmony, nothing is going to knock us off our self-satisfied perch. Except maybe the Klingons.

MAJOR SOURCES

Cayce, Edgar Evans. *Edgar Cayce on Atlantis*. New York: Warner Books, 1996.
Center for Millennial Studies web site: http://www.mille.org.
Criswell. *Criswell Predicts*. Anderson, SC: Droke House, 1968.
Hogue, John. *The Millennium Book of Prophesy*. San Francisco: Harper, 1997
Jenkins, John Major. "The How and Why of the Mayan End Date in

2012 A.D." Internet web site: http//www.levity.com/eschaton/
Why2012.html.

Lindsey, Hal, and C. C. Carlson. *The Late, Great Planet Earth*. New
York: Harper, 1992.

Noone, Richard W. *5/5/2000*. New York: Three Rivers Press, 1997.

Unarius Society Internet web site: http://www.unarius.org/et.html.

Van Impe, Jack. "Overview of Major Events" Internet web site: http://
www.jvim.com/timeline.html.

42

The Shroud and
the Scrolls

On April 18, 1998, Jesus returned.

Not the Man himself, of course. A picture of him. In fact, it's probably the most detailed picture of Jesus Christ ever produced. If you had scored a ticket to Turin, Italy, and a reservation for the two-month exhibit, you would have been lucky enough to come as close as you ever will to staring straight into the face of Western history's greatest superstar.

The Shroud of Turin came out of its shell.

The shroud goes on display very rarely. The last public exhibition came twenty years earlier and drew 3 million people. For those who need to ask—*heathen swine!*—the shroud is a large linen sheet at least several hundred years old, perhaps as ancient as two thousand years. The cloth bears the faint (and getting fainter) image of a bearded, long-haired, and frankly rather large nosed man who—even hard-core skeptics agree— has suffered the wounds associated with death by crucifixion. In fact, the wounds seem very close to those described in that international bestselling anthology of ancient literature known as the Bible as having been inflicted on the one and only Big C, though the more cautious refer to him as, simply, the Man of the Shroud.

Or as we'll call him, in keeping with 1990s *X-Files* jargon, Shroud Man.

The unfortunate figure on the shroud bears puncture marks along the forehead, presumably from a "crown of thorns." The back is marked by flogging lacerations. Shroud Man even bears a wound to the right side of his chest, exactly where Jesus, according to the Gospel of John, took a lance poke from a Roman centurion as he hung on the cross. The cloth is flecked with what appear to be ancient bloodstains from all of these wounds.

Admittedly, it seems unbelievable that the shroud is, as tradition and common belief has it, the actual burial cloth of Jesus. On the other hand, the shroud's very existence in a relatively intact state in the year 1998 indicates that there's something special about it. Most burial cloths from that time and place rotted away aeons ago. If the shroud in question really is two thousand years old, people from that time on must have taken a certain amount of care with it. Another question: How did the remarkably realistic image get on the thing, anyway?

The shroud's authenticity has been in doubt since it was first "discovered." The first recorded mention of the shroud, in a letter written by Bishop Pierre d'Arcis in 1389, condemns it as fake! D'Arcis even asserts that the forger had been caught—and had confessed. The bishop, however, appears to be off the mark. However the shroud was created—and the method of its making remains mysterious—it was surely a sophisticated process. Given the madness of the Middle Ages for relics—mementos not only of Jesus but of anyone associated with him—why would the inventors of this technological marvel stop at forging a Jesus shroud? Why not other images of Jesus? Or Mary? Or James? Or any of the apostles? Surely any of them would have fetched a hefty sack of shekels.

But there is only the shroud.

Does anyone know what the shroud really is? A British shroud researcher in 1960 made a potentially startling find: the manner in which Shroud Man was buried was exactly the same way in which bodies were buried by a small sect of ancient Isarelites who wrote the Dead Sea Scrolls.

The scrolls open up a whole maw of conspiracy and cover-up. As with all cover-ups, some powerful players were protecting their collective tuchis. The purpose of this particular conspiracy (if we may be so bold as to call it that) was public relations. Or more precisely, image control—Jesus' image, that is. Was he the docile, if divinely conceived, carpenter-cum-rabbi that we all know and love? Or was he, in fact, a tough-talking, hard-core political revolutionary more interested in fomenting riots than forming new religions?

Upon their discovery, the scrolls resided where they had apparently been sitting at least since that first-century, anti-Roman riot that razed Jerusalem. They sat inside a set of urns stashed in several dank cliffside caves beneath the rubble of an ancient burg called Qumran.

The settlement, of which a bare outline remains, sits thirty-three miles from the hilltop fortress of Masada, where a cadre of Jewish rebels resisted the Romans until their situation became drained of all hope and they all ran each other through with their swords.

The scrolls consisted of a wide variety of scribblings, some in Hebrew, some in Aramaic. Some were alternative renderings of biblical episodes. Some were scriptural apocrypha. Then there were the controversial "sectarian" writings that described life in the Qumran colony and turned out to record some very interesting events indeed.

The Qumran sect, though it existed for at least a century before Jesus, adhered to recognizable early Christian ritual and doctrine. This, of course, runs counter to the orthodox Catholic tenet that there was no Christianity before Jesus came on the scene. Kind of an important tenet when you think about it.

The suggestion that Christianity evolved from a faction of Judaism was the least of the heresies drawn from a close reading of the scrolls by scholars outside of the "international team." Which is probably why de Vaux's little cabal almost never let anybody read them. Well over half of the extant scrolls remain unpublished. (A scroll underground has long been active, allowing certain documents to see the light of modernity.) The "international team" plodded along at an excruciating pace, at the same time refusing independent researchers so much as a peek at the material.

In their book *The Dead Sea Scrolls Deception*, drawn largely from the work of Robert Eisenman, an American scholar whose efforts have been instrumental in wresting the scrolls from the monopolistic, monolithic, and indeed rather petty clutches of the "international team," Michael Baigent and Richard Leigh (best known for their wild and wacky theories about Those Christ Kids) draw the following key conclusions:

• The reputedly pacific, hermitish inhabitants of Qumran were Zealots, that most militant and violent of Jewish revolutionary groups—kind of an ancient Hebrew Vietcong—founded shortly before the birth of Jesus.

• Though the Qumran dwellers, under the orthodox scroll-scholar "consensus," were isolationist, uninvolved in political and religious issues, the authors of the scrolls display a keen interest in affairs at the Temple of Jerusalem, the center of Jewish civilization at the time. The Qumran community, which deposited its scrolls in the cliffside caves, was also in close contact with the Masada sect that repelled the Romans for six years in its mountaintop fortress before committing mass suicide. Some of the Qumran dwellers may have died at Masada.

• The Zealots, generally thought of as "freedom fighters," were more than that; they were religious fanatics who broached no deviation from biblical law. The Masada self-immolators were Zealots. The teachings of Jesus, the alleged "prince of peace," were heavily influenced by Zealot thought and in turn influenced Zealotry.

- It is therefore not unreasonable to infer that Jesus was a Zealot or at least a political revolutionary sympathetic to the Zealot movement. In any case, he was not the ethereal figure pictured in the Gospels and certainly never considered himself the leader of a new religion that would break away from Judaism. (Even the Gospels refer to Jesus' disciple Simon as "Simon Zelotes," i.e., Simon the Zealot, proving that Jesus carried at least one Zealot in his entourage.)

- The "Teacher of Righteousness," described in the scrolls as leader of the Qumran community, and James the brother of Jesus, mentioned in the Gospels, are one and the same.

- Qumran is "the early church" referred to in the Acts of the Apostles in which it is named "Damascus." This is the same "Damascus"—not the Syrian metropolis—where the Roman assassin Saul is heading when he experiences his sudden conversion to "Christianity" and becomes the new faith's leading evangelist, taking the name "Paul."

- The "Liar" in the scroll narrative, the adversary of the "Teacher of Righteousness," was none other than Paul. The scroll story chronicles the conflict within the "early church" between the followers of Jesus, the messianic revolutionary, and the followers of Paul, the hit man turned evangelist who never knew Jesus yet claimed a more intimate familiarity with his thought than Jesus' own disciples—and his own brother.

- Paul may have been deliberately planted by the Romans as an agent provocateur to disrupt, defuse, and depoliticize the new movement.

To say that these points add up to a revisionist view of Christianity is an understatement. They turn the history of that religion on its head, and because Christianity arguably has been the most influential force in molding Western civilization, the

Dead Sea Scrolls, if ever properly investigated and interpreted, could skew the whole Western world. These are high stakes.

If the shroud has a connection to the Qumran community and the shroud is Jesus, the implications are incredible. The secret of the shroud may be the secret history of Western civilization.

But enough about the secret history of Western civilization. The most important question about the shroud is a simple one: Real or fake? If the shroud is really 2,000 years old, where was it for the first 1,350 years of its existence? Skeptics who believe that the shroud was fabricated in the mid-fourteenth century get really smug when they point out that there is no mention of the shroud prior to that time.

According to Ian Wilson, there are not only mentions of the shroud; it was one of the most venerated objects in Christendom and in fact was a direct influence on artistic representations of Jesus from the sixth century on.

As Wilson, a devotedly pro-shroud journalist who has devoted his career to verifying the shroud's veracity, notes, in the first several centuries after the death of Christ, the big guy was usually painted as sort of a Tiger Beat pinup. He was short-haired, fresh-faced, and clean-shaven—a damn fine-looking young man.

Suddenly, the painted image of Jesus changes. He is no longer Leonardo DiCaprio. He's an older man with long hair parted in the middle. He has a beard that splits below his chin into a distinctive "fork." His nose is long. He is, to put it succinctly, Shroud Man.

The skeptics say, "So what?" The hirsute sage was the popular image of Jesus in the fourteenth century. Of course the shroud forger—some mad monk, presumably—would have copied it. But as the saying goes, God is in the details. Portrait after portrait of Jesus from centuries prior to 1350 bear distinctive features that correspond to the most minute features of Shroud Man's face: an odd *V* shape between the eyes, a line across the throat (corresponding to a crease in the shroud's linen); a mark on the forehead (a bruise, it seems).

According to Wilson, the shroud is actually the Edessan icon—a hypothesis that would give the shroud a traceable history possibly as far back as the fourth century. Edessa (now the Turkish city of Urfa) was a center of early Christiantity in what was then Syria. The Christians there were nuts about a piece of cloth that bore the image of Jesus' head. Wilson says that this icon was the shroud itself, folded to reveal only the head.

For the conspiracy-minded, the shroud offers even more mysteries. For a period of about 150 years, beginning in 1204, the shroud may have been in the possession of the Knights Templar, legendary guardians of the Holy Grail. (See chapter 39 for more info on the Templars and graildom.) Some writers theorize that the shroud itself is the grail. For centuries, the shroud was displayed only in a box with a grill-patterned cover. Occasionally, the cloth would be unfolded, just enough to reveal the head of Jesus.

The Templars adopted a variety of heretical practices for which they were eventually persecuted and destroyed. One of these odd habits was their devotion to the image of a head called "Baphomet." No one's sure what that word means, but it may be a corruption of *abufihamet*, an Arabic word that means "Father of Wisdom." Baphomet, according to some reports, was the head of a bearded man. Long after the Templars met their grisly fate, researchers found a bust of Baphomet in a decaying Templar stronghold in England. The bust, it is reported, bore an uncanny resmblance to Shroud Man.

The image on the shroud is itself a head scratcher. It appears similar to a photographic negative. However, it usually takes a camera to make a photograph, and they just didn't have fun gadgets like that two thousand years ago, or even seven hundred years ago, which is when most scientists believe the shroud was actually created.

In 1988, the Catholic church for the first time allowed researchers to snip small swatches from the crumbling cloth. After several tests, conducted independently by three teams of scientists residing in separate corners of the globe, the researchers found that the shroud was created no earlier than 1260, perhaps as recently as 1390. Those results were obtained via carbon-14 dating, the process of measuring decaying radioactive isotopes in any formerly living piece of material (such as the flax fibers from which the cloth was woven). Once you die, your isotopes decay at a fixed rate, so some future archaeologist who digs up the mess of scattered bones and grit that used to be you can tell roughly how long you've been dead. This procedure will come in especially handy if, like Shroud Man, your bones and grit cannot be located but you do happen to leave your full-body image imprinted on a bedsheet before you die.

Another scientist, in an unrelated experiment back in 1978, determined, after more than a decade of study, that the image on the shroud is, in fact, a painting. He found traces of pigments on the cloth. But shroud supporters counter that those flecks likely dropped from other paintings which, over the centuries, were pressed against the shroud in attempts by their artists to sanctify them. And other scientists say they've found no evidence of paintbrush strokes, which, after all, are as necessary to a painting as a camera is to a photograph.

And even the carbon-14 results have been questioned by shroud-positive scientists who say that the 1988 swatches were corrupted by the presence of a "bioplastic coating" that could throw off the dating process by as much as thirteen hundred years! Conveniently, that would put the cloth's origin at just about *two thousand years ago*.

Suffice it to say, while the scientific evidence probably weighs on the side of a sophisticated Middle Ages fabrication, the shroud's exact origins remain extremely murky. Even if the thing was slapped together by a mischievous monk who wanted to create the ultimate relic (big business in those days), the question remains—how? The extraordinary detail and realism of the image seem atypical of the era, and if the image is not a painting, what is it? For that matter, if it is a painting, why paint a negative?

And what about the blood all over the cloth? According to chemist Alan Adler, quoted in that prestigious journal of religious archaeology *Time* magazine, the blood has not only been proved to be real in chemical tests; it actually contains a fluid that comes only from *clotted* blood. Of course, the mad monk of the hypothetical painting scenario could have decided to add extra realism by bleeding on the cloth. But would he wait for his blood to clot before secreting it onto the bogus shroud? Back then no one even knew what a blood clot was, much less that it contained substances different from ordinary blood. Our mad monk must indeed have been ahead of his time.

In any case, like all good mysteries and conspiracies, the truth of the shroud will always remain lost in the shadowy depths of history.

MAJOR SOURCES

Baigent, Michael, and Richard Leigh. *The Dead Sea Scrolls Deception*. London: Corgi Books, 1992.

Baigent, Michael, Richard Leigh, and Henry Lincoln. *Holy Blood, Holy Grail*. New York: Dell, 1983.

Drews, Robert. *In Search of the Shroud of Turin*. Totowa, NJ: Rowan and Allanheld, 1984.

McCrone, Walter C. *Judgment Day for the Turin Shroud*. Chicago: Microscope Publications, 1997.

Nickell, Joe. *Inquest on the Shroud of Turin*. Buffalo, NY: Prometheus Books, 1983.

Stevenson, Kenneth E; and Gary R. Habermas. *Verdict on the Shroud*. Ann Arbor, MI: Servant Books, 1981.

Van Biema, David. "Science and the Shroud." *Time*, 20 April 1998.

Wilcox, Robert. *Shroud*. New York: MacMillan, 1977.

Wilson, Ian. *The Shroud of Turin*. New York: Doubleday, 1978.

————. *The Blood and the Shroud*. New York: Free Press, 1998.

43

The Protocols *Fraud*

As a historical document it is an absolute fraud. As a conspiracy theory it is utterly spurious and without merit. Nevertheless, the so-called *Protocols of the Elders of Zion* has insinuated itself into many latter-day conspiracy theories, perpetuating the myth that Jews control the world just as a virtuoso manipulates the strings of his violin.

That racist, anti-Semitic theory can be found in "New World Order" theories that posit that all-powerful Jewish bankers are the string pullers behind global events. As ridiculous as it sounds, this bogus scenario recently found its way into popular theories in Malaysia and Japan, stating that Jews had sabotaged the Asian economies, forcing them to collapse. (As usual, there was no evidence to back this theory.)

Exactly how the myth of the global Jewish conspiracy became so entrenched around the globe—even in the Far East, where Jews are indeed scarce—is a fascinating story. It also remains a popular theory among anti-Semites in Europe, America, and the Middle East. In fact, it's rather ironic that the racist

330

canard known as the "International Zionist Conspiracy" sprouted from a political tract having nothing at all to do with Jews. In its earliest form, that tract appeared shortly after the French Revolution.

The apocryphal document that has promoted the racist canard of the Jewish conspiracy for nearly a century is called the *Protocols of the Elders of Zion.* The origin of the *Protocols* myth is instructive: It is an amalgam of fictional documents, plagiarized political pamphlets, and innuendo that fermented in Europe during the nineteenth century. The earlist germ of the myth can be found in a 1797 book by the French Cleric Abbé Barruel on the revolutionary Jacobins. This book, which became a bestseller in Europe and America, posited that the secret societies known as the Illuminati and Freemasons were the gray eminence behind the French Revolution.

But Barruel made no mention of the Jews in the book. The Jews were folded into the myth in 1806, when Barruel received a letter from a retired army officer living in Florence, one J. B. Simonini. Simonini warned Barruel about a "Judaic sect" that was "the most formidable power, if one considers its great wealth and the protection it enjoys in almost all European countries." Simonini claimed that he uncovered their nefarious plot by disguising himself as a Jew and infiltrating a conspiratorial gathering of Piedmontese Jews in northern Italy. According to Simonini, the Jewish plotters confessed to him that they had founded the Illuminati and Freemasons and also had infiltrated the ranks of Christian clergymen. What's more, they were planning to install a Jew as pope.

This conspiratorial notion resurfaced seventy-five years after the Simonini letter in a novel written by an official in the Prussian postal service (Sir John Retcliffe, a pen name of Hermann Goedsche). This fictional work contained a chapter called "In the Jewish Cemetery in Prague" that described how every one hundred years, the elders of the twelve tribes of Israel gathered at the grave of the most senior rabbi to plot the enslavement of the Gentile world. This chapter was reprinted as a pamphlet in Russia and France, and over time it came to be accepted as fact.

The full-blown *Protocols of the Elders of Zion* appeared in Russia at the turn of the century. The book plagiarized from both Retcliffe's novel and an 1865 pamphlet attacking Napoleon III called *Dialogue aux Enfers entre Montesquieu et Machiavel,* by Maurice Joly. In essence, the *Protocols* fused a French political tract to the fantasy of a Jewish plot to control the world. Spanning twenty-four chapters and twelve hundred pages, the *Protocols* consisted of a series of written lectures in which a member of the secret Jewish world government—the Elders of Zion—outlined the Jewish scheme for world domination. The *Protocols* claimed that because people are incapable of governing themselves, what the world needed was a Machiavellian despot.

Moreover, the *Protocols* claimed that the Jews, in preparation for a worldwide revolution, had been pitting Gentile citizens against their feckless leaders. After the revolution, the Jewish overlords would keep the Gentiles in line by imposing a social welfare state based on centralized government, full employment, taxation in proportion to wealth, public education, and support for small business. According to the *Protocols,* the Elders of Zion would dangle the carrot of liberty before their subjects but never deliver on its promise.

In Russia this counterfeit document helped fuel the anger and hysteria that led to the pogroms. (Another version was later used by the czar's secret police just before the Russian Revolution to justify a crackdown on revolutionaries living outside Russia.) The *Protocols* soon circulated in Germany, finding an audience eager to believe its claims: The German defeat in World War I was already being blamed on the Jews. British newspapers reviewed and commented on the document, further advancing its renown. The Nazi party would later fold the *Protocols* into its twisted ideology.

During the 1920s in America, the *Protocols* found their

biggest champion in automobile pioneer Henry Ford. According to historian Leo P. Ribuffo, the *Protocols* came to Ford via one of his representatives, who acquired the document from a Russian émigré, who claimed to have information on Jewish plots throughout Europe. The *Dearborn Independent* began publishing a series of articles on the "International Jew."

As a scapegoating document, the *Protocols* have always reflected the concerns of the group that adopts them. As Ribuffo notes, the document in America came to represent concerns different from those it had in Russia. In Russian hands, the *Protocols* were used to justify the right-wing oligarchy's attempts to retain power—by blaiming that country's turmoil on the Jews. In Ford's hands, the *Protocols* were used to explain the widespread and daunting social changes that were under way in post–Civil War, rapidly industrializing America. The rise of workers' unions, the influx of new immigrants, the growth of "big government"— all of these unsettling new developments were blamed on the Jews. Ford also emphasized the *Protocols* claim that Jews controlled the world's financial institutions and spread political radicalism. The *Dearborn Independent* went so far as to claim that Christopher Columbus had been manipulated by Jews.

The *Protocols* found their way to Japan in 1917. According to David G. Goodman and Masanori Miyazawa, authors of *Jews in the Japanese Mind,* Japanese soldiers dispatched to the Russian Far East after the Bolshevik Revolution picked up copies of the document from counterrevolutionary White Russian troops and carried them home. Thus would the seeds of the myth of the international Jewish conspiracy sprout in Japanese soil, as always reflecting the fears and concerns of the host nation. According to Goodman and Miyazawa, the anti-Semitic myth in Japan has served to strengthen the Japanese sense of self, an image defined by "ethnic nationalist xenophobia." Just as it did in America, the *Protocols* myth has fueled conspiracy theories that attempt to define outside threats by giving them a Jewish face.

UNIFIED FIELD THEORIES

Sadly, it is the flexibility of this myth, the way it can be twisted to appeal to the collective national fears of any country, that keeps it alive. As the trend toward economic globalization continues to destabilize economic nationalism, the spurious myth of the international Zionist conspiracy will undoubtedly continue to rear its ugly head time and again.

Major Sources

Cohn, Norman. *Warrant for Genocide*. New York, Harper and Row, 1969.

Goodman, David G., and Masanori Miyazawa. *Jews in the Japanese Mind*. New York: Free Press, 1995.

Ridgeway, James. *Blood in the Face*. New York: Thunder's Mouth Press, 1990.

VII

Conspiracy, Inc.

44

The White House Putsch

F ew Americans know it, but during the Great Depression, a cabal of millionaire bankers and industrialists hatched a conspiracy to hijack the U.S. government and install a fascist dictatorship. It was, in the words of contemporary journalist John L. Spivak, "one of the most fantastic plots in American history."

Spivak's assessment in his 1967 book, *A Man in His Time*, certainly continues to hold true sixty years after the fact: "What was behind the plot was shrouded in a silence which has not been broken to this day. Even a generation later, those who are still alive and know all the facts have kept their silence so well that the conspiracy is not even a footnote in American histories."

Although a congressional committee confirmed the allegations, the findings were hushed up amid murmurs of a coverup. No wonder. The plotters were brand-name American financiers in the Morgan and Du Pont commercial empires, right-wingers bitterly opposed to Franklin Delano Roosevelt's New Deal and the president's sympathies toward organized labor.

Perhaps Americans would know all too much about the plot, and even celebrate it on "President Duce Day," if it weren't for a

337

patriotic military man, Major General Smedley Darlington Butler. In the summer of 1933, the putsch plotters approached Butler, the retired commandant of the U.S. Marines and a popular war hero affectionately known as "the fighting Quaker." They offered him the job of transforming the American Legion veterans group into a 500,000-man marauding army, which was to spearhead an American coup d'état.

Unfortunately for facism, Butler's appeal to the plotters also turned out to be the conspiracy's downfall. The conspirators apparently chose the former general because of his enormous popularity with rank-and-file soldiers; but it was Butler's antielitist leanings and reputation for honesty that had made him a populist favorite. In short, the conspirators couldn't have selected a candidate more unlikely to agree to lead a fascist takeover. Shrewdly, Butler decided to play along, feigning interest in the plans in order to draw the plotters into the daylight and expose the scheme to Congress.

As he told the House of Representatives' McCormack-Dickstein Committee, which was investigating Nazi and communist activities in America, Butler was first approached by one Gerald G. MacGuire, a bond salesman and former commander of the Connecticut American Legion. As journalist Spivak described him, "MacGuire was a short stocky man tending toward three chins, with a bullet-shaped head which had a silver plate in it due to a wound received in battle."

According to the former general, MacGuire described to Butler "what was tantamount to a plot to seize the government, by force if necessary." MacGuire, said Butler, explained that he had traveled to Europe to study the role played by veterans' groups in propping up Mussolini's fascist Italy, Hitler's Nazi Germany, and the French government. MacGuire lauded France's Croix de Feu as "an organization of super-soldiers" with profound political influence. Then the man with the silver plate in his cranium announced that "our idea here in America" is to "get up an organization of this kind" because "the political setup has got to be changed a bit."

According to Butler, MacGuire elaborated on the plot: "Now, did it ever occur to you that the president is overworked? We might have an assistant president; somebody to take the blame." MacGuire called the new super Cabinet official a "secretary of general affairs." And, he said, "You know the American people will swallow that. We have got the newspapers. We will start a campaign that the president's health is failing. Everybody can tell that by looking at him, and the dumb American people will fall for it in a second...."

Although MacGuire denied Butler's account under oath, corroborating testimony came from Paul Comly French, a *Philadelphia Record* reporter. Butler had asked French to look into MacGuire's plot and shed some light on "what the hell it's all about."

After checking with Butler, the voluble MacGuire agreed to see French. French testified that MacGuire told him, "We need a fascist government in this country...to save the nation from the communists who want to tear it down and wreck all that we have built in America. The only men who have the patriotism to do it are the soldiers, and Smedley Butler is the ideal leader. He could organize a million men overnight."

French continued: MacGuire "warmed up considerably after we got under way and he said, 'We might go along with Roosevelt and then do with him what Mussolini did with the King of Italy.'" If Roosevelt played ball, French summarized, "swell; and if he did not, they would push him out."

According to French, MacGuire dropped names to give the impression that American Legion brass were involved in the plot.

To impress Butler, MacGuire had flaunted a bank book itemizing deposits of more than $100,000 available to pay for "expenses." Later, he flashed a wad of eighteen $1,000 bills and boasted of "friends" who were capable of coughing up plenty more dough where that came from.

One of those friends was Robert Sterling Clark, a prominent Wall Street banker and stockbroker. When Butler demanded that MacGuire produce his superiors, the tubby intermediary made the introductions. According to Butler's testimony, Clark spoke of spending half his $60 million fortune in order to save the other half. What's more, Clark purportedly waxed ominous about the misguided FDR: "You know the president is weak. He will come right along with us. He was born in this class, and he will come back. He will run true to form. In the end he will come around. But we have got to be prepared to sustain him when he does."

Amazingly, the McCormack-Dickstein Committee (a forerunner of the infamous House Un-American Activities Committee) never bothered to haul Clark in for questioning. And the committee's members—who exhibited considerably more zeal ferreting out two-bit commies than they did big-shot American fascists—failed to grill a half-dozen other suspects named by Butler and French. In fact, the committee suppressed many of the names, even though French's newspaper articles caused a stir by naming the well-heeled conspirators (at the height of the Depression).

In addition to MacGuire and Clark, the leading plotters included:

- Grayson Murphy, a director of Goodyear, Bethlehem Steel, and a panoply of Morgan banks. Murphy was the original bankroller of the American Legion, which he and other wealthy military officers formed after World War I to "offset radicalism." He was also MacGuire's boss at the New York brokerage firm.
- William Doyle, former state commander of the Legion and purportedly the architect of the coup idea.
- John W. Davis, former Democratic candidate for president of the United States and a senior attorney for J.P. Morgan and Company.
- Al Smith, former governor of New York, a Roosevelt foe, and codirector of the newly founded American Liberty League, an organization described by MacGuire as the matrix on which the plot would be executed.

Other prominent businessmen lurked in the background, including Smith's codirector at the American Liberty League, John J. Raskob, who was a former chairman of the Democratic Party, a high-ranking Du Pont officer, and a bitter enemy of FDR, whom he classified among dangerous "radicals." And in even deeper shadows was right-wing industrialist Irénée Du Pont, who established the American Liberty League. Grayson Murphy—MacGuire's boss—was treasurer of the same group. Clearly, this was no penny-ante whiner's club. Most astonishing was the presence among the plotters of heavy-hitting politicos from FDR's own party.

Mysteriously, though, the congressional probe expired with a whimper. The McCormack-Dickstein Committee released heavily edited excerpts from Butler's testimony but claimed it had uncovered "no evidence" other than "hearsay" linking prominent Americans to a fascist plot.

Had the committee backed down rather than take on a klatch of power-drunk millionaires? Did high-ranking Democrats— possibly one in the White House, as some reports had it—put the kibosh on the investigation for similar reasons, or to stave off political embarrassment, or to protect Democratic muckamucks who were in on the scheme?

All of the above would seem likely, for in fact the McCormack-Dickstein Committee's public report was utterly contradicted by its internal summation to the House. That document might have been lost to history had Spivak not somehow managed to liberate a copy. Contrary to the public whitewash, privately the committee acknowledged Butler's accuracy and MacGuire's lying. The report concluded:

> In the last few weeks of the committee's life it received evidence showing that certain persons had made an attempt to establish a fascist organization in this country....
> There is no question that these attempts were discussed, were planned, and might have been placed in execution when and if the financial backers deemed it expedient....

CONSPIRACY, INC.

MacGuire denied [Butler's] allegations under oath, but your committee was able to verify all the pertinent statements made to General Butler, with the exception of the direct statement suggesting the creation of the organization. This, however, was corroborated in the correspondence of MacGuire with his principal, Robert Sterling Clark, of New York City, while MacGuire was abroad studying the various form of veterans' organizations of Fascist character.

Alas, as is so often the case, when truth finally emerged it was greeted as yesterday's news—or worse, as last year's outmoded fashion, which clashed with the committee's public dismissal of the charges. Spivak's reporting appeared in a small left-wing publication where it went largely unnoticed. After all, *Time* magazine—hardly what you would call antagonistic toward right-wing industrialists—had already dismissed the allegations as a joke.

"The fighting Quaker" went on national radio to denounce the committee's deletions of key points in his testimony, but history's loaded die had already been cast.

Ultimately, the plot's failure owes as much a debt to Butler as it does to the hubris of the super-wealthy. Lacking a Mussolini-calibre proxy, but swimming in ample cash to buy one, America's elite fascists dispatched the man with a plate in his head to build a better Duce. Of course, the revolution went south when, in an act of inspired stupidity, they decided to buy a dictator who happened to be a notorious democrat with a small *d*.

MAJOR SOURCES

Archer, Jules. *The Plot to Seize the White House*. New York: Hawthorn Books, 1973.
Seldes, George. *Even the Gods Can't Change History*. Secaucus, NJ: Lyle Stuart, Inc., 1976.
Spivak, John L. *A Man in His Time*. New York: Horizon Press, 1967.

45

The Candy-Coated Conspiracy

As any local reporter who's ever covered a small-time city council meeting knows, the specter of fluoridation still haunts the public agenda. There's always some crotchety old buzzard who shows up, sheaf of documents clenched in fist, ranting about the impurity of precious bodily fluids. You'd think *Dr. Strangelove* had put the issue to rest once and for all.

In essence, the issue is "purity of essence," as the mad general Jack D. Ripper phrased it in Stanley Kubrick's 1964 flick (subtitled *How I Learned to Stop Worrying and Love the Bomb*). Beginning in the late 1930s, ostensibly as a public health measure, various academics, physicians, and bureaucrats began advocating the artificial enrichment of public water supplies with fluoride, a mineral known to prevent tooth decay.

To say this apparently public-spirited project was greeted less than warmly is an understatement. For the next forty years a significant lobby emerged dedicated to the proposition that fluoridation of public water supplies was not only unnecessary

343

and potentially harmful, it was an insidious plot hatched by the worldwide communist conspiracy. Or something. At best, the plot's aim was to poison the U.S. public. At worst—to dissipate what President Kennedy might have later termed American "vigah."

The psychosexual subtext of this fear simmered barely beneath the surface. Somehow, this effort to improve the nation's dental health (widespread fluoridation has the potential to render cavities as passé as whooping cough) was being interpreted as an attempt to turn the home of the brave into a nation of gay blades.

Kubrick flayed fluoride paranoia with his General Ripper, for whom the pinko plot against "our precious bodily fluids" was but an excuse for his own impotence and implied homosexuality. But despite its pointed satire *Strangelove* left the anti-fluoridators undeterred.

As always, however, even with an issue this ridiculous, there is another side. The merits of government-mandated chemical modifications to the public drinking supply are certainly debatable. But is it really all part of a perfidious plot?

"In the words of the Communist Party itself," writes Phoebe Courtney in her 1971 tract *How Dangerous Is Fluoridation?* "anyone who promotes and supports fluoridation can be considered a 'radical'!"

Actually, what the *Daily World* article quoted by Courtney really said was that "such a well-documented and simple improvement in public health should be avidly supported by all who consider themselves radicals." Not that anyone who supports fluoridation is a radical. But logic was never the fluoride-baiters' strong point.

"An Ominous Precedent: Can Water Supplies be Used for Sinister Purposes?" Courtney asks in the title of just one of fifteen chapters in her 158-page paperback. Before you know it, nefarious liberals and cold-hearted physicians will be employing the water supply for "compulsory birth control" and the dissemination of "anti-hostility drugs."

"Perhaps 1984 is closer than we realize," warns the author. Perhaps indeed.

Among her other imprecations:

- "Fluoride pollution causes massive fish-kill."
- "The public seldom hears of it, but fluorides damage water-pipes as well as people.... Automobile radiators were eaten out by fluoride corrosion."
- "It is common knowledge among all chemists and people interested in this particular subject that fluoride is one of the most electronegative active elements known to man."
- "Claim of 65 percent reduction in cavities not true!"
- "In his article in the March 1968 issue of *American Opinion* [a John Birch Society magazine], David O. Woodbury referred to sodium fluoride as 'violent enough in high concentrations to be the standard rat and roach killer and a first-rate pesticide.'"
- "Mrs. M.H., aged fifty-seven, a nurse, and Mrs. E.K., aged thirty-eight, had been in the habit of drinking one to two glasses of water before breakfast. For some unknown reason, they suddenly experienced abdominal cramps and vomiting immediately after their customary morning drink."

To combat the menace of fluoridation, Courtney suggests buying "extra copies of this book for your personal distribution. You may wish to send or give copies to: Officials of your city; Leaders of Parent-Teacher Associations, womens' clubs, fraternal and civic organizations; voters groups and patriotic groups; water works officials; the editor of your local newspaper as well as radio and TV commentators; your personal physician and dentist."

Incidentally, we also suggest that readers purchase extra copies of this book for distribution to physicians, water works officials, and patriotic groups.

As with so many of these theories, even the wackiest ones, there are two sides to the story. Courtney tends to play down the commie-conspiracy angle in favor of an even more nefarious culprit.

"For the sugar and candy interests, fluoridation was a heaven-sent proposal," Courtney writes. "Mothers who become convinced that fluorides strengthen their children's teeth and make them resistant to decay, are not afraid to allow them to eat all the candy and sweets they want. And this is exactly what the candy manufacturers planned when they endorsed fluoridation."

MAJOR SOURCE

Courtney, Phoebe. *How Dangerous Is Fluoridation?* New Orleans: Free Men Speak, Inc., 1971.

46

Reefer Madness

What if there was a plant that could feed and clothe the world, end global deforestation, replace smutty fossil fuels in the gas tank of your car, and offer salubrious therapy for dozens of ailments? What if George Washington and Thomas Jefferson had grown it, were required by law to grow it, so useful was this miracle shrub? Well, then, it stands to reason that a combine of jealous industrialists, shrieking demagogues, and yellow journalists would scurry to stomp the "demon weed" out forever and purge its distinguished legacy from the history books.

The name of this botanical martyr? The Founding Fathers, who drafted the Declaration of Independence on paper made from the plant, knew it as hemp. You may know it by another of its many appellations: Indian hemp, true hemp, bhang, dagga, ganja, muggles, muta, grefa, tea, boo, goo, gauge, herb, weed, "the kind," cannabis, reefer, buds, grass, pot—to wit, *marijuana*.

Beginning to get the picture? In his eminently civilized book, *The Emperor Wears No Clothes*, Jack Herer has exposed the

347

"malicious conspiracy to suppress not a 'killer weed,' but the world's premier renewable natural resource, for the benefit of a handful of wealthy and powerful individuals and corporations." Herer is the founder of a group called HEMP (Help End Marijuana Prohibition). He sees the sixty-year war on pot as more than a pox on tokers: It's a latter-day Inquisition, a pernicious reprise of the Dark Ages, and, not least, "a conspiracy against mankind."

As do so many, this conspiracy began in smoke-filled board rooms—and you can bet the smoke wasn't a mellow sinsemilla haze. The year was 1937, and with the advent of new mechanical fiber stripping technology, hemp was poised to make a grand comeback as the nation's favorite, most versatile textile. But as Herer relates it, an unholy trinity of hemp enemies orchestrated the notorious prohibition of this "member of the most advanced plant family on Earth."

First, a brief history lesson, necessary because the story of hemp has indeed been obscured by a half century of suppression: Before the invention of the cotton gin in the early 1800s, hemp products made from the fiber of the plant's reedy stalk were everywhere in America—and the world. The word *canvas* comes to us from the Dutch pronunciation of the Greek *kannabis*. From the fifth century B.C. through the late nineteenth century, ships' sails and rigging were made from hemp. For thousands of years, cannabis fibers had been the chief source of the world's clothing, tents, carpets, rope, bedding, and flags—including Old Glory. As Herer helpfully reminds us, Washington and his troops would have frozen to death at Valley Forge were it not for their hemp threads. The Conestoga wagons that trekked across the American prairies were covered with cannabis canvas, and the settlers' Bibles were likely to have been printed on reefer paper. For thousands of years, hemp-seed oil did yeoman's duty as lamp fuel and even food. And during the nineteenth century, patent medicines utilizing the plant's more familiar chemical attributes were imbibed by God-fearing Americans of all stripes.

By the late 1930s, *Popular Mechanics* and other magazines were hailing technology that promised to make hemp, the strongest of the natural fibers, a "new billion-dollar crop." But there were those who connived to bury hemp's illustrious history under a mountain of slander, vilifying "marihuana" as the killer weed smoked by murderous Mexicans and insolent Negroes.

The first powerful player in the anti-hemp triad identified by Herer was William Randolph Hearst. The millionaire magnate deployed his sprawling Hearst newspaper chain in a hysterical crusade against marijuana.

The second, and most strident, figure in the plot to assassinate hemp was a corrupt hypermoralist named Harry J. Anslinger. Described in Albert Goldman's book, *Grass Roots*, as "a bull-necked, bald-headed, slab-shouldered cop" with "the demagogue's flair for sloganlike phrases," Anslinger was the spear carrier in the war on pot. His crude propaganda, laughable today, popularized spurious myths about pot in (Hearst) articles with headlines like MARIHUANA—ASSASSIN OF YOUTH and MARIHUANA MAKES FIENDS OF BOYS IN 30 DAYS: HASHEESH GOADS USERS TO BLOOD-LUST. Ax murderers, rampaging gunmen, and suicidal motorists were "depraved creatures" motivated by "reefer madness." In one publicized speech, Anslinger warned, "If the hideous monster Frankenstein came face to face with the monster marihuana, he would drop dead of fright." (Like many a morality cop, Anslinger was also a first-class hypocrite. He later admitted to illegally supplying morphine to the Red-baiting and drug-addicted Senator Joseph McCarthy. During World War II Anslinger helped the OSS, forerunner to the CIA, in unsuccessful experiments with a hashish derivative they hoped to use as a truth serum on spies.)

Forming the third flank in Herer's conspiracy theory was the powerful Du Pont corporation. All three had reasons for extinguishing the hapless weed.

Although most historians have explained the Anslinger-Hearst assault on pot as a product of the prohibition era, paranoia over creeping immorality, and old-fashioned Jim Crow racism, Herer has thrown an economic theory into the mix.

It seems that the Hearst Paper Manufacturing Division, with its sprawling timber acreage, was threatened by a new milling process devised by the U.S. Department of Agriculture to convert the woody stalks of hemp into reams of high-grade paper, cardboard, and fiberboard. Incidentally, the process produced fewer toxic chemicals than wood-pulp manufacturing and, according to the government, would save four acres of fragile forest for every acre of hemp cultivated. Concludes Herer: As far as Hearst and the wood-pulp-based paper industry were concerned, "Cannabis hemp would have to go."

As for Du Pont's motives, Herer postulates that hemp's natural fibers imperiled that company's mad dream of clothing the world in polyester.

In the campaign to assassinate hemp, Anslinger and the Hearst papers weren't above race-baiting. The bull-necked narc often described marijuana users as "ginger-colored niggers" with big lips, whose "satanic" music and demon weed drove white women "to seek sexual relations with Negroes." He warned Congress that most of the reefer fiends were "Negroes and Mexicans," or, worst of all, "entertainers." Hearst articles depicted languid, pot-smoking Mexicans who could turn into homicidal lunatics at the snap of a fried synapse. According to Herer, Hearst hammered (and misspelled) the Mexican slang term *marijuana* into the public consciousness in a campaign designed to confuse folks who might otherwise discover that the demon weed and the historic fiber were one in the same.

Soon enough the fix was in. Anslinger's Treasury Department bosses held closed-door meetings that yielded sneaky legislation to slap an exorbitant $100 tax on unregistered dealers selling hemp. (Anslinger, notes Herer, owed his job to his "uncle-in-law," Andrew Mellon, owner of the nation's sixth largest bank, who also happened to be...*a Du Pont banker*.) Thanks to the influence of House Ways and Means Committee chairman Robert L. Doughton, a dyed-in-the-wool (make that *poly-blend*)

Du Pont ally, the anti-marijuana law (posing as a tax law) breezed through Congress over the weak objections of hemp producers and the American Medical Association. Thus was born the Marihuana Tax Act of 1937, which effectively outlawed the drug—and the rest of the plant—in America.

And sure enough, shortly after the 1937 marijuana ban, Du Pont unveiled its "plastic fibers," which came to dominate markets previously served by hempen goods. The following year, Du Pont patented Nylon and a new super-polluting wood-pulp process.

As if to rub Rayon in hemp users' faces, in 1939 Lammot Du Pont boasted in *Popular Mechanics* of "conserving natural resources by developing synthetic products to supplement or *wholly replace natural products*" (emphasis added).

Maybe all of this is not exactly irrefutable proof, but as the *Emperor Wears No Clothes* points out, thanks to the governmental ban on cannabis, Du Pont continues to be the nation's "largest producer of man-made fibers, while no citizen has legally harvested a single acre of textile-grade hemp in over fifty years." Perhaps it's the price of progress: The snuffing of a versatile, clean, renewable resource paved the way for the Du Pont dynasty, dioxin, timber clearcutting and, of course, the leisure suit.

MAJOR SOURCES

Goldman, Albert. *Grass Roots: Marijuana in America Today*. New York: Warner Books, 1979.

Herer, Jack. *The Emperor Wears No Clothes: Hemp and the Marijuana Conspiracy*. Van Nuys, CA: Hemp Publishing, 1992.

47

New World Order

During the heady days of the Persian Gulf War, President George Bush dusted off an ancient phrase that immediately set teeth on edge—that is, the grinding teeth of conspiracy trackers.

"I hope history will record that the Gulf Crisis was the crucible of the new world order," Bush intoned in the wake of his greatest triumph, the American-led victory against Iraq. *New World Order*. The phrase had tripped from the president's lips at least half a dozen other times before and after American smart bombs had transformed the former "wimp" into a short-term war hero.

Of course, the *real* meaning of the term—bandied about for decades by a phalanx of elite bankers and industrialists— couldn't have been clearer to ultra-right-wingers of the John Birch Society ilk. Simply put, *New World Order* was code for "one-world government," a megalomaniacal communist plot to enslave the planet. In the words of the late Gary Allen, the prolific Birch Society author, "Communism is an arm of a bigger conspiracy to control the world by power-mad billionaires." Bush, the ultimate establishment insider, was clearly an agent of these crypto-capitalist/communist forces—as had been every sell-out president since FDR.

Lest we dismiss such concerns as the ranting of survivalist kooks, it's important to note that the New World Order is an equal opportunity conspiracy theory. Left-wingers were just as exercised by Bush's words, although progressives tended to see the preppy president more as a champion of capitalism run amok than as a creeping commie.

In fact, right-wing or left, suspicions about the New World Order are actually quite rational. The champions of the "NWO" are indeed a cadre of powerful industrialists, bankers, academics, and politicians who for three quarters of a century have been a gray eminence behind the governance of Britain and America. More to the point, perhaps, they *are* the governors of the Western world. Call them what you will, they are the "Establishment." Through vastly influential organizations like the Council on Foreign Relations and the Trilateral Commission, these elites formulate tomorrow's public policy today and staff the ship of state with their own.

If this network is something less than the Red devil depicted in many a right-wing conspiracy theory, it is nonetheless a kind of big business cabal that helps the elite of the private sector, if not "rule the world," then at least run it like a business.

The self-appointed historian of this power brokerage was Georgetown University professor Carroll Quigley, a distinguished scholar whom right-wingers regard as a smoking gun personified. In his massive history of the modern era, *Tragedy and Hope*, the late Professor Quigley wrote that there "does exist, and has existed for a generation, an international Anglophile network which operates, to some extent, in the way that the radical Right believes the Communists act."

Quigley admitted that he "had been close" to this "semisecret organization" of international manipulators—indeed, admired its goals—and had been allowed to examine its "papers and secret records."

According to Quigley, the network's benevolent aim is "nothing less than to create a world system of financial control in private hands able to dominate the political system of each country and the economy of the world as a whole"—thereby assuring peace and prosperity and, of course, profit.

This network grew out of secret political societies hatched by diamond baron/stealth fanatic Cecil Rhodes (Rhodesia, Rhodes scholarships) and a clutch of bleeding-heart imperialists resolved to prevent the sun from setting on the British Empire. By 1908, Rhodes was dead, but his dream and vast wealth lived on to sire the furtive Round Table Groups.

During the early part of this century, the aristocratic Round Tablers—who set up franchises in South Africa, Australia, the United States, and Canada—yearned to "civilize" native subjects of the British dominion. If properly instilled with liberal Oxford values and presumably an appreciation of cricket, even the most "backward" races could learn to be contented, perhaps "autonomous," citizens of empire. A connected dream was to yoke all of the English-speaking nations (America included) into a confederation of Atlantic states, with the capital in Washington, D.C.! (To Birchers' ears, this is an early echo of the dread "one-world government.") If their grander schemes flopped rather obliquely, the Round Tablers achieved a failure of spectacular proportions when they led the drive to appease Hitler.

In America, the Rhodes groups and J. P. Morgan banking interests incorporated the Council on Foreign Relations (CFR) in 1921 as a Round Table "front." According to Quigley, CFR and other Round Table cutouts became "a power structure between London and New York which penetrated deeply into university life, the press, and the practice of foreign policy" in both countries. This is the famous "Eastern Establishment" that continues to hold sway over the U.S. government, academia, Wall Street, and major American media outlets, including the *New York Times* and *Washington Post*.

The American arm of the network flourished under the

patronage of billionaire benefactors, including the Morgan and Carnegie interests—and of course the ubiquitous Rockefeller family.

Ah, the Rockefellers! Dons of the financial underworld! Godfathers of the commie/capitalist internationale! That, anyway, is what many a right-wing conspiracist believes. In Bircher fulminations, the four R's—Rhodes, Rothschilds, Rockefellers, and Reds—are demons that turbocharge the dry facts of Professor Quigley.

The radical-right theories were never synthesized more impressively than in Gary Allen's 1971 call to arms, *None Dare Call It Conspiracy*. Merging nativist strains of anticommunism, antielitism, and "gold standard" conservatism, Allen argued that the Rockefeller-CFR-Establishment cabal—dubbed the "Insiders"—had toiled for decades to "abolish the United States" and establish an "all powerful world socialist superstate."

Allen wasn't suggesting that supercapitalists like the Rockefellers were sincere Marxists, but rather that they used socialism "as the bait...the excuse to establish the dictatorship." According to Allen, the Rockefellers, the British Rothschild clan, and their various corporate agents had not only financed Lenin and the Bolshevik revolution, but David Rockefeller may have been the "paymaster" who later fired his employee, Soviet premier Krushchev! How did "the Rockefeller Foreign Office" keep unruly Moscow in line? Allen muses that the Insiders might have used "SMERSH, the international Communist murder organization described in testimony before congressional committees and by Ian Fleming in his James Bond books."

Allen's vision was nothing if not dramatic. In a successful effort early in the century to hijack the American economy and political arena, he reports, the Insiders established a central bank (the Federal Reserve System), lorded over by international bankers; they followed up by saddling citizens with the income tax, thereby fulfilling two key planks of Marx's *Communist*

Manifesto. The Insiders then "scientifically engineered" the stock market crash of 1929. They managed to top that feat by starting World Wars I and II (the latter through their appeasement of Hitler) *and* the Vietnam debacle, profiteering in all cases by arming both sides. Oh yeah, they also invented the nefarious United (communist) Nations as the keystone of their relentless New World Order.

In a rare instance of giving the Rockefellers a bit of a break, Birchers revived the old right-wing theory that the real powers behind the Insider throne—both communist and "cartel capitalist"—were those standby conspiracy bugaboos, the Illuminati, a secret Freemasonic society that definitely existed, albeit in eighteenth-century Bavaria.

(In an effort to cast the Illuminati as a "Zionist" cabal, anti-Semites—and Allen wasn't one—often invoke the Jewish Rothschilds and the old lie that the Bolshevik revolution was all a Jewish plot. Allen dismissed that "thinking," and typically had a more interesting angle: The Insiders themselves covertly promoted such anti-Semitic falsehoods in an effort to tar all their critics as racists. Of course, Allen offered no evidence for this theory, but perhaps he was on to something. More than one modern blowhard of the "there-are-no-conspiracies" school has offhandedly broadbrushed conspiracy theorists by yoking them with Holocaust apologists.)

Although the conspiratorial tapestry woven by the Birchers was a bit, well, *busy*, even the staid Professor Quigley grudgingly acknowledged that it contained "a modicum of truth." For one thing, the so-called Insiders "had no aversion to cooperating with the Communists," per Quigley. After all, big business is big business, and what better way of acquiring access to untapped natural resources than being neighborly? Likewise, the CFR-dominated U.S. Department of State was indeed very influential in midwifing the UN. And the Round Tablers did push for the income tax and the Federal Reserve.

As for the Rockefellers, the family *has* played a major role in the network since its early days. David Rockefeller, chairman of the CFR board, founded the Trilateral Commission in the early 1970s (same Euro-American "internationalists" but with the additional membership of Japanese power players). Another Rockefeller-Insider group arose as the retiring Round Tables passed the torch to the CFR (either that, or went deep underground, a hunch of many conspiracy theorists): This was the Bilderberg Group, named for the location of its first annual meeting, the hotel Bilderberg in Oosterbeek, Netherlands.

A super-secret riff on the CFR, the Bilderberg roll call featured Rockefellers and hordes of American officials, including U.S. State Department/CFR stalwarts Henry Kissinger, George Ball, Dean Rusk, and Dean Acheson. Its European contingent was infested by royals, including the founding Bilderberg chairman, Prince Bernhard of the Netherlands.

As we've seen, the CFR-Trilat-Bilderberg membership rolls were brimming with American officials and politicians eager to suck up to the power establishment. Even Richard Nixon, whose animus for the Eastern elite was famous, joined the CFR and later hired Rockefeller protégé Henry Kissinger. (Birchers haven't forgotten that President Nixon invoked the spooky phrase "new world order" during his trip to *Red* China.) Other U.S. presidents who were Insiders included Gerald Ford (CFR, Bilderberg), Jimmy Carter (CFR, Trilat), George Bush (CFR *board director*, Trilat), and even Bill Clinton (CFR, Trilat, *and* Bilderberg).

During the Carter era 284 CFR/Trilats held administration positions. Key Insiders included Vice President Walter Mondale, national security advisor Zbigniew Brzezinski (director of the Trilateral Commission), Secretary of State Cyrus Vance and CIA Director Stansfield Turner. By the end of Reagan's two terms, the number had risen to 313. Reaganite Insiders included secretaries of state Al Haig (a favorite candidate for Watergate's Deep Throat) and George Shultz (the tenth consecutive CFR alumnus to hold that job) and CIA Director William Casey.

Under Bush, "the conspiracy president," the number sky-rocketed to 382, including national security advisor Brent Scowcroft and the attorney general, Richard Thornburgh.

As for the Clinton administration, little has changed as far as CFR faces go. Secretary of State Warren Christopher, all five of his undersecretaries, and many of *their* underlings are CFR-ites. So are Clinton's national security adviser and CIA director, and so is his Republicrat aide, David Gergen.

Gergen is only one point of light in a constellation of media stars absorbed into the CFR. A partial list includes the late Walter Lippman (a CFR director in the 1930s), CIA propagandist/*Life* magazine publisher C. D. Jackson (who helped set up the Bilderberg Group), *New York Times*man Leslie Gelb (current CFR president), Dan Rather, Tom Brokaw, and Jim Lehrer, the non-Canadian half of the *MacNeil/Lehrer NewsHour*.

Though the CFR/Trilat connection runs deep into the blue veins of the Establishment, predictably its members scoff at the suggestion that they hold excessive influence over American "democracy" and world affairs. David Rockefeller once sniffed at what he called these "foolish attacks on false issues." With perhaps excessive modesty, he assured the skeptics that his Trilateral Commission is just "a group of concerned citizens interested in fostering greater understanding and cooperation among international allies."

Well, apparently all groups of concerned citizens are not created equal. As journalist Bill Moyers put it in a 1980 TV documentary: "David Rockefeller is the most conspicuous representative today of the ruling class, a multinational fraternity of men who shape the global economy and manage the flow of its capital. Rockefeller was born to it, and he has made the most of it. But what some critics see as a vast international conspiracy, he considers a circumstance of life and just another day's work."

If the New World Order isn't a blueprint for the "world super-state" of Bircher nightmares, it may simply mean a world more "orderly" for transnational big business. The implications are just as ominous, for although Trilats don't aim to raze Capitol Hill to make way for a U.N. high rise, they have made it clear that democracy often hampers their terribly important work. Not only have the Round Table progeny pushed for "limited," strongman "democracy" in third world countries, they have openly complained about the surfeit of liberty for the little people in this country.

A 1975 Trilateral Commission report concluded that the United States was plagued by an "excess of democracy," when "what is needed is a greater degree of moderation in democracy," to improve "governability." Trilat co-founder Brzezinski recommended a study on "Control Over Man's Development and Behavior" to devise "new means of social control," especially "in advanced societies."

In the coming New World Order, the natives apparently have yet to be civilized.

MAJOR SOURCES

Allen, Gary. *None Dare Call It Conspiracy*. Rossmoor, CA: Concord Press, 1971.

McManus, John F. *The Insiders: Architects of the New World Order*. Appleton, Wisconsin: John Birch Society, 1992.

Quigley, Carroll. *Tragedy and Hope: A History of the World in Our Time*. New York: MacMillan Company, 1966.

Sklar, Holly, ed. *Trilateralism: The Trilateral Commission and Elite Planning*. Boston: South End Press, 1980.

Wilgus, Neal. *The Illuminoids: Secret Societies and Political Paranoia*. Santa Fe, NM: Sun Publishing Company, 1978.

VIII

Tragedy and Trauma

48

This Means War

On the evening of December 6, 1941, Franklin Delano Roosevelt, the president of the United States, received a message intercepted by the U.S. Navy. Sent from Tokyo to the Japanese embassy in Washington, the message was encrypted in the top-level Japanese "purple code." But that was no problem. The Americans had cracked the code long before that.

It was imperative that the president see the message right away because it revealed that the Japanese, under the heavy pressure of Western economic sanctions, were terminating relations with the United States. Roosevelt read the thirteen-part transmission, looked up and announced, "This means war."

He then did a very strange thing for a president in his situation.

Nothing.

The Japanese secret declaration of war never reached the people who needed to hear it the most—Admiral Husband E. Kimmel, commander in chief of the United States Pacific Fleet at Pearl Harbor, Hawaii, and the unit's commanding general,

Walter Short. Pearl Harbor, it was common military knowledge, was where the Japanese would strike. If they struck.

At dawn the next morning a Japanese squadron bombed Pearl Harbor and the surprise attack was just that, a complete surprise. At least to Kimmel and Short and the 4,575 American servicemen who died.

It may not have been such a surprise to Generals George C. Marshall and Leonard T. Gerow and Admirals Harold R. Stark and Richmond Kelly Turner. They were the military's top brass in Washington and the only officers authorized to forward such sensitive intelligence to outlying commanders. But the decoded war declaration did not reach Kimmel and Short until the morning, with the attack well underway off in the Pacific.

Marshall and Stark, supreme commanders of the U.S. Army and Navy respectively, later testified that the message was not forwarded to Kimmel and Short because the Hawaiian commaders had received so many intercepted Japanese messages that another one would simply confuse them.

Internal army and navy inquiries in 1944 held Stark and Marshall derelict of duty for keeping the Hawaiian commanders in the dark. But the military buried those findings. As far as the public knew, the final truth was uncovered by the Roberts Commission, headed by Justice Owen Roberts of the Supreme Court, and convened eleven days after the attack. Like another investigative commission headed by a Supreme Court justice on a different topic more than twenty years later, the Roberts Commission appeared to have identified its culprits in advance and gerrymandered its inquiries to make the suspects appear guilty. The scapegoats were Kimmel and Short, who were both publicly crucified, forced to retire, and denied the open hearings they desired. One of the Roberts Commission panelists, Admiral William Standley, would call Roberts's performance "crooked as a snake."

There were eight investigations of Pearl Harbor altogether. The most spectacular was a joint House-Senate probe that reiterated the Roberts Commission findings. At those hearings,

Marshall and Stark testified, incredibly, that they could not remember where they were the night the war declaration came in. But a close friend of Frank Knox, the secretary of the Navy, later revealed that Knox, Stark, and Marshall spent most of that night in the White House with Roosevelt awaiting the bombing of Pearl Harbor and the chance for America to join World War II.

A widespread coverup ensued. A few days after Pearl Harbor, reports historian John Toland, Marshall told his top officers, "Gentlemen, this goes to the grave with us." General Short once considered Marshall his friend, only to learn that the chief of staff was the agent of his frame-up. Short once remarked that he pitied his former pal because Marshall was the only general who wouldn't be able to write an autobiography.

There were multiple warnings of the Pearl Harbor attack concealed from the commanders at Pearl Harbor. The Winds Code was perhaps the most shocking. That was an earlier transmission, in a fake weather report broadcast on a Japanese short-wave station, of the words *higashi no kaze ame*. Which means, "east wind, rain." The Americans already knew that this was the Japanese code for war with the United States. The response of top U.S. military officials? To deny that the "winds" message existed and to attempt to destroy all records of its reception. But it did exist. And it was received.

Completely apart from the cloak and dagger of cryptography, the Australian intelligence service, three days before the attack, spotted the Japanese fleet of aircraft carriers heading for Hawaii. A warning went to Washington where it was dismissed by Roosevelt as a politically motivated rumor circulated by Republicans.

A British double agent, Dusko Popov, who siphoned information from Germany, learned of the Japanese intentions and desperately tried to warn Washington, to no avail. And there were others.

Why would Roosevelt and the nation's top military commanders sacrifice the U.S. Pacific Fleet, not to mention thousands of servicemen—an act that could justifiably be deemed treason? They had concluded long before Pearl Harbor that war against the Axis powers was a necessity. The American public disagreed. A strike against American territory would surely bring the public around.

"This was the president's problem," wrote Rear Admiral Robert A. Theobald who commanded Pearl Harbor's destroyers, "and his solution was based upon the simple fact that, while it takes two to make a fight, either one may start it."

"A small group of men, revered and held to be most honorable by millions," wrote Toland, "had convinced themselves that it was necessary to act dishonorably for the good of their nation—and incited the war that Japan had tried to avoid."

MAJOR SOURCES

Theobald, Robert A. *The Final Secret of Pearl Harbor*. Old Greenwich, CT: Devin-Adair, 1954.

Toland, John. *Infamy: Pearl Harbor and Its Aftermath*. New York: Doubleday, 1982.

49

The Lost Boys

The flag adopted by America's POW/MIA movement tells a provocative story: A downcast soldier languishes behind barbed wire, while an armed sentry looms in a distant watchtower. This mournful image, superimposed against a field of black, flies at veterans centers and lodges nationwide like an article of faith—but perhaps also as a symbol of *lost faith*.

This is because the banner also conveys another message: American prisoners of war were abandoned in Vietnam, "betrayed" by their own government, which for dark reasons continues to suppress evidence that live POWs remain behind enemy lines. The only thing missing from the flag is a cackling U.S. bureaucrat.

In recent years a ground swell of opinion has borne the theory of the "lost boys" out of America's conservative heartland and into the mainstream. But skeptics disparage the "MIA myth" as a mass pathology, a Rambo fantasy, a symptom of the jingoistic "Vietnam syndrome." Is it?

In the debit column, no living POWs have emerged from the jungles of Vietnam, Laos, or Cambodia in recent years to tell harrowing tales of abandonment. The "evidence" that vaults periodically into newspaper headlines is usually countered by government "experts": The photograph of three aging MIAs? A not-so-clever forgery. The Soviet "smoking gun" document referring to some seven hundred American prisoners never released by Hanoi? Probably a tally of "allied" POWs from Asia, not red-blooded American boys.

But the debunkers tend to ignore an inventory of bizarre, hard-to-explain details, incidents, and reports that do, in fact, make an interesting case for "conspiracy."

Kiss the Boys Goodbye, the 1990 book by former *60 Minutes* producer Monika Jensen-Stevenson and her husband, espionage author William Stevenson, makes one of the more persuasive arguments for the "lost boys" theory. "Hundreds of refugees reported seeing Americans in all parts of Communist Southeast Asia in the early postwar years," long after the government announced that all American POWs had been released, they write. Reportedly, American soldiers and intelligence officers on covert missions in Indochina continued to report sightings of U.S. prisoners in Vietnam and Laos throughout the 1980s. The former head of the Pentagon's Defense Intelligence Agency (DIA), General Eugene Tighe, claimed publicly that the secretive DIA had intelligence to prove "there *are* live Americans over there."

A key report came from a U.S. Marine private named Bobby Garwood, who had been captured by the Viet Cong at China Beach in 1965. Fourteen years later—at a time when there were supposedly no American POWs in Indochina—the Vietnamese government set Garwood free. Though Garwood claimed that other live POWs remained in Vietnam, the military rather hastily branded him a traitor, effectively discrediting his story. (Years later, the government would quietly acknowledge it had made a mistake in labeling Garwood an enemy quisling, but by then his claim about live Americans was hardly timely news.)

How many POWs were wasting away in the jungle? Jerry Mooney, a National Security Agency analyst who had monitored American prisoners throughout Indochina up until 1976 (three years after President Nixon assured Americans that all POWs had been accounted for), claimed that he had tracked more than three hundred.

Douglas Applegate, a congressman from Ohio, announced in 1984 that he had obtained "very disturbing" CIA documents listing hundreds of "reports of live American prisoners in Laos." The DIA interceded and had Applegate's words stricken from the *Congressional Record*, supposedly because he had referred to satellite photographs showing Caucasian inmates—a breach of technological secrecy.

When POW/MIA families began requesting declassified documents, the military moved, strangely, to reclassify them. The official word remained that "there is no evidence to indicate that any live American POWs from the Indochina conflict remain alive."

Privately, though, the Reagan administration apparently thought otherwise. Reagan's National Security Counsel point man on POW families, Richard Childress, warned Jensen-Stevenson that her pursuit of the story "could jeopardize the lives of the prisoners still there." Huh? There weren't any POWs, yet Jensen-Stevenson was nevertheless endangering their "lives"?

President Reagan, himself, contradicted the official line (hardly a surprise, that), acknowledging in a letter to the wife of an MIA that his administration had planned a military rescue mission in 1981.

In 1986, the *Wall Street Journal* added a few details: That rescue mission had evolved after Hanoi offered to sell fifty-seven *live* American hostages to the United States for a price of $4 million. Reportedly, the Reaganites rebuffed the offer, unwilling to pay a ransom for hostages—if true, an ironic reluctance given the later Iran-Contra arms-for-hostage deals. According to the *Wall Street Journal*, Richard Allen, Reagan's crafty national security advisor, proposed an alternative: a Rambo-like rescue mission into Laos with the goal of retrieving live American prisoners. For some unexplained reason, though, the raid had failed.

According to a group of veterans who confronted Allen after the news story appeared, the Reagan aide said: "I know they're there, and it is my firm belief that live POWs are still being held in Indochina." By the time the mission got underway, Allen explained to the angry vets, the prisoners had all been moved.

But an assemblage of commandos and intelligence vets told a slightly different story. Yes, there had been a government-approved reconnaissance and rescue operation in 1981, but it had been scuttled—or sabotaged—at the last minute. Enter Colonel James "Bo" Gritz, the real-life Green Beret Rambo who inspired Sylvester Stallone's commie-crushing action hero. (One difference between fiction and reality was that Stallone wasn't known for making anti-Semitic remarks.) A super-stealth group within the Pentagon known as the Intelligence Support Activity (ISA) had indeed sponsored a Gritz mission to Laos, which was to supplement a larger Delta Forces raid. Before the Delta commandos got off the ground, though, the Pentagon shut the operation down. Then it shut off Gritz's mission.

But the cigar-chomping Green Beret had a plan B, and he launched his operation Velvet Glove, anyway. But as Gritz and his Special Forces troopers later told it, they arrived in Laos to discover their cover had deliberately been blown by the Voice of America, the U.S. government's propaganda broadcast. By the time Gritz trudged back to civilization, the international press was calling him a rampaging renegade. That's how it appeared, but it just wasn't true. The ISA continued to insist that its support of Gritz had been sanctioned by the Pentagon's joint chiefs; whatever else it was, Velvet Glove was not a "rogue" mission.

Given such wildly mixed signals from public officials, the conspiracy theorists were hardly unjustified when they began getting "paranoid." Wasn't the government acting mighty hinky, privately claiming there were live POWs in Indochina but publicly doing all it could to discredit anyone who tried to prove it? It seemed that every respected military official, competent government employee, straight-laced soldier, or inquiring reporter who broke ranks with the official line on POWs instantly became persona non grata, or worse, was dismissed as a "true believer," a crank, a nut, paranoid, even unpatriotic.

General Tighe, the former DIA chief whose internal Pentagon commission concluded that American POWs were being held in secret camps throughout Indochina, was publicly excoriated by Pentagon brass and privately maligned as maybe having a screw loose.

Journalists who stubbornly stuck with the story were getting threatening phone calls and being harrassed rather unsubtlely. Jensen-Stevensen's briefcase and notes were snatched in an airport; a BBC reporter was targeted by DEA officers who told him that somebody wanted to send him a warning; a Montana journalist looking into the suspicious death of an intelligence veteran involved in a POW mission received a scary phone call from a man warning her, "It's not in your best interests to investigate. Take it how you like. Do you need me to come out there and persuade you?"

The reaction to anyone claiming there were live POWs was so vitriolic, so over the top, it naturally inflated small suspicions to Brobdingnagian proportions.

Which brings us to that most famous of POW hunters, Texas billionaire and superpatriot H. Ross Perot. Perot had been hunting for POWs since the late Nixon epoch. In 1973, he financed a mercenary raid into the jungles of Laos and Vietnam, which failed despite the support of straight-shooting cowboys John Wayne and Clint Eastwood. According to the *New Republic*, Perot tried—and failed—again in 1983, this time with Bo Gritz wearing the fatigues. (Other reports have it that the ISA was in on the Perot-Gritz mission, which wouldn't be all that surprising considering Perot's eager-beaver support

of Ollie North schemes during the early eighties, but Perot has
denied these charges.)

Apparently in appreciation of his open billfold, Ross was
given a spot on Reagan's Foreign Intelligence Advisory Board.
There he could look into the POW issue as a "special investigator," and he later claimed that the government had current
evidence of live POWs.

At some point, for whatever reason, the Reaganites got less
cooperative with pesky Perot. The NSC snubbed his offer of "a
hundred million dollars to buy back prisoners from Hanoi,"
and the White House also rejected his proposal to broker a deal
with Hanoi. Perot jetted to Hanoi anyway and haggled with
Vietnamese apparatchiks. "They said something to me that
went so much to the heart of the matter," Perot told Jensen-
Stevenson. "It confirmed...*the men are there*." But the official
U.S. delegation that followed Perot's opening, including POW
point man Richard Childress, steered the negotiations to the
subject of remains—teeth, bones, uniforms—sidestepping the
issue of live prisoners, according to other delegates. Perot's
advance work, apparently, was for naught.

But the last straw for gung-ho Perot seems to have been Vice
President George Bush. For some reason, Perot had the odd
impression that good ol' George, the former CIA director, was
"a Boy Scout" who would jump at the chance to help an ol' pal
save the Pee-Oh-Dubble-yuh's. But, if Perot is to be believed,
Bush turned out to be the immovable object to H. Ross's
irresistible force.

Clearly, Perot's falling out with his idol Bush over the POW
issue set the stage for the billionaire's 1992 crusade for the
presidency, which was as much Perot's personal vendetta
against Bush as a strike against the tassel-loafered conspirators.

It all fell apart thus: Perot had gone to the thrifty and
trustworthy Bush to spill the beans about the real stumbling
block in the POW quest. "Well, George," Perot had explained,
"I go looking for prisoners, but I spend all my time discovering
the government has been moving drugs around the world and is

involved in illegal arms deals...I can't get at the prisoners because of the corruption among our own covert people."

That was the breaking point, Perot claimed; thereafter, he was "instructed to cease and desist" in his official capacity as a presidential investigator. But according to the *New Republic*, what really steamed Perot was that Bush had ignored the billionaire when he fingered the man he believed to be gumming up the POW search, Richard Armitage, who at the time was an assistant secretary of defense in charge of POW issues. Taking a leaf from the liberal Christic Institute (see page 310), Perot reportedly thought that Armitage was near the center of an old-boy network of intelligence vets who had dealt drugs, run guns, and left POWs out in the cold, among other conspiracies. (A federal judge subsequently threw out the Christics' lawsuit, which named Armitage and others, as frivolous.)

Drugs and illegal arms deals tied to the POW coverup? Was Perot off his King-size rocker?

Well, maybe. But that was precisely the underground story being traded by an assortment of clandestine operatives and government veterans. The sordid tale supposedly began during the Nixon administration.

"We negotiated the prisoners away," submitted Roger Shields, the Pentagon man responsible for POW/MIA affairs between 1971 and 1976. Shields wouldn't elaborate, but he told Jensen-Stevenson to ask Henry Kissinger, Nixon's secretary of state, why there had been such haste at the time of the 1973 Vietnam peace accord to remove the names of missing American soldiers and pilots from the official POW/MIA roster. Kissinger has maintained that no live Americans were left behind.

But the figures never quite added up. The answer to the puzzle, Perot and others believed, lay not in Vietnam, but in neighboring Laos, where the CIA and the U.S. military had fought a secret war against the communists for close to three decades. Although the North Vietnamese released 591 Americans in early 1973, they continued to refer to prisoners in Laos not covered under the Kissinger negotiations. On the eve of the accords, Pentagon books listed 317 men missing in Laos, men never accounted for, dead or alive.

"We can't make use of what we know about those lost in Laos because the whole war there was secret," claimed one of the sources, Nick Rowe, an army colonel and veteran of special intelligence operations.

The CIA's secret wars in Laos and Cambodia are a matter of record. Rowe, Gritz, and other military insiders described the secret wars, which, they claimed, had rendered the missing expendable:

- The illegal covert wars in Indochina continued even after the official end of the Vietnam conflict—and well into the late 1980s. Many of the missing in Laos disappeared during clandestine missions deployed *after* the 1973 armistice with Vietnam. Ergo, these secret soldiers drafted from the rank and file of the regular military were subject to "plausible deniability."
- The CIA helped fund its covert wars in Southeast Asia via sales of arms and narcotics, the latter produced by Laotian warlords in the opium fields of the Golden Triangle region, America's largest supplier of contraband heroin. (The CIA's involvement in Southeast Asian drug running has been well-documented through the years.) According to Ed Wilson, the CIA operative convicted for selling explosives and arms to Libya, those snooping around the MIA issue were bound to discover all sorts of embarrassing projects: heroin running; offshore banks set up by the CIA to fund "privatized" covert ops, à la Ollie North's Iran-Contra network; the arming of anticommunist guerrillas; etc.
- The government's official POW/MIA efforts—with offices and operatives on the ground in Southeast Asia—may have been used as a cover for continuing the secret wars and running the drugs that funded proxy armies. This might explain why several military rescue efforts planned during the early 1980s were scuttled before they got off the ground.

Bolstering the charges of secret warfare was the government of Thailand, which claimed it was used as a staging area for CIA-military covert training of guerrillas.

In early 1993, Senator John Kerry's select committee on POW/MIA affairs wrapped up its year-long investigation into the fate of American POWs. Their inconclusive conclusion—that they found no evidence of living POWs, but also that they couldn't disprove the theory—was embraced by the debunkers as the final nail in the coffin of the conspiracy theorists.

However, the Senate committee did produce evidence that supported part of what the conspiratologists had been saying all along: that the Reaganites, in their zeal to "roll back" global communism, used the POW/MIA issue as a cover for funding a covert guerrilla war in Laos. What's more, Senate investigators suspected that a private support group of POW families—backed by, yes, Childress and other Reagan officials—had raised private cash for an illegal war in Laos under the guise of funding POW reconnaissance missions.

If Perot and company weren't 100 percent on the mark in their suspicions, at least they were on the right track. Which begs an alternative conspiracy theory, the one favored by lefties who aren't inclined to sentimentalize heartland ideals like nationalism, valor, and the fallen warrior. To wit: *There never were any surviving POWs.* The Reagan-Bush administrations foisted the myth of the "lost boys" on its own constituency, the patriotic right, as a cynical hoax intended to rally cash and cover for yet another secret jungle war.

If you buy this theory, the sources claiming knowledge of live POWs fall into two categories: outright frauds spreading disinformation and deluded but well-intentioned believers. Certainly, there were some troubling super-sources navigating the POW/MIA waters, including Scott Barnes, a self-professed CIA contract agent who claimed to have restaged the aborted Bo Gritz mission. According to Barnes, he and his partner found American POWs in Laos—and were ordered to "liquidate the merchandise," a command they refused. Barnes's partner had been killed as a result of such insubordination, but, as luck would have it, Barnes lived to tell the tale.

A semiomniscent source peddling a number of conspiratorial tales, Barnes has been denounced as a charlatan and self-promoting scam artist. But he has bent the ears of many a POW tracker, including the cabal-sniffing Perot. Which, interestingly, may have helped undo the down-home billionaire's bid for the presidency. For Barnes was the guy who persuaded Perot he was the target of a Republican dirty-tricks campaign, a news flash that sealed Perot's image as a paranoid neurotic convinced that GOP malefactors were out to airbrush lesbians into photographs of his daughter. After Perot's self-destructing performance on *60 Minutes*, voters seemed to decide that maybe he wasn't the guy you'd like to think of as having his finger on "the button." Perot's credibility implosion certainly turned out to be good news for Bush, which makes Barnes a very interesting character indeed. It gives one cause to wonder who benefited from Barnes's hard-to-believe tales of POW double crosses.

Which isn't to say that all evidence on the POW front has been an outright swindle, as the lefties and centrists who disparage the lost boys theory like to claim. When *Kiss the Boys Goodbye* coauthor William Stevenson called on Vietnamese officials to ask about prisoners, they seemed blunt enough. "We had thousands of Americans after the release of 1973," offered the former chief of the secret police. "Until 1985, I knew about groups of Americans in several locations."

Submitted Truong Chinh, at one time the gray eminence behind Ho Chi Minh: "It is possible we shall embarrass the American government some day by sending some back."

It's been said that the discovery of aging American soldiers in Vietnam would prove embarrassing to both countries as they move toward normalizing relations. As the former Vietnamese chief of secret police put it to Stevenson, "It would help nobody today, not us nor the Americans, to let go of captured soldiers now. They're better dead."

Even if the theory of the lost boys is true, more than twenty years have elapsed since the (official) U.S. pullout from the Vietnam War. Even if the government was lying ten years ago when it said there are no living Americans POWs in Southeast Asia, when it says the same thing today it just might be telling the truth.

MAJOR SOURCES

Blumenthal, Sidney. "Perotnoia: The Strange Journey of Ross Perot." *New Republic*, 15 June 1992.

Jensen-Stevenson, Monika, and William Stevenson. *Kiss the Boys Goodbye: How the United States Betrayed Its Own POWs in Vietnam*. New York: Dutton, 1990.

Parfrey, Adam. "Bo Gritz Interrogated." *Flatland*, no. 10, 1993.

"Evidence Hints at Reagan Bid to Aid Laos Rebels." *San Jose Mercury News*, 24 January 1993.

50

The Evil Empire Strikes Back

W hen the Cold War's Reagan phase was in its most fevered stage, a Soviet fighter pilot made a badly timed boo-boo. He uncorked a missile at a Korean Air 747 and sent the plane with its 269 passengers swirling into the icy blackness of the Japan Sea.

The airliner had strayed 365 miles off course and was flying over not only Soviet territory, but some of the USSR's most sensitive military installations. It was the early morning of September 1, 1983.

In the Soviet Union, Yuri Andropov, chief of the feared and loathed KGB, was now premier. Back home, Ronald Reagan's "evil empire" rhetoric still rang fresh in American ears and the MX missile awaited congressional approval. Funding for the new missile system appeared in trouble, but after the KAL shootdown it sailed through as smoothly as an airliner through the calm Asian morning.

Within hours of the tragedy, Reagan, Secretary of State

378

George Shultz, and U.N. Ambassador/anticommunist poster lady Jeanne Kirkpatrick made public presentations defining the U.S. version of the tragedy: In cold blood the Soviets had fired on a civilian craft with no attempt to warn the plane's crew. If right-thinking Americans, at that point, needed further confirmation of the Soviet commies' callous contempt for human life, there it was.

As always occurs when the government manufactures an instant orthodoxy, a dissenting view also took shape. According to this theory, KAL 007 was the Reagan cold war's *Lusitania:* a civilian vessel sent on a provocative military mission—deliberately placed in harm's way and its inevitable destruction justified by the government's own aggressive intentions.

In other words, a provocation.

There was precedent. Seymour Hersh, one of the most honest and penetrating investigative reporters on intelligence and military affairs, details a lengthy history of U.S. sorties into Soviet space for purposes of testing Soviet defenses. As both Hersh and conspiracy proponent R. W. Johnson (an Oxford University Fellow in Politics) report, for a Korean airliner to wander into Soviet space for mysterious reasons was far from unprecedented. One had been shot down five years earlier.

And there was a motive for KAL to participate. Korean Air, whose financial survival depended largely on special favors from the U.S. government regarding routes and landing rights, was always willing to play ball with Uncle Sam. According to torts lawyer Melvin Belli, who represented relatives of some of the passengers, 007's pilot said to his wife shortly before departing, "Never again. This is the last trip. It's too dangerous."

A strange remark for an experienced airline pilot to make about a routine jaunt from Alaska to Seoul (a Korean Air 747 still takes the same route every day, though the flight is no longer numbered 007).

There is no question that the U.S. government conspired, as it were, to publicize a story that made the Soviets look as fiendish as possible—facts be damned. Even if KAL 007 was deliberately off course, nothing justifies shooting down a civilian airliner (though the U.S. government had little problem five years later when an American warship shot down an Iranian airbus, but that's another conspiracy).

But if the United States put KAL 007 over the Soviet Union on purpose, then the Soviet action seems more like lethal incompetence than unmitigated evil. The United States itself must share blame for the violent death of its own citizens.

The only piece of information about the flight and fate of KAL 007 that seems certain is that a Soviet fighter did indeed shoot it down—despite some conspiracy theories that hold that the United States deliberately bombed the plane (Robert Cutler's self-published *Explo-007* argues that hypothesis). More than ten years after the attack, the most important question about flight 007 remains open: Why did the plane wander into the most dangerous area in the militarized atmosphere?

Was it an accident, as argued by Hersh and, several years later, in a *New Yorker* magazine article written by Murray Sayle? Or was the plane, as Johnson believes, on some sinister, secret, and ultimately catastrophic mission?

According to Johnson, KAL-007 was sent at the behest of the Reagan administration-run CIA to trigger Soviet defenses. This would allow the numerous U.S., NATO, and Japanese electronic surveillance posts monitoring the Far East, a patch of the globe dotted with the highest of high-tech electronic intelligence collection stations, to get a good look at the Big Red Machine in action.

Not all the vantage points were Earthbound. A surveillance satellite orbited over the Sea of Japan at the time of the shootdown and—weirdly—the space shuttle Challenger, which two years later met its own untimely end, also flew over the Japan Sea four times during KAL-007's trip.

For some reason, the Challenger's cargo, a 3.5-ton satellite, had been replaced at the last minute with a "dummy satellite" of the same considerable bulk. Johnson has no evidence about the "dummy," but he suggests that it was in fact some kind of military monitoring device.

The CIA behaved strangely after it heard about the downing. Already knowing that the plane was in Davy Jones's locker, the agency put out the story to relatives of the dead passengers that the flight had landed safely on the Soviet-held island of Sakhalin.

The most persuasive counterpoint to the provocation theory (it should be noted that Johnson was merely the most articulate and credible proponent of that theory; its popularity was wide, helped along by some rather shameless Soviet propaganda) came after the end of the Cold War with the former Soviet intelligence and military agencies suddenly displaying a refreshing candor.

In an attempt to lay the conspiracy theory to a final rest, Murray Sayle presented the "error" case in his December 13, 1993 *New Yorker* piece cover-tagged, "A Cold War Case Closed." Unlike Johnson and Hersh he wrote with the benefit of access to Soviet information.

According to Sayle's piece, the Soviets recovered the plane's "black box" flight recorder (which was actually, Sayle seems pleased to point out, bright orange). The Soviets had always denied finding the recorder, but in the light of Boris Yeltsin's new dawn, the recordings found their way into the public domain.

Of course, no one would claim that Yeltsin is above a little trickery, but Sayle did not investigate the authenticity of the tapes.

"The voices can only be the real thing," he announces, as if pounding a gavel. He pursues the possibility of forgery no further.

That caveat dismissed, Sayle reports that the tapes reveal a sleepy, inattentive flight crew mumbling about the dinner menu and the pros and cons of exchanging currency at the airport. Not the stuff of Frederick Forsyth novels.

But no mild-mannered *New Yorker* reporter is qualified to interpret the contents of a flight recorder, so Sayle's "case closed" relies primarily on the conclusions of a French investigating unit working for the International Civil Aviation Organization (ICAO).

The ICAO team decided that the whole tragic problem stemmed from the captain's failure to engage the plane's inertial navigation system (INS), drowsily permitting the 747's "suicidally unreliable" magnetic compass to guide the plane.

That error is not unknown even to experienced pilots. But it is quite uncommon, despite Sayle's misleadingly phrased assertion that of "more than a hundred airline navigation errors involving the INS between September of 1978 and May of 1983" almost twelve percent were due to letting the compass rather than the INS itself guide the aircraft.

In other words, in a five-year period during which there were hundreds of thousands of commercial airline flights, the error apparently committed by the KAL 007 crew occurred approximately twelve times.

In his book *Shootdown*, Johnson dealt with the "drowsiness" issue long before the black-box tapes became available. He contends that the crew would have had to miss more than one blinking light to allow the plane to wander more than three hundred miles off course.

The pilots must have been feeling admirably casual given their flight path through perhaps the world's most heavily surveilled region. To allow their mistake to go uncorrected, they had to disregard their craft's ground-mapping radar, which would have revealed that the plane was flying over solid land, not sea as laid out in the flight plan.

The airliner, according to Johnson, made a sharp turn as Soviet fighters approached, presumably caused by the coincidental impulse of this highly improvisational flight crew to reprogram its computer at that moment.

If they knew they were in danger the flight crew would have reported this fact to its ground controllers. It didn't. Not then, or even after it was hit and began swirling downward toward the water.

Not only did the pilot never say "Whoops!" he didn't even say "Uh, oh."

Johnson also notes one last piece of bizarre evidence: a fuzzy tape analyzed as the voice of KAL's first officer talking to Tokyo in the last seconds of KAL 007's existence.

The contents of the tape are barely intelligible and still uncertain, but some analysts think they hear the officer asking not for an air traffic controller but for a "director," as in "mission director." Only a military or intelligence flight requires a "director." The voice on the tape also refers to "bogies," a military term for enemy aircraft.

But scariest of all are the last words on the tape, according to analysts, recorded thirty-eight seconds after missile impact and delivered by the first officer, or Johnson suggests, someone in a nearby plane observing the confrontation, with unnerving calm.

"Gonna be a bloodbath," the level voice says. "You bet."

MAJOR SOURCES

Hersh, Seymour. *The Target Is Destroyed*. New York: Random House, 1986.

Johnson, R. W. *Shootdown*. New York: Viking Penguin, 1987.

51

Pan Am Flight 103

Four days before Christmas 1988, a Pan Am 747 was ripped from the sky by a powerful wad of plastic explosives. Perhaps it was happenstance that five CIA agents were among the 259 human beings who died in the crash. Perhaps it meant nothing that another squad of CIA agents showed up in Lockerbie, Scotland, a few hours after the aircraft splattered the country village with gruesome debris.

That the CIA agents on the crash scene, some posing as Pan Am employees, walked away with a mysterious briefcase seems somewhat more significant. It belonged to one of their downed men. By confiscating the case, they interrupted the sacrosanct "chain of evidence," imperiling prospective prosecutions. The half-million dollars found by two Scottish farmboys seems noteworthy as well. Detectives surmised that the cash also belonged to the deceased CIA team.

The ill-fated spies had traveled from Beirut. Their mission, investigators believe, was to locate American hostages held there by Islamic fundamentalist kidnappers. Pan Am flight 103, had it followed the bombers' schedule, would have exploded over the Atlantic ocean, but the bomb went off too soon. Wreckage, bodies, and passengers' personal effects all landed on the ground and meticulous Scottish investigators recovered everything except the briefcase. Among the fallout were two cryptic documents, both property of the CIA.

One was an intricate drawing of the interior of a Beirut building. Two crosses marked the map. The CIA agents had located two hostages. They may have intended to negotiate for the hostages' release, using the $500,000 to purchase information. Or, it is possible, the team headed by Charles McKee, an army major, was doing advance work for a rescue raid.

The other document was a Christmas card with a message either in intelligence cant or some kind of code. Investigators deduced the meaning of the message. It was addressed to one of the CIA agents and said that whatever they were planning would happen on March 11, 1989.

The bomb cost not only 270 lives (including the eleven Lockerbie dwellers who perished on the ground), but may have cost at least some of the hostages their immediate freedom. It undoubtedly impeded U.S. intelligence efforts in the Middle East. Recall that earlier, Beirut CIA station chief William Buckley had been grabbed, sent to Iran, and tortured to death in interrogation. Iran was the first suspect in the bombing of 103.

The CIA presence was publicly reported, though not widely known. A March 1990 *New York Times Magazine* excerpt from the book *The Fall of Pan Am 103* failed to mention the CIA officers, though the book itself goes into detail about who they were and why they were there. The *Times* version blamed the disaster on "bungling" German police.

Most media reports on the Pan Am 103 bombing endorsed the stereotype of irrational terrorists motivated by revenge. That there may have been a strategic and, by the warped logic of clandestine warfare, "rational" reason to bomb the plane—beyond retaliation for the shootdown of an Iranian airbus or the bombing of Tripoli (depending on who's getting blamed that day, the Iranians or the Libyans)—is not generally discussed. Admitting a motive (other than inscrutable fanaticism) for such a monstrous crime implies that the target of the crime, the United States, was involved in skullduggery of its own.

Far more incendiary were the conclusions of a private investigator, self-described former Israeli intelligence agent Juval Aviv. His New York firm, Interfor, conducted an investigation for Pan Am's insurance company. The Interfor report contains the grimmest conspiracy allegations in the Lockerbie case.

For two years the Interfor report circulated hand to hand in fax/Xerox form on the conspiracy circuit. The report went largely ignored by major news organizations. Then *Time* magazine suddenly discovered it and set off a bitter and highly personal internecine journalistic confrontation—all ignited by the following tale of intrigue, as told by Interfor:

A separate CIA team, stationed in Frankfurt and referred to as CIA-1 by Interfor, was also trying to free the hostages, Aviv reported. Because CIA-1 was an unauthorized "off the shelf" covert operation controlled from Washington, not from CIA headquarters in Langley, Virginia, it was at cross-purposes with the McKee team. The unnamed operatives hooked up with Monzar Al-Kassar, a Syrian arms and drug merchant, brother-in-law to Syria's intelligence chief (Syrian intelligence is a major terrorism sponsor) and paramour of Syrian fascist despot Hafez Al-Assad's niece. Not surprisingly, Al-Kassar was also deeply into terrorism, the politically correct thing to do for Syrian arms runners.

Al-Kassar, according to Interfor, assisted the French government in freeing French hostages. If he'd do the same for them, CIA-1 offered Al-Kassar, they'd protect his drug-smuggling route, which they had had under surveillance for some time.

"Al-Kassar agreed to the deal," says Aviv's report, "but continued his terrorism activities and told his cohorts that their smuggling through Pan Am/Frankfurt at least was now protected and safe to the U.S."

At the same time, Al-Kassar, who'd once been hired by Iran-

Contra conspirators Richard Secord and Albert Hakim to ship weapons to the Nicaraguan Contras, helped the Frankfurt-based CIA group by shipping weapons to Iran. The Americans hoped, once again tragicomically, to trade arms for hostages. According to Interfor, the drug-and-gun runner kept arms flowing to the Contras as well. In an effort to keep his American patrons happy, he even financed some of the Contra shipments with his own drug profits. "CIA-1 gave Al-Kassar a free hand," wrote Aviv.

Because CIA-1 was an unofficial operation run out of Washington, dealing arms for hostages and striking bargains with drug smugglers, comparisons to the Iran-Contra "enterprise" managed by Oliver North are inevitable. CIA-1 operated in 1988, when North was long since fired and CIA Director William Casey, the father of Iran-Contra, was dead from a brain tumor. Neither, then, could have been CIA-1's "control."

So who was? Much of Iran-Contra was coordinated, it now appears, from Vice President George Bush's office. Could former CIA chief Bush or his underlings be the "control" for CIA-1? Interfor doesn't touch that subject.

While CIA-1 was messing around with terrorists and heroin merchants, the official CIA and the State Department, blissfully unaware of its off-the-shelf counterpart's activities, sent the McKee team to Beirut. According to Aviv, their mission was, in fact, reconnaissance for a rescue mission. They found and photographed buildings where the hostages were incarcerated.

"After some time, the special team (McKee) learned of Al-Kassar and started investigating him," Aviv reported. "They also realized some CIA unit was protecting his drug smuggling into the U.S. via Frankfurt airport.... They had reported back to Langley the facts and names, and reported their film of the hostage locations. CIA did nothing. No reply."

While under surveillance, Al-Kassar and his associates in Syrian intelligence were surveilling the McKee team right back. When McKee and his cohorts became "frustrated and angry and made plans to return to the U.S.," Al-Kassar was watching.

He knew that the agents booked themselves a connecting flight in London: Pan Am flight 103, originating in Frankfurt. A week before that plane went down, Al-Kassar told CIA-1 of his problem, ratting out the McKee team, travel schedule and all.

All during this period, for political reasons of their own, Al-Kassar's terrorist overlords were plotting to bomb an American plane. They'd originally selected American Airlines as the victim. The target soon changed.

Warnings flowed in from every direction. German intelligence, the Mossad, and CIA-1 got word of a bomb attack in the making. No one did anything about it. The McKee team was in the dark and way out in the cold. Al-Kassar's associates slipped a compact "Semtex" device onto Pan Am 103, under cover of Al-Kassar's CIA-secured drug route. A German agent assigned to watch the route noticed that the drug suitcase was of a different make than usual. This agent heard the warnings. He knew right away that he wasn't eyeing dope, but a bomb.

The agent alerted CIA-1 to the bomb. CIA-1 called its Washington control. Control's reply: "Don't worry about it, don't stop it, let it go."

After its stopover in London, where it picked up a group of Syracuse University students returning home from a semester abroad, various American tourists, and the five CIA agents who knew where the hostages were held, the 747, nicknamed Maid of the Seas, exploded in mid-air.

The Interfor report first surfaced courtesy of James Traficant, an eccentric Ohio congressman with a populist's nose for conspiracies. He reportedly got it from Victor Marchetti, former aide to longtime CIA director Richard Helms. Marchetti, though his whistleblowing book *The CIA and the Cult of Intelligence* is now a classic, works for the ultra-right-wing Liberty Lobby these days and therefore has credibility problems.

Maybe, then, the Interfor report received scant publicity due to the questionable leanings of its leakers. More likely, the scandalous nature of its allegations are to blame. Much of the report gibes with public reality: the ignored warnings, for instance, and the botched raid by German police on a bomb-making enclave in October 1988. If properly carried out, that raid might have preempted the bombing.

The CIA-complicity charges erupted in April 1992. *Time* ran a rather lurid cover story, "Why Did They Die?" which conflated the Interfor allegations with additional details apparently from a dubious source named Lester Coleman. The story had a number of faults. The most glaring was its misidentification of a Christian Broadcasting Network cameraman (with photo!) as the traitorous CIA agent who sold out the McKee team.

Predictably, the story drew a torrent of attacks, particularly from Christopher Byron who wrote two major debunking pieces for *New York* magazine and from CNN correspondent Steven Emerson (in the *Washington Journalism Review*), co-author of his own book on Pan Am 103.

In his book, *The Fall of Pan Am 103*, Emerson dismisses the Interfor report as a "spitball," a hodgepodge of fact and unfounded speculation worthless as intelligence. The report had been echoed briefly on network news long before the *Time* story. On the day before Halloween 1990, NBC News reported that terrorists had infiltrated a Drug Enforcement Administration undercover operation to plant the Pan Am 103 bomb. Substitute *CIA* for *DEA* and the story mirrored the Interfor account. (Interfor did note that CIA-1 was working with the DEA.) The story was picked up by major dailies, including the *New York Times*, then quickly "investigated" and denied by the DEA.

In his attack on the *Time* piece—which followed Byron's closely—Emerson charged that *Time* "ignored evidence that contradicted its story." Both Emerson and Byron found some sizable holes in the *Time* story—though both spent an inordinate amount of ink on ad hominem attacks against Aviv and Coleman. They also made much of the fact that *Time*'s story appeared one week before a lawsuit against Pan Am was scheduled to go to trial.

Part of the problem was that *Time*'s story—perhaps thanks to the overzealous "hoaxster" Coleman—fleshed out the Interfor report with some questionable assertions that its critics were quick to seize upon.

Conspicuous by its absence from both Byron's and Emerson's articles was any mention of Monzar Al-Kassar. The omission was especially glaring because a key point of both attacks was the supposed mystery of how the bombers knew which flight the McKee team would take. According to the Interfor report, the information came from Al-Kassar.

Right about the time when Bush was recruiting Syria into the "allied coalition" against Iraq, the CIA shifted blame for the bombing from Syria to Libya, obviating more than two years of work by a multitude of investigators, from the Scottish police to ABC News, all of whom pointed to Ahmed Jibril and his patrons, Syria and Iran. Absolving Syria, of course, negates the Interfor scenario.

Late in 1991, the U.S. government indicted two Libyan intelligence agents for the bombing, and briefly, newspapers brimmed with bluster about the dire consequences to Libya if the pair weren't handed over. The legal tussle had not been resolved as of early 1994.

On the fifth anniversary of the bombing, in December 1993, the BBC aired a documentary, *Silence over Lockerbie*. The BBC debunked the CIA's Libya-damning evidence and, while not ruling out Libyan involvment, the documentary shifted blame back to the original suspects, Syria and Iran.

There are other conspiratorial tales to explain the mass murder aboard Pan Am flight 103. One, which briefly surfaced in the Italian press, puts the infamous, neofascist, quasi-Masonic P2 Lodge at the center of the conspiracy. But none are as detailed and internally consistent as the Interfor report. That doesn't mean Aviv got it right. It means only that the real story lies buried somewhere in the graveyard of geopolitics.

MAJOR SOURCES

Emerson, Steven, and Brian Duffy. *The Fall of Pan Am 103*. New York: Putnam, 1990.

Johnston, David. *Lockerbie: The Tragedy of Flight 103*. New York: St. Martin's Press, 1989.

Pan American Insurance Investigator's Report (copy in authors' possession).

52

The Jonestown Massacre

On November 18, 1978, in a cleared-out patch of Guyanese jungle, the Reverend Jim Jones ordered the 913 members of his flock to kill themselves by drinking a cyanide potion, and they did.

The cultists were brainwashed by the megalomaniac Jones, who had named their jungle village after himself and held them as virtual slaves, if not living zombies. Jones himself was found dead. He'd shot himself in the head, or someone else had shot him. Square-jaw, jet black hair and sunglasses, looking like a secret service agent on antipsychotic drugs, Jones takes his place alongside Charles Manson in America's iconography of evil.

But was Jones really a lone madman as Americans are so often advised about their villains? Is it plausible that more than nine hundred people took their own lives willingly, simply because he told them to? Or is there another explanation?

Not long after the slaughter in Jonestown, whispers began, strange hints of human experiments in mind control, even genocide, and the lurking presence of the CIA. At the very least, these stories maintained, the U.S. government could have prevented the Jonestown massacre, but instead it did nothing.

At worst, Jonestown was a CIA-run concentration camp set up as a dry run for the secret government's attempt to reprogram the American psyche. There are suggestions of parallel "Jonestowns" and that the conspiracy did not end with the deaths in Guyana.

Jim Jones was born May 13, 1931, son of a Ku Klux Klansman in Lynn, Indiana. His mother, he claimed, was a Cherokee Indian. That has never been verified.

An unsupervised child, Jones became fascinated by church work at an early age. By 1963 he had his own congregation in Indianapolis: The People's Temple Full Gospel Church. It was an interracial congregation, something then unheard of in Indiana. Young Jim Jones crusaded tirelessly on behalf of blacks. He also suffered from mysterious fainting spells, heeded advice from extraterrestrials, practiced faith healing, and experienced visions of nuclear holocaust.

Certain that Armageddon was imminent, that Indianapolis itself was to be the target of attack, Jones sought guidance. He found it in the January 1962 issue of *Esquire* magazine. An article in the occasionally ironic men's mag named the nine safest places in the world to get away from the stresses and anxieties of nuclear confrontation. One of those retreats was Brazil. Intimations of Jones's link to the CIA begin all the way back there.

According to an article in the *San Jose Mercury News*, Jones's neighbors in Belo Horizonte, Brazil (where he lived before moving to Rio De Janeiro), remembered his claim to be a retired navy man who "received a monthly payment from the U.S. government." They also remembered that Jones—who later claimed that he was forced to sell his services as a gigolo to support his family—"lived like a rich man."

"Some people here believed he was an agent for the American CIA," one neighbor reported.

Neighbors' recollections notwithstanding, Jones's biographer Tim Reiterman says that the Jones family "lived simply" in

Brazil, subsisting on rice and beans. When he returned to the United States, shortly after President John F. Kennedy was assassinated, Jones told his followers that he had spent his time in Brazil helping orphans. Eventually, he moved his church to Ukiah, California, then to San Francisco, where it became a fundraising force courted by local politicians.

Before Jones arrived in Brazil, he'd stopped in Georgetown, Guyana. Though his stop there was a quick one, he managed to garner some ink in the local media by publicly charging churches with spreading communism. According to Reiterman, it appeared a calculated attempt to "put himself on the record as an anticommunist."

Fifteen years later, he would tantalize his Jonestown flock with promises to move the People's Temple from Guyana to the Soviet Union. In a 1979 book, one former Jones devotee, Phil Kerns (whose mother and sister died at Jonestown), raises the possibility of a Soviet conspiracy behind Jonestown.

"Jones was a Marxist," Kerns wrote, "who had numerous contacts with officials of both the Cuban and Soviet governments." Among other suspicious facts, Kerns notes that shortly before the massacre two People's Temple members spirited $500,000 out of the cult's colony to the Soviet embassy.

Jones's deputies did meet frequently with Soviet officials—so frequently, in fact, that they became a running joke in Guyana's diplomatic circles. Jones told his followers that the CIA had "infiltrated" Jonestown.

Later, as we'll see, others raised the possibility that Jonestown *was* the CIA.

The temple's dalliance with the Soviets, however, is a wholly plausible point of contact between the cult and the Agency. Reiterman, a skeptic of the conspiracy theory, points out that "the CIA's presence in socialist Guyana...could be assumed." They certainly would have taken an interest in the temple's Soviet contacts.

Why exactly was Jones interested in the Soviets? He must have known that his professed dream of moving the temple to the U.S.S.R. was only that, a dream. He dropped it quickly in favor of mass suicide (a follower asked Jones, shortly before the suicides, if it weren't possible to forget the whole thing and escape to Russia; Jones said it wasn't). If the CIA had infiltrated the temple, or if the temple was, even in part, a CIA operation, then members' sojourns to the Soviet embassy would have had a more pragmatic purpose.

The CIA was first with news out of Jonestown, reporting the mass suicides. The suicides followed an attack, ordered by Jones, on a party led by Congressman Leo Ryan, in Guyana to investigate alleged human rights abuses at Jonestown. The gunmen struck at Port Kaituma airfield, as the Ryan party was preparing to depart. Ryan was assassinated in the attack. Four others died as well. Several more were shot, including Reiterman, then a reporter for the *San Francisco Examiner*. Among the wounded was U.S. embassy official Richard Dwyer.

Wounded, but ambulatory.

Did Dwyer stroll back to Jonestown after the airstrip assault? Was he there during the massacre? Reportedly, at one point on a tape recorded as the killings began, Jones's own voice commands, "Get Dwyer out of here!" Reiterman assumes that this was a "mistake" on Jones's part, that Dwyer was not actually there. If he was, however, the implications are chilling.

Dwyer was an agent of the CIA.

For his part, Dwyer neither confirms nor denies that he was a CIA agent, but he was identified in the 1968 edition of *Who's Who in the CIA*. A month after the massacre the *San Mateo Times*, a Bay Area newspaper (hometown paper of Leo Ryan), reported that "State Department officials acknowledge that a CIA agent was dispatched to Jonestown within minutes of the airstrip assault." Dwyer denied to the *Times* that he was there at the time. According to one report, Dwyer's next stop after Guyana was Grenada.

Nor was Dwyer necessarily the only intelligence-connected character in Guyana. The U.S. ambassador himself, John Burke, later went to work for the "intelligence community staff" of the

CIA. Richard McCoy, another embassy official, has acknowledged his counterintelligence work for the U.S. Air Force. The socialist government of Guyana had piqued the interest of U.S. intelligence for years. If there were covert operations going on there, no one should be surprised.

Leo Ryan's aide Joseph Holsinger feared that the CIA might have been running a covert operation there so sinister it would shock even hardened CIA-watchdogs. In 1980 Holsinger, who'd already discovered Dwyer's presence at Jonestown, received a paper from a professor at U.C. Berkeley. Called "The Penal Colony," the paper detailed how the CIA's mind-control program, code-named MK-ULTRA, was not stopped in 1973, as the CIA had told Congress. Instead, the paper reported, it had merely been transferred out of public hospitals and prisons into the more secure confines of religious cults.

Jonestown, Holsinger believed, was one of those cults.

There were large amounts of psychoactive, i.e., mind-control, drugs found on the site of the suicides. Larry Layton, the Jones lieutenant who became the only person charged in any of the killings (he was in the airstrip hit team, and somehow survived the Jonestown massacre), was described as sinking into a "posthypnotic trance" as he sunk ever deeper under Jones's spell. Layton's own father called him "a robot."

Layton's brother-in-law, the man who arranged the lease on Jonestown with the Guyanese government for Jones, was reportedly a mercenary for the CIA-backed UNITA rebels in Angola. Layton's father, according to Holsinger, was the biochemist in charge of chemical warfare for the U.S. Army at its Dugway Proving Ground in Utah.

Jones himself, the supposed Soviet sympathizer, was once a fundraiser for Richard Nixon, around the same time Jones declared himself the reincarnation of both Jesus and Lenin.

Then there was the problem of the bodies. The Jonestown body count jumped by about four hundred within two days after the suicides, leading to speculation that escapees may have been hunted down and killed. In any case, Guyanese coroner

Leslie Mootoo testified that as many as seven hundred of the dead appeared to have been forcibly killed, not "suicides" at all.

"I believe that it is possible that Jonestown may have been a mind-control experiment," Holsinger said in a 1980 lecture, "that Leo Ryan's congressional visit pierced that veil and would have resulted in its exposure, and that our government, or its agent the CIA, deemed it necessary to wipe out over nine hundred American citizens to protect the secrecy of the operation."

The "operation," if there was one, may have continued after the suicides. There have been attempts to repopulate Jonestown with Dominican and Indochinese refugees, backed by the Billy Graham organization. There was a Jonestown doppelgänger in Guyana even while Jones was still in business. Self-styled "Rabbi" David Hill, with his eight thousand-member Nation of Israel cult, was powerful enough to earn the nickname "vice prime minister" in his travels through the country.

One final, weird note: A memo that allegedly passed between Jones and People's Temple lawyer Mark Lane (who escaped the massacre) showed the two pondering the relocation of Grace Walden to Jonestown. Walden was a key witness to the assassination of Martin Luther King, Jr. Lane represented King's accused assassin, James Earl Ray. When the memo turned up, Lane denied that he had discussed moving Walden. (He claims that the memo was part of an "army intelligence coverup" of the King assassination, ostensibly an attempt to discredit him and, through him, Walden.) Most of the People's Temple rank-and-file were black. Most of the leadership was white. Joyce Shaw, a former member, once mused that the mass suicide story was a coverup for "some kind of horrible government experiments, or some sort of sick, racist thing...a plan like the German's to exterminate blacks."

In 1980, the House Permanent Select Committee on Intelligence announced that there was "no evidence" of CIA involvement at Jonestown.

MAJOR SOURCES

Kerns, Phil. *People's Temple, People's Tomb*. Plainfield, NJ: Logos International, 1979.

Kilduff, Marshall, and Ron Javers. *The Suicide Cult*. New York: Bantam Books, 1978.

Krause, Charles. *Guyana Massacre: The Eyewitness Account*. New York: Berkley Books, 1978.

Moore, Rebecca. *A Sympathetic History of Jonestown*. Lewiston, NY: Edwin Mellon Press, 1985.

Reiterman, Tim. *Raven: The Untold Story of the Reverend Jim Jones and His People*. New York: E. P. Dutton, 1982.

This chapter owes a debt to research assembled by John Judge.

53

AIDS: The Pentagon's Plague?

Dr. Donald MacArthur, a high-level defense department biological research administrator, showed up at a June 9, 1969, meeting of a House subcommittee on military appropriations begging for cash to carry out an unsavory endeavor.

"Within five to ten years," he prognosticated, "it would probably be possible to make a new infective microorganism which would differ in certain important aspects from any known disease-causing organisms. Most important of these," he continued—and this is the ominous part, "is that it might be refractory to the immunological and therapeutic processes upon which we depend to maintain our relative freedom from infectious disease."

This new germ, the one Dr. MacArthur desired so sincerely to whip up in his lab, would destroy the immune system. The good doc proffered the most hackneyed of Cold War rationales for this odious ambition.

"Should an enemy develop it there is little doubt that this is an important area of potential military technological inferiority in which there is no adequate research program."

He got his coveted taxpayer funding. In 1977 and 1978, at the tail end of Dr. MacArthur's time frame, the first cases of Acquired Immune Deficiency Syndrome (AIDS) emerged in Africa.

As smoking guns, or smoking petri dishes, go, the MacArthur transcript leaves something to be desired. But the coincidence is undeniably provocative. Is AIDS the ultimate in biological warfare? This is a case with so many conundrums that the JFK assassination seems like a District Court drunk-driving rap by comparison.

U.S. representative Theodore Weiss—a New York congressman with a large gay constituency—speculated in 1983 that "as far fetched as it may seem, given the attitudes toward homosexuals and homosexuality by some segments of society, the possible utilization of biological weapons must be seriously considered."

The demographics of AIDS also encourage the biowarfare notion. Though no one is immune, several groups have been especially hard hit: gays, Africans, drug users. Could those groups have been deliberately targeted in some Pentagon-operated biotech chamber?

Support for this biowarfare thesis is scanty at best. But then the same holds true for the "official" explanation of how AIDS entered the human population—that green monkeys spread it, somehow—which rests on a rather flimsy foundation itself.

The generally accepted cause of AIDS is a virus labeled HIV (Human Immunodeficiency Virus) "discovered" in 1984 by Dr. Robert Gallo and, more or less simultaneously, by a team of French scientists (the French doctors charge, apparently with some justification, that Gallo ripped off their research—but that's a conspiracy for another book). From what corner of the ecosystem the virus arose remains an open question.

Gallo et al. note the similarity between a simian-borne virus (STLV-III) and HIV. They muse that at some point the *Cer-*

copithecus aethiops carrying this virus transmitted it to an African human being. Within a few years thousands of people dropped dead from having sex and from blood transfusions.

It is barely worth scrolling down the litany of assumptions required to support this untested bit of fabulism (not the least of which is the massive and presumably instantaneous mutation of the simian virus). 'Nuff said that the green monkey scenario is at best an educated guess.

There are some gaping improbabilities in the AIDS-biowarfare mise-en-scène as well. Perhaps AIDS is indeed a biological bomb aimed to eradicate the world's useless eaters. The military and its politico-industrial cronies have certainly pulled some nasty stunts in their time. But who in their right mind would unleash a highly insidious, unstoppably lethal pathogen into the same population that includes oneself and one's All-American family?

A brief history of the U.S. biological warfare program appears elsewhere in this volume (see page 40). It includes on-the-record instances of military assaults on U.S. cities, unleashing various germs and toxins, though none as deadly as HIV (by a long shot). Nonetheless, there are some noteworthy examples of verifiable ruthlessness. Take the fiendish Tuskegee Syphilis Study. The U.S. Public Health Service ran the study on four hundred syphilitic black men, denying them not only treatment for their ailment but any information that they had the disease at all. This proceeded for forty years.

Then there was the 1931 Puerto Rico cancer experiment; self explanatory. A number of Puerto Ricans were deliberately infected with cancer by the Rockefeller Institute and thirteen died. Chief pathologist Cornelius Rhoades's justification?

"The Porto [sic] Ricans are the dirtiest, laziest, most degenerate and thievish race of men ever inhabiting this sphere....I have done my best to further the process of extermination by killing off eight and transplanting cancer into several more....All physicians take delight in the abuse and torture of the unfortunate subjects."

TRAGEDY AND TRAUMA

None too politically correct, that Dr. Rhoades. No one prosecuted him, though. They brushed him off as "mentally ill." The U.S. government must have disagreed. It placed Rhoades in charge of two large chemical warfare projects during the 1940s, granted him a seat on the Atomic Energy Commission, and pinned him with the Legion of Merit.

Though biowarfare research was legislatively banned in 1972, the Pentagon's "Department of Loopholes" took immediate action and research pressed on. One of the germs that intrigues military researchers is the *canis* strain of *brucella*. Symptoms of this disease include headaches and fevers, malaise, muscle aches, pharyngitis, and lymphadenopathy—the same roster seen in AIDS-Related Complex, the precursor to full-blown AIDS.

The first published charge of an AIDS-biowarfare connection came in the *Patriot*, a newspaper in New Delhi. The July 4, 1984, report cited articles from an official U.S. Army research publication about "natural and artificial influences on the human immune system."

The Indian paper reported that scientists from Fort Detrick— home of the National Cancer Institute's Frederick Cancer Research Facility but until 1969 known as the Army Biological Warfare Laboratory—ventured into darkest Africa in search of "a powerful virus that could not be found in Europe or Asia." The data from this excursion "was then analyzed at Fort Detrick and the result was the isolation of a virus that causes AIDS."

The U.S. government immediately labeled the article Soviet disinformation, a case not harmed by the subsequent relentless coverage given the story in Soviet media. A *Pravda* editorial cartoon showing a doctor standing on a pile of corpses, and handing a general a vial marked *AIDS virus* did draw a whine of protest from the U.S. embassy. But it wasn't until a major British newspaper splashed the story all over its tabloid pages that American authorities began to react, their objections echoed slavishly by the ever-enterprising U.S. media.

Next came the 1986 pamphlet *AIDS: USA Home-Made Evil* by two French-born East German scientists, Jakob and Lilli Segal. The pamphlet, with no listed publisher, floated freely throughout the English-speaking regions of Africa. Not an orthodox means of scientific publication, but the Segals' arguments formed the basis for much of the subsequent discussion, such as it was, of the AIDS-biowarfare theory.

HIV, the enigmatic Segals enigmatically claimed, is a genetically engineered hybrid of the visan virus (cause of a sheep-borne brain disease) and a virus called HTLV-I (HIV was originally named HTLV-III), which causes white blood cell cancer.

The Segals, too, fingered Fort Detrick as the lab that invented the virus. There has never been any hard evidence that HIV was synthesized at Fort Detrick—or anywhere else—but it can't hurt to inquire why the National Institutes of Health asked the army researchers at Fort Detrick, not the "civilians" there, to help develop a cure for AIDS.

In February of 1987 army colonel David Huxsoll, taken by a scoffing fit while discussing the AIDS-biowarfare charges, blabbed an intriguing bit of information.

"Studies at army laboratories have shown that the AIDS virus would be an extremely poor biological warfare agent," quoth the colonel.

What studies? Pentagon PR tells us that the military wants to put an end to AIDS in our lifetimes, not an end to our lifetimes. Huxsoll later denied making the statement. The reporter who wrote it down stands by the story.

The first American AIDS outbreaks—then confined almost exclusively to the gay male population—coincided with the onset of Reaganism and its attendant bitter backlash against gays. The biowarfare theory assumes that gays were singled out for destruction, or, at the very least, for scapegoating. But how?

In 1978 more than a thousand nonmonogamous homosexual adult males received experimental vaccinations against hepatitis B, courtesy of the National Institutes of Health and the Centers for Disease Control. Within six years 64 percent of those men had AIDS.

Coincidence is of course possible, even likely in this case. Under the conventional view of AIDS-transmission, non-monogamous homosexual adult males are prone to the disease anyway.

There was another vaccination program, for smallpox this time, in Africa. The World Health Organization ran the show. The regions where W.H.O. administered its program later became the most AIDS-wrecked in Africa. Again, however, the notion that this could be a coincidence is quite plausible, though among adherents of the AIDS-conspiracy theory the smallpox program stirs considerable alarm. But it's hard to knock the W.H.O.'s largely successful attempt to eradicate smallpox—a far worse killer than AIDS.

There are variations on the AIDS-biowarfare theme: Some rest on the argument that HIV, on its own, does not cause AIDS. Dioxins (used by the military in Vietnam) and dengue virus (used by the CIA in Cuba) have found mention as possible culprits, as has a mutated form of syphilis. Any of these would be simpler than a synthesized virus to administer as a weapon.

There's only one certainty: The epidemiology of AIDS is one case where neither the official nor the conspiratorial explanations comes off as particularly satisfying.

MAJOR SOURCES

Krupey, G. J. "AIDS: Act of God or the Pentagon?" *Steamshovel Press* no. 4 (Spring 1992).

Lederer, Robert. "Chemical-Biological Warfare, Medical Experiments and Population Control." *Covert Action Information Bulletin*, no. 28 (Summer 1987).

Lehrman, Nathaniel S. "Is AIDS Non-Infectious? The Possibility and Its CBW Implications." *Covert Action Information Bulletin*, no. 28 (Summer 1987).

Rappoport, Jon. *AIDS Inc.: Scandal of the Century*. Foster City, Calif.: Human Energy Press, 1988.

54

Bombshells in Oklahoma City

More than any other event in recent years, the terrorist bombing of the Alfred P. Murrah federal building in Oklahoma City has galvanized the paranoid psyche. Suspicious minds on the right—the "Patriot" or "militia movement," as the media has dubbed them—view the event as a heinous act of government perfidy, a terror trick used to justify a crackdown on American civil liberties or, worse, the opening salvo in a Washington-sanctioned invasion of America from abroad. Meanwhile, paranoids in government and in the media and among leftist watchdog groups that find themselves increasingly adrift in the ideological murk of the post–Cold War era, have imposed their own political semaphore on the same event. In their view, the Oklahoma bombing represents an act of terror perpetrated by zealots of the nativist right wing—a rising menace composed of those dangerously nutty militias and racist hate groups.

Somewhere amid all the feverish speculation emanating from

both polar extremes lie the facts, which suggest that neither view of the terror attack in Oklahoma City is dealing with reality on a first-name basis. In fact, as presented in the popular press, the government case against a handful of Patriot extremists (which, at this writing, has yet to go to trial) makes as little sense as the convoluted conspiracy theories traded on the Internet and talk radio.

In the cloud of suspicion hanging over the site of the former Murrah building we have a genuine mystery.

This much about the bombing is undisputed: At 9:02 A.M. on April 19, 1995, a massive explosion literally ripped the north face off the federal building in downtown Oklahoma City. As the smoke, dust, and debris settled, the devastating magnitude of the blast immediately became evident: One third of the building had collapsed, and the bomb (or bombs) had left behind a crater thirty feet wide and eight feet deep. As the days passed and rescue crews probed through the detritus, the body count would rise to 169 people, including 19 children who had been attending a day-care center for federal employees on the second floor. Among the government agencies located in the Murrah building were the Bureau of Alcohol, Tobacco and Firearms (ATF), the FBI, the Drug Enforcement Administration (DEA), the Defense Investigative Service, the Social Security Administration, and the U.S. Army and Marines recruiting offices.

Federal investigators hastily announced that the explosive had been an ammonium nitrate and fuel oil bomb, the same type of home-brewed "fertilizer" explosive as used in the 1993 bombing of the World Trade Center by Middle Eastern terrorists. The FBI initially estimated that the bomb had weighed 1,000 to 2,000 pounds, the payload probably packed in a car; however, in an effort to account for the bomb's massive destructive force, authorities soon upgraded their estimates to hypothesize a 4,800-pound bomb, most likely delivered via a truck. The fertilizer–fuel oil mixture, composed of commercially available materials, had been packed in twenty blue plastic barrels. Officials described the method of detonation as a hand-lit safety fuse. Several eyewitnesses on the scene just before the explosion reported seeing a yellow Ryder truck approach the front entrance of the building, halting in a no-parking zone. They described two men in blue jogging suits exiting the truck and getting into a car. There may have been a third person driving the car. A woman driving on Northwest Fifth Street near the Murrah building reported that she nearly ran into a man, later identified by authorities as a suspect in the bombing, who was walking away from the building. Another witness claimed to have seen two men peeling away from the scene of the crime in a yellow Mercury.

Sifting through the debris, law enforcement officials soon announced that they had discovered a truck axle, which contained a vehicle identification number that they traced to a Ryder truck rented in Junction City, Kansas. This lucky discovery became the first break in the case. Meanwhile, the second breakthrough was about to drop onto the investigator's laps in the town of Perry, Oklahoma, sixty miles north of the erstwhile Murrah building. At about 10:20 A.M., a Perry police officer pulled over a 1977 yellow Mercury Marquis that had been speeding at more than eighty miles per hour. Officer Charles Hanger noticed that the car had no license plates. Exiting his squad car, Hanger approached the driver's side of the vehicle; he reported seeing the telltale bulge of a shoulder holster under the driver's jacket. The driver—twenty-six-year-old Timothy James McVeigh, about to enter the annals of conspiracy theory, informed Hanger that he was packing a gun. Pointing his own gun at McVeigh's head, Hanger confiscated the driver's .45-caliber Glock pistol, loaded with hollow-point "cop killer" bullets, and a sheathed hunting knife.

Hanger arrested McVeigh, who calmly—dispassionately, per Hanger—cooperated with his captor. Booked in Noble County on charges of illegally transporting a loaded weapon, carrying a concealed weapon, and driving a vehicle without license plates, McVeigh, a former army sergeant who had served with distinction in the Persian Gulf War, sat in a courthouse jail cell for two days. By Friday morning following Wednesday's bombing, he would be charged in the worse terrorist incident ever carried out on American soil. There were several strong links between McVeigh and the crime in Oklahoma City, including that his appearance matched eyewitness descriptions of John Doe number one, a tall man with a military-style crewcut. Moreover, a former coworker of McVeigh's had called the FBI, reportedly offering evidence that connected McVeigh to the bombing. McVeigh is also alleged to have dropped a business card in the squad car after his arrest; the card, advertising Paulsen's Military Supply in Wisconsin, had scrawled on it, "more five-pound sticks of TNT by May 1." According to other news reports, the FBI also discovered in the glove compartment of McVeigh's rented car a letter to a friend vowing revenge for the 1993 federal raid on the Branch Davidian compound in Waco, Texas.

McVeigh was also carrying a phone debit card issued by *The Spotlight*, the conspiracy-minded newsletter of the anti-Semitic Liberty lobby. Purportedly, the government case against McVeigh relies heavily on the record of phone calls made with this card, which link McVeigh to suppliers of the fertilizer and plastic barrels allegedly used in the manufacture of the bomb.

In addition to McVeigh, the FBI had issued sketches of the so-called John Doe number two, believed to have been an accomplice in the Oklahoma bombing. The famous sketch of John Doe number two depicted a dark-haired man, perhaps of Middle Eastern extraction, wearing a baseball cap. Witnesses reported having seen this man with McVeigh at the bombing site and earlier at the Ryder rental franchise in Kansas. Initially, reports stated that the second suspect arrested in the bombing, Terry Nichols, was the same man seen in the familiar sketch of John Doe number two. But Nichols, an army buddy of McVeigh's, didn't look anything like the sketch. (McVeigh had implicated Nichols and Nichols's brother, James, having upon his lockup in Noble County listed James as his next of kin.)

Strangely, the FBI and federal prosecutors soon proffered a revised story, suggesting that John Doe number two, whoever he had been, was no more, most likely having been incinerated in the explosion. Terry Nichols further implicated McVeigh in the bombing, telling the FBI that McVeigh had called him from Oklahoma City the Sunday before the bombing, asking for a ride. Nichols drove from his home in Herington, Kansas, to Oklahoma City, then drove McVeigh to Junction City, Kansas. According to Nichols, during the drive McVeigh offered a cryptic statement: "Something big is going to happen," he said. "Are you going to rob a bank?" Nichols asked. McVeigh didn't elaborate but merely repeated the first statement: "Something big is going to happen."

A search of Terry Nichols's farm by the Federal Bureau of Alcohol, Tobacco and Firearms reportedly turned up bomb-making materials—blasting caps, sixty-foot Primadet detonator cords, ammonium nitrate, nitrogen fertilizer, and 55-gallon blue plastic drums. The prosecution's case tightened when it was learned that the Nichols brothers had made appearances at meetings of the Michigan Militia, an Armageddon-ready phalanx of right-wing patriots convinced that the United Nations was plotting an imminent invasion of America. And McVeigh, it has been alleged by several witnesses, was seen in the company of Michigan Militia leader Mark Koernke, acting as his bodyguard.

It certainly seems as though federal prosecutors have sewn up an airtight case against McVeigh and Terry Nichols. Still, a number of extremely puzzling and as-yet-unexplained events undermine the simplistic case presented in the popular media. For starters, certain persons in surprising places seem to have had foreknowledge of the bombing. According to the Portland *Oregonian* of April 20, 1995, Judge Wayne Alley, whose office was across the street from the Murrah building, was advised by unidentified government "security specialists" several days before the bombing to take "special precautions." Conspiracy trackers have had a field day with this peculiar bit of news,

which seemed to take on even more significance because (a)
Alley is a former U.S. Army general and (b) the judge was
scheduled to preside over the trial of McVeigh and Nichols
before the court venue changed to Denver.

Judge Alley wasn't the only person to receive advance warning of the bombing. In *OKBOMB!*—Jim Keith's anomaly-
packed book on the conspiratorial dimensions of the bombing—Keith chronicles a number of other instances where elect
individuals were warned to stay away from the Murrah building. David Hall, the general manager of KPOC-TV in
Oklahoma claims that he has videotaped interviews with eight
workers in the federal building who assert they were told to
expect a bombing on April 19. Per Hall, two days before the
blast, a secretary to a state center received the same warning.
Keith also reports that Oklahoma State representative Charles
Key has claimed that "he knows of two witnesses who heard
ATF employees mention that they had been warned not to come
to work on the day of the bombing." Key has urged Congress
and the state of Oklahoma to investigate these claims, but so far
without success.

Without a formal investigation into such claims, it's difficult
to distinguish rumor from fact, but a handful of other people in
Oklahoma City have made similar assertions. Several claim that
the ATF had warned its employees to stay away form the
building on April 19. Although ATF maintains that five of its
fifteen agents assigned to the Murrah building were on the
premises during the tragedy, and that all five were injured, other
reports (including one from an ATF agent and another in the
New York Times) suggest that no agents were on site at 9:02
A.M. that morning.

Twenty miles away from the blast, seismographs at the
University of Oklahoma recorded not one, but two explosive
"events" just after 9:00 A.M. on April 19, within ten seconds of
each other. The Omniplex Science Center in Oklahoma City
recorded the same dual disturbance, the second one stronger
than the first. The second tick of the seismograph needle has

been dismissed by skeptics as a mere "echo" of the main event. However, Dr. Charles Mankin, director of the University of Oklahoma Geological Survey, held a press conference shortly after the bombing and told an assembly of journalists that the seismograph readings more likely indicated two explosions, rather than, as debunkers often assert an "air blast" caused by the collapse of the building or an earthquake. As Mankin put it to the fourth estate, "The news media, itself, even reported two bomb blasts initially, but later changed their story."

The twin blast theory gets even more interesting in light of several other little-reported details. For one, eyewitnesses—including rescue workers on the scene just after the explosion—reported that the bomb squad detail had discovered another bomb, apparently unexploded, amid the rubble. According to David Hall, the general manager of KPOC-TV in Oklahoma, local fire chief John Hanson told him that "they had found two undetonated bombs in the building as well as one rocket launcher in the building." These accounts of multiple bombs recovered on the site are at odds with the official version of events that eventually emerged—that a single 4,800-pound fertilizer bomb was to blame for the massive damage to the Murrah building.

The nature of the bomb itself is another contentious issue. More than one demolitions expert has commented that a homemade fertilizer bomb—even if prepared under ideal conditions, which this one wasn't—packed inside a truck parked outside of the federal building could never have mustered the destructive force of the Murrah bomb or bombs. Brig. Gen. Benton Partin, a retired U.S. Air Force officer with considerable knowledge of military ordinance, believes he smells a rat: "When I first saw the picture of the truck bomb's asymmetrical damage to the federal building...my immediate reaction was that the pattern of damage would have been technically impossible without supplementary demolition charges at some of the reinforced concrete column bases (inside the building)—a standard demolition technique." Partin went on to say that "the

gross asymmetry in the federal building damage pattern is ipso
facto evidence that there was an inside bomb effort and a[n
outside] truck bomb effort."

Which leads us to the inside-job theory. Did the truck bomb
terrorists have help from personnel with access to the building,
perhaps government employees within the building? Here we
begin to tread into a minefield of speculation, and with the
government holding its evidentiary cards close to the vest,
there's no way of proving that particular conspiracy theory.
However, this hasn't inhibited conspiracy trackers from march-
ing into the rhetorical blast zone. And on their way in, they
brandish a curious *New York Daily News* story reporting that
several hours into the search and rescue operation after the
bombing, "some rescue workers were ordered to stop searching
for survivors while federal officials removed boxes of documents....Groups of 40 to 50 federal agents spent much of the
night carrying dozens of boxes from the seventh and ninth
floors, where the federal Drug Enforcement Administration and
Bureau of Alcohol, Tobacco and Firearms have offices." This
delay of the rescue operation occurred despite that people were
still buried alive in the rubble. What if the feds were trying to
remove unexploded ordnance, using the cover story of document retrieval? ask inquiring minds.

Same inquiring minds found at least partial corroboration
from Oklahoma State representative Charles Key, who dredged
up a sheriff's department film that referred to an "arsenal
room" inside the Murrah building. Apparently, at the time of
the bombing, weapons were being stored in that room. Per Key,
the sheriff's film "establishes, beyond a doubt, that the ATF was
maintaining an arsenal room in the Murrah building the day of
the bombing and that [the] arsenal room was ruptured by the
initial blast from a truck bomb." Key pointed out that the
pattern of damage was worse in the area of the alleged arsenal
room. According to several eyewitness reports, bomb squads
removed an assortment of ordnance from that room, including
undetonated explosives and even an anti-tank TOW missile. To

date, Key's calls for a full investigation of these stories have gone unheeded by state and federal officials.

More peculiarities revolve around the key suspects, McVeigh, Nichols, and the mysterious John Doe two. According to KPOC-TV's David Hall, a month after the bombing the FBI had a suspect matching the description of John Doe two under surveillance. Early in its investigation, the FBI had referred to a videotape showing McVeigh and John Doe two leaving the crime scene in a brown Ford pickup. On the day of the blast, the police had issued an all-points bulletin for a brown Ford pickup with two occupants. KFOR-TV, another local station, tracked down a truck answering to that description parked outside a "northwest Oklahoma City business." In a June 7, 1995, report, KFOR correspondent Jayna Davis showed a digitally obscured picture of an employee at that business. "Law enforcement officers," she said, "agree with us [that he] strongly resembles the FBI sketches of John Doe two. We know who he is, but we can't show you his face at this time because he has not been arrested or charged. However, we have witnesses who identified him in the company of Timothy McVeigh just days before the blast and just a few miles away from the Murrah building."

The next day, KFOR described the man as an Iraqi national who had served in Saddam Hussein's Republican Guard during the Gulf War. The addition of a Middle Eastern accomplice to the crime scenario certainly complicates federal prosecutors' simple story of right-wing nuts gone amok. But for now, at least, the question of why they apparently lost interest in the second John Doe remains a mystery. So, for that matter, do the early reports of video footage shot at the scene of the crime. What happened to that footage, if indeed it ever existed?

KPOC-TV's David Hall tells another strange story that the federal authorities have yet to explain or adequately debunk. Hall says that on the Friday following the Wednesday bombing, while listening to his police-band radio scanner, "I heard a broadcast coming over from the Oklahoma Highway Patrol that they had a car on I-35 and that the car, most likely, had been involved in the bombing." Hall dispatched a camera crew, which arrived at the scene to find a woman claiming she had witnessed the arrest of a man at 1:30 P.M. She said that Highway Patrol officers had removed a suspect from his car and put him in a "military helicopter." According to Hall, several other bystanders reported having witnessed the same scene, helicopter and all. Did the police actually pick up McVeigh on Friday, rather than Wednesday, as we've been told?

Not surprisingly, in the absence of a straightforward story from federal officials, an assortment of even more way-out conspiracy tales have spawned to fill the gaps in what we know. Most outlandish are several well-publicized theories attributing the bombing to agents of the Japanese government, as payback for the earlier gas attack on Tokyo subways (chapter 55), which in this epic scenario was a CIA-orchestrated plot. Not much more useful is the theory spouted by jailed tale-spinner Michael Riconosciuto (see chapter 24), who claims that the bomb used in the blast was a military fuel-air explosive, which Riconosciuto also claims he invented. Other speculations revolve around the many McVeigh "sightings" made before and after his arrest. (These theories came to a boil when *Soldier of Fortune* readers dug up a picture of a Waco ATF agent who bore a passing resemblance to the crew-cut boy bomber of Oklahoma City.) Did someone deploy a series of McVeigh doubles to confuse the investigative trail or to draw attention to McVeigh *before* the bombing? Was McVeigh set up to be the patsy? If this speculative possibility sounds familiar, you've done your homework on the JFK assassination, which abounds in stories of CIA-deployed Lee Harvey Oswald doubles gallivanting across the Northern hemisphere.

Clearly, some variety of conspiracy informs the muzzy events of the Oklahoma bombing—indeed, federal prosecutors have charged McVeigh and Nichols with conspiracy. But what was the precise nature of the conspiracy? Are we to believe the official version of events, that McVeigh and Nichols and perhaps unindicted co-conspirators from the militia movement

teamed up to strike back at the feds for whatever reason—
revenge for Waco or fear of a pending United Nations invasion?
That theory is certainly plausible. But there may be more to the
story than we've been led to believe, given the unconfronted
evidence we've detailed in this chapter. Did McVeigh and
Nichols get assistance from someone or *someones* within the
government, making the Oklahoma blast an "inside job"? Of
course, in these days of hyperbolic suspicion, it's as easy to
imagine crazed "rogue agents" of the government pulling off
the OK caper as it is to imagine nutty right-wing zealots behind
the bombing. But the fact is, the inside-job theory lacks a
convincing motive. The theory popular among paranoid Patriots—that elements of the government used McVeigh and
company to launch a latter-day Reichstag fire, a provocation to
be blamed on the enemy (Patriots)—doesn't gel because the
payoff for evil feds is so minuscule compared to the risks. In
other words, the feds don't need a heinous crime to pin on right
wingers to justify a crackdown on civil liberties. Law enforcement and conservative courts have been cracking down on civil
liberties successfully for years without having to resort to a
terror bombing.

Yet another Patriot theory ascribes motive this way: Inside
government jobbers used the bomb to destroy Waco evidence
that would have incriminated the ATF. But this theory falls
apart when you invoke one simple word: *shredder.*

There's another option for theorists that seems to make more
sense: Could a federal agency be attempting a more "benign,"
after-the-fact cover-up of its own bungling? An agency that had
advance knowledge of the bombing but failed to thwart it
would be staring a monumental PR disaster in the face, the kind
that might lead to dissolution of that agency. Was the ATF
illegally storing high explosives and other dangerous materials
in a public building, and did that gross negligence literally add
fuel to the fire?

On June 14, 1997, Timothy McVeigh was convicted of
murder, conspiracy to commit murder, and weapons-related

charges and was sentenced to death two months later. In April 1998, he filed to appeal the ruling. In a separate trial, Terry Nichols (who cooperated with the authorities) was convicted on December 23, 1997 of conspiracy to use a weapon of mass destruction and involuntary manslaughter. He was sentenced to life in prison and a fine of $14.5 million in restitution to the U.S. government. It appears that it is better to eliminate messy uncertainties from your case before it goes to trial. Much easier to convict a conspiracy of two or three guys.

MAJOR SOURCES

Keith, Jim. *OKBOMB!: Conspiracy and Cover-up.* Lilburn, GA: IllumiNet Press, 1996.
Parfrey, Adam. *"Finding Our Way Out of Oklahoma,"* in *Cult Rapture.* Portland, OR: Feral House, 1995.

55

Wake Up and Smell the Gas

Sarin to be sprayed in major city.
Russian Navy assault squad to land in Japan.
Aum to take over Japan.
 —Scribbling found in notebook kept by
Aum Shinrikyo "intelligence Minister" Yoshihiro Inoue

When police, following a trail of melons, finally caught up with the Guru of Gas, they tried to take his pulse. All he said was, "Don't touch me. I don't even let my disciples touch me."

Shoko Asahara may not have permitted his 40,000 followers to lay hands on him, but he did let them drink his used bathwater. Even his blood and his semen. For a price. The bathwater, known to members of Asahara's Aum Shinrikyo as "miracle pond," was one of the few beverages permitted to the cultists. Asahara let it go for about 200 bucks a pop. His blood

was somewhat pricier. A few swallows went for over $10,000—
the same price as the special electrode-fitted cap on sale at
Aumsters that let them tune in to their master's brainwaves.

But those heady days are over, now for the members of Aum
"Supreme Truth" (the rough English translation of Shinrikyo).
The Japanese press had been eagerly anticipating Tuesday, May
16, 1995, as "X-Day," the day that Japan's police descended on
an Aum-owned building called "The Sixth Satian." They found
40-year-old Asahara, self-proclaimed "Holy Pope" of the religious sect-turned-doomsday-cult-turned-latter-day-I.G.
Farben, lying prostrate in a cramped capsule hanging from the
third floor ceiling. On the floor of the little compartment was
over $10,000 worth of Japanese cash. Asahara clung to his wad
of yen as it were a teddy bear as police dragged him away.
Almost two months after the March 20 poison gas attack on
Tokyo's subways killed 12, sickened 5,000, and disrupted the
morning commute for countless others, the bad guy was, at last,
busted.

According to the countless "leaked" confessions of Aum
initiates under arrest, Asahara dispatched five two-person com-
mando teams onto separate subways, each carrying plastic bags
filled with deadly nerve gas. The gas was later identified as
sarin, an odorless, invisible concoction invented by the Nazi
Germans in 1938 and supposedly 500 times more lethal than
cyanide. The five trains were scheduled to converge in or near
Kasumigaseki Station, Tokyo's deepest subway station and one
of its most centrally located. Kasumigaseki is close to several
government offices, including Japan's National Police Agency.

According to reported confessions, the Aum hit squad placed
their inconspicuous-appearing gasbags on the train floor at a
designated time and punctured them with umbrellas. They they
got off as the gas dispersed.

Once the police figured out that Shoko Asahara was hiding
somewhere in the Sixth Satian, it still took them four hours to
dig him out. They located Asahara sealed inside a coffinlike
cubicle suspended from the ceiling. One of the clues that keyed

the cops to Asahara's presence in the building was the Holy Pope's sweet tooth for melons. His disciples aren't allowed to eat them, but he couldn't contain his craving. Asahara recklessly and repeatedly dispatched his flunkies to a local fruit stand, to satisfy his urge to snack.

Four days after his arrest, Asahara protested to his interrogators that he was being misrepresented in the media as some kind of fanatical melon nosher. Not so! said he. "I not only like melons," he told police, "but all fruits." When police took Asahara into custody they also, for some reason, opened his family refrigerator (Asahara's wife headed Aum's "Telecommunications Ministry" and his 12-year-old daughter is listed as "Secretary General to the Pope"). They found it stocked with melons. They also found such verboten-to-believers delicacies as deep-fried prawns, junk food, and orange juice.

Asahara also disavowed all meat and fish products found in the fridge as not for him. "I don't eat any kind of meat," the guru declaimed.

Of course, those were but the most amusing of the many morsels turned up in the course of the eight-week-anti-Aum law enforcement onslaught. Asahara prophesied that Aum would run Japan by the turn of the century, and they were not skimping on preparations for the coup d'état. Inside buildings designated as religious facilities were full-scale chemical and biological warfare laboratories.

At one location, Aum's scientists were attempting to cultivate botulism, and if the allegations against the cult hold up, it looks like they succeeded in synthesizing sarin. In the eleven years since Asahara—then known by his given name of Chizuo Matsumoto—opened a health food shop and yoga school in Tokyo, his family business has exploded into an international war machine and country-within-a-country in Japan. Police turned up nearly everything else from AK-47s to a bioengineering facility that was set up to manufacture botulism—a small vial of which, properly disseminated, would wipe out all of Tokyo. He's like Dr. No come to life. Police even found a stainless steel tank suitable for storing acid in a secret basement under an Aum building and they wonder if that answers the question of how Aum disposed of the bodies of its kidnap victims.

Aum was spooky from the start. According to Japanese press reports, Aum commandos received paramilitary training from elite Russian military units. The mostly blind Asahara was first arrested soon after opening his health food business for peddling an "all-purpose elixir" that consisted of little more than ground-up orange peels. Changing his name to something more ethereal sounding than Chizuo Matsumoto, he spread the word that he'd studied Buddhism in the Himalayas and become the first Japanese to attain enlightenment. It was his enlightened state that, more recently, allowed his occasionally emaciated followers to excuse his excesses of appetite. After one attains enlightenment, according to the word of Aum, it's chow time.

The sect seemed innocuous enough until November of 1989. Just three months after Aum received the official government OK as a bona-fide religious group, a lawyer for clients who had a beef with Aum vanished from his home along with his wife and infant son. The following year, Asahara and a bunch of other high-level Aumsters formed their own political party, called the True Teaching Party, and ran for parliament. At their rallies, hundreds of devotees would show up wearing plastic masks of Asahara's hirsute, pudgy mug. This was not much of a campaign strategy. Come election day, the Aum contingent was soundly thrashed.

After their political humiliation, Aum began to metamorphose from, in the words of Japanese journalist Shoko Egawa, "a bunch of naive people enthusiastic about their religion to a group of gloomy but aggressive paranoids."

After his arrest, Asahara said little. When police raised the subject of the subway gassing, he replied by griping about his supposed liver ailment. He had a habit of flattering his interrogators, telling them they "look cool, like detectives on a TV drama."

As the guru gangboss nestled in his cubbyhole, a horde of

reporters camped out for several days around the Sixth Satian (*satians* are supposedly the elemental truths of Hinduism, but Aum's satian buildings weren't exactly what the Hindus had in mind; the Seventh Satian, was revealed during police raids as a covert chemical warfare facility). When Asahara was finally loaded into a police van, crowds gathered on highway over-passes to watch it go by and TV helicopters followed its progress from their vantage point in the skies. All very O.J.-esque.

But at the same time America was fixing its gaze on the football star and his messy domestic dispute, folks in Japan had a little more to fret about in Aum. The subway gassing was neither the first nor the last act of terror attributed to the killer cult. According to the relentlessly leaked confessions of arrested Aum bigshots, the cult was behind the March 30, 1995, shooting of National Police Agency chief Takaji Kunimatsu (he was badly wounded, but recovered and returned to the job several months later) and the mail bombing aimed at the governor of Tokyo which, on X-day itself, deprived one of the governor's aides of most of his fingers.

When the gas attack struck Tokyo's subways, police had already been planning a crackdown on the group, spurred on by the daylight abduction of a Tokyo notary worker who had tried to talk his sister out of joining the cult. Two days after grabbing the guru, police picked up Takeshi Matsumoto, the Aum stalwart who's the chief suspect in that kidnapping.

The day after Asahara's arrest the sect's chief doctor, Ikuo Hayashi, dropped a bombshell. He admitted, police say, that not only was the cult responsible for kidnapping the notary worker early in 1995, but that the man died while being held captive by Aum. Hayashi said he was ordered to kill the man by lethal injection but found him dead before he could stick the needle in.

Hayashi was one of the most vocal Aum devotees now in custody when it comes to recounting the sarin attack. In an admission that can't help but restore one's faith in human nature, Hayashi admitted that "my conscience really stung me" before puncturing his sarin bag. "I looked around and saw all those commuters and I thought, 'I'm a doctor. I work to save people's lives.'" But the cardiac specialist and graduate of one of Japan's best med schools went ahead and released the gas anyway.

There were also incidents throughout the spring of 1995 of mysterious, nauseating fumes wafting through Yokohama station, sending 400 people to the hospital. But most unsettling of all, on May 5, 1995, two burning bags of toxic chemicals were found in a men's room in Shinjuku Station, Tokyo's downtown crossing and the busiest train station in the world. Had the two bags burned far enough, they would have combined to produce cyanide gas with potential to kill 10,000 people.

The aroma of Aum had been sniffed before, most notably in Matsumoto, Japan, a small town where seven people had died of poison gas in June 1994. Also in 1994, residents in Tokyo near one of Aum's buildings complained that noxious fumes from the structure were causing an outbreak of illnesses in the area. Then, a month after the Matsumoto incident, people in Kamikuishiki—home of Asahara's headquarters where he was eventually arrested—noticed a nasty stench from one of Aum's buildings. No one died or even became very sick. But leaves around the town began to turn brown. Investigators found traces of phosphorous around the offending building, though they wouldn't search the place because Aum still claimed religious exemption.

A picture of Aum emerged that made it look less like a zany, quasi-Buddhist mega-commune and more like an all-too-real plot to overthrow Japan's government. The possibility also exists that Aum was only one part of such a plot.

From the various confessions they've taken, the cops say that the subway attack scheme was hatched two years in advance, as a way to help fulfill Asahara's doomsday prophecies. But as public as it became, to the point where its doe-eyed telegenic spokesman Fumihiro Joyu gave wet dreams to teenage girls across Japan (he won the hearts and minds of the nation when he declared that Asahara's teachings had given him the inner strength to swear off masturbation), Aum remains mysterious. Asahara has generally been portrayed as sort of a roly-poly Japanese Charles Manson, luring Japan's disaffected youth from the drudgery of the workaday world with promises of freedom and enlightenment but instead turning them into servants for his own evil plots. But just as speculation persists that Manson had some kind of weird connections, Asahara may not have been operating as a lone nut.

The cult seems to have had some sort of protection. Tokyo-based Aum-watcher Tim Romero notes that "it is very hard to accept incompetence alone as a sufficient explanation" for the hands-off police attitude toward Aum in the years before the Tokyo gassing. Nor does *New Yorker* reporter Murray Sayle's explanation that Japan is so eager to prove its recently acquired taste for religious tolerance to the world that it ignores the abuses of even the craziest cults.

Romero points out that more than sixty people escaped from Aum's home base between 1991 and 1995, all telling horror stories of abuse. Some of these stories were later borne out by captured cultists' confessions, including Poe-like tales of people being dipped in vats of boiling oil, stabbed in the heart, strangled, and in some cases, microwaved (doubtful that Poe would have thought of that last one).

Police did nothing in response to the escapees' stories. Nor did the cops move when, in three separate instances, runaway cultists were kidnapped back into the cult right out in the open as horrified onlookers gaped, powerless. One woman was dragged off a train, beaten up on a crowded platform, then thrown in a car registered to Aum and driven back to the compound. In one case, the kidnappers wore the distinctive Aum headgear that supposedly lets members tune in to Asahara's brainwaves.

Equally strange was the police obstinance after the Matsumoto gassing. They accused a local man of somehow synthesizing sarin "accidentally" in his backyard fishpond while trying to cook up a homemade weed killer. Despite the utter absurdity of this accusation—noted by chemists the world over—the police stuck to their story and the major Japanese press went along. A year later when it came out through cultists' confessions that Aum had sprayed the sarin from the back of a specially modified van, the biggest newspapers in the country (and the world; Japanese national dailies have circulations eight to ten times that of the *New York Times*) apologized to the unfortunate local resident, whose wife was severely injured in the sarin attack.

But what should really have attracted the attention of the authorities was that, somehow, this yoga instructor accrued an empire valued at over a billion U.S. bucks in just a few short years. While it's true that Aum pulled the old "turn over your worldly possessions" trick on its followers—mostly the housewives and elderly women among them—there's no way that bilking little old ladies (nor selling his semen) could have allowed Asahara to amass the sums required to build the arsenal of weaponry and ultrasophisticated chemical and biological warfare facilities that have been uncovered.

Two Japanese politicians, though not members of Aum, gave large donations, according to ex-Parliamentarian Koichi Hamada, who made the charge in a book called *Hamako's Emergency Statement*. He names those two but does not name a third who he says, introduced Aum leaders to top Russian officials. The *Sunday Mainichi* magazine also reported that Asahara developed his connections to Russian bigwigs with the help of a Japanese Parliamentarian. One of the politicians named by Hamada, Shintaro Ishihara, resigned shortly after the police began their raids on the Aum compound.

Even more intriguing, Shin Kanemaru, the onetime political kingmaker who used to receive bribes so vast that the cash had to be delivered in a wheelbarrow, owned a number of gold bars that didn't bear the official government seal. Aum was in possession of similarly unstamped gold bars, which has led the press to wonder if the same forces that backed Kanemaru's reign also financed Aum. The mystery of Kanemaru's gold died with him in March 1996, but many in Japan wondered if the gold came from North Korea.

The Korean connection—North and/or South—arises often in theories about the secret history of Aum. The Japanese weekly press (the weeklies are Japan's sole bastion of crusading and every-so-often reckless journalism) was filled with speculation about Aum's connection to the South Korea–based Unification Church—the Moonies, which itself has long had strong ties, even its origins, in the Korean CIA. This same speculation has extended beyond the pulpy pages of the weeklies. Journalist Takashi Tachibana asserted the Moonie-Aum connection, as well as widespread links between Aum and prominent politicians, in a TV interview. Tachibana didn't cite any evidence, but he does have his credibility to ride on. He's the journalist whose revelations played a leading role in bringing down the government of Lockheed-scandal-connected prime minister Kakuei Tanaka. It was also reported that, when the crackdown on Aum began, the cult gave some of its assets to another, unnamed religious organization for safekeeping. The Moonies, perhaps?

There has been speculation aplenty that Asahara, whose 30,000 Russian devotees were thrice the total of his Japanese disciples, had something on Boris Yeltsin. Could Aum have been channeling cash to the boisterous Russian neocapitalist? Asahara seemed welcome in Moscow, where he was negotiating to buy laser weapons technology and other goodies. His visits were backed by a major Russian university and he used to do a radio show from Russia that would reach Japan. The day after the subway gassing, there was a fire in Aum's Moscow office.

The connections grow ever more sinister. The cult had verified links to the military. Something like sixty members of Japan's Self-Defense Force (the de facto military under Japan's postwar pacifist constitution) belonged to the Aum organization and some are suspected of tipping Asahara to the coming police raids. At least two, according to the weekly *Shukan Bunshun* operated within the cult's "chemical unit." One thirty-eight-year-old officer—the same one who gave Asahara a nonclassified chemical weapons textbook—also allegedly handed the guru a classified document with information on the SDF's helicopter brigades and missile capabilities. The cult owned an enormous Russian military helicopter and was looking to buy more, leading police to the fairly obvious conclusion that Asahara envisioned his own helicopter strike force.

The shooter who hit Japan's national police chief, unconfirmed reports would have it, was one of Aum's Self-Defense Force members. The number of soldiers who belonged to Aum is a more than a little disconcerting. As London *Independent* Tokyo correspondent Richard Parry noted in a May 31 column in the English language *Daily Yomiuri* newspaper, the SDF connection harkens back to another bizarre episode that kept Japan captivated: the public suicide of Japan's greatest novelist turned right-wing fanatic, Yukio Mishima, in 1970.

Mishima maintained his own private army that was allowed to train using SDF facilities. He had some high-level supporters in the SDF until he embarrassed everyone involved by commandeering an SDF barracks in Tokyo, holding a general hostage, then delivering a semisane speech to an assembly of soldiers, urging them to stage a military coup. He concluded this little spectacle by going back into the general's office and committing *seppuku*, ritual auto-disembowelment.

Parry writes that "at least one close observer of the Tokyo sarin affair believes the Mishima and Aum affairs have plenty in common." He cites journalist Masaski Shimosato, who has the distinction of having called attention to Aum's chemical warfare efforts long before the subway incident. Shimosato, says Parry, "believes firmly that the 'Armageddon' which the cult predicts in its literature is more than just a vague religious apocalypse, but a deliberately planned uprising against the Japanese state, a coup d'etat, carried out in collaboration with thousands of sympathizers in the Self-Defense Forces." While as Parry points out, this may turn out to be just "the stuff of cheesy conspiracy theories," Aum's already-established links to the SDF—as well as to Russia and the yakuza—only deepen the Aum mystery.

The matter of Aum's accomplice is not much discussed in the daily Japanese press, but it was the focus of an interview with an anonymous public security official that appeared in the August 15, 1995 edition of *Weekly Playboy* (no relation to Hef's baby), one of Japan's stack of muckraking weekly magazines. If the information in the interview is accurate, it would rend the whole Aum case into shreds.

The "public security" department is a highly secretive internal force that operates apart from Japan's National Police Agency and the Tokyo Metropolitan Police (which, in another mystery, has been handling most of the Aum case even though many incidents fall well outside the Tokyo jurisdiction; the NPA has been frustrated in its attempts to get involved in the investigation). This unnamed official claims that "60 percent" of the Aum info leaked to the media is flat-out false. Many of the Aum members in custody who, according to the press and police, have been squawking their lungs out have actually been maintaining soldierly silence, the official told the magazine.

The press, not surprisingly, has relied far too heavily on police sources, said the official. But more intriguingly, another reason for the duplicity may be that some other entity helped, or perhaps ordered Aum to sarinfy the subways. The *Weekly Playboy* interview suggests that "a sample of sarin was delivered to (the cult) from someone on the outside, and that the cult was able to develop its own sarin based on an analysis of that sample."

How Aum was able to manufacture sarin in its own makeshift labs has always been a bit of a puzzle. The London *Sunday Times Magazine* had an engineer, Yohei Fukuzawa, check out the cult's supposed sarin labs—bearing in mind that sarin is one of the most difficult of all chemical weapons to manufacture. Fukuzawa described the Aum lab as "a place for cooks, not scientists." Other experts who looked at the Aum facilities either firsthand or in photographs reached similar conclusions. The cult's scientific capabilities were far too crude to have produced the deadly gas, they say.

The nameless, faceless security official interviewed by *Weekly Playboy* also asserted that the cult's murdered science "minister," Hideo Murai, was in fact "assassinated" to keep him from spilling the beans, not on Aum but on Aum's silent accomplice.

The Murai murder may be the Rosetta Stone to all this craziness. Aum's "science and technology minister" was stabbed to death on April 23, 1995. Murai, thirty-six, was an accomplished chemist who left academia to join Aum and head its chemical production facilities. He was killed—on live TV, no less—by Hiroyuki Jo, a Korean member of a four-person far-right group who was allegedly motivated by outrage at Aum's dirty deeds. The far-right group turned out to be a sham.

The biggest story to come out relating to Murai's death was that, as his blood was draining away, he whispered to a paramedic that he had been murdered by "Judas." The Korean killer had ties to Japan's entrenched organized crime syndicate, the yakuza. He later admitted that the order for the killing came from a yakuza member who told Jo that he'd have "nothing to worry about" once he'd iced Murai. Jo owed the mob a lot of money.

The Japanese far right and the yakuza have been cozy for decades and yakuza-ultraright influence is often the unseen force guiding Japanese politics where men like Kanemaru and Yoshio Kodama—a gangster with CIA connections who ruled Japanese politics from behind the scenes until the Lockheed scandal brought him down—call the shots.

In addition to Jo, police arrested Kenji Kamimine, a top member of the Hane-gumi syndicate, in connection with Murai's stabbing. The Hane-gumi is (or was—it disbanded on May 14, 1995 after Kamimine's arrest) a subsidiary of the

Yamaguchi-gumi, the top yakuza crime family. (*Gumi* means, essentially, "gang.")

According to police, Jo worked at Yamaguchi-gumi head-quarters and may have been a member of Hane-gumi.

Jo also had connections to Aum. He ran an events-promotion firm and had done business with Aum on four occasions. One of the Japanese tabloids, *Tokyo Sports*, reported that Jo or someone who looked just like him, had actually been sighted at an Aum gathering a few years ago. The more credible *Tokyo Shimbun* daily reported that a cult member had been in contact with Jo prior to the murder. Later, Japanese television reported that an unidentified top member of Aum told police that the cult's number-two man, Kiyohide Hayakawa, had commented shortly before Murai's murder that he had "taken care of everything."

The story was that the cult leadership had not been at all amused at Murai's public admission that foul odors emanating from an Aum building were the result of chemical experiments. Murai said they were making fertilizer, but even that was too close to the truth for comfort and, according to the source, Asahara and his top henchmen decided to shut up their chief scientist for good. One of the many types of chemicals Aum allegedly produced was an amphetamine-like stimulant. One theory has it that Aum sold these drugs to the yakuza.

There are a number of oddities about Murai's murder that call the Zapruder film to mind. The tapes show that Jo stabbed Murai first in the arm, which startled the chemist but didn't stop him. Murai was surrounded by Aum bodyguards, but even as the bewildered chemist examined his bloodied arm for several seconds, his protectors did nothing. Some observers claim that the tape shows one bodyguard actually extending an arm to block Murai's path after the first, nonfatal stab. Rumors are floating around Tokyo that some of the bodyguards were seen talking to Jo, who'd been hanging around the Aum offices all day, earlier that afternoon.

Revelations about the cult's ambitions grew freakier by the day. On May 25, the national *Yomiuri Shimbun* daily reported that six Aum members journeyed in March to the Nikola Tesla Museum in Belgrade, Yugoslavia. According to police, Aum's internal newsletters often discussed Tesla's theories—Tesla, of course, being the overlooked genius of modern engineering whose discoveries, his devotees say, could revolutionize the industrial world. Aum was especially interested, according to the police sources, in Tesla's theories about how to trigger earthquakes artificially. Asahara interpreted the January 17, 1995 Kobe earthquake as the first shot of World War III—he figured that it had been artificially triggered—and perhaps was looking to strike back.

As if that wasn't weird enough, a TV report said that an Aum group had also visited Zaire last December and that Aum publications showed a keen interest in the Ebola virus. Presumably, this was another attempt to make a biological weapon. The group also fooled around with anthrax, the granddaddy of all twentieth-century germ weapons (see chapter 5).

In the familiar M.O. of all cults, from LaRouchies to militias, conspiracy theories serve as a unifying force against the hostile outside (some might say, "real") world. Asahara's conspiratological rants took on a decidedly anti-American tone. The U.S. military was putting Aum under nonstop assault, Asahara preached. But his paranoia bore a peculiar twist. He was obsessed with gas.

"We've been under deadly gas attacks since 1988," he said in an April 1994 sermon. "Gases are sprayed from helicopters or planes wherever I go." But maybe that wasn't such a terrible fate. In a sermon a month earlier, he'd called it a "heavenly principle" to "terminate one's life by using sarin and other gases developed during World War II."

In a radio broadcast that December, Asahara informed his followers, "I come under a gas attack wherever I travel and jet fighters from U.S. forces fly around Mt. Fuji." More than all talk, Asahara apparently acted out his theories. On January 4,

1995, Aum's attorney announced that the sect's headquarters had been subjected to "a mustard gas attack from outside." A gaseous PR blitz followed, with Aum releasing to major media outlets a forty-eight-minute video titled, "Slaughtered Lamb: A Record of Poison Gas Oppression."

The video showed visual evidence of the gas attack—a lot of scorched earth around the cult's compound. Police now say that Aumsters sprayed their own lawns with weed killer. No mustard gas was ever found. Even so, four days after the Tokyo subway gassings, Asahara was quoted in an Aum handbill claiming to be "very sick now because of poison gas attacks on me."

Perhaps Asahara finally decided to retaliate and unleash a gas attack of his own. Two days after his arrest Asahara was taking a "they weren't just following orders" approach to his defense. He blamed his rogue underlings over whom, he protests, he cannot maintain full-time supervision.

"I have so many followers. I don't keep track of everything they've done," he reportedly told his interrogators. One might think that gassing thousands of people on a crowded subway might be a detail that would merit some attention.

Despite the guru's silence and denials (he faces hanging if convicted), his henchmen flipped like burgers at Jack in the Box. Police say that Aum's chief physician, the man who surgically removed fingerprints from top Aum officials, has confessed to the umbrella-and-baggie sarin attack. Aum's top chemist (at least the top one left alive), Masami Tsuchiya, copped to brewing sarin—and to using it in Matsumoto. Police failed to link Aum to that gas attack, even though the cult owned large swaths of property in the town, much to the consternation of the locals. After the Matsumoto incident, Asahara went public, accusing the U.S. Navy of spraying the gas. He fingered Murai (an easy target at this point) as the man giving direct orders not only to make the Nazi nerve gas but to "try it in Matsumoto."

In October 1995, there seemed to be a huge break in the case.

The key word is "seemed." First, NHK-TV, the Japanese equivalent of the BBC, reported that Asahara had broken down and confessed to "everything." Confessions are the usual means by which the Japanese police solve crimes, and while in the United States they are easily recanted and don't carry too much weight, in Japanese criminal law confessions are everything. So Asahara's alleged opera act could have been a blockbuster. Except no one's sure if it really happened or not. The police denied it, at least publicly. And so did Asahara's lawyer, Hiroshi Yamamoto.

On the other hand, how would Yamamoto know? The police denied him permission to visit his client in jail ever since Yamamoto smuggled a tape-recorded message from Asahara to his followers. Though there is no provision in Japanese law for denying a prisoner his right to counsel, Tokyo District Court said the cops were in the right because "it would be inappropriate for Yamamoto to meet with Asahara in view of his close ties to the cult."

The Great Man himself, of course, was not exactly available for interviews.

Nonetheless, just a day or so after the confession controversy subsided, one of the most-sought Aum fugitives showed up at a police station in Saitama prefecture, just north of Tokyo, and handed himself over.

Masahiro Tominaga, twenty-six, is the chief suspect in a May 12, 1995, parcel bombing aimed at Tokyo governor Yukio Aoshima, a former TV comedian.

When Tominaga strolled into the police station he announced, "I'm Tominaga of Aum and I feel sorry for having caused you so much trouble." Uh-huh.

The police, despite their earlier hesitance, rounded up hundreds of Aum members after the gas attack in the subway. Perhaps Tominaga knew that he'd be better off coming in from the cold and expressing remorse—a very important aspect of Japanese justice—than running.

On September 5, 1995, the first conviction in the Aum case

was meted out. Cult "construction minister" Takayuki Oikawa received a one-year suspended prison term and three years probation for trespassing. His offense: parking his car in someone else's space.

MAJOR SOURCES:

This chapter is based primarily on accounts appearing in Japan's daily and weekly press—both English language and Japanese (with the aid of a translator)—mostly in the six months after the March 20, 1995, Tokyo subway attack. Other sources include the following:

Dalrymple, James. "The Day Japan Lost its Nerve." *The Sunday Times Magazine*, 13 August 1995.

Fukunaga, Hiroshi. "AUM Sweet Home." *Tokyo Business Today*, June 1995.

Japan Times, *Terror in the Heart of Japan*. Tokyo: Japan Times Ltd., 1995.

Sayle, Murray. "Nerve Gas and the Four Noble Truths." *New Yorker*, 1 April 1996.

Van Biema, David. "Prophet of Poison." *Time*, 3 April 1995.

The anonymous interview with a public security official appeared in *Weekly Playboy*, August 15, 1995, in Japanese. It was summarized in English in "60 Percent of What's Reported About Aum Is Crap," *Mainichi Daily News*, August 6, 1995.

56

Smart Bomber

If the cabin-dwelling mountain man Ted Kaczynski really is the "terrorist group FC," as the Unabomber referred to himself in his missives to the media, he offers an interesting lesson in how to elude the FBI. Stay put. If indeed the literate bomber and the hermitlike, if not hermetic, ex-math professor Theodore John Kaczynski are one and the same, then this most-wanted fugitive dwelled in the same Montana shack for twenty-five years. For darn near the last eighteen of those years, the Unabomber has been blowing up stuff and, rather unfortunately, people that he considered representative of techno-evil industrial society. Until early 1996, the feds were pretty well stumped as to who or where the bomber might be. They arrested Ted Kaczynski in his hut—which lacked all modern amenities, even a toilet—on April 3, 1996, after staking him out for several weeks on a tip from Kaczynski's younger brother.

A few months later, on June 25, 1996, Kaczynski appeared in a Sacramento, California, court to answer the indictments against him. Several days before that hearing he had been formally indicted in four of the sixteen Unabomber attacks, including two of the three fatal bombings.

He entered a not guilty plea. It was the first time he had made any kind of public assertion of his guilt or innocence—and he didn't even make it. His lawyer spoke for him at the hearing. Kaczynski is an enigmatic fellow to say the least. The details of his life have been covered quite thoroughly, yet no one's exactly sure why be became the Unabomber. According to various speculations, he was embittered after a romantic rejection, he failed to get an article published in a journal and he was inspired by the Joseph Conrad novel, *The Secret Agent* (in which a university professor quits to make bombs). He remains as much of a mystery in custody as the Unabomber was prior to Kaczynski's arrest.

Christened for his early tendency to hit universities and airlines (which assumes that all of the attacks linked by the FBI are indeed the work of the same perpetrator), the Unabomber began what the media is fond of calling his "reign of terror" on May 26, 1978, when a bomb intended for a Northwestern University professor injured a security guard. Since then, there have been an additional fifteen bombings or attempted bombings credited to the Unabomber. The bombs killed three, though the first fatality didn't occur until 1985.

The bomber's victims included an advertising executive, a timber industry lobbyist, a few academic scientists, and a computer store owner. But the bomber really became a media star in 1995 when he went public, as it were, with a series of notes to the media. In June, he threatened to blow up a plane at Los Angeles International Airport, then quickly followed up with a missive declaring the threat "a prank."

The publicity blitz climaxed when the *Washington Post* acquiesced to the bomber's demand that it (in conjunction with the *New York Times*) publish what came to be called "The Unabomber Manifesto." Actually titled, "Industrial Society and Its Future," the 35,000-word monograph outlined a primitivist-anarchist philosophy opposed to all forms of modern technol-

ogy and advocated dismantling modern industrial society. If
that actually happened, the rest of the world would be living
exactly how Kaczynski himself lived.

The bomber always identified himself (or herself) as a
"group"—the aforementioned "FC," which according to the
bomber's own assertion stood for "Freedom Club." He en-
graved the letters on his bombs, making sure the signature
would survive any blast. But the authorities always believed the
incendiary campaign was the work of one man.

The FBI had the Unabomber pegged as highly educated, and
Kaczynski fit that bill. He enrolled in Harvard at the age of
sixteen, graduated before he turned twenty, and was a rising
star on U.C. Berkeley's math faculty at the age of twenty-five.
He left Berkeley abruptly and under vague circumstances. Some
press accounts quote colleagues as recalling Kaczynski's saying
he wanted to pursue "social causes," though no one could recall
which causes (blowin' up stuff may or may not count as a
"cause").

And though he lived alone in the woods, he wasn't exactly
living underground. He was reasonably well-known in Lincoln,
Montana, though no one claimed to know him very well. He'd
hang out at the town library and venture in for supplies at local
shops every now and then. While his solitary lifestyle, living off
his garden and off of deer and porcupines he'd shoot with a .22
must have afforded him a great deal of freedom from prying
eyes, it also enhances the mystery of how this indigent Harvard-
grad-turned-Grizzly Adams-emulator managed to scoot all over
the country dropping bombs in the post from the Bay Area or
planting them in person (in the case which led to the famous
Unabomber sketch) behind a Utah computer store.

Kaczynski is proving to be a strange criminal, but one aspect
of his case that was hardly strange was the flow of leaked
information from law enforcement authorities to the media.
The government built its case against Kaczynski in the press.
Par for the course.

For anything resembling the real story of the Unabomber to

come out will take quite some time. Certainly the length of Kaczynski's trial. Until then, the extent of the evidence the government actually has against the Nutty Professor remains unknown. The evidence may well prove incontrovertible. After-all, the government has had almost two decades to amass its case.

But without benefit of that evidence on the public record, one has to wonder if the FBI really has anything to nail Ted Kaczynski. From the moment Kaczynski was arrested the leaks from inside the FBI began and dozens of them proved unreliable or in some cases just plain false. If the FBI has real, hard evidence against Kaczynski, why has so little of that been leaked while the stream of bad information seems endless?

One answer to that question could simply be the ineptitude of an overeager press. Whatever the case, there was, without a doubt a "rush to judgment" (to ressurect that hoary old conspiracy slogan) to pin the Unabomber rap on Kaczynski.

So frequent and egregious were the leaks that Kaczynski's court-appointed lawyers petitioned a judge to throw out the case altogether, saying all potential grand jurors had been poisoned against Kaczynski by the FBI's leaking campaign. The judge nixed the idea, though he did say that there had been a lot of leaks.

A spokesman for the Justice Department told the *Washington Post*, "There are times when we informally try to prevent something which is grossly untrue form being published or broadcast, but in this case I felt I couldn't even do that."

According to the *New York Times* and the other major news outlets, federal investigators located an "original" copy of the Unabomber manifesto in his tiny Montana cabin. That would appear to seal it, as far as circumstantial evidence goes. But when the FBI released an inventory of over 700 items seized from Kaczynski's tiny home, the manifesto wasn't listed, nor were any original copies of Unabomber correspondence. The inventory did list "documents." But that could mean anything.

Of course, no one in the media reported seeing the captured

manuscript for themselves. All of the reports were based on unnamed federal sources.

Two days after Kaczynski's arrest, the Associated Press (along with most other major news outlets) reported that a manual typewriter found in the mountain man's tiny shack "appears to be the one the Unabomber used to type his letters and his grand manifesto about the evils of technology, a federal official said."

Regardless of whether a "federal official" said it, that damning assertion—especially coming so quickly—should have induced at least a smattering of incredulity. Sure enough, the *New York Times* reported that "sophisticated tests conducted on two typewriters found early in the search of the Montana cabin had led them to discount the likelihood that either machine had been used to type the Unabom manifesto."

Oh.

Apparently, it must come as a surprise to the *Times* and its fellow big media outlets that "sophisticated tests" are in fact required to determine whether a particular document came from a particular typewriter. You can't just eyeball it.

Lo and behold, the feds found a third typewriter near where they found the Unabomber manuscript. "Officials said Friday that they were relieved that preliminary tests had confirmed that the type on the third machine matched the typewriting of the manuscripts," the *Times* reported on April 8, 1996.

What is the nature of these "preliminary tests?" The *Times* doesn't say. While on the one hand, it looks as if the FBI's got their man, it's still worth bearing in mind the shaky reliability of media reports and the government's—for all of its teeth-gnashing over the constant leaks to the media—knowledge that building a solid case in the press is important to keeping the case solid in court—and to making the FBI look good.

On April 8 most dailies, following the lead of *Times* reporter David Johnston, ran stories saying that Kaczynski had been spotted by a hotel manager in Sacramento around the times that two bombs were mailed from the California capital. But faced with a media request to open some sealed files on the case, the

FBI asserted that releasing such evidence in public could "taint" witnesses. The FBI cited, as an example, the hotel manager who identified Kaczynski. When interviewed earlier by the G-men, it turns out, he could not ID a photo of the suspected Unabomber. After the stories appeared the FBI went back to the man and found that "he had no records" to support the assertions quoted in the press and he "told the FBI he had no records of hotel stays."

The *Los Angeles Times* buried the hotel manager's recantation deep inside a story asserting that the FBI found a "hooded sweatshirt and aviator sunglasses" that look like the ones worn by the culprit in the famous Unabomber sketch. Now there's evidence!

In the initial stages of the investigation, when Kaczynski's picture was flashed so widely across the print and broadcast media (not to mention the Internet) that he had to be approaching O.J.-equivalent recognizability, no one came forward with a reliable sighting of him near any of the locations where bombs were planted or mailed. (Quite a few people reported sightings, but none could be described as reliable.)

A head scratcher of a detail noted by researcher Ross Getman on the "Truth is Redacted" Web site: according to the Harvard Alumni Directory, Kaczynski was in Afghanistan in 1982. Perhaps giving this address was Ted's idea of a joke. But if it's true, it probably counts him out as the Unabomber—at least with regard to the two bombings attributed to UNABOM that year and probably the attempted attacks in 1980 and 1981.

Among other leaked info: the FBI's alleged discovery and defusion of a live bomb in Kaczynski's cabin along with loads of chemicals that could be used to make bombs, books on bomb building, and "meticulous" (that word gets used a lot) notes on building explosives. None of those incriminating items were ever spied by anyone else who dropped by Kaczynski's mountain shanty, including a census taker, and a fellow hunter named Glen Williams who describes himself as the closest thing Kaczynski had to a friend.

According to Williams, who was interviewed by the *Boston Herald* newspaper, Kaczynski left his property for more than a few days just one time, in the mid-1980s. Of course, this "friend" may have memories that are less than perfect and probably wasn't hanging with Kaczynski around the clock, but if his recollection is accurate, that would leave the alleged bomber little time to pull off his trips to the Bay Area.

The feds also said that Kaczynski forayed fifty miles to a Helena hotel "at least twenty-five times; four of the stays roughly coincided with five bombings blamed on the Unabomber," according to AP. The bombs weren't mailed from Helena, however (at least they weren't postmarked there) so the connection between Kaczynski's hotel stays and the bombings beyond mere temporal coincidence has yet to be clarified. And what about the other twenty-one times he stayed at the hotel that did not "roughly coincide" with Unabomber attacks?

No one in the general public can say for certain whether Kaczynski really is the feared author of the best anarcho-luddite diatribe ever to appear in the *New York Times* and *Washington Post* (namely, "Industrial Society and Its Future"), though from what's been reported in the press the prognosis for the fifty-three-year-old essayist is not a happy one. But the FBI must come up with answers to some pretty tough questions. A few key queries, as phrased by the *Boston Globe* would include "how a reclusive former professor living without electricity, a car or a telephone in one of the remotest parts of America could track his intended bombing victims, gather ingredients to make sophisticated explosives, then shuttle them off in envelopes that generally bore West Coast postmarks."

No minor points, those. *U.S. News and World Report* reported that Kaczynski's family sent him "thousands of dollars" over the years, which would explain how he could afford to travel—but not how he'd keep up on current events to the point where he could choose his targets as selectively as he obviously did. Kaczynski himself reportedly told the few people whom he talked about such things with that he subsisted on

$300 per annum. Over twenty-five years that adds up to $7,500, which qualifies, nominally, as "thousands," but isn't enough to finance repeated cross-country sojourns.

One speculation that didn't appear too widely in early press accounts but has made its way into the Unabomber-devoted Internet newsgroup *alt.fan.unabomber* is that Ted the K had an accomplice. He purchased his Montana property with his somewhat more outgoing brother, David, the guy who ultimately dimed out the alleged Unabomber. David Kaczynski had lived in a back-to-nature cabin himself, in Texas, until a few years earlier when he moved to Schenectady, New York (near Albany) to get hitched to his high school sweetheart. That, of course, is not at all to imply that David Kaczynski is Unabomber II—far from it—but the possibility of an accomplice certainly can't be ruled out. In his letters to the media, the Unabomber always referred to himself as a "group," which may well have been nothing more than a lame attempt to throw investigators off the track or the wish-fulfillment fantasies of an intensely lonely mind.

With the reasonable doubt piled high in Kaczynski's case (investigators may have found lot of circumstantial evidence—even, they claim, a live bomb; but tying Kaczynski to any specific bombing is another whole project), any speculation on a possible playmate for him would fall under the category of "wild." One avenue that conspiracy researchers might want to explore is the theses propagated on the Internet by Ross Getman. A few months prior to Kaczynski's arrest, Getman circulated his paper, "The Unabomber and the Planned March on Skokie," in which he speculated that the bomber may have ties to the neo-Nazi National Socialist Party of America. That was the group that staged a 1978 "march in the heavily Jewish Chicago suburb of Skokie, Illinois, home to more than 7,000 Holocaust survivors."

The first Unabomber attack came at the height of the furor over the planned Nazi march. In 1995 the FBI went to a Skokie high school following Unabomber leads. Note that the bomber's first four attacks came out of the Chicago area. The first two were at Northwestern University where, according to Getman, "two years earlier an assistant professor in the computer science and engineering area had written a controversial book arguing that the Holocaust was a hoax." Then a bomb was planted on an American Airlines flight from Chicago to Washington. The fourth was mailed to United Airlines president Percy Wood's Chicago-area home.

The National Socialist Party of America was headed by one Frank Collin (note the initials). Getman finds a heavy use of "Nordic symbolism" in the Unabomber's work, with repeated references to wood and ice. The bomber not only made his bombs out of wood, in one case sending a cherry twig with his package, but in 1980 sent a bomb to the aforementioned airline executive Mr. Wood. The bomb was concealed in a book called *Ice Brothers*. Earlier package bombs had been plastered with Eugene O'Neill stamps—O'Neill being known for his classic play "The Iceman Cometh." The bomber used the O'Neill stamps again on the bomb aimed at Wood.

The novel *Ice Brothers*, Getman explains, takes place during World War II and is set on a patrol boat named *Valkyrie*, a reference to the proto-Nazi composer Richard Wagner's *Ring Cycle*, an epic opera based on the same Teutonic myths that later formed an integral part of Hitler's mystical philosophy. In that same mythology, the raven is a sacred bird. "Hitler passed a special law to protect ravens," notes Getman. The Unabomber once used "Ravenswood" as the return address on a bomb.

"The attempted use of chaos and anarchy by anti-Semites has a long tradition," says Getman, who theorized that the Unabomber was "a sick individual carrying on the legacy of Frank Collin."

Does Ted Kaczynski fit that description? At this point, he's not talking, and despite some rather thorough biographical pieces on him in various magazines, the origins of his political predilections remain an utter mystery.

Another highly speculative, conspiratorial possibility, unlikely though it may be: Is Kaczynski a fall guy for some sort of weird conspiracy to drive a nail into tree-spiking environmentalist havoc wreakers like Earth First!? ABC News reported on April 5 that Kaczynski showed up at an EF meeting at the University of Montana in Missoula in 1994. According to ABC, he went on the FBI's list of suspects at the time. A so-called hit list published in a radical environmental newspaper called *Live Wild or Die* may have been the Unabomber's source for finding victims, investigators believe—though the list was published in 1990 and just four of the bomber's sixteen attacks have come since then.

In May of 1990 Earth First! activists Judi Bari and Daryl Cherney were injured by a pipe bomb in their car. The FBI blamed the bombing on the two Earth First!ers themselves, but never established any evidence to back up that claim and never brought any charges. Earth First! for its part charged that the FBI was trying to frame and discredit the environmental "direct action" group, best known for its program of placing metal spikes in trees to prevent loggers from cutting them down. Or worse, that the bombing was an assassination attempt that the FBI either tacitly or explicitly sanctioned.

While we're at it, we might as well link the Unabomber to the CIA, too. It's all pretty tenuous. For that matter, it may have been just a law enforcement leak to make the FBI look closer than it was to getting its man. But on July 30, 1995, the *Los Angeles Times* reported that forty-eight-year-old fugitive James William Kilgore is a "possible suspect" (how's that for iffy?) in the Unabomber case.

Kilgore, notes the paper, "is best known for his connections to the Symbionese Liberation Army."

According to conspiracy theory pioneer Mae Brussell's reality map, there was something odd about the SLA all along, even before it kidnapped Patty Hearst. Its leader, Donald "General Field Marshal Cinque" DeFreeze—career crook and informer for the LAPD—emerged from the California penal system's Vacaville Medical Facility, where he'd come under the tutelage of CIA-connected Colston Westbrook, a psychological warfare specialist, according to Brussell. Westbrook enlisted DeFreeze into his Black Cultural Association. He offered lessons in "communism" but riveted inmates' attention by displaying in the classroom a succession of, as he put it, "fine looking chicks." Usually the women were for display purposes only, but reportedly, DeFreeze was later allowed conjugal visits with women of his choice—a perk that goes only to married inmates in most cases.

Armed robber DeFreeze obtained early release from Vacaville by performing "a favor" for prison authorities. Brussell asserts that, "a 'favor' at Vacaville Medical Facility usually means submitting to medical research on the brain." Was DeFreeze another psychomanipulated patsy, Mae Brussell wonders? "Were electrodes or transponders inserted into DeFreeze's brain?"

It is true that Brussell does not exactly prove her case in her rhetorical-question-ridden 1974 article "Why Was Patricia Hearst Kidnapped," but she makes several unsettling points. The SLA seemed to come out of nowhere, with no known ties to any radical group or movements. In fact, among Bay Area activists, the SLA was suspected of being a band of police provocateurs.

Its mostly white middle-class members were virtually devoid of previous political experience of any kind. Some came out of the military, including Foster's co-killer Joseph Remiro. Others were waifs and naifs, drug-addled "good kids" gone astray, not unlike Charlie Manson's disciples. The impressionable type. Then there was Donald "Cinque" DeFreeze with his CIA mentor and cozy relations with California prison authorities.

If some shadowy government agency, restless with merely infiltrating authentic leftist movements, did want to create its own phony "radical terrorist" group, it probably would look a lot like the SLA.

If Kilgore had some connection to the Unabomber, and if the SLA was indeed some kind of CIA front—well, the conspiratorial implications would be dizzying.

But it's all a pretty big stretch. According to the *Los Angeles Times*, the FBI was never very hot on Kilgore's heels, "to the frustration of some critics of the UNABOM probe." His name first came up in April 1995 in an L.A. TV news report, which the FBI "repudiated" while still noting Kilgore as "someone they'd like to interview."

The ex-SLAer had been on the lam for nineteen years. The Unabomber had been active for eighteen. Kilgore is wanted on a charge of unlawfully possessing an explosive device, and supposedly his fingerprints were lifted from an SLA-manufactured pipe bomb. He hails from Marin County. The FBI suspected that the Unabomber hung out in the Bay Area or in nearby Sacramento. Kilgore is the son of a lumber broker. Many of the Unabomber's attacks have had "wood" themes. Kilgore supposedly fit the Unabomber's physical description—though that's hard to say because no one has seen him since 1976.

Ted Kaczynski's trial as the Unabomber was almost as dramatic as his life on the outside. As the 1996 pretrial processes continued, Kaczynski's mental health was at the forefront. Both the prosecution and the defense were going to use Kaczynski's journal entries, isolation, and personal statements to indicate his mental disorder. Angry, Kaczynski protested his legal representation (since they were going to plead not guilty by reason of insanity) and wanted to represent himself at his trial. In the meantime, there was discussion of administering capital punishment, which his brother David hotly protested (he had turned in Ted on the condition that he not be given the death penalty). During the argument over whether or not the prosecution would seek the death penalty Ted Kaczynski attempted suicide in jail. After a psychological evaluation it was determined that Kaczynski was competent to stand trial but he was also probably a paranoid schizophrenic, as his lawyers had originally claimed. The judge finally rejected Kaczynski's request to represent himself. Ultimately, on January 22, 1998, Kaczynski plead guilty and was sentenced to life in prison.

MAJOR SOURCES

Information about evidence against Ted Kaczynski comes from press
accounts in the weeks immediately after his arrest.

Douglas, John. *Unabomber*. New York: Pocket Books, 1996.

Much information about Kaczynski comes from dozens of press
reports. The most important articles are:

Associated Press, "Kaczynski's Spiral—Boy Genius to 60s Wallflower
to Embittered Hermit." 20 April 1996.

Howe, Rob. "The Lone Stranger." *People* 15 April 1996.

Johnston, David. "Long and Twisted Trail Led to Unabom Suspect's
Arrest." *New York Times,* 5 April 1996.

McFadden, Robert D. "From a Child of Promise to the Unabom
Suspect." *New York Times,* 26 May 1996.

Mueller, Mark. "Friend: I Liked Having Him Around." *Boston
Herald,* 6 April 1996.

Talbot, David. "Kaczynski Linked to Radical Group." *Boston Herald,*
6 April 1996.

Thomas, Evan. "Blood Brothers." *Newsweek,* 22 April 1996.

Thomas, Evan. "Probing the Mind of a Killer." *Newsweek,* 15 April
1996.

Van Biema, David. "The Mounting Evidence." *Time,* 22 April 1996.

57

The Jet, the Net, and the Missile

A scant eleven minutes after 230 people settled in for a sleepy, seven-hour night flight to Paris from New York's JFK International Airport on July 17, 1996, their Boeing 747-100 burst into a fireball and plummeted, two-and-a-half miles into the Atlantic ocean, off Long Island. No one survived.

Over two years later, the known facts of the TWA Flight 800 calamity remain sketchy. Investigators have no idea what caused the explosion. They do say, however, that they know what did not cause it: conspiracy!

Did a missile, fired by a U.S. Navy vessel, blast the civilian airliner? Did the government cover up the accident? Or wasn't it an accident? That was the conspiracy theory, and thanks to the Internet and the growing spell it casts over the mainstream media, the TWA 800 "missile theory" became one of the most frantically publicized and publicly debated conspiracy theories ever.

Unlike most pre-Internet conspiracy theories, the missile

theory made a swift impact on the major media. In mid-September, with little else besides the rampant discussion of the theory on the Internet to go on, reporters began quizzing crash investigators about the "friendly fire" scenario.

Of course, it was not the first time major media have fed off the conspiracy-theory underground. *Time* magazine's controversial 1992 cover story alleging that the bombing of Pan Am Flight 103 was somehow connected to a U.S. undercover operation grew out of a theory that had been circulating for more than three years. The missile theory took less than two months to surface. As powerful a medium as the Internet is, it still takes a mainstream source to get a conspiracy theory off the ground. The net, however, facilitates the synergy between the two spheres.

Though conspiratorial murmuring began almost immediately after the crash, it was an article in the *Jerusalem Post* three days later that fueled the theory. The *Post* posed a "what if" scenario to anonymous sources in the French Defense Ministry. The sources said that if the plane were indeed brought down by a missile, then it would have to be a U.S. miltary missile. A terrorist weapon just wouldn't have the punch. They gave no further support for their hypothetical assertion.

In the past, a single article in an Israeli newspaper would have had little effect on the American *Zeitgeist;* these days thousands of newspapers have web sites. The *Jerusalem Post* is one of the thousands. Digitized dittos of the *Post* story were flying around cyberspace within hours.

Using a quick survey of Internet web sites and news-group postings as a political barometer, it appeared in August 1996 that President Clinton was not only headed for a crushing defeat in November but probably for federal prison and the gas chamber. Clinton is a certified conspiracy-theory superstar, as his repeated presence in this very book attests.

TWA 800 conspiracy theorizers certainly didn't spare the ubervillain from Hope. On July 23, 1996, J. Orlin Grabbe—best known for his thirty-seven-part web-published series on

Vince Foster—confidently asserted on his web site that Syrian-backed terrorists shot down the plane. Not "friendly fire" at all but a friendly cover-up. Clinton suppressed the truth, Grabbe said, because he wanted to blame Iran or Iraq so he could triumphantly bomb one country or the other as an election-commandeering October Surprise. As if he needed one.

Grabbe didn't pause long enough from his omniscient narrative to explain how he knew all this.

The next day, a Usenet posting, attributed to Gene Hilsheimer of Panama City, Florida, revealed that two Arkansas state troopers were on TWA 800, on their way to Paris to spill dirt on Clinton in an interview with the French daily *Le Monde*. The source of this ante-upping information: the *Miami Herald*. But after a week of giddy on-line debate over "TWA Troopergate," the *Herald* ran a story exposing the posting as a "cyberhoax." The *Herald* never published such a story, and there were no troopers on the plane.

But the missile theory really got moving in November 1996. Pierre Salinger, the stogie-chomping expatriate and ex-newsman, set flight from his Paris pad and launched himself into the national U.S. headlines.

Salinger, the respected journalist and onetime press secretary to President Kennedy, was seventy one years old at the time, and like many seventy-one-year-olds, he didn't do much Internet surfing.

It was a weird incident that, if nothing else, shows why journalists need to get their toes wet in cyberspace (though many of them take a perversely smug pride in their Internet illiteracy). Salinger announced that he had a government document proving that TWA Flight 800 was blasted out of the sky by a U.S. military missile in a catastrophic training accident. The document, Salinger told French television and the numerous U.S. reporters who called him at his hotel in France, "was written by an American, but it was given to me by someone in French intelligence in Paris."

Well, leave it to the French. If, in fact, it was a French

intelligence agent who passed on the document, then the United States really shouldn't worry too much next time it catches a French agent snooping because the allegedly explosive document had been floating around on the Internet since late August. But Salinger unwittingly passed it off as exclusive, suppressed information.

The document, penned by former airline pilot and crash investigator Richard Russell, is the Rosetta stone of the "friendly fire" theory. In a nutshell, the document claimed inside knowledge of the investigation—and that the higher-ups knew the true cause of the TWA 800 crash. A missile, natch.

In an interview with us, Russell copped to authorship of the document—a fact also noted in *Newsweek* and *USA Today*. He said that he wrote it as a private E-mail using his America Online account and fired it off to a dozen or so friends. Apparently, one or more of them must have fired it off to a few friends of their own, because before you could say "kaboom" the message was all over the Internet, posted in several Usenet news groups, e-mailed from coast to coast and around the world, and even faxed into major newsrooms.

Russell claimed that he based his message on high-level sources, but he won't name them, and no one has come forward, even anonymously, to corroborate the information. As for Russell, he seemed a bit tired of the whole affair (and this was just a few months after the crash; the controversy continues even now!), saying, "I'd rather be a nonentity in this thing."

Can't say the same for Salinger, however.

A World War II vet, Salinger, in addition to his stint as JFK's spokesman, had a run as a U.S. senator and media personality. He appeared as Lucky Pierre on the Adam West *Batman* series. But drawing on his experience as a bon vivant and connoisseur of large cigars, he found that his large network of contacts in high places would serve him well as a reporter. ABC gave him a job, and Salinger has since been out front on numerous international stories. His 1992 book *Secret Dossier* is a minor classic for the way it spelled out the behind-the-scenes conspiring between the CIA, Kuwait, and Iraq that led up to the Gulf War. (See chapter 7 for more details.)

So when Salinger announced that he had proof of this heinous "friendly fire" accident and subsequent, massive cover-up, the world listened. Unfortunately, Salinger put his foot deep into his mouth. In a phone call after he made his startling announcement, a CNN producer who had received the Russell document by fax about two months earlier read it to the veteran foreign correspondent and transcontinental jet-setter. "Yes. That's it. That's the document," said an astonished Salinger. "Where did you get it?"

Well, Pierre, if you'd get a little Net savvy, you'd figure it out.

After that egg-in-the-face episode, one would imagine that Salinger would be loath to pursue the matter further. But there he was again, in March 1997, waving his latest article for *Paris Match* magazine. In this one, Salinger presented stills from a radar videotape, said to have been recorded off an air-traffic-control system monitoring the doomed flight. That tape, Salinger says, shows an unexplained blip heading directly toward the plane at high velocity and converging with the plane right at the time when the blast would have, well, blasted.

Needless to say, the immediate reaction to Salinger's "new evidence" was not exactly warm and welcoming. FBI mouthpiece James Kallstrom's retort was pretty typical, calling Salinger's salvo "a joke" filled with "inaccuracies, distortions, and inventions."

There are a couple of curious aspects of the affair. All of a sudden, Salinger was working with self-proclaimed "nonentity" Russell. The missile-theorizing former pilot, who claims to have access to inside info, was, in fact, the source of the radar tape. According to the *New York Times*, Russell tried to pawn the video off on ABC News—for a million bucks. Russell wasn't taking phone calls, so the *Times* didn't confirm that rather damning assertion with Russell himself. But what is known is this: The FBI subpoenaed the tape, went down to Florida, and seized Russell's copy.

While Salinger was generally being presented as a lone nut, as many as 150 eyewitnesses were convinced that they saw a streak of light headed toward the plane seconds before it exploded. Add that to an Associated Press report that a National Guard helicopter pilot, Captain Chris Baur, was in the air near the explosion and upon returning to his base "told officials immediately he thought he saw a missile." Apparently, Baur repeated that claim to officials numerous times but wouldn't comment publicly (so at least no one can say the guy's just out for publicity).

The usual response to the missile eyewitnesses has been to bring out the old saw which holds: "Eyewitness testimony is notoriously unreliable." But isn't that kind of a misleading argument? The testimony of any single eyewitness is often unreliable, but a preponderance of corroborating eyewitnesses, many of whom have no direct contact with each other, is powerful evidence. Ask any cop.

Let's be honest. We'd have loved to hitch our ever-rising star to Salinger's caboose (on second thought, *yuk!*) and join in the TWA missile hunt, but dammit, we know our readers expect integrity. (Koff! Koff!) So all we can say is that the TWA "friendly fire" missile theory is at best an open question in our minds.

We are certain that our friends in "the corporate media" weren't exactly giving it a fair airing. Take, for example, the March 12, 1997, *CBS Evening News* report on the missile theory. There were three sources, all of them government investigators, quoted in the all-too-brief report. No alternative point of view; for that matter, no nongovernmenatal point of view. If we were strident, ultraleft, angry-at-the-world types like Noam Chomsky, we'd call that propaganda! But we're not, so we won't.

We do know for a fact that CBS had ample opportunity to present a nongovernmental point of view because the producers of that same report sent a camera crew to *70 GCAT*'s (*70 Greatest Conspiracies of All Time*) spacious East Coast headquarters and spent considerable time interviewing a highly placed source within the *70 GCAT* braintrust. But we ended up on the cutting-room floor.

Perhaps the best investigative piece supporting the missile theory to appear in print in the months following the crash came from the *Riverside Press-Enterprise* on October 4, 1996. The piece noted that all of the friendly-fire allegations had been unambiguously denied by everyone in a position to deny them, including allegations (in the Russell document and elsewhere) that special "warning zones" off Long Island had been activated on the night of the crash, July 17. If those zones were activated, it could mean that naval exercises were taking place in that area, possibly firing live missiles.

An "ex-navy officer who used to supervise warning areas" told the paper (anonymously, of course) that "the plane was the victim of an exercise gone awry." But even that nameless source characterized his own information as secondhand. And, of course, it was denied. But more intriguingly, the *Press-Enterprise* uncovered "documents showing the activation of vast military exercise areas...that contradict earlier official denials."

Those navy and Federal Aviation Administration records showed, according to the *Press-Enterprise* story, that "scheduled operations July 17 turned large chunks of airspace into danger zones for civilian aircraft." When the paper showed copies of those records to navy spokesmen, the navy stopped talking to the *Press-Enterprise* and bounced all calls to the FBI and National Transportation Safety Board, the main agencies in charge of the crash investigation.

While the *Press-Enterprise* article was almost entirely speculative, very thin on workable fact, it notes that "a special 7,790-square-mile area became off-limits at 8:00 P.M., about the time TWA 800 was backing away from the passenger gate." That area is known as W-105 (and, interestingly, is mentioned in the Russell message).

There was, the navy acknowledges, a P-3 submarine-detecting plane flying through the area at that time. The article asserts that W-105 would not have been activated for something as simple as a "P-3 fly through." Quoting a "retired senior Pentagon officer"—again nameless—as saying "this had to be a command and control exercise or exercise to qualify somebody to do something or whatever" (how's that for specificity?), the *Press-Enterprise* speculates that the exercise involved "the Army's special forces" or something similarly sinister. Such exercises could have involved dummy or low-yield missiles, one of which could have hit the plane.

Shortly after Salinger's radar tape went public, a writer named James Sanders turned up another piece of, as they say in the conspiracy biz, "best evidence." As reported in his 1997 paperback *The Downing of TWA Flight 800*, Sanders uncovered a few pieces of foam from the destroyed 747's seat cushions. On the foam there was a mysterious reddish stain. Upon analysis, Sanders asserts, the stain turned out to be missile fuel.

So what happened to that evidence? Sanders received it from an inside source he calls, slipping into *X-Files* mode, "Hangar Man." Then he sent it on to a trusted producer at CBS News. CBS, always hot for a good story, promptly turned it back over to the FBI. And that was the last we heard of it. Sanders also says that the FBI searched his house and he feared for his safety.

All pretty damning stuff, at least on the surface. But the government investigators didn't think so. More than fourteen months after TWA Flight 800 crashed off the coast of Long Island, investigators, not exactly moving with the speed of a heat-seeking missile, were close to a final solution to that vexing question of what caused the 747 to erupt in a catastrophic fireball at eleven thousand feet.

And the answer is—ready now?—nobody did it! And, oh, yeah, that mysterious "streak of light" you saw, if you were one of 244 witnesses who gave statements after the crash—that was just a leaky fuel tank.

The latest move toward this definitive answer in which no

one is to blame came when the CIA and FBI, one of those Marvel Comics—like team-ups, issued a joint report on the so-called missile theory that has generated nearly a year's worth of press and on-line speculation. In the joint report, the two spook agencies said that while it's true that all those people saw a "streak" that appeared to be headed for the plane, what they really saw was the plane itself, already in the process of inexplicably falling apart. The light streak was actually fuel that ignited as it streamed out of the aircraft.

After fending off questions about the TWA 800 missile theory for more than a year, the FBI, with help once again from the CIA, finally closed down their criminal investigation of the exploding 747 in late 1997. The spy agency produced a computer-animated video showing, hypothetically, how the plane blew up (no missile in sight), and that was that.

But wait! The CIA cartoon didn't convince everyone. Hard to believe, we know. But there are always a few nuts, crackpots, and lunatics out there who just like to contradict everything! In this case the nut was former Joint Chiefs of Staff (JCS) chairman Adm. Thomas H. Moorer!

You may not have heard this story, though on the face of it Moorer, one of the nation's top retired navy men, who made missile warfare his area of expertise during his distinguished career, would merit some media attention. Not that a spiffy resumé makes the man right, but at least it ought to earn him some ink. Imagine if Colin Powell had come out and said that he believed that "all evidence would point to a missile" in the TWA 800 disaster. Although that's exactly what Moorer said, his comments garnered no more than a few hundred words (if that) in a January 9 squib on the Gannet News Service wire.

But that wasn't good enough for Moorer, who, according to the Gannet story, "expressed grave suspicion over the FBI's 18-month investigation of the disaster."

"It absolutely deserves more investigation—a lot more," the admiral opined. "This time I wouldn't let the FBI do it."

Why didn't Moorer's comments attract a little more atten-

456

TRAGEDY AND TRAUMA

tion? Probably because the media was sick of the story and the conspiracy stigma that hangs all over it like a dirty shirt. If Moorer's plea leads to calls for a new "missile theory" investigation, mark our words, Sunday morning pundits will first offer sonorous proclamations about the need to "put this behind us." Then they'll write Moorer off as a crank and shake their heads over how badly he's lost it since he was JCS chairman.

The lengths to which the government and its pals in the press have gone to debunk this whole missile problem will no doubt only further the suspicions that have been floating around since the plane went down. And who knows? Perhaps with good reason. Is the government covering up the fact that the navy downed the plane with a training rocket? The way this investigation's gone, it's almost as if they're simply covering up for everyone, navy or not. The investigators still say there is no hard support for any hypothesis—missile, onboard bomb, or the government's favorite, "mechanical failure." The latter appears to be the most blame free, but someone's got to be responsible for a technological screwup. We're frankly surprised that the investigators haven't opted for the "meteor theory," which has also found some adherents. Heck, if a meteor brought down the 747, then it really is not anybody's fault. And we can all go home.

The CIA-FBI report may or may not be a definitive debunking of missilophilia, but it raises or ignores as many questions as it answers. What about the other pilots who have also reported missiles or at least "streaks" near their own planes. In September 1996, 220 miles south of the TWA crash site, an American Airlines pilot reported seeing a missile whiz by his 757 aircraft. Then, in November, a Pakistan Airlines pilot flying very near the Long Island crash scene swore he saw a "streak of light" whiz by his plane. That same night, a TWA flight was flying behind the Pakistani plane and verified the report. But officials dismissed the streak of light as—a meteor! (We're not kidding.)

And just why the heck did the CIA suddenly surface as a player in the crash investigation? We're no experts, but last we checked, the CIA wasn't supposed to be involved in domestic affairs. Maybe the fact that this was an international flight gives the spy bureau some jurisdiction. But we hadn't heard of their involvement up to this point.

Finally, with the glut of Internet conspiracy theories about pretty much *everything* lately (we're thinking, in particular, of the Princess Diana no-brainers), it's worth mentioning that this "friendly fire" theory does conform to the our exacting standards of what constitutes legitimate conspiracy theorizing. Unlike the Diana theories, which arose *ex nihilo* after a not-unusual event (the violent crash of a speeding car), there is actually something to spark speculation in the TWA case. A streak of light! The solid safety record of the 747! The plodding, seemingly aimless investigation!

Is that "evidence?" Sure—at least enough evidence to ignite a conspiracy theory. Whether the evidence turns out to be legit or not, we can't say.

Guess we'll just have to trust the CIA.

MAJOR SOURCES

Hendrix, David E., et al. "New Data Show Missile May Have Nailed TWA 800." *Riverside Press-Enterprise,* 10 March 1997.
Hosenball, Mark. "The Anatomy of a Rumor." *Newsweek,* 23 September 1996.
O'Sullivan, Arieh. "France: Airliner Possibly Shot Down by Missile." *Jeruslam Post,* 21 July 1996.
Purdy, Matthew. "No Missile on Radar Tape, TWA Investigator Says." *New York Times,* 13 March 1997.
Sanders, James. *The Downing of TWA Flight 800.* New York: Zebra Books, 1997.
Vankin, Jonathan, and John Whalen. "How a Quack Became a Canard." *New York Times Magazine,* 17 November 1996.

58

Crack Shots

Back in the Watergate glory days, it was the *Washington Post* against the world, fearlessly exposing a scandal that could bring down the government while its competitors scoffed. Those were the days when the *Post* all but invented "investigative reporting." By 1996, the roles were, as pundits at places like the *Post* enjoy saying, flip-flopped. Now the *Post* does the scoffing as another, smaller paper plows through a lid-blowing investigative effort.

The background: In August the *San Jose Mercury News* began running a series by reporter Gary Webb that certainly sounded familiar to the select few who actually paid attention during the Iran-Contra scandal or to anyone who had read earlier editions of this book and others like it. Namely, that the CIA was somehow behind the flow of cocaine into the United States in the 1980s, using the profits to bankroll Nicaraguan right-wing Contra guerrillas.

Specifically, the stories alleged that two Nicaraguan drug merchants, Danilo Blandon and Norvin Meneses, raised money for the Contras, with the CIA's rubber stamp, by selling coke to legendary L.A. cocaine impresario "Freeway" Ricky Ross. Freeway Rick, in turn, converted the cocaine into low-priced crack and spread it through the black community in Southern California, and beyond.

Webb even dug up a picture of CIA-backed Contra leader Adolfo Colero sitting in a kitchen, hanging out with Meneses, providing visual verification of the CIA-Contra cocaine connection. When the *Post* and other big papers ran their attacks on Webb, one of the main points was that Contra leaders were not actually CIA agents but merely paid "assets," thereby absolving the CIA of responsibility.

Webb's story seemed to confirm the long-held belief within the African-American community that the CIA had deliberately flooded U.S. cities with crack. The motive: racial annhiliation. Webb's story, it is important to note, never made any such allegation. If you were looking for it, though, you could easily read the story and see what you wanted to see. The "conspiracy" charge was the core of the attacks on Webb and the *Mercury News*.

CIA drug smuggling was not a new story, however. The now-forgotten but once-infamous Christic Institute's "Secret Team" lawsuit, smartly summarized in chapter 60 of this very volume, focused on the Agency's long-documented and always denied narcotics connection. Nor were the crusading Christics the first to hit upon this sinister connection. Author James Mills spent five years following U.S. drug-enforcement agents around the world for his groundbreaking (and at more than eleven hundredplus pages, imposing) tome *The Underground Empire*.

"You don't have to be a CIA-hater," Mills wrote, "to trek around the world viewing one major narcotics group after another and grow amazed at the frequency with which you encounter the still-fresh footprints of American inelligence agents."

You sure don't. For those who glean their news from sources other than the *Washington Post* and the *New York Times,* the Webb series provided a drug-addled stroll down memory lane. Flashback (in a good way, of course) to the late 1980s, when U.S. senator John Kerry ran a subcommittee investigation into Contra-cocaine connections. He concluded that at least some CIA officials knew that cocaine smuggling was an integral part of the Contra-arming effort.

Kerry's investigation, needless to say, received a healthy snubbing in the mainstream media, though it was splattered all over front pages in alternative publications, such as the Chicago-based weekly *In These Times.* But it did rear its head every now and then on the national airwaves. The now-defunct CBS newsmagazine *West 57th* did a couple of shows on the Contra-cocaine link (on April 6 and July 11, 1987).

But the *Mercury News* story was the first time a major (the *Mercury News* has two Pulitzer Prizes under its belt) newspaper actually pursued the CIA-dope connection with any, as JFK would say, "vigah!" And the *Mercury News* put another twist on the story. The cocaine brought into the country by CIA-backed Nicaraguan drug dealers went straight to the L.A. 'hood, where it became "crack." The crack plague of the 1980s (and 1990s) is actually, at least tangentially, a CIA operation.

The *Post,* however, set out to debunk its cross-country counterpart's story. On October 4, 1996, it ran a piece entitled "The CIA and Crack: Evidence Is Lacking of a Contra-Tied Plot." As so often occurs with this type of debunking journalism, the bigger paper's "investigation" (at least as published) amounted to little more than a series of denials by the very people who would probably be indicted if the *Mercury News* story panned out. The *Post* also asserted that the crack plague was a "broad-based phenomenon," painting Webb as reductionist for appearing to ascribe the whole thing to the Contra-CIA connection (a charge Webb doesn't make).

Despite the big boys' best efforts, the *Mercury News* series gave the CIA-drugs story new credibility.

To most anyone following the CIA-drugs story in the alternative and conspiracy press for the previous decade, therefore, Webb's revelations were powerful, if not very surprising. What was surprising, though in retrospect it shouldn't have been, was the counterstrike against Webb from his supposed journalistic "colleagues." The *Los Angeles Times* also ran its own "investigation" of Webb's investigation and found, shockingly enough, that there was nothing there. *Phew!* Good thing the big guys didn't get scooped.

The pressure from its better-known counterparts eventually weighed heavily on the *Mercury News*. Editor Jerry Ceppos penned a *mea culpa* on May 11, 1997, in which he, for all intents and purposes, retracted Webb's stories and apologized for ever running them. In fact, Ceppos said that he, the editor of the paper, had not read the obviously explosive series prior to publication.

Back in the 1980s, when Kerry's subcommittee found its own evidence of CIA involvement in cocaine trafficking, the agency pretty much ignored it. But this is the age of the Internet and the *Mercury News* story exploded across the country faster than you could say, "Beam me up, Scotty!" This time the CIA went ahead with an internal probe of itself (and we all know how much fun that can be). Now, a year later, the CIA has finished probing internally, and they found—are you sitting down?—*nothing!*

The report has not been released to the public, natch. According to a December 18 piece in that same *Los Angeles Times* the investigation was "described as the most intensive in [the CIA's] history," and it concluded that charges of CIA links to cocaine traffickers were "without foundation."

But there's a catch. The investigation was basically a joke. Retired CIA agent Duane "Dewey" Clarridge, a veteran counterintelligence man who was CIA chief of covert operations in Latin America during the 1980s, called the questions submitted to him by the CIA "nonsense" and refused to answer them. The *Times* quotes ex-CIA officials who were interviewed as part of the probe as saying that the questions posed by the Agency were softballs.

According to former CIA officer Donald H. Winters, the CIA began its interview with him by stating, "They had no substantive evidence that any of the allegations in the San Jose article had any basis." The CIA interviewer then simply put Winters "through the motions of touching all the bases."

Now there's an investigative technique! "Uh, excuse me, O.J. We know you're innocent as the day you were born, but why not give me that golfing-on-the-front-lawn story, anyway, just for the record."

When Clarridge was sent a written CIA questionnaire (investigation by questionnaire, another time-honored sleuthing secret), he sent it back blank. Other non-CIA figures, such as Robert Owen, who blew the whistle on CIA-drug connections as early as 1985, were not contacted at all.

Concludes the *Times*, "The report is unlikely to put to rest all the questions about CIA complicity with cocaine trafficking in Central America's turbulent 1980s."

No. Really?

MAJOR SOURCES

Hackett, Thomas. "The CIA-Crack Story: Anatomy of a Journalistic Train Wreck." *Salon*, May 30, 1997.
McManus, Doyle. "The Cocaine Trail." *Los Angeles Times*, 20–22 October 1996.

McManus, Doyle, and James Risen. "CIA Probe Absolves Agency on L.A. Crack." *Los Angeles Times,* 18 December 1997.

Mills, James. *The Underground Empire.* New York: Dell, 1987.

Solomon, Norman. "Snow Job: The Establishment's Papers Do Damage Control for the CIA." *EXTRA!,* January/February 1997.

Suro, Robert, and Walter Pincus. "The CIA and Crack: Evidence Is Lacking of Contra-Tied Plot." *Washington Post,* 4 October 1996.

Webb, Gary. "Dark Alliance." *San Jose Mercury News,* 18–20 August 1996.

IX

State Secrets

59

The Return of Hitler's Spy

World War II had been kaput scarcely a week when a U.S. Army DC-3 touched down outside of Washington, D.C., ferrying a top-secret German cargo. Stepping off the plane, possibly disguised as an American general, was Nazi legend Reinhard Gehlen, Hitler's master spy.

His slight physique—five feet eight, 130 pounds—belied his strategic importance to the U.S. officials who welcomed him with open arms. As chief of the Third Reich's Foreign Armies East, Gehlen had been Hitler's most senior officer on the Russian front. He had run an elaborate network of Nazi spies against the Soviet Union—the new villains in the budding Cold War.

Though he was forty-three years old, and Germany lay in ruin, Gehlen's best years were still ahead of him. He was about to make an offer that America's military and governing elites couldn't refuse: He would put his clandestine nexus of Nazi SS officers, underground fascist sympathizers, fugitive war crimi-

467

nals, and encyclopedic Soviet files into the service of Uncle Sam.

A shrewd survivor, Gehlen had buried his organization's plenary files on the USSR in the Austrian Alps as soon as Nazi Germany's collapse became imminent. Gehlen knew that the battle against communism would replace the war against fascist Germany as the overriding military and political goal of the capitalist West. "My view," he wrote in his memoir, "was that there would be a place even for Germany in a Europe rearmed for defense against Communism. Therefore we must set our sights on the Western powers, and give ourselves two objectives: to help defend against Communist expansion and to recover and reunify Germany's lost territories." (Apparently, Gehlen's bargaining chip was so valuable, his hosts were willing to overlook the general's still-current ideas about *Deustchland über alles*.)

Shortly after Germany's surrender to the Allies, Gehlen had descended from his Alpine retreat, audaciously turning himself over to American authorities. "I am head of the Section Foreign Armies East in German Army headquarters," he announced in his prepared speech. "I have information to give of the highest importance to your government."

"So have they all," snapped an army captain, who sent the arrogant, hot-tempered general packing to the camp at Salzburg with the rest of the Nazi prisoners. But he wouldn't stew there for very long. Within a month, with the Soviet Union demanding custody of Gehlen and his files, Hitler's spy master began to receive a stream of important American visitors.

At Fort Hunt near Washington, where an NCO butler and several white-jacketed orderlies catered to his needs, Gehlen conferred with President Truman's national security advisor, a gaggle of army intelligence generals, and Allen Dulles, a giant in America's wartime intelligence outfit, the Office of Strategic Services (OSS). Later Dulles would take the helm of the CIA.

After a year in Washington, Gehlen returned to the Fatherland—not as a prisoner, but as an influential agent in America's anticommunist war of nerves with Russia. Gehlen took command of his old organization and became America's foremost intelligence source on the Soviet Union. His influence over American policy would be sweeping; and like the proverbial Faustian pact, there would be later reverberations: His exaggerated reports of Russian military strength would escalate the Cold War to dangerous peaks.

How the U.S. government came to collaborate with Gehlen and hundreds of other high-ranking Nazis is a rarely told chapter of American history. American officials, increasingly paranoid about the threat of Soviet influence in postwar Europe and around the world, found expedient soul mates in the Nazi scientists and SS officers they recruited. After all, Nazi Germany's fascists were vehemently opposed to communism, too. Invoking the exigencies of the Cold War, Dulles explained away any misgivings about hiring Gehlen: "He's on our side, and that's all that matters."

Even as the U.S. military was hunting down Nazi war criminals, other branches of the U.S. government were quietly enlisting many of the same fugitives. Project Paperclip was the U.S. War Department's code name for its secret importation of Nazi scientists, using sanitized, rewritten "records" to sneak the Germans through U.S. immigration. In Germany, many of those scientists had benefited from fatal experiments performed on prisoners at Dachau and from slave labor at other concentration camps. During the early 1980s the U.S. Department of Justice identified numerous Nazi veterans who were still living in America.

Truman's National Security Council issued classified directives sanctioning the use of former Nazi collaborators. The paper trail was subject to a massive coverup, and the complete history of America's dalliance with Nazis remains partially obscured. They may not have saved Hitler's brain, as the B-movie conspiracy theory had it, but the Führer's intelligence apparatus found a new host, transplanted onto America's spy and military agencies. It's ironic that when President Truman demobilized the OSS, he warned against setting up a permanent

"Gestapo-like" intelligence agency, even as his administration was dotting the *i*'s and crossing the *t*'s on its make-work program for former and possibly not-so-former Nazis and their quislings.

Among the notorious Nazi fugitives quietly pardoned and employed by the postwar American government for intelligence work was Klaus Barbie, the SS "Butcher of Lyon." Barbie worked with Gehlen after the war and even lived for a time in the United States.

Though Gehlen promised his handlers, "on principle," that he wouldn't recruit former SS and Gestapo men, he immediately broke his official word, hiring at least six SS and Sicherheitsdienst (SD) veterans. And America's intelligence elite looked the other way.

Two of Gehlen's notorious postwar hires were Dr. Franz Alfred Six and Emil Augsburg, SS intelligence veterans involved in the mass extermination of Jews. They were both fugitive war criminals.

Franz Six was described by Adolf Eichmann as "a real eager beaver" when it came to the genocide of Jews. "The physical elimination of Eastern Jewry would deprive Jewry of its biological reserves," Six had announced at a conference on the so-called Jewish Question. He put his plan into practice in Smolensk, where his unit murdered some two hundred people in cold blood, among them "thirty-eight intellectual Jews who had tried to create unrest and discontent in the newly established Ghetto of Smolensk," he reported to headquarters.

Emil Augsberg, a staffer under SS chief Himmler, also had led a murder squad in Russia. According to his Nazi Party records, he achieved "extraordinary results...in special tasks," an SS euphemism for mass murder of Jews. Gehlen would find good use for Augsburg's specialty: overseeing assassinations behind "enemy" lines.

For the Gehlen Organization, both Six and Augsberg reactivated their Nazi spy networks in the Soviet Union and hired unemployed German intelligence veterans, many of whom were fellow fugitives. Gehlen must have realized that unofficial Allied policy favored the employment of war criminals: Augsberg was simultaneously moonlighting for several other U.S. intelligence agencies and a French government clandestine group, all the while serving in a private network of ex-SS officers.

When the U.S. Army's Counter-Intelligence Corps (CIC) caught up to Six, he was convicted of war crimes and got a twenty-year sentence. (Augsberg was luckier: the CIC didn't arrest him—it *hired* him.) After only four years in prison, though, Six won clemency—and U.S. permission to rejoin the Gehlen Organization as a valuable asset to Western security.

Gehlen's group not only formed the core in America's absorption of Hitler's espionage elite, it also helped midwife the newborn CIA: During the early postwar years, all of the Agency's anti-Soviet assets in Eastern Europe were managed and mastered by Gehlen. Sometimes his reports were retyped verbatim on CIA stationary and passed along to Truman. Gehlen also held great sway over NATO's intelligence and strategy. According to one estimate, the master spy generated 70 percent of NATO's information on the Soviet Union, Eastern Europe, and Europe.

In effect, the West's bulwark against the USSR was utterly dependent on information flowing from an operation run by former Nazis—and said information was often spurious, at that.

In his sobering book on America's recruitment of Nazis, *Blowback,* Christopher Simpson notes that Gehlen's alarmist reports helped ratchet up tensions between the United States and the Soviet Union during the Cold War: "Gehlen provided U.S. Army intelligence and later the CIA with many of the dire reports that were used to justify increased U.S. military budgets and intensified U.S./USSR hostilities," Simpson writes.

Gehlen's exaggerated reports about an imminent Soviet attack—when in fact the Russians were still licking their postwar wounds—came close to touching off war several times. According to Gehlen biographer E. H. Cookridge and others, in 1948

Gehlen nearly convinced the United States that the Soviets were about to launch an assault on the West. He advised that the West would be wise to strike first. Later, during the 1950s, his erroneous claims that the Soviets had outpaced America in the military buildup fueled fears about the so-called missile gap, which helped stoke up anticommie feelings to feverish levels.

"The [CIA] loved Gehlen because he fed us what we wanted to hear," former CIA officer Victor Marchetti told Simpson. "We used his stuff constantly, and we fed it to everybody else: the Pentagon; the White House; the newspapers. They loved it, too. But it was hyped up Russian boogeyman junk, and it did a lot of damage to this country."

Ironically, the Org also damaged the CIA's anti-Soviet work. The Org's underground groups were so riddled with Soviet double agents, that Western intelligence was compromised for decades. John Loftus, formerly the chief prosecutor of the Justice Department's Nazi-hunting section, summed up the Soviet infiltration of anti-East Bloc groups this way: "It really shows how Soviet intelligence was able to keep communism afloat for the last seventy years."

Intentionally or not, Gehlen undermined the very "national security" that had justified his recruitment in the first place.

Which brings us to some interesting, yet unsubstantiated, speculation. Some researchers propose that Hitler's haughty spy master had a plan B, an ulterior motive beyond the personal survival instinct and rabid anticommunism. Conspiracy researcher Carl Oglesby contends that Gehlen's postwar organization operated as a cover for the Odessa, an international underground set up by deputy führer Martin Bormann to preserve the defeated Nazi Reich. Oglesby calls Gehlen's group "by far the most audacious, most critical, and most essential part of the entire Odessa undertaking." Military intelligence historian (and espionage veteran) Colonel William Corson seconds this notion.

The Gehlen Org, Oglesby argues, provided a haven for fleeing Odessa members by putting them on the American intelligence payroll—a brilliant gambit. More than a few of Gehlen's operatives were indeed Odessa members.

Oglesby's evidence is curious, if not entirely convincing. A declassified CIA document from the 1970s reports that while he was in a U.S. Army VIP prison camp in Wiesbaden, "Gehlen sought and received approval" for his deal with the Americans from Hitler's appointed successor, Admiral Karl Doenitz. "The German chain of command was still in effect," Oglesby concludes, "and it approved of what Gehlen was doing with the Americans."

Whether or not the Gehlen Org was a diversion to preserve an underground Nazi empire is an open question. But Gehlen did manage to attain his goal of splitting away from U.S. intelligence to serve the fledgling West German government. Gehlen's Org continues to live on, as Germany's BND intelligence service.

The Org's legacy also survives in America. The forty-year defense buildup that helped transform America into the world's largest debtor nation, as well as the ongoing exploits of Gehlen's godchild, the CIA, in the expedient realms of political assassination, propaganda, and covert operations certainly owe a debt to Hitler's master spy, and the men who signed him up to "our side."

MAJOR SOURCES

Cookridge, E. H. *Gehlen, Spy of the Century.* New York: Random House, 1971.

Gehlen, Reinhard. *The Service.* New York: World, 1972.

Higham, Charles. *American Swastika.* New York: Doubleday, 1985.

Loftus, John. *The Belarus Secret.* New York: Paragon House, 1989.

Oglesby, Carl. "Reinhard Gehlen: The Secret Treaty of Fort Hunt." *Covert Action Information Bulletin,* no. 35 (Fall 1990).

Simpson, Christopher. *Blowback.* New York: Weidenfeld & Nicolson, 1988.

Whiting, Charles. *Gehlen: Germany's Master Spy.* New York: Ballantine Books, 1972.

60

The Secret Team

A true period piece and document of an era, the Daniel Sheehan Affidavit even inspired a graphic novel—appropriately, because the document is less a court filing than a work of art; a Francis Ford Coppola-esque epic of secrets and subterfuge and omnipresent danger.

The affidavit was filed in December 1986 by Daniel Sheehan, a longtime activist-lawyer—he had worked, for example, on the Karen Silkwood case and for the Native Americans besieged at Wounded Knee. By the mid-eighties he was chief council for the Washington, D.C.-based Christic Institute, "an interfaith, public interest law firm and public policy center."

Wielding the unwieldy Racketeer Influenced and Corrupt Organizations statute (RICO) usually employed by prosecutors to bag mob bosses, Sheehan tried to nail an entire "secret team" of spies, mercenaries, gun runners, and their White House basement buddies by implicating them in the bombing of a renegade Contra leader's press conference in La Penca, Costa Rica.

The Contra, Eden Pastora, had tired of CIA hands-on

management of the anti-Sandinista rebellion. He called the press conference to explain his reasons for breaking with other Contra groups who paid greater homage to the CIA than to the cause. As soon as Pastora started to blab—boom!

The Christic clients were two journalists scarred in the blast. With the broadly drawn RICO statute, if Sheehan could tie the bombing to the activities of this secret team, he could bring down the entire shadow government.

The affidavit came out around the same time that the Iran-Contra scandal hit the news and as the scandal unfolded some of its key names turned out to be among those men listed as the Christic Institute's twenty-nine defendants. Names like Richard Secord, Oliver North, John Hull, and Theodore Shackley; Thomas Clines, Albert Hakim, John Singlaub, and Edwin Wilson—all of them CIA operatives, military officers, arms dealers, or some combination thereof—populate Sheehan's counter-reality.

The affidavit, arising from Sheehan's own investigation involving seventy sources, spins the tale of an arms-for-drugs-for-guns-for-money enterprise extending from the far reaches of Southeast Asia three decades ago to Central America in the 1980s. The narrative picks up against a *Godfather Part II* backdrop of rip-roaring Havana circa 1959, overtaken by socialist revolution. Conspiracies unfurl posthaste. Richard Nixon meets with security-specialist-cum-private-spy Robert Maheu to discuss means of undermining the new Cuban government.

Maheu contacts the underworld elite: John Roselli, Sam Giancana, Santos Trafficante. They assemble a team of assassins to "supplement" the supersecret National Security Council "Operation 40," aimed at toppling Castro.

Members of Operation 40 also smuggle drugs into the United States from Cuba. Use of the Mafia leads to some "problems of control," but the operation carries on.

A few years later Operation 40 leadership relocates to Laos, the new frontier. The CIA's "Blonde Ghost," Shackley, and his chief lieutenant Thomas Clines form a new assassination squad using Laotian Hmong tribesmen.

The hit squad's commander is General John Singlaub, later founder of the ultra-right-wing World Anti-Communist League. North and Secord both served under Singlaub.

The unit backs an opium lord named Van Pao in a territorial war against two competitors in the Laotian jungle.

The fortunate Mr. Pao, with a little help from his friends, emerges victorious after his drug trade rivals are "mysteriously assassinated." Soon Van Pao meets in a Saigon hotel with Santos Trafficante and another drug-importing contract is finalized, according to Sheehan's allegations.

These types of activities proceed apace throughout the Vietnam era, most of the time with some kind of official sanction from the CIA or the military. The Phoenix Program, under which forty thousand Vietnamese local and municipal leaders were assassinated, was one such fully approved program of questionable ethical status. But good things come to an end. When Phoenix reached the end of its mandate, Shackley, Clines, and Richard Armitage—whom the affidavit describes as the "bursar" for this unusual quasi-corporation—"began a highly secret non-CIA authorized program setting up their own private anticommunist assassination and unconventional warfare program."

The secret team was born.

That, anyway, is the story according to Dan Sheehan. Opium-sales money "secretly smuggled out of Vietnam in large suitcases by Richard Secord and Thomas Clines—and carried into Australia where it was deposited in a secret, personal bank account," provided the wherewithal for the "Team's endeavors."

The affidavit contains any number of serious allegations against these men—who needless to say have denied them ad infinitum. It accuses Secord of brokering arms to Middle Eastern countries through middleman Albert Hakim in a scam that let the secret team skim profits away from the government—and into more secret team shenanigans.

Illegal? Sure. But good business. When the Reagan administration hit upon the "neat idea" of pawning off overpriced artillery to the "Islamic fanatics" in Iran—who were then engaged in a volley of mass slaughter with Iraq—and sending the skim to the "freedom fighters" in Nicaragua, the secret team got the job.

Not content with war profiteering, the secret teamsters turned also to their old standby, dope dough. Planes that flew weapons to the Contras sailed back packed with Colombian cocaine.

Among the accoutrements of death purveyed by the secret team, according to the Christic Institute affidavit, were liberal dollops of a plastic explosive called C-4, sold to (among other charming characters) Libyan terrorists. C-4 was the plastique of choice in a plethora of terrorist acts including the bombing of Pan Am 103. Sheehan swears that his evidence implicates one such Libyan using secret-team-supplied C-4 in the La Penca bombing.

But even more intriguing than the conspiracy described in the Christic Institute lawsuit was official reaction to the suit itself. Sheehan's case has been criticized, even by his ideological allies, for containing inaccuracies and (yawn) for taking an overly "conspiratorial" view of recent history. But Sheehan never had a chance to answer his critics in the one forum where his theories could have been laboratory-tested, the courtroom.

Judge James King threw the Christic's case out of the federal court in February of 1989, and he went a step further. He leveled a $1 million judgment against the underfunded Christic Institute on the grounds that the lawsuit was "frivolous." Given the non-profit group's precarious budget, the judgement amounted to an assassination attempt against the Christic Institute—until an anonymous fatcat came up with the cash.

The Christics' appeal was also rebuffed. Though the institute scrapes by, it has been crippled with discreditation, enduring the same treatment dispensed to, it seems, almost anyone who mounts a substantive challenge to U.S. covert operations. The case offers an instructive lesson in why conspiracy theories usually remain merely that: theories.

"If we were back in Vietnam in a fire fight," General Singlaub once remarked of his supposedly frivolous legal adversaries, "then I'd ask for an air strike to blow the bastards away."

MAJOR SOURCE

Affidavit of Daniel P. Sheehan, 12 December 1986.

61

Meet the New Boss...

Bill Clinton's presidency, like that of the previous Democrat in the White House, Jimmy Carter, has provided a bounty for right-wing conspiracy theorists. You know, cranky, disgruntled, out-of-touch-with-reality types like, say, Senate minority leader and presidential candidate Bob Dole.

Shamelessly, considering the Republicans' Iran-Contra imbroglio, Dole spearheaded the call for a special prosecutor to investigate the so-called Whitewater scandal. Named for a real estate deal in which the Clinton couple invested and lost a fair amount of cash about a decade before Mr. Bill came to Washington, dark allegations eddied around the case for months—charges ranging from influence peddling to assassination—but somehow, no one seemed to pin anything on the president and his supposedly equally culpable spouse.

The January 24, 1994, *Newsweek* declared, with remarkable candor, that "in the Whitewater scandal, Clinton's real problem may be letting his frustration overcome his judgment." Which, according to most judicial precedents has yet to become a punishable offense.

A few months later, a March 27 *New York Times* piece pored over the Clintons' tax returns, scouring for scuz. Clinton's lawyer, and Clinton himself, had acknowledged an error in reporting his Whitewater losses. Again, no big scandal. The best the *Times* could come up with was that the error "raises new questions about how the Clintons responded in 1992 to potentially damaging news accounts suggesting that Whitewater might have been a sweetheart deal."

"Questions" about "potentially" damning news stories "suggesting" that something "might" have been fishy: not exactly what you'd call "nailing down the story," but that's about what the "scandal" came to—not a question of Clinton's misdeeds, but how the First Couple handled their bad press. Whitewater looked more like a conspiracy against the president than one he was involved in.

Nonetheless, in June 1994 the Senate voted to hold limited hearings into the Whitewater affair. Muscling out a Republican proposal for drag-on-forever hearings, Democrats held the day, allowing the inquiry to zero in on just a few issues—including the suicide of Clinton crony Vincent Foster, which some on the Right (onetime Moral Majoritarian Jerry Falwell is tops among them) claimed was actually a Clinton-sanctioned rubout.

Most of the fussing over Whitewater came from the opposition party, the Republicans, who after twelve years found themselves squeezed out of the White House as well as outnumbered in Congress. But it all seemed rather hypocritical given their years of self-righteous posturing over the far more substantial and serious Iran-Contra affair. Republican reluctance to reopen that still festering wound may explain why they didn't seize on another Clinton peccadillo that makes Whitewater seem like a cartoon by comparison—one that could tie Clinton to Iran-Contra.

While the dovish draft dodger Clinton doesn't mingle so comfortably with the Ollie North clique, there is one noteworthy case that hooks him into an arms-for-drugs operation.

Seems that one of the secret airstrips from which the CIA—or someone—dispatched planes to Central America that carried weapons to the Contras in Nicaragua and, apparently, cocaine back into the United States, was located in a small Arkansas burg called Mena.

It was from this airstrip, in October 1986, that a plane carrying Eugene Hasenfus departed. Shot down over Nicaragua, Hasenfus survived to expose the CIA's part in the Contra insurgency (which until then had been sold to the public by the Reagan administration as the underdog effort of a ragtag troop of freedom-loving patriots).

The Mena coke smuggling endeavor was real. Massachusetts Senator John Kerry's Senate subcommittee examined the evidence and deemed it "sufficient for an indictment on money-laundering charges." Clinton was governor of Arkansas while this covert operation was underway. Nothing suspicious about that. But allegedly he knew about Mena and took no action—in fact, he is said to have aided the coverup.

"I have never seen a whitewash job like what has been executed in this case," said Arkansas congressman Bill Alexander, who, in what could be construed as a publicity stunt, sent Iran-Contra prosecutor Lawrence Walsh two boxes of the state attorney general's investigatory files on Mena. "There has been a conspiracy of the greatest magnitude that has not been prosecuted."

Pressed by Alexander in 1991, as he was gearing up to run for president, Clinton made his first public announcement regarding Mena. He claimed to have authorized a $25,000 allocation for a grand jury investigation of Mena way back in 1988. But the prosecutors who would have received the money deny that any such allocation was offered, and even the governor's office was forced to fess up that no record of any such funding authorization exists. After Clinton's statement and its subsequent failure to be borne out by reality, Alexander requested that the federal Justice Department allocate the $25K. According to a report in the *Village Voice* the money was granted to Arkansas authorities but never reached the police authorities in charge of the investigation.

What would possess Clinton to go along with a coverup of the Mena operation and then apparently fabricate a butt-covering tale about it? That is a matter for the imagination, since no further link between the then-governor and the drugs-and-guns operation has ever been established or even suggested by evidence. Hard to believe he was protecting George Bush, who probably knew a thing or two about Mena.

The best guess comes from Mark Swaney, grad student and leader of a grass-roots group that once filed a one thousand-signature petition demanding that the state look into Mena. Swaney's hypothesis, as recounted in the *Voice*, involves one Larry Nichols, a Contra enthusiast whom Clinton, for equally unknown reasons, appointed to head the Arkansas Development Finance Authority (ADFA). The ADFA under Nichols's stewardship, according to information Swaney gleaned from a couple of shadowy informants who may or may not have intelligence connections, might have been attempting to win black-budgeted government programs for Arkansas. This policy could have tangled state authorities up with the Mena covert operators.

The ADFA might even have been used to launder drug money, which would clearly pose a PR problem for Clinton and his wife, whose law firm counseled ADFA.

Clinton eventually sacked Nichols for allegedly making unauthorized phone calls to his Contra pals in Central America and sticking the state with the phone bill. Nichols in turn sued Clinton for defamation of character, and from that lawsuit emerged revelations of Clinton's extramarital dalliance with a cheesy blonde who later praised the governor's cunnilingual prowess to *Penthouse* magazine.

All quite interesting, indeed. But perhaps shedding light on Clinton's bizarre behavior in the Mena scandal may have performed a greater public service.

Mena has produced not a peep from the Republican side, but when it came to Whitewater, Republican leader Dole rather sanctimoniously called on the attorney general to investigate the president, "for the president's sake and for the sake of the integrity of the attorney general's office."

Similar pleas were notably absent from the Republican side in the days of George Bush's malfeasance-ridden regime (from the Democratic side, too). Coupled with the barrage of playing-to-the-peanut-gallery charges of sexual hijinks aimed at Clinton from various shadowy corners (calling to mind the stories that toppled Gary Hart, who had the best shot of beating Bush in 1988), Dole's unctuous pronouncement makes one wonder if Clinton's presidency may not be the victim of sabotage—betrayed by the very cabal he's worked all his life to join.

Clinton acknowledged his ascendance into this cadre in his nomination acceptance speech at the 1992 Democratic convention when he coupled Professor Carroll Quigley with President Kennedy as the two most notable influences on his political development, thus acknowledging his affinity with the global banking-and-business elite that aspires to rule the world—at least in the minds of John Birchers and those of amenable perspective—who look upon Quigley's magnum opus *Tragedy and Hope* as the confessional that consummates their conspiracy theory (see chapter 47).

Quigley was a scholar, man of letters, and Clinton's favorite prof during his Georgetown University days. There aren't many politicians who'd use the most important speech of their careers to laud an author whose masterwork promoted the interests of a clandestine organization working to "create a world system of financial control in private hands able to dominate the political system of each country and the economy of the world as a whole." But Clinton did.

The same putative Anglo-American Establishment (to cop the title of Quigley's other major work) spewed forth Bush, who surprised Birchers not at all when he suddenly became infatuated with the phrase, "new world order."

Right wingers have built a cottage industry in imprecations against the "new world order." The late Gary Allen, author of the Birch classic *None Dare Call It Conspiracy,* titled his final paperback tract *Say "No" to the New World Order.* That was in 1987 when the Bush presidency was but a gleam in George's shifty eye.

Paranoia on the right was not only prescient, but substantive. The Council on Foreign Relations and related blue-blood cabals have been pushing for a "new world order" in their journals and symposia for years. Quigley was the self-appointed and highly affectionate historian of this meta-aristocracy. And Clinton announced to the world that he loves the guy. New world order redux.

Clinton always had more in common with Bush than he let on. Granted, he ran against Bush as an outsider. But where Bush was once a card-carrying member of the Council on Foreign Relations and the Trilateral Commission, Clinton notched those two plus the dread Bilderberg Group on his curriculum vitae. The difference, such as it is, is that while Bush was born into the Eastern Establishment his preppy portfolio prefabbed, Clinton—hailing from a town called Hope with a drunken dad and a gaggle of illegitimate siblings—is strictly a made guy.

Even Clinton's Rhodes scholarship seems sinister, taken in context. Cecil "Rhodesia" Rhodes, the zillionaire imperialist who endowed the scholarship fund, founded the Round Table, a British precursor to the Council on Foreign Relations. The idea behind the scholarships was to solidify British imperial dominion by inculcating the best and brightest from the colonies with British values at Oxford, then shipping them home to perpetuate the Empire among their native people.

The scholarships were "one component of Rhodes's plan to create a one-world government," writes conspiracy researcher Jim Martin.

Whitewater may not stick, but Clinton's credentials as a one-worlder are beyond reproach.

MAJOR SOURCES

Bainerman, Joel. *The Crimes of a President*. New York: S.P.I. Books, 1992.

Martin, Jim. "Quigley, Clinton, Straight and Reich." *Steamshovel Press*, no. 8 (Summer 1993).

Snepp, Frank. "Clinton and the Smugglers' Airport." *Village Voice*, 4 April 1992.

Kenn Thomas provided research for this chapter.

62

It's Not Missionary Work

From Costa Rica to Cambodia, Italy to Iraq, Ecuador to Australia, if you can get a Fodor's travel guide on it, chances are the CIA has found its way there as well.

Foreign political leaders, some freely elected, some not, have been relieved of their responsibilities—and occasionally of the burden of life—courtesy of Uncle Sam's good neighbor policy. The CIA's various plots against Fidel Castro (see chapter 2) all fell short and functioned mainly to bolster the self-effacing Keystone Spooks image that the CIA likes to present for itself. Because it's better to look silly than sinister. At least if you're vying for congressional funds and trying not to run afoul of those pesky oversight committees.

In Ecuador, American-inspired conspiracies helped toss out two chief executives, first in 1961, then, with a special repeat performance, in 1963. In Nicaragua, Reagan's cronies master-minded a civil war that eventually wore down the population to the point where they voted out the otherwise well-liked Sand-inista government. In Greece, Washington bankrolled a military coup for which President Lyndon Johnson offered the Greeks the following cogent justification: "Fuck your parliament and your constitution."

Washington has always offered a helping hand to nations threatened by their governments' determination to make decisions without checking in with Washington first, whether in El Salvador, Angola, Germany, Korea, the Philippines, or anywhere. The U.S. attitude was best summarized in another gem from quotemeister Henry Kissinger—explaining why the United States funded the Iraqi Kurds to destabilize the government of that country through civil war—only to abandon them to Saddam Hussein's genocide when their purpose had been fulfilled.

"Foreign policy," quipped Hank the K, "should not be confused with missionary work."

The ruins of governments overthrown speckle the globe. A 1973 coup against Chile's elected president Salvador Allende climaxed a decade-long effort to keep Allende out of power. The popular Marxist politician fell just percentage points shy of winning the 1958 election. The CIA stepped in and assumed covert control of the 1964 campaign with an election-rigging operation that one intelligence operative described as "blatant and almost obscene."

On a per-voter basis the CIA's $20 million Chilean election budget topped the Lyndon Johnson and Barry Goldwater campaigns combined. The bulk of the cash paid for propaganda that dwelled on the theme of Allende's "godless atheist communism."

Johnson took some Stateside heat for implying in his "Daisy" TV spot that Goldwater sought to incinerate toddlers in a nuclear maelstrom. But in Chile the CIA paid for a radio ad backing Allende's opponent. The ad featured a machine gun rat-a-tat-tatting to a woman's agonized shriek, "They have killed my child—the Communists!"

U.S. taxpayer dollars also subsidized magazine and newspaper articles and their sneaky placement in Chile's mainstream press. For that matter, the CIA entered the newspaper business itself with several start-up papers, one described by the State Department as graphically "magnificent...a Madison Avenue product far above the standards of Chilean publications."

Allende suffered an electoral massacre in 1964, in retrospect a far kinder fate than would be inflicted upon him, and the Chilean population, later. After Allende's victory in 1970, the uppermost officials of the U.S. executive branch—President Richard Nixon, National Security Adviser Henry Kissinger, Attorney General John Mitchell, and CIA chief Richard Helms— confabbed in Washington. Helms took notes: "Save Chile... not concerned with risks involved...$10,000,000 available...make economy scream."

Eventually the CIA recruited some Chilean military brass into a coup cadre, a project impeded by what the CIA described as the Chilean army's "constitutional-oriented inertia." Dang that constitutional inertia!

But on September 11, 1973, the coup got its act together. Allende was killed and a military dictatorship seized power and soon earned global recognition for its mass executions, liberal use of torture, and Nazi-style book burning.

"I don't see why we need to stand by and watch a country go communist because of the irresponsibility of its own people," proffered the always pithy Kissinger.

Nor for that matter should the United States stand by when one of its closest allies gets sick of the CIA's hijinks and tries to close down its shop. Under CIA pressure in 1975, Australia's "governor general" Sir John Kerr, the queen of England's representative, fired the country's prime minister Edward Whitlam.

Strictly speaking, Kerr's coup d'état was legal. Whitlam had declined to dissolve parliament after the opposition-controlled senate, in an equally unprecedented move, refused to approve the government's budget. The senate was unabashedly trying to force Whitlam out, but he refused to go.

Whitlam's true transgression was dismantling U.S. intelligence operations in Australia and divorcing Australia's intelligence service from the CIA (or at least trying to). The two were cooperating in various trouble spots, including Chile. The CIA was busy in Australia itself, both with sanctioned activities such as running spy satellites from Australian stations and more questionable ones, like infiltrating labor unions.

Kerr himself worked for a number of CIA front groups before becoming Australian governor general. The CIA labeled him "our man."

"We" had several men in Japan. U.S. intelligence organizations, recently declassified records show, cut secret deals with suspected war criminals who went on to become some of the most powerful men in Japanese politics. The program of intervention in Japanese politics skewed Japan's postwar stab at democracy, propping up the inaptly named Liberal Democratic Party—which supported the Japan–U.S. security treaty and remained firmly anti-Communist—and undermining the opposition Social Democratic Party of Japan, who leaned more to the left and opposed the security deal.

Like so many such programs, the Japan endeavor brought the CIA into alliances with some, shall we say, questionable characters. The three central figures in the operation, on the Japanese side, were two *kura maku* (a Japanese term referring to men who wield power behind the scenes) and their friend, a prime minister.

All three—Yoshio Kodama, Ryoichi Sasakawa, and Nobusuke Kishi—were jailed after World War II as class-A war criminals but were suddenly and inexplicably released in December 1948. Kodama's CIA connections came to light years ago when he was a central figure in the Lockheed scandal. In addition to his work for the CIA, Kodama was a Lockheed lobbyist who helped the multinational military contractor sell its wares by less than aboveboard means to Japan. He was also a leading power in the *yakuza*, Japan's organized crime syndicate, who made unimaginable fortunes in drugs, guns, and other contraband before the war with his Shanghai-based Kodama Kikan. The Kikan was also a center of Japan's intelligence operations, so Kodama was no stranger to government spookery.

Sasakawa was another billionaire power broker. He was named in a 1992 PBS *Frontline* documentary as a major founder of the "Moonie" Unification Church, itself by some accounts an arm of the Korean CIA. And the KCIA was founded in large part by the U.S.'s CIA back in 1961.

In January of 1995, Japan's Kyodo News Service found documents showing that one-time war crimes suspect Sasakawa was earmarked as an informer by military intelligence. This happened in February 1948, just two months after Sasakawa's release from prison and less than a year after an internal military memo dubbed Sasakawa a "man potentially dangerous to Japan's political future."

More documents came to light, with Kishi the subject this time. According to Japan's biggest newspaper, the *Yomiuri Shimbun*, the documents show that Kishi was "singled out" for U.S. backing, thanks to his sturdy opposition to communism at a time when it was feared that Japan was ready to start sucking up to China.

No one's yet sure of the extent of the CIA's Japan operation, but it was large. Late in 1994, documents were discovered that revealed as many as sixty CIA operatives in Japanese politics, mainly there to spy on and disable the more left-leaning Socialist Party, Japan's second-largest political organization.

In October of 1994, the *New York Times* found documents showing payment of "millions of dollars" to the LDP, Japan's ruling party, over a period of three decades.

"The principle was certainly acceptable to me," said U. Alexis Johnson, a former American ambassador to Japan quoted in the *Times*. "We were financing a party on our side."

In the Dominican Republic, Rafael Trujillo was also "on our side"—until we shot him. As with Panama's Manual Noriega decades later, Washington simply grew weary of Trujillo's despotism. Circa 1961, Trujillo's continued presence posed a threat to U.S. interests for two reasons. First, Castro had only recently tossed out the corporate-friendly tyrant Batista in Cuba; Washington feared a repeat unless it could place a more "responsible" dictator in power.

Second, President Dwight Eisenhower and some of his foreign policy poohbahs developed a certain sense of embarrassment over the increasingly obvious fact that the United States fiercely opposed left-wing governments, yet gave right wingers plenty of slack. This conundrum was later solved by the Reagan administration, which cleverly drew a distinction between "authoritarian" (right wing) and "totalitarian" (dirty commie) governments, declaring with a certain degree of caprice that the latter are worse.

The Eisenhower boys were never that inventive. They figured that whacking Trujillo was their sole option. As it turned out, the plan didn't reach fruition until the Kennedy administration when a group of right-wingers blasted the dictator out of existence with shotguns.

Reporter Jim Hougan, of *Credentials*, described Trujillo as "a decadent paranoid whose sensual appetites were rivaled only by the sadistic excesses of his favorite son, Ramfis, a psychopath who relished other people's pain."

A charming pair. Perhaps, one might surmise, Trujillo deserved his buckshot shower. But wait! Who flew in from Paris to take the reins of power but dear little Ramfis. Luckily for the Dominicans and the world, that madman eventually lost power and gave up the ghost in a drunken car crash.

Not all madmen meet American standards. In 1953, Secretary of State John Foster Dulles presented a plan for ousting "that madman Mossadegh" from the premiership of Iran. Granted, Mossadegh was an eccentric sort, but he was committed to a form of democracy, anyway. More to the point, he felt an obligation to nationalize foreign oil companies whose Iranian business was among their most rewarding.

One night, the young figurehead shah of Iran, with prodding from the CIA, staged a coup that met with derisive laughter from the jolly and well-liked Mossadegh. The shah fled to

Europe, but CIA official Kermit Roosevelt (grandson of Theodore), who had drawn up the Dulles plan, declared the coup a success.

It turned out to be a self-consciously self-fulfilling prophecy. The CIA brought the shah back into the country, and after a nine-hour battle between pro- and anti-Mossadegh army factions, the monarch assumed absolute rule. Not that Mossadegh's troops lacked resolve. But the Shah's forces were well supplied. It's matériel was, as one American military officer testified to congress, "furnished through the military defense assistance program."

How thoughtful of them.

Ah, but lately life for the once free-spirited, rollicking CIA has not been quite so devil-may-care. A small sampling of its handiwork came back to haunt the fun-loving agency via the Guatemalan route. That the agency had long backed Guatemala's rampaging and somewhat sadistic military is no revelation, but when a U.S. congressman found out that a CIA contract agent in that Central American country had personally done in an American citizen as well as a Guatemalan revolutionary leader who was married to an American, well, the sparks sure did fly.

In July 1995, New Jersey Democratic representative Robert Torricelli—who sat on the House Intelligence Committee—found out that one Col. Julio Alberto Alpirez was on the CIA payroll and also, incidentally, was the murderer of Michael DeVine, an American who ran an inn in the Guatemalan rain forest. Alpirez was also involved in the torture-slaying of Efrain Bamaca Velasquez, a guerrilla leader and husband of U.S. lawyer Jennifer Harbury.

The CIA responded to this revelation with its usual contrition. Its own inspector general compiled a 700-page report that found the agency innocent of complicity in the murders. The report even suggested that Alpirez may not have been the killer, despite its own information having pegged him as such. In other words, the agency picked the lesser of two screwups, choosing to say that one of its officers got his facts wrong rather than to accept that one of its operatives snuffed out an American.

The scandal then was somehow spun away from the fact that the CIA, either by omission or commission, had a hand in murdering an American citizen, to the shameful conduct of Torricelli in making this fact public. The connection between the CIA and the murders was, unsurprisingly, classified. No one, least of all congressional intelligence overseers, is supposed to spill classified data. The person thought to have leaked the investigation to Torricelli, Bill Clinton adviser Richard Nuccio, found himself under criminal investigation. The House ethics committee for a while considered discipline against Torricelli, but decided against it.

MAJOR SOURCES

Blum, William. *The CIA: A Forgotten History*. London: Zed Books, 1986.

Hougan, Jim. *Spooks*. New York: Bantam Books, 1978.

Marchetti, Victor, and John Marks. *The CIA and the Cult of Intelligence*. New York: Dell, 1975.

X

Random Shootings

63

Who Slew the Walrus?

T he scene outside New York's spooky old Dakota apartment building on the evening of December 8, 1980, was as surreal as it was horrifying. John Lennon, probably the world's most famous rock star, lay semiconscious, hemorrhaging from four flat-tipped bullets blasted into his back. His wife Yoko Ono held his head in her arms and screamed (just like on her early albums).

A few yards away a pudgy young man stood eerily still, peering down into a paperback book. Moments earlier he had dropped into a military firing stance—legs spread for maximum balance, two hands gripping his .38 revolver to steady his aim—and blown away the very best Beatle. Now he leafed lazily through the pages of the one novel even the most chronically stoned and voided-out ninth grader will actually read, J. D. Salinger's *Catcher in the Rye*.

The Dakota doorman shouted at the shooter, Mark David Chapman, "Do you know what you've done?"

"I just shot John Lennon," Chapman replied, accurately enough.

It was a tragedy of Kierkegaardian pointlessness. There was only one apparent way to squeeze any sense from it; write it off as random violence by a "wacko."

"He walked past me and then I heard in my head, 'Do it, do it, do it,' over and over again, saying, 'Do it, do it, do it,' like that," Chapman, preternaturally serene, recalled in a BBC documentary several years after going to prison. "I don't remember aiming. I must have done, but I don't remember drawing a bead or whatever you call it. And I just pulled the trigger steady five times."

Chapman described his feeling at the time of the shooting as "no emotion, no anger...dead silence in the brain."

His unnatural tone sounded all-too-familiar. British lawyer/journalist Fenton Bresler took it as a tip-off. Chapman was a brainwashed hit man carrying out someone else's contract.

"Mark David Chapman," writes Bresler, "is in many ways as much the victim of those who wanted to kill John Lennon as Lennon himself."

Prosecutors, at a loss for motive, opted for the cliché: Chapman did it for the attention—the troublesome American preoccupation with grabbing that elusive fifteen minutes propels many a daily-newspaper-journalist-cum-pop-sociologist into raptures of sanctimony. But Arthur O'Connor, the detective who spent more time with Chapman immediately following the murder than anyone else, saw it another way.

"It is definitely illogical to say that Mark committed the murder to make himself famous. He did not want to talk to the press from the very start....It's possible Mark could have been used by somebody. I saw him the night of the murder. I studied him intensely. He looked as if he could have been programmed."

O'Connor was speaking to Bresler, and publicly for the first time. Bresler's book *Who Killed John Lennon?* offers the most cogent argument that Lennon's murder was not the work of yet another "lone nut."

Conspiracy theories abounded after the Lennon assassination, many rather cruelly fingering Yoko as the mastermind.

Another focused on Paul who, by this line of reasoning, blamed Yoko for engineering his arrest in Japan on reefer charges. The Lennon conspiracy turns up on radio talk shows with some frequency, where hosts fend off callers with the "Why bother to kill that guy?" defense.

Only Bresler's thesis, that Chapman was a mind-controlled assassin manipulated by some right-wing element possibly connected to the newly elected (and not even inaugurated) Reagan apparatus of reaction, transcends the confines of pure speculation, extending into the realm of actual investigation.

Even so, Bresler's book a little too often substitutes rhetorical questions ("What does that steady repetition of a voice saying 'Do it, do it, do it,' over and over again in Mark's head sound like to you?") for evidentiary argument. We can forgive him for that failing. Bresler tracked the case for eight years, conducted unprecedented interviews, and extracted a ream of previously unreleased government documents. But unlike researchers into the assassinations of the Kennedys and Martin Luther King, he did not have volumes of evidence gathered by any official investigation, even a flawed one, to fall back on. The New York police had their man, the case was closed the very night of the murder—and, anyway, what political reason could possibly exist for gunning down the composer of "I Am the Walrus"?

In building his case, Bresler establishes some key points that put the lie to any "Who would want to kill an aging rock star?" brush-off.

Richard Nixon, his administration and other right-wing politicians (including ultraconservative ancient Senator Strom Thurmond, who personally memoed Attorney General John Mitchell on the matter) were fixated on what they saw as the Lennon problem. To them, the politically outspoken singer-songwriter was an insidious subversive of the worst kind, the famous and beloved kind.

- J. Edgar Hoover shared their concerns. One page of Lennon's FBI file bears the handwritten, block-lettered, underlined words, ALL EXTREMISTS SHOULD BE CONSIDERED DANGEROUS.

- The government went all-out to deny Lennon his longed-for permanent U.S. residency, and more than that, to deport him altogether (that was the subject of Thurmond's memo).
- Lennon's FBI file—at nearly three hundred pages as chubby as Hoover himself—reveals that he was under "constant surveillance." Nor did the G-men keep a particularly low profile around the ex-Beatle, apparently attempting to harass him into silence or at least drive him nuts, similar to the tactic they had used on Martin Luther King, Jr., a few short but eventful years earlier.
- In late 1972, when the "surveillance" was at its peak, Lennon told humorist Paul Krassner, "Listen, if anything happens to Yoko and me, it was not an accident."
- The FBI and the CIA tracked Lennon at least from his "Free John Sinclair" concert in 1969 until 1976—even though by then Lennon had won his immigration battle and dropped out of not only political activism but public life altogether into what turned out to be a five-year period of seclusion. His apartment was watched, he was followed, his phone was tapped.

Placing a person under "constant surveillance" and ordering that person executed are admittedly two different things. Nevertheless, Bresler's point is that the government did not consider John Lennon a harmless rock 'n' roller whose awkward entrance into the world of political activism often carried a high cringe factor (as in his Montreal "bed-in").

He was viewed as a dangerous radical who needed to be stopped.

And in a way that official paranoia might have been justified, because as embarrassing as Lennon and Ono's political publicity stunts occasionally became, John Lennon was always capable of seizing the spotlight and speaking directly to millions of young people who venerated him.

With unfettered access to the media, his power was immense, at least potentially so, and recognized by more experienced radicals like Jerry Rubin and Abbie Hoffman, who linked themselves to Lennon, clinging so close that they made the rock star uncomfortable.

Lennon was killed just four years after the intense FBI/CIA surveillance ceased. In those intermittent years, Jimmy Carter was president—a Democrat who kept the two gestapo-ish agencies more or less in check.

But in December 1980, when John Lennon's first album in half a decade was high on the charts, Carter was a lame duck chief executive, having lost his reelection bid to Ronald Reagan. Reagan's campaign was managed by career secret agent William Casey, who under President Reagan became the CIA's most freewheeling chief since Allen Dulles. The new far-right administration would reassemble the intelligence services and grant them a cheerful carte blanche.

The forces that tried desperately to neutralize Lennon for at least seven years lost power in 1976. Lennon's government dossier ends in that year. In 1980, as those forces were preparing to retake control of the government, "dangerous extremist" John Lennon emerged from retirement. Within a few months he was murdered.

The paper trail that might support the conspiracy theory is a little thin, however. It doesn't extend much beyond the airline ticket found in Chapman's hotel room; a Hawaii-New York connection departing December 5. But Chapman had actually purchased a Hawaii-Chicago ticket to depart December 2, with no connecting flight. The ticket found after his arrest had apparently been altered. None of his friends knew that he traveled on to New York. They thought he went to Chicago for a three-day stay.

Bresler concludes that the Lennon assassination, which, as Chapman himself noted in a rare interview, "ended an era," bears similarities to another assassination that took place twelve years earlier: the murder of Robert F. Kennedy.

RFK's apparent lone killer, Sirhan Sirhan, and Chapman (coincidentally?) shared a defense psychiatrist. But while Dr. Bernard Diamond couldn't skirt the obvious fact that Sirhan was under hypnosis (Diamond wrote it off as self-hypnosis), he labeled Chapman a "paranoid schizophrenic."

The court disagreed. Chapman even now has never had more than routine psychiatric care since entering his guilty plea. He was not sent to a mental hospital, but to Attica State Prison. He was judged legally "rational."

Bresler clears up a few widely disseminated misconceptions about Mark David Chapman:

- While any mention of his name is now accompanied by the phrase "deranged fan," Chapman was anything but. He was no more or less ardent a Beatles/Lennon fan than anyone of his generation. His real rock hero was Todd Rundgren, a cynical studio craftsman who could not be further from Lennon in artistic sensibility.

- Notwithstanding Chapman's announcement months after the murder that he "killed Lennon to gain prominence to promote the reading of *The Catcher in the Rye*," Chapman never exhibited strong feelings about the novel until shortly before the shooting. (*Catcher*, Bresler muses, may have been used as a device to trigger Chapman's "programming.")

- After the murder, major media ran bizarre stories of Chapman's supposed growing identification with John Lennon— at one point he even "rebaptized" himself as Lennon, according to *Newsweek*. These stories were all quite fascinating, but there was no evidence to back any of them up. (It is true that when Chapman quit his last job he signed out as "John Lennon," then crossed the name out, but Bresler interprets this, reasonably, as Chapman saying, "John Lennon, I am going to kill you," rather than "John Lennon, I am you.")

- Chapman was not a "loner." He was for most of his life a

normally social individual and a camp counselor who had a special rapport with kids.

Bresler also notes that when Chapman signed up for a YMCA overseas program, he selected an odd destination: Beirut—a perfect place, says Bresler, for Chapman, a once gentle soul, to be "blooded," that is, desensitized to violence.

A final note to the mystery of Mark David Chapman: As he was ready to go to trial and his diligent public defender was winding up six months spent assembling Chapman's defense, the accused killer suddenly decided to change his plea to guilty. His lawyer was perplexed and more than a little perturbed. But Chapman was determined. He said he was acting on instructions from a "small male voice" that spoke to him in his cell.

Chapman interpreted it as the voice of God.

MAJOR SOURCE

Bresler, Fenton. *Who Killed John Lennon?* New York: St. Martin's Press, 1989.

64

Potshots From the "Bushy Knoll"?

Talk about a small world! At about 2:30 in the afternoon of March 30, 1981, it became positively microscopic.

Crouching on the sidewalk in front of the Washington Hilton, a young man who modeled himself on Robert DeNiro's not-so-right Travis Bickle character from the movie, *Taxi Driver*, drew a bead on the new president. Steadying his .22-caliber pistol in both hands, John Hinckley, Jr., began firing explosive "devastator" bullets at Ronald Reagan. In the ensuing pandemonium, the sixth slug found its mark.

Apparently, before Secret Service agents could muscle the elderly president into his bulletproof limo, a shot had ricocheted off the armored sedan's fender, plowing into Reagan's armpit and puncturing the Gipper's lung. Had Hinckley scored a more direct hit that day, Vice President George Bush almost certainly would have ascended to the presidency, sloughing off his second-banana status eight years ahead of schedule.

Small world, indeed. For that very same day, John Hinckley's older brother, Scott, had a dinner date with an old friend of the

family: Neil Bush, son of the vice president. What some saw as
merely an odd coincidence prompted more conspiratorially
attuned eyebrows to arch like divining rods. After all, what are
the odds of the president's constitutional successor and the
president's would-be assassin knowing each other? Probably
zero.

But the Bushes and Hinckleys went way back, to Texas of the
1960s, where both George Bush and John Hinckley, Sr., had
amassed personal fortunes in the booming oil industry. Both
were blue bloods who circulated in the same privileged circles,
which the transplanted aristocrats liked to call their "Texas Raj."

Of course, socializing with the prominent family of a would-
be assassin is hardly a hanging offense. Still, in the foggy nebula
of a forming conspiracy hypothesis, circumstantial details have
a way of radiating suspicious import:

- In the NBC special reports aired immediately after the
  shooting, correspondent Judy Woodruff said that at least
  one shot was fired from the hotel, *above* Reagan's lim-
  ousine. She later elaborated, saying a Secret Service agent
  had fired that shot from the hotel overhang. Could Reagan's
  wound have been inflicted by friendly fire? Or, more
  ominously, did Woodruff glimpse a bona fide "second
  gunman"—à la JFK in Dealey Plaza? Either way, Woodruff's account might explain how a slug managed to strike
  Reagan when his limo's bulletproof door stood between
  him and Hinckley. Sizing up the Hinckley-Bush nexus,
  conspiracy researcher John Judge has theoretically dubbed
  this "the shot from the Bushy knoll."
- According to conspiratologist Barbara Honegger, White
  House correspondent Sarah McClendon made the somewhat more subjective comment that Reagan's Secret Service
  retinue wasn't in its "usual tight formation" around Reagan
  in front of the Hilton. Were the Gipper's bodyguards out to
  throw the game?
- Then there was Hinckley, himself. The Jodie Foster–obsessed

space cadet had been prescribed psychoactive drugs by a hometown psychiatrist. According to press reports, at the time of the shooting he was dosed with Valium. Before targeting Reagan (supposedly to gain the "fame" that would redeem him in the eyes of Foster and the world), Hinckley had stalked Senator Ted Kennedy and President Jimmy Carter. He devoured books on Sirhan Sirhan, Robert Kennedy's assassin (suspected by many conspiracy researchers to have been hypnotically programmed), and Arthur Bremer, who shot George Wallace. Theorists ask the inevitable question: Was Hinckley a mind-controlled assassin, a Manchurian Candidate programmed to "terminate with extreme prejudice"? They point to the CIA's longtime obsession with mind control and the fact that during the 1980 presidential primaries, Bush—the former director of Central Intelligence—enjoyed the zealous support of Agency regulars, who preferred their former boss to Reagan.

• For an antisocial pariah, Hinckley sure got around. In October 1980, he had flown to Nebraska in an attempt to contact a member of the American Nazi Party. Columnist Jack Anderson later claimed that Hinckley had ties to an American faction of the pro-Khomeini "Islamic Guerrilla Army." According to conspiracy author Barbara Honegger, a member of that group told Anderson he had warned the Secret Service about Hinckley's designs on Reagan—two months before the shooting. If Anderson's source is to be believed, the Secret Service did nothing to stop the Jihad-happy gunman.

• The day after his Nazi-seeking mission, Hinckley flew to Nashville to stalk Jimmy Carter, but was arrested at the airport when authorities discovered three handguns in his suitcase. Oddly, after only five hours in custody, this unstable character—who had attempted to transport weapons across state lines and into a city soon to be visited by the president of the United States—was fined and released without further ado. Even more oddly, the authorities apparently didn't bother to examine his journal, which in Dear Diary fashion, detailed Hinckley's plans to kill Carter. Was this a case of bumbling negligence or something more ominous?

- Finally, a pall of suspicion quite naturally fell over George "Poppy" Bush, the preppy achiever and future president whose spooky pedigree was longer than a Texas limo. Bush's father, Prescott Bush, Sr., had served as an army intelligence operative during World War I. Perhaps determined to prove himself a chip off the old block, George, like pater Bush before him, joined Skull and Bones, the elite Yale "society" that weaned more than a few powerhouse pols, Wall Street lions, and CIA superstars. Of course, everyone knows that much later in his life, Bush leap-frogged the career spies and became director of the CIA, where he deftly curtailed congressional investigations into various Agency misdeeds that had begun to ooze into public view following the wildcat gusher that was Watergate.

Of course, there is circumstantial evidence—denied by Bush—that he did in fact pay his dues to the Agency long before becoming its head honcho spook. As a young oilman, Bush founded the Zapata Offshore Oil Company, which, according to one former CIA operative, was used by the Agency as a front for clandestine operations during the early 1960s. "I know [Bush] was involved [with the CIA] in the Caribbean," the ex-CIA man told the *Nation* in 1988. Interestingly, according to retired colonel Fletcher Prouty, who acted as liaison between the Pentagon and CIA during the 1961 Bay of Pigs invasion, that disastrous operation was code-named Zapata, while two Navy ships assigned to the attacking armada had been rechristened *Houston* and *Barbara*. Could these have been sentimental references to Bush's adopted home and the future First Lady?

More evidence that George Bush had been a spook with portfolio as far back as the early 1960s would surface during the 1988 presidential campaign. Joseph McBride, writing in the

Nation, caused a stir when he reported on an interesting FBI memorandum signed by director J. Edgar Hoover, addressed to the State Department, dated November 29, 1963, and bearing the subject heading, "Assassination of President John F. Kennedy November 22, 1963." In it, Hoover reports that the FBI had briefed "Mr. George Bush of the Central Intelligence Agency" about the reaction of anti-Castro Cubans in Miami to the assassination. Twenty-five years after Hoover sent his memo, Bush would deny that it referred to him. "Must be another George Bush," a campaign flack muttered.

The CIA agreed, and, breaking with its longstanding policy of "neither confirming nor denying" the identity of its personnel, claimed that the employee referred to in the memo was "apparently" one George William Bush, who had left the CIA in 1964. Journalist McBride managed to track down the less famous Bush, who acknowledged that he had in fact worked for the CIA for about six months in 1963–64. But he certainly wasn't the George Bush of the memo, he said, because as a short-term "lowly researcher and analyst" he had never been briefed by the FBI or any other government agency, for that matter. "Is that the other George Bush?" he asked.

Indeed, there's another espionage link between George *Herbert Walker* Bush and outré characters orbiting the assassination of JFK. When Lee Harvey Oswald moved to Texas, the socially maladroit young man made an unlikely friend in the suave Baron George De Mohrenschildt, a White Russian emigré connected to the oil industry and, some suspect, the CIA. In 1978, Gaeton Fonzi, an investigator for the House Select Committee on Assassinations, called on De Mohrenshildt to question him about his unlikely friendship with Oswald. The baron's daughter told Fonzi that De Mohrenshildt wasn't home, so the investigator left his business card and said he'd call again. Later that day, Fonzi learned that De Mohrenshildt had returned home, gone upstairs, and lethally blasted his head with a .20-guage shotgun. (That is, if he wasn't "suicided.") When the police found him, the Baron had Fonzi's card in his pocket. In

De Mohrenshildt's address book, Fonzi found this entry: "George H. W. (Poppy) 1412 Ohio also Zapata Petroleum Midland."

If George Bush—the Skull and Bonesman who moved with equal ease among Eastern elites, Western oil tycoons, and Republican Party bosses—had also been a lifelong member of that fusty men's club of veteran intelligence operatives, his later fraternizing with the likes of Manuel Noriega, the Iran-Contra boys, Bay of Pigs/Watergate godfather Dick Nixon, and "new Hitler" Saddam Hussein would certainly make a lot more sense.

Of course, Bush's potentially Janus-faced background doesn't prove anything about the Hinckley hit. But it does suggest an underrated capacity and talent for deception, which is what keeps conspiracy trackers focused on the Bushy knoll.

So where was George, the future conspiracy president, on the day of Hinckley's dirty deed? Out of town, on official vice presidential business. Hmm.

OK, you could probably demolish the whole Bush-Hinckley theory by posing a simple question: Assuming the vice president had "foreknowledge," why on earth would Poppy's son risk meeting with a Hinckley sibling on the *very day* of the coup? Then again, we *are* talking about Neil Bush, whose common-sense deficit would later embarrass Dad when the Savings and Loan scandal made him its official poster child.

MAJOR SOURCES

Clarke, James W. *On Being Mad or Merely Angry: John W. Hinckley, Jr., and Other Dangerous People.* Princeton, NJ: Princeton University Press, 1990.

Fonzi, Gaeton. *The Last Investigation.* New York: Thunder's Mouth Press, 1993.

Honegger, Barbara. *October Surprise.* New York: Tudor Publishing Company, 1989.

McBride, Joseph. "The Man Who Wasn't There, 'George Bush,' CIA Operative." *Nation,* 16 July 1988 and 13 August 1988.

Vankin, Jonathan. *Conspiracies, Cover-Ups, and Crimes.* New York: Dell Publishing, 1992.

65

The Bulgarian
Concoction

On a spring day in 1981, the almighty Cold War blasted its way into St. Peter's Square, Vatican City. Mehmet Ali Agca, a twenty-three-year-old Turkish terrorist and international fugitive, trained his pistol above the heads of the faithful and began to pump 9-mm slugs at the Holy Father himself, Pope John Paul II. Hit twice in the chest, the pope slumped in his popemobile, hemorrhaging blood. Police quickly wrestled the gun from Agca and collared the would-be assassin.

As did so many international incidents during the Cold War, the attempted assassination of John Paul II spawned dueling conspiracy theories. Version one, promoted by a consortium of anticommunists, vintage Western spooks and "terrorologists," proclaimed the assault a Soviet plot. Version two, proffered by critics on the Left (left behind in the American media's rush to endorse version one) argued that if there was an East versus West conspiracy, it had been launched not by communists, but

510

by a clutch of Western cold warriors *after* the assassination attempt: a disinformation plot to frame the Soviets.

Which version was closer to the truth?

Agca, as the international press initially reported, apparently had nothing to do with the Soviets. In fact, the terrorist's background and associations all pointed quite clearly to a network of neofascist Turks—the terrorists behind Agca's earlier assassination of a liberal Turkish journalist and perhaps also the convicted killer's mysterious escape from prison.

The prospects for the Red conspiracy theory didn't begin to perk up until more than a year after the assault in St. Peter's Square. It was then that Agca confessed, from his Italian prison cell. Three Bulgarians living in Rome had put him up to the nefarious deed, he claimed. The anticommunist faction rallied to the cause and dubbed the affair, the Bulgarian Connection, a catchy title worthy of a Robert Ludlum spy novel.

To wit: the evil Kremlin, through its proxies in communist Bulgaria, plotted to assassinate the pope in an effort either to a) destabilize Turkey and NATO, or b) demoralize uppity Poland, the Holy Father's communist-infested homeland. According to this theory, the Bulgarians had activated Agca and his fascist cadres to execute the plot, thereby maintaining Soviet "deniability."

Yet apart from Agca's tardy "confession," there was little credible evidence to support the Bulgarian hypothesis. In fact, a fair reading of the evidence favors conspiracy theory number two: The Red conspiracy was a red herring.

For starters, the two key "journalists" promoting the so-called Bulgarian Connection in the American media had backgrounds as right-wing disinformationists. "Terrorologist" Claire Sterling had worked for the CIA-sponsored newspaper, *Rome Daily American,* and even Agency veterans found her books "linking" the Soviet Union to "international terrorism" notoriously unreliable, naively laden with CIA-planted propaganda canards.

The other Bulgarian Connection tout was Paul Henze, a

"former" propagandist and CIA veteran who had run the Agency stations in Ethiopia and Turkey.

But even before Henze and Sterling stoked up their Red Scare Redux, the Bulgarian-KGB theory had suspicious origins: Just six days after Agca's assault on the pope, Italy's corrupt intelligence agency, SISMI, produced a document claiming that a Soviet official announced at a meeting of the Warsaw Pact powers that Agca had been trained in the Soviet Union. The document later proved to be a forgery, but it helped buoy the anti-Soviet conspiracy theory.

Other "evidence" was equally chimerical. Sterling relied on a melodramatic cast of unnamed "insiders," such as the mysterious Bulgarian "Colonel X" whose "knowing Eastern eye could spot telltale signs" of commie conspiracies. In other words, Colonel X had a hunch that the Russians did it. Henze's supposed proof included vague rumors circulating in Italy, suspicions that the Vatican blamed Moscow, and assurances that a future defector with knowledge of the plot "is almost certain to turn up one of these days." (Ah, if only undiscovered theoretical future evidence were admissible in a court of law.)

Henze and Sterling, of course, were hardly deterred by the actual, *existent* evidence, which suggested that Agca's assassination effort had been sponsored by the neofascist Gray Wolves, the youth arm of Turkey's extreme-right Turkes party. Agca's neo-Nazi confreres generously supplied him with cash *and* the gun used against the pope. Undaunted by this superior evidence, Henze and Sterling speculated (without a scintilla of proof) that high-ranking members of the Gray Wolves, a fascist organization whose motto is "death to communists," decided to chuck their fanatic ideology and collaborate with the Bulgarian commies.

Yet there was always Acga's confession to fall back on. Or was it, too, suspect? In fact, there was plenty of evidence, largely unreported in the American press, that Agca had been cajoled and bribed to implicate the Bulgarians.

According to various sources, officials from the notoriously shifty SISMI pressured Agca during jail-house visits. During the

1985–86 trial of the Bulgarians implicated by Agca, a state witness accused former SISMI officials of hatching a plot to coerce Agca into implicating the Bulgarians. One of the named SISMI spooks, Francesco Pazienza, denied any complicity, but confirmed that *other* SISMI officials had in fact put the squeeze on Agca.

Pressure to blame the Soviets reportedly came from other quarters as well, including the prison's Catholic chaplain. (At one point, Agca fired off a stinging letter to the Vatican complaining of death threats from a Vatican emissary.) Also applying powers of persuasion were a Mafia leader incarcerated in the same prison (he claimed that SISMI pressured him to menace Agca) and the Italian magistrate who prepared the case against the Bulgarians.

Despite Agca's cooperation (or perhaps because of it) the long-awaited trial of the Bulgarians was something of a letdown for partisans of the Red Conspiracy theory. Agca set the tone for the proceedings when he promptly declared himself to be Jesus Christ. He continued to contradict, retract, and change his previous testimony, as he had done all along.

One example from many: Before the trial, Agca claimed to have attended a meeting at the Rome apartment of one of his supposed Bulgarian masters, Sergei Antonov. Agca described the apartment in detail. But when later challenged, Agca reversed his story, claiming that he had never visited Antonov's apartment, after all. The strange thing was that he had described the Antonov suite to a T—with the exception of one salient architectural detail present in every other apartment in the complex, but not Antonov's. If Agca had never been to chez Antonov, as he now claimed, how did he manage to describe it earlier? The fact that he screwed up one key detail suggests that Agca was coached by someone who had cased a neighboring flat.

Ultimately, the court dismissed the case against the Bulgarians for utter lack of evidence. Assessing the judicial fiasco, a major Italian newspaper commented that "Only one thing is clear: Agca is a liar."

In fact, the concerted efforts of Red-baiting journalists and investigators to pin the blame on the Soviets suggest a propaganda operation aimed at fomenting anticommunist sentiment worldwide and certainly in Poland, where the upstart Solidarity movement had been suppressed by the communist government. Although Cold War conservatives in the CIA pushed the Russkie conspiracy theory, a contingent of Agency analysts who had examined all the data argued that there was little, if any, credible evidence for Soviet involvement. (Future CIA director Robert Gates found himself in hot water when it was revealed during his Senate confirmation hearings that he had misrepresented the analysts' report in an effort to demonize the Evil Empire.)

As for Agca's motive in whacking the pope, some have suggested that the ultra-nationalist Gray Wolves intended to spread terror and chaos in Turkey and abroad in order to build support for a fascist putsch. Interestingly, this was the modus operandi of Italy's own neo-Nazi underground, which practiced the so-called "strategy of tension," in which neofascists bombed train stations and committed other acts of terror which were then blamed on the Left to build support for the far-Right.

Indeed, there are accounts of meetings between members of the Gray Wolves and Italy's right-wing terrorist groups, including the P2 quasi-Masonic lodge and Ordine Nuova (new order). Further, in the mid-1980s, Italians learned that P2 members had burrowed into prestigious positions in the press, government, and especially SISMI, the Italian intelligence agency accused of pressuring Agca to finger the Soviets. The 1980 terrorist bombing of the railway station in Bologna, initially blamed on the left, later resulted in indictments of P2 luminaries like Francesco Pazienza (the ex-SISMI official accused of helping to coach Agca), and Italy's public enemy number one, neo-Nazi terrorist Stefano della Chiaie.

On the lam from Italian authorities, Pazienza was later apprehended in the United States. He told U.S. customs officials of a Miami meeting in April 1981, a month before the assault on the pope. According to Pazienza, the meeting was attended by Gray Wolves, including Oral Celik—who reportedly accompanied Agca to St. Peter's Square—and Stefano della Chiaie.

Although Pazienza's claim hasn't been corroborated, the attempted assassination of the pope makes more sense in the context of the Italian ultra-Right's "strategy of tension": like the Bologna bombing, a neofascist provocation blamed on the Left.

Finally, there are indications that Western intelligence agencies had some foreknowledge of Agca's plot—but did nothing to stop it. According to several reports, the CIA had thoroughly infiltrated the Gray Wolves. West German and Swiss authorities monitored Agca's phone calls as he passed through their countries—and apparently didn't bother to arrest the fugitive. Most interestingly, in the months before the Agca's attack, Count Alexandre de Marenches, the rightist chief of the French clandestine services, reportedly spread word of an East Bloc plot to kill the pope. Did de Marenches already know about the Gray Wolves plot or that cold warriors would subsequently attempt to frame it on the Soviets?

There isn't evidence to prove definitively that Western spooks looked the other way, or even supported the Gray Wolves plot, but it is clear that ideologues exploited the outcome. And continue to do so. What propaganda/CIA veteran Henze wrote about the Soviets might also be read another way: "Disinformation can have a long shelf life."

MAJOR SOURCES

Henze, Paul B. *The Plot to Kill the Pope.* New York: Charles Scribner's Sons, 1985.

Herman, Edward S., and Frank Brodhead. *The Rise and Fall of the Bulgarian Connection.* New York: Sheridan Square Publications, 1986.

Herman, Edward S., and Noam Chomsky. *Manufacturing Consent: The Political Economy of the Mass Media.* New York: Pantheon Books, 1988.

XI

Twilight of the Idols

66

The Lincoln Conspiracies

$\mathbf{A}$s conventional history tells it, the conspirators who plotted the assassination of President Abraham Lincoln met justice at gun-point and on the business end of a hangman's noose. John Wilkes Booth, the actor who fired a derringer ball into Lincoln's brain at point-blank range, was shot dead by federal troops near Bowling Green, Virginia, two weeks after his grand exit from the scene of the crime at Ford's Theater. Later, four of Booth's coconspirators went to the gallows.

Yet from the moment of the president's murder on that drizzly Good Friday, suspicions about the actual nature of the conspiracy began to fester. Did the government have foreknowledge of Booth's plot? Was Booth a pawn of high-ranking officials? Inevitably, 125 years after the crime of the nineteenth century, fact and lore are more than a little tangled. Still, given the abundance of odd "coincidences" and curious admissions of the players, in many ways America's first presidential assassination remains a genuine mystery.

The Booth plot, which included the attempted butchering of Secretary of State William H. Seward (he lived) and the planned assassination of Vice President Andrew Johnson (never executed, thanks to a coconspirator with cold feet), involved nine ne'er-do-well Northerners (including Booth) who harbored Southern sympathies. But the bitter Civil War had only tentatively concluded, so it fell upon the Northern government to blame the plot on the South, not sparing Confederate president Jefferson Davis from indictment. Of course, the North didn't let a minor obstacle like lack of evidence hinder its case; at the trial of Booth's peon cohorts, the government suborned testimony to implicate "the dirty Rebs."

Trumped-up evidence not withstanding, Booth did in fact have provocative links to Southern brass. A rabid advocate of the Confederacy (yet unwilling to don a uniform and fight), the egocentric actor used his celebrity as a cover for smuggling medicine to the South. Consequently, some historians have claimed that Booth was a Confederate secret agent.

During an October 1864 trip to Montreal, Canada, Booth conferred with Jacob Thompson, chief of the Confederate secret service. At about the same time, Booth had been recruiting for his grand plot to kidnap Lincoln, hoping to trade his eminent hostage for Confederate POWs. "Did Booth propose his kidnap scheme to Jacob Thompson?" asked historian Theodore Roscoe. "Probably. Did he suggest Lincoln's assassination...?" Roscoe thought that possible as well.

Another item often cited as evidence of a Southern role in the Booth plot is a note found in Booth's steamer trunk and signed by a "Sam." The note referred to seeing how Richmond, the capital of the Confederacy, would feel about some unspecified affair.

During the nineteenth century, a steady stream of pamphlets linked Booth to the Copperheads—Northern Democrats seen as Southern-symps—and their secret society, the Knights of the Golden Circle. The Jack Ruby of the Lincoln affair, Boston Corbett, the soldier who shot Booth in a burning barn, purportedly was a religious nut who had castrated himself to achieve spiritual purity. Though later locked away in a mental institution, he managed to escape and vanish without a trace. The altar on which the long-haired Corbett supposedly offered his eternal chastity? The Russian Skoptsi sect, a pagan goddess cult whose priests wore women's clothing. A pagan cult? Ah, cue the Illuminati: For conspiratologists who like to posit that all-powerful eighteenth-century Bavarian secret society at the center of history's nastiest moments wonder if the Illumined Ones had a hand in the Lincoln murder. If so, can we be sure that Brother (or is it Sister?) Corbett really killed Booth?

The more enduring—and earthbound—theories assert that Booth was working for traitors among Lincoln's own cabinet, that he escaped with their assistance, and that the rakish actor lived to a ripe old age on a handsome government pension.

"There was one man who profited greatly by Lincoln's assassination," historian Otto Eisenschiml announced in 1937. "This man was his secretary of war, Edward M. Stanton." A member of the Radical Republican faction that bitterly opposed Lincoln's lenient reconstruction plan for the South, Stanton stood to consolidate his own power if the North imposed a hard-line military occupation instead.

As Eisenschiml and other revisionist historians saw it, Stanton's behavior immediately preceding the assassination, and also after, was highly suspicious.

* Stanton refused a request by Lincoln to allow the secretary of war's assistant, Major Thomas Eckert, to accompany the president to the fateful performance at Ford's Theater. The implication, according to Eisenschiml, is that Stanton knew something Lincoln didn't.
* Despite the profusion of death threats against Lincoln— and an earlier kidnap attempt by Booth in which the actor shot the famous stovepipe hat clean off Abe's head—only one bodyguard accompanied the president to Ford's Theater. And he was hardly a stellar specimen at that, abandon-

ing the president in his hour of need to indulge in a snort at the corner pub. Apparently the bodyguard was never reprimanded for his gross negligence.

- The night of the assassination, commercial telegraph lines in Washington—controlled by the government during wartime—apparently went dead, delaying the news of Booth's escape. Some see this mysterious event as evidence that government insiders abetted the assassin in his flight.

- There is also the curious matter of Booth's diary, which disappeared into a Stanton safe after the assassination. It wasn't until several years after the conspiracy trial that the journal was made public, a revelation that caused a political tempest. Curiously, there were at least eighteen pages missing. Lafayette C. Baker, the scheming chief of the National Detective Police (NDF), forerunner of the modern Secret Service, testified that when his men turned the diary over to Stanton, all the pages had been intact.

  Others have explained Booth's vanishing diary in terms of a less sinister conspiracy. Thomas Reed Turner suggests that the government suppressed the diary, which detailed the failed kidnap plots, to avoid raising embarrassing questions about its own inaction in the wake of Booth's less-than-subtle abduction attempts. According to Turner, "There was more than just a suspicion that the government was aware of Booth's plot.... The fact that the government was able so rapidly to get on the track of the main conspirators indicates that this was a group it had under surveillance." Still, if this is true, the question remains: Why *didn't* the government put Booth and company out of business before all hell broke loose?

- In a strange cipher message written by NDF chief Baker (himself the object of many a suspicion) three years after the assassination, the corrupt top cop issued what some believe to be a rhyming confession: "In New Rome there walked three men, a Judas, a Brutus, and a spy. Each planned that he should be the kink [sic] when Abraham should die ... As the fallen man lay dying, Judas came and paid respects to one he hated, and when at last he saw him die, he said 'Now the ages have him and the nation now have I.'"

"Judas" obviously refers to Stanton, who rushed to the scene of the crime and uttered his famous "Now he belongs to the ages" quote. Brutus may refer to Booth's father, the famous actor Junius Brutus Booth; to Booth himself; or to Lincoln's close friend, Ward H. Lamon, the U.S. marshal for Washington, who had often warned Lincoln about assassination plots, but was out of town on that fatal evening. *Et tu*, Lamon? Whatever its real meaning, Baker's doggerel declaration concludes thus: "But lest one is left to wonder what has happened to the spy, I can safely tell you this, it was I. Lafayette C. Baker 2–5–68." Even anticonspiracist historians like Thomas Reed Turner concede that the text and signature seem to be authentic.

Baker died several months after penning that cryptogram, "at the robust age of forty-four." His wife believed he had been poisoned by government operatives.

Dead men tell no tales, of course.

It fell upon Schick Sunn Classic Productions, producers of searching documentary films on Bigfoot and Noah's Ark, to rejuvenate such arcana. *The Lincoln Conspiracy*, a 1977 book and feature film, is less the catalog of verities it professes to be and more of an imaginative compendium of assassination possibilities. Drawing on controversial "never before published documents," authors David Balsiger and Charles E. Sellier proposed a superconspiracy in which four separate (and not necessarily congenial) groups sponsored Booth's kidnap and assassination plots: Stanton and his Radical Republican confreres, who planned to seize the government with the aid of Baker; Jacob Thompson, the Confederate spy master, and his Graycoat superiors in Richmond; Northern bankers and cotton speculators, who made a mint on wartime contraband and hated to see the good times end; and Maryland planters whose malevolence toward the Negro-coddling Lincoln knew no bounds.

But Balsiger and Sellier managed to top even that ambitious theory by rallying the enduring legend of Booth's survival and escape from the massive federal dragnet. *The Lincoln Conspiracy* claimed that the man killed in the Garrett barn was not Booth, but a second Rebel-agent-cum-fugitive who had nothing to do with Booth's plot. His name was Captain James William Boyd, a man who, unfortunately for him, "bore a striking resemblance to Booth."

Lucky for Booth this amazing body double (who stood a full six inches taller than Booth) bore a number of other convenient similarities, including the initials J. W. B., which even *more* conveniently were tattooed on his arm. According to Balsiger and Sellier, both J. W. B.'s were hobbled by seriously injured legs. (Booth snapped his when he leapt from the president's box to the stage at Ford's Theater; Boyd's old war wound had flared up.) And as luck would have it, both men were accompanied by fugitive sidekicks, who themselves shared an uncanny resemblance. Not only that, but in his flight the hapless Boyd managed to team up with a bona fide Booth coconspirator.

When NDF chief Baker informed Stanton that his men had killed Boyd, and not Booth, the coverup began. This theory, like other tales of Booth's survival, draws on genuinely peculiar details surrounding the identification and disposal of the body, which were conducted in ironclad secrecy. Few saw the body; an official photograph of the corpse was consigned to oblivion; and Booth's own doctor had trouble identifying his former patient, who had never sported reddish hair *before*. (The folks at Sunn Classic tell us that Boyd had...reddish hair!)

Balsiger and Sellier's claims about body doubles and synchronized limping are a bit hard to swallow, as are their "newly discovered" documents, which include transcripts (yet not the originals) purporting to be the missing pages of Booth's diary.

However improbable, though, the legend of Booth's survival is incontestably deathless. During the 1920s, the mummified remains of a derelict painter, John St. Helen, billed as the once-worldy Booth, enjoyed a mildly successful postmortem career as a carnival sideshow. Before that, the latter half of the nineteenth century had been rife with accounts of a gracefully aging Booth, lately back from Europe, India, or points more mysterious, dropping in on relatives, or spouting deathbed "confessions" in unglamorous places like Enid, Oklahoma.

To loosely paraphrase Booth's often-alleged overboss, the redoubtable Secretary of War Stanton: Now the Lincoln conspiracies belong to the ages.

MAJOR SOURCES

Balsiger, David, and Charles E. Sellier, Jr. *The Lincoln Conspiracy.* Los Angeles: Schick Sunn Classic Books, 1977.

Howard, Michael. *Secret Societies: Their Influence and Power in World History*. Rochester, VT: Destiny Books, 1989.

Roscoe, Theodore. *The Web of Conspiracy: The Complete Story of the Men Who Murdered Abraham Lincoln*. Englewood Cliffs, NJ: Prentice-Hall, 1960.

Turner, Thomas Reed. *Beware the People Weeping: Public Opinion and the Assassination of Abraham Lincoln*. Baton Rouge, LA: Louisiana State University Press, 1982.

67

The Long Aim of the Law?

It was just after 6:00 on April 4, 1968, and Martin Luther King, Jr., was standing on the second-floor balcony of Memphis's Lorraine Motel when a sniper's bullet cut through the evening air. Playfully bantering with his driver one moment, King was on his back the next, a pool of blood expanding around his head. Minutes later, the civil rights leader was dead.

The ostensible assassin, captured months later, was James Earl Ray, a petty crook who hadn't shown a previous aptitude for any criminal enterprise more elaborate than gas station stickups and a prison escape. As the result of a deal between his attorney and the prosecution, Ray pleaded guilty and received a ninety-nine-year sentence. But he immediately recanted and, insisting his innocence, has attempted to secure a retrial ever since, without success.

Did Ray kill Martin Luther King? Two and a half decades after the fact, a small mountain of accumulating evidence tends to corroborate Ray's broadest claim that he *didn't* fire the fatal shot. What we now know of that indelible day in Memphis shifts suspicion rather dramatically.

In the days and hours leading up to King's murder, an extraordinary phalanx of government agents, informants, soldiers, and spies quietly filed into Memphis. Their business remains murky, purposefully so—government documents that might shed light on the case are still stubbornly classified.

However, they clearly had little interest in *protecting* King. His increasingly vocal opposition to the Vietnam War and outreach to impoverished whites had begun to stoke fears of revolution in the streets. Army intelligence, which had spied on King for decades, considered him to be a subversive and possibly a communist. Now they clambered to develop plans that might undercut King's agenda, especially his upcoming March on Washington, billed in a panicky Pentagon intelligence report as "a devastating civil disturbance whose sole purpose is to shut down the United States government." King was the domestic equivalent of the enemy being fought overseas: "a Negro who repeatedly has preached the message of Hanoi and Peking."

Against this martial backdrop, King had returned to Memphis, vowing to restage a nonviolent march in defense of striking sanitation workers. The previous week, a King rally there had erupted into a riot that injured sixty and left one person dead. Egged on by FBI director J. Edgar Hoover's hysterical "blind" leaks to the press, the media was now billing King's return as a "dress rehearsal" for looting and rioting in Washington.

Enter the feds, surreptitiously, almost as if they had declared war on King:

- In advance of King's visit, the army's 20th Special Forces Group, based in Alabama, had dispatched Green Beret soldiers to various cities in the South, including Memphis. Their mission: Making street maps, identifying landing zones for antiriot troops, and scouting sniper sites—*sup-*

posedly to crush civil disorder. But the 20th was chock full of Special Operations Group vets, who in Vietnam had worked with the CIA in clandestine operations, including assassinations. According to a former army counterintelligence major quoted in the *Memphis Commercial Appeal*, "They couldn't let a lot of these crazy guys back into the States because they couldn't forget their training." So the army "dumped" them in Birmingham's 20th SFG. "The rural South was 'in-country,'" the major said, "and at times things got out of hand." The Ku Klux Klan became the 20th's domestic intelligence network, dubbed "Klan Special Forces."

- According to army records obtained in 1993 by the *Memphis Commercial Appeal*, on April 3 army agents from the 111th Military Intelligence Group arrived in Memphis, where they shadowed King's "movements and monitored radio traffic from a sedan crammed with electronic equipment."
- On the day of King's assassination, "eight Green Beret soldiers from an 'Operation Detachment Alpha 184 Team' were also in Memphis carrying out an unknown mission," per the *Commercial Appeal*.
- According to then-Memphis police detective Ed Redditt, "an hour and a half, no more than two hours" before King's assassination, he was summoned from his command post adjacent to the Lorraine Motel and whisked away to police headquarters. Redditt was one of only two officers assigned to protect King. In the police chief's office, "It was like a meeting of the Joint Chiefs of Staff," he later told author Mark Lane. "In this room, just before Dr. King was murdered, were the heads and the seconds in command of I guess every law enforcement operation in this area...The sheriff, the highway patrol, army intelligence, the national guard. You name it. It was in the room."

Redditt was introduced to a U.S. Secret Service agent who claimed to have flown out from Washington to warn him that a group in Mississippi had put a contract on his head. Redditt, an African American, was ordered to relinquish his post and go home. The supposed "death threat," Redditt learned years later, turned out to have been a false alarm.

- The first person to reach the mortally wounded King was Marrell McCullough, supposedly a black radical, but in reality an undercover cop keeping tabs on the minister's entourage for the Memphis police and the FBI. According to Mark Lane, shortly after the assassination McCullough was also working for the CIA.
- The local cops behaved plenty suspiciously, too. Memphis's director of police and fire services removed the two black firemen stationed at the firehouse adjacent to the Lorraine Motel. That firehouse, Station 2, became the stakeout where Detective Redditt would surveil and protect King— until Redditt, too, was yanked from the site.

According to FBI documents, the Bureau had recently heard of some fifty threats against King's life, the latest just three days before his death. Despite the warning signs, the local police withdrew their tactical units several blocks away from King's motel. They also failed to seal off streets or issue an all-points-bulletin after the shooting. Consequently, the killer—or killers—had an open escape route.

The assassination was immediately dubbed the work of that familiar American archetype, the nonpolitical loner. And two months after the murder, London authorities arrested James Earl Ray, the leading suspect. Ray, a forty-year-old white fugitive, had indeed fled Memphis moments after the fatal shot was fired. Without a doubt, he had some connection to the killing—a fact he has never contested.

The evidence aligned against Ray certainly looked convincing, perhaps too convincing. It included fingerprints on a .30–06 rifle with sniper's scope, which was found on the sidewalk outside a seedy rooming house opposite the Lorraine

Motel. Ray had in fact checked into a room there under an alias earlier that day. Bundled with the gun were an assortment of Ray's personal items, including his prison-issued radio taken during his escape from lock-up the previous year.

Witnesses at the boarding house reported seeing a dark-suited man, presumed to be the new "tenant," rushing through the second-floor hallway moments after the shot rang out. He was described as carrying a long package. A minute or so later, patrons in a record store beneath the boarding house saw a similarly clad man rush by the store window, dropping the package onto the pavement with a conspicuous thud. Moments later, they saw a man in a white Mustang bolt away from the curb in a screech of burning rubber.

It didn't look good for Ray, to put it mildly. Not only did the window in Ray's room face the Lorraine Motel balcony, but so did the window in the common bathroom on the same floor, where several witnesses claimed the gunshot originated. The furniture in Ray's room had been rearranged to facilitate access to the window, and among Ray's personal effects ditched on the sidewalk below was a pair of binoculars he had purchased that afternoon.

Ray's inarticulate claims didn't help his case. He insisted that he had been the dupe in a plot organized by a mysterious character named Raoul, whom he described variously as a "blond Latin," a "red-haired French Canadian," or an auburn-haired "Latin Spanish." According to Ray, Raoul had hired him in Montreal the previous year as a courier in a gun-smuggling venture.

As Ray told it, he had purchased the damning rifle and binoculars at Raoul's behest. The rifle was to be a demo model for prospective illegal buyers. Although his boss told Ray to stay near his car parked below the flophouse, Ray claimed that he had driven to a nearby gas station. When he returned to the boarding house, he later asserted, pandemonium was in full swing. Assuming that Raoul's gun deal had gone awry, Ray claimed that he hightailed it out of town, only learning later that King had been gunned down.

Though the official version of events seems to present an open-and-shut case against Ray—bolstered by his initial guilty plea—there are more than a few discrepencies:

- Numerous witnesses reported that there were two white Mustangs parked outside the fleabite boarding house in Memphis. Could a man of a similar physical build and attire have impersonated Ray, conspicuously dropping the rifle for the benefit of bystanders, and then peeling away in a car just like Ray's?
- For Ray to pack his easily traced personal effects with the supposed murder weapon is the height of criminal stupidity. For him to then dump the incriminating package in plain view of witnesses, a few steps away from his car, is just plain unbelievable. On the other hand, someone trying to frame Ray might do just that.
- Only one "witness," Charles Stephens, identified Ray as the man seen fleeing from the boarding house. At first Stephens denied that Ray was the man who rushed from the bathroom, but after languishing in jail for a spell as a "material witness," Stephens changed his story. Later, however, he recanted and complained that he was coerced into signing a false affidavit.

  According to Grace Stephens, her husband wasn't even in the building when the shot rang out. It was *she* who saw a man fleeing down the hall, not her husband. "There's no doubt in my mind," Mrs. Stephens claimed from the beginning. "That wasn't James Earl Ray. It was an entirely different man."

  To be sure, the Stephenses aren't the most reliable of witnesses; at the time both were drinking heavily. In a move that certainly seems suspicious, though, soon after her husband was jailed, Grace was illegally confined to a

mental institution. According to her lawyer, she was "shuttled off" to the nuthouse because her loud claims threatened
the Memphis prosecutor's case against Ray.

• Though the rifle and sundry items packed around it were
covered with Ray's fingerprints, uncharacteristically it took
the FBI weeks to match them to Ray the escaped convict.
And none of Ray's prints were found in his room, nor on a
box filled with bullets.

There are other mysterious occurrences that belie the lone-
nut scenario: On the lam in Toronto, while he was holed up in a
boarding house, Ray was visited by a person who has come to
be known as "the fat man." The fat man hand-delivered an
envelope to the frightened fugitive. Apparently Ray wasn't
concerned that this supposed stranger might be a policeman,
for according to the hostel keep, her reclusive guest uncharacteristically met the man at the front door. It would seem that the
mysterious stranger delivered a wad of cash, for the very next
day Ray bought a plane ticket to London.

Canadian authorities later located the fat man, who rattled
off an implausible story that nonetheless satisfied the police: He
had stumbled upon an envelope bearing Ray's address and
decided to return it to its owner. But when author Philip
Melanson tracked him down and confronted him years later,
the fat man said that he had refused to testify in 1968 in order to
avoid getting "a bullet in my head." Later, he added, without
elaborating, "Ray and those people are gangsters. They'll kill
anyone."

But the best and spookiest evidence of a conspiracy consists
of Ray's use of sophisticated aliases during the months leading
up to the assassination and directly thereafter.

All four of Ray's aliases have one very crucial connection:
they were names of real people living in close proximity to one
another in Toronto, Canada. But Ray visited Toronto only once
in his life: while on the lam, just *after* King was assassinated.
Yet he had been using several of the false identities months

before the assassination. How had Ray come by these names? Typically, Ray's explanations have been evasive.

Melanson tracked down the Canadians, and the scenario he details in his 1989 book, *The Murkin Conspiracy*, is downright chilling. Months before the assassination, Ray was using the alias, "Eric Starvo Galt." Melanson discovered that, during the same period, the Toronto man named Eric Galt was signing his middle name, St. Vincent, as "St. V.," scribbling lopsided circles for the periods, so that the full name looked to the uninitiated like "Eric Starvo Galt." In an impressive bit of detection, Melanson found that at some point, the real Eric St. Vincent Galt changed his signature, and began signing documents and personal checks as Eric S. Galt. At about the same time, the recidivist American crook James Earl Ray changed his alias to "Eric S. Galt." And this was months before Ray's first and only visit to Toronto!

There were other uncanny parallels between Ray and the Canadians whose names he apparently filched—especially Galt. Ray bore a striking resemblance to Galt. Both had scars above their eyes. In fact, the other Canadians also had facial scars. Four months before the assassination, Ray—the two-bit holdup man—underwent plastic surgery, which modified his "very distinctive pointy nose," according to Melanson, and made him look even more like the real Galt. Moreover, the Canadian Galt was a skilled marksman who often toted guns in his car to and from the shooting range and who had visited cities of the American South frequented by Ray.

Melanson's point is very persuasive: These parallels cannot possibly be coincidences. Was someone trying to draw attention to these four hapless Canadians? In fact, that's just what happened. During the search for King's assassin, they became unwitting victims of Ray's aliases. At the time of "the greatest manhunt in history" Galt saw his name blazoned in banner headlines. Had the FBI not identified Ray's prints on the rifle, the innocent Galt would almost surely have become the prime suspect.

What was the point of this sophisticated legerdemain with Ray's aliases? According to Melanson, Galt was the key. "Galt was more than simply a cover: He was a man who could be implicated in the crime, at least temporarily, while Ray made his escape." The other two Canadians lived conveniently near Galt, and police might erroneously conclude that the real Galt had stolen his three "aliases" from them. In short, the unsuspecting Galt was set up to be the "wrong man."

The parallels "were surely the result of conspiratorial planning rather than coincidence," concludes Melanson, adding that "This was beyond the capacities of a small-time loser like Ray."

Melanson argues that the conspirators probably selected Galt and cribbed his vital stats by gaining access to his top-secret security clearance file. For Galt was an employee at a Canadian defense firm working on a classified missile project for the U.S. military. His file was kept by the Royal Canadian Mounted Police (RCMP).

The CIA routinely trades information with the RCMP, raising the possibility that American intelligence had a hand in Ray's elaborate odyssey—and the murder of Martin Luther King, Jr.

While some assassination researchers believe that Ray was a completely innocent "patsy," others suggest that he played a part in the plot, albeit maybe not as the triggerman. Melanson, who belongs to the latter school, suggests that had Ray reached his ultimate destination, Angola, he would have been discreetly murdered.

Which brings us full circle to the quasi-chimerical "Raoul," Ray's purported master. Ray had supposedly met Raoul in Montreal. In 1968 a Canadian journalist tracked down a "Raoul-like" character in that city. Named Jules Ron "Ricco" Kimble, this American expatriate also was known as "Rolland" or "Rollie."

Although the House Select Committee on Assassinations report stated that Kimble denied any evidence of the murder, in

1989 he told reporters John Edginton and John Sergeant that he had in fact been involved in the conspiracy that killed King. According to Kimble, the plot involved agents of the CIA and FBI, the "mob," and Ray. (Kimble is serving a double life sentence in El Reno, Oklahoma, for two murders he says were political.)

Kimble now claims responsibilty for introducing Ray to a CIA operative in Montreal who arranged for Ray's aliases. But was Kimble, himself, the mysterious Raoul? Unfortunately, the story gets murkier, for reporters Edginton and Sergeant cite an anonymous "ex-CIA agent" as confirming that the Agency employed a Canada-based operative who specialized in creating false identities. That operative's name? Raoul Maora.

The evidence of government involvement in the King assassination is admittedly circumstantial. But taken together—the massive presence of U.S. intelligence and law enforcement operatives in Memphis, the discrepencies in the evidence against Ray, the Canadian aliases, and the fact that Ray seems to have had a sophisticated support network that kept him on a payroll—the scenario gets, well, curiouser and curiouser.

The FBI's alleged absence from the scene of the crime is particularly odd. The Bureau claimed that it hadn't had King under surveillance in Memphis. For years, however, he had been the target of Hoover's pathological crusade to destroy the "Black Messiah," as King was known in Bureauspeak. That the FBI would innocently call off its unrelenting dogs just as King's "threat" to law-and-order types was cresting stretches credulity to the snapping point.

Did the FBI's illegal campaign against King go beyond its well-documented character assassination? An FBI memo dated less than a year before King died in Memphis seems prescient: It stated that a CIA informant "feels that somewhere in the Negro movement, at the top, there must be a Negro leader who is 'clean' who could step into the vacuum and chaos if Martin Luther King were either exposed or assassinated."

No heir apparent ever emerged—although ultrasuspicious

conspiracy trackers note Jesse Jackson's public appearance soon after the shooting in a shirt stained with the fallen martyr's blood—but by hook, crook, or sheer dumb luck, Hoover and his bully boys got their wish.

MAJOR SOURCES

Edginton, John, and John Sergeant. "The Murder of Martin Luther King, Jr." *Covert Action Information Bulletin*, no. 34 (Summer 1990).

Lane, Mark, and Dick Gregory. *Murder in Memphis: The FBI and the Assassination of Martin Luther King*. New York: Thunder's Mouth Press, 1993.

Melanson, Philip H. *The Murkin Conspiracy: An Investigation Into the Assassination of Dr. Martin Luther King, Jr.* New York: Praeger Publishers, 1989.

68

RFK Must Die!

The killing of Robert F. Kennedy, the senator who would have surely been president had he not been gunned down, is at the same time an ostensibly simpler yet more mysterious crime than the assassination of his brother, the president.

The many possible keys to the JFK assassination lie in documents, events, and witness testimony, much of it accrued by two separate government commissions. The interlocking intelligence, military, and underworld operations that seem somehow to bear on the Dallas events speak more or less for themselves. Lee Harvey Oswald may have taken the final secret of JFK to his premature grave, but he left a paper trail behind him.

The secrets of Robert Kennedy's assassination lie locked in the most secure vault of all—a man's mind. Sirhan Bashira Sirhan, who still sits in jail today, his sentence commuted from death to life, has never been able to remember what happened the night of June 5, 1968, when he lunged out of a crowd and opened wild fire in Kennedy's general direction. Unlike the politically preoccupied Oswald, Sirhan never had any strong political convictions. And unlike Oswald, the globetrotting marine whose biography is a cryptogram of curious connections, Sirhan's life leading up to the assassination is remarkable only for its unremarkability. No satisfactory motive for his action has ever been revealed because even he does not know why he shot Kennedy—or even if he did.

First, the facts. Then, the questions:

On California's primary election night, Bobby Kennedy—senator from New York, former U.S. attorney general, and, of course, younger brother of the president slain four and a half years earlier—celebrated his crucial victory in that large state with a speech at his campaign headquarters in Los Angeles's fashionable Ambassador Hotel. The win in California looked certain to propel him past Hubert Humphrey—Lyndon Johnson's waffling vice-president—and fuzzy-minded liberal Eugene McCarthy into the Democratic presidential nomination when the party convened that summer in Chicago.

After rousing his supporters with the exhortation, "On to Chicago! Let's win there!" Kennedy made his way off the podium through a pantry in the kitchen of the Ambassador. The place was jammed with warm bodies. These were the days before the Secret Service received a mandate to guard presidential candidates as well as the president, and for some reason the Los Angeles Police Department (LAPD) was off the case (the department would later claim that Kennedy had ordered them away, a claim never substantiated and apparently designed, like any number of notions promulgated by defenders of the official version in the *first* Kennedy assassination, to somehow hold the victim responsible for his own death).

As Kennedy pushed through the throng, a dark-skinned young man—later identified as the partial amnesiac Sirhan—leaped at the senator and shouted, "Kennedy, you son of a bitch!" Flailing a .22 caliber pistol, he squeezed off a string of shots. Kennedy crumpled, blood oozing from the back of his head and spreading smoothly into a pool on the pantry floor.

A day later he was dead.

Five months later, Richard Nixon, who eight years beforehand had lost the narrowest election in U.S. history to Kennedy's older brother, defeated Kennedy's replacement on the Democratic ticket (Humphrey) by the second smallest margin.

The Los Angeles Police Department, at that time the most respected municipal law enforcement agency in the country thanks to its spiffy *Dragnet* image, took over the investigation, forming a task force dubbed Special Unit Senator. Determined not to repeat "the mistakes of Dallas," the LAPD formulated an impenetrable case against the lone assassin who was subsequently easily convicted.

But there were discrepancies and omissions from the official version. Some of the most important:

- The blood seeping from Kennedy's head came from a wound behind his right ear. Powder burns indicated that the shot came from no farther than two or three inches away. Sirhan was at all times in front of Kennedy. Even granting the ad hoc (and false) explanation that Kennedy suddenly turned his head away from the gunman, Sirhan never got closer than a few feet. Given that single piece of evidence there is no physical possibility that Sirhan could be the sole assassin. The coroner who ascertained the position of the fatal wound, Thomas Noguchi, was fired and had to sue to get his job back.
- Based on evidence of bullet holes and bullets found in the pantry, at least thirteen shots were fired. Sirhan's pistol held just eight shots and they were accounted for, having been recovered from Kennedy's body and the bodies of other wounded victims. The LAPD explained some of the extra bullet holes as "dents caused by food carts" and suppressed photographs of its own officers examining other holes. Ceiling panels and door jambs where extra bullet holes were sighted and photographed were destroyed.
- At least five witnesses—according to police reports—saw a

woman in a polka-dot dress fleeing the scene of the assassination. Some of the witnesses—notably a young Kennedy campaign worker named Sandra Serrano—heard the woman shouting, gleefully, "We shot him!" Serrano asked the mystery woman whom they shot. "Senator Kennedy," the woman replied, on her hurried way out. A couple identified only as "the Bernsteins," who were interviewed briefly by a patrolman, told the same story, but they were outside the hotel, about one hundred feet down a staircase from Serrano's position when they had a brief exchange with the woman who was still screaming "We shot him! We killed him!" The "Bernsteins" (who could not be located later) also asked the woman "Who was shot?" and received the same reply.

Sirhan has always maintained that prior to being hauled to the ground by, among others, pro football player Rosy Grier, who was Kennedy's bodyguard that evening, his final memory of the evening was of drinking coffee with a young woman. Serrano and another witness, Thomas DiPierro, reported seeing Sirhan in the company of the polka-dot woman before the shooting.

The LAPD responded to their statements by dispatching Enrique "Hank" Hernandez to administer polygraph examinations designed not to ascertain the truth of their stories but to browbeat them into recanting, which, under Hernandez's relentless and often abusive pressure, they both did.

The patrolman's report of "the Bernsteins'" account vanished from the LAPD files. The police investigators claimed the woman in the polka-dot dress was Valerie Schulte, an attractive coed from U.C. Santa Barbara who was also a Kennedy hanger-on. Schulte was there and wearing a polka-dot dress, but the dress and its attendant dots were the wrong color and she did not fit the description given by Serrano and DiPierro (both of whom noted that the polka-dot-dress woman had a "funny nose"). Nor, presumably, did Schulte, something of a Kennedy groupie, flee the scene shrieking "We shot him!" in a fit of joy.

These three points by themselves should have been enough to first of all, point the investigation in the direction of an assassination conspiracy; and just as important, to take it away from the LAPD, which clearly decided in advance that its own interests were best served by closing off any embarrassing avenues of inquiry that might reveal a plot to kill the probable next president of the United States hatched within their own inviolate jurisdiction. After all, shouldn't the hypercompetent godchildren of Joe Friday have ferreted out such a nefarious caper before it came to fruition?

Besides face-saving, there are other possible—though more highly speculative—reasons why the LAPD would stymie rather than expand on conspiracy leads. The chief investigator for Special Unit Senator, the man who made all the decisions, was Manny Pena, an LAPD officer brought out of "retirement" for the occasion. In fact, he had never really retired. He was working for the CIA.

The intelligence agency had a cooperative deal with the L.A. cops and Pena allegedly had engaged in numerous assignments for the CIA under cover of the Agency for International Development (AID). Supposedly known to insiders as the CIA's "Department of Dirty Tricks," AID-cover units were said to specialize in assassination techniques.

Through Pena—and possibly Hernandez, who also boasted of taking part in secret operations overseas—the CIA becomes a suspect in the whitewash of facts that point toward conspiracy. Why the coverup?

Sirhan himself is the strangest element of a strange case. Not that the lad himself was terribly odd. But his memory blackouts; his "automatic writing" including the repeated scrawl, "RFK must die!" scribbled randomly in notebooks that the LAPD for some reason saw fit to label "diaries"; the analysis of a former army intelligence officer who gave Sirhan a Psychological Stress Evaluation; and the testimony of a witness in a later civil trial who quoted acquaintances of Sirhan's as describing him in "a trance"—they all add up to one bizarre but unavoidable conclusion: when he shot Robert Kennedy, Sirhan Sirhan was hypnotized.

The defense psychiatrist, Dr. Bernard Diamond, explained away the diagnosis he could not deny by speculating that Sirhan must have hypnotized himself. After Sirhan was placed on death row, Dr. Eduard Simson-Kallas—then chief of the prison's psychological evaluation program—spent thirty-five hours examining Sirhan. In an interview with FBI-agent-turned-investigative-reporter William Turner, Simson-Kallas labeled Diamond's diagnosis "the psychiatric blunder of the century."

Quoted in Turner's book *The Assassination of Robert F. Kennedy*, Simson-Kallas asserts that self-hypnosis never runs so deep that it induces memory blocks, and while partial amnesia can result from schizophrenia, Sirhan showed no other indication of that mental malady.

Turner and his coauthor Jonn Christian argue that Sirhan was a Manchurian Candidate assassin, the "robot of another," firing at Kennedy not of his own twisted but otherwise free will, but as a result of a posthypnotic suggestion. They also believe, based on the basic physical evidence, that Sirhan did not actually shoot Kennedy (in fact, unspent .22 shells were found on Sirhan's person, leading Turner and Christian to believe that Sirhan fired no bullets at all—only blanks).

The fatal shot was likely fired, the authors (and any number of assassination researchers) hold, by a security guard named Thane Eugene Cesar who was stationed right behind Kennedy and admitted drawing his gun—and even privately admitted firing it. Cesar somehow lost his clip-on necktie during the confusion. In the famous photo of a dying RFK sprawled on the pantry floor, a stray clip-on tie lies just a foot or so from Kennedy's clutching right hand.

With the number of bullets flying around the pantry, however, Turner and Christian also believe that there must have been a third gun somewhere on the scene. Sirhan was nothing but a decoy; a mind-controlled patsy.

One deficiency in most Manchurian Candidate conspiracy theories is the absence of any identified programmer for these "hypnoprogrammed" assassins. Turner and Christian find a candidate, though their evidence is rather thin.

They zero in on William Joseph Bryan, "the world's leading expert" on hypnosis—or so Bryan claimed. Bryan's moment of greatest acclaim came when he helped solve the Boston Strangler case by hypnotizing the suspect, Albert DiSalvo. Sirhan's notebooks contained—among other ostensibly senseless jottings—the name "DiSalvo" written over and over again. Confronted with this "diary entry" Sirhan was baffled and said the name was meaningless to him.

When a journalist (an attractive female journalist, which with a character like Bryan is not an insignificant detail) asked the effusively self-promoting hypnotist for his opinion on Sirhan, the world's leading expert on hypnosis became inexplicably enraged.

"I'm not going to comment on that case because I didn't hypnotize him," Bryan snapped, then terminated that interview.

Bryan's dead body turned up in a Las Vegas motel room in 1977. Two call girls who "serviced" him regularly for the final two years of his life told Turner and Christian that Bryan not only boasted to them about hypnotizing Sirhan, but also about working for the CIA on "top secret projects."

It may well have been bluster. But whoever hypnotized him, the fact that Sirhan was hypnotized is not really in doubt. Whether he was a subject of some CIA MK-ULTRA-related mind-control program or whether, as has been occasionally speculated, he was affiliated with some sort of occult group— another form of mind control—or both or neither, is one of those secrets locked and perhaps now lost in the cozy confines of Sirhan Sirhan's securely sealed mind.

MAJOR SOURCES

Charach, Ted. *The Second Gun*. Film documentary, 1973 (video copy in authors' possession).

Kaiser, Robert. *RFK Must Die!* New York: E.P. Dutton Co., 1970.

Turner, William, and Jonn Christian. *The Assassination of Robert F. Kennedy: The Conspiracy and Coverup.* New York: Thunder's Mouth Press, 1993.

69

JFK: Conspiracy of Confusion

Michael Scott's father, Winston, had been chief of the CIA's Mexico City station from 1956 until his retirement in 1969, so in 1985 when Scott dropped in at CIA headquarters in Langley, Virginia, he was greeted more cordially than one might expect from the not-entirely-inviting spy agency.

Scott's father, a career secret agent, died in 1971, apparently from complications of a household accident. At the time of his passing he had just put the finishing touches on a memoir of his cloak and dagger career. He planned a trip to Washington to voluntarily (even enthusiastically) have the text vetted by his former boss, director of Central Intelligence, Richard "Man Who Kept the Secrets" Helms. But due to his demise, the elder Scott's travel plans were canceled. Within hours after Mrs. Scott found her husband's body drooping over the breakfast table, the CIA's legendary and consummately creepy counterintelligence chief James Angleton showed up on the Scott family doorstep in Mexico City, searching for the manuscript.

In 1985, Michael Scott was making ends meet as a Hollywood producer. Out of curiosity, he asked to see the never-published book. He hoped it would help him better understand his father's mysterious life. An inquiry to the CIA prompted the invitation to Langley. As he told the story to reporter Dick Russell, Scott was introduced to a "high-ranking officer who had obviously read the manuscript," who told him that "they had been forced to delete portions of the manuscript for national security."

What portions? the surviving Scott inquired.

"Well, there was some mention of Lee Harvey Oswald in some area," the CIA officer said, "and we don't want to make that public."

The CIA treated the son of one of its veteran officers no differently than it treated Congress and the American public. It held back or destroyed who-knows-how-many documents that could have illuminated the background of the JFK assassination—many relating to its formerly supersecret alliance with the mob to clip Castro.

Helms lied to the Warren Commission when he testified that the CIA never "contemplated" using Oswald as a contact. In fact, in 1960, according to internal CIA memos, the Agency "showed intelligence interest" in the then-obscure Oswald. During his condolence call at the Scott residence, Angleton scooped up a tape recording, purportedly of Oswald. The CIA tape came from Oswald's now-famous visit to Mexico City in the summer of 1963, just a few months before the Kennedy assassination.

Oswald—or someone pretending to be Oswald or someone identified as Oswald—went to the Cuban and Soviet embassies in Mexico City petulantly and obstreperously demanding a visa to Castro's Cuba. He also reportedly met with Soviet intelligence agents and tried to obtain a visa back to the Soviet Union where he had once defected (and returned to the United States strangely unmolested). Why? There are a number of theories. Perhaps Oswald was a disaffected nut smitten by delusions of Marxist grandeur (who later took out his private frustrations on JFK). Or perhaps he was working for an intelligence agency in an anti-Cuban operation. There were many underway at the time.

Or perhaps someone was trying to make Oswald look like a communist so that, the theory goes, the Soviets could take the blame for the subsequent assassination. After the assassination, there was an attempt by CIA operatives and powerful right-wingers (led by oilman H. L. Hunt) to finger Castro and/or Kruschev as the kingpin.

In any case, Oswald's voice was recorded in Mexico City and Winston Scott saved one of the recordings in his home. He kept it even after he retired. The CIA did not admit that such a recording existed until 1976. Then it lied that the recordings were all destroyed before the assassination. The FBI later said that the voice on the tapes was not Oswald's at all.

Someone impersonating Oswald prior to the assassination?

The Mexico City episode is crucial to any portrayal of Oswald as an emotionally volatile crank, but in a 1978 debate with attorney and pioneering conspiracy researcher Mark Lane, the CIA's former Western hemisphere chief David Atlee Philips announced that "there is no evidence to show that Lee Harvey Oswald visited the Soviet embassy." If he didn't, who did? Lane described Philips's startling statement as a "confession."

Philips was the CIA spokesman before Congress about the Oswald tapes. This is the same David Philips suspected by the House Select Committee on Assassinations of doubling as "Maurice Bishop," CIA controller of the Cuban "Alpha 66" anti-Castro brigade. The same David Philips in charge of exculpating the CIA in the Oswald-Mexico City incident may have engineered the "Mexico City scenario" in the first place, according to Lane, who has made a legal and literary career out of blaming the CIA for JFK's death.

Alpha 66's Cuban leader, Antonio Veciana, claimed that at one of his hundred or so meetings with "Bishop," Oswald was there, not saying anything, just acting odd. "I always thought

Bishop was working with Oswald during the assassination,"
Veciana told reporter Russell.

Veciana's cousin worked for Castro's intelligence service.
After the assassination, Bishop wanted Veciana to bribe his
cousin into saying that he met with Oswald, in order to
fabricate an Oswald-Castro connection.

Investigators never established for sure that Bishop and
Philips were one and the same, but descriptions of Bishop's
appearance and mannerisms mirrored Philips's. A police artist's
sketch of Bishop based on Veciana's description jogged the
memory of Senator Richard Schweiker, a member of the
assassination committee, as being the spittin' image of Philips.
When the select committee's ace investigator Gaeton Fonzi
finally brought Veciana and Philips together, the two started
acting weird around each other. After a short conversation in
Spanish, Philips bolted. Witnesses to the encounter swear that a
look of recognition swept Veciana's visage, but Veciana denied
that Philips was his case officer of more than a decade earlier.

"But," Veciana added cryptically, "he knows."

Veciana's reluctance to make the ID, Fonzi theorized,
stemmed from two unfortunate events that had befallen the
Cuban of late: one, he was convicted of running drugs and
suspected that Bishop set him up; two, he was shot in the head.

Later Fonzi put the question to Veciana in a more comfortably roundabout way. "Would you have told me if I had found
Maurice Bishop?" he asked. "Well, you know," said Veciana
with a smile, "I would like to talk with him first."

Russell interviewed a retired army colonel named, coincidentally, Bill Bishop, who claimed to be a CIA-employed hit man
(in his talk with Russell, Bill Bishop took credit for pulling the
trigger on Dominican Republic dictator Rafael Trujillo). Bill
Bishop said that he worked for the CIA's Mexico station with
Philips and that he and Philips ran Veciana together. He later
produced a tape recording of a phone call between Veciana and
himself in the mid 1980s. The two clearly know each other.

There was definitely something the CIA did not want publicized about Lee Harvey Oswald. The Veciana saga might contain at least a clue. However, because no conspiracy theory has been more widely written about than the JFK assassination, no conspiracy theory has come in for more strident attacks. The credibility of the attacks rests on the lack of credibility of one Lee Harvey Oswald, a personage painted as so twisted and pathetic that he is precluded from even unwitting participation in any act more complex than a temper tantrum.

That view finds its most recent outlet in Gerald Posner's pompous book, *Case Closed*. To make sure that readers get his point, Posner gives his Oswald chapters such subtle titles as "He Looks Like a Maniac," "Our Papa is Out of His Mind," and "His Mood Was Bad."

When his treatise came out in 1993, marketed to coincide with the thirtieth anniversary of President Kennedy's death, the enterprisingly smug Posner supplanted the Warren Commission as the final arbiter of JFK truth as far as the major media were concerned.

Jonathan Kwitny, himself a journalist of notable repute, explained the media's attraction to *Case Closed*.

"All the good young reporters and public officials who mistakenly swallowed the official FBI-CIA line on the assassination thirty years ago have been waiting all this time for someone to relieve them of the self-doubt they are too smart not to have suffered under," Kwitny wrote in the *Los Angeles Times*, giving Posner a rare negative review.

Posner's method of evading evidence that punctured his thesis was to obfuscate with unsupported assertions stated in a tone of unshakeable authority. The counterevidence was usually buried in a footnote. Nowhere was his technique more apparent than in his treatment of the incendiary Veciana-Bishop/Philips-Oswald story.

Posner states that "there are doubts" about whether Maurice Bishop ever existed. He does not state the source or substance of these "doubts," nor does he note that former CIA director John McCone did say that a "Maurice Bishop" worked for the

agency. And in fact, a number of other CIA employees interviewed by Fonzi said the same, including one who spontaneously named Philips as "Bishop."

"The CIA denied that any case officer had ever been assigned
to Veciana," says Posner. So what? The House Select Committee
in its report "found it probable that some agency of the United
States assigned a case officer to Veciana." Given the CIA's deep
involvement in anti-Castro plots at the time, that agency was
most likely the CIA.

It is true, as Posner (foot)notes, that the committee in its
report said it "could not...credit Veciana's story." It also said,
as Posner does not report, that "no evidence was found to
discredit Veciana's story" and "there was some evidence to
support it." In a footnote of its own, the committee acknowledged that it "suspected Veciana was lying, when he denied that
[Philips] was Bishop." At the same time, said the report, Philips
"aroused the committee's suspicions" by claiming that he didn't
recognize Veciana, especially because Philips "had once been
deeply involved in Agency anti-Castro operations."

The committee, mainly through its penchant for vacillation
and its unwillingness to offend the CIA, created more confusion
than it cleared up. Confusion has indeed been the one consistent
quality of the now three-decade-plus JFK case. Posner's ag-
gravating work simply stirred the fog.

So who killed JFK? The CIA? Anti-Castro fanatics? The
Mafia? The military? A cabal of wealthy right-wing extremists?
Or were they all somehow in league? There is evidence for any
of the above. And all. Perhaps there were multiple plots against
Kennedy that coalesced into one gigantic coverup with each
party protecting its own interests but not necessarily cognizant
of its counterparts' involvement.

Dick Russell writes that there were three plots against JFK in
1963. His primary source is a man named Richard Case Nagell
who tells of working for an array of intelligence agencies,
domestic and otherwise. The first plot was to bomb JFK's

speech at the Orange Bowl in Miami. The alleged CIA hit man Bill Bishop corroborated that story.

Plot number two—also corroborated independently by Bill Bishop—was scheduled for Los Angeles. Nagell's involvement was to shadow a Los Angeles leftist named Vaughn Marlowe who was "considered for recruitment to hit JFK," Nagell told Russell. The recruiters were L.A. members of Alpha 66. Marlowe didn't know he had been, potentially, the original Oswald until years later when Russell informed him. But he did know that Nagell was shadowing him. During New Orleans district attorney Jim Garrison's highly publicized investigation of the JFK case, Marlowe wrote Garrison to tell him about Nagell.

Nagell was also aware of the third plot—so aware that Russell believes he was hired by the KGB to terminate the plot by terminating Oswald. Instead, Nagell deliberately got himself arrested by firing a gun inside a bank in El Paso on September 20, 1963.

According to the recollections of Nagell's arresting officer, Nagell said, upon being taken into custody, "I'm glad you caught me. I really don't want to be in Dallas."

"What do you mean by that?" the policeman asked.

"You'll see soon enough," Nagell replied. Two months and two days later, in Dallas, President Kennedy was shot and killed.

Russell, unlike Posner, makes no claims to unimpeachable veracity. Far from it. But starting with Nagell, Russell winds through a menagerie of grim characters who fit in all of the categories mentioned above. Among the scariest and most powerful was Retired General Charles Willoughby, formerly intelligence chief for General Douglas MacArthur, but whose political leanings made MacArthur look like, well, JFK. MacArthur once described his underling as a "little fascist." Self-described hit man Bill Bishop also worked as an "intelligence aide" to MacArthur, according to a document turned up by Russell. "If true," Russell emphasizes, "that would mean Bishop had served under MacArthur's intelligence chief, Charles Willoughby."

Willoughby formed an ultra-rightist network whose most visible spokesman was fire-and-brimstone preacher Billy James Hargis and which included Texas oil baron H. L. Hunt and CIA-agent-turned-journalist Edward Hunter (credited with inventing the word "brainwashing"). Willoughby stayed in close touch with Allen Dulles, director of the CIA later fired by Kennedy—and subsequently appointed to the Warren Commission to investigate the slaying of the president who had fired him.

In 1975, after Russell wrote an article about the assassination for the *Village Voice*, he received an anonymous letter identifying "a famous American general who was born in Heidelberg, Germany, in 1892" as "having masterminded the assassination." The odd letter named this "famous general," cryptically, as "Tscheppe-Weidenbach."

Years later, while Russell was reading the book *The Origins of the Korean War* by Bruce Cumings, he came across "an obscure mention that Adolf Tscheppe-Weidenbach of Heidelberg, Germany, had changed his name, upon arrival in the United States shortly before World War I, to Charles Willoughby."

Finally there is the story, recorded by Fonzi, of Dave Morales, a self-proclaimed CIA assassin who one night, with only close friends present, went into a boozy diatribe against Kennedy for sacrificing his CIA-trained comrades at the Bay of Pigs.

"Suddenly he stopped," Fonzi writes, "and remained silent for a moment. Then as if saying it only to himself he added: 'Well, we took care of that son of a bitch, didn't we?'"

MAJOR SOURCES

Fonzi, Gaeton. *The Last Investigation*. New York: Thunder's Mouth Press, 1993.
Hurt, Henry. *Reasonable Doubt*. New York: Henry Holt and Company, 1985.

Lane, Mark. *Plausible Denial*. New York: Thunder's Mouth Press, 1991.

Posner, Gerald. *Case Closed: Lee Harvey Oswald and the Assassination of JFK*. New York: Random House, 1993.

Russell, Dick. *The Man Who Knew Too Much*. New York: Carroll and Graf, 1992.

Summers, Anthony. *Conspiracy*. New York: Paragon House, 1989.

Any writing about the JFK assassination owes a debt to the work of hundreds of researchers. Some, but by no means all, of the most important are: Peter Dale Scott, Jim Garrison, Jim Marrs, Sylvia Meagher, and Carl Oglesby.

70

Die, Princess Di!

Nothing proves the potency of instant Internet paranoia better than the sudden, shocking death of Britain's Princess Diana. Even after the massive public mourning over the death of Diana had abated, conspiracy theories of her "murder" raced along on-line like a drunk driver on speed.

The conspiracy theories run the gamut from the mundane (Diana as a threat to the royal family) to the mondo (Diana as sacrificial Satanic princess). The idea that Diana was murdered became so powerful that the billionaire Mohamed al-Fayed, the father of her also-dead boyfriend Dodi Fayed, espoused it himself.

Mohamed al-Fayed's craving for proof that Diana and Dodi were assassinated by British intelligence in cahoots with the CIA led to the case of an Austrian man attempting to peddle bogus documents to Fayed—that supposedly "proved" the plot.

That arrest led to the even odder occurrence of the CIA issuing an official denial that it had anything to do with Diana's death. Naturally, to many conspiracy theorists, the CIA's denial was taken as confirmation. And who can blame them?

On the other hand, here are the basic facts:

Diana Spencer, princess of Wales, died in a car accident on August 31, 1997. She had just finished dinner at the Ritz-Carlton Hotel in Paris with her latest love interest, the previously noted Dodi Fayed. Dodi was the affable ne'er-do-well son of equally aforementioned, ridiculously wealthy Egyptian émigré Mohamed al-Fayed. The hotel was owned by Dodi's father.

Diana was always under intense surveillance by the press. Pictures of the princess in a candid situation commanded megadollars on the world tabloid-newspaper market. Since her romance with Fayed went public just weeks earlier, the pressure from photographers had grown even worse.

Seeking to avoid the media horde, Diana and Dodi sneaked out the rear of the Ritz into an idling Mercedes. They were accompanied by Diana's bodyguard, Trevor Rees-Jones, and a driver hired by Fayed's family, Henri Paul.

After the accident, investigators found that Paul had a huge level of alcohol in his blood. Also, he was taking antidepressant drugs, which, investigators concluded, had nothing to do with his state of intoxication. However, the presence of those drugs could indicate something about Paul's state of mind and why he might take chances with his own life and the lives of his passengers.

Paul also apparently had, in addition to the large quantities of booze in his bloodstream, large quantities of cash in his bank account, deposited shortly before the fatal day.

Diana's car did not dodge the photographers. A group of them spotted the car and followed it. For some reason, the driver reached speeds reported as high as two hundred kilometers per hour. When the car entered the Point de l'Alma Tunnel, it went out of control. Everyone in the car died except for Rees-Jones, who was wearing a seatbelt, which proves a whole other point.

At the time of her death Diana was easily the most famous woman in the world (sorry, Madonna), thanks to her "fairy tale" marriage to Britain's future king and the seemingly ceaseless sequence of sordid scandals that brought the fairy tale to a grim end. As beloved as she was by the public, she was despised by her royal ex-in-laws. For the price of a mere twelve years of marital agony, Diana won a permanant voice on the world stage.

But someone wanted to shut her up.

That is, if you buy the conspiracy theories. And there's a wide selection available for purchase. The theories range from the mundane to the bizarre. In the former category, the rather ho-hum theory that Diana was killed because the British royal family doesn't like Muslims and Diana, apparently, was about to get hitched to one. She had finally found a serious beau after her breakup with Prince Charles (and the previous boyfriends she'd cheated on him with). But Dodi wasn't a beau deemed proper for a princess.

Dodi Fayed's father owns London's famed Harrod's department store. The Fayeds always craved acceptance from the British aristocracy, but for the white-bread British establishment (not to mention the ultrastuffy royals) they were just too, well, swarthy. However, if Dodi had succeeded in wooing Diana, the Fayeds would finally have their entrée. Rather than risk having to treat these undesirables as equals, the powers behind the British scenes simply killed both Dodi and Di.

One of the most vocal proponents of the "anti-Muslim conspiracy" theory was Sherman Skolnick. In fact, Skolnick is one of the most vocal proponents of almost any conspiracy theory. He started as a Kennedy-assassination researcher and over the years has branched out. His writings on almost any subject (e.g., he wrote that the collapse of Britain's Baring's Bank bore the clandestine stamp of the pope!) can be found on the Internet these days.

Skolnick said that he had spoken to numerous British and European journalists in the days following Diana's death and they all told him basically the same thing.

"Diana was assassinated," he reports. "And the simple reason for the murder is, British intelligence is pledged to protect the monarchy. The monarchy was not going to have a new step-father for the heir to the throne, Prince William. They weren't going to have a Muslim."

Of course, one could ask the question, why not just kill Dodi? Why also whack Diana? But these sorts of conspiracy theories always leave a lot of loose ends.

In any case, Skolnick's is an example of a not-so-imaginative theory. Many of the Diana conspiracy theories were considerably more exotic. An anonymous writer using the pseudonym "Ru Mills" proposed the theory (on the Internet, of course), that "whoever controls Princess Diana controls the world."

In this murky concoction, Mr. Mills (or maybe Ms. Mills; it's difficult to tell) argues that a "Cult of Diana" has existed for many centuries, going back to ancient Rome. This particular Diana was a part of that legacy. Her sons, William and Harry, carry divine blood.

"The current British Royal Family are impostors," writes Mills. "The House of Windsor is a fraud. But the lineage of Lady Diana Spencer goes back to Charles II of the House of Stewart. The House of Stewart is of *true* royal blood."

And what is the origin of that "true royal blood?" It dates back, according to Ru Mills, to the Merovingian dynasty, a family of French royalty who ruled from about A.D. 500 to 750.

The history of the Merovingians, much like that of Britain's King Arthur, relies less on documentation than on legend, mystery, and mysticism. There is, however, one popular theory about these supposedly magical kings, a theory that we explore in chapter 39 and that Ru Mills buys without hesitation.

"All true European royalty is descended from the Merovingians," says Ru, "which are believed to be descendants of Jesus Christ."

Heavy! Diana, a great-great-great-great-etc.-granddaughter of the Big C himself! In other words, that car crash was more than just a tragic drunk-driving mishap. It was a crucifixion.

Diana was sacrificed, says this theory (if you can call it a "theory"). She left the masters of the New World Order no choice, see? They wanted her to take a husband. They had a certain man in mind. And that man?

None other than Bill Clinton.

Yes, according to this master plan, Bill Clinton divorces Hillary (or just kills her, which might have been easier), then weds Diana. The princess, says Ru Mills, was having none of it. She refused to marry Bill Clinton. (Good thinking!)

Her sons, William and Harry, now carry on the Merovingian legacy. They will start a new religion that will control the world. So whoever controls them rules the world. And with Diana's death, they are controlled by the British royal family— the same family that saw Diana as an impertinent rebel.

The idea that the British royal family runs, well, everything is not new. (See chapter 38, "Anglophobia," for the straight skinny on the queen conspiracy.) In chapter 33, "The Royal Ripper," we check out the possibility that the British royals are all Free-masons who commit murder in the name of their secret rituals.

Masons? Maybe. But Satanists? Apparently nothing is too evil and sordid for these royals. Kitty Kelley had nothing on a conspiracy theory that turned up (attributed to an anonymous author) in the winter 1998 issue of *Paranoia* (a magazine whose outlook is pretty much as advertised).

"If you think that the assassination of Diana was a tiff inside the Royal family—or a racist plot to keep the Egyptians out of Britain—you are wrong...The assassination was an act of ritual, and the ritual is so very effective because you are never looking out for it."

In other words, the "murder" of Diana was a Satanic rite. And because no one could ever believe anything so far-fetched, the conspirators are safe.

The anonymous author identifies an international cult of Satanists in high places. Not surprisingly, Bill Clinton is among them. British prime minister Tony Blair (the British Bill Clinton) is another devil worshiper, as is Gen. Colin Powell, whom the article identifies as "the voodoo prince."

What possible evidence could exist that a routine (but for its victims) drunk-driving accident was the work of Satanists? One big tip-off, according to this conspiracy theory, was that Diana was killed on the last day of August and "last days of the month are significant in Satanism."

Uh-huh.

The anonymous author then lists a series of photographs which, he or she says, show Diana before her death dressed in occult attire—subtly. In one photo "she is wearing a dress decorated with sequined pentagrams, exactly 13 are visible on the top part of the dress." The author's conclusion: "Diana seems dressed as the bride of Satan."

Those two theories are among the most far-out and consequently the most interesting. Because most of the Diana conspiracy theories were simply, well, boring.

The first hint in the mainstream media of conspiracy theorizing surfaced a couple of days after Di's unfortunate joy ride when that zany party dude Qaddafi came up with a whacked-out theory that made the Reuters wire. Way to go, Mu'ammar! But we were way ahead of good old Mr. Green Book. Since the first edition of *70 Greatest Conspiracies* came out, we've been running an Internet World Wide Web site (http://www.conspire.com). All that our readers have to do is click on an E-mail link to beam whatever perverse notions occupy their minds directly to the gleaming, eight-by-ten-foot high-definition screen at *60 GCAT* Central.

We received our first Diana-conspiracy E-mail within minutes (yes, that's right, *minutes*) of the initial news bulletins. That one was followed by dozens more. Elsewhere on the Internet, a handful of web sites and an entire news group (alt.conspiracy.princess-diana) cropped up and was immediately filled with thousands of postings. Most of them focused on rather conventional themes. The "anti-Muslim conspiracy" was popular, as was the rather illogical notion that Prince Charles wanted Diana out of the way so that he could be "free" to wed his longtime paramour, the rapidly aging Camilla Parker-Bowles.

Then there's the "theory," such as it is, that Diana was killed by agents of the international arms cartels to stop her crusade against land mines (though far more people are now aware of that crusade than ever were before her demise).

Yet another version of the conspiracy scenario has it that Diana faked her own death. Kind of like our own king here in the United States—Elvis! (There's some profound insight to be drawn from that analogy. We're just not sure what it is.)

Frankly, we're a little disheartened by this whole phenomenon. This is a paint-by-numbers, prefab conspiracy theory if ever there was one. Back in the good ol' days when conspiracy theorists were still considered crackpots, it actually took some kind of evidence to get this type of frenzy under way. But somewhere along the line, in the last few years, it became cool to be a conspiracy theorist. Now anytime some poor sap drops dead every frat boy with an Internet account races to be the first in his quad to post the conspiracy of the moment.

The first move is usually ascertaining a motive behind the postulated homicide—and because everyone's got a motive to kill *somebody,* this is the easy part. And then that motive is offered up with a knowingly cocked eyebrow as implicit proof that a conspiracy must have occurred.

Ironic, isn't it? When we started writing this book, it seemed to us that people too often took what they read in the paper or heard on the nightly news as gospel. And, we felt, that's exactly what the big media wanted.

Think for yourselves! we cried out without much success. But now conspiracy theorists themselves have become just as predictable as any TV news anchorman interviewing a congressman.

We suppose we have to share some small amount of credit for the current conspiracy vogue, and needless to say, we're not complaining. But this bandwagon is feeling a little bit crowded lately.

MAJOR SOURCES

Anonymous. "The Murder of Princess Diana." *Paranoia,* Winter 1998.
"Lots of Cash in Driver's Account." Reuter News Service, 4 February 1998.
"Princess Diana: 1961–1997." *Newsweek,* 8 September 1997.
Sancton, Thomas, and Scott MacLeod. *Death of a Princess: The Investigation.* New York: St. Martin's Press, 1998.

XII

Madness for a
New Millennium

71

911

When the Twin Towers of Manhattan's World Trade Center (WTC) collapsed after the terrorist air strikes of September 11, 2001, they threw up a cloud of impenetrable smog. The buildings pulverized into dust and ash and millions of tons of debris blinded all of lower Manhattan. But there was another cloud of smog that spewed from the cataclysmic attacks now instantly identifiable by the telephonic moniker "911," a cloud of conspiracy theory and speculation issuing from an utter sense of disbelief that something this deadly, gory, and traumatic could happen to the United States of America.

There were millions of tons of conspiracy theories too, but most were, frankly, outrageous nonsense—maybe even dangerous nonsense. A quick cruise of the Web finds sites devoted to the following ideas, among others:

- The four hijacked planes were not hijacked but flown by remote control.

- The WTC towers were brought down by bombs planted in advance or by a laser beam.
- A plane never hit the Pentagon at all, it was a missile or a truck bomb.

For anyone interested in digging for truth through the rubble of 911, the proliferation of inane, insane, or merely misguided conspiracy theories obscured real investigation of true U.S. government conspiracies, a covert history that may have played a part in 911 reaching back into the murky depths of Reagan-era weirdness when the zeal to defeat the Soviet "Evil Empire" was so great that it led to a bizarre plot in which the CIA may have been funding the KGB.

Why did 911 spawn such a glut of conspiratoriology? The easy answer is that the bigger the disaster, the bigger the disbelief. And there had never been a disaster like 911. The trickier answer is that many of the conspiracy theories were not "theories" at all, but propaganda. 911 was a paradigm-shattering event in a number of ways. A certain segment of the conspiracist population subscribes to the paradigm that the United States is never a victim in world affairs, only an oppressor and aggressor. Of course, that's not a paradigm without some basis in reality, but when the tables were turned, when the United States suddenly became the victim, the result, to that group, simply did not compute. When your paradigm is attacked, there are only two responses: shift your paradigm or shift the facts to fit your paradigm. Spin the truth to fit your point of view.

Many conspiracy theorists chose the second option, creating theories in which the United States was somehow complicitous in the attacks, actually perpetrated them, or, in the most extreme theories, that the attacks never happened at all! 911 was all a massive hoax. In any of those cases, we're not looking at "theory," we're looking at spin.

In the Internet age, especially since the TWA Flight 800 crash (see chapter 57) and the death of Princess Diana (see chapter 70), conspiracy theories materialize seemingly out of nowhere, instantaneously. Predictably, it took about a week for the basic 911 party line to emerge. The Web site Voxnyc.com spelled out the boilerplate version on September 19:

> A thorough scientific analysis of the swirl of events, people, nations, motivations, propaganda, personalities and histories involved in this current moment in history, leads to only one conclusion: that clandestine forces aligned with George Bush Sr. are planning to attack the US population, blame it on Islamic terrorists and use the attacks as a pretext for a total clamp-down on dissent, basic civil liberties, normal democratic processes and in the confusion that will follow they will wage unchecked war and aggression against Iraq, and other nations, Islamic and otherwise, who have natural resources and particularly oil reserves that this shadowy group of petrochemical and arms industrialists are thirsting for.

How exactly a "thorough scientific analysis of the swirl of events, people, nations, motivations, propaganda, personalities and histories involved" could have been performed in less than eight days remains unclear.

Trying to go point-counterpoint with the 911 insta-theories is nothing but, as one journalist put it, "a mug's game." How can you debate with people who insist on having all their arguments both ways? On the one hand, they'll claim (with considerable basis) that the U.S. government ignored numerous warnings that Osama bin Laden was about to attack a major U.S. target. On the other hand, they'll claim (with almost no basis) that bin Laden is innocent.

Canadian author and college professor Michel Chossudovsky (author of *War and Globalisation: The Truth Behind September 11*), one of the big-time 911 conspiracy guys, goes the "Osama is innocent" route, declaring, "A few hours after the terrorist attacks on the World Trade Center and the Pentagon, the Bush administration concluded without supporting evidence, that Osama bin Laden and his Al-Qaeda organization were prime suspects."

Without supporting evidence? The myriad warnings *were* the evidence. When you've received alert after alert—for half a decade—that bin Laden's organization is planning to hit you, then you get hit, who do you think did it?

Conspiracy theories of this genre are tautologies, in which evidence that flatly contradicts the theory is labeled "disinformation" and therefore taken as *confirmation*. A theory that is confirmed by *everything* can't be confirmed at all. Either the United States had the warnings or it didn't. Either way, according to this particular conspiracy theory, bin Laden's innocent.

There's only one conclusion regarding this line of reasoning: The person doing the reasoning has his or her mind made up in advance. If reality contradicts your opinion, deny reality! To call many of the 911 conspiracy theories *"conspiracy theories"* is to give them too much credit. They are just denials, not much different in form (nor sometimes, disturbingly, in content) from Holocaust denials.

If we sound annoyed at these new theories, it's because we are. At one time, not too long ago, conspiracy theories were a challenge to orthodox, "establishment" opinion. In the past few years, we've seen a new generation of conspiracy theory that has become an orthodoxy of its own, as monolithic and impervious to dissent as the media-industrial opinion complex itself.

If we didn't know better, we'd think that the government itself disseminated these nonsense theories as disinformation to discredit anyone raising legitimate questions about the events of 911. The Bush administration has not exactly gone out of its way to discourage the crazy theories. When Bush, in November 2002, appointed none other than Henry Kissinger to lead an "independent inquiry" into 911, cries of "Warren

Commission II!" came not only from the conspiracy theorists, but from some "mainstream" commentators as well. Kissinger quickly resigned rather than reveal a list of clients served by his consulting and lobbying firm, Kissinger Associates. He would have been compelled to open his closely guarded list for public viewing because, potentially, Kissinger's clients included governments who may have had 911 terrorist connections.

In the end, Kissinger decided that protecting his clients was more important than protecting his country. He recused himself from probing the mysteries of 911. Why Bush thought that Kissinger, of all people, was the man to get to the bottom of it all is a mystery unto itself.

The tiresome and frustrating denial theories accomplish nothing except to make an even more confounding mess of an event so confusing and contradictory that it makes the JFK assassination look like a model of clarity. So our little public service announcement would be: "Please theorize *responsibly*."

The same people, such as the aforementioned Professor Chossudovsky, who would tell us that there is "no evidence" to support blaming bin Laden's network for 911, also inform us, at great length, that bin Laden was somehow a puppet of the CIA. (Again, wanting it both ways. If bin Laden is innocent, why is it relevant that he's a CIA creation?) The prolific Jared Israel of the Emperors-Clothes.com Web site tells us, "Bin Laden et. al. were CIA employees, given the best training, arms, facilities and lots of cash for many years." Really? Bin Laden a CIA *employee*? "That's what the [*New York*] *Times* reported on August 24, 1998," says Israel.

Impressive sourcing, diminished only by the fact that the *New York Times* reported no such thing. What the paper did report, and what has been documented at tremendous length during the decade prior to 911, and since, is that during the Soviet war in Afghanistan, which dragged on from 1979 to 1989, the CIA shuttled funds to the Afghan mujahideen guerilla forces who struggled desperately to hold off the Soviet military machine.

Bin Laden, with millions of dollars at his disposal and a fanatic's will to dwell in mountain caves in service of his cause, was a well-known figure within that resistance.

This ersatz syllogism—the CIA funds Afghan opposition, bin Laden is part of the Afghan opposition, therefore, the CIA funds bin Laden—has been accepted as an article of faith and cornerstone of most 911 conspiracy theories. But is such a thing possible? Could the CIA really be in league with the world's number one terrorist, the man who slaughtered more American civilians in a single day than any enemy in history? Is it really that evil?

Even reputable authors have stated that the CIA "trained" bin Laden's forces, sometimes referring to them as "the CIA's Muslim mercenaries." A small newspaper in Canada, the *Vancouver Courier*, ran an article on October 1, 2001, asserting that the "U.S. nurtured radical Islam." It didn't take long before *that* piece was all over the World Wide Web.

The situation is considerably murkier than the conspiracy theorists make it seem, and certainly more ambiguous than (on the other side of the informational coin) apologists for U.S. policy would have the world believe.

There were at least six factions of Afghan resistance fighters in combat against the Soviets in the 1980s. They were not all "Islamic fanatics" or "terrorists," though some certainly were. Then there were the "Afghan Arabs," which was bin Laden's group. The "Afghan" part of their label referred only to their geographical location and their cause. Most of them were Arabs, and other Muslims, from places like Saudi Arabia, bin Laden's home. The Afghan Arabs were quite fanatical and have since morphed into bin Laden's Al Qaeda terrorist organization. They came to Afghanistan as mercenaries, but their motivation was not money but religious extremism. It was their holy calling to drive the heathen Soviets out of the Islamic land of Afghanistan.

Some of the native Afghan mujahideen felt the same religious zealotry, but most wanted nothing more than their country back. They wanted the Soviets to stop slaughtering their people and go home. These "moderate" (for lack of a better term) Afghans had little use for the Afghan Arabs, who had even less use for them.

Bin Laden operatives assassinated Ahmad Shah Massoud, the Afghan general most effective in battling the Soviets. Massoud's militia held off nine separate Soviet offensives during the decade-long war, but suicide bombers eliminated him just two days before the 911 attacks.

The CIA could have thrown 100 percent of its support behind Massoud in the 1980s, but it didn't. Massoud wasn't exactly Thomas Paine when it comes to upholding democracy, but as TV news producer Richard Mackenzie, who spent months riding with Massoud's troops, put it, "he would have been a voice for fairness and a more democratic state in Afghanistan."

Massoud himself didn't disguise his revulsion at bin Laden's freelance force of fundamentalists. "We don't need armed Arabs wandering around our country," he told Mackenzie. "They have no place here. They should leave."

While the CIA left Massoud largely to his own devices, a huge percentage of the American taxpayer money pouring into the region went to the most extreme Islamic fundamentalist of all Afghan militia commanders, a man who, according to journalist Peter Bergen, "worked closely together" with bin Laden.

Why?

The CIA operation in Afghanistan was convoluted. The CIA set up shop in Pakistan and funneled its money to Pakistan's shadowy, shady intelligence agency, the Inter-Services Intelligence (ISI). In inimitably obtuse fashion, the CIA agents on the scene, under directive from President Ronald Reagan's CIA director William Casey, entrusted their whole operation to their Pakistani counterparts.

"By simply handing ISI some $3 billion of American tax-payers' money," writes Bergen, "the CIA handed the Pakistanis complete control of how the funds were distributed."

The Pakistanis threw their support behind an Afghan war-lord named Gulbuddin Hekmatyar, who was indeed an Islamic extremist and who supported Zia-ul-Haq, Pakistan's own Islamist dictator at that time. Hekmatyar received $600 million in U.S. taxpayer funds, "by the most conservative es-timates," reports Bergen.

The Reaganites, blindly obsessed with eradicating the Soviet threat, were blithely oblivious to the threat that was to come from Hekmatyar and his extreme-Islamist ilk. The bloodthirsty warlord rarely fought against the Soviets, pre-ferring to murder his fellow Afghans. Hekmatyar was always an Islamist ultrazealot. He did not need "nurturing" in that worldview from the CIA, and it is an incredible exaggeration to say that the CIA "created" him. Through its alliance with Pakistan's ISI, what the CIA did manage was to give Hekmatyar far more stature and power than he ever should have received. In Afghanistan's environment of total war where the guy with the biggest bombs wins, the ISI made sure that Hekmatyar was that guy. Under Reagan and then President George Bush, the CIA never raised a peep of protest.

After the Soviets pulled out, a coalition of Afghan factions formed a government in the country's capital of Kabul. Hekmatyar was named prime minister, but his main achieve-ment while in office was to bombard the capital city with rockets. Those were the same rockets purchased for him by the ISI with CIA cash. The attacks were an attempt to oust Massoud from power in Kabul.

At one point, Hekmatyar's forces reportedly massacred 1,800 people in a single town in a single day. By 1996, Hek-matyar was allegedly responsible for killing 50,000 of his countrymen.

Hekmatyar joined the Taliban when it took over the Afghan government in 1996, but soon turned against it—only to rejoin its forces when the United States attacked Afghanistan in the aftermath of 911. Finally, it was left to the CIA under President George W. Bush to rectify the havoc wrought by the recipient of its largesse. In May 2002, the CIA fired one of its own rockets at Hekmatyar, but missed. It was a classic case of blowback: the CIA attempting to assassinate a killer who owed much of his power to the CIA. As of this writing, Hekmatyar's whereabouts are a mystery, as are bin Laden's.

The ultimate irony of the CIA's involvement with Hekmatyar may have been that, all along, he was working for the Soviets, rather than against them. The Revolutionary Association of Women of Afghanistan (RAWA) believes that Hekmatyar was on the KGB payroll all along and that a conspiracy between the Soviet spy agency and the Islamist warlord was behind the assassination of RAWA's leader in 1987. Documents made public by an ex-Soviet archivist in 2002 failed to support the Hekmatyar-KGB connection (at least according to the *Washington Post*), but they did prove that the KGB infiltrated many Afghan militia groups, provoking them to attack each other. The infighting was, not surprisingly, a serious impediment to the Afghan struggle against the Soviets, and no Afghan commander killed his fellow Afghans with greater enthusiasm than Hekmatyar.

The CIA, especially if RAWA's claims are correct, was paying to disrupt the anti-Soviet resistance it was eagerly supporting. Such are the vicissitudes of covert action. Sometimes, real conspiracies are far more insane than any conspiracy theory.

In any event, just because a theory is paranoid doesn't always mean it's insane. If this book proves anything, it's that a theory can be wrong without being crazy. Separating the ludicrous theories of 911 from the genuine mysteries is more than a little difficult, because the ludicrous theories often include the genuine mysteries of that bright blue morning, September 11, 2001, when four commercial airliners slammed into, respectively, the WTC Twin Towers in lower Manhattan, the Pentagon, and an open field in rural Pennsylvania.

As became immediately evident, the aircraft had been hi-jacked. They were commandeered by nineteen Arab terror-ists who somehow took total control of the jets, their crews, and cockpits, armed only with "box cutters," a type of razor.

The terrorists killed more than 3,000 people, as well as themselves. The WTC attacks stole the show that day. (The Pentagon attack and the United Airlines Flight 93 crash oc-curred out of view of TV cameras.) When the second plane smashed into the south tower at top speed, disintegrating in a massive fireball, live TV was on the scene to broadcast the horror worldwide.

The initial spectacle of destruction was surpassed about an hour later when both towers of the WTC—quarter-mile-high signatures of the Manhattan skyline for three decades—col-lapsed, disgorging a gargantuan plume of acrid soot into the autumnal New York air and blacking out the sun. Within minutes, the WTC Plaza became "Ground Zero," a towering mound of mangled metal and a graveyard for thousands.

Very quickly, responsibility for the attacks was assigned by these same official sources to the previously discussed bin Laden, a multimillionaire exile from Saudi Arabia who had over the past decade used his ample bank account to create and finance a global network of Islamic "holy warriors," known as "Al Qaeda," dedicated—as per bin Laden's own public statements—to slaughtering Americans and Jews any-where they could find them. Bin Laden was behind several major terrorist attacks in the 1990s, but those were all carried out abroad—the bloodiest being the near-synchronous bomb-ings, on August 7, 1998, of U.S. embassies in Kenya and Tanzania.

The U.S. government's initial, official position was that it was taken completely off guard by the 911 attacks. They were, literally, a bolt from the blue. President Bush affirmed this position when he stated, on September 16, "Never did anybody's thought process about how to protect America, never did we ever think the evildoers would fly not one but four commercial aircraft into precious U.S. targets. Never."

The two men charged with protecting U.S. national security from within and without, respectively—FBI director Robert Mueller and CIA director George Tenet—backed up the president.

Quote Mueller, "There was never even anything saying, 'Something is planned in the United States.' "

Similar protestations of helpless ignorance were uttered by Tenet, who added (in Senate Intelligence Committee testimony) that he did not really consider this massive and utterly unexpected attack on the territorial United States to represent a "failure" of U.S. intelligence operations. "Failure means no focus, no attention, no discipline," he explained.

Any reasonable suspicion or conspiratorial speculation begins with those statements, from the exact people who should have known that an attack of 911 magnitude was on the way, because Bush, Mueller, and Tenet are all self-evidently full of crap.

Beginning in 1998, there were dozens of indications and even some direct warnings that an attack on the scale of 911 was in the works. Here are just a few from the congressional Joint Inquiry Staff report issued in September 2002:

- June 1998: U.S. intelligence learns that bin Laden is planning attacks inside the United States itself, with Washington, D.C., and New York as possible targets.
- August 1998: Spy agencies relay information to the FBI and Federal Aviation Administration (FAA) that a group of Middle Eastern terrorists planned to fly an explosives-packed plane from a foreign country and slam it into the WTC.
- December 1998: An intelligence report on bin Laden states that the terrorist leader is "keenly interested in striking the U.S. on its own soil."

- March 2001: A source tells U.S. intelligence that a group of bin Laden agents planned an attack within the United States in April of that year.
- June 2001: The CIA's Counter-Terrorism Center learns that key bin Laden operatives are "preparing for martyrdom."
- August 2001: Immigration officials in Minneapolis detain Zacarias Moussaoui, whose suspicious conduct while enrolled at a flight school there made FBI agents believe he was planning a terrorist attack.
- September 2001: On September 10, the National Security Agency intercepts a pair of communications in another country, discussing an imminent terrorist attack. On September 12, the intercepts are translated.

The same report also detailed numerous earlier intelligence reports on terrorists who planned to use aircraft as flying bombs by crashing them into buildings and public spaces. As early as 1994, Algerian Islamists hijacked a French airliner, declaring that they were going to crash it into the Eiffel Tower. In 1995, then-fugitive WTC bomber (from the 1993 bombing) Ramzi Yousef was nabbed with plans to crash a plane into CIA headquarters. In 2000, a source told the FBI that he'd trained with Al Qaeda in Pakistan and that he was part of a plot to hijack a 747, with trained pilots among the hijackers. In August 2001, U.S. intelligence discovered that bin Laden planned a plane-crash attack on the U.S. embassy in Nairobi, Kenya.

"Despite these reports," said the congressional Joint Inquiry Staff, "the Intelligence Community did not produce any specific assessments of the likelihood that terrorists would use airplanes as weapons."

(An interesting side note: an alternative plan was to bomb the Nairobi embassy from the air. When Al Qaeda attacked an Israeli resort hotel in Kenya in November 2002, bombs were apparently dropped from a plane overhead, in addition to the suicide bomb-truck that crashed into the hotel lobby.)

There were other warnings. The "Phoenix memo" on July 10, 2001, came from (appropriately) the FBI's Phoenix, Arizona, office. It warned FBI headquarters that numerous Middle Eastern men with possible links to terror groups were training at flight schools in the United States. If the FBI had heeded that memo, the hijackers-to-be who had indeed studied at U.S. flight schools almost certainly would have been discovered and the 911 plot quashed.

Bush himself, through his mouthpiece Ari Fleischer, later admitted that his previously quoted denial of the "evildoers'" intentions was fudged. Bush did, Fleischer admitted, receive a briefing in August 2001 where he was told bin Laden disciples were targeting American airliners for hijacking. The earlier denials, Fleischer said, referred only to specific warnings about a suicide attack planned for September 11, of which there were none.

Perhaps most shocking, according to a September 7, 2002, report in London's *Independent* newspaper, the United States received a warning from within Afghanistan's then-ruling Taliban junta. The regime's foreign minister learned in July 2001 that bin Laden was planning a massive, spectacular attack inside the United States, an attack that the Taliban official feared would lead to American military retaliation and the destruction of the Taliban itself. He was right about that. According to the British paper's story, he sent an emissary to pass the word to American officials in Pakistan, then to the United Nations wing in Kabul. The emissary pleaded for a "Mountain Storm" to drive Al Qaeda out of Afghanistan, similar to the "Desert Storm" that drove Iraq out of Kuwait a decade earlier.

According to the newspaper, not only did U.S. and UN officials scoff at his call for a U.S. attack, they simply brushed aside his warning of a catastrophic terrorist strike. The warning was never passed along.

The United States was evidently so woefully unprepared for an attack it had every reason to see coming that, when it happened, even its last-resort line of defense was nowhere to be found. Air Force jet fighters from the North American Aerospace Defense Command (NORAD) routinely "scramble" in response to suspicious aviation incidents. According to NORAD's own account, it received word from the FAA that American Airlines Flight 11—the first plane to hit the WTC—was hijacked at 8:40 A.M., and it didn't order fighters into the air until 8:46. By that time, the plane had already crashed into the first tower.

At 8:52, the F-15 fighters—which can fly almost 1,900 mph at top speed—finally got into the air. They took off from Otis Air National Guard Base in Massachusetts and (again, by NORAD's own account) zoomed straight for New York City, 153 miles away. Even if they'd averaged only *half* their top speed, they should have arrived split seconds before United Airlines Flight 175 made its horrifying, live-TV hit on the second tower.

Incredibly, the fighters did not arrive until eight minutes later, at 9:10. If the NORAD time line is accurate, the planes were inexplicably flying at just 510 miles per hour.

"For a long time I wondered what would have happened if we had been scrambled in time," said one of the pilots, interviewed a year later by the BBC. "I don't know what we could have done to get there any quicker."

Well, how about *fly faster*, for starters?

A NORAD officer said that planes were flying between 1,100 and 1,200 mph. That would have put them at the WTC more than a minute and a half before the second plane hit—plenty of time to disrupt the rogue airliner's flight or blast it out of the sky.

Why the fighters didn't reach the WTC in time to save the second tower—or at least have a chance at saving it—remains mysterious. Either they were flying at a strangely leisurely pace, or NORAD's time line is wrong. And if NORAD's time line is in error, there must have been a huge delay getting the planes in the air. Neither possibility is very encouraging.

Nor does either scenario explain why the FAA waffled for eighteen minutes before notifying NORAD at all. The first indication that something was askew on Flight 11 (the flight stopped sending out its normal "beacon signal") occurred at 8:20.

Fighters would have had less time to cut off the Pentagon plane, United Airlines Flight 77. NORAD received word of that hijacking at 9:24 and got its planes in the air six minutes later. The plane hit the Pentagon seven minutes after that. The fighters had taken off toward New York and turned around to head for Washington, but they didn't get there for another *twelve minutes*.

Not only did the intelligence services fail prior to 911, but also the national defense failed as the events were unfolding that day. Were these dual debacles the result of incompetence, negligence, and bureaucratic intransigence? Or was something darker and deeper at work? The conspiracy theorists would tell us that these failures were not failure at all: the attacks were *deliberately* allowed to happen!

But why? The answer depends on the conspiracy theorist. Here are a few:

- The Bush administration needed an excuse to go to war in Afghanistan to secure a prospective natural gas pipeline.
- Right-wingers in the government wanted a pretext to strip Americans of their civil liberties, with the justification of "national security."
- The United States is attempting to commit genocide against Arabs and Muslims for the benefit of its client-state Israel, and the phony terror attacks give a reason to go ahead.
- Or worse, Israel perpetrated the attacks itself.

These are the ad hoc, evidence-free speculations that back up the conspiracy theories, anyway. The last one is undoubtedly the most noxious, the point where 911 denial intersects with Holocaust denial. Regardless of what one thinks about the Israeli-Palestinian conflict, the idea that Israel would commit an act of all-out war against its closest ally in the world can only be described as an absurd canard. Where does this madness come from? Shortly after the attacks, a story floated around the Internet that, somehow, 4,000 Israelis were warned not to come in to work at the WTC that day. They all called in sick.

"4,000 Israelis" became an instant urban myth, spreading at cyber-velocity. Unsurprisingly, the story is completely untrue, which should have been self-evident as it rests on the improbable notion that 4,000 Israelis actually worked in the WTC.

The story originated on a Lebanese TV station six days after the attack and was picked up by a Pakistani newspaper as well as the Russian news service *Pravda* (which later apologized for running the story), both of whom posted it on their Web sites. The story was off and running. The curiously specific "4,000" number probably derived from statements issued by the Israeli consulate on 911 expressing concern for the 4,000 Israelis employed in *all of New York City*.

Another story cited to support the "Israel did it" myth: Five Israelis were taken into custody on 911 allegedly for "puzzling behavior." It was said that these five were seen on a nearby rooftop laughing and celebrating—and filming with a video camera—as the Twin Towers burned.

The facts: five young Israelis were arrested that day, but on the George Washington Bridge. A rooftop wasn't involved, and neither were the Israelis. They were held for two weeks under conditions that, they alleged, amounted to "a nightmare." They were beaten by police and threatened with death. At one point, a guard opened a cell door to let other inmates into the cell where one Israeli was held. The guard told the other inmates that the Israeli was "the terrorist responsible for the World Trade Center," leading the other prisoners to rush into the cell.

The Israeli five were picked up because the FBI, it claimed, had a warning that someone in a white van was going to blow up the bridge. These five Israeli citizens were driving a white van across the bridge. Wrong place, wrong time, wrong complexion.

It hardly comes as a shock that the Lyndon LaRouche organization finds the "blame Israel" scenario quite attractive. In late August 2002, LaRouche's now-venerable house organ *Executive Intelligence Review* "reported" that Israeli Prime Minister Ariel Sharon "is about to covertly launch a Sept. 11-type terrorist attack, targeting the United States—in order to drag President George W. Bush into a war against Iraq."

None of the "Israel did it" scenarios address, in any remotely plausible fashion, the question of why Israel would want to stage a major terrorist attack against its most staunch and supportive ally. Even if the idea were to transfer blame to Arab patsies, wouldn't the risk outweigh the reward? Wouldn't these hypothetically evil Israelis worry about being found out? Wouldn't they understand that if their involvement leaked (as it surely would have if they were willing to warn 4,000 of their own citizens and if five of their "agents" were careless enough to be seen laughing it up on a nearby rooftop as the WTC burned), that would be the end of the State of Israel, once and for all?

While it's easy, and likely accurate, to impugn the motives of those who concoct "Israel did it" theories, other variations on the "Osama's Just a Patsy" theme make equally little sense.

In arriving at the hypothesis that there were "no suicide pilots" on board any of the four hijacked planes, Carol A. Valentine—who holds the title of "curator" at the Waco Holocaust Electronic Museum (a Web site devoted to conspiracy theories of the Waco Branch Davidian raid in 1993; see chapter 7)—starts by listing a few basic facts about the Northrop Grumman Global Hawk, a state-of-the-art unmanned spy plane "with the wingspan of a Boeing 737." (While it's true that the Global Hawk has, actually, a somewhat larger wingspan than a 737, it is a considerably smaller plane, less than half the length, and it is much smaller than a 757 or a 767, two each of which were hijacked and crashed on 911.)

Valentine also cites a couple of articles stating that it is possible, with existing technology, to fly and land a commercial airliner by remote control from the ground. After 911, President Bush called for this system to be installed on commercial aircraft. This would allow ground controllers to, in effect, rehijack a hijacked plane, thwarting the plans of terrorists to crash into large buildings. A great idea, except that the cost of fixing up the entire existing fleet of commercial airliners with such a system could run as high as $300 billion.

"Technically speaking," writes Valentine, "we could have a 'suicidal' airplane fly into a building without a suicidal pilot. Robotics and remote control technology has developed to the point that a high-altitude Global Hawk (or a low-altitude Tomahawk cruise missile) can be guided into collision with a target without a Kamikaze pilot in the cockpit."

Thus endeth the hard evidence. And there begineth the suspiciously leading questions that pass for evidence. As another conspiracy site (The World Trade Center Demolition and the So-Called War on Terrorism) put it, "Since it is possible to control a Boeing 757 or 767 by means of remote control, might not the jets which hit the Twin Towers and the Pentagon (assuming that more than one did) have been remotely controlled?"

Maybe the Twin Towers themselves were demolished by remote control, too!

"Did a laser beam weapon cause the collapse of the World Trade Center?" wonders Christopher Bollyn of the Web site American Free Press. "American Free Press has interviewed a German physicist who believes a laser beam weapon, employing infrared technology originally developed in the Soviet Union, may have caused the collapse of the towers," he continues.

If it wasn't anything as cool as laser beams, how about bombs? Someone got into the WTC and placed explosive devices in crucial positions sometime prior to 911. The buildings came down due to a "controlled demolition."

As bomb theory maven Peter Meyer states, "the Twin Towers were designed to withstand the impact of a Boeing 707, which is very similar to a Boeing 767." Well, except that a 767 is a lot bigger and weighs about 50,000 pounds more. Nor could anyone really know that the Twin Towers would withstand the impact of even a 707. A 707 never impacted them. The buildings' designers did their level best, no doubt, but the technology they were using three decades ago couldn't tell them for sure what kind of punishment the buildings could withstand. The original designers of the WTC buildings have acknowledged that if they knew in the late 1960s what they know today they could have prevented the collapse.

Other than the fact that the bomb theory defies common sense, not to mention Occam's Razor (the simpler a theory, the more likely it is to be right), one has to wonder why the conspirators didn't detonate the WTC bombs immediately after the planes hit. Wouldn't that have been more dramatic, inflicting something like 30,000 fatalities rather than a paltry 3,000? Conversely, if the bad guys simply wanted to demolish the buildings and inflict minimum loss of life, why not wait another hour or so until everyone could get out of the buildings?

For that matter, why bother with the charade of crashing planes into the buildings at all? Why not just bomb them?

You could still use "Arab terrorists" as scapegoats, if that was your plan.

Thierry Meyssan, author of the French best-seller *L'Effroyable Imposture* (in America, *911 The Big Lie*), does the bomb-in-the-WTC crowd one better. His book *Pentagate* "documents" his thesis that the Pentagon was also damaged by bombs, not a crashing jet, and that no jet ever crashed into it at all! How his book became a best-seller is a far bigger mystery than what happened to the Pentagon, which was, sorry to say, struck by a Boeing 757-200 traveling at about 350 miles per hour, as reported by dozens of witnesses. We are not talking about witnesses who think they may have heard a shot from the grassy knoll, or was it the book depository? We are talking about witnesses who stood and watched as a 255,000-pound, 178-foot-long aircraft smashed into one of the country's most recognizable buildings.

But Meyssan presents a series of photos that supposedly defy the "official" explanation. He displays a photo of the wrecked outer wall of the Pentagon and asks (those suspiciously leading questions again!), "Can you explain how a Boeing 757-200 . . . only damaged the outside of the Pentagon?"

The answer is simple. It didn't. The plane damaged the entire structure, penetrating deep into the Pentagon and blowing up in a hellish fireball. This accounts for the seeming absence of airplane debris on the Pentagon lawn, another highly incriminating bit of evidence according to Meyssan. The problem is, there is debris evident in some photos, just not the ones that Meyssan chooses, at least not on his Web site. Much of the remainder of the plane entered the building and, in all likelihood, vanished in the massive fire, just like the WTC planes.

Meyssan and his online apostles apparently expect that when a jumbo jet crashes at high speed into a massive, powerfully reinforced steel-and-concrete building, large portions of the plane will remain intact. Look at photos from almost any air disaster—few if any of which involve building collisions—and you'll see that there's hardly anything left! Most of what remains of a crashed plane and, tragically, its passengers, is unrecognizable rubble. Mix that with debris from a demolished building and what you've got is, well, a mess. How anyone can look at a photograph of a disaster on the scale of the Pentagon crash and make any definitive statement about anything is baffling.

While it's hard to know what an otherwise respected journalist like Meyssan thinks he's doing, his ideas have the intellectual quality of Holocaust denial, or more charitably, Moon-landing denial. (As far as we know, Meyssan does not subscribe to either of those denials.) The same goes for the bomb-in-the-WTC theorists. With zero evidence to actually support their case, you simply rely on denying the validity of *any* evidence that backs the "official" story.

For example, when an e-mailer to Peter Meyer's site asks Meyer to explain why aircraft debris was photographed on the Pentagon lawn if in fact no plane hit the Pentagon, the response comes, "there is obviously something rather suspicious about this piece of 'evidence.' . . . One cannot exclude the possibility that this thing was placed at the scene precisely to provide 'evidence' that what hit the Pentagon was an American Airlines jet."

The fact that Flight 77 was hijacked, that passengers made cell phone calls from within the plane describing what was going on, that dozens of people with nothing apparently to gain by lying said they saw the plane flying toward the Pentagon and then hitting it—all of that evidence means nothing. The plane was never hijacked. It was a remote-controlled drone. The cell calls were fabricated. The witnesses may have seen something, but they don't know what. The witnesses are wrong.

This willful, almost gleeful flight from all rationality is exasperating, to say the least. When those airliners crashed into the WTC, the towers collapsed and along with everything else in their path, crushed a noble American tradition of creative suspicion. The greatest conspiracy theories, represented throughout this book, represent the sincere pursuit of truth by minds that refuse to follow the party line, even when the party line seems like the only route through the darkness. In the aftermath of 911, conspiracy theory formed its own party line. Sincere pursuit of the truth behind the greatest public trauma in anyone's living memory is getting lost, and that's nothing but another tragedy of 911, among thousands.

MAJOR SOURCES

Alexander, Yonah, and Michael S. Swetnam. *Usama bin Laden's al-Qaida: Profile of a Terrorist Network*. Ardsley, NY: Transnational Publishers, 2001.

Bergen, Peter. *Holy War, Inc.: Inside the Secret World of Osama bin Laden*. New York: The Free Press, 2001.

Bodansky, Yossef. *Bin Laden: The Man Who Declared War on America*. Roseville, CA: Prima Publishing, 2001.

Cooley, John K. *Unholy Wars: Afghanistan, America and International Terrorism*. London: Pluto Press, 1999.

Labeviere, Richard. *Dollars for Terror: The United States and Islam*. New York: Algora Publishing, 2000.

Reeve, Simon. *The New Jackals: Ramzi Yousef, Osama bin Laden and the Future of Terrorism*. Boston: Northeastern University Press, 1999.

72

Neither Rain, nor Sleet, nor Snow . . . Just Anthrax

Sixteen months after the anthrax terror letters of 2001, the FBI seemed to be running in circles. The G-men had zeroed in on a "person of interest"—the Justice Department's euphemism for "suspect" in the post–Richard Jewel era—and had spent the holiday season conspicuously tailing him as he ran various dull errands in and about suburban Maryland.

At least superficially, the suspect—er, *person of interest*—fit the FBI's "behavioral assessment" of the anthrax terrorist, that person (or persons) unknown who had unnerved an already traumatized nation in the weeks following September 11, 2001, by mailing at least four letters containing deadly anthrax spores. In addition to killing five people and sickening more than a dozen others, the noxious letters provoked widespread anxiety bordering on hysteria, forced the evacuation of major federal government buildings, temporarily crippled the U.S. postal system, and made Cipro a household word.

Early in its investigation, the FBI had eliminated foreign terrorists from its short list of suspects. Instead, the sons of J. Edgar Hoover were hunting for the sort of perpetrator they'd always been most comfortable dealing with: that species of antisocial adult American male often better known as the "lone nut." Underscoring its belief that the guilty party was a native son, the FBI had dubbed its investigation "Amerithrax." The behavioral profile posted on the FBI's Web site described the likely culprit as having a "scientific background," a high comfort level working with hazardous materials, and a job that gave him access to anthrax.

That description more or less applied to Steven J. Hatfill, a forty-eight-year-old biowarfare defense research scientist who by the winter of 2002–2003 had become the most visible person of interest in the FBI's investigation. Most significantly, Hatfill had worked for two years, between 1997 and 1999, as a civilian researcher at the U.S. Army Medical Research Institute of Infectious Diseases (USAMRIID) at Fort Detrick in Maryland. As the army's premiere biodefense research lab, Fort Detrick happened to be the main repository of the army's Ames strain of *Bacillus anthracis*, the same all-American "brand" of the virulent bacteria found in the terror letters of 2001.

By the close of 2002, the FBI had already searched Hatfill's apartment twice, subjected him to a lie-detector test, scoured a family property in Florida, and sawed holes in a frozen pond near his apartment to dredge for discarded lab equipment. According to Hatfill, who took his complaints to the press, the FBI was habitually in his rearview mirror.

The FBI had already questioned and administered polygraph tests to some 80 scientists at Fort Detrick and 200 more at the army's Dugway Proving Ground in the Utah desert. But Hatfill seemed to be of special "interest."

Few outside the concrete ramparts of the J. Edgar Hoover Building concurred. In fact, in the absence of leads, tips, or evidence of a material nature, a swarm of alternate theories had long ago germinated in the fertile minds of amateur sleuths, flack-jacket journalists, and just about everyone else with access to Web "blog" technology. Speculation, it seems, abhors a vacuum.

Before the speculation, however, came the basic facts of the case, which, for the most part, have never been in dispute. About a week after Al Qaeda terrorists slammed highjacked jets into the World Trade Center (WTC), someone deposited anthrax-laced letters into a mailbox in Trenton, New Jersey. Two of the letters, later recovered, were addressed in block letters to NBC News anchor Tom Brokaw and to the *New York Post*. (Judging from the subsequent outbreaks, there may also have been anthrax letters mailed at the same time to Dan Rather, Peter Jennings, and American Media, Inc.—publisher of *The National Enquirer*, *The Sun*, and other gossip tabloids—although no envelopes or notes were ever recovered from those locations.)

Each of the envelopes contained a dusting of brownish, granulated anthrax spores. Each envelope also contained a one-page note. Both notes were photocopies of the same unsigned, handwritten message, printed in block letters. Headlined "09-11-01," the punctuation-free message read:

THIS IS NEXT
TAKE PENACLIN [*sic*] NOW
DEATH TO AMERICA
DEATH TO ISRAEL
ALLAH IS GREAT

On October 3, fifteen days after the letters were postmarked, the first confirmed case of anthrax exposure surfaced, in Boca Raton, Florida. A photo editor at *The Sun* had been diagnosed with the rare inhalation form of the disease. Two days later, he was dead—the first known death from inhalation anthrax in the United States since 1975. At about the same time, another American Media employee—this one working in the mailroom—contracted inhalation anthrax. Meanwhile, others had already taken ill with infections that would later be diagnosed as the somewhat less virulent cutaneous form of anthrax. The victims included another American Media employee, two postal workers at different New Jersey post offices, an editorial assistant at the *New York Post*, Brokaw's assistant, and the seven-month-old son of an ABC News producer.

On October 9, four days after the first death in Florida, someone mailed two more anthrax-laced letters from Trenton. Addressed to Democratic senate majority leader Tom Daschle and Democratic senator Patrick Leahy, these envelopes also contained Ames-strain anthrax spores. However, this time the powder proved to be more refined and thus more potent than the first batch. Because it was misrouted through a State Department mail facility in Sterling, Virginia, the Leahy letter was delayed (thereby exposing more postal routes and government offices to the spores, which were fine enough to leak through the microscopic pores of the envelope). On October 15, someone in Daschle's office opened the letter addressed to the senator. The return address on the envelope seemed innocuous enough: "4th GRADE, GREENDALE SCHOOL. FRANKLIN PARK NJ 08852." No such school exists in Franklin Park. The message, block-printed by the same hand as the media letters (but this time with punctuation), was somewhat more specific than the media letters had been:

09-11-01
YOU CAN NOT STOP US.
WE HAVE THIS ANTHRAX.

YOU DIE NOW.
ARE YOU AFRAID?
DEATH TO AMERICA.
DEATH TO ISRAEL.
ALLAH IS GREAT.

The Leahy letter, recovered later, reportedly contained a photocopy of the same note (and 23,000 anthrax spores, enough to kill 100,000 people). Oddly, the FBI has yet to release photographs of the note, leading many a conspiracist to speculate that the feds are hiding something. More on that in a moment.

By mid-October, twenty-eight cases of anthrax exposure had been confirmed. By the end of the month, there were four more fatalities, bringing the total to five: two Washington postal workers, a New York City hospital worker, and a ninety-four-year-old woman in Oxford, Connecticut. All had contracted inhalation anthrax, most likely through cross-contamination of the mail. Many others working in the Senate Hart office building were exposed to the anthrax spores, but they took their Cipro antibiotics and either recovered or never developed symptoms.

By early November, several competing schools of anthrax conspiracy theory had emerged:

The guys-with-foreign-accents theory: In many ways the weakest of all the competing suppositions, the theory that Al Qaeda terrorists or agents of Iraq (or both) masterminded the anthrax mailings proved to be one of the most persistent guesstimates. And for obvious reasons: (1) Osama bin Laden's Al Qaeda network had, just weeks prior to the anthrax deliveries, launched the most devastating terrorism attack in the history of the world. To anxious mailbox owners, the anthrax assault certainly *looked* like phase two of "911." (2) The anthrax letters were headlined "09-11-01" and showcased anti-American sloganeering of a fanatical Islamist flavor. And (3) Advocates of this theory tended to be orotund, international affairs experts, the sort of wonkish hawks who monopolize the guest-panel chairs on Sunday morning news shows. Consequently, their opinions, though every bit as speculative and hunch-based as those of other conspiracy theorists, carried more weight in the arena of popular opinion.

The FBI and the CIA had spent months looking for a foreign connection, but turned up nothing. As an unnamed "senior intelligence official" told the *New York Times*, "We looked for any shred of evidence that would bear on this, or any foreign source. It's just not there."

In the absence of evidence, proponents of the theory offered a number of dubious "proofs." For instance, in June 2001 Ahmed Alhaznawi, one of the soon-to-be 911 suicide highjackers, visited a Florida doctor, who treated a dark lesion on the man's leg. After the anthrax letters became major news, federal investigators tracked down the doctor, who, although he had not diagnosed Alhaznawi with anthrax, conjectured that the lesion "was consistent with cutaneous anthrax." It was guesswork at best, but it has since become a staple "proof" in the foreign-perp theories. Yet even if Alhaznawi's lesion was caused by anthrax, that still doesn't explain who mailed the anthrax letters after the WTC terrorists were dead and buried under tons of rubble.

Onward, then, to the right-wing militia nutter theory: Given recent history's bustle of proactive "anti-gub'mintism" on the far, nativist right, it wasn't much of a stretch to imagine a platoon of don't-tread-on-me "patriots" firing off the anthrax letters from a weekend warrior retreat or hateful coffee klatsch. According to this theory, the Islamist posturing of the letters might have been an intentional misdirection, perhaps a racist attempt to pin the blame on "no-account ferriners." What's more, the targets of the mailings—network TV anchormen and two liberal Democratic senators—hold a special place of contempt in the hearts of the far-right activists.

The FBI nurtured this theory early on (and may continue to have feelings for it). However, after genetic analysis of the anthrax powder revealed the spores to be a highly refined grade of the Ames strain, the home-grown haters theory suddenly looked less likely. The arcane scientific skill set required to obtain and process weapons-grade spores seemed to rule out rural revolutionaries.

Which brings us to the military-industrial-espionage complex theory: Pupils of the "inside-job" school of suspicion posited the theory that either the military, the CIA, the George W. Bush administration, or defense contractors—or a supercharged admixture thereof—committed the evil deed. Their motive? To provoke the nation into a self-defensive, antiterrorist, promilitary posture, thereby ushering in a new era of civil liberties attrition, war adventurism, defense spending, and so on. Of course, ultravigilant cabal detectors had already tried to tailor the same basic theory to fit the entire 911 catastrophe (see chapter 71). Taken literally and in its broadest articulation, this theory certainly pushes the envelope of credibility (even *our* envelope of credibility).

An interesting corollary theory combines the lone-nut and government-cabal hypotheses. Which takes us full circle, back to person-of-interest Steven J. Hatfill:

Late in 2001, a microbiologist named Barbara Hatch Rosenberg, speaking at an international conference in Geneva on biological and toxic weapons, asserted that the recent anthrax attacks had been unleashed "by an American using a weaponized biological agent." Rosenberg's theorizing—one more note in the rising arpeggio of instant hypotheses—might have gone unnoticed were it not for the fact that she is chairwoman of the Federation of American Scientists' working group on biological weapons.

When she returned to the United States, Rosenberg elaborated in a series of postings on the Federation of American Scientists' Web site, describing the likely perpetrator as "an American microbiologist who has access to recently-weaponized anthrax or to the expertise and materials for making it." He probably worked in the USAMRIID at Fort Detrick, Rosenberg speculated, and his motive "was not necessarily to kill, but to create public fear, thereby raising the profile of [biowarfare]." In other words, the culprit was a lone zealot eager to educate Americans on the importance of a strong biodefense program, and all the funding that it entails, even if it meant *becoming* a bioterrorist to make his point.

In Rosenberg's thesis, the U.S. government was also complicit, at least secondarily, as it provided the culprit with the "unwitting assistance of a sophisticated government program."

As Rosenberg continued to update her posts, it became clear that she had a specific biochemist in mind. This unnamed biochemist was a person "who fits the FBI profile in most respects," she wrote. As she would later report, she and at least five "inside experts" had given the FBI the name of "one specific person as the most likely suspect." In February 2002, Rosenberg accused the FBI of "dragging its feet" in pursing this lead, and her speculation began to take on a more conspiratorial edge: As a USAMRIID insider, might the suspect know "something that he believes to be sufficiently damaging to the United States to make him untouchable by the FBI?" she wondered. That forbidden knowledge, Rosenberg seemed to be suggesting, might entail secret U.S. germ warfare projects expressly forbidden under the 1972 Biological Weapons Convention. Rosenberg was insinuating that the FBI or other official departments of the U.S. government had possibly engaged in a cover-up conspiracy, letting the perp off the hook in exchange for his continued silence.

Among Rosenberg's regular readers were journalists who began to air her theories in the press. They never specifically named her preferred suspect, but they dropped enough clues along the way to make it clear who Rosenberg had in mind. *New York Times* editorial columnist Nicholas D. Kristof all but spelled it out in his May 24, 2002, column, paraphrasing Rosenberg's description of "one middle-aged American who has worked for the United States military bio-defense program and had access to the labs at Fort Detrick, Md. His anthrax vaccinations are up to date, he unquestionably had the ability to make first-rate anthrax, and he was upset at the United States government in the period preceding the anthrax attack."

In a June update to her online profiling, Rosenberg revealed more details, including her speculation on a possible motive. During the summer of 2001, "the Suspect" she wrote, "had a career setback that challenged his high ambitions and left him angry and depressed." Perhaps, Rosenberg suggested, he had mounted the anthrax attacks as revenge on the government.

Of course, Rosenberg's pet suspect was Steven J. Hatfill, the biochemist who had spent two years at the USAMRIID. Hatfill's resume and background as an apparent military buff certainly caused his more liberal critics' antennae to twitch. According to his own resume, in 1975 Hatfill had served with the U.S. Army Institute of Military Assistance while simultaneously joining the Special Air Service in the white supremacist regime in Rhodesia. According to his own curriculum vitae, Hatfill had also served in Rhodesia's white-led counterinsurgency forces, the Selous Scouts, and obtained his medical degree in apartheid-era South Africa, where he subsequently served in the South African military medical corps. According to some of Hatfill's associates, he had boasted of having been a double agent in South Africa, although for whom (Rhodesia? The U.S. Army? The CIA?) he apparently did not say.

Whether it was all empty braggadocio of a resume padder or not, Hatfill's self-generated mystique soon came back to haunt him. By now, Rosenberg was ready to speculate about even darker conspiratorial motives, "Perhaps the letters were actually an official assignment," she wrote, a government-sponsored experiment or political provocation. Which, of course, takes us back to the now-familiar and claustrophobic military-industrial-espionage complex theory.

In June 2002, Rosenberg briefed staff members of Senators Daschle and Leahy about her suspicions, and in short order the proverbial fire under the collective G-man ass had been lit. Within days, the formerly sluggish special agents swooped down to search chez Hatfill. Before mounting its search of his apartment, however, the FBI thoughtfully invited the press and its action-news helicopters, if only to demonstrate once and for all where the buck, and the foot-dragging, stops.

The search failed to turn up any damning evidence, but the press it generated damned Hatfill to a rather hellish existence. Whereas the media previously kept Hatfill's identity, well, under their collective hat, the *New York Times* now felt comfortable naming him in print. After that, as Hatfill put it, his life was "destroyed." For the rest of the summer, Hatfill was hounded by reporters at all hours, vilified on the Internet (one Web site referred to him as "Steven 'Mengele' Hatfill, Nazi swine"), and widely discussed on TV and radio talk shows.

In August, an indignant Hatfill convened a press conference to deny the allegations that he was in some way connected to the anthrax letters and to rebut Rosenberg's claims against him:

He had never worked with or cultivated anthrax at Fort Detrick or anywhere else, he said. In fact, his field of expertise was virology, not bacteriology.

He was *not* up to date on his anthrax booster shots, and his last anthrax vaccination had been in December 1998.

He had not been, as Rosenberg had suggested, disgruntled, angry, or depressed in the summer of 2001. Rosenberg had referred to a "career setback," and indeed Hatfill had lost his security clearance after taking a CIA lie-detector test. At the time, Hatfield was employed by Science Applications International, a biodefense contractor that did work for government agencies, including the CIA. As a prerequisite to participating in a CIA project, Hatfill took a polygraph test. Apparently, the CIA was not satisfied with his responses to questions about his resume—*that* resume. Even though he failed to obtain clearance, Hatfill insisted, he continued to work on unclassified projects at the private firm.

In the wake of the press conference, the FBI refused to comment on Hatfill's rebuttals, so there's really no way to measure the accuracy of his counterclaims. Was Hatfill the proverbial wrong man, a mildly eccentric character whose background led overzealous critics to the wrong conclusion? Or might he have been an outright patsy who had been framed by the real perps? That possibility apparently occurred to the FBI, who had asked Rosenberg as much when they visited her in August 2002, just before tossing Hatfill's apartment a second time. "They kept asking me did I think there might be a group in the biodefense community that was trying to land the blame on Hatfill," Rosenberg told a *Washington Times* reporter.

It's an interesting question because part of the supposed "evidence" against Hatfill was a hoax anthrax letter mailed from London to Senator Daschle late in 2001. The letter, postmarked in London, has been described in media accounts as being "much like the real one," whatever that means. As Rosenberg was quick to report, Hatfill had been in England (but not London) on the same day, attending a high-profile British biodefense conference. If Hatfill had indeed sent the hoax letter, effectively leaving an obvious trail of bread crumbs in his wake, he'd probably qualify as one of the dumbest terrorists of all time. However, if someone else mailed the letter knowing that it would appear to implicate Hatfill, well, the case for conspiracy gets more interesting.

Speaking of frame-ups, another bizarre episode may hold a potential clue to the mystery of the anthrax letters. In September 2001, before anyone realized the first anthrax letters were moving through the U.S. mail, someone posted an anonymous letter to Quantico Marine Base fingering an

Egyptian-born former USAMRIID scientist at Fort Detrick as a potential bioterrorist. After the anthrax outbreaks became headlines, the FBI questioned the scientist, Ayaad Assaad, and cleared him, deciding that the letter was probably a hoax. Assaad later told the *Hartford Courant* that he suspected someone was trying to frame him and that the timing of the note makes its author a suspect in the anthrax attacks. According to the *Courant,* Assaad thought that the "details of his work contained in the letter mean the author must be a former Fort Detrick colleague."

Rosenberg has interpreted this possible attempt to frame Assaad as yet another piece of evidence against Hatfill, who started working at the USAMRIID the same year Assaad was laid off due to "downsizing." But the *Hartford Courant* also turned up some interesting details that certainly widen the field when it comes to persons of interest. In 1992, an internal inventory at the USAMRIID revealed that twenty-seven specimens, including anthrax spores, Ebola virus, hanta virus, and two classified agents, had gone missing. Apparently, only one of the lost samples was ever recovered. The same audit uncovered various episodes of suspicious activity in the labs, including "unauthorized research" late at night and tampering with equipment to conceal the fact that it had been used.

According to the *Hartford Courant,* documents from the inquiry showed that one of the unauthorized night visitors was Lieutenant Colonel Philip Zack, a former employee who at the time no longer worked at Fort Detrick. "A surveillance camera recorded Zack being let in at 8:40 P.M. on Jan. 23, 1992, apparently by Dr. Marian Rippy, a lab pathologist and close friend of Zack's," the *Courant* reported. Zack had voluntarily left Fort Detrick in late 1991, amid allegations that he, Rippy, and others in the pathology division had "formed a clique that was accused of harassing . . . Assaad, who later sued the Army, claiming discrimination."

Currently, the mystery of the anthrax letters lingers, seemingly impervious to investigative efforts of both professional and amateur sleuths, not unlike the nastily resilient pathogen itself.

MAJOR SOURCES

Dolan, Jack, and Dave Altimari. "Anthrax Missing From Army Lab." *Hartford Courant,* 20 January 2002.

FBI. "Amerithrax Investigation" Web site, www.fbi.gov/ anthrax/amerithraxlinks.com.

Gugliotta, Guy, and Gary Matsumoto. "FBI's Theory on Anthrax Is Doubted." *Washington Post,* 27 October 2002.

Jackman, Tom. "Ex-Army Scientist Denies Role in Anthrax Attacks." *Washington Post,* 11 August 2002.

Johnston, David. "Search of Biologist Is Uneventful." *New York Times,* 26 June 2002.

Lake, Ed. "The Anthrax Cases" Web site, www. anthraxinvestigation.com.

Kristof, Nicholas D. "Connecting Deadly Dots." *New York Times,* 24 May 2002.

Rosen, Laura. "Who Is Steven Hatfill?" *The American Prospect Online,* 27 June 2002, www.prospect.org.

Rosenberg, Barbara Hatch. "Analysis of the Anthrax Attacks." Federation of American Scientists Web site, www.fas. org/bwc/news/anthraxreport.htm.

United Press International. "FBI Is Tracking Hatfill." Newsmax Wires, 24 December 2002.

73

Votescam 2000

The 2000 U.S. presidential election lasted so long it should have been sponsored by Viagra, though it ended not with a bang but with a supreme whimper. And immediately after the thirty-seven days from vote until final decision, if calling a halt to the counting of votes can be described as a "final decision," the American people raised their voice as a collective statistic to render a swift and decisive judgment. That's what happens in this era of insta-polling. In this case, the American people were represented by 633 adults surveyed by an overnight CNN-Gallup poll.

Speaking for the other 250 million of us, as reported on CNN, a whopping 80 percent of those adults accepted George W. Bush as "the legitimate president." A less overwhelming but still alarming 53 percent agreed with the U.S. Supreme Court decision that sent thousands of uncounted ballots cast by other adult Americans to the circular file, awarding Bush the presidency.

What the 633 adults perhaps did not realize was that for Bush to be installed as president, Americans had to be stripped, officially and legally, of their right to vote. Maybe that was fitting, as Bush's own father had been removed from office by a decisive margin of votes eight years earlier.

For that matter, Americans have no right, none, to vote for the "electors" who actually pick the president under the archaic and slightly arcane system known as the "Electoral College." That, anyway, was the edict from the highest court in the land, the final arbiter of all things legal and constitutional in the United States.

"The individual citizen has no federal constitutional right to vote for electors for the President of the United States," wrote the Court in its curiously unsigned opinion, "unless and until the state legislature chooses a statewide election as the means to implement its power to appoint members of the electoral college."

The Court is correct. The Constitution does not speak a syllable regarding the right to vote. In the early days of the republic, Congress selected the president, all on its own. Now, one might have thought that the last 200-plus years of history, during which the right to vote has gained a slight toehold in American political tradition, might count for something. Apparently not. The Court has returned us to the eighteenth century.

Democracy, we hardly knew ye.

How did this happen? The brief background is as follows: the Democrat, Vice President Al Gore, and the Republican, Texas governor/eponymous son of former president George Bush, offered the American electorate very little to choose from. Throughout the entire 2000 campaign, polls placed them in more or less a dead heat. And by gosh, this time the polls were right. When voting booths drew their shutters for the night on November 7, the election was too close to call.

That didn't stop the shadowy, monopolistic Voter News Service (VNS) and its TV-network clients from calling it. But that's a part of the Grand Conspiracy we'll approach in greater detail momentarily. What's important for now is that the electoral vote, which would determine the next president, came down to one state: Florida.

And so it came to pass that the governor of the State of Florida was Jeb Bush, brother of George W. Bush who, if Florida's electoral votes went his way, would become president. Assuming the land's highest office, for G. W. Bush, would complete one of the most shockingly swift and seemingly inexplicable ascents in American political history: from failed oilman, to Major League Baseball owner, to Texas governor, to president in less than a decade.

So Bush's fate was in the hands of his own brother. Mere coincidence? Perhaps. But even in the most charitable, non-conspiratorial interpretation, it was a fortuitous coincidence for Bush. Well before November 7, political expert-types believed that Florida would be the hinge on which the election turned. Those twenty-five electoral votes in a state split between conservative natives and liberal northeastern transplants would decide the election. And everybody knew it. That's why Gore spent the final thirty hours of his campaign stumping sleepless through the night in that state. During that same time, George Bush dozed.

Bush may not have yet opened his eyes when the polls opened that day, and Gore may have been fighting to keep his from closing, but in Florida the curious occurrences commenced bright and early and continued apace throughout election day.

In the sure-fire-Gore county of Palm Beach, the design of the so-called "butterfly" or "facing-page" style of punch-card ballot proved "confusing." As a result, thousands of voters, most of them Democrats and Jewish, punched their ballots for Pat Buchanan, the third-party candidate who is also the nation's leading defender of accused Nazi war criminals. Either that, or they double punched their ballots, mistakenly voting for Buchanan then also punching the hole next to Gore's name. A ballot with two votes doesn't count for any and thus those voters disqualified themselves.

In the days that followed, talk-show hosts and pundits across America had great fun ridiculing the astigmatic, Alzheimer's-inflicted Jewish voters of Palm Beach County—aren't elderly Jewish people a scream?—but no one argued that those voters did not intend to vote for Gore. In other words, Bush won Palm Beach County—and as a result the state and the presidency—by mistake.

Or was it a mistake? Radio and TV interviews with Palm Beach County voters yielded a description of the ballot that didn't match up with the ballot reproduced in the media. It seems that when the computer-card ballot was slipped into its holder, the holes didn't line up the way they were supposed to. Apparently no one checks for those things.

In other counties, there were allegations that African American voters, likely Gore-backers, were intimidated by police, with roadblocks set up near their polling places. More than a year after the 2000 election, Bush's own Justice Department announced that it was investigating charges that black voters were shut out of polling places.

Returning for a moment to Palm Beach County, of the 28,000 votes that were trashed for improper punches, nearly half came from predominantly black or elderly precincts. In the mostly black precincts, nearly 16 percent of ballots went uncounted, double the total in white precincts. The *Times* of London reported that many of the discarded double-punched ballots were actually prepunched before anyone voted on them. The *Times* quoted Democratic officials saying that if true, the allegation of prepunching indicated "organized corruption." No kidding.

And let's not forget the *X-Files*-ish tale of Volusia County, where the vote count was described by the *Washington Post* as "a tragicomedy of errors." At ten p.m. that oh-so-fateful election night, Gore's tally suddenly plunged by 16,000 votes while an obscure Socialist Party candidate mysteriously gained 10,000. Even odder, this abrupt shift in fortunes occurred entirely in a single voting precinct that had only 600 voters.

The eye-opening reversal of fortune was written off to a computer "glitch." But that wasn't the only glitch in Volusia County. In one precinct, an election worker took off with two uninspected bags of ballots. During a recount the next day, a different election worker walked in with a bag of ballots that he'd left in his car overnight. A few days after that, workers found one bag of ballots unsealed, another with a broken seal, and a third open with ballots spilling out. And to top off this extravaganza of ineptitude, many African American college students protested that they had been barred from polling places despite being properly registered as voters.

One of Bush's own lawyers fretted that "from a practical standpoint, nobody has any faith in the system." Meanwhile, a Gore attorney predicted that "television movies" will be made about how "the election was stolen in Volusia County" and that the county would become the new "Grassy Knoll gunman" for conspiracy theorists.

Perhaps. On the other hand, a good conspiracy theorist could identify a whole army of grassy knoll gunmen in the 2000 Bush coup.

There was the aforementioned Jeb Bush, governor of the decisive state. And there was Florida's secretary of state, Katherine Harris, a Republican and active Bush supporter, whose job is to "certify" election results. Midway through the recount process in November, with thousands of votes still in doubt, Harris "certified" the election results in favor of Bush. She had a legal deadline, though she also had the power to extend that deadline. She chose not to. Once she certified in Bush's favor, the election was effectively over. At the very least, Bush had powerful ammunition against further recounts or legal challenges—and he gained a solid upper hand in the public relations battle.

There was James Baker, the subject of *Godfather* metaphors ad infinitum. He's the "Bush family consigliere." The metaphor is not inappropriate. A trusted advisor (and secretary of state) to President Bush the elder, Baker appeared out of nowhere to "supervise" the Florida recount for the Bush forces. He was about to embark to Europe with former president Bush when he got the call. Quickly, he was there, appearing on podiums and, in a largely successful effort to discredit the human recounts of computer ballots, making statements to the effect that machines are better than people.

How about John Ellis, overseer of the "decision desk" at the conservatively bent Fox News Channel? Charged with "fair and balanced" (as per Fox's much-repeated slogan) reporting of election results, Ellis was in fact first cousin to the Bush brothers. They called him often on election night and he fed them information before it went out over the air, doing little for the credibility of network news reporting in this whole mess.

The previously alluded to VNS also figures in what may, in the end, turn out to be a conspiracy of incompetence as opposed to a preplanned plot. Could anyone be as smart, or as dumb, as would be required to chain together the surreal circumstances of that night with malice aforethought?

VNS is the direct descendant of News Election Service, named by the late Jim and Ken Collier as the axis of evil in a conspiracy to rig elections ongoing since 1960. This time, however, VNS seems to have been guilty of total stupidity, rather than premeditated malfeasance. Before eight p.m. (that is, before polls had closed), the TV networks acting on information from VNS exit polls "called" the Florida vote for none other than Al Gore. The mistake happened when someone at VNS recorded a vote total of "4,302" for Gore as "43,023." VNS also made numerous goofs in tabulating its own exit poll findings. VNS and the networks soon rescinded their "Gore wins" pronouncements. Six hours later, they "called" Florida again. This time for Bush. (Perhaps it was no surprise that after VNS blew it again during the 2002 midterm elections, producing no election-night projections whatsoever, the media companies that sponsored it finally

brought the ax down and put the consortium out of business.)

All of that chaos was mere preface to the anarchy that set
in over the next five weeks, anarchy the Bush team was able
to exploit far more adroitly than its Gore-supporting adversaries. Once Bush was the projected and certified winner, the
Bush Squad's top priority was clear: *stop the vote count!*
That meant cutting thousands of people out of the democratic process, but Bush, Baker, and the rest of the garrison
under their command didn't care about the voters, only the
result.

Though their candidate lost the popular vote and would
have lost the electoral vote had at least 20,000 Gore voters
not mistakenly cast ballots for Buchanan, the Bush team
moved forward with its grab for power. The circumstances
may not have been premeditated, but the grab itself was.
Bush's own people admitted that if Gore won the electoral
vote while losing the popular vote, they had a plan to spark
a popular uprising against the Electoral College system with
a talk-radio blitz and media ad campaign. Constitution be
damned.

No need for a conspiracy theory. The conspiracy was right
out in the open. As recounts bulldozed ahead, the Bush team
organized "demonstrations" and near-riots aimed at halting
them—through intimidation, if nothing else worked. In Miami-
Dade County, John Sweeney, a Republican congressman from
New York, barked commands at a mob of Republican vigi-
lantes inside a county building and directly outside the room
where the recount was taking place. "Shut it down!" ordered
Sweeney, and the angry throng did just that.

The final coup de grace of the coup d'etat took place not
in the streets or in the crowded halls of some county administration building, but in the U.S. Supreme Court. On
December 13, five of the nine justices voted to halt all recounts and declare Bush the next president. Their grounds
for doing so were virtually nonexistent, legally speaking.

Their decision rested mainly on the "equal protection" clause of the Fourth Amendment, reasoning the justices themselves had earlier rejected in a preliminary ruling.

This coup was amazing, because it was carried out in plain sight. Unlike most juicy conspiracies, the plotters paid no regard to secrecy or cover-ups or clandestine activity of any kind. The five pro-Bush justices offered no apologies for transforming the Court, quite openly, into an arm of the Bush campaign. Their own written language attests to that fact. Justice Antonin Scalia wrote that allowing recounts to continue would risk "irreparable harm" to Bush by "casting a cloud upon what he claims to be the legitimacy of his election."

In plain English, if the recounts continued, Bush might lose. They must be stopped.

Is it a hyperbole to call Bush's ascent to the presidency a "coup"? Paranoid? Hysterical? The *American Heritage Dictionary* defines "coup d'etat" as "a sudden, decisive exercise of power whereby the existing government is subverted without the consent of the people."

When votes cast by actual people are ignored and an election is decided by a court that publicly acknowledges its support for one candidate, what else do you call it but a "sudden, decisive" power grab? Bush's defenders and media-types, desperate to appear "evenhanded," have accused Gore of engaging in the same ruthless, conspiratorial tactics as Bush. That may be true. It could be that Gore got out-couped. But nothing changes the fact that Bush did everything possible to overturn and subvert the process of democratic elections for no other reason than lust for power.

It may have been an accident that put the Bushites in the position of stopping vote counts and the Gore group in the position of counting votes until it could count no more. But despite what the 80 percent of 633 adults said hours after the Supreme Court handed down its decision, that accident doesn't make the election legitimate.

MAJOR SOURCES

ABCNews.com Staff. "Irregularities Alleged." ABCNews.com, 8 November 2000.

Ackerman, Bruce A., ed. *Bush v. Gore: The Question of Legitimacy*. New Haven, CT: Yale University Press, 2002.

Bugliosi, Vincent. *The Betrayal of America: How the Supreme Court Undermined the Constitution and Chose Our President*. New York: Thunder's Mouth Press/Nation Books, 2001.

Greenberg, David. "Was Nixon Robbed?" *Slate*, 16 October 2001.

Jensen, Elizabeth. "In This Ballot, Voter Service Is the Loser." *Los Angeles Times*, 14 January 2003.

Kaplan, David. *The Accidental President*. New York: William Morrow and Company, 2001.

Milbank, Dana. "Tragicomedy of Errors Fuels Volusia Recount." *Washington Post*, 12 November 2000.

Tapper, Jake. *Down and Dirty: The Plot to Steal the Presidency*. New York: Little, Brown & Co., 2001.

74

www.illuminati.com

The Internet is a great place to shop for spycams and pornography, refinance your mortgage, or sign up for penis enlargement. It's also been touted as a forum for exchanging the gift of knowledge. But what if the promise of a brave new pixilated world of "information empowerment" merely cloaks the Web's true agenda, a plot far more sinister than, say, making Harry Knowles employable?

We've all heard about the peculiar origins of the Net as a project spawned by the U.S. Defense Department back in 1969: In case of a nuclear war, even after the red rain began to fall on the barren wasteland that was once North America, the military needed to be sure that its top brass could send e-mail to one another. Of course, no one in 1969 had the slightest idea what e-mail was (remember, The GAP was barely off the ground at that point). Thus, bursting with can-do attitude, the true-blue (and also khaki) boys of the Defense Department invented it. Of course, back then it was called "IP-based ASCII text messaging," a phrase that required considerable "shakedown" before it was ready to roll off the tongue as

"You've got mail!" But then what would transmit this new-fangled "e-mail" from place to place? Why, the Internet, naturally. So they invented *that* too.

Paranoid savants who "get" the big picture tend to look at the Internet's military origins as a sort of smoking microchip; from their Imax-sized vantage point, they see the conspiracy extending well beyond a paltry plot to invade your privacy by tracking your credit card spending.

The congenitally "aware" see through the smokescreen (and often smokescreensavers) to espy a devious group that includes businesspeople, politicians, and intellectuals manipulating world events, working toward the goal of a quasi-fascistic, one-world government. This cabal has a name: No, not "AOL." We're referring to the Illuminati.

As they are behind so many other great developments—including the Age of Enlightenment, modern democracy, and funny Masonic hats—it stands to reason that the Illuminati (see chapter 36) are also behind the Internet, right? But why?

Here are a few of the reasons that we have been told about:

- To spy on you: "Their purpose," says Anthony Hilder, who has produced hundreds of video and audiocassette programs outlining the Illuminati plot, "is not simply a source of control but a recovery of information from all people, knowing that people would become involved around the world and voluntarily supply information which could be used against them."
- To cloud your mind with naughty thoughts: The belief that the Illuminati uses sexual symbolism as a means of mind-control is another key element of the conspiracy theory. And the Internet is nothing if not rife with sexual symbols (often in streaming video format). Even "WWW" is a sexual symbol. "Come on!" you say? Check it out: "W is the 23rd letter in the alphabet,"

notes Robert Sterling, whose Konformist.com site is one of the Web's best-known repositories of conspiracy theory research. "And 23 times three, of course, equals 69. So you've got the whole psycho-sexual thing going on."

- To hail Satan: Are the Illuminati agents of the Antichrist, the "Beast" prophesied in the Bible who will cause the end of the world? Some researchers believe the "number of the beast," 666, is used as a signal by the Illuminati to indicate their true purpose. Aaron Johnson, a southern California conspiracy researcher and self-described "patriot," believes that the letters "WWW" reveal the link: "The letter *W* is the sixth letter of the Hebrew alphabet," Johnson says. "The three Ws—World Wide Web. That's not by accident. To me it means 666. It's another part of the infrastructure of control of society and the world."

(It should be noted that in the Hebrew alphabet letters are assigned numerical values, and "Vav," a close equivalent of the letter "W," is indeed the number 6. But in Hebrew numerology "Vav-Vav-Vav" translates not as "666" but as "18," the numerical value of the word "Chai," which means "life." In fact, 18 is one of the most important "lucky numbers" in the Jewish religion.)

While we're on the subject of portals (or "Windows") to hell, let's not forget everyone's favorite demonic Internet presence: Bill Gates. Prophecy Central is a fundamentalist Christian Web site that casts the geek-overlord as a sinister player in the events leading up to the biblical End Times. As the organization's "Bill Gates Watch" warns, the Master of Microsoft is "of interest to prophecy students who are expecting a world-wide computer network to be in place in the possibly near future to make Antichrist's economic dictatorship possible. NOTE: The focus is on the information, not the person." In other words, though Gates may not necessarily be Damian Thorne incarnate, he is a kind of indicator species of evil, and as such, the man to watch.

In fact, one vigilant Gates watcher on another Microsoft-bashing/Jesus Christ–esteeming Web site shrewdly located a pertinent passage in the book *World War III: Coming Soon to Your Neighborhood* by Jack B. Otto. According to Otto, "Few Masons know that Albert Pike, the Prince Adept, was also the head of the Palladists, another semi-secret society that worshipped Satan." The name of Microsoft's current copy-protection scheme? Palladium. Quote the Web master, "Because the elite sickos are so crazed about symbology, it would not be too outrageous to believe that Gates (elite) would call his proposed software 'Palladium.' How appropriate for such a system, which seems to be that of total control over anyone with a computer using the Internet or e-mail (once they've brought in their 'New World Order')."

But we're getting off topic, just like the kind of people who post opinions on the (Illuminati-controlled) Internet. Back to the list of reasons why the Illuminati seeks to control the Internet:

- To drug you into submission: Sterling wrote the article "The Web and the Pentagon," in which he compares the creation of the Internet to the military's well-documented use of LSD in mind-control experiments. "Could the Web be merely the twin companion of LSD?" asks Sterling in the article (which appeared in the anthology *Cyberculture Counterconspiracy,* vol. 2). "The final key in an occultic project created to destroy the existing order and establish a new one?"

Sterling, however, has less in common with "patriot" conspiracy theorists like Hilder and Johnson than he does with the late psychedelic guru Timothy Leary, who believed that the Internet, like LSD before it, can be a liberating force, rather than an oppressive one, in spite of its possibly conspiratorial genesis.

"Of course the Internet is a conspiracy," says Sterling. "It was created by the Defense Department. But then again the Defense Department also created LSD. That doesn't mean you don't take it."

MAJOR SOURCES

Bill Gates Watch Web site, www.bible-prophecy.com/pcu8.htm#article.
Freeworld Alliance Web site, www.freeworldalliance.com.
Konformist Web site, www.konformist.com and www.konformist.com/hilder/nwotapes.htm.
Sterling, Robert. "The Web and the Pentagon." Reprinted in *Cyberculture Counterconspiracy,* vol. 2, edited by Kenn Thomas. Escondido, CA: Book Tree, 2000.

75

The Ship That Wasn't There

If by now you haven't heard of the whispered "Philadelphia Experiment," it's not for lack of vocal projection on the part of the whisperers. Some sixty years after an event that may or may not have happened, the story of a U.S. Navy warship's "teleportation" from Philadelphia to Norfolk, Virginia, and back again has lodged itself squarely in the national gullet. Flip through the edutainment cable channels on any off-Shark Week, and you're bound to encounter an exposé on the secret World War II–era invisibility experiment previously exposed by a fleet of paranormal researchers, large-print authors, recovered-memory eyewitnesses, and weekend relativity theorists.

Whether true or not, the story of the USS *Eldridge*'s fantastic voyage has taken on the mythic proportions of modern folk legend. Like Roswell—another touchstone of "suppressed" twentieth-century history—accounts of the Philadelphia Experiment have, over the years, accumulated a wealth of details and spawned dozens of elaborative narratives, some more imaginative than others.

Still, the basic outline of the legend has remained fairly fixed: In 1943, the Office of Naval Research (ONR) is said to have conducted a top-secret experiment in "electronic camouflage" at the Philadelphia Navy Yard. As to whether the project's objective was simple radar invisibility or the much more over-the-top, naked-eye-style invisibility often depicted in comic books and short-lived television series, accounts vary. However, this much is agreed on: Rather than conduct the ultrasensitive test within the secure confines of a remote laboratory, the navy decided to perform its experiment in broad daylight, in a bustling wartime shipyard, with plenty of eyewitnesses on hand. So much for military "intelligence."

Under the guidance of several name-brand scientists (Albert Einstein and Nicolai Tesla among them), the ONR outfitted a manned destroyer escort—the *Eldridge*—with several tons of highly classified electronic equipment. At the appointed hour, a switch was thrown, and "magnetic resonance" generators of some sort began to radiate a powerful electronic force field around the ship. The field quickly grew in intensity, enveloping the *Eldridge* and its men in an eerie green fog, until ship and crew completely vanished, leaving behind only the compellingly specific aroma of burnt ozone.

It was at this point that the experiment suddenly hurdled out of the major-historical-breakthrough column into unequivocal *Holy-Shit!* territory: An instant or two after it disappeared from Philly, the *Eldridge* reappeared 230 miles away at a port in Norfolk, Virginia. Obviously, the navy had gotten much more than it bargained for—invisibility is one thing, but the physical teleportation of many tons of matter is quite another, no matter how stiff your epaulets. At any rate, before the flabbergasted crew could take advantage of the unscheduled layover in Norfolk, the *Eldridge* disappeared yet again, only to rematerialize instantaneously, or thereabouts, back in Philadelphia.

Not surprisingly, all this rapid ethereal transit led to some bizarre side effects: According to most accounts, half the crew emerged from the strange cruise "mad as hatters," the usual outcome of paranormal catastrophes. At least madness proved to be a kinder fate than that suffered by several other sailors, who apparently rematerialized inside the ship's solid steel bulkheads. Navy brass were aghast at the unintended consequences, so the project was quickly scuttled. The government committed the stark-raving seamen to appropriate institutions, hushed up the entire affair, and wisely moved on to developing safer and saner secret weapons, like the A-bomb.

Or so the story goes.

Of course, the Department of the Navy has consistently denied involvement in any invisibility or teleportation scheme, whether in Philadelphia, Norfolk, or any other hyperspace coordinate. And in an example of military efficiency, the navy's public relations office long ago drafted a form letter for inquiring minds, dismissing the so-called experiment as a "myth" more suited to the "realm of science fiction" than to the overbooked debunking schedule of a busy public relations officer. (You can save time and postage by looking up the form letter on the Internet.)

To be sure, the physical evidence in support of the Philadelphia Experiment is about as vaporous as the vanishing ship itself. There really was a World War II–era destroyer escort called the USS *Eldridge*, which ushered supply convoys through the U-boat-infested waters of the Atlantic. But, as the navy points out, there are no official records placing the *Eldridge* in Philadelphia during 1943, the time frame for the alleged experiment. What's more, the ONR didn't even come into existence until 1946, three years *after* the tale has it masterminding the ill-starred invisibility project.

Perhaps a more rewarding line of inquiry can be found in tracing the roots of the legend. The first public peep from anyone about the tale seems to have come from a rather oddball drifter named Carlos Miguel Allende (aka Carlos Miguel

Allenda, aka Carl M. Allen). In 1955, Allende struck up a
mail correspondence with UFO researcher Morris K. Jessup.
A part-time UFOlogist and sometime auto parts salesman,
Jessup had recently published *The Case for the UFO*, an
earnest inquiry into the then-novel flying saucer phenomenon. In a series of rambling, handwritten letters that were
certainly "paranormal" in a grammatical sense, Allende regaled Jessup with a tale he described as "A TRUTH TOO
HUGE, TOO FANTASTIC, TO NOT BE TOLD."

And indeed, Allende's story lived up to all the capital letters. In October 1943, Allende claimed to have witnessed a
navy experiment that resulted in the "complete invisibility of
a ship, Destroyer type, *and all* of its crew" (Allende's emphasis). According to Allende, he had watched the action from
the deck of the SS *Andrew Furuseth*, a merchant ship trolling
in the same waters during the experiment.

If the high concept didn't immediately hook Jessup,
Allende's tale was peppered with vivid specifics, recognizable
names, and impressive techno-babble: Based on certain hushed
up practical applications of Einstein's unified field theory
"privately" confirmed by "Dr. B. Russell"—as in the famous
logician Bertrand Russell—the experiment generated a
"Force-Field" of "oblate spheroidal shape" around the ship.
In addition to driving the crew "Stark Raving, Gibbering,
Running MAD," the project had other dramatic complications. For instance, for years after the experiment the stricken
seamen tended without warning to become "frozen" in
"TIME"—that is, locked in a cigar store–Indian pose, unable
to move a muscle. Others, Allende insisted, found themselves
turning invisible at the most inopportune moments. One
cursed crewman "just walked 'throo' His quarters Wall in
sight of His Wife & Child & 2 other crew Members [and]
WAS NEVER SEEN AGAIN." Two other men abruptly
burst into flame and "BURNED FOR 18 DAYS." Overall, it
was apparently a pretty bad scene.

As near as Jessup and subsequent researchers were able to

determine, Allende had indeed served on a merchant marine ship called the *Andrew Furuseth* in 1943, and the vessel had been to Philadelphia during that same period. But that was the only element of his story solid enough to be confirmed. The other "facts" of the tale proved to be as elusive as Allende himself, whose letters often featured a Pennsylvania return address but postmarks from Texas, Mexico, and other points south. To his credit, Jessup remained only cautiously interested in Allende's tale up until the spring of 1957. At that point, something unusual happened, and Jessup found himself increasingly pulled into Allende's storytelling force field, a circumstance that would ultimately end in tragedy.

The something unusual was a letter from the ONR inviting Jessup to Washington. When Jessup arrived at ONR headquarters, he was shown a dog-eared paperback copy of his book. Inside were extensive annotations handwritten in three different colors of ink, as if by three different individuals commenting back and forth on Jessup's text. The annotator or annotators purported to have extensive knowledge of UFOs, their propulsion systems, undersea alien cities, and other fantastic whatnot. At the height of the Cold War and the UFO "flaps" of the 1950s, the ONR evidently believed that the outré scrawlings—which spoke authoritatively of "motherships," "scout ships," "telepathing," and other pulp sci-fi concepts— might have national-security ramifications.

The ONR officers explained that the book had arrived anonymously in the mail eighteen months earlier (stamped with a Texas postmark). When asked for his reaction, Jessup commented that the handwriting closely resembled Allende's. The navy wanted to see that correspondence, so Jessup obliged. The ONR apparently concurred that the marginal notes were Allende's. The navy subsequently republished Jessup's book, complete with the strange annotations, in a limited-press edition for internal ONR distribution. Printed by the Varo Manufacturing Company, a Texas-based navy contractor, the spiral-bound copy also included the Allende letters to

Jessup about the disappearing ship. (An angry Allende would later burst into the Varo offices and demand his share of the proceeds from "my book.")

Whether or not you believe the Philadelphia Experiment actually happened, it's clear that the navy's wide-eyed interest in Allende's scribblings elevated an otherwise obscure story into a larger arena. In the process, the navy, nautically speaking, hoisted itself by its own petard, because the rare "Varo edition," soon to become a hot collectible in the UFOlogy circuit, was taken by many to be prima facie evidence of a naval connection to the rumored Philadelphia Experiment. Authors and lecturers of a Fortean bent began alluding to the Allende letters and the hyperspace-tripping navy ship, invoking the Varo edition as a smoking gun.

Unfortunately, the navy's interest in Allende's scrawlings also had a profound effect on Jessup. With an ONR imprimatur (of sorts) on Allende's UFO *Cliff Notes*, Jessup suddenly began to take his itinerant correspondent more seriously. According to friends and associates, Jessup became increasingly occupied with making sense of Allende's theories, or at least squaring them with his own views. Of course, he failed, and as a result seems to have grown increasingly despondent.

Fellow UFO researcher Ivan Sanderson, a close friend, described Jessup as "an ebullient enthusiast . . . almost too enthusiastic and confident of his theories," but who "seemed to suddenly doubt everything" in the wake of the Allende letters, including his own abilities as a UFO theorist. A psychic friend was more succinct: His "vibrations," she observed, "had taken on . . . a sort of astral B.O." In concert with a string of personal setbacks, including a divorce from his wife, his publisher's rejection of several book manuscripts, and a serious car accident, the Allende affair apparently helped nudge Jessup over the edge emotionally.

Finally, on April 20, 1959, Jessup drove to a rural park not far from his home in Coral Gables, Florida, attached one end of a garden hose to his car's exhaust pipe and fed the other end through a side window. The official cause of death was self-inflicted carbon monoxide poisoning, which certainly gibed with a letter Jessup had mailed to a friend just days earlier. The friend described it as a "straight suicide note."

Of course, Jessup's demise only fueled further speculation in conspiracy-minded circles that he had been "suicided" to enforce his silence. The evidence behind such conjecture was exceedingly diaphanous and most often couched in the passive tense ("Perhaps he was allowed to die," suggested one suspicious acquaintance). Still, a good conspiracy narrative demands a martyr, and Jessup had inadvertently filled the bill.

Perhaps Jessup would have chosen a different path had he lived long enough to hear his roving pen pal retract his tales. A decade later, in the summer of 1969, Allende stormed into the offices of a citizen's UFO research group in Arizona and declared that his letters to Jessup and the Varo edition annotations were bilge. Peeved that just about every chronicler of the unexplained had been cashing in on "his" story of the vanishing navy ship—everyone but him, that is—Allende had decided to put the brakes on the legend. He claimed that the point of his hoax was to "scare the hell out of Jessup." Scribbled as a new annotation in a coveted copy of the Varo edition, Allende's mea culpa characterized his descriptions of the sailors' side effects as "the carzyest [sic] pack of lies I ever wrote." True to form, however, Allende's "confession" was itself contradictory and failed to retract the claim of the disappearing ship. In that omission, future contributors to the narrative would find a loophole big enough to steam a destroyer escort through.

Winged but not mortally, the legend hobbled along for another decade, occasionally surfacing as an aside in books of the Bermuda Triangulating variety. Then, in 1979, along came *The Philadelphia Experiment: Project Invisibility* to rescue the story from the fringes of Big Foot and Atlantis scholarship. Written by Minnesota schoolteacher/"investigator of the unexplained" William L. Moore "in consultation with" best-selling Bermuda Triangle author Charles Berlitz, the book sold like unidentified flying flapjacks—or whatever the paranormal equivalent of hotcakes. It soon inspired a Hollywood movie, which in turn seems to have encouraged a whole new generation of "eyewitnesses" (more on them in a moment) to "step forward," the preferred locomotion of whistle-blowers.

Moore and Berlitz recapped the familiar Allende-Jessup saga, but also seasoned an already thick stew with new ingredients, including a spicy extraterrestrial angle. One mysterious informant is said to have appeared in a park, circa 1970, to spontaneously brief a pair of young airmen on the navy's wartime "invisibility experiment." This particular stranger suggested that some of the sailors might have "passed into another world and . . . seen and *talked* to strange alien beings." A well-informed carpenter from Canada had it from high-ranking U.S. officials that the American government had been in touch with alien beings since 1943, when "contact was apparently made . . . during a naval experiment involving radar invisibility." Future Philadelphia Experiment theoreticians would take this newly revealed UFO connection much, much further.

Most of the new sources introduced in the book fell into the "friend-of-a-friend, once-removed" category. However, Moore and Berlitz scored a coup of sorts in tracking down the evasive and peripatetic Allende, who by then had apparently made a full recovery from his earlier retraction. In fact, Allende was now willing to offer additional details, asserting that he had been close enough to the experimental ship to shove his arm into the force field (avoiding mental injury, one must assume).

The authors' almost preternatural investigative agility also led them to a dramatic, Deep Throaty character identified as "Dr. Rinehart." It was, Moore and Berlitz explained, "a name given to him in a fictionalized version of the Philadelphia

Experiment published recently." Now, this is a bit confusing: Moore and Berlitz were referring to the suspense novel *Thin Air*, penned by George E. Simpson and Neal R. Burger and published a *full year* before Moore and Berlitz's tome hit the revolving bookstands. Obviously inspired by Allende's tale, *Thin Air* told the now-familiar story of a destroyer escort made to disappear in a secret 1943 navy experiment.

At a key point in that novel, an intrepid naval investigator (our hero) tracks down a reclusive old scientist named Rinehart, who obligingly acknowledges his role in the 1943 invisibility experiment. At a key point in Moore and Berlitz's nonfiction book, an intrepid investigator of the unexplained (Moore) also tracks down a reclusive old scientist named "Rinehart," who also obligingly acknowledges his role in the 1943 invisibility experiment. Moore and Berlitz never explained how a couple of hack novelists found out about Moore's secret meeting with the real Rinehart and then duplicated that scene—down to the detail of Rinehart nervously peering out the window of his cabin—a year before it happened! Perhaps, there are explanations for this uncanny synchronicity simpler than, say, *reference-librarian time travel*, but we won't hazard a guess. At any rate, it wouldn't be the last time that the lines separating fiction and reality would "go invisible" in the always-evolving saga of the disappearing ship.

If, after plowing through two-thirds of Moore and Berlitz's book, readers were thinking, "Well and good, but where is the breakthrough in all this?" Moore and Berlitz were ready with an answer! "Now," they declared on page 244, "with the writing of this book, it is finally possible to announce a breakthrough . . . in the mystery." Moore and Berlitz had secured from an anonymous source a rare photocopy of an undated clipping from an unidentified newspaper, which was now locked in "a secure safety deposit box" at a location that they prudently left unspecified. And in its unassailable strongbox, Moore and Berlitz were happy to report, the clipping "has managed to survive all efforts to discredit its authenticity."

Headlined "STRANGE CIRCUMSTANCES SURROUND TAVERN BRAWL," the clipping apparently corroborated a key claim in Allende's original letters to Jessup. To wit: Allende had counseled Jessup to search for a newspaper article he remembered reading at the time of the experiment. He couldn't remember the exact date or name of the newspaper, but the story had mentioned something about rowdy sailors in a dockside "gin joint" suddenly disappearing. Jessup never managed to locate the news report, but Moore and Berlitz had it before deadline. According to Moore and Berlitz's transcript, a navy shore patrol sent to stop a barroom scuffle arrived to find the joint "empty of customers." A "very nervous waitress" told the military police that two sailors "just sort of vanished into thin air . . . right there," adding, "and I ain't been drinking either!" It may have lacked a publication date, but the story did feature 1940s-appropriate hardboiled dialogue; one skeptic dismissed the waitress's claims as "a lot of hooey from them daffy dames down there."

Modern skeptics might be inclined to suspect that *The Philadelphia Experiment: Project Invisibility* itself contained a dash or two of "hooey." They would soon find other reasons to take Moore and Berlitz's reporting with a destroyer escort–sized grain of salt. In the mid-1980s, after coauthoring an oft-disputed book on Roswell, Moore wound up at the center of the Majestic 12 (MJ-12) controversy. That donnybrook concerned eight pages of supposedly leaked government documents "proving" that President Harry Truman had created a secret task force of twelve to facilitate treaties with space aliens. The documents may or may not have been hoaxed. (Uberskeptic Phillip Klass went so far as to accuse Moore, himself, of forging the papers—probably an overreach on the part of the typically bombastic debunker.) The debate rages on, at least wherever saucer seekers congregate. Finally, in the late 1980s, Moore secured his reputation as a bête noire of saucerology by confessing at a UFO convention that he had willingly sowed UFO disinformation at the behest of the government.

None of that seems to have put a damper on the legend of the Philadelphia Experiment, however. Hollywood snatched up the film rights to Moore and Berlitz's book and in 1984 mustered a low-budget sci-fi movie of the same name, reupping with a sequel a decade later. If Hollywood's *The Philadelphia Experiments* (I and II) disappeared from movie houses faster than the original ship from its watery vortex, the films made waves with at least one viewer: After seeing the first film in 1988, a retired electronics engineer named Al Bielek began to recover hitherto forgotten memories of his *own* role in the actual, non-VHS Philadelphia Experiment of 1943. Unfortunately for Bielek, his date of birth was such that he would have been a mere seventeen in 1943, a tender age he definitely recalled spending in high school. It was a logistical stumbling block, to be sure, but it was no match for the inrush of reclaimed memories. For, as Bielek soon recalled, he was in reality another man entirely: Edward A. Cameron II.

Try to keep up, but watch your step, the gangplank gets a bit slippery here: Born Edward A. Cameron II in 1916, the man who would later become Al Bielek was in 1943 a Harvard-trained physicist working alongside Tesla on the USS *Eldridge* "radar-invisibility" project. Cameron survived the horrors of the ship's accidental teleportation, but lost a brother, who "disappeared" from 1943 and *traveled forward* in time to 1983. After the war, Cameron wound up working on a continuation of the accidental invisibility/teleportation/time travel project at a military base at Montauk Point in Long Island.

Still with us? Then let's give Bielek the floor: "From that

point," he explained to *Connecting Link* magazine, "I was time shifted to 1983. Once there, I was given a super brainwashing—all memory was removed. Additionally, I was age-regressed (reduction of physical age and size from a 30-year old to approximately one year of age) and then, at a physical age of one year, sent back in time to 1927 to be plugged into a new family as a substitute for a dead son. This new family—the Bieleks—became my only known parents for over half a century!"

If you're confused, we suggest renting a VHS copy of *The Philadelphia Experiment*. After all, it worked for Bielek/Cameron. As a matter of fact, versions of the legend predating the movie never mentioned anything about time travel. That was a Hollywood innovation—and apparently an extremely accurate one, because in the film, two sailors are transported through time from 1943 to 1983. Exactly as Bielek/Cameron subsequently remembered it happening!

So here was that division between fiction and reality "blinking out" again, and perhaps even accidentally traveling forward in time, who knows? Bielek coauthored a book about his time-and-thought-warping adventures, then hit the New Age lecture circuit, where he remains a staple.

If, by the late 1980s, the narrative stew was verging on a too-many-cooks situation, the 1990s would make a potluck of it. Bielek's recovered memories must have been contagious, because an armada of witnesses began cruising into port. The first to translate their reclaimed memories into a book-writing franchise were Preston B. Nichols and Peter Moon. In 1992, the duo published *The Montauk Project: Experiments in Time*, which they followed up with at least three sequels. Taking up where Bielek had left off, Nichols and Moon recalled that they, too, had worked on the project after it was transferred from Philadelphia to Montauk Point. Like Bielek, they had been superbrainwashed to remove all memories of the gig.

Nichols and Moon were generous enough to include Bielek/Cameron in their aeon-leaping chronology, and also his aforementioned time-slipping brother, who became the chief psychic at Montauk, opening and closing time tunnels with his computer-assisted mind.

Throughout all these fantastic episodes, Einstein's wasn't the only unified field theory in effect. With the benefit of time travel, Nichols and Moon were able to fashion a unified field map of conspiracy theories. You name the cover-up, they've teleported into the palpitating heart of it. The Pyramids of Mars? Been there, saw Martians. Nazi UFOs? Photographed 'em. Alien UFOs? Reverse-engineered 'em. Mass abductions of children? Did 'em (in order to draft the waifs into expendable time-travel teams). You get the idea.

If, by the twenty-first century, the legend of the Philadelphia Experiment (and beyond) seemed to be sagging under the weight of its own invention, well, thus it ever was. A disclaimer of sorts appears in the preface of *The Montauk Project: Experiments in Time*. It could just as easily apply to the entire sprawling mythology launched so many years ago by the peculiar Allende, "This work is being presented as non-fiction. . . . However, it can also be read as pure science fiction if that is more suitable to the reader."

Major Sources

Moore, William L., and Charles Berlitz. *The Philadelphia Experiment: Project Invisibility*. New York: Fawcett Crest, 1991.

Nichols, Preston B., and Peter Moon. *The Montauk Project: Experiments in Time*. New York: Sky Books, 1992.

Simpson, George E., and Neal R. Burger. *Thin Air*. New York: Dell Publishing, 1978.

Steiger, Brad, Alfred Bielek, and Sherry Hanson Steiger. *Phila-

delphia Experiment and Other UFO Conspiracies*. New Brunswick, NJ: Inner Light Publications, 1990.
Vallee, Jacques. *Revelations: Alien Contact and Human Deception*. New York: Ballantine Books, 1991.

76

The Most Dangerous Game

He struck four times over a period lasting less than one year. He killed just five people, which is five too many, of course. But his death toll was not nearly as prodigious as many other serial killers who've received far less publicity. So how did the Zodiac killer become an icon of American evil, with two new books about him and a Hollywood movie in the works more than thirty years after he committed his last known crime?

He was never caught. That's a good first step toward evil-icondom. More important to the legend, and more just plain evil, he wrote twenty letters, mostly to newspapers, not only naming himself ("This is the Zodiac speaking . . ."), but also trademarking himself by signing each missive with a cross superimposed over a circle, resembling a sniper's crosshair— or something. In his block-lettered scrawl, rife with misspelled words, odd phrasings, and paraphrases from *The Mikado,* Zodiac gleefully recounted minute details of his crimes, threatened to shoot schoolchildren, and seemed to be having a jolly good laugh at the expense of the cops trying to catch him. This is the stuff of which evil icons are made.

Even eviler, Zodiac sent several sophisticated ciphers, most of which proved nigh impossible to crack. Zodiac promised that the ciphers contained his true identity, but even when they were solved, they revealed nothing. They were just another way for Zodiac to enhance his mystique, his reputation for the macabre, and, in all likelihood, amuse himself. Now that's evil.

As comes with the territory for icons of evil, Zodiac has been the topic of conspiracy theories aplenty. They range from the mundane—he had a single accomplice—to the way, way out. Was Zodiac an "agent provocateur" dispatched to wreak terror as part of a "strategy of tension," paving the way for a law-and-order fascist crackdown?

This conspiracy theory might work if we meld it together with another theory elsewhere in this book, because one of the more popular Zodiac conspiracy theories would have us believe that Zodiac was a member of the Manson Family.

For conspiracy theorists, this would open up whole new vistas. We outlined the Manson Family conspiracy theory in chapter 34: the Family may have been connected to drug dealing, organized crime, and even intelligence agencies. Connecting Zodiac to Manson might give credence, under this uber-conspiracy scenario, to the covert operation theory. If Manson took orders from someone connected to intelligence and Zodiac took orders from Manson, well, the paranoid mind reels. We'll warp our way into that weird world momentarily. But first, let's present the known and undisputed facts of Zodiac's terror spree.

Zodiac struck first on December 20, 1968. He shot a teenage girl and boy on their first date, as they parked on Lake Herman Road, a Lover's Lane area in Vallejo (a small city north of San Francisco). Zodiac killed them both, shooting with remakable accuracy, though the night was pitch black. Months later, in a letter, he explained that he had taped a flashlight to the barrel of his gun. But following this attack, nothing was heard from the killer.

Minutes after midnight on July 5, 1969, in another "parking" area in Vallejo for young couples (outside the Blue Rock Springs golf course), Zodiac opened fire on another young couple. He had been following them as they drove to the parking lot. Darlene Ferrin died. Her companion, Mike Mageau, survived. Half an hour later, the killer phoned Vallejo police to "report a double murder," adding, "I also killed those kids last year." He left the phone off the hook and police traced the call to a phone booth a block from the Vallejo police station and across the street from Ferrin's house.

On July 31, Zodiac followed up with a letter. Three letters, actually, packed with technical details that only the killer could possibly know: the exact number of shots fired, the brand name of his "ammo," and descriptions of the victims' clothing.

He also included, in each letter, one portion of a three-part cipher. A high school teacher in Salinas, California, solved it. The message read, in part, "I like killing people because it is so much fun . . . because man is the most dangerous animal of all to kill." The cipher described killing people as "the most thrilling experience . . . even better than getting your rocks off with a girl." It explained that Zodiac believed (or said he believed) that his victims would become "slaves for my afterlife."

Another letter followed a week later, giving further intimate details. The killer gave himself a name. The letter opened with what became his signature salutation, "This is the Zodiac speaking." He signed his letters with a cross-in-circle symbol.

Zodiac committed his third and most ghastly attack on September 27, 1969. Changing his modus operandi, he bound and stabbed a young couple, Cecila Shepherd and Bryan Hartnell, in broad daylight and on the shore of Lake Berryessa.

The two college students were relaxing under a tree on a peninsula when a man approached them, wearing a meticulously designed costume, like a comic-book villain. The main feature was a jet-black hood, squared off on top with eye holes covered by clip-on sunglasses. The frontpiece draped all the way to the man's belt and on the front was stitched in white the cross-in-circle logo of Zodiac. He held a gun.

In an curious touch, Zodiac told them he was "an escaped convict from Deer Lodge, Montana."

Zodiac tied the couple with cable he carried on his belt. Then he announced, in monotone, "I'm going to have to stab you people." Zodiac plunged a hunting knife into Hartnell's back seven times. Then he turned to the girl, let out a freaky gasping sound, and stabbed her ten times, including once in the groin and in each breast. Hartnell recovered, but Shepherd died. Before leaving the scene, Zodiac wrote on the door of Hartnell's station wagon the dates of the previous two killings and of this attack, followed by the words "by knife."

Zodiac killed for the last time—the last confirmed time—on October 11, 1969. Again, he changed his MO. In San Francisco, he hailed a cab, took it to a destination in the upscale Presidio district, and methodically executed the cab driver, twenty-nine-year-old Paul Stine, with a single shot to the temple. Zodiac calmly moved to the front of the cab and cut away a piece of Stine's blood-soaked shirt. Later, he would snip swatches from the bloody shirt and mail them to police.

There are other killings attributed to Zodiac. Author Robert Graysmith, who wrote not one but two books on the killer, lists forty-nine "possible" Zodiac victims. In letters, Zodiac occasionally took credit for crimes that he did not commit. He claimed a body count that increased with each letter, topping out at thirty-seven. Yet there's no hard evidence linking Zodiac to any crimes other than the four attacks already listed.

Graysmith believes that Zodiac was Arthur Leigh Allen, a onetime schoolteacer and convicted pedophile who lived in

Santa Rosa and died of diabetes-related complications in 1992 at age fifty-eight. In both of his books, Graysmith piles up gigabytes' worth of circumstantial evidence that seems to connect Allen to the crimes. Allen closely fits witness descriptions and he, Graysmith reports, gave strong hints to people who knew him that he was, in fact, the Zodiac killer.

There's no "smoking gun," but from the evidence Graysmith compiles, it sure looks like Allen was the Zodiac killer. But even in Graysmith's work there are open questions, hints, and suggestions that Allen may not have been acting alone. Graysmith has said in interviews that he long suspected Allen may have had an accomplice.

That suspicion was strengthened, in Graysmith's mind, when in October 2002, the San Francisco police crime lab finally obtained partial DNA samples off of a few of Zodiac's thirty-year-old envelopes. They also had Allen's DNA from a sliver of his brain that had been preserved after his death.

The DNA did not match.

News accounts declared that the DNA tests ruled out Allen as a suspect. In fact, the tests ruled him out only as the letter writer. And, in more fact, Allen's handwriting never matched the letters anyway, nor did that of any of the police's suspects from whom handwriting samples were obtained. Allen, like the witness descriptions of Zodiac, was a heavyset, round-faced man in his midthirties at the time of the killings. But there was another man, in his early twenties and slender, also described in connection with Zodiac. Shortly before the Stine murder, another San Francisco cabbie was robbed, but not killed, by this other man. Short of pulling the trigger, police thought their MO's so similar that they assumed the robber was Zodiac himself.

Graysmith hypothesizes that Zodiac had a "young accomplice," not involved in the murders, but who "ran interference" for Allen. Graysmith also notes that Zodiac's letters were printed, often with odd spacings between words, as if the writer were taking dictation. In the 2002 book *"This Is the Zodiac Speaking"*: *Into the Mind of a Serial Killer,* psychologist David Van Nuys concludes that Zodiac was a victim of multiple personality disorder, based on analysis of the Zodiac communiqués. But rather than postulating that this unknown person suffered from a very rare mental disease that made him seem to be more than one person, wouldn't it make more sense to assume that Zodiac was, simply put, more than one person?

Before we get to the Zodiac-Manson connection, let's make a brief digression into what we could call a "conspiracy of one" theory. Under this belief, Zodiac was one person, but two different killers. The Zodiac killer was the same person as the Unabomber.

Could Theodore John Kaczynski, the infamous bomber who terrorized scientists and corporate executives with mail bombs for almost two decades, have been the same man who terrorized the Bay Area in the late 1960s? Kaczynski lived in the area at the time (he was a professor at the University of California, Berkeley). Both the Unabomber and Zodiac were prolific correspondents with the media, indicating that their crimes were motivated by a desperate need for attention. Kaczynski was intensely isolated and sexually frustrated, which fits Zodiac's probable psychology. Remember that for Zodiac, killing people was "better than getting your rocks off with a girl." Which sounds like precisely the type of thing you'd hear from someone who never got his rocks off with a girl.

Kaczynski tells of developing the desire, as early as 1966, to kill anyone who annoyed him. He built bombs and started setting them off in the late 1970s, several years after Zodiac disappeared from the scene. Zodiac wrote about building a bomb and even drew a diagram of the bomb he supposedly constructed.

These superficial similarities have to be written off as coincidences, however. Kaczynski never matched the description of Zodiac, and the nature of his crimes was radically different. Kaczynski was a chilly intellectual who took extreme pains to justify his murders, constructing a complex political worldview that culminated in his 40,000-word "manifesto," all aimed toward explaining the logic behind his hobby of cold-blooded murder.

Zodiac, on the other hand, killed "because it is so much fun." He didn't bother making excuses for himself. Quite the opposite. His whole platform consisted of generating as much attention for himself as possible. He murdered up close and personal, even cradling Stine's bloodied head in his lap after blowing the cab driver's brains out. The icily detached Kaczynski preferred to deal death by remote control. He was hundreds of miles away when his bombs went off.

Charles Manson and his followers were anything but icily detached. They enjoyed sticking their fingers in their victims' blood. Manson girl Susan "Sadie" Atkins, the murderess of Sharon Tate, declared that she experienced an earth-shaking orgasm as she plunged her knife over and over again into Tate's pregnant body. Now that's personal.

Self-published writer Howard Davis and conservative Christian author and Web site proprietor Bill Nelson are the chief architects of the Zodiac-Manson hypothesis. This theory holds that Manson's "chief lieutenant," Bruce Davis, was Zodiac. The Zodiac murders were one element in Manson's helter-skelter master plan, the theory holds.

In 1972, Davis was convicted of two "other" Manson murders, unrelated to the more famous Tate-LaBianca massacres. He's still in prison for those murders today. Unfortunately for the imaginative among us, the evidence linking the homicidal Davis to Zodiac is skimpy.

The author Davis demonstrates that the Manson family killer Davis (not related) bears an uncanny resemblance to two different Zodiac witness sketches. On Howard Davis's Web site, he displays a handwritten letter from onetime Mansonite Larry Melton, in which Melton states that Manson girl Sandra Good sewed the Lake Berryessa Zodiac costume for Davis. The letter, however, is recent and written in response to claims made by Nelson, so chances are that Melton is simply parroting Nelson.

For his part, Nelson claims on his own Web site that "actual items of the Zodiac murders were located and found by surprise in the belongings of Bruce M. Davis."

If true, that discovery would seem rather incriminating, to say the least. But, Nelson adds, "this will not be made public until after a retirement from a law enforcement person who told the story!"

Okay.

While it's typical of many conspiracy theories to rely on the fallacy of unrevealed evidence, it's still not evidence. Beyond that, the Davis connection, like the Kaczynski connection, relies on a number of very thin coincidences. For example, Zodiac used certain phrases in his writings that were typically British, leading some investigators to take him for an Anglophile. Bruce Davis traveled to England at Manson's behest.

One of the Zodiac letters was dated October 5, 1970, Bruce Davis's twenty-eighth birthday.

Manson and the Family were arrested October 12, 1969 (for car theft). Even though Davis was not with them, he was also arrested on the same day. The murder of Paul Stine took place on October 11, 1969.

Zodiac's executioner-style get up during the Lake Berryessa attack is reminiscent of costumes worn by Satanists and other occultists. Manson, as discussed in the aforementioned chapter 34, was supposedly connected to the Satanic Process Church of the Final Judgment and, according to "Family" author Ed Sanders, to an occult group in northern California that reputedly practiced human sacrifice.

Zodiac undoubtedly had occult influences. He claimed in his letters that the purpose of his killings was to collect souls who would become his slaves in "paradice [*sic*]."

That's the type of "evidence" Howard Davis and Bill

Nelson present for their "Bruce Davis as Zodiac" hypothesis. As explored in our chapter "Hello From the Gutters," investigator Maury Terry links Manson and the Process Church to New York's 1975–1976 Son of Sam killings, which bore some similarities to the Zodiac spree six years earlier on the other coast: young women killed in parked cars at close range, rambling, taunting notes to police and the media, and the killer giving himself an eerie nickname.

It seems unlikely, however, that Manson can be linked to Zodiac. Terry's links between Manson and Son of Sam are tenuous enough. But if, let's say, the links are there, what was the motive behind this ongoing conspiracy of random terror?

According to Mae Brussell and her disciple Dave Emory, it's the National Security State in action. The idea is to spread fear and terror throughout the populace, thus igniting a movement for greater police power and control of the general public.

Quote Emory, "You take a society and you unleash all of these horrendous screwball killers—or killers we're told are screwballs—it has the effect of driving the political spectrum to the 'right.' People want 'law and order.' They want stronger laws, more cops, more jails, quicker capital punishment. And in general, it predisposes them to accepting the incredible. It's just, 'Well with all those "nuts" out there, you never know who's gonna do what.' "

In October 2002, the screwball killer scenario was playing itself out again, three decades after Zodiac. The Beltway sniper terrorized the greater Washington, D.C., area, picking off people seemingly at random and following up with hostile, threatening notes to police. There was even a touch of the occult, with the killer apparently leaving a "death" Tarot card at the scene of at least one shooting.

The result: The military got involved in the investigation, there was talk of bringing the National Guard into the streets, and motorists were stopped and questioned in massive "dragnets."

And almost every day on TV the sniper was compared, by at least one of the ubiquitous experts, to Son of Sam and the Zodiac killer. National security? When they arrested a suspect in the sniper case, he turned out to be an ex-soldier.

MAJOR SOURCES

Davis, Howard. *The Zodiac/Manson Connection*. Costa Mesa, CA: Pen Power Publications, 1993.

Gorightly, Adam. *The Shadow Over Santa Susana: Black Magic, Mind Control and the Manson Family Mythos*. Lincoln, NE: iUniverse, 2001.

Graysmith, Robert. *Zodiac*. New York: Berkley Books, 1987.

___. *Zodiac Unmasked: The Identity of America's Most Elusive Serial Killer Revealed*. New York: Berkley Books, 2002.

Kelleher, Michael D., and David Van Nuys. *"This Is the Zodiac Speaking": Into the Mind of a Serial Killer*. Westport, CT: Praeger Publishers, 2002.

Manson Murders Web site, www.mansonmurders.com.

Zodiac Killer Web site, www.zodiackiller.com.

The Zodiac-Manson Connection Web site, www.zodiacmurders.com.

77

Knowledge Is Power

Somewhere in one of the Pentagon's numerous corners—let's take some poetic license and call it a dark one—sits an office marked with the logo of the All-Seeing Eye. In true Illuminati fashion, the Eye floats above a pyramid, glaring down godlike on a floating image of Planet Earth. A beam of light emanates from the Eye, suspending the earth in its glow.

This odd logo would be nothing but a curiosity if it were not the official symbol of an agency with an ominously Orwellian name: the Information Awareness Office (IAO). The function of this new military agency is more disturbing than either its logo or its name. The job of the IAO is to collect every piece of data possible about you. Yes, you, the American citizen. Your credit card use, your medical data, travel history, phone bills, driving history. If you've done it, the All-Seeing Eye of the IAO wants to know about it.

The office was created at the start of 2002 as part of a new program designed, ostensibly, to root out terrorists in the aftermath of the September 11, 2001, terrorist attacks. The program was christened "Total Information Awareness" (TIA), another touch of George Orwell.

TIA came into existence, officially, in January 2002, but the public didn't catch wind of it until later in the year when the *New York Times* and other publications mentioned it.

Not until January 2003 did Congress take note of TIA's troubling possibilities. Oregon congressman Ron Wyden (a Democrat) sponsored legislation, passed without debate, that requires that the TIA's creators produce a report delineating the program's goals and capabilities. By the time Congress got around to taking this rather obvious action, TIA had already graduated from the experimental phase and had a prototype up and running.

The program was newsworthy not only for its projected, paranoia-inducing capabilities, but for the man President George W. Bush selected as the Master of Total Information: Admiral John Poindexter, the man in charge of the Iran-Contra operation, who admitted concealing information about his illegal covert actions from the president. He was later convicted of lying to Congress about it. (The conviction was tossed out on a technicality.)

As a private citizen, Poindexter joined Syntek Technologies, a defense contractor that worked directly with the Defense Advanced Research Projects Agency (DARPA, best known as the creator of the Internet). The IAO is an arm of DARPA.

Poindexter ran the Syntek team that created Genoa, a computer program designed to spy on other computers. Genoa infiltrates unsuspecting hard drives and, like an info-vampire, sucks information into its own massive database. Bush took Poindexter, this consummately clandestine man, and appointed him the officer in charge of nosing around in other people's business. He's America's Butt-insky-in-Chief.

Exactly how Total Information Awareness plans to achieve totality remains, naturally, secret. One may assume that the very software Poindexter helped to whelp will do much of the work. But it's also likely that the office of the All-Seeing

Eye will rely on the All-Seeing Computer Network, the top-secret international spy-tech system referred to in knowing whispers as *Echelon*.

Echelon purportedly intercepts every phone call, every fax, every e-mail and downloads them into a vast network of superduper-computers called "Dictionaries." The Dictionaries comb intercepted transmissions for certain keywords. For example, an e-mail that said "Bmb NYC tmw, Allah B przd" would send the Dictionaries into a tizzy. Like the National Security Agency (NSA) itself—America's black-budgeted directorate of worldwide electronic surveillance—Echelon remains shrouded in mystery, but the shroud has been lifting since the late 1990s, albeit incrementally.

Echelon, as it turns out, is one case where reality is nearly as disturbing as conspiracy theory. The system known in popular parlance as "Echelon" is actually the United Kingdom–USA Communications Intelligence Agreement (UKUSA). Signed in 1947, the pact set ground rules for cooperation between the electronic intelligence agencies of the United States and the United Kingdom, with Australia, New Zealand, and Canada joining up in later years.

"The major English-speaking nations of the world were joined in a highly secret agreement to eavesdrop on the rest of the world, friend as well as foe," explains James Bamford, author of not one but two definitive books about the NSA. "As a sovereign nation has a body of laws, so UKUSA has a body of secrets."

Those secrets encompass not only the massive intelligence files accumulated by UKUSA members, but also the rules and regulations that govern the community of high-tech voyeurs, their code words, their "indoctrination oaths"—everything.

In his aptly titled book *Body of Secrets*, Bamford recounts that, in the 1970s when the rules were finally well established, America's NSA set out to merge the UKUSA agencies into a "virtual nation" that shared not only information, but also a gargantuan, single computer network. The network received the code name "Platform" and comprised fifty-two formerly unconnected computer systems worldwide. Now, they needed a highly sophisticated software program to make the computers work together so that, according to Bamford, "everyone would be able to share in the take—to dip their electronic ladles into the vast cauldron of intercepts and select what they liked."

The code name for the new software: Echelon.

And with that, the legend of Echelon, the All-Seeing Eye in the sky, came into being.

There are U.S. laws forbidding the NSA from eavesdropping on American citizens inside the United States, but Great Britain and the other UKUSA partners are not constrained by such domestic regulations. Using Echelon, it would be a small matter for the NSA to get around the laws (assuming it obeys the laws in the first place) by "dipping its electronic ladle" into the intercepts collected by the British, Australians, or Canadians. The other countries, with similar, restrictive laws against spying on their own people, could do the same.

In the book *Spyworld*, ex-Canadian intelligence agent Mike Frost recounts that the British prime minister did just that in 1983. Margaret Thatcher, having her doubts about a couple of high government officials, went to Canada's equivalent of the NSA, the Communications Security Establishment, and let the Canadians do her dirty work.

In the 1980s when the Reagan administration was obsessing over Nicaragua, the NSA intercepted phone calls from Congressman Michael Barnes of Maryland and certain Nicaraguan officials. The law allows the NSA to pick up international phone calls, but as Barnes said at the time, "to use it for domestic political purposes is absolutely outrageous and probably illegal."

UKUSA has also targeted international activist organizations such as Amnesty International and Greenpeace, according to a London *Observer* article from 1992. Allegedly, the *Observer* itself was also the victim of UKUSA spying dur-

ing the Thatcher era, after the paper published a story asserting that Thatcher's son, Mark, took bribes in an arms deal
with Saudi Arabia.

The NSA has also, at the behest of the president, been used
for commercial espionage. In incidents that were later reported in the mainstream media, Bill Clinton used the NSA
(and the CIA) to spy on Japanese auto manufacturers. The
info collected by the spies went not only to Washington, but
also to Detroit. It also went to U.S. trade rep Mickey Kantor,
who was facing down Japanese car companies in trade negotiations. Clinton later used the NSA to listen in on Asia-
Pacific Economic Conference delegates when their meeting
came to Seattle in 1997.

Clinton was far from the only commander in chief who
commanded his spy agencies to go after foreign business.
George Bush, in 1990, used data gleaned by the NSA to
wrest part of a big satellite contract away from the Japanese
corporation NEC and into the hands of American corporation AT&T. Commercial spying by the snoops who are supposed to be trying to figure out when the next terrorist attack
is coming, and other mildly important national security functions, dates back at least to the Nixon epoch. As does the use
of this same high-tech spy apparatus to keep an All-Seeing
Eye on political dissenters, activists, and other pesky trouble-
makers.

Until now, however, UKUSA-Echelon surveillance of private individuals not involved in politics, activism, or international trade was probably more paranoid fantasy than
reality. Sure, UKUSA has had the power to listen to your
phone calls and read your faxes for a long time. But what
would be the point?

Well, now there is a point. Or so we are told. The point is
to stop terrorism. Total Information Awareness, under the
command of admitted liar and rogue operator John Poindexter,
is apparently the blunt instrument to make that point. Once
TIA is up and running, everything that Echelon or anyone

else can get on you goes into that database. Potentially, anyway. As the Latin inscription under the Eye in the Pyramid that marks the IAO says, *"Scientia Est Potentia."*

In English: *Knowledge is Power.*

MAJOR SOURCES

Bamford, James. *Body of Secrets: Anatomy of the Ultra-Secret National Security Agency.* New York: Doubleday, 2001.

Manjoo, Farhad. "Total Information Awareness: Down But Not Out." *Salon,* 28 January, 2003.

Poole, Patrick. "Echelon: America's Secret Global Surveillance Network." *Free Congress Foundation Report,* 2000.

Rosen, Jeffrey. "Total Information Awareness." *New York Times,* 15 December 2002.

Sutherland, John. "No More Mr. Scrupulous Guy." *The Guardian,* 18 February 2002.

78

Kraemer vs. Kraemer

Conspiring minds want to know: Who, exactly, is Fritz Kraemer? Little known outside of Washington power circles, the German-born military strategist achieved the rarified status of gray eminence among America's military and policymaking elites during the Cold War era. According to those who sought his advice, Kraemer exerted a "profound influence" on Pentagon generals, White House luminaries, and "Army officers by the hundreds." As plans officer to the army chief of staff and an implacable anticommunist, he left an indelible mark on a crucial chapter of American history.

At the same time, he consciously sought to leave as few fingerprints as possible on the public record. It was only at the height of his career during the 1970s that knowledge of Kraemer's central role in American Cold War history began to trickle into the mainstream. In a worshipful 1975 profile, the *Washington Post* dubbed Kraemer "the Iron Mentor of the Pentagon," describing him as "an institution unto himself" at the center of America's military brain trust. He had "molded" the likes of Henry Kissinger and Alexander Haig.

("Henry does not come to me for advice," Kraemer thundered to the *Post*, "He comes for *absolution!*") Management guru Peter F. Drucker, an old college acquaintance, went even further, extolling the redoubtable Teuton he'd first met in Weimar Germany as no less a personage than "The Man Who Invented Kissinger."

Commentators of a more apprehensive bent have been less charitable. After reading the *Washington Post*'s profile, late conspiracy tracker extraordinaire Mae Brussell (see chapter 8) felt her hyperattuned synapses sparking. The March 2, 1975, story—centerpiece of the *Post*'s Sunday magazine—recounted the incredible career of an eccentric, but apparently brilliant, Prussian refugee from prewar Nazi Germany whose flight to America precipitated his meteoric rise within the American military establishment.

His story read like a surreal American fairytale. Here was the monocled, aristocratic, thirty-four-year-old "doctor of laws" drafted as an alien into the U.S. Army. Here was Kraemer, swinging his swagger stick as he lectured his fellow soldiers on the evils of Nazism, in stentorian tones more often associated with a Prussian officer than a buck private. Here was Private Kraemer taking a green recruit named Heinz "Henry" Kissinger under his wing, quickly graduating from rifleman to army intelligence officer (and taking his new protégé with him), heroically pursuing Germans in France, single-handedly forcing a Rhineland city's surrender, interrogating Nazis at the Battle of the Bulge, ferreting out Gestapo officers after the war, and reuniting with the wife and son he'd left behind in Nazi Germany. Ultimately, he returned to America with a bronze star and a battlefield commission to steer Kissinger's illustrious career, advise presidents, and counsel joint chiefs of staff on the most crucial matters of strategic Cold War policy.

And here was Brussell furiously bombarding Pentagon press officers with demands for a photograph of this phenomenal, yet oddly obscure, military genius, this Horatio

Alger with a thick German accent. What had set Brussell's cortex atwitter, apart from the improbable sweep of the story arc, were a number of peculiar parallels between the wartime itinerary of Fritz G. A. Kraemer—future Iron Mentor of the Pentagon—and that of another, contemporaneous Fritz Kraemer.

That other Kraemer had last been seen in the historical record during the early summer of 1946 as prisoner number 33 at the famous Dachau trials of Nazi war criminals. This particular Kraemer—Brigadefuehrer (Brigadier General) Kraemer, chief of staff of Adolf Hitler's Sixth Panzer Army— was among seventy-four Waffen SS officers charged with murdering more than seventy unarmed American prisoners in cold blood during the Battle of the Bulge, in what later came to be called the "Malmedy massacre" in Ardennes, Belgium. While the military tribunal handed down death sentences to some of the more culpable Nazi officers, and life sentences to others, Brigadefuehrer Kraemer received a relatively lenient ten-year term at the U.S. Army's Landsberg prison in Germany. Strangely, at least in Brussell's view, that was the last the world would hear of Brigadefuehrer Kraemer.

Until Brussell came along, that is. A one-woman war crimes tribunal in her own right, the queen of conspiracies soon took to the airwaves in her weekly radio broadcast to pose the slightly leading question, "When will monocled Fritz Kraemer be fingerprinted and compared to Hitler's SS Kraemer?" After all, the U.S. military and espionage establishments had eagerly imported Nazi scientists, spooks (see chapter 59), and outright war criminals for use in its then-blossoming Cold War with the Soviet Union. Why not a brilliant military tactician with direct experience fighting the Soviets?

Brussell plunged into researching the lives of both Kraemers. If she found no smoking swastika, she did dig up several unusual biographical lacunae, as well as some intriguing geographical intersections in her tale of two Kraemers.

First off, Brussell found the American Kraemer's humble aversion to publicity rather suspicious. In the *Washington Post* feature, the caption under a rare candid (and unclear) photograph of Kraemer read, "Dr. Fritz Kraemer refused to be photographed or to provide any photographs for this story because of his feeling that a civil servant should not seek publicity. All sources checked at the Pentagon turned out to be oddly bare of Kraemer pictures." To Brussell, Kraemer's camera shyness was, as they say in poker, "the tell." What was he hiding?

Brussell also found the official records on Brigadefuehrer Kraemer to be oddly bare. Although the Allied forces had amassed a welter of official records on most convicted Nazi war criminals, the available Kraemer papers documented in detail only the period of his career between 1943, when he was a colonel in the First SS Panzer Corps, and 1946, the time of his sentencing for war crimes. This dearth of detail seemed particularly strange, given that, after his arrest, Kraemer had cooperated with the U.S. Army by writing several well-regarded analyses of German battlefield tactics during the Battle of the Bulge. One of those manuscripts does contain a brief biographical paragraph sketching out a few background details, including his date and place of birth (December 12, 1900, in Stettin, Pommerania—now part of Poland), his prewar career (police lieutenant in Stettin and later Berlin), and the year in which he began his two-year course of studies at the Berlin War Academy (1934).

Various military histories describe Brigadefuehrer Kraemer as a talented, "capable," and "elegant" ex-Wehrmacht officer whose induction into the Waffen SS had more to do with the Nazi command's desperate need for professional soldiers on the front lines than with personal ideological zeal on Kraemer's part.

As we've noted, Brigadefuehrer Kraemer's disappearance from the public record after his sentencing at Dachau in 1946 struck Brussell and subsequent conspiracy trackers as somewhat unusual. On the other hand, given the stigma attached to such a legacy in postwar Germany, it's certainly not hard to imagine a former Nazi war criminal maintaining a low profile during the waning years of his life. Various military histories report, without getting specific, that after his release from prison, the ex-SS general lived in Höxter, Germany, until his death on June 23, 1959. And that about covers what is known of the Nazi Kraemer.

In contrast, Brussell found the Americanized Fritz Kraemer's life story to be rendered in vivid technicolor detail, despite the man's aversion to personal publicity. Both the *Washington Post* profile, penned by the late journalist Nick Thimmesch, and Drucker's memoir *Adventures of a Bystander* painted an already larger-than-life character in the broadest of strokes. (So cinematic was the story line of Kraemer's life that he once declined a "lucrative offer from MGM to do a movie of his life," according to Thimmesch.)

Born in 1908 or 1909, presumably in the Ruhr region of Germany (accounts are unclear on that point), young Fritz enjoyed a privileged, if unconventional, upbringing. His mother, an iconoclast who ran a children's home in Wiesbaden, had inherited the wealth of her father, a successful manufacturer of paraffin and chemical dyes. Kraemer spent much of his youth in British, German, and Swiss boarding schools, honing his native intellect, mastering half a dozen languages, and developing a patrician's self-flattering sense of noblesse oblige.

Kraemer's father, although of plebeian stock, proved to be an ambitious lawyer capable of lifting himself by his wife's bootstraps into a comfortable living as a moderately important civil servant. Apparently a "stern monarchist" and admirer of Kaiser Wilhelm II, he later allied himself with the emerging Nazi movement. Young Fritz reportedly despised the Nazis (and, by extension, his father, who had separated from his mother early in the marriage). In Weimar Germany, the rabble-rousing Nazis were an affront to Kraemer's elite sensibilities—proletarian thugs led by that "miserable Bohemian corporal," incapable of graciously accepting their lowly station in life. If there was any group to be held in even greater contempt, it was that other mob of order-opposing revolutionaries, the communists.

By all accounts, Fritz had acquired relatively early in life a somewhat romantic obsession with the chivalric conservatism that embodied the old—and by then long gone—Prussian empire. It was both a self-image and a political philosophy, and it would serve him throughout his life. He went so far as to adopt the style and mannerisms of an aristocratic Prussian officer: sporting a monocle and riding boots and brandishing a crop, sword, or swagger stick. According to Drucker, he affected the "languid accent" of a Prussian guard, energetically lecturing any and all within earshot on the virtues of old-world conservatism, Lutheran stoicism, and fealty to the old German Reich.

In fairytale fashion, young Fritz seemed to lead a charmed life. He studied at the London School of Economics, earned his doctorate in international law at the University of Frankfurt, and embarked on a promising career as a lawyer in the German Civil Service. But in 1933, "that miserable Bohemian corporal" came into power. Without hesitation, Kraemer packed his bags and his new bride, a Swedish girl named Britta, and exited Germany for Italy. According to Drucker, Kraemer's "code of honor did not permit him to maintain any relationship with so dishonorable and lawless [a] regime."

Kraemer spent the next five years earning a doctorate in political science at the University of Rome and working for the League of Nations. But Benito Mussolini's alliance with Hitler in 1937 sent honor-bound Kraemer packing yet again, this time for America. Oddly, though, Kraemer first delivered Britta and their infant son, Sven, back to Germany to lodge with his mother until he settled in America. Sending his loved ones back into the belly of the beast seems a strange decision for a gentleman who stood on lofty antifascist principles the way lesser men might squat on a stepladder. But Kraemer would later justify the decision to journalist Thimmesch as yet another self-sacrificing moral stand, "I knew one day the allies would shell and bomb Germany and my family would be there. BUT NAZIISM WAS ETHICALLY WRONG FOR GERMANY, THE U.S. AND WORLD! THIS WAS NOT TO BE A CHARMING TEA PARTY! I HAD TO STAY WITH THE SIDE THAT WAS RIGHT!" (Apparently, Kraemer tends to speak in all caps.) At any rate, war soon broke out in Europe, leaving Britta and Sven stranded in Nazi Germany.

And that, as they say in Hollywood, is the backstory. But the plot thickened in the second act of Kraemer's chronicle, when as a U.S. Army private, his reported route through Europe took him unusually close to Brigadefuehrer Kraemer. It may all amount to little more than sheer coincidence. As Drucker pointed out in his tribute to his friend, "Kraemer is a very common German name." Still, the two Kraemers seemed to share more in common than just the same name:

- Private Kraemer arrived in Europe in the aftermath of D-day, at about the same time that Brigadefuehrer Kraemer had been transferred from the eastern front to fight the Allied assault on the western front.
- In December 1944, Privates Kissinger and Kraemer— now both working for military intelligence—were reportedly dispatched into the midst of the Battle of the Bulge, to interrogate Nazi troops posing as Americans. Brigadefuehrer Kraemer was at that very moment in the thick of the same battle, on the *other* side, providing strategic support to Operation Greif, a secret plan involving Nazi troops posing as Americans.
- After the war, the Americanized Kraemer and Kissinger

were both assigned to the U.S. Army Counter Intelligence Corps, working at first on the de-Nazification
program and later in the recruitment of ex-Nazi
intelligence officers to spy on Soviets and other communists. It's not all that much of a stretch to imagine
a decorated, experienced eastern front general of
Brigadefuehrer Kraemer's caliber being sought for recruitment by the likes of Kissinger.

• Perhaps the most interesting connection between the
two Kraemers is this: According to Drucker, by the
end of the war the Americanized Kraemer had advanced in just months from a private to "either a
colonel or brigadier general on [General George S.]
Patton's staff." The imprecision of Drucker's reporting
is intriguing enough, especially given that the enemy
Kraemer also held the rank of brigadier general. But it
becomes even more interesting when we learn that the
captured enemy Kraemer was also, in a manner of
speaking, on Patton's staff. According to Ladislas
Farago's book *The Last Days of Patton*, the famous
general had been ordered to produce a series of historical reports on the battlefield tactics and techniques
used by both sides in the latter days of the war. In a
village thirty kilometers north of Frankfurt, Patton
had assembled "the great captains of the defunct
German army . . . picking the best brains the Wehr-
macht had," including "stars like former Panzer general . . . Fritz Kraemer."

Patton would have known both Kraemers—or, as Brussell
believed, the one-and-only Kraemer. According to Thimmesch,
the Americanized Kraemer asked Patton for permission to
retrieve his family from Wiesbaden. He found them healthy
and untouched by the Nazi rabble, an amazing circumstance
indeed given Kraemer's claim that his mother had harbored
refugee Jewish children at her school throughout the war.

As Drucker tells it, Kraemer resigned his military commission to become "the political adviser on Europe for the Chief of Staff of the U.S. Army." (It was a job that the captured Brigadefuehrer Kraemer, having fought the Soviets on the eastern front, might have been eminently qualified for, perhaps even more so than the comparatively inexperienced "doctor of law" turned army private.)

In keeping with his predilection for maintaining a low profile, Kraemer's official title was rather modest: senior political analyst. However, as Drucker notes, "'political analysts' are not sent to the U.S. War College; that's for general officers or better." And Kraemer not only attended the prestigious officers school, he taught at it—a rather amazing accomplishment for a former soldier with limited military experience.

Though his office in the Pentagon was small and unadorned, its location belied the political analyst's importance to the Cold War military complex: a private door connected Kraemer's cubicle to the office of the army chief of staff.

Of course in Brussell's view, the American patriot and anticommunist Kraemer were one and the same. Brussell believed the colorful personal history of Fritz G. A. Kraemer to be nothing more than an elaborate cover story designed to account for the man's peregrinations through postwar Germany. Brussell also suspected that Kissinger's connection to Kraemer grew out of the latter's work as an army intelligence recruiter of ex-Nazis. Time and again, in the official Kraemer story, Kissinger's wartime advancements (and also his postwar career) are brokered thanks to the influence of his avuncular, monocled mentor. In a large military bureaucracy during the confusion of a major war, how influential can an army private with minimal experience be? On the other hand, if young Kissinger had hitched his star to a valuable German "defector," it stands to reason that doors would suddenly begin to open for the unseasoned and awkward lad. "The Man Who Invented Kissinger," indeed.

Of course, all of Brussell's evidence was circumstantial, and her somewhat strident *"j'accuse!"* was highly speculative.

She did eventually receive a response to her demand for a picture of the Pentagon's camera-shy Fritz Kraemer. It was an eight-by-ten, black-and-white publicity photo of a highly decorated army officer presenting a plaque to a middle-aged civilian who calls to mind Erich von Stroheim with a comb-over. The plaque was inscribed, "Department of the Army/ Decoration for Exceptional Civilian Service/Dr. Fritz G. A. Kraemer."

Although Brussell believed that the man in the Pentagon bore an uncanny resemblance to official photographs of Dachau trial prisoner number 33, others disagreed. For one thing, prisoner number 33 had angular, almost pointy ears with no lobes. The man in the Pentagon picture sported rounded ears with large lobes. And the aggressive proboscis of the specimen in the Pentagon photo easily outdistanced the wedge-like snout of the captive brigadefuehrer. Of course, in the world of conspiracies photos are made to be doctored. Hence, Brussell's continued and, alas, officially un-heeded calls for the unambiguous evidence of fingerprints.

Kraemer outlived Brussell, who died of cancer in 1988. Currently, Kraemer, now in his nineties, lives in low-key re-tirement in the Washington area. His son, Sven, proved to be a chip off the old block; during the 1970s, he went to work for Kissinger on the National Security Council, where he ex-ercised his ardent anticommunist philosophies. Later, he played a role in the Reagan administration's Iran-Contra scandal, ensuring, at least in the darting eyes of Brussell's fol-lowers, the endurance of the Kraemer conspiracy dynasty.

MAJOR SOURCES

Drucker, Peter F. *Adventures of a Bystander*. New York: Harper & Row, 1979.

Eisenhower, John S. D. *The Bitter Woods*. New York: Putnam, 1969.

Farago, Ladislas. *The Last Days of Patton*. New York: McGraw-Hill, 1981.

Information Network Against War and Fascism. "Fritz Kraemer: WCPL 504." San Francisco: Hand-bound collection of documents, publication date unknown.

Thimmesch, Nick. "The Iron Mentor." *Washington Post*, 2 March 1975.

Various National Archives documents in the authors' possession.

Whiting, Charles. *Ardennes: The Secret War*. New York: Dorset Press, 1985.

79

Power to the People

The summer of 2001 was not a particularly hot one in California. The good people of the Golden State made no exceptional demands on their air conditioners or other appliances. Why, then, was 2001 the summer of the "rolling blackouts"? Why did a sudden "energy crisis" sweep California and threaten to overwhelm the country? And why did the "shortage" vanish as quickly and mysteriously as it had appeared, leaving behind nothing but grossly inflated energy prices and justifiably disgruntled consumers?

We all need energy, of course. We need it all the time, and we need it bad. Energy turns everyone into a little child. We need to nurse at the bosom of the gigantic energy corporations, and we never wean off. People need power, and that makes power companies the most powerful companies. Because energy is a universally demanded commodity, those giant corporations can do pretty much what they want. They've always understood that it's better not to compete with each other, because there's plenty of money in it for all the players. That is why the energy business, more than any

655

other, functions like a conspiracy. The phony California "crisis" was largely the result of just that—the fix was in.

No company better illustrated the shady business of power, in both the physical and political senses, than a Texan entity known as Enron, who played a major role in engineering the California "crisis." Enron's friends occupied the White House itself as well as hundreds of seats in Congress. Unlike most power players, Enron got its comeuppance, but as is always the case in the energy world, we all paid the price. All of us, that is, except the Enron executives who escaped with fabulous fortunes intact.

Enron's spectacular financial detonation rocked the entire U.S. economy. Enron was the definition of a conspiracy: a small group of elite insiders working behind the scenes and on the margins of legality for their own profit and power— and everyone else can go screw themselves.

The most immediate victims of Enron's mind-boggling corruption were its own rank-and-file employees. Enron had invested their retirement plans heavily in its own stock, which was dumb enough. Then the top Enron bosses crossed the line from "dumb" to "malevolent" when they put a "freeze" on their employees' ability to dump their stock, even when the bosses knew it had a one-way ticket to worthlessness. The Houston-based energy-and-other-stuff trading company was skidding toward the largest bankruptcy in American business history.

Enron's captains of industry leaped for their gold-encrusted lifeboats and forced the crew to go down with the ship. In the four years leading up to the Enron disaster, company Chairman Kenneth Lay cashed out $205 million in the same stock that his employees were prohibited from unloading. The employees lost everything.

Enron began life as a pipeline company, a steadily profitable business. But in the swollen bubble of the 1990s, Enron decided it was better, or at least sexier, to become a "trading" company. "Trading," in today's economy, is the business of buying and selling things you don't own with money you don't have.

For most of the late 1990s, Enron operated like a Mafia "bust-out" scheme, leveraging everything and camouflaging massive losses behind bogus account books and sham, scam "partnerships" that existed simply to launder money.

The busted-out employees must have been delighted to learn that some of Enron's top execs controlled the money-laundering "partnerships" and profited from them immensely. Enron's finance boss Andy Fastow collected about $50 million off just two of those partnerships, which he ran. At the same time, Enron shifted its lost money, hundreds of millions of dollars, to these "off-the-books" partnerships, effectively hiding from shareholders and regulators the potentially unsettling fact that the company was doomed. Everything was rosy in Enron's "on-the-books" enterprise. Seemed so, anyway, with Enron amassing huge profits. Ah, but there's the rub. Despite its "profits," Enron made almost no actual money!

How? With a type of accounting practice known as "mark to market" that allowed Enron to take a wild guess at how much money it would make years down the road and count that guessed-at sum as "revenue" *now*. Welcome to the zany world of high finance.

President George W. Bush bailed out of the Enron disaster faster than anyone. Enron boss Lay was known to Bush, in an affectionate, male-bonded sort of way, as "Kenny Boy." Mr. Boy and his fellow Enronians gave so much money to Bush's campaign that Bush owed his presidency to Enron more than anyone (other than those five U.S. Supreme Court justices; see chapter 73). Yet once the Enron scandal broke, and the extent of the company's monetary funny business went public, Bush disavowed his old buddy. He asserted, with what one assumes was a straight face, that when he ran for governor of Texas in 1994, Lay supported his *Democratic opponent.*

What Bush and his even more energy-industry-enmeshed

Vice President Dick Cheney were not telling is that top Enron executives were key in formulating U.S. energy policy, meeting behind closed doors. Cheney later refused to release the records of those meetings.

Cheney was a vociferous doomsayer when it came to the energy crisis. Just seven months before Enron finally choked out its last breath (the company filed for bankruptcy on December 2, 2001), Cheney declared the energy situation to be "a storm cloud over the horizon" and he predicted that California-style rolling blackouts would plague the nation in years to come.

Cheney's solution to this alleged problem: get more energy! Drill more wells! Mine more coal! Split more atoms! And so on. (It did not mean, according to Cheney, conservation, which he dismissed as nothing more than a "personal virtue.")

This was not a surprising position for Cheney to take, given that prior to becoming vice president, Cheney headed up Halliburton, Inc., a Texas "oil services" company. Under his stewardship, Halliburton became the largest concern of its kind in the world. What's good for the oil business is good for Halliburton, and energy crises are definitely good for the oil business. Interestingly, under Cheney—who, as defense secretary for President George Bush, helmed the war against Iraq in 1991—Halliburton was growing its business by supplying services to Iraq's petrol industry.

Asked about the Iraq dealings when he was campaigning for the nation's second-highest office, Cheney simply lied. He claimed they did not exist. (The dealings were documented by the *Financial Times* of London.)

Cheney and his cronies had an obvious interest in manufacturing an "energy crisis" that would require wildly jacked up prices and relentless drilling. So they did. "As a country, we have demanded more and more energy," Cheney announced, "but we have not brought online the supplies needed to meet that demand." Sounds scary, but as no less a source than

Forbes magazine, the self-appointed "Bible of Capitalism," pointed out, Cheney was spouting falsehoods again.

"Between 1980 and 2000," the magazine recounted, "despite a 90 percent increase in real gross domestic product, energy consumption increased by just 25.6 percent." The United States, it turns out, is an extremely energy-efficient nation. The "crisis" in California was the result "not of fuel shortages, but of a half-baked attempt at deregulation."

But the "half-baked attempt" was more than a laughable legislative snafu. Deregulation opened the energy market to deliberate manipulation by unscrupulous energy companies. Chief among those companies, who else? Enron.

In late 2002, on-the-record evidence of the Enron energy conspiracy began leaking into the public record. One ex-Enron trader pled guilty to a "conspiracy to commit wire fraud" charge and in so pleading admitted that he (as reported in the *L.A. Weekly*) lied about the amount of energy available to California and how much his company, Enron, could provide.

"The artificial shortages," the *Weekly* reported, "drove energy prices to 10 times the cost of production."

Around the same time, an Enron-controlled utility in Oregon admitted in public filings that it placed phony orders for California power to create "congestion" in the power lines. Enron then charged whopping "congestion fees" for coming to the rescue.

And what about President Bush, the frustrated oilman who owed his political career to Enron? In the year before Enron's final flameout, according to *Time* magazine, "Bush had quietly performed a host of political sacraments for the Texas company." Among them,

> the energy policy Vice President Dick Cheney drafted in 2001 after meetings with Enron officials, portions of which seem to have sprung directly from Enron's wish list; there were the ex-Enron chiefs and consultants

salted around the Bush Administration, from the Army Secretary Thomas White to the U.S. Trade Representative Robert Zoellick. Bush chose Pat Wood—a man strongly backed by Lay—to be his top energy-price regulator.

In 1973, the world faced its first "energy crisis," when OPEC nations cut off the supply of oil. The "shortage" led to many cries—echoed three decades later by Cheney—that the earth was running short of energy resources. Then, as now, it's just not true. What the world does face is an energy market that can be fixed like a Mafia card game by countries, cartels, and companies, like Enron, with aid from its allies in government. Many of those allies previously drew paychecks from Enron and other energy companies. The ongoing energy scam may be yet another case of "none dare call it conspiracy." But whether you call it "conspiracy" or "politics as usual," it amounts to the same thing: Power in the hands of the *pezzonovante* (as Michael Corleone would say). The rest of us empty our wallets at the gas pumps and keep the thermostats affordably chilly.

MAJOR SOURCES

Ackman, Dan. "There Is No Energy Crisis." *Forbes.com*, 2 May 2001.

Bryce, Robert. *Pipe Dreams: Greed, Ego and the Death of Enron*. New York: Public Affairs, 2002.

Cruver, Brian. *Anatomy of Greed: The Unshredded Truth From an Enron Insider*. New York: Carroll and Graf, 2002.

Duffy, Michael, and John F. Dickerson. "Enron Spoils the Party." *Time*, 4 February 2002.

Fineman, Howard, and Michael Isikoff. "Lights Out: Enron's Failed Power Play." *Newsweek*, 21 January 2001.

Rappleye, Charles. "A Switch for Enron." *L.A. Weekly*, 25 October 2002.

80

Acid Drop

No one saw Frank Olson plunge to his death from the thirteenth story of New York's Statler Hotel. No one, at any rate, willing to admit it. Not the man from the CIA who was in room 1018A with Olson when the forty-three-year-old biochemist and father of three crashed through a closed, shuttered window and tumbled to the cold sidewalk below. To believe the CIA man, he either awoke in his bed some time after midnight to see his roommate charge the window and throw himself through the thick plate glass, or, as he told it on another occasion, he awoke *after* Olson had already defenestrated, startled from sleep by the sound of shattering glass.

The CIA man with the shifting story was Robert Lashbrook, deputy to the CIA's wizard of mind-control and exotic assassinations. Despite its many inconsistencies, the CIA account of what happened during the early morning hours of November 28, 1953, would become the official story of Olson's death: It was an unfortunate suicide triggered by a small dose of LSD that was secretly administered to Olson in a mind-control experiment gone awry.

Fifty years after the fact, conventional history records Olson's death as perhaps the most infamous repercussion of MK-ULTRA, the CIA's illegal quest to "modify an individual's behavior by covert means" using hypnosis, electroshock treatment, and psychotropic drugs such as LSD (see chapter 1). According to this interpretation, Olson's fatal fall was the result of a "bad trip," a tragic, yet accidental, consequence of the CIA's Cold War wet dream of developing a magical brainwashing elixir.

But could the Olson story have an even simpler, albeit darker, explanation? Is it possible that the accidental death scenario—however embarrassing to the CIA at the time of its disclosure during the mid-1970s—served as a cover story to conceal a more disturbing truth? To wit: Was Olson deliberately assassinated?

Two decades after the bizarre tragedy, Olson's eldest son, Eric, would begin to dispute the official account. His search for answers would ultimately span three decades, becoming a personal obsession that would drain his finances, upend his relationships, and derail his once promising career as a Harvard-trained psychologist. No obstacle would deter him from his mission, not even the taboo of unearthing his father's bones. (The Shakespearean parallels weren't lost on the scholarly Eric, "Think *Hamlet,*" he liked to say, "but on the order of *years,* not months.") Eventually, Eric would uncover tantalizing evidence suggesting that his father, far from being the victim of a "drug experiment gone awry," may have been murdered as the proverbial man who knew too much.

Yet, in the aftermath of that ill-fated Thanksgiving weekend in 1953, and for a numbing twenty-two years afterward, the Olson family had been given no explanation at all for Olson's mysterious death.

* * *

It was still dark outside when two grim visitors arrived at the Olson house in Frederick, Maryland, two days after Thanksgiving. Alice Olson roused her nine-year-old son, Eric, from bed and led him into the living room. The sleepy boy immediately recognized the two men as the family doctor and Lieutenant Colonel Vincent Ruwet, his father's boss at U.S. Army Camp—later Fort—Detrick, just down the road from the Olson home.

Ruwet delivered the terrible news: Alice's husband was dead. Earlier that morning, Olson had "fallen or jumped," as Ruwet put it, from the window of a New York City hotel room. Calling it a "work-related accident," Ruwet explained that the family would be eligible for government compensation. (On the compensation form he subsequently filed on behalf of the family, Ruwet wrote that Olson had died of a "classified illness.")

Exactly what kind of work Olson had been engaged in at the time of his "accident" wasn't a part of the morning's ad hoc grief counseling. Alice, a thirty-eight-year-old housewife, had only a vague knowledge of her husband's classified work at Camp Detrick, where he was the director of planning and evaluations in the U.S. Army Chemical Corps' Special Operations Division (SOD). She knew that, as a biochemist, Olson's specialty during World War II had been the airborne delivery of biological toxins and bacteria, including anthrax. Before the end of the war, a painful stomach ulcer had forced Olson to seek a medical discharge from the army. But he had stayed on at Camp Detrick as a civilian scientist.

In consoling the Olsons, Ruwet made no mention of the nature of the work at Camp Detrick. Nor did he ever mention LSD or the CIA.

As Eric struggled to absorb the devastating news, Alice composed herself enough to tell her two other children, seven-year-old Lisa and five-year-old Nils, that their father would not be coming home. Compounding the family's sense of shock was the seeming improbability of the tragedy. That Olson had taken his own life just didn't square with the devoted husband and caring father they knew. It made no sense. And in the absence of a reasonable explanation—the missing *how* and *why*—a kind of numbness began to set in. As Eric would later recall, "In that moment when I learned that my father had gone out a window and died, it was as if the plug were pulled from some central basin of my mind and a vital portion of my consciousness drained out."

Yet, Alice knew that her husband had been troubled by something of late. A deeply moral and religious man, Olson had been grappling with an ethical dilemma related to his work. Whenever a group of lab monkeys died after completion of a successful experiment, Olson would come home depressed and withdrawn. At one point, he had said to Alice rather enigmatically, "If the Germans had won the Second World War, my colleagues and I would have been prosecuted for war crimes."

The casket, draped with an American flag, remained closed at the funeral four days later. The government explained to the family that even though the body had been embalmed, it was badly disfigured from the fall. Among the mourners at the ceremony were two CIA men: Lashbrook and his boss, Sidney Gottlieb, the architect of the CIA's MK-ULTRA program and the spy agency's mastermind of bizarre assassination techniques employing lethal biological agents ranging from anthrax to shellfish toxin (see chapter 2).

As the coffin was lowered into the ground, the CIA men might have felt an odd sense of relief. After all, the mystery of what killed Olson—and, perhaps, *who* killed him—was buried on that day along with the body.

The mystery would remain underground—literally—for the next twenty-two years. In the absence of "closure," the Olsons' personal trauma would also remain buried, in a state of unspoken denial. As Eric would later explain, "So great was the shock experienced by the family that we did not grieve our loss at all; it was as if nothing had happened." But as they often do, calm surfaces belied turbulent undercurrents. By the 1960s, Alice had developed a drinking problem that eventually led to the loss of her job as a teacher and to a drunk driving arrest on Christmas Eve. Unable to broach the subject of their father's death with their mother, the Olson children were left to grapple with a legacy of shame and pain. To their friends, they would explain that their father had died of a "fatal nervous breakdown."

It was long after the Olson children had grown up—and Alice had recovered from alcoholism—that the ghost of the father returned. On June 11, 1975, startling new details turned up on Alice's front doorstep in the morning edition of the *Washington Post*. A front-page story headlined "SUICIDE REVEALED" zeroed in on a sensational item from the just-released report of the Rockefeller Commission, the first of the post-Watergate inquiries into CIA misdeeds. According to the report, an "Army scientist" had leaped to his death from the thirteenth floor of a New York City hotel room in 1953 after being dosed with LSD by the CIA.

Though the report didn't name the victim, the family recognized their father in the details. A check with Ruwet confirmed it.

According to the report in the *Washington Post*—based on the official findings of an internal CIA investigation conducted after the incident—a "civilian employee" of the army had been dosed with LSD during a government retreat in western Maryland. As the Rockefeller Commission summarized, "This individual was not made aware he had been given LSD until about 20 minutes after it had been administered. He developed serious side effects and was sent to New York with a CIA escort for psychiatric treatment. Several days later, he jumped from a tenth-floor window of his room and died as a result." (Actually, room 1018A was on the thirteenth floor.)

In the weeks following the *Washington Post* story, no one

from the government bothered to contact the Olsons. Frustrated and understandably indignant, the family—and their lawyers—held a press conference in their backyard. Now, the bizarre story had a face and a name, and journalists flocked to the event. Eric, by then a thirty-year-old graduate student working toward his doctorate in clinical psychology at Harvard, recalls brushing elbows with the likes of *Rolling Stone* magazine's Hunter S. Thompson and Leslie Stahl of CBS News. The Olsons took turns reading from a family statement demanding full disclosure from the government. "We feel our family has been violated by the CIA in two ways," Eric declared. "First, Frank Olson was experimented on illegally and negligently. Second, the true nature of his death was concealed for twenty-two years. . . . In telling our story, we are concerned that neither the personal pain this family has experienced nor the moral and political outrage we feel be slighted."

That evening and the following day, stories about Frank Olson and his family dominated network news broadcasts and newspaper headlines. Suddenly, information so long denied the Olson family began to dribble in. Two days after the press conference, Armand Pastore contacted the family. In 1953, Pastore had been the night manager at the Statler Hotel. He explained that at around two a.m. on November 28 of that year, a panicky busboy had summoned him out to the sidewalk in front of the hotel. Lying on the pavement, bloodied and broken, was Frank Olson. Looking up thirteen floors, Pastore saw a dangling blind flapping through an open window frame. Amazingly, Olson was still alive. "He was trying to mumble something," Pastore later told reporters, "but I couldn't make it out. It was all garbled, and I was trying to get his name." Pastore called for a priest and an ambulance. By the time the ambulance arrived, Olson was dead.

Pastore recalled that immediately after the incident someone had made a phone call from Olson's hotel room to a number in Long Island. According to the hotel switchboard operator, who had listened in, it was a short conversation consisting of only two lines:

"Well, he's gone," a man in the hotel room had said.

"That's too bad," a man on the other end of the line had replied before hanging up.

Pastore told Alice that he had always been disturbed by the "unusual circumstances" of her husband's death. As he later elaborated to reporters, "In all my years in the business, I never encountered a case where someone in the middle of the night jumped through a closed window with the shades and curtains drawn."

Pastore wasn't the only interested party to take note of the recent news headlines. Less than two weeks after their backyard press conference, the Olsons were summoned to the White House for a personal meeting with President Gerald Ford. In the Oval Office, Ford offered the family an official government apology. In a photograph taken during the 1975 meeting, Alice and her grown-up children—Eric, thirty, Nils, twenty-seven, and Lisa, twenty-nine—look at ease and, more to the point, relieved, as they stand with the president. At the time, it must have been a reassuring, and even heady, experience. After years of government silence on the subject of Frank Olson's death, the family had finally achieved recognition—and, most important, a promise of full disclosure.

The Olsons had been considering legal action, but White House attorneys advised the family against it, telling them, Eric recalls, that "the law was not on our side." Instead, the government lawyers promised that the White House would support a private bill in Congress to pay the family a settlement. The family signed a waiver releasing the CIA from liability, and in return the Olsons were eventually awarded $750,000 in compensation. The family decision not to file suit, made in deference to Alice's desire to bring the twenty-two-year ordeal to closure, would prove to be a mistake.

Yet at the time, the family believed that full disclosure was finally at hand. Five days after the Oval Office session, the Olson family met with CIA director William Colby at the spy agency's headquarters in Langley, Virginia. Over a lavish multicourse luncheon in the director's dining room adjacent to his seventh-floor office, Colby offered the Olsons his apologies. The meeting was as awkward as the food was elegant. In his memoirs, Colby later referred to the encounter as "one of the most difficult assignments I have ever had." At the end of the hour, the CIA chief gave the family an inch-thick file of declassified documents, calling it the complete dossier on the death of Frank Olson.

Though heavily redacted, the file fleshed out the narrative bones of the *Washington Post* story. On November 19, 1953, Olson had joined nine colleagues for a three-day working retreat at Deep Creek Lodge, a rustic cabin in the secluded woods of western Maryland. Five of the attendees were SOD men from Camp Detrick, including Olson and his boss Ruwet. The remaining four were CIA officers from the Technical Services Staff (TSS), commonly known inside the CIA as the "dirty tricks department." The official purpose of the gathering was to discuss MK-NAOMI, a top-secret joint program of the SOD and TSS to develop germ weapons to infect enemy spies in the field. To maintain absolute secrecy, the participants had been instructed to remove all Camp Detrick tags from their automobiles and to adopt the occupational "camouflage" of sports journalists.

Assisted by his deputy Lashbrook, Gottlieb, head of the TSS Chemical Division, led the sessions in the lodge's chestnut-paneled living room, opposite a roaring fire in a stone hearth. A brilliant chemist with personality tics numerous enough to satisfy a novelist's appetite for the aberrant (Norman Mailer and Barbara Kingsolver have immortalized him in their fiction), Gottlieb at the time had not yet been dubbed "the CIA's Dr. Strangelove." But a few decades of diligent work—and a congressional inquiry or two—would eventually remedy that oversight.

Born with two clubfeet, Gottlieb spent much of his life almost compulsively adapting himself to the external world. According to a cousin, Gottlieb's mother screamed when the blanket covering his feet was removed in the hospital. Unable to walk, he spent his earliest years in her arms. As a child, he underwent foot surgery three times. Although he remained handicapped for life, he compensated by teaching himself to become a graceful square dancer. A habitual stutterer, Gottlieb exhibited the same zeal for self-improvement and personal reinvention in every other aspect of his life. He excelled in his studies and eventually earned a doctoral degree in chemistry from the California Institute of Technology.

After joining the CIA in 1951, he quickly proved himself to be an ardent Cold War patriot. As his CIA recruiter later noted, "He always had a certain amount of 'guilt' . . . about not being able to be in the service during World War II like all his contemporaries because of his clubfoot, so he gave an unusual amount of patriotic service to make up for that." Working in the CIA's chemical group, Gottlieb impressed his superiors as a resourceful, inventive administrator.

By early 1953, Gottlieb had been given control of MK-ULTRA, the CIA's newly minted mind-control program. At the same time, he ran the research efforts in germ warfare being conducted out of Camp Detrick. Later, he would become the CIA's expert in better assassination through chemistry. Some colleagues saw Gottlieb, in his single-minded ardor for his work, as something of a "wild man."

In less than a year on the job as steward of MK-ULTRA, Gottlieb had already established a rather wild and arguably unscientific methodology that involved dosing unsuspecting CIA men at Langley with LSD and then watching them freak out. According to the official CIA account, Gottlieb performed the same experiment on the men at Deep Creek Lodge.

After dinner on the second night, Gottlieb or one of his CIA men secretly slipped LSD into seven glasses of Cointreau liqueur. If Gottlieb and Lashbrook are to be believed, each of the seven men received a relatively modest dose of seventy micrograms. (Ten years later, Hollywood luminaries such as Cary Grant and James Coburn would regularly ingest doses of 200 micrograms under the supervision of a handful of Los Angeles psychiatrists who briefly dabbled in LSD therapy.) The meeting quickly devolved into laughter and random psychedelic incoherence. Though Gottlieb eventually got around to telling his guinea pigs that they had been drugged, several of the men remained uneasy. Olson reportedly had the worst trip. As the biochemist's SOD colleague Ben Wilson would later tell author John Marks, "Olson was psychotic. He couldn't understand what happened. He thought someone was playing tricks on him."

Olson and several others spent a sleepless night under the effects of the drug. The next morning, their nerves frayed, the men decided to adjourn early. When Olson returned home, Alice found her husband to be uncharacteristically withdrawn. After a silent dinner, he told his wife he had made a "terrible mistake" at the retreat. He refused to elaborate, and he didn't mention anything about Gottlieb drugging him.

Over the weekend, Olson remained quiet and emotionally remote, his thoughts as impenetrable as the dense November fog that hung over the landscape outside. He and Alice spent much of that weekend sitting on the couch, holding hands, quietly looking out the window at the obscuring mist. At one point, Alice asked Olson whether he had falsified information. He said he hadn't. When she asked if he had broken security, he replied, "You know I would never do that." Although he revealed little more, he did tell his wife that he planned to resign from his job and retrain himself as a dentist. Alice said that if he felt it was necessary, she would support his decision.

On Sunday night, the couple took in a movie, *Martin Luther*, the just-released biopic on the sixteenth-century Protestant reformer. As Alice would later note, it wasn't the best choice of movies, given her husband's mood. The film, which chronicles Luther's struggles against moral corruption in the Catholic Church and his ultimate break with Catholicism, greatly upset Olson. At the end of the film, Luther nails his ninety-five theses to the door of the castle church in Wittenberg, officially severing his ties to the Catholic Church.

Early the next morning, Olson appeared in his boss's office to tender his resignation. Ruwet reassured Olson that he had done nothing wrong at the retreat and persuaded his employee to stay on. But the next morning, Olson, still agitated and determined to quit, was back in Ruwet's office. According to Ruwet, Olson said he felt "all mixed up" and questioned his own ability to perform his duties. Ruwet decided that Olson needed "psychiatric attention." But instead of sending him to the base hospital, Ruwet called Lashbrook at the CIA.

Lashbrook and Gottlieb hastily made arrangements for Olson to see Harold Abramson, a New York doctor and allergist who had parlayed a fascination with behavior-modifying drugs into lucrative MK-ULTRA contract work. (In one of his "experiments," Abramson had dosed goldfish with LSD to see their reaction.) The fact that Abramson was not a psychiatrist apparently didn't bother Gottlieb, who later sought to justify the peculiar patient referral on national security grounds, that last refuge of panicky civil servants: Abramson, who had considerable experience dosing himself and others with LSD on behalf of the CIA, was already vetted for secrecy.

Ruwet phoned Alice on Tuesday morning to tell her that he and a colleague were taking her husband to New York for treatment because they were "concerned that Frank might become violent with you." According to Eric, this statement "completely shocked my mother, because she had seen no indications of anything remotely like violent tendencies." Eric now believes that Ruwet was lying, in an effort to frighten Alice and thereby "preempt the possibility that she might object in any way to their plans."

Later that day, Alice drove with Olson to Washington, D.C.,

where he was to catch a flight to New York with Ruwet and Lashbrook. The couple stopped for lunch at a coffee shop just outside the Capitol, but Olson wouldn't touch his coffee. "I can't drink this," he said. He grew anxious that someone might have tampered with the beverage, a not entirely paranoid concern given his earlier secret LSD dosing. A half-hour later, Olson boarded a flight to New York. It was the last time Alice would ever see him.

According to the CIA file, Olson saw Abramson for the first time later that day. By then, Olson had become increasingly "paranoid," as the CIA report put it, and was convinced that the CIA was putting Benzedrine or some other stimulant into his coffee to keep him awake.

The next day, Lashbrook and Ruwet took Olson to the home of John Mulholland, a professional magician whom the TSS had hired to write a manual adapting "the magician's art to covert activities." Gottlieb had tasked Mulholland with developing sleight-of-hand techniques that CIA agents could use to slip drugs into drinks. Although Lashbrook later asserted that he was only trying to amuse Olson, the visit had an opposite effect: it freaked him out. If anyone had wanted to unhinge a guy already convinced that he was being drugged against his will, they probably couldn't have done better than to commission an impromptu magic show by a known conjurer of CIA Mickey Finns.

Cutting the visit with Mulholland short, Lashbrook and Ruwet hustled Olson back to Abramson's Long Island office. The CIA allergist talked to Olson for about an hour, then gave him permission to spend Thanksgiving with his family. Olson and his two escorts had an evening to kill before their flight back to Washington the next morning, so the trio took in a Rodgers and Hammerstein musical. But Olson became agitated during the first act, believing, according to Ruwet, that people were waiting outside the theater to arrest him. Ruwet took Olson back to the Statler Hotel. That night while he slept in the adjacent bed, Olson slipped out of the room and wandered the streets of New York. According to Ruwet, Olson proceeded to tear up his paper money and throw his wallet away, purportedly under the delusion that he was following orders. Ruwet and Lashbrook claimed to have found Olson sitting in the Statler lobby early the next morning.

In Ruwet and Lashbrook's version of events, the three flew back to Washington later that morning. However, during the drive from National Airport back to Frederick, Maryland, Olson purportedly grew alarmed. If Ruwet is to be believed, Olson said he was "ashamed" to see his family in his present condition and worried that he might become violent with his children. Lashbrook supposedly contacted Gottlieb, interrupting his boss's Thanksgiving dinner, and the CIA men decided it would be best to take Olson back to Abramson in New York. Ruwet agreed to return to Frederick and notify the family that Olson wouldn't be coming home for the holiday.

Later that day, Lashbrook escorted Olson to Abramson's office, and the nonshrink finally decided to get Olson qualified professional help. According to the CIA's version of events, Olson agreed to check himself into Chestnut Lodge, a Maryland sanitarium staffed by psychiatrists who allegedly had special security clearance. (In fact, Eric would later discover that the doctors at Chestnut Lodge had no special security clearance, a fact that begs the question: Why did the CIA lie about this?) According to Lashbrook, he and Olson were unable to get a departing flight until the weekend, so they settled for Thanksgiving dinner at a Horn and Hardart Automat, then checked into room 1018A of the Statler Hotel.

At some point on Friday—the last day of Olson's life—Abramson showed up at the hotel with a bottle of bourbon and the sedative Nembutal. To say the least, it was an odd prescription for a man who already believed—irrationally or not—that the CIA was trying to drug him. The CIA report offers no more details about Olson's doings on that Friday. However, we do know that Olson called his wife on Friday evening. It was the first time they had spoken in three days, and Alice was relieved to discover that his mood had improved (a state of mind in stark contrast to the angst-ridden portrait depicted by the CIA). They spoke for several minutes, and Olson told his wife that he was looking forward to seeing her and the kids the next day. By two a.m. Saturday morning, just hours after the phone call, and hours before his scheduled flight back to Washington, Olson was dead.

When police arrived on the scene, they found Lashbrook sitting on the toilet in room 1018A, cradling his head in his hands. The CIA man immediately began to tell lies. First, he claimed that he worked for the Defense Department. Then he insisted he had no clue as to why Olson jumped, but added, irrelevantly, that the dead man had "suffered from ulcers." Police initially suspected a homicide with homosexual overtones, but they dropped the matter after Ruwet and Abramson backed Lashbrook's account and hinted at classified government connections.

While the CIA's Office of Security went to work scrubbing New York clean of any telltale evidence linking Olson's death to the CIA, Lashbrook and Abramson got their own cover stories straight. Lashbrook dictated the specifics of Olson's alleged psychiatric symptoms while Abramson took notes. Lashbrook went so far as to claim that Alice had urged her husband to seek psychiatric help months before the LSD dosing—a bald-faced lie, according to Alice.

Despite Lashbrook's pathetic attempts to deflect blame by trumping up a bogus psychiatric history for Olson, CIA inspector general Lyman Kirkpatrick officially (but secretly) concluded that Olson's "suicide" had been "triggered" by the LSD dosing. Kirkpatrick recommended stern censures for Gottlieb and his immediate TSS superiors, but CIA director Allen Dulles interceded, reducing the reprimand to a weak hand slap that did no harm to Gottlieb's career as the CIA's Cold War alchemist.

Although the CIA documents that Colby had given the Olson family filled in some missing details, it raised as many questions as it purported to answer. In fact, the *New York Times* called the file "elliptical, incoherent, and contradictory." It was, the newspaper concluded, "a jumble of deletions, conflicting statements [and] unintelligible passages." For one thing, despite LSD's tendency to provoke mercurial responses in distressed individuals, Olson's bad trip—a week-long psychosis escalating to suicide—seemed out of proportion to the small dose he supposedly swallowed. Then there were several contradictory statements made by Abramson in the report. In one memo, he wrote that Olson's "psychotic state . . . seemed to have been crystallized by [the LSD] experiment." But in another document, he characterized the LSD dose as "therapeutic" and an amount that "could hardly have had any significant role in the course of events that followed."

Even more puzzling were the report's numerous references—with all details blacked out—to the CIA's Project ARTICHOKE. As the precursor to MK-ULTRA, ARTICHOKE focused on the search for a "truth drug" to aid in interrogation. But the top-secret program had also involved other interrogation methods, including torture and attempts to induce amnesia in "blown agents" who knew too much. If Olson's death was indeed the unintended result of an MK-ULTRA experiment, as the report concluded, then why all the cryptic references in the document to ARTICHOKE?

Unanswered questions or not, the family wanted to believe—needed to believe—that vindication and justice had prevailed. It was time to move on. But, it seemed, the curse of the past wouldn't let go. In 1976, Eric's sister Lisa, her husband, and her two-year-old son took off from Frederick in a small plane bound for the Adirondacks, where they planned to invest Lisa's share of the settlement money in a lumber mill. The plane crashed and no one survived.

That same year, Eric moved to Sweden, the birth country of his father's parents, hoping to put some distance between himself and the family curse. In Stockholm, he worked to develop the psychotherapeutic technique he had begun at Harvard: the "collage method," a process that involved clipping pictures and pasting them into photomontages. Eric found that when patients assembled a collection of nonverbal images in a tableau, they often gained powerful insight into suppressed emotions and memories. (Eric's own collages often featured images of men tumbling from buildings.) During what would become a decade-long sabbatical in Sweden, Eric fathered a son, Stephan, with a woman he did not marry.

But his new life abroad offered little insulation from the past. Ironically, Eric's retreat to a "neutral and very quiet country" only sharpened his resolve to exorcise the old family ghosts. "Sweden gave me a great deal of distance from the whole CIA business," he explained. "And it was precisely the new-found calm which enabled me to see that, objectively, the CIA's version of events made no sense. My effort was not to hold on to the issue, but to put it behind me. The problem was that every time I turned over another rock, I discovered another snake."

The serpents were in the details. In his spare time, Eric continued his labors to "decode" the meaning of the Colby documents. It was a process not unlike the collage method: piecing together seemingly fragmentary data, but often uncovering deeper or hidden connections.

Back home in the United States, some of those deeper connections had begun to surface on their own. In late 1975, summoned by the U.S. Senate, Gottlieb returned from semi-retirement as a hospital volunteer in India (he dedicated the latter portion of his life to charitable pursuits, almost as if doing penance for earlier sins). In secret testimony before the Senate Church Committee on Assassinations, the former CIA chemist admitted to his key role in CIA assassination plots against foreign leaders. In 1960, for instance, Gottlieb himself had hand-delivered an "assassination kit" to the CIA station chief in the Congo, with instructions that it be used to eliminate Congolese leader Patrice Lumumba. The kit consisted of a lethal toxin—possibly anthrax—concealed in a tube of toothpaste. When the Church Committee published its findings, Eric realized that Gottlieb had been involved in work much darker than mere "experimental drugging."

In 1978, an even bigger shocker surfaced: In his memoir, former CIA chief William Colby admitted that Olson was more than an "Army scientist," as the official story claimed. At the time of his death, in fact, Olson had been a full-fledged "CIA employee" and a "CIA officer."

Clearly, in its postmortem investigation, the CIA had attempted to conceal the fact that Olson was one of its own. But why? Eric wondered. Ransacking the Colby documents for the umpteenth time, Eric stumbled on a new, possibly telling clue. One of the reports submitted by Abramson, the CIA allergist, described the drugging at Deep Creek Lodge as "an experiment [that] had been done to trap" Olson. This description of the fateful session as a "trap" obviously contradicted the official CIA story that Olson had been one of seven human guinea pigs in a simple LSD experiment. Given the many references in the Colby document to ARTI-CHOKE, Eric began to wonder if the Deep Creek Lodge dosing had been part of an interrogation targeting his father.

In 1984, Eric returned to the United States. His first order of business was to visit room 1018A at the Statler Hotel (by that time, renamed the Pennsylvania Hotel). Standing in the tiny room, Eric was struck by the physical impossibility of the official scenario. There wasn't room enough for a running start, and the window sill was high and blocked by a radiator. Says Eric, "I knew that my father couldn't have jumped out through that closed hotel window even if he wanted to."

That same year, Eric, Nils, and Alice paid a visit to Gottlieb at his secluded farmhouse in Rappahannock County, Virginia. The sixty-six-year-old former master assassin was now devoted to two of his presumably less lethal passions, goat farming and communal living. He greeted the Olsons warily. "Oh, my God," he said. "I'm so relieved to see you all don't have a gun." The night before, he told them, he had dreamed that the Olsons had shot him dead. The family wanted answers, but Gottlieb, true to his espionage training, was evasive. He said that he regretted the incident, but denied that Olson was pushed out the window. At the end of the meeting Gottlieb snapped to Eric, "I can see you're still wrapped up in your father's death. I recommend that you join a support group for children whose parents have committed suicide."

The family also called on Lashbrook, by then retired, at his home in Ojai, California. Eric recalls that Lashbrook was uncommunicative and nervous, claiming to have forgotten key details. The one useful item he revealed was that Gottlieb had been with Olson in New York the week before he died, a fact Gottlieb had failed to mention.

If the CIA's cult of secrecy remained the proverbial immovable object, by the early 1990s Eric had become its unstoppable force. Eric's avocation had become a fixation that had eclipsed his career; having returned to the United States for good, he gave up his work as a clinical psychologist to focus full-time on his father's case. To bankroll his investigation, he became adept in the art of nonprofit fund-raising. But he also borrowed money from friends and family, maxed out half a dozen credit cards, and began to sink into debt. Personal relationships faltered. Friction grew between Eric and Nils, a successful dentist who had helped Eric financially in his quest, but who now worried that Eric had gone off the deep end.

Concern for his mother, who by the early 1990s had developed pancreatic cancer, held Eric back from taking the next logical step in his investigation. But after Alice died in

1993, Eric, with the consent of Nils, decided to exhume his father's body. In June 1994, forty-one years after Olson's burial, Eric watched as a steam shovel began to dredge up the earth at his father's grave. Supervising the disinterment was Professor James Starrs, a criminologist and forensic scientist at George Washington University who had previously unearthed and reexamined the corpses of Jesse James and Carl Weiss, the alleged assassin of Senator Huey Long. After two hours of digging, Starrs' men hauled the rusted casket out of the hole and transported it to a nearby police lab.

As he prepared to unseal the lid, Starrs warned Eric not to watch. The sight of his father's shrunken corpse might prove disturbing. "I'm seeing this!" Eric shot back. When Starrs raised the lid, Eric was surprised to find Olson's body remarkably well preserved. The skin was brown and shriveled, but the face was still recognizable.

After Eric left the lab, Starrs began his autopsy. He quickly discovered that the New York medical examiner's report from 1953 was dead wrong. That report had described multiple facial lacerations caused by the impact with the glass. But Starrs was looking at an undamaged face, devoid of cuts. Even more remarkable than what he did not find was what Starrs *did* find: A large bruise over Olson's left eye, which suggested to Starrs that the victim had been smashed on the head *before* plunging through the window. Starrs concluded that the forensic evidence was "rankly and starkly suggestive of homicide."

"I am exceedingly skeptical of the view that Frank Olson went through that window on his own," Starrs said at the end of his investigation. The evidence suggested that someone had knocked Olson over the head either while he slept or during a struggle and then tossed him out the window.

Three years later, Eric discovered that a CIA assassination manual written in late 1953, the period of his father's death, prescribed exactly that technique. The manual, declassified by the CIA in 1997, contained the following eerie passage:

"The most efficient accident, in simple assassination, is a fall of 75 feet or more onto a hard surface. Elevator shafts, stairwells, unscreened windows and bridges will serve . . . The act may be executed by sudden, vigorous [redacted] of the ankles, tipping the subject over the edge." The manual recommended a sharp blow to the victim's temple: "In chase cases it will usually be necessary to stun or drug the subject before dropping him."

Eric had other reasons to believe that his father had been the victim of a CIA assassination. Investigative writer H. P. Albarelli Jr., who had been conducting his own research into the Olson death, claimed to have contact with retired CIA agents in Florida. According to these unnamed sources, the CIA had hired contract killers associated with the Trafficante mob family to murder Olson in room 1018A. Citing confidentiality agreements with the CIA, these sources have thus far declined to go public with their claims.

Though armed with a mountain of circumstantial evidence, Eric remained hamstrung by the waiver he and his family had signed promising not to sue the CIA. Barred from pursuing the case in civil court, he turned to the criminal justice system. In 1996, Eric asked Manhattan district attorney (D.A.) Robert Morganthau to open a new investigation. Morganthau agreed, assigning the task to his "cold case" unit. Almost immediately, though, the investigation encountered a major setback. A week after the case was reopened, William Colby, a key witness, vanished. After an intensive ten-day search of the Wicomico River in southern Maryland, where he had last been seen canoeing by himself, the former CIA chief's body washed ashore. The death was ruled accidental.

Meanwhile, ex-CIA man Robert Lashbrook fought Morganthau's attempts to interview him; he eventually submitted to a deposition. But the D.A.'s attempts to question Sidney Gottlieb, who was to become a central target of the investigation, hit a terminal snag in 1999 when the ailing Gottlieb died, taking whatever secrets he still guarded to his grave.

Although their cold case proceeded to get colder, the D.A.'s office did manage to dislodge a number of interesting leads. Most notably, a source with connections to Israeli intelligence told the investigators that for years the Mossad had used the Olson case in its operative training program as an object lesson in the "perfect murder."

But as the new millennium ushered itself in, it was becoming clear to Eric that the New York D.A. was losing interest. Eric inundated the cold case unit daily with potential leads, but few were being checked out. Then in early 2002, to Eric's dismay and frustration, the D.A. quietly dropped the case (the New York D.A.'s office has declined to comment, citing grand jury secrecy). In an angry letter to Morgenthau, Eric and Nils accused the D.A.'s office of being "corrupted [by] and . . . knuckl[ing] under to federal pressure to back off from any real examination of the facts and motives involved" in the Olson case. In another letter to Assistant D.A. Stephen Saracco, Eric wrote, "I know that you have reason to believe (no—that is too weak a way of putting it; to 'know' is more like it) that my father was murdered. You have made that abundantly clear on numerous occasions. . . . Looking back, I realize that it was when you returned from California [to depose Lashbrook] that everything changed. You stopped taking any initiative, you stopped gathering evidence."

For Eric, the D.A.'s dumping of the Olson case was yet another in a long line of betrayals by the state. But even the worst setbacks can be instructive. He now realized he had been naïve to expect justice from the same government that had committed the crime in question. After all, he observed, "The CIA has never been convicted of any crime in this country."

Ironically, the Olson case itself may have played a key role

in fortifying the CIA's ability to commit felonies with im-
punity—the equivalent of a get-out-of-jail-free card. Eric
later uncovered an official "memorandum of understanding"
between the CIA and the Department of Justice essentially
excusing the CIA from having to report crimes committed by
its own personnel when doing so might compromise "highly
classified and complex covert operations."

The timing of the memo was interesting. It was drafted in
early 1954, shortly after Olson's death, contemporaneous to
the CIA's internal probe into the Olson affair, and in anticipation of then-pending legislation requiring government
agencies to report criminal violations of its employees to the
Justice Department.

The memo remained under wraps and officially off the
books for decades, until the Olson case erupted again in
1975. The day after President Ford apologized to the Olsons
in the Oval Office, a congressional subcommittee headed by
Bella Abzug met to question Lawrence Houston, the former
CIA general counsel who had drafted the 1954 memo. In the
transcript of the hearing, Abzug presses the ex-CIA lawyer to
explain the genesis of the memo. When the lawyer hems and
haws, Abzug rather astonishingly asks whether the memo
might have been used to cover up murder in the Olson case.

ABZUG: It may very well have been a State offense if
there was foul play. Was [the Olson case] ever referred
to the New York Police Department or State authorities
for consideration?

HOUSTON: Not that I recall.

ABZUG: In other words, this memorandum of understanding in your judgment gave authority to the CIA to ...
give immunity to individuals who happened to work for
the CIA for all kinds of crimes, including possibly murder.

Failing to get a straight answer, the indomitable congress-woman presses harder, and Houston finally yields:

HOUSTON: It could have that effect, yes.

ABZUG: Did it have that effect?

HOUSTON: In certain cases it did.

By the time Eric unearthed the hearing transcripts, Abzug had passed away. So it's not possible to know for sure whether she had any specific reason—other than a well-oiled suspicion of the CIA—to suspect that Olson had been mur-dered.

Eric later wondered whether Houston's "memo of under-standing," or another backroom agreement, had played a role in the abortive investigation by the New York D.A.'s of-fice. As Professor Starrs had once summed up the mystery, "When you pull on the Frank Olson case you feel that some-thing very big is pulling back."

Embittered, cynical, frustrated, and utterly undeterred, Eric pressed ahead with his own private investigation. Now living by himself in the family home his father built, he sur-rounded himself with stacks of documents and bits of evi-dence accumulated in his decades-long pursuit of justice. What little money he managed to scrape together he funneled back into the investigation. Meanwhile, without proper main-tenance, the Olson home had fallen into disrepair, its paint peeling and roof sagging. It was, in a sense, a house haunted by its own history.

Although Eric was convinced that his father had been the victim of a CIA assassination, the possible motive behind a murder had long remained the weak link in his theories. But new sources were emerging. One of them was a former CIA pimp named Ira "Ike" Feldman. A squat, muscular fellow who played the tough guy card to the hilt, Feldman had worked as a federal narcotics agent during the 1950s. Most of his historical foot-notoriety, however, stems from his free-lance work using prostitutes to lure unsuspecting "johns" to a CIA safehouse in San Francisco, where the unwitting pleasure-seekers would instead be dosed with MK-ULTRA acid. Feldman told Eric that Olson had been murdered.

As Feldman elaborated in a 2002 documentary about Olson aired on German television, "The source that I have was the New York City Police Department, the Bureau of Narcotics agents and the CIA agents themselves. They all say the same thing: that [Olson] was pushed out of the window and did not jump. People who wanted him out of the way said he talked too much and he was telling people about the things he had done, which are American secrets. If you work on a top government secret . . . and it spills out to people who should not know, there is only one way to do it: kill him."

To be sure, as a CIA scientist working on some of the nation's most secret Cold War projects, Olson was in a position to know things that, if exposed publicly, would prove embarrassing to the government. But, Eric wondered, what sort of secrets might his father have known? Another clue arrived when a European investigator and journalist contacted Eric and told him of a trip his father had made to England, Germany, and Scandinavia during the summer of 1953. The investigator had interviewed William Sargant, the English psychiatrist and consultant to British intelligence (and author of an early book on brainwashing). Olson had met with Sargant to discuss a moral crisis: He had been horrified to witness "terminal experiments" conducted by the CIA on human subjects: Nazi prisoners and suspected spies who had been plied with the various, sometimes lethal, ARTICHOKE interrogation techniques.

Olson's special diplomatic passport confirmed that he had indeed traveled on government business to Europe during that time frame. Eric recalled family descriptions of Olson's state of mind after returning from the European junket. According to Eric's uncle, who spoke to Olson during the summer of 1953, he had undergone an ethical crisis of some sort. At one point, Olson had commented to his wife that Americans were just as responsible for "war crimes" as the Germans had been.

In the spring of 2001, Eric heard from one of his father's colleagues at Camp Detrick, Norman Cournoyer, a man Eric had assumed was dead. Cournoyer had worked with Olson during World War II to design the protective clothing worn by American soldiers during the invasion of Normandy. He had remained close to Eric's father after the war, when Olson had been recruited into the CIA. Cournoyer had recently seen an article about Eric in the *New York Times Magazine*. "Eric," he said, "you've got everything right except for one thing."

"What's that?" Eric replied.

"The historical context."

Eric asked him to elaborate but the old man demurred. "I am eighty-two years old and I'm no longer afraid," he said. "I'm going to tell you the truth. But I don't want to do it on the phone."

A week later, Eric flew to Massachussets to meet Cournoyer in his home. The man who greeted him at the door was physically frail, confined to a wheelchair as the result of a stroke, but still sharp of mind. Cournoyer directed Eric into his dining room, instructing him to remove all the paintings from the wall to make room for the eight-foot-long historical time line Eric had brought with him, a chronological collage.

Cournoyer got right to the point: "Yes, your father worked for the CIA. He told me that directly." Cournoyer explained that Olson had revealed sometime in 1946–1947 that he was "on a new path" as a CIA employee. That path involved "information retrieval," an intelligence euphemism for interrogation techniques pioneered under the ARTICHOKE project.

Cournoyer affirmed that Olson had returned from Germany

during the summer of 1953 feeling "troubled." Later, in the documentary aired on German TV, Cournoyer elaborated, stating that "the people [Olson] saw in Germany [at the CIA interrogation center] went to the extreme. He said: " 'Norm, did you ever see a man die?' " I said, 'No.' He said, 'Well, I did.' "

Olson told Cournoyer that CIA interrogators were using experimental techniques first employed in Nazi drug experiments during wartime. Now, the Americans were testing the same techniques on captured Germans and others. "They were using Nazis," Cournoyer said, "they were using prisoners, they were using Russians."

But terminal ARTICHOKE experiments weren't the only matters weighing heavily on Olson's conscience during the summer of 1953. Pointing to the section on Eric's time line spanning the early 1950s, Cournoyer offered a laconic statement: "Korea is the key." This was the historical context he had referred to in the phone conversation.

"Your father," Cournoyer explained, "was horrified to discover that the Americans were using biological warfare in Korea."

According to Cournoyer, through his work at Camp Detrick, Olson had acquired direct knowledge of illegal biowarfare experiments being conducted by U.S. armed forces and the CIA on Korean soldiers and civilians. One of the virulent agents deployed was none other than airborne anthrax, Olson's area of expertise. Cournoyer's assertions resonated strongly with Eric. He recalled his mother telling him that Olson had been concerned that the United States was using biological weapons in Korea.

The U.S. government has always denied allegations that it sprayed Korean soldiers with anthrax and dropped a number of other lethal germ warfare agents, including Bubonic plague-bearing fleas. However, the allegations have proved persistent, and, thanks in large part to a 1952 international study into the matter, are generally taken as a given everywhere in the world outside the 202 area code.

Did Olson—hardly reticent about his growing ethical dilemma—become a perceived security risk? Did his superiors fear he might turn whistle-blower, exposing dangerous knowledge about America adopting the killing techniques of German and Japanese war criminals? Cournoyer believed so. "This," he told Eric, "is quite probably what got your father murdered."

As Eric spoke with his father's old friend and colleague, Cournoyer's gardener interrupted them. "There's something out there," he said, pointing at the window overlooking the lawn. The men moved to the window. From behind a tree in the middle of the lawn, a huge mountain lion emerged. Padding slowly, it crossed the yard while the men gazed in astonishment. A third-rate novelist couldn't have ordered up a more obvious literary trope: The cat was indeed out of the bag.

As he continued to assemble his postmortem collage, Eric also encountered signs and symbols of a less fantastical nature.

There was the peculiar memo in Olson's personnel file at Camp Detrick, which indicated that the CIA did indeed see him as a potential security risk. In 1994, an Associated Press reporter discovered the typewritten memo, which quoted an earlier, handwritten note forwarded to Camp Detrick in 1975 by a person described only as "retired Army and retired DAC" (army shorthand for "Department of the Army Civilian"). The handwritten note, headlined "RE - DR. F. W. OLSON," suggested further investigation into Olson's background in connection to his death. One item on the list suggested that someone look into "Trip to Paris and Norway in 1953(?) and possible fear of security violation. Sources — F. W. Wagner, H. T. Eigelsbach, Robert Lashbrook, and Dr. [Abramson]."

That the CIA had much to hide became dramatically evident during the summer of 2001, when Eric obtained documents from the Gerald Ford Presidential Library in Ann Arbor, Michigan. Among the papers were memos written by senior White House staffers and attorneys who were concerned about the possibility of an Olson family lawsuit and the inevitable public disclosure it would entail. White House attorney Roderick Hills wrote to White House deputy staff director Dick Cheney (yes, *that* Dick Cheney) stating, "Dr. Olson's job [was] so sensitive" that in a trial the government would refuse to reveal it.

Another of the memos, written by Cheney on July 11, 1975, the day after the Olson family press conference, and addressed to his boss Donald Rumsfeld (yes, *that* Donald Rumsfeld), raised concern for the possibility that it might become necessary to disclose highly classified national security information in connection with any court suit, or legislative hearings."

Such a revelation was to be avoided at all costs, the internal correspondence stated. What exactly was this "highly classified national security information"? MK-ULTRA? As far as that program was concerned, disclosure was already well underway. Was the big secret that Olson was a CIA employee? That hardly seems shocking in the context of an accidental LSD dosing. In fact, it might be argued that, public relations–wise, a CIA employee dying in a bungled CIA drug experiment is somewhat less scandalous than an innocent army civilian as fall guy. If, however, the "highly classified" secret concerned a CIA-ordered hit on one of its own, the aggresive, decades-long cover-up begins to make sense.

Fifty years after the fact, Eric came to believe that he had finally pried loose the carefully guarded state secret of his father's death. In the summer of 2002, he and Nils were finally ready to lay their father, and the mystery, to rest. Nine years after unearthing Olson's body, Eric and Nils put their father's cursed bones back into the ground (the tissue remains in

Professor Starrs' lab). They now rest in a plot beside the remains of Alice, their sister Lisa, her husband, and her child.

The day before the reburial, the surviving Olsons held one last backyard press conference. It wasn't exactly the sort of closure the Olson family had sought for so many years; after all, no one from the D.A.'s office was on hand to announce an official finding, or even to call for a congressional inquiry. And no government panel would be publishing a report acknowledging that Frank Olson had been murdered. Nevertheless, it was a kind of justice—hard-fought and self-won.

"Frank Olson did not die as a consequence of a drug experiment gone awry," Eric said, addressing a small huddle of TV cameras. "He died because of security concerns regarding disavowed programs of terminal interrogation and the use of biological weapons in Korea. This secret was so immense that even twenty-two years later the White House had been enlisted to maintain it."

Finally, the fall that had begun forty-nine years earlier was over. It had held the family suspended in a kind of weightless limbo, captives to the pull of their own unrevealed and unresolved history. And like bodies in motion around a distant, immense, and barely visible object, their destination was forever falling away from under them. But on the day Eric put his father to rest for the second time, the son seemed to have found his footing again. At last, he said, he was ready to move on. "Today," he announced, "Frank Olson finally hit bottom." Eric Olson might just as well have been talking about himself.

MAJOR SOURCES

Albarelli Jr., H. P., and John Kelly. "The Strange Story of Frank Olson." *Weekly Planet*, 6 December 2000.
Conversations and correspondence with Eric Olson.
Fischer, Mary A. "The Man Who Knew Too Much." *Gentlemen's Quarterly*, January 2000.

Olson, Eric. Frank Olson Project Web site, www.frankolson
    project.org.
Gup, Ted. "The Coldest Warrior." *Washington Post Magazine*,
    16 December 2001.
House of Representatives. Hearings Before a Subcommittee on
    Government Operations, 94th Cong., 1st sess., July 22, 23,
    29, 31 and August 1, 1975.
Ignatieff, Michael. "What Did the CIA Do to Eric Olson's
    Father?" *New York Times Magazine*, 1 April 2001.
Koch, Egmont R., and Michael Wech. *Codename: ARTICHOKE*.
    Egmont R. Koch Filmproduktion. First aired on German tele-
    vision August 12, 2002.
Marks, John. *The Search for "The Manchurian Candidate."*
    New York: Norton, 1991.

XIII

Disinformation, Please

81

Sink the Lusitania!

When a German U-Boat commander, one foggy morning in 1915, while stalking the southern coast of Ireland, ordered a single torpedo launched at a British luxury liner, he knew he was about to piss off everyone in Western Europe who wasn't German.

But it's pretty safe to say he didn't comprehend the contribution he was making to the history of conspiracy theory. What he launched on that May 7 morning, wasn't just a torpedo, but a prototype for a new kind of conspiracy theory that's in heavy rotation almost one hundred years later.

The luxury liner was the RMS *Lusitania,* the most popular, grandest ship of its era. We remember the RMS *Titanic* better today, mainly because that ship was even bigger and more tricked out than the *Lusitania* but sank on its very first voyage in a highly avoidable accident. The *Lusitania* was launched in 1907, crossed the Atlantic safely and (for its day) speedily more than two hundred times and never ran into trouble.

Never, that is, until at the peak of World War I German

submarine captain Walther Schwieger, enjoying lunch on the conning tower of his U-Boat as it floated on the Atlantic surface, spotted smoke from the giant liner's stacks on the horizon.

Just about every war, including the cold one and the rather nebulous one "on terror," features a provocation of some sort—a criminal atrocity committed by an enemy (actual or imagined) that gets everyone all riled up and into a nice, feisty, kill-the-bastards kind of mood. In 1941, Pearl Harbor jolted the American public into World War II. In 1983, the Soviet shootdown of Korean Air Flight 007 reignited the U.S.-Soviet conflict for the Reagan years after the mushy, détente-laden Carter era. And of course, 2001 gave us the September 11 (9/11) attacks. World War I, at least the United States' entry into it, had the sinking of the *Lusitania*.

In every case, the conspiracy theory would have it, the victims of these attacks were actually the perpetrators of them. It usually takes a catastrophe, a national trauma, to catalyze a country to war. So why not set one up yourself?

According to the conspiracy theory—most famously argued in a 1972 bestseller by *London Times* correspondent Colin Simpson—the sinking of the *Lusitania* was just such an inciting incident for the United States entry into World War I. The British government desperately desired U.S. doughboys on the front lines. Therefore, the reasoning goes, the British government set up the sinking of the *Lusitania*. The inevitable American outrage, the British believed, would force the United States into the war.

There are some torpedo-sized holes in the theory. The biggest hole being that the United States did not enter the war, or even break diplomatic relations with Germany, for another two years after the *Lusitania* slid beneath the sea. If the sinking was indeed a plot by the British government to lure the United States into the war by letting almost 1,200 civilians be murdered, it was a spectacular failure.

There were 128 Americans sailing on the *Lusitania* including millionaire (back when being a millionaire was actually

pretty impressive) Alfred Vanderbilt and theater mogul
Charles Frohman (the man behind *Peter Pan*), both of whom
perished. But U.S. president Woodrow Wilson's reaction to the
atrocity was no more than a call for the various warring
countries to quit sinking each other's passenger ships, which
could be read as the early-twentieth-century equivalent of
George W. Bush's "get Hezbollah to stop this shit" remark.

Wilson followed with a proclamation that would be in-
comprehensible today. He announced that America was "too
proud to fight."

Yes, the mood of the country was just a wee bit different
back then. But the inclination toward conspiracy theory remains robust today, particularly given these *Lusitania*-style
calamities. It should not be surprising that as such incidents
recur, conspiracy theories recur as well. In truth, the sinking
of the *Lusitania* has more than passing similarities to 9/11,
86 years later—beyond the obvious of both being attacks on
civilian targets.

In both incidents, there were significant warnings that an
attack was pending—warnings that were ignored. In the
Lusitania's case, the warnings were none too subtle. The
German government took out an ad in fifty major American
newspapers a week before the *Lusitania* sailed, declaring its
intention to sink the famous liner and advising Americans
not to travel on board. But the U.S. State Department scuttled the ad.

This action shows evidence of complicity by the U.S. government itself, which apparently must have been bursting its
britches to get its butt into the war, despite the isolationist
convictions of its president. However, a subsequent warning,
again placed by the Germans, did appear in newspapers directly adjacent to advertisements for the *Lusitania*'s final transatlantic crossing: "Vessels flying the flag of Great Britain, or
any of her allies, are liable to destruction."

Can't get much clearer than that. As one might imagine,
the passengers already booked on the *Lusitania* were a little

rattled. The *Lusitania*'s captain, William "Bowler Bill" Turner (so nicknamed, of course, in honor of his preferred headgear, rather than any kegling prowess in the lanes) assured them that the ship was safe from torpedoes due to its lightning speed. Making the voyage across the pond in just over a week, the *Lusitania* was indeed the fastest passenger ship of its size in the water.

Turner had the rotten luck to survive the sinking, thus unwittingly appointing himself the focus of all the blame and scandal. For one thing, he believed the *Lusitania* could outrun a German torpedo. Oops. Turner was a replacement captain. The ship's regular captain bowed out because of a case of nerves from nonstop torpedo warnings.

The *Lusitania* disaster has another eyebrow-cocking similarity to 9/11. As with 9/11 in which the worst damage was caused not by the impact of the planes but by the subsequent collapse of the buildings, the sinking of the *Lusitania* was not caused by the impact of Schwieger's lunchtime torpedo, but by a massive explosion in the ship's forward cargo hold– an explosion so tremendous that the *Lusitania* was completely underwater after just eighteen minutes.

What caused this secondary, but devastating blast? That mystery has never been solved, at least not in any satisfactory way. In 1993, explorer Robert Ballard took an expedition to the *Lusitania*'s final resting place. It was Ballard who discovered the wreck of the *Titanic* in 1985, more than 2½ miles deep in the vast North Atlantic. The *Lusitania* presented a considerably easier challenge, lying beneath just 295 feet of water, puddle depth really, right off the Irish coastline. Turner had been speeding her toward port at the time of the torpedo hit and second blast.

Ballard's investigation yielded a benign theory: the torpedo strike had ignited coal dust in the ship's hold. But the coal dust scenario seemed improbable, especially in light of the long-held belief that the *Lusitania* was carrying illegal munitions and that it was those armaments that blew up and sunk the ship.

Here's where the conspiracy theories start to take on water. Okay, in column A we have the theory that the Brits, in their stereotypically sinister Brit fashion, carefully plotted the sinking, making unwitting and unwilling martyrs of nearly two thousand British subjects to cause an ever-expanding war.

In column B we have the hypothesis that the *Lusitania* was an illegal munitions transport, used by the British to import arms from America immune from German attack, with its civilian passengers as human shields.

The two theories can't both be true. Unless we had multiple plots surrounding the poor *Lusitania*, which just wanted to get from New York to Liverpool unmolested. Usually, and in Simpson's definitive book, the conspiracy is laid at the door of the British admiralty—specifically with Admiral Winston Churchill. So was Churchill involved in both the arms-smuggling conspiracy and the conspiracy to destroy those illegal arms?

The "*Lusitania* as military vessel" theory seems designed more to absolve the Germans of responsibility for the disaster than it does to pin it on the British—much like the idea that if Korean Air Flight 007 were actually a covert spy plane, it would absolve the Soviets of guilt for shooting it down. A military vessel makes for a legitimate military target. And as it turns out, the *Lusitania* was carrying arms, but nothing powerful enough to have caused the fatal explosion.

Investigators after Ballard concluded that steam from the ship's boilers ignited. But the true cause of the second blast will never really be certain.

Back in Germany, while all of Europe and a good part of the United States erupted in anger, the government minted a Franklin Mint–style commemorative medallion with an engraving of the ship sliding beneath the waves. Schwieger was celebrated as a national hero. Of course, the United States did enter the war in 1917. And on May 7, 1919, four years to the day from when Schwieger ordered that single torpedo launched into history, the allies handed the defeated Germans the Treaty of Versailles, officially ending the World War and, in the highly punitive conditions it imposed on the Germans who were barred from the treaty negotiations, planted the seeds of the next one.

MAJOR SOURCES

Bailey, Thomas A., and Paul B. Ryan. *The Lusitania Disaster: An Episode in Modern Warfare and Diplomacy*. New York: Free Press, 1975.

Ballard, Robert D. *Exploring the Lusitania: Probing the Mysteries of the Sinking That Changed History*. With Spencer Dunmore. New York: Warner Books, 1995.

Beesly, Patrick. *Room 40: British Naval Intelligence 1914–1918*. New York: Harcourt Brace Jovanovich, 1982.

Clarkson, Grosvenor B. *Industrial America in the World War: The Strategy Behind the Line 1917–1918*. Cambridge, MA: Houghton Mifflin, 1923.

Devlin, Patrick. *Too Proud to Fight: Woodrow Wilson's Neutrality*. New York: Oxford University Press, 1975.

Du Pont Company. *Du Pont: The Autobiography of an American Enterprise*. Wilmington, DE: Du Pont Company, 1952.

———. *A History of the Du Pont Company's Relations with the United States Government, 1802–1927*. Wilmington, DE: Du Pont Company, 1928.

Engelbrecht, H. C., and F. C. Hanighen. *Merchants of Death: A Study of the International Armament Industry*. New York: Dodd, Mead and Company, 1934.

Ferrell, Robert H. *Woodrow Wilson and World War I, 1917–1921*. New York: Harper & Row, 1985.

Kenworthy, J. M. *Sailors, Statesmen—and Others: An Autobiography*. London: Rich & Cowan, 1933.

———, and George Young. *Freedom of the Seas*. London: Hutchinson & Co., 1928.

Lansing, Robert. *The War Memoirs of Robert Lansing, Secretary of State*. Indianapolis, IN: Bobbs-Merrill, 1935.

Link, Arthur. *Woodrow Wilson and the Progressive Era, 1910–1917*. New York: Harper & Row, 1954.

"*Lusitania* Controversy." Great War Primary Documents Archive Web site, www.gwpda.org/naval/lusika04.htm.

Simpson, Colin. *The Lusitania*. New York: Ballantine Books, 1974.

82

Unhappy Chemtrails to You (Until We Meet Again)

Glance up at the sky any day of the week, and you're likely to see at least one gossamer vapor trail lingering in the wake of a high-flying aircraft. Maybe you'll see more than one of these wispy filaments still hanging overhead long after the commercial or military jets that made them have disappeared over the horizon. If you're like most people, you probably won't give them a second thought. Or, at the very least, you might mentally register them as aircraft contrails—condensation trails of tiny ice crystals formed in the slipstream of jet engines.

But whether you happen to subscribe to the *chemtrail* branch of conspiracy speculation (or just listen to a lot of late-night AM radio), you may see something far more sinister: a

700

systematic government effort to seed the skies secretly with trails of noxious chemicals.

In the annals of alternative exegesis, chemtrails (aka aerosol crimes) are a fairly recent concern, first widely publicized by Canadian journalist, author, and videographer William Thomas in the late 1990s. In articles penned for holistic lifestyle journals and as a frequent guest on Art Bell's paranormal-focused late-night radio program, *Coast to Coast AM*, Thomas alerted listeners to chemical trails "spread by fleets of jet aircraft in elaborate crosshatched patterns [which] are sparking speculation and making people sick across the United States" and Canada.

Thomas's emphatic warnings of "poison from the sky" helped ignite those sparks of speculation into surging arcs of suspicion. By the early aughts, chemtrail angst had become about as commonplace on Internet conspiracy sites as the toxic vapors were allegedly in the skies overhead. Distinct from the relatively benign phenomenon of high-altitude water vapor contrails, chemtrails were described as "aerosol anomalies," streams of chemicals and particalized metals deliberately released by military and commercial aircraft, often at low altitudes too warm for the formation of contrail ice crystals.

The evidence of a government plot to pump pathogens into the air remains largely anecdotal—and heavily based on eyewitness reports from sky gazers in fourteen NATO nations and also across forty-eight states. These concerned citizens have observed unnaturally hazy skies suspiciously filled with too many jets. "They look like they're playing tic-tac-toe up there," warns a typically anonymous whistle-blower in the first chapter of Thomas's confidently titled 2002 book, *Chemtrails Confirmed*. Thomas also relays the health complaints of landlocked citizens unlucky enough to find themselves underneath a smoky overflight—complaints that include "flu-like symptoms . . . pneumonia, heart problems, even death."

Distilling the crisis to its essential nut, Thomas writes, "Someone is stealing our skies."

On that point, most chemtrail trackers are inclined to agree. However, when it comes to the *who and why*, several schools of thought have emerged.

Even though the concrete evidence is thin to the point of gaseous (we'll get to that in a moment), most chemtrail blazers see a U.S. government hand on the poison-pen skywriting, often with complicit commercial aviation interests ably assisting. However, because the chemtrail phenom is often alleged to be global in scope (remember: sightings in fourteen NATO nations), many chemtrail theorists suggest a much larger international conspiracy centered on NATO or some other secret alliance of governments. Thomas, who favors this hypothesis, knowingly asserts that "Croation chemtrails began the day after that country joined NATO."

As for motive—the *why?*—theorists posit several alternative possibilities of varying degrees of plausibility. In his earliest reports on the mystery air dusting, Thomas focused on the health issues allegedly plaguing those underneath the flight vectors. Writing in the summer of 2000, Thomas theorized that at least some of the chemtrails might be part of clandestine biowarfare simulations conducted by the U.S. government. Pointing to the well-documented history of such previous secret experiments (see "The Sickening Secret", p. 35), Thomas and others speculated that the federal government might be sliming civilians with untold pathogens, chemicals, and fungi as part of a renewed (and therefore highly illegal) biowarfare test program.

The evidence? Several newspaper accounts of "overfilled hospital emergency rooms" in various states, which, Thomas surmised, must be connected to chemtrails. That and samples of "gel-like" fallout from chem ground zero collected by "one of my researchers" and analyzed by a "government-licensed lab," which found the goo to contain a *"cocktail of pathogenic moulds and fungi"* [Thomas's emphasis]. This is QED, more or less.

Building on Thomas's speculation, a portfolio of even more

dramatic theories soon began to circulate in the marketplace of conjecture: might chemtrails be a form of government-assisted Darwinism, a genocidal means of population control aimed at the weak and infirm? "If the chemtrails *contain biological agents*," suggested ChemtrailCentral.com, "then people already *weakened* by other factors [might die] . . . as a result of the additional strain on their systems." [original emphasis].

Or perhaps chemtrails might simply be a covert form of socialized medicine (seriously) intended to inoculate unsuspecting citizens from future biological and chemical attacks by America's (post-9/11) enemies. Once again, we yield the floor, and the emphasis text, to ChemtrailCentral.com: "Some propose that the government may be quietly releasing *bioagents to vaccinate* citizens via the air. . . . Municipal water supplies might not be universal enough [for vaccine delivery] . . . but everyone breathes the air. And the *federal* government *rules* the air."

What about mind control? There *has* to be a theory about chemtrails and mind control, right? Relax. *Of course*, there is. But the route there is a bit choppy, so keep your seat belt fastened. (Flight attendants, secure the door.)

In a 2001 feature article published in a weekly entertainment tabloid *Columbus Alive*, a "scientist working at Wright-Patterson Air Force Base who insisted upon anonymity," revealed to the greater central Ohio movie- and club-going readership that he was indeed "familiar with chemtrail experiments." According to the unnamed scientist, the government has been spraying various substances into the atmosphere, most notably aluminum oxide and barium stearate. What's more, the off-the-record (and untraceable) insider scientist elaborated that one of the Wright-Patterson experiments was conducted "in conjunction with the military's High-Frequency Active Auroral Research Program (HAARP) in Alaska." The secret experiments involved using the airborne barium to reflect HAARP's 3-gigawatt electromagnetic beam in order "to

take 3D images of the ground far over the horizon." Still in
your seat? The landing strip is in sight. Because it's been an
article of faith in some conspiracy theorist circles that
HAARP is all about government schemes to "disrupt mental
processes" via pulsed radio frequency transmissions, it didn't
take long for chemtrail theories to crossbreed with mind-
control scenarios. To be fair, most dedicated chemtrail theorists dismiss the hypnochemtrails scenario as ludicrous. But
the theory does have more than a few avid fellow travelers.

The barium-HAARP scenario also led to speculation that
the chemtrails might have a less provocative purpose—as part
of the wireless communications and radar studies that the
military had already acknowledged to be part of the Alaska-
based high-frequency radio wave project.

And then there was the most obvious, and in many ways,
most *plausible*, hypothesis: weather modification. Think
about it. It's well documented that NASA has conducted research into how jet contrails affect weather patterns. Moreover,
cloud seeding is an established reality, a technique used for
decades to boost rainfall during droughts, disperse fog over
airports, and increase snowfall over ski resorts. So how implausible is it to assume that the government might have advanced beyond sprinkling silver iodide or dry ice into stubborn
cumuli to coax a little moisture? Not very, apparently, for into
this theoretical low-pressure zone rushed a front of stormy
supposition. Once again, HAARP reared its High-Frequency
Active Auroral head. After all, hadn't HAARP's patent state
that "weather modification is possible by . . . altering solar
absorption patterns by constructing one or more plumes of
particles which will act as a lens or focusing device." Particles?
Did someone say *barium-dust chemtrails*? Yes, William
Thomas, to name one of many.

By the mid-2000s, weather and climate-modification theories
had become the dominant branch of, well, let's call it *aerosol
criminology*. Evidence may have been as nebulous as ever,
but by now a number of intriguing, if far from definitive,

leads had surfaced: "Weather as a Force Multiplier: Owning the Weather in 2025," a 1996 research paper commissioned by the United States Air Force, anticipated "intervention techniques to modify the weather" by "infusing either energy or chemicals into the meteorological process." Though vague on specifics, the paper advocated using "technology [that is already] there, waiting for us to pull it all together."

A 1992 paper by the National Academy of Sciences offered several possible solutions to "mitigating" planetary warming, including using "aircraft to maintain a cloud of dust in the low stratosphere to reflect sunlight."

In 1998, Dr. Edward Teller (yes, *that* Dr. Edward Teller: father of the H-Bomb and, later, senescent advocate of Ronald Reagan's Strategic Defense Initiative) had proposed injecting tiny shards of metal into the atmosphere to create a sunshield that would put the brakes on global warming. In an article for the *Wall Street Journal*, Teller dubbed his brainstorm a "sunscreen for planet earth." At about the same time, several other scientists proposed a similar "geoengineering" solution to climate change: dispersing sunblocking particles through the exhaust systems of commercial airliners.

Though far from slam dunk evidence, all this academic theoretical speculation about flooding the skies with sunblocking particles was—interesting. The only thing for certain is that the pathological skeptics and voluminous debunkers who predictably brayed about improbable conspiracy theories had failed yet again to read the scientific literature and see that the improbable had become quite plausible.

MAJOR SOURCES

Chemtrail Central. Chemtrail Web site, www.chemtrailcentral.com.
Conway, Bruce. "The Chemtrail Smoking Gun: Proof of Global Geoengineering Projects." Lightwatcher Web site, www.lightwatcher.com/chemtrails/smoking_gun.html.

Fitrakis, Bob, and Fritz Chess. "Stormy Weather: The Government's Top-Secret Efforts to Control Mother Nature." *Columbus Alive*, 22 December 2001.

Robinson, Arthur B., Noah E. Robinson, and Willie Soon. "Environmental Effects of Increased Atmospheric Carbon Dioxide." *Journal of American Physicians and Surgeons*, 22 September 2007.

Thomas, William. *Chemtrails Confirmed*. Carson City, NV: Bridger House Publishers, 2004.

———. "Chemtrails: Covert Climate Control?" *Nexus Magazine*, October–November 2001.

83

Are UFO Whistle-blowers Government Disinformation Artists?

Could it be that the great bulk of UFOlogy is based on disinformation from the U.S. government, perhaps using UFOs to cover up unavoidable sightings of futuristic flying weapons under development by a ubiquitous military-industrial complex? Could be.

It does seem as if many UFO whistle-blowers are "former" employees of the government. Others appear to have gotten their information directly from an Uncle Sam spokesperson. Let's review the cast of characters. You decide whether there's a Big Picture, and Big Brother is behind it. At the risk of mixing metaphors, according to author Michael Benson, here's the starting lineup of whistle-blowers with connections to a certain five-sided building in Washington, D.C.

First up is *Jaime Shandera*—a Los Angeles TV producer and UFO researcher, who publicized documents purporting to acknowledge the existence of a secret U.S. government panel to investigate UFOs called MJ-12 (Majestic-12). Shandera's story began in December 1984, when he received a package with an Albuquerque postmark and no return address.

At that time Shandera was working with writer/researcher Bill Moore who made a deal with U.S. intelligence to exchange what he believed to be top secret documents for his services as a government mole in the UFO community. Inside the package was a role of film that when developed showed an eight-page document that appeared to be a briefing paper dated November 18, 1952, to President-elect Dwight D. Eisenhower from Vice Admiral Roscoe Hillenkoetter regarding the recovery of two crashed UFOs. The document goes on to say that at the site of the first UFO crash, in July 1947, the dead bodies of four humanoids, apparently from outer space, were recovered. Attached to this memo was another document. This appeared to be a presidential order written by Truman, creating a super-secret investigation unit to study the crashed airships and the humanoid remains. The document says the group was to be called "Majestic-12."

In an attempt to verify authenticity, Shandera and Moore later visited the National Archives in Washington, DC, and discovered a memo dated July 1954, from the president's as-sistant General Robert Cutler to President Eisenhower stating that a meeting of MJ-12 was scheduled for the White House on July 16, 1954. Shandera and Moore did not make the MJ-12 memo public until 1987 when they learned that British UFO researcher Timothy Good had acquired a copy of the memo and was going to publish it. Not wanting to be scooped, Shandera went public.

Dr. Richard J. Boylan was a behavioral scientist who'd been known to hypnotize patients with perfectly normal mental problems only to learn that they'd been abducted by aliens. Boylan claimed Shandera was a member of a group called Aviary, a small group of individuals with extremely high security clearances, who since the 1970s have worked on various aspects of UFO research and policy. The members of Aviary, Boylan claims, refer to one another by code names, often the names of birds. Other members of Aviary reportedly included:

- Dr. Christopher Green, the chief of the Biomedical Sciences Department of General Motors, and reportedly former head of the CIA's UFO files at the "Weird Desk." Dr. Green's nickname was "Blue Jay."
- Ron Pandolfi, CIA Deputy Director for the Division of Science and Technology and custodian of UFO files at the "Weird Desk." Nickname: "Pelican."
- Dr. Bruce Maccabee, a well-known UFO expert and research scientist in optical physics and laser weapons applications at the U.S. Naval Surface Weapons Lab, Silver Springs, Maryland. Maccabee was a physics /photointerpretive consultant for the Mutual Unidentified Flying Object Network (MUFON). Nickname: "Sea Gull."
- Hal Puthoff, physicist with the Institute for Advanced Research in Austin, Texas. Nickname: "Owl."
- Lieutenant Colonel John Alexander, Ph.D., U.S. Army Intelligence and Security Command. Alexander is director of the Non-Lethal Weapons Department, Los Alamos National Laboratory. Nickname: "Penguin."
- Commander C. B. Scott Jones, Ph.D., U.S. Navy (Ret.), former Office of Naval Intelligence Officer with thirty years service in U.S. intelligence overseas; involved in the Defense Nuclear Agency, Defense Intelligence Agency, Defense Advanced Research Projects Agency, and other organizations. Nickname: "Chickadee."

- Jacques Vallée, Ph.D., former astrophysicist with GEPAN, the French government's UFO investigative agency. He later worked as principal investigator with the U.S. Defense Department computer network projects. Dr. Vallée has written many books about UFOs. Nickname: "Parrott."
- Dan Smith, civilian UFO researcher who, apparently on a volunteer basis, has served as a liaison between CIA and non-CIA UFO sources. Nickname: "Chicken Little."
- Captain Bob Collins, U.S. Air Force (Ret.); Special Agent, Air Force Office of Special Investigations. Nickname: "Condor."
- Gordon Novel, CIA employee who was living in New Orleans in 1963 and who was questioned by the FBI on five separate occasions following JFK's assassination. While investigating a conspiracy in the JFK assassination in 1967, New Orleans district attorney Jim Garrison subpoenaed Novel, but Novel fled to Ohio where Garrison failed to obtain his extradition. Boylan believed Novel later investigated alleged ET energy technology and titanium aluminide metallurgy for their investment potential. Nickname: "Buzzard."
- Sergeant Richard "Dick" Doty, U.S. Air Force (Ret.); Special Agent, Air Force Office of Special Investigations; reported to have engaged in UFO disinformation projects. Nickname: "Falcon."
- Dale Graff, UFO-related technology specialist and former contracts overseer for the Defense Intelligence Agency (DIA) at Wright-Patterson Air Force Base. Nickname: "Harrier."
- Jack Verona, before he disappeared in the late 1990s, was involved in Project Sleeping Beauty, which researched ways to disable enemy "target" personnel using directed precise-frequency radiated electromagnetic-energy fields. Nickname: "Nightingale."
- Jaime Shandera's nickname was "Woodpecker."

Batting in the second slot in our lineup of government-affiliated whistle-blowers is *John Lear*—a former CIA pilot, who flew missions over Vietnam, and the son of William P. Lear, the developer of the Lear jet. In 1988, Lear, a resident of Nevada, released a nine-page letter to the UFO research community saying that "we must face the shocking facts . . . [t]he 'horrible truth' the government has been hiding from us over forty years. Unfortunately, the 'horrible truth' is far more horrible than the government ever imagined. . . . In its effort to protect democracy, our government sold us to the aliens. And here is how it happened. But before I begin, I'd like to offer a word in the defense of those who bargained us away. They had the best of intentions. . . . Germany may have recovered a flying saucer as early as 1939. General James H. Doolittle went to Sweden in 1946 to inspect a flying saucer that had crashed there in Spitzbergen. . . . The 'horrible truth' was known by only a very few persons: They were indeed ugly little creatures, shaped like praying mantises and who were more advanced than us by perhaps a billion years. Of the original group that were the first to learn the 'horrible truth,' several committed suicide, the most prominent of which was General James V. Forrestal. . . . General Forrestal's medical records are sealed to this day. . . . President Truman quickly put a lid on the secret and turned the screws so tight that the general public still thinks that flying saucers are a joke. Have I ever got a surprise for them. . . . In 1947, President Truman established a group of 12 of the top military scientific personnel of their time. They were known as MJ-12. Although the group still exists today, none of the original members are still alive."

The letter goes on to say that our scientists and the aliens cut a deal: in exchange for some of the aliens' advanced technology, the scientists agreed to ignore their abduction of humans and their mutilation of cattle.

Lear writes, "The EBEs [Extraterrestrial Biological Entities] assured MJ-12 that the abductions . . . were merely the ongoing monitoring of developing civilizations."

The letter then said that the EBEs had deceived MJ-12 and that their plans actually included "parasitical consumption of human biological matter," the killing of humans who got in their way, and the crossbreeding of humans and aliens.

Forrestal, who was the first U.S. Secretary of Defense (previously the position had been known as the Secretary of War), told a friend fifteen months before the beginning of the Korean War that American soldiers would soon be fighting in Korea. He had apparently been troubled by the fact that, during the first years following World War II, top officials in the U.S. government were making concession after concession to the Soviet Union. President Harry Truman asked for Forrestal's resignation on March 2, 1949. In May 1949, Forrestal was taken to Bethesda Naval Hospital for what was called a routine examination. Days later, Forrestal's body was found in a room. A noose was around his neck. His death was called a suicide. Forrestal's diary was held for more than a year before officials released an edited version to the public.

The existence of MJ-12 is seemingly corroborated by scientist Robert I. Sarbacher, a consultant for the U.S. Department of Defense Research and Development Board. An expert on instrumental physics and communications engineering, Sarbacher researched guided missiles for the Pentagon. He was also a high-ranking official at the Washington Institute of Technology. Sarbacher said that MJ-12 possessed the bodies of dead aliens. Though he never saw the dead aliens, he had seen lightweight but strong metallic material from a crashed craft, presumably material confiscated from Mac Brazel [a rancher who recovered the material] in Roswell, New Mexico, in 1947.

Sarbacher said, "[The] instruments or people operating these machines were also of very light weight, sufficient to withstand the tremendous deceleration and acceleration associated with the machinery. I remember in talking with some of the people at the office that I got the impression these 'aliens' were constructed like certain insects we have observed on earth, wherein because of the low mass the inertial forces involved in operation of these instruments would be quite low."

Writing on November 29, 1983, Dr. Sarbacher said, "I still do not know why the high order of classification has been given and why the denial of the existence of these devices."

According to Sarbacher's documents, members of MJ-12 included:

- Scientist Vannevar Bush, who was then head of the U.S. Department of Defense Research and Development Board.
- Secretary of Defense James V. Forrestal, who served as a member until his death on May 22, 1949.
- General Walter B. Smith, who replaced Forrestal starting on August 1, 1950. Smith, born in 1895, served as chief of staff to General of the Army Dwight D. Eisenhower, the Supreme Allied Commander in Europe, during World War II. Eisenhower called him "the general manager of the war." Does the CIA have its own "X-Files"? Smith thought that UFOs could have national security implications and ordered a study to be done. The results remain classified.
- Gordon Gray (1909–1982), a lawyer who from 1937 to 1947 was a newspaper publisher (the *Winston-Salem Journal* and the *Twin City Sentinel*). He was chairman of the board of the Piedmont Publishing Company. Gray was appointed in 1950 as special assistant to President Truman on National Security Affairs. He became national security director of the CIA's Psychological Strategy Board in 1951.
- Top American scientist J. Robert Oppenheimer (1904–1967) was a famous physicist known as the father of the atomic bomb.
- Thornton Page, former professor of astronomy at the University of Chicago; deputy director of the Johns Hopkins Operations Research Office.

- H. P. Robertson, CIA physicist and director of the Weapons Systems Evaluation Group in the Office of the Secretary of Defense. During January 1953, worried that the Soviet Union might attempt to destabilize the United States with tales of a UFO invasion, Robertson suggested to a CIA panel investigating UFOs that the U.S. Air Force start a "debunking" campaign using celebrities saying that they didn't believe in UFOs and we shouldn't either. He also suggested that police keep a close eye on UFO research organizations, since such groups could easily be used for "subversive purposes."
- Sidney W. Souers. President Truman appointed Souers as the first Director of Central Intelligence on January 23, 1946, one day after Truman signed the presidential directive that gave birth to the Central Intelligence Group.
- Dr. Detlev Wulf Bronk, a biophysicist whose specialty was the human nervous system. Bronk was, according to some reports, the leader of an autopsy team for aliens supposedly found near a UFO crash near Roswell, New Mexico, in July 1947.
- John Von Neumann, top American scientist during the 1940s and 1950s.

Does MJ-12 still exist—if indeed it ever existed? Dr. Steven Greer, Director of the Center for the Study of Extraterrestrial Intelligence (CSETI), has reported that the MJ-12 Group is now designated PI-40.

Up third in our whistle-blowing batting order is *Robert Lazar*—he claims to be a former government scientist who had been employed for approximately six months at a secret facility known as S-4 (and nicknamed "Dreamland") within Area 51. He was paid by the U.S. Navy. Lazar says that nine retrieved flying saucers were stored at S-4 and his job was to duplicate "gravity-wave amplifiers" and "anti-matter propulsion systems" used in advance technology flying machines.

Lazar says that the technology comes from extraterrestrials who exist in Area 51 where they work in conjunction with top U.S. scientists and military personnel. He says that there are nine flying saucers of "extraterrestrial origin" kept in a hangar, and that the "gravity-harnessing" machine he was working on used as fuel an element (#115) both unknown and impossible to synthesize on Earth. His experiments and research were done using approximately a quarter ton of element #115 that had been gathered from the flying saucers.

Lazar's story received big exposure because of a November 6, 1989, Las Vegas, Nevada, KLAS-TV UFO documentary produced and narrated by George Knapp.

Because of the fantastic nature of his story, Lazar's credibility was closely scrutinized. That credibility took a hit in 1990 when he pleaded guilty to pandering in connection with his installation of a computer and security system in a Nevada brothel. Of course, his desire to get a whorehouse onto the information superhighway does not make him a liar.

Perhaps the most bizarre of the government employees turned whistle-blowers/disseminators of possible disinformation is our cleanup and fourth hitter: *Milton William "Bill" Cooper*. Cooper's story is told in his best-selling book of hysteria, *Behold a Pale Horse*, which includes lots of words in all caps.

"Most of this knowledge comes directly from, or as a result of, my own research into the TOP SECRET/MAJIC material WHICH I SAW AND READ between the years 1970 and 1973 as a member of the Intelligence Briefing Team of the Commander in Chief of the Pacific Fleet. Since some of this information was derived from sources that I cannot divulge for obvious reasons, and from published sources which I cannot vouch for . . . (this) must be termed a hypothesis. I firmly believe that if the aliens are real, THIS IS THE TRUE NATURE OF THE BEAST. It is the only scenario THAT ANSWERS ALL THE QUESTIONS and places the various fundamental mysteries in an arena that makes sense. It is the only explanation which shows the chronology of events and demonstrates that the chronologies, when assembled, match perfectly," Cooper writes.

Cooper's theory goes like this: Between January 1947 and December 1952 at least sixteen flying saucers crashed on Earth, thirteen of them in the United States. Recovered were sixty-five bodies and one live alien.

"An alien craft was found on February 13, 1948, on a mesa near Aztec, New Mexico. Another craft was located on March 25, 1948, in White Sands Proving Ground. It was 100 feet in diameter. A total of 17 alien bodies were recovered from those two crafts. Of even greater significance was the discovery of a large number of human body parts stored within both of these vehicles. A demon had reared its head and paranoia quickly took hold of everyone 'in the know.' The Secret lid immediately became a Top Secret lid and was screwed down tight. THE SECURITY BLANKET WAS EVEN TIGHTER THAN THAT IMPOSED UPON THE MANHATTAN PROJECT. In the coming years these events were to become the most closely guarded secrets in the history of the world," Cooper writes.

Cooper's story synchs in perfectly with the MJ-12 disinformation, with Secretary of Defense James Forrestal losing his life because he favored disclosing the "alien secret." Truman formed the National Security Agency to help protect that secret. The living alien, Cooper said, had been captured following the Roswell crash and was named EBE, short for Extraterrestrial Biological Entity. EBE loved strawberry ice cream, but got sick and died after a couple of years of captivity. When Cooper listed the sites of the alien crashes, many of them were on or in the vicinity of United States Air Force bases or research-and-development areas for state-of-the-art military aircraft.

Later more aliens came, hideous praying mantis aliens. Cooper believed in the U.S. government's alliance with these aliens that, in exchange for advanced technology such as Velcro and microchips, were allowed to abduct unwilling human subjects for some of the good ol' orifice probing and some efficient harvesting of biological material. It was all terrifying, of course, to the poor individual from whom the material was being harvested. It happened a lot to chubby girls.

In the same mold as Cooper is fifth-place batter, retired Command Sergeant Major Robert O. Dean who wrote in the May/June *Perceptions Magazine* in 1996 that while on duty on the General Staff of Strategic Headquarters, Allied Powers Europe, he observed a "Cosmic Top Secret" briefing that acknowledged the existence of UFOs and a surviving alien captured at Roswell.

Dean claims that technology exists beyond what is publicly known, and that around 1984 "they did indeed pull off a sustained, controlled fusion reaction at Los Alamos, using lasers. In itself, this little piece of scientific knowledge can blow the world up in terms of global economics."

Fusion meant limitless inexpensive power. The oil companies, auto industry, steel industry, and world economy would all be in real trouble.

"To me it's clear as it can be, but I don't know how to get this info out to the masses of people. A few others in this effort and I are trying as best we can, in our limited way, to do it. But we're at a crucial moment in our history as a species and as a race," Dean concluded.

Batting sixth, UFO investigator Bruce Maccabee, Ph.D., was for thirty years a research physicist for the U.S. Navy. He has made much of his reputation reporting information given to him by other military men, such as the stories he was told in the mid-1980s regarding a dogfight between the United States Air Force and a flying saucer told to him by an air force officer whom he only ID'd as "Hawk."

Batting seventh, the whole French space agency. In 2007, the agency effectively blew the whistle on itself and released onto the Internet what they claimed were all 100,000 documents in their files regarding UFOs. Of these, they noted, only twenty or thirty sightings could be corroborated by other evidence; that is, the objects caused marks on the ground or radar picked them up as actual objects. Of those, the most noteworthy was a supposed January 1981 sighting of a flying saucer over Trans-en-Provence, a village inland from the French Riviera. The object was eight feet across and left marks on the ground when it landed. An analysis of the marks indicated that the object had heated up the earth there. The object, it was determined, must have weighed hundreds of pounds and caused plant life in its vicinity to undergo biological changes. Oo-wee-oo.

Whistle-blowers in other parts of the world tend to be former or current government employees as well. Of course, you might say, who else would know these secrets? And that is true enough, but it also leaves open the possibility that those people are still under orders when they go rogue.

Eighth-place hitter Nick Pope, the British "Mr. X-Files" used to work for the British government. And batting ninth is the man who toured the world discussing the Belgium UFO phenomenon, a retired major general in the Belgium army named Wilfred De Brouwer.

Out in the bullpen are the spokesmen for Chilean UFO investigations, Rodrigo Bravo, a captain and pilot for the Aviation Army of Chile, and Dr. Anthony Choy, a disseminator of info regarding UFOs in Peruvian skies and a lawyer for the Peruvian air force.

Time after time, information-hungry UFOlogists have been led by the hand by a full squad of government-connected whistle-blowers whose claims can never quite be proven. Honest researchers often come to the conclusion, as did Nick Redfern, author of *Body Snatchers in the Desert* and *On the Trail of the Saucer Spies*, that "the data I was supplied with suggested that the 'alien' angle of the UFO puzzle is a smoke screen, behind which sensitive military projects (sometimes of a distinctly dark and dubious nature) can be effectively hidden."

MAJOR SOURCES

Benson, Michael. *Inside Secret Societies: What They Don't Want You to Know.* New York: Kensington Publishing, 2005.

Boylan, Dr. Richard J. "Birds of a Feather No Longer: Policy Split Divides 'Aviary' UFO-Secrecy Group." Dr. Boylan Web site, *Drboylan.com.*

Cooper, William. *Behold a Pale Horse.* Flagstaff, AZ: Light Technology Publications, 1991.

"France's Space Agency Puts Its Secret UFO Archive on the Web." *International Herald Tribune—Europe.* 23 March 2007.

Koppang, Randy. "UFO Whistleblower Robert O. Dean Speaks Out." UFO Evidence Web site, www.UFOEvidence.org.

Randle, Kevin D. *Case MJ-12: The True Story Behind the Goverment's UFO Conspiracies.* New York: HarperTorch, 2002.

Redfern, Nick. "UFO Whistleblowers." UFO Mystic Web site, *www.Ufomystic.com.*

84

Darth Cheney: Dr. Evil for the New Millennium?

During the eight years when the president of the United States was a poster boy for nepotism and frat house high jinks, and the VP was, by far, the most powerful and influential man ever to hold that position, people had a right to wonder who was really in charge.

We're talking about George W. and Darth Cheney, of course—and for eight years, it was the common belief Cheney was the one calling the shots from his undisclosed location while stroking his hairless kitty—Dr. Evil for the new millennium, the Man in Charge, the leader of the so-called Free World.

Cheney's agenda, the theory goes, included throwing tasty bone after bone to the corporation he "used to run," jacking up oil prices, and creating record profits for Big Oil. It involved prosecuting two war efforts that borrowed money from the federal trust and funneling it directly, do not pass Go, into the pockets of the military-industrial complex, a white-collar crime that made Enron look like sidewalk three-card-Monty.

Money poured so hard into the funnel that it overflowed. Billions of dollars were missing, licked up by the quickest and most opportunistic reptilian businesspersons. There were sergeants coming home from Iraq with seven figures' worth of cash on them.

So when you're looking for the biggest and greatest conspiracies, you have to take a cool look at how Richard Bruce Cheney acquired so much power and what he did with it once he had it.

He was born in Nebraska, grew up in Wyoming, and earned a masters degree at the University of Wyoming. He joined the Nixon administration at twenty-eight years of age. In 1977, he was elected to the congress representing his home region in Wyoming, then returned to the White House as White House Chief of Staff for President Ford.

Cheney returned to Congress during the Reagan administration. According to some reports, Cheney was trained to run a secret government during the Reagan years, perhaps spent some time inside Mount Weather (see "Underground Bases," Chap. 96.).

According to *www.shoestring911.blogspot.com*, during the 1980s, Dick Cheney and Donald Rumsfeld were key players in a highly classified program. They had great covers, Cheney as a Republican congressman, Rumsfeld as head of the pharmaceutical company G. D. Searle. At least once per year, they both left their day jobs for periods of three or four days and headed to Andrews Air Force Base, near Washington, DC. There they were taken to a secret, possibly underground location within the United States, along with forty to sixty federal officials and one member of the Reagan cabinet. While they were gone, none of their work colleagues, or even their wives, knew where they were.

Cheney served five more terms in Congress, receiving his annual secret government training before becoming secretary of defense for the first president Bush. In that role, he got his hooks into the Pentagon, directing two huge military campaigns in Panama and the Persian Gulf. He oversaw the Pentagon at a time when the Pentagon was in a state of flux, adapting to the post–Cold War age. Cheney put his stamp on the U.S. military.

Some of the fleecing of the Treasury was done right out in the open. When George W. asked Cheney to be his VP, Cheney was forced to step down from his day job running Halliburton, a huge energy company. When 9/11 forced America into retaliation against al-Qaeda and, for reasons largely manufactured, Iraq, Halliburton received billions in government contracts. They were even in charge of feeding the troops. Cheney told the world he was no longer affiliated with Halliburton in any way, all a coincidence, but CBS News in 2003 reported that Cheney's ties with the company remained.

"I've severed all my ties with the company, gotten rid of all my financial interest. I have no financial interest in Halliburton of any kind and haven't had, now, for over three years," he said.

Truth was, at the very least, he retained stock options in the company and received deferred compensation, a money sum reportedly twice as large as his salary when he was CEO. When he left Halliburton, he received a $1 million bonus, and in return, he gave Halliburton the contract to "restore Iraq's southern oil fields." A study into Halliburton's behavior after it received the defense contracts, conducted by Representative Henry Waxman, determined that the company was systematically overcharging the taxpayer and had been "accruing exorbitant costs at a rapid rate."

Halliburton was paid $40 million for providing housing and transportation for teams searching for nonexistent weapons of mass destruction in Iraq. When Democrats tried to investigate Cheney's activities, Cheney went straight to the Supreme Court and asked that the investigations be shut down, arguing that he was above such scrutiny, dealing as he was with matters of national security.

Torture camps for suspected terrorists and illegal wiretaps of U.S. citizens are earmarks of the Dr. Evil Cheney years, but those who believe in these things know that's just the tip of the iceberg.

Many believe Cheney was in Israel's hip pocket, on the take, and corrupt down to his pores. The war in Iraq hadn't been about weapons of mass destruction, of course. It hadn't even been about ending the brutal regime of dictator Saddam Hussein. That was all PR, baby. The idea was to turn Iraq into the new Texas while gaining a foothold in a region that posed a dire threat to Israel. But none of that was ever said out loud by the Bush administration or the Pentagon—or the mainstream press, for that matter—but that was the belief of millions.

From 2001 to 2009, the world was run by one man with a terrifying sneer. He was a man who worked in a subterranean way, the leader of the shadow government, the puppet master of the New World Order: Darth Cheney.

MAJOR SOURCES

Chapman, Bob. "Crimes of Halliburton: Fraud, Fraud & More Fraud." Conspiracy Planet Web site, www.conspiracyplanet. com.
"Cheney, Rumsfeld, and the Secret Government." Shoestring Web site, www.Shoestring911.blogspot.com.
Curry, Tom. "Cheney's Day Before Supreme Court." MSNBC Web site, www.msnbc.com.
Murphy, Jarrett. "Cheney's Halliburton Ties Remain." CBS News Web site, www.cbsnews.com.

85

Kaspar Hauser: Paranormal Feral Boy

Was the biological heir to the House of Baden spirited away as an infant so that a man named Leopold would instead ascend to the throne?

In 1828, in Nüremberg, Germany, a very strange teenaged boy was discovered. Dressed like a peasant and sounding drunk and dumb, the boy carried two letters to the captain of the local cavalry regiment. The first letter, purportedly from the boy's adoptive father, asked that he be trained as a rider. The letter said that the boy had never been allowed to leave the house, and if he didn't join the cavalry, he would end up beaten to death and hung from a chimney.

The second letter appeared to be from the boy's mother. It said his name was Kaspar, he'd been born on April 30, 1812, and his real father was dead, so whoever took him in should feel free to supply him with a second name of his or her choice. The mother claimed that she was a "poor little girl who could not feed herself."

A close look at the two letters revealed that although an effort had been made to disguise the fact, the same hand wrote both. The captain took the boy in and noticed that his feet had no calluses and were soft like a baby's. The boy, though healthy, lacked manual dexterity and walked like a toddler. He ate only bread and butter, choking up everything else, and seemed unaware of gender differences. He showed no embarrassment when the captain's wife bathed him, and it would be interesting to know how often that happened.

At first his only words were "boy," which referred to himself, and "horse," which referred to his only toy. In the beginning, he called all animals horse. He had a gentle disposition and became upset if any living thing was harmed, even an insect. The first time he saw a candle, he stuck his finger in the flame, then cried out with pain as he was unexpectedly burned.

Shown a mirror, Kaspar tried to touch his reflection and tried to look behind the mirror to see where the image was coming from. Shiny objects grabbed his attention.

A physician was called in to give the boy a thorough examination. The doctor determined that the boy was not dull witted as had been feared, but was suffering from a complete lack of sensory experience. The boy would always be more comfortable in the dark, and indeed seemed to others to be able to see in the dark because he had been kept without light for the first part of his life.

The doctor also discovered that there was an abnormality in Kaspar's knees caused by his inability to stand up for many years. Eventually, he learned to speak in broken sentences and said that he remembered previously seeing only one person. He'd lived in a coffin-shaped box, seven feet long, three feet wide, and a foot and a half high. There was no light. He had straw to sleep on, and the meals were bread and water.

When the water was bitter, he would fall asleep and wake up with fresh clothes on and trimmed nails.

One day, he recalled, a man taught him to write the words "Kaspar Hauser" and then carried him outside. The light and the air caused the boy to faint, and when he awoke, he was in Nürnberg with the notes in his pocket.

The boy, now known as Kaspar Hauser, became a well-known curiosity and the city's dignitaries all came to visit. He drew crowds. People came from miles around to see Kaspar eat or sleep. Some noted that the boy bore a tremendous resemblance to the family of the Grand Duke of Baden, a man whose two heirs to the throne both supposedly died as infants.

When the duke died in 1830, his successor was Grand Duke Leopold, who got the job because the previous duke, so it was said, had no sons. To prevent any questions, Leopold granted custody of Kaspar to his friend Lord Stanhope and notified the world that the boy was a fraud, a Hungarian with no ties to the previous duke.

But the well-known German jurist Anselm Ritter von Feuerbach theorized that Kaspar was the son of the duke, who had been stolen away as an infant so someone else could become duke. He said that Kaspar had been exchanged for the dead baby of a peasant.

Feuerbach died under suspicious circumstances in 1833, starting rumors that he had been poisoned because he had discovered proof of Kaspar's heritage. Despite the rumors, no proof ever surfaced.

That same year, Kaspar himself was lured out into the open by a promise of evidence regarding his real father. But it was a trick, and when Kaspar showed up for the clandestine meeting, he was stabbed.

This was not the first time Kaspar had been attacked. He had survived an 1829 incident in which he had been attacked while sitting alone in an outhouse.

He stumbled home from his clandestine meeting and died from his wounds three days later. The story went that the Grand Duchess of Baden, Kaspar's supposed mother, wept for days upon hearing of his death.

According to Dr. Bruce D. Perry in his book *Childhood Experience and the Expression of Genetic Potential*, Kaspar's body was autopsied, and his brain was found to be unusual. Kaspar had a small cortical size and few nondistinct cortical gyri, all consistent with cortical atrophy.

"In 1996," Mysterious People reported, "DNA analysis of bloodstains found on Hauser's clothes was undertaken at the laboratories of Forensic Science Service in Birmingham, England, and in the LMU Institute of Legal Medicine at the University of Munich. An attempt was made to match Hauser's DNA to living Baden descendants. Results showed no link. Apparently, Kaspar wasn't the Prince of Baden." But wait. "In 2002, it was discovered that the original samples used for the testing had not, as claimed, been from Hauser's clothes. New samples were obtained from the boy's hat, trousers, and hair curls in the Feuerbach collection of Hauser artifacts, and this time DNA tests were positive. Results showed a 95 percent match to the DNA of Astrid von Medinger, a descendant of Stephanie de Beauharnais." Kaspar was a prince who'd been plucked from his destiny by a history-altering conspiracy.

MAJOR SOURCES

Bonderson, J. *The Great Pretenders*. New York: Norton, 2005.
"Feral Children: The Unsolved Mystery of Kaspar Hauser—Wild Child of Europe." Mysterious People Web site, www.mysteriouspeople.com/Hauser1.htm.
Feuerbach, Anselm Von. *Kaspar Hauser, An Account of an Individual Kept in a Dungeon, Separated from All Communication with the World, from Early Childhood to About the Age of Seventeen*. London: Simpkin and Marshall, 1833.

"Kaspar Hauser." www.feralchildren.com/en/showchild.php?
    ch=kaspar.
Masson, Jeffrey Moussaieff. *Lost Prince: The Unsolved Mystery
    of Kaspar Hauser.* New York: Free Press, 1996.
Newton, Michael. *Savage Girls and Wild Boys: A History of
    Feral Children.* London: Faber and Faber, 2002.

86

Frankenfood: Is Your Dinner Genetically Engineered?

"**I**t's alive! *It's aliiive!*" Worse, it's on our dinner plate. Flee! Frankenfood! Fleeee!

The term "Frankenfood" refers to food derived from genetically modified plants and animals. Yum. Scientific meddling might be socially acceptable when it comes to creating living beings out of an assemblage of dead parts, but when scientists playing the role of God start mutating what's on our dinner plate. Well, it's enough to give you the willies.

As Mary Shelley pointed out, when you mess with nature, nature messes back—often in grotesque ways. Brrrrr.

K. C. Cole of the *Los Angeles Times* once wrote, "It's only natural that we cringe at the artificial: it goes against the grain. So it's no real wonder that many people are feeling

729

uncomfortable about the recent proliferation of genetically engineered crops."

Genetic engineering means that scientists have changed the DNA of a living organism, the fingerprint of the organism, the thing that makes it specific—unique. The scientists are molecular biologists, and they accomplish this amazing feat by using enzymes instead of a scalpel to perform microsurgery. Strands of DNA are cut in some places and attached in others, using the enzymes. The desired result is always to make that plant or animal produce the most food. But changing one aspect of the organism's makeup without disrupting the others is a tricky business. By changing the DNA of a plant or animal scheduled to become food, we change what it is on the most fundamental level.

The current research concerns vectors, which are strands of DNA that can, like a virus, enter a living cell and insert copies of itself into its DNA. Scientists hope to one day be able to create their own designer vectors, which can then be inserted into an organism, making it different in the desired way. The fruit from a tomato plant will be more plentiful and larger, perhaps even quicker to ripen or more resistant to frost. To make a tomato plant thrive in the cold, the biologist might find an organism that has this trait, such as a trout that thrives when swimming in near frozen water, isolate the DNA strain that gives the organism that trait, duplicate it, and insert it as a vector into the DNA of the tomato plant.

Okay, enough of the science lesson. Let's get to the dangers of this kind of research—the dangers, grotesque and otherwise. First of all, there's always the chance that the insertion of foreign DNA will kill the organism. When DNA is formed through traditional breeding, the mating organisms are usually similar, and the DNA is joined in entire strands, in a fixed sequence. The result is usually predictable. Not so when scientists often try to link two types of dissimilar genes; the genetic engineering can't even approximate the kind of specificity accomplished every minute of every day by the birds and the bees. Currently, scientists are fairly precise at plucking out the proper DNA for transplantation, but they still can't pinpoint where the DNA strand will attach itself in its new host. The DNA affixes itself in a random fashion, and the plant, instead of growing huge fruit, might grow huge roots and drown itself.

It is this impreciseness in the cause and effect of even the most modern experiments that has led experts to say genetic engineering is like performing heart surgery with a shovel.

When dealing with food, there is always the potential that an unwanted change caused by a designer vector attaching itself in an unexpected spot might render the food without nourishment or make it poisonous. The danger could be both to the people who consume the mutated food and to the land in which the crops are grown. Bulbous roots might suck all of a key nutrient out of the soil, leaving the land barren until it can be artificially replenished.

And the poisonous tomato might look perfectly normal. It might look, smell, taste, and smell like a perfect tomato, yet be mutated in a deadly way. Those who created and distributed these tomatoes wouldn't know there was something wrong until tomato eaters began to drop—or grow a second set of teeth. An unwanted result of a mutation might be an affected immune system. Entire crops might be wiped out by a previously harmless fungus.

There is also the very real threat that if a mutation did turn out to be harmful, it might be difficult to stop. The wind, insects, and birds all carry seeds from one place to another. Pollen from mutated plants could find its way into unaffected plants, causing a multigenerational mutation with dire consequences.

From a consumer point of view, deception might be a concern as well. Simply using a billion digital calculations, scientists may be able to design plants and meat to appear fresh long after their expiration date. Cosmetically, the food might stay attractive longer, but that doesn't mean its healthfulness and nutritional value hasn't suffered as usual from not being fresh.

Another concern involves the organisms from which the vectors will be plucked. If the donor organism isn't part of the food chain, will resulting mutations be inedible?

A lot of the conspiracies in this fat book you're reading might be considered, ahem, a little paranoid. You know, a little—but not so this one. Back in the early 1990s, a genetic engineering experiment did go wrong. A genetically engineered bacterium was used to create a substance called tryptophan, best known as the amino acid in turkey that makes everyone fall asleep in front of the football game on Thanksgiving. Scientists wanted to make the substance, called "Nature's Prozac," in quantity. Unfortunately, to put it mildly, the man-made tryptophan created by the mutated bacteria had a bad effect on people—a possibility that wasn't considered until the pills, manufactured in Japan and on sale everywhere, left 37 people dead, 1,500 partially paralyzed, and 5,000 more temporarily disabled.

One improvement scientists hoped to make in crops through genetic alteration was to make them more resistant to the poisons farmers use to kill weeds and parasites. The unexpected side effect is that farmers, confident now that the pesticides and herbicides won't hurt their crops, are using the poisons in more plentiful quantities, causing environmental problems.

The bottom line is that scientists have approached genetic engineering as if it were just as natural as normal breeding. But there's no evidence to support that thinking. And if you think this should be nipped in the bud, it's already too late. A huge percentage of our processed foods now contain a genetically altered soybean that can be produced cheaply and in great quantity. Remember that guy who ran onto the stage when Dylan was singing at the Grammies many years ago? He had SOY BOMB written on his naked upper torso. Well, now you know what he was protesting against. Speaking for most humans, soy residue now permeates from our every cell, so saturated are we with the bean and its by-products. The growing number of people with soy allergies (gee, wonder why that's happening) now find themselves with a very short menu.

Genetic engineering and germ warfare research are not mutually exclusive. As the mutant tryptophan demonstrated, a scientist seeking a balm for people's anxieties can end up killing them in agonizing ways.

In order to get to an organism's DNA, some breaking, entering, and asexual reproducing is required, and bacteria and viruses are the critters that know how to bust into a cell and, like the world's fastest Xerox machine, copy themselves a billion times over.

Can scientists control the bacteria and viruses they use when they genetically alter a crop? No. Not even close. And the technology that is being developed with the food experiments can be used to create diseases. Why would a scientist want to create a disease? Two reasons: One, he wants to turn it into a weapon and use it during war. Or he is doing legitimate medical research, in essence seeking the vaccine for a disease that does not yet exist. In either case, the possibility for disaster is extreme.

A product of genetic engineering that conspiracy theorists fear might end up hurting a lot of people is aspartame, which some claim causes illness in those who use enough of it. The product was developed by Searle, which was being run at the time by Donald Rumsfeld, long associated in conspiracy theories with the Shadow Government and the New World Order.

The story goes that the FDA (Food and Drug Administration) only okayed the product—despite a 1971 study that showed it caused lesions on the brains of infant mice—because of the powerful people behind its creation, manufacture, and distribution.

Aspartame was developed back in the 1960s by a Searle

chemist named James Schlatter, who was trying to develop an ulcer drug at the time. The stuff was two hundred times sweeter than sugar but had no calories.

The first safety tests didn't go well. Lab monkeys and mice who took the stuff developed bleeding brains and cancer. The stuff ate away at the nervous system, caused malignancies, and, for good measure, showed signs of being highly addictive.

Yet, when it came time to get approval from the FDA, Searle handed over the results of one hundred tests, all of which indicated that the fake sugar was safe.

The head of the FDA at that time, a Reagan appointee, was Dr. Arthur Hull Hayes Jr. who had been involved in chemical-warfare studies while working for the Defense Department. At the time of his appointment, Dr. Hayes had conducted tests in Maryland on army volunteers regarding the effects of a mind-disorienting drug. One of Hayes's first decisions as head of the FDA was to approve aspartame. Since then, more than three quarters of the complaints to the FDA have concerned products containing aspartame.

In Europe today there is a major push by an agricultural company called Monsanto, developers of innovative farming products, to feed the world with its new genetically mutated "maize" (corn). The push continues despite studies that show animals who feasted on the science fiction maize showed statistically significant changes to their blood and vital organs. The study was followed by a concerted effort to suppress the results. The decision should be simple. The stuff isn't good. Back to the drawing board. But that's not the way it works. Just like the soy bomb and aspartame, there seems to be a certain inevitability that, before long, the genetically mutated maize will be in everything we eat, an invisible new factor in our deteriorating human ecology.

Major Sources

Cole, K. C. "Genetically Altered Food Unnatural? Not Really." *Los Angeles Times*, 21 October 1999.

"Frankenfood." Word Spy Web site, www.wordspy.com.

Hightower, Jim. *Let's Stop Beating Around the Bush*. New York: Viking Press, 2004.

"Monsanto GM Maize Conspiracy Revealed." GM-Free Ireland Web site, www.gmfreeireland.org.

"What Are the Dangers: Fundamental Weaknesses of the Concept." Safe Food Web site, www.safe-food.org/-issue/dangers.html.

87

The "Miracle" at Fatima

Any attempt to rationalize the miracles of Fatima, which took place in Portugal during World War I, must fly in the face of the Catholic Church, which has recognized the occurrences here as genuinely miraculous. The Catholic Church does not recognize miracles every day, so why this one?

It's because the ultimate event, the dancing of the sun, took place before an estimated 70,000 spectators—about the same number of live eyewitnesses to each year's Super Bowl.

But those 70,000 showed up at Fatima to see a miracle, and they would have been greatly disappointed if they hadn't. Whether some trick was behind the dancing sun, the expectations of the crowd may be important. In its yearning to believe, suspending their disbelief would have been like taking candy from babies.

For skeptics, the real trick was to get a crowd that big

gathered in one place with such a common expectation. The hype must be examined, skeptics believe. Who had the charisma to convince that many people, many strangers, that a miracle was about to occur?

For that answer, we'll have to take a closer look at the little girl whose word all those people were taking when they traveled to that pasture on October 13, 1917, and the events, all of which centered around her, that led up to the dancing sun.

Lucia dos Santos began claiming that strange things were happening to her during the summer of 1915 when she was only eight. While saying the rosary with three other girls, on three separate occasions, the girls claimed to see "a white man without a head floating in the air."

The girls further described the apparition as resembling "a statue made of snow rendered almost transparent by the rays of the sun." No one believed the girls. Even Lucia's mother called it "childish nonsense." The children were taunted by other children because they had "seen things."

During March of the following year Lucia—now with her two cousins Jacinta and Francisco, both of whom were subservient to Lucia and would remain at Lucia's side for the duration of the miraculous sequence—were playing by the side of Cabeço Hill.

While watching the wind sway the tops of nearby pine trees, Lucia and her cousins saw a transparent boy about fifteen years old who said, "Don't be afraid. I am the angel of peace."

The children saw the angel twice. The first time he told them to pray, and the second time he gave them Communion, a Catholic ceremony whereby a worshipper symbolically consumes, internalizes, the body of Christ by eating a wafer of bread.

After seeing the angel, Francisco complained of fatigue: "I like very much to see the angel, but afterwards we can't do anything. We can't walk or talk. We don't know what's wrong."

On May 13, 1917, Lucia, now ten years old and her two cousins, Francisco, nine, and Jacinta, seven, were at the Cova da Iria, a pasture said to be the site of an ancient cult of Isis.

There was a flash of light that startled the two girls. Francisco could not see it. Then a "cloud of light" appeared over a holm oak tree. The cloud gradually focused itself into the image of a beautiful woman.

The vision said, "Don't be afraid, I won't hurt you. I am from heaven."

The vision told them they should return to that spot on the thirteenth of each month and she would return. She promised that she would reveal her identity at the end of a six-month span.

She told the children that all three of them were going to go to heaven, but that Francisco would have to say many rosaries. When Lucia relayed the message to the boy, Francisco could suddenly see the woman, but he still could not hear her voice. The woman instructed the children to pray for an end to the Great War.

Just before the vision went away, she held up the palms of her hands, from which came strong beams of light. The light filled the girls' bodies, and they dropped to their knees under its power. The vision told them to say the rosary and they felt great joy. The figure, in the meantime, "vanished into the sky."

Initially, the girls agreed to keep the strange occurrence a secret, but Lucia was barely home when the whole story came pouring out of her. Only now she was positive that the visitation had come from the Virgin Mary herself!

While her mother, as usual, raised a skeptical eyebrow, many townspeople now took the children seriously—at least seriously enough to take a stroll over to the oak after a month rolled around. On June 13, about fifty curious townsfolk accompanied them.

The spectators did not see any beautiful woman in the sky. They saw the children oohing and ahhing as the Virgin Mary floated downward from heaven and hovered amid the holm oak's branches. Afterward, Lucia reported that a strange door appeared, and the woman disappeared through it.

The witnesses did report some strange phenomena, however. It was said that during the time the children were in the presence of the ecstatic vision, the others could hear a strange buzzing sound.

A "thunderclap" that sounded as if it came from beneath the ground could be heard just before the vision left. Some eyewitnesses reported seeing some of the branches on the oak tree being bent as if by invisible forces. Those branches, it was said, remained bent downward for an hour after the vision had left, before returning to their normal upright position.

The eyewitness reports were such that the crowd was much bigger for the July 13 appearance, estimated at 5,000 people, at which time the lady—again visible only to the children—told Lucia a "special revelation" that she forbade the girl to reveal. Lucia was instructed to tell the crowd that they should all come back on October 13 because she was going to perform a miracle that will affirm everyone's belief in God.

Skeptics wonder how Lucia, a child, could possess the powers of illusion to promise a miracle that will fool thousands of spectators—and then pull it off?

At this point it becomes necessary to believe in a conspiracy, an organized mind-control program, in order to claim that nothing supernatural occurred. The only alternative is to believe that somehow Lucia used the power of suggestion alone to convince 70,000 eyewitnesses that they were seeing the sun dance in the sky. You have to admit, it isn't the sort of con job you see every day.

The conspiracy notion takes on some credence when you take into account the strong political motive to modify Portuguese belief systems. Portugal was "plagued" by increasing anticlerical sentiments in the midst of a world war and a Russian communist revolution. The Vatican—largely because of its vulnerable location, location, location—considered the choice between fascism and communism a no-brainer. With the rise of communism in Europe and its antireligion stance, any attempt to pump power into the Catholic Church in Europe would have to be interpreted as anticommunist.

During that July visit to the oak tree, eyewitnesses reported seeing a white cloud emerge from the tree. Now the reports were coming with poetic embellishment. Again the vision, invisible only to the pure children, bent the branches "as if in going away the Lady's dress had trailed over them."

The children were not allowed to visit the oak tree on August 13. Instead, the police from the nearby town of Ourém arrested the children and kept them in jail for the entire day. When they were released, the children claimed that the police had threatened to boil them in oil if they did not admit that they were behind all of the trickery at the Fatima holm oak. But the children stuck to their guns and maintained that their story was true.

Despite the children's absence, another large crowd had gathered at the tree, and they were treated to a light show that only further whipped up anticipation of the promised October miracle.

First the crowd heard a loud clap of thunder. Then some saw a "luminous globe wandering in the sky." The clouds took on all the colors of the rainbow and reflected light such that it colored the faces of the spectators looking up at them. "Flowers of light" were said to fall from the sky. One witness heard "the roar of a rocket." If Lucia was solely responsible for a hoax, how did she, in jail under threat of torture, create a light show like the one described by the eyewitnesses?

On September 13, at least 30,000 spectators showed up at the pasture for what was being billed as the visitation of the Blessed Virgin Mary. It was a Happening, a festival of exaltation. Again the globe of light was seen wandering around the sky, only the children—who were not taken into custody a second time—predictably saw the globe as the figure of a woman.

A stream of light globules was seen pouring from the sky. The globules reached the ground and instantly dissolved into nothing. This final happening whipped the Portuguese public into a frenzy.

By October 13, the date of the promised miracle, the entire area surrounding the holm oak was packed with people. The crowd probably would have been bigger but for a torrential downpour throughout the morning. A buzz went through the crowd when the three children arrived and took up their customary place near the tree. A long, long ninety minutes went by before anything happened.

Then, Lucia screamed, "Look at the sun!"

As the crowd looked up, a globe of light, described by some as the sun, began to do strange things in the sky. Some said that it pinwheeled in the sky and shot colors outward. It was called a "catherine wheel" and likened to a "spinning bicycle wheel." Once again these lights were so bright that they were said to color the faces of the spectators.

A professor of natural sciences at Coimbra University was at Fatima at the time of the miracle and wrote that he saw "a disc with a clear-cut rim, luminous and shining, but which did not hurt the eyes. It looked like a glazed circular piece cut from a mother-of-pearl shell."

Others said that it swung in the sky from side to side. Once again the flowers of light rained their petals to the earth, but this time the globules dissolved before striking the ground.

Those who have tried to explain the Fatima occurrences away as some sort of natural phenomenon ignore the unlikelihood that Lucia would have been able to predict such a thing.

Skeptics also point out that people in other parts of the world, illuminated as they were by the very same sun, saw nothing unusual in the sky at the time of the Fatima miracle.

However, those skeptics ignore reports coming from as far as twenty miles away from Fatima that there was a strange object hovering in the sky. Of course, it was the crowd's

assumption that the object in the sky—sophisticated fire-
works or something—was the sun to begin with. Most reports would indicate that the object was not in the correct
portion of the sky to be the actual sun, and remember it was
a stormy day with a thick cloud cover overhead.

In the meantime, the crowd was near panic with fear. Many
were convinced that the world was about to end. Folks collapsed in prayer, convinced that they were about to die.

A reporter for a local newspaper who was on the scene
filed this report the following day: "The sun appeared like a
dull silver plate spinning around in a circular movement as if
moved by electricity." A competing newspaper referred to
the object in the sky as "a shining disc of dull silver."

While the crowd saw the dancing sun, again only the children claimed to see the Virgin Mary. Lucia told the crowd
that the woman had identified herself before them as "the
Lady of the Rosary."

It has long been believed that Lucia announced to the crowd
that the Blessed Virgin Mary had given her several predictions
during her October visit. But it is important to note that the
first mention of these predictions come in Lucia's memoirs,
which were written between 1935 and 1941, long after the
predictions had come to pass. Anyway, according to Lucia,
the Virgin Mary told her of the predictions during her July visit.
The first was that neither Jacinta nor Francisco had long to
live. Both died in the influenza epidemic of 1919 and 1920.
(It has been said that Lucia spoke of the predictions regarding the deaths of her cousins before she wrote about it in her
memoirs, but no one claimed Lucia spoke of predictions before 1927, seven years after both of her cousins had passed
away.)

In her written memoirs, Lucia also claimed that during the
July visit the Virgin Mary made the Earth transparent so that
she and her cousins could look straight down into hell.

The Virgin Mary had also predicted that the Great War
would end but that there would be a second worse world war

if mankind (i.e., the Communists) did not cease offending God by ignoring the laws of the Catholic Church.

There was one more secret that the Virgin Mary allegedly gave to Lucia, but she was sworn never to reveal it. Legend has it that Lucia wrote the last secret down and put it in a sealed envelope, which the Vatican keeps locked up to this day.

Theories about the contents of the last prediction range from scenarios for the end of the world to the "anti-Christ shall become Pope." Stories once circulated that Pope John Paul I, who died only a month after becoming pontiff, had a heart attack and expired when he read what was in the envelope. Still another story says that he threatened to reveal the prediction to the world, and he was murdered. There is no evidence to support either theory.

The two cousins, when first asked about the Marian visitations (an occurrence in which the Blessed Virgin Mary appears to one or more people), said that they didn't understand the words the lady had spoken but that Lucia understood them. Later, after the impressionable cousins had heard Lucia talk of what the vision said, they too quoted the visitor as if they had heard her.

The impression that the cousins were merely following Lucia's lead occurred to others, including Lucia's mother who expressed concern that her daughter was a fake and that she was misleading half the world.

According to Sandra L. Zimdars-Swartz in her 1991 book *Encountering Mary*, "All accounts agree that [Lucia] was the only one of the three seers to interact with both her vision and with the crowd, carrying on conversations with both while her two cousins stood by silently. She has said, moreover, and probably not incorrectly, that Francisco and Jacinta had been accustomed to following her directives before the apparition began, that they turned to her for guidance afterwards, and that it was she who convinced them that they had to be very careful in their experiences."

Today we can see how similar this incident is to modern UFO sightings. Eyewitness descriptions at the site of silver discs in the sky make this comparison inevitable. The Fatima incident took place at the dawn of aerial warfare. An early wartime strategy theorized that if you made an aerial attack appear sacred to the enemy, the enemy would not shoot it down. We don't know what method could be used to make a bomber plane look sacred, and we don't know whether the theory was ever tested, but if it was, the occurrences at Fatima fit the bill as a feasibility study—one with a strong anticommunist message built in.

MAJOR SOURCES

"The Fatima Network: Our Lady of Fatima Online." Fatima Web site, www.fatima.org.
Fernandes, Fernando, Joaquim Fernandes, and Raul Berenguel, comps. *Fatima Revisited: The Apparition Phenomenon in Ufology, Psychology, and Science*. San Antonio, TX: Anomolist Books, 2008.
Warfield, Benjamin B. *Miracles: Yesterday and Today, True and False*. Grand Rapids, MI: Eerdmans, 1965.
Zimdars-Swartz, Sandra L. *Encountering Mary*. Princeton, NJ: Princeton University Press, 1991.

88

The Birth of Nuclear Terrorism: The Poisoned Russian Spy

Got something nasty to say about the Russian government? You'd better think twice. Despite the breakup of the Soviet Union, the fall of the Iron Curtain, and the end of the Cold War, the Kremlin uses assassins to rid the world of its critics.

You remember the old days, when *Time* magazine called the Soviet KGB "one of the most ruthless organizations on earth" with functions equivalent to the CIA, the FBI, the Secret Service, and the Pentagon combined. Back then, the whole world was afraid of the KGB, and Russians knew better than to badmouth Soviet officials or communist ideology. Such trash talk had to be uttered with the utmost discretion. The KGB was everywhere and their assassins never lacked for targets.

There was a soaking of liquid affairs (murder and assassination, hands wet with blood). Both Nikita Khrushchev and Leonid Brezhnev had brought with them an early phase of hope, but those promises went unfulfilled. It remained a country that could put satellites in space but couldn't build a decent refrigerator—and new moaners and groaners surfaced faster than assassins could liquidate them.

The KGB remained busy, and its violence was both public and publicized. There could be no doubt: if Russians wanted to stay safe, they thought like everyone else and did what they were told. The KGB numbered a half million, with plenty of "special-purpose forces" with licenses to kill. Its expertise was in *mokrie deal* or "wet affairs." The assassins worked for the KGB's Department V, the organization's "Executive Action Department."

But when the Soviet Union crumbled, a naïve and dangerous myth permeated the United States: The "Big Bad Bear," the evil empire, was no more, and in its stead was a Russia eager to chant the *koans* of democracy as their new twenty-first-century mantra. The oppression of the old days was gone, and Russians were experiencing freedom of speech and thought just as we sometimes enjoy here in America. With the Cold War over, the Pentagon's budget was cut. Everything, thanks to Ronald Reagan, was beautiful, man.

Like most myths, this one was substantially wishful thinking. To expect Russia's security forces to change that completely so rapidly, was unrealistic. Russia remained a battle-scarred nation, whose borders had been repeatedly invaded throughout its history. It remained suspicious, even paranoid. The enemy without was always a hazard, but so was the enemy within. If Russia was to survive, everyone still needed to remain on the same page. Thus, dissidents continued to be disposed of just like in the old days.

But assassins no longer worked exclusively in bullets and arsenic. For the New Age they developed a new technique, one so closely associated with terrorism that the implications to possible future dissidents—as well as to other super-powers who might consider bully tactics—was clear: the big bear still had its teeth and its claws. It was still home to countless nuclear weapons and the technology to deliver them to their targets.

The deaths never really stopped. Georgi Markov, a dissi-dent writer, was dispatched with a poison pellet from an um-brella, perhaps a death blow administered by Dealey Plaza's iconic "Umbrella Man." Ukrainian presidential candidate Viktor Yushchenko was poisoned. An anti-Russian American business writer named Paul Klebnikov was shot down mob style.

That said, our story starts on November 1, 2006, when a former Russian spy named Alexander Litvinenko was poisoned in London. He survived for three weeks before succumbing. During those weeks, Litvinenko said he had been poisoned after meeting with a contact who claimed to have informa-tion connecting the Russian government with the Moscow shooting death of journalist Anna Politkovskaya, a frequent critic of Russian president Vladimir Putin and the Kremlin. Litvinenko fell ill only hours after that meeting, which took place in a London sushi restaurant. The poison worked slowly, however, and the victim was able to talk intermittently for fifteen hours with Scotland Yard investigators.

Doctors couldn't be sure at first what was killing the man, but his combination of symptoms—yellowish skin, sunken eyes, hair loss, dehydration, and heart complications—tended to indicate radioactivity or thallium exposure. Initial tests were inconclusive.

Litvinenko was, during the last years of the Soviet Union, a KGB agent. He subsequently became a colonel with the Russian Federal Security Service. His specialties were counter-terrorism and the infiltration of organized crime. In 1998, he accused his supervisors of being behind the assassination of Russian tycoon Boris Berezovsky. He was arrested for insub-ordination and ended up fleeing Russia in 2000. The United

Kingdom granted him and his wife Marina political asylum but, obviously, not security. He was a stubborn and courageous man, who continued his dissident behavior from his new home in England. Financed by a sympathetic Russian tycoon, Litvinenko lived in a London suburb with his wife and son and chased a career as a freelance writer. His wife Marina was a ballroom dance teacher, and his son Anatoly was enrolled in an international school.

Litvinenko had been a vocal supporter of anti-Moscow Chechen separatists. The victim accused Moscow of bombing a series of apartment buildings as a pretext to Russia's 1999 invasion of Chechnya and of killing opponents of Putin. The Kremlin denied having anything to do with Litvinenko's death and suggested that some of his London underworld connections might have poisoned him.

The victim had gone out of his way to earn Putin as an enemy. Going well beyond criticizing the president's policies, Litvinenko wrote a published article that accused Putin of being a pedophile, claiming that the evidence was clear once one examined the "blank spots" in Putin's biography. The article was unsubstantiated.

On his final day of good health, according to his wife, he planned to spend the day at a series of meetings in central London and return home to a home-cooked meal. That evening, at home after dinner, he began to feel queasy, a nausea that would, as it turned out, never go away. It wasn't until the second day of pain that the victim began to suspect he'd been poisoned. Marina took him to the hospital where doctors at first thought he was suffering from a gastric flu. Only after symptoms persisted did they diagnose poisoning.

He endured twenty-two days of intense suffering. Many men would not have lasted that long, but Litvinenko maintained the superb physical fitness he had known since his days as a secret agent.

The deaths of Litvinenko and Politkovskaya were another patch on a Russian quilt of death—a continuation of a pattern that indicated to the outside world how Russia's handling of dissidents wasn't much different in the twenty-first century than it had been for most of the twentieth century. In 2004 in Qatar, Russian agents killed the president in exile of the breakaway republic of Chechnya with a car bomb. The agents were captured, tried, and convicted—then given a hero's welcome when they were returned to Moscow.

It was eventually determined that it *was* radioactivity that killed Litvinenko, specifically exposure to the extremely rare Polonium 210. (That substance, by the way, is also the possibly deadliest substance found in cigarette smoke.) It was a horrible, slow, and painful way to die. London police told the press that the case set a new precedent as far as they were concerned—the first case of nuclear terrorism. The murder could not have been more cruel. Along with news of the murder, every newspaper in the world carried a photo of the victim, lying hairless and gray in his hospital bed, eyes clouded with pain and despair.

According to Paul Joyal, a security consultant and expert on Russia, quoted on MSNBC, the message sent to the world by Litvinenko's bizarre murder was clear. It was, Joyal said, that "if you speak out against the Kremlin, no matter who you are, where you are, we will find you and we will silence you—in the most horrible way possible."

MAJOR SOURCES

Curry, Ann. "Last Days of a Secret Agent: Who Killed Alexander Litvinenko?" MSNBC Web site, www.msnbc.com.
"Poisoned Spy Accused Putin of Being a Paedophile." *London Daily Mail*, 20 November 2006.
"Russian Former Spy Dies." CNN Web site, www.cnn.com.
"Secret Emperors and Shadowy Assassins." *Time*, 18 February 1985.

89

Beware the Vril Overlords: Infiltration of the Lizard People

Here's a conspiracy that's downright creepy—and slithery, and with a forked and flicking tongue.

Reptile aliens—on two legs, like humans, have become, since the 1980s, a staple in UFOlogical conspiracy theories. How the reptoids arrived on earth varies depending on the theory. Some believe they've been here for thousands of years, perhaps leftovers from a prehistoric civilization, living a parallel existence to humans. Others believe they are more recent arrivals, extraterrestrials dropped off by a flying saucer. But no matter how they got here and what we call them, they're hideously ugly, and their presence is mad malevolence.

Men who resemble lizards or amphibians have been part of man's mythology dating back to funky, funky, chic days of the ancient Greeks when it was believed that Cecrops I, the first mythical king of Athens, was half human, half snake. Medusa had John Holmesian snakes growing out of her scalp rather than hair. Pausanias was a winged Greek god who, like many men on an intoxicated prowl, flew with serpents between his legs.

In India, there is the legendary Naga, reptile people who live underground and ocassionally interact with man on the surface. Naga, it is said, once lived on a continent in the Indian Ocean, a huge land mass that, like Atlantis, was swallowed by the sea.

In Japan, some believe in *kappa*, lizard men who live along rivers and feed off human passersby.

In China and Korea, there is the belief that a strain of humans exist whose ancestors, some of them at least, were dragons. The Book of Genesis features a talking serpent, who had Eve's ear and was instrumental in setting the Bible's plot into motion.

And the list goes on and on—but is any of this even scientifically feasible? The answer is a resounding maybe—but only if you are willing to squint your third eye and let your intellect blur.

We'll wait. Ready? Here goes.

Paleontologist Dale Russell has theorized that had the Chicxulub meteorite not wiped out the dinosaurs, existing dinosaurs might have evolved into intelligent, even human-like, beings who walked on two legs. Russell's vision of the dinosauroid had three fingers on either hand, one partially opposed, and large eyes. Like people, these creatures would have navels, but unlike male humans, all genitalia would be internal. Their language would sound like the songs of birds.

Modern sightings of reptile people are as common as they ever were. Residents of South Carolina have been periodically spotting a "lizard man" for decades. The most recent of these reports came in February 2008 when a Bishopville, North Carolina, woman named Dixie Dawson reported that "the whole front half of our van is chewed up. There are bite marks right through the front grill. Both sides of the van above the wheel wells were bitten and the metal is bent like a piece of paper."

Although sightings date back to 1972, the most famous occurred in 1988 when seventeen-year-old Christopher Davis, who was changing a tire on a deserted road at 2:00 A.M., reported, "I looked back and saw something running across the field toward me. It was about twenty-five yards away, and I saw red eyes glowing. I ran into the car, and as I locked it, the thing grabbed the door handle. I could see him from the neck down—three big fingers, long black nails, and green rough skin. It was strong and angry. I looked in my mirror and saw a blur of green running. I could see his toes and then he jumped on the roof of my car. I thought I heard a grunt and then I could see his fingers through the front windshield where they curled around on the roof. I sped up and swerved to shake the creature off."

Then there's the Loveland Frog, a reptoid among reptoids. Residents of Thetis Lake, Canada, love their half man half frog, sighted around Loveland, Ohio, for the past sixty years.

On March 3, 1972, a cop drove down Riverside Road at one in the morning, when he saw something on the icy road. At first he thought it might have been a dog. The cop pulled over on the shoulder, his headlights on the beast, which stood erect before heading down an embankment and out of sight. The cop described the creature as three and a half feet tall and maybe sixty-five pounds. He and another officer returned to the scene later that night and saw scrape marks on the hill going down into the river. They did not file an official report. Other sightings followed.

Then there's the "Lizardman" of Wayne, New Jersey, the "Giant Lizard" of Milton, Kentucky, and the list goes on.

Since World War II, stories of reptilian humanoids have become cross-pollinated with UFO stories. Many sightings of such creatures in modern times are by those who also claim that aliens have abducted them.

UFO investigator John Carpenter, onetime head of MUFON, believes that not all abductions are perpetrated by small gray humanoids, but that some are also done by six- to eight-foot-tall reptile people who are ugly, mean, and aggressive. These reptile people prefer to abduct humans from their homes rather than from the regions of UFO sightings.

Perhaps the first abductee to report reptoids was Herbert Schirmer, an Ashland, Nebraska, cop who—during the early morning hours of December 3, 1967—was driving down the road on the edge of town when he saw a football-shaped UFO hovering over the road no more than forty feet from him. When the incident was over, Schirmer realized that there were fifteen minutes that he could not account for. Afterward, Schirmer suffered unexplainable anxieties and headaches that wouldn't respond to medication. Schirmer's experience came to the attention of the United States Air Force–sponsored Condon committee who saw to it that Schirmer was placed under hypnosis. The hypnosis was performed by Dr. Leo Sprinkle, no relation to Annie. While in a trance, the police officer recalled for the first time that he had been taken aboard the UFO. He said that he even "briefly communicated" with the UFO's commander who was shaped more or less like a human, though only about five feet tall with a thin reptilian face and gray skin. During the encounter, he felt a few seconds of body tingling and then a sharp stabbed-with-a-needle pain just behind the base of his ear. Schirmer told Sprinkle that he knocked back steaming cups of coffee as if they were water after his encounter. Schirmer told UFO researcher Jacques Vallée years after the event that he remembered being taken from his car into the UFO, where the head "operator" gave him a tour.

A similar incident was reported thirteen years later by Alan Godfrey. On November 28, 1980, Godfrey, a West Yorkshire, England, policeman, was patrolling the outskirts of

Todmorden, a Pennine hill town. At 5:00 A.M. he saw lights on the road that he thought at first were coming from a bus. As he got closer to the object, he saw that it was a dome-shaped UFO with a row of windows around the middle. He saw his patrol car's headlights reflecting off the surface of the object as it hovered just above the road. Then the object was suddenly gone. When Godfrey got back to the police station, he realized that there was fifteen minutes that he could not account for. Only under hypnosis could Godfrey "remember" what happened during the missing time. He recalled that his car was hit by a beam of light that caused the car to lose power. He was taken inside the object where reptilian humanoids with gray-white faces communicated with him telepathically and gave him a medical examination. Before releasing Godfrey, they told him that they would be contacting him again in the future.

Reptoids.com, the official website of the Reptoid Research Center run by longtime reptilian-humanoid expert John Rhodes, states matter-of-factly that a variety of "bipedal, up-right-walking reptoids have been reported. These fit for the most part into three categories: (1) reptilian humanoids, (2) winged Draco reptoids, and (3) reptilian-gray crossbreeds. Of the three, type 1 is the most common. These reptilian hu-manoids vary in height from five to nine feet in height. Their bodies are "lean and firm" and their arms are heavily muscled. They have three long fingers, an opposable thumb, three large toes, and one smaller toe away from the others on the out-side of each foot. They are greenish-brown in color, they lack lips, and they have canine teeth longer than the others giving the appearance of fangs. The eyes come in two types: large and black or white with flame-colored, vertical-slit pupils. Their heads are cone shaped with two bony ridges from their brows to the back of their heads. There is no bridge between the eyes, no ears—although witnesses have seen holes where human ears would have been—and no hair.

The Dracos, type 2, can grow to be twelve feet tall but

otherwise are similar in appearance to type 1, except they have sharp horns—and wings, which are usually held in a retracted position. Reports of Dracos flying are rare. Skin is leathery and blackish-brown in color.

Dracos are the jocks of the alien community. Their build is more athletic, as if they might have been designed by Jack Kirby. They are both athletic and right-wing, like waaaaaaay right, and have been spotted in the company of beings who are members of a subterranean Nazi superrace with telekinetic powers. As most of you know by now, that is the very worst kind—a superrace in turn associated with the group known as Vril.

Vril was supposedly the language, composed of oral sounds and clicks, spoken by the people of Atlantis. (Atlantis being the mythical island in the Atlantic Ocean where a great civilization is said to have existed before it sunk to the bottom of the sea.) The Vril Society, also known as the Luminous Lodge, was a secret society that formed in Germany following World War I.

The story goes that the society traces its origin back to 1917, with the war still ongoing, when four people—three men and a woman who was a "spiritual medium"—met in secret and discussed a "magical violet black stone" and methods of making contact with worlds of faraway and long ago. They believed that this could be achieved through the power of the Black Sun, the light from which was real but could not be seen by the human eye. The emblem for the Vril Society was a Black Sun, although the idea did not originate with the Vril Society. Black Suns were part of the symbology of Babylon and Assyria. According to Vril Society lore, the group—now working in conjunction with the Thule Society—was successful in channeling information from extraterrestrials.

The Thule Society was known in Germany as *Thule-Gesellschaft*, or the *Germanorden* (German Order). This group started out near the end of World War I as a literary discussion group, founded by Baron Rudolf Freiherr von Sebottendorff.

It evolved into an anti-Semitic pro-Germany organization that believed in the occult. The Thule Society was greatly influenced by another occult group known as the Theosophical Society. Critics of the society during the 1920s said that the theologists were not a study group but a propaganda group. The group was named after a mythic and arctic land called Ultima Thule, which was supposedly the original homeland for the Germanic people. These people were superior to other humans, and it is believed, because they were extraterrestrials who, over the years, lost knowledge of their origins.

The Thule Society's emblem is a swastika over a sword. According to some, an inner core of Thule members worship Satan and believe that an increased awareness of evil raises their consciousness. There is also a story that the Thule Society was determined to return those of the Merovingian bloodline—supposedly descendants of Jesus and Mary Magdalene—to the thrones of Europe. Adolf Hitler and his Nazi party stepped in and prevented this from happening. In the years after World War II, it is believed that members of this group continued Hitler's policies of ethnic cleansing under the guise of "sacrifices," murdering hundreds of people believed to be Jews or Communists. According to historian Trevor Ravenscroft, the Thules are a "Society of Assassins."

Thule Society lore says a German writer named John Van Helsing discovered a crashed flying saucer in the Black Forest in 1936. He said the craft was back engineered by members of the Thule Society. This information, in combination with information gathered by the Vril Society through channeling, allowed the first German flying saucer, known as the Haunebu 1, to be flown in August 1939. It is said that secret SS files contain details of the craft, saying that it was seventy-five feet in diameter.

One person who claimed to believe in the Vril Society was a man named Kerry Thornley, who shows up in literature regarding President Kennedy's assassination in a variety of contexts. According to Michael Benson, author of *Inside Secret*

Societies, Thornley, a suspected Oswald look-alike (even though he was several inches taller than Oswald) was the only man to write a book (albeit a novel) about Lee Harvey Oswald *before* Kennedy's assassination. Thornley's number of connections with the assassination is well above the national average. He was in the Marines at the El Toro Annex in California in 1959 when he met Oswald. He wrote the novel *The Idle Warriors* in 1962. The novel was about a disgruntled Marine who defects to the Soviet Union. Thornley called his Oswald-based hero Private Johnny Shellburn. The book was not published until 1991.

After the assassination, Thornley did publish a book about the assassination, but it was a nonfiction account. After meeting Oswald, Thornley became obsessed with him, and from that point on their lives formed an interesting parallel. Thornley was stationed in Atsugi, Japan. So was Oswald (although not at the same time). FBI agents interviewed Thornley two days after Kennedy's assassination. The FBI was drawn to him because of the manuscript he had been vigorously shopping to publishers. Thornley testified before the Warren Commission about knowing Oswald in the Marines and about what the accused assassin was like. Thornley saw to it that a copy of his manuscript was placed in the National Archives. He told the Commission that he was a "close acquaintance" but not a "good friend" of Oswald in the Marines. His testimony helped establish the accused assassin as having Marxist leanings.

According to Michael Benson, author of *Who's Who in the JFK Assassination*, Thornley moved to New Orleans after being discharged from the Marines, as had Oswald. Oswald and Thornley simultaneously lived in New Orleans. Thornley, however, claims he never ran into Oswald there. Regarding his and Oswald's proximity in New Orleans during the summer of 1963, Thornley wrote that Oswald "was even reputedly stopping in now and then at a bar where I hung out. We may have passed each other on the street, but if so, we didn't recognize each other. Only after the assassination did I realize that Oswald had been right under my nose for over two weeks."

New Orleans District Attorney Jim Garrison didn't believe this to be true. Garrison said there was at least one eyewitness—a woman named Barbara Reid—who placed Thornley and Oswald together in a New Orleans restaurant just weeks before the assassination. Garrison called Thornley as a witness at the Clay Shaw trial and later charged Thornley with perjury. Garrison's claims against Thornley were that (1) Thornley and Oswald were involved together in covert CIA operations, (2) Thornley impersonated Oswald as early as 1961, and (3) Thornley's writings about Oswald were actually CIA disinformation. Garrison eventually dropped the perjury charge, although claim 2 is worth considering, in light of the fact that Thornley made a short visit to Mexico City in September 1963, just as Oswald was supposed to have done. Thornley, while living in New Orleans, became an admitted acquaintance of assassination suspects Guy Banister and David Ferrie.

After living in New Orleans, Thornley moved to Los Angeles where he got a job as a doorman at the building where mobster Johnny Roselli lived. It was while living in Atlanta that Thornley told authorities that back in New Orleans before the assassination he had been told by a man named Gary Kirstein that Kennedy and Martin Luther King Jr. would be murdered. Thornley came to suspect that Kirstein was actually E. Howard Hunt. After telling this story, Thornley claimed he was pistol-whipped by ski-masked intruders at a friend's birthday party. The only thing the intruders stole was Thornley's identification.

According to the *New York Press*, Thornley believed, at least publicly, that "he and Lee Harvey Oswald were products of genetic tests carried out by a secret proto-Nazi sect of eugenicists, the Vril Society . . . that a bugging device was implanted in his body at birth, and that both he and Oswald were secretly watched and manipulated from childhood by shadowy, powerful Vril overlords." On the February 25, 1992, edition of the TV program *A Current Affair*, Thornley said that he was part of a conspiracy to assassinate Kennedy and that his co-conspirators were men he called "Brother-in-law and Slim."

MAJOR SOURCES

Benson, Michael. *Inside Secret Societies*. New York: Citadel, 2005.

———. *Who's Who in the JFK Assassination: An A-to-Z Encyclopedia*. New York: Citadel, 2003.

"'Lizard Man' returns?" WISTV Web site, www.wistv.com.

"South Carolina Lizard Man." American Monsters Web site, www.americanmonsters.com.

"The Loveland Frog." Weird Encyclopedia Web site, www.weird-encyclopedia.com.

"What Do Reptoids Look Like?" Reptoids Web site, www.reptoids.com.

90

Silencing X

The religious sect known as the Nation of Islam was made popular by Elijah Muhammad, who was born Elijah Poole around October 7, 1897, in a rural part of Georgia known as Sandersville. In April 1923, Elijah took his family north to Detroit, Michigan, where he got a job working on an automobile assembly line. In 1930, Elijah met the founder of the Nation of Islam (then known as the Temple of Islam), Wallace D. Ford, who preached that it was time for black people to return to Islam, the religion of their ancestors, according to Michael Benson, author of *Inside Secret Societies*.

When Elijah met him, Ford was selling silk products door to door, but he said he was a prophet who came from Africa to help blacks understand their heritage. The black race, according to Ford, was the superior "original race," and black Americans were Islam's lost sheep. His job was to bring them back home. Ford taught that in the early days of the world, black men were in charge. Black scientists, Ford claimed, created the seas and the mountains. They were in contact with nine-foot-tall men from Mars who caused the moon to blast into orbit around the Earth from its previous place beneath the Pacific Ocean.

Elijah became Ford's chief aide and devoted disciple. Ford gave Elijah his Muslim name, Muhammad. In 1934, Elijah was arrested for encouraging Black Muslim parents to send their children to Muslim schools, which were not considered legitimate schools by the Michigan State Board of Education. Elijah did not serve jail time, but his schools were closed down. In response, Elijah, along with Ford, moved to Chicago, Illinois.

Benson wrote that Ford disappeared on February 26, 1934, and to this day, no one knows what happened to him. After his disappearance, Elijah took control of the Nation of Islam. The next year, Elijah moved to Washington, DC, after hearing rumors of death threats against him. In 1942, during World War II, Elijah was arrested, along with many other Black Muslims, for draft evasion. Elijah was imprisoned, even though he was forty-five years old—too old to be drafted. He was not released from prison until World War II ended in 1945.

In the years following the war, the Nation of Islam went on a membership drive, preaching the message of black power to people in ghettos and prisons. During the 1950s, one of the men recruited by the Nation of Islam while serving a prison term was Malcolm Little, who would later declare his surname, his slave name, bogus and call himself Malcolm X. During the 1960s, the most famous recruit of the Nation of Islam, was the World Heavyweight Boxing Champion Cassius Clay, who changed his name to Muhammad Ali.

Malcolm left the Nation of Islam in 1964 after he learned that Elijah had been unfaithful to his wife and had fathered children out of wedlock. Malcolm became a member of the Islamic religion, which is not associated with the Nation of Islam. The Nation of Islam immediately declared that Malcolm was its enemy.

Nation of Islam spokesman Louis Farrakhan allegedly told a reporter from the newspaper *Muhammad Speaks*, "Only

those who wish to be led to hell, or to their doom, will follow Malcolm. The die is set, and Malcolm shall not escape,
especially after such evil, foolish talk about his benefactor.
Such a man is worthy of death and would have been met with
death if it had not been for Muhammad's confidence in Allah
for victory over his enemies." Farrakhan has since denied that
he ever said those words, but they were printed.

Those who actually conspired to murder Malcolm must
have read that with delight. Farrakhan, or someone speaking
for him, was laying down the legend to be the perfect false
sponsor.

On February 21, 1965, Malcolm was scheduled to speak
on behalf of his new organization—Muslim Mosque Incorporated—at the Audubon Ballroom on West 160th Street in
Harlem, across the street from Columbia-Presbyterian Hospital. Four hundred folding wooden chairs had been set up in
the ballroom. Security was surprisingly light. This was partially by Malcolm's design. He had forbidden high-security
measures such as searching all guests at the door. He said all
that frisking made folks uncomfortable. Usually, he kept his
family away from his controversial religious activities, but
on this day, he invited his pregnant wife Betty and his four
daughters to come hear him speak. As was normal for Malcolm during the meeting, he wore a dark suit, a white shirt,
and a slender tie. During the preliminary speakers, he sat
backstage and worked on his remarks. He peeked out and
saw there were a few empty seats. There was about a three-
quarter house. On this day he planned not to talk about the
black man's struggle with the white man. He would talk instead about the foolishness of black men fighting other black
men.

When it was his turn, he moved to the front of the room
and said, "*Asalaikum* [peace be with you], brothers and sisters." Before he could begin his speech, however, a commotion
broke out in the audience, and almost everyone, including
Malcolm, looked out into the seats to see what was going on.

"Take your hand out of my pocket," a man yelled.

Malcolm tried to calm the situation down. "Hold it! Hold it! Don't get excited," he said. A smoke bomb was set off at the back of the auditorium. Someone poured water on the bomb and put out the fire before the smoke could fill the ballroom.

A man sitting in the front row stood up, pulled a sawed-off shotgun from beneath his coat, and fired into Malcolm's chest. Two other men with handguns ran forward and pumped more bullets into Malcolm's body.

Malcolm was struck sixteen times with a combination of shotgun pellets and revolver bullets, mostly in the chest. One struck his cheek and another the middle finger of his left hand. Malcolm's hand went to his chest when the firing started. Then his other arm flew up. As he fell over backward on the stage, his head hit the stage hard and he knocked over two chairs.

Betty covered her daughters with her body until the shooting stopped. Chaos erupted. Betty ran onto the stage screaming, "They're killing my husband!" By the time she got to him, she knew he was gone.

The shooters scattered in different directions. No two witnesses saw the same thing. One of the shooters, later identified as Talmadge Hayer, was chased from the ballroom by an armed member of Malcolm's security force. The security guard shot the assassin in the leg. Dragging his leg, like John Wilkes Booth, Hayer made it to the sidewalk, but angry spectators began to kick him. The crowd might have killed him if police officers hadn't come to his rescue.

The police officers who were supposed to be stationed outside the ballroom for Malcolm's meeting were nowhere to be seen. But two policemen cruising by in a patrol car stopped when they saw the angry mob kicking the assailant. Someone ran to the hospital across the street and returned with a stretcher. Malcolm was carried into the hospital where he was pronounced dead on an operating table.

According to the official version of the assassination tale, one of the conspirators escaped from the Audubon Ballroom through a bathroom window, and another was knocked down by an undercover policeman named Gene Roberts, an officer of the NYPD's Bureau of Special Services. The undercover policeman had been covering Malcolm for a long time, and he was known as Brother Gene to Malcolm's staff and followers. Roberts paid little attention to the man he decked in the confusion, so busy was he trying to get to Malcolm. Roberts desperately tried resuscitation.

The assassins left hardware behind. Police recovered the sawed-off shotgun, a .45 pistol, a 12 gauge shotgun, and more than thirty shell casings from the pistol and from a 9-millimeter automatic that the assassin either escaped with or disposed of so well that it was never found.

The next day, Elijah commented on Malcolm's death, saying, "Malcolm died according to his preaching. He seems to have taken weapons as his god. Therefore, we couldn't tolerate a man like that. He preached war. We preach peace."

Within two weeks of the assassination, two more men were arrested for the shooting. They were Norman 3X Butler and Thomas 15X Johnson, both members of the Nation of Islam. After that the police stopped investigating, and there are several reasons to doubt whether the NYPD fully solved the case. Initial reports indicated that at least five men were involved in the shooting, three who fired weapons and two who created a diversion. When the police had arrested the alleged shooters, they stopped looking for the others.

Hayer, from the time he first confessed to shooting Malcolm, insisted that Johnson and Butler had nothing to do with it. It is puzzling that Malcolm's personal security guards did not notice Johnson and Butler entering the auditorium since they were known followers of Elijah. Hayer, on the other hand, was not a Black Muslim, and he denied that the Nation had paid him to kill Malcolm. He did admit that he had committed the crime for money, but he never identified who paid him or who his accomplices were.

Conspicuous in his absence at the trial of Butler and Johnson was Gene Roberts, the undercover police officer who knocked an assassin down in the rush that followed the shooting.

By the time of Malcolm's death, the Nation of Islam had spread to more than sixty cities in the United States and to Ghana, Mexico, and Caribbean countries. In 1972, Elijah appointed Farrakhan as the Nation's new spokesman. Farrakhan was born Louis Eugene Walcott on May 11, 1933, in Roxbury, Massachusetts, and was raised by his mother, a native of St. Kitts, an island in the Caribbean Sea.

A child prodigy, by age thirteen he had played with the Boston College Orchestra and the Boston Civic Symphony. The following year, he became nationally famous when he won a talent contest on the *Ted Mack Amateur Hour*, a popular TV show at the time, similar to today's *American Idol*. As an entertainer, he became known as "The Charmer." In February 1955, while appearing on a show called Calypso Follies, Farrakhan was invited by Malcolm X to visit the Nation of Islam's Temple Number Two. Soon afterward, Farrakhan joined the organization, and he became known as Louis X. He gave up show business and became a minister for the Nation of Islam's Boston temple in 1956. At first Farrakhan was a devoted follower of Malcolm, even patterning his speaking style after Malcolm's. But when Malcolm split from the Nation of Islam, Farrakhan turned on him, calling him a traitor. (Today Malcolm's family says that Farrakhan turned on Malcolm earlier than he admits.)

After Malcolm was assassinated, Farrakhan became head of the Nation's Harlem mosque. He quickly became the Nation's number one spokesman and continued to promote Elijah's teachings even after Elijah died in 1975. Farrakhan has been the spokesman for the Nation of Islam for thirty-five years. Under his leadership, the Black Muslims have thrived.

In 1995, Farrakhan organized the successful Million Man March in Washington, DC. Hundreds of thousands of black

766 DISINFORMATION, PLEASE

men attended the march and vowed to renew their commitment to family, community, and personal responsibility.

While the Nation of Islam works to create healthier black individuals and communities, it has been heavily criticized for its hateful teachings against white people, especially Jewish people. Many black leaders have condemned Farrakhan's anti-Semitic remarks. The Nation still talks of Martians being involved in the creation of the world. In 1995 Farrakhan told a gathering that he had had a vision of a UFO. He said that Martians had abducted him and taken him to the mother ship, where he met Elijah, who gave Farrakhan the idea for the Million Man March. Unlike Malcolm, who never had any money of his own, Louis Farrakhan lives in luxury in a mansion in Michigan. He is the father of nine children and has many grandchildren and great grandchildren.

The assassination of Malcolm was a well-conceived conspiracy. The chaos and disorientation caused by the diversion at the rear of the room, kept to a minimum the number of people who saw Malcolm being shot. It was a well-timed op, a tough feat to pull off in a room that holds three hundred people. Our ability to determine what really happened is further muddied by the conflicting reports that eyewitnesses offered. Police and news reports both included happenings that did not become a part of the official version. Early reports maintained that two men had been arrested at the scene, but it turned out to be only one. For days reports indicated that at least five men had been involved in the assassination, but that number went away and could not be remembered once it became clear that only three men were going to be arrested and tried.

Of course, the confusion involves not only who fired the automatic and who threw the smoke bomb but who designed the scheme and who sponsored it. Who was Master Cylinder? One theory was set forth by *Washington Post* writer Karl Evanzz, who digested hundreds of thousands of pages of FBI and CIA documents regarding the Audubon assassination and concluded that Master Cylinder was John Ali, a former intelligence agent who, Malcolm believed, had been responsible for his ouster from the Nation of Islam.

Evanzz discovered that the first man to find out the truth about John Ali was an African American journalist named Louis E. Lomax who died, as whistle-blowers so often do, in a car accident due to brake failure. Evanzz also discovered that the NYPD as well as the U.S. intelligence agencies were routinely using undercover agents to infiltrate and weaken "subversive political organizations." Malcolm and his followers would have made the list of organizations to be infiltrated with ease. The man was shaking hands with Martin Luther King in front of cameras. He was talking Pan-African economy. That shit was dangerous.

The co-author of Malcolm's autobiography, Alex Haley wrote, "The more I keep thinking about this thing . . . I'm not at all sure it's the Muslims. I know what they can do and what they can't, and they can't do some of the stuff recently going on. . . . I think I'm going to quit saying it's the Muslims."

MAJOR SOURCES

Bell, Walter. "Malcolm X." True TV Web site, www.trutv.com. (www.trutv.com/library/crime/terrorists_spies/assassins/malcolm_x/4.html)

Benson, Michael. *Inside Secret Societies*. New York: Citadel, 2005.

―――. *Malcolm X*. Minneapolis, MN: Lerner Publications, 2002.

Breitman, George, Herman Porter, and Baxter Smith. *The Assassination of Malcolm X*. New York: Pathfinder Press, 1991.

Goldman, Peter. *The Death and Life of Malcolm X*. New York: Harper & Row, 1973.

Malcolm X. *The Autobiography of Malcolm X*. With Alex Haley. New York: Ballantine Books, 1964.

91

Subliminal Messages

The concept of using subliminal messages to influence the masses first became part of Western civilization's *gestalt* during the 1950s when it was revealed that advertisers had been inserting single frames of film promoting their products in the middle of feature films playing in theaters. The result: the ad flashed before the audience at a speed that could not be perceived by the conscious mind, but worked instead on the subconscious mind. For no apparent reason, the theory went, everyone watching the movie would simultaneously thirst for a Coke—or whatever the subliminal message was pushing.

Using the same theory, the artists who designed print ads often arranged their images to communicate a concept covertly. Most famous, the word sex is often hidden in the design, such as in the cracks of an ice cube over which backlit brown liquor is being poured.

Do subliminal messages work? It's never been proven conclusively to have much of an effect, but the very idea of subliminals—that it's what you can't see, the thing below the "threshold of awareness," that influences you the most—appeals to paranoid minds, and that includes most of ours.

Not all subliminals were visual. On TV, they could be inserted in the narration of a commercial, using methods learned by advertising agencies after years of psychological and social-scientific research.

James Vicary was the guy who was caught inserting images into theater prints of feature films. He claimed that, in test runs, he made soda sales increase by almost 20 percent, and popcorn by a whopping 58 percent.

None other than Aldous Huxley found the notion of subliminal messaging terrifying. "I feel very strongly that we mustn't be caught by surprise by our own advance in technology. This has happened again and again in history with technology's advance, and this changes social conditions and suddenly people have found themselves in a situation which they didn't foresee and doing all sorts of things they didn't really want to do," Huxley said. The FCC warned against subliminal messages in broadcasting, but didn't actually ban it.

Doubts about the power of the subliminal message were raised in February 1958 when KTLA reportedly inserted the words "Telephone Now" into a half-hour TV program. No one called, the station later claimed. Five hundred viewers were subsequently quizzed, and only one expressed an urge to phone.

According to conspiracy theorists, however, subliminals are effective, and in this world of shadow and reflection, any claim to the contrary was disinformation. The public was lied to so that the technique could be used for really important things, like controlling the minds of TV viewers around the world. Some believe the Freemasons have used the technique to control, well, everything.

During the 2000 U.S. presidential campaign, a TV ad for George W. Bush showed an image of his opponent, Vice President Al Gore, and then flashed for a split second the word RATS across the screen. The designer of the ad, Alex Castellanos, known for his attack ads, was asked how the subliminal message got there. Castellanos said it was accidental. Then he backed off from that, saying that the letters were designed to be a "visual drumbeat" to attract your eyes to the word "bureaucrats" that lingers on the screen long enough to be registered by the conscious mind. No matter how influential the word RATS might have been as a subliminal, it was surely trumped by its being revealed and its subsequent controversy during which the word RATS and the opponent Al Gore were mentioned in juxtaposition repeatedly by friends and foe alike.

Rock albums have long been considered a hotbed of sub-liminal activity, beginning with the most famous case, the "Paul is dead" clues that were seemingly embedded in the images and sounds of Beatle albums. A voice says "I buried Paul" at the end of "Strawberry Fields Forever." "Revolution #9" back-ward says "Turn me on, dead man."

And as if Anton LaVey had his devil-worshipping hooks into Jimmy Page himself, play Led Zeppelin's "Stairway to Heaven" backward and you hear, "Oh here's to my sweet Satan." There's a commercial for dope too. Play "Another One Bites the Dust" by Queen backward and you hear, "It's fun to smoke marijuana."

No one has ever fessed up to putting these messages on the records, and some argue they are merely auditory tricks ex-ploiting our natural tendency to form words out of garble.

Law enforcement has attempted to use subliminals to cap-ture criminals. In the famous BTK serial-killer case in Wichita, Kansas, around 1980, police appeared on TV and asked view-ers to call in and talk about the still-on-the-loose serial killer. They did this in hopes that the murderer himself would watch. During the broadcast, they subliminally flashed a drawing BTK had sent to one of his intended victims. Then they flashed a drawing of an Indian chief in full headdress and a picture of a telephone dial. This was supposed to communicate to the killer, "BTK, call the chief," as in the chief of police. It didn't work. BTK, in fact, remained free to kill repeatedly for another twenty-five years after the subliminal was broadcast.

In 1992, inventor Oliver M. Lowery of Georgia patented a "Silent Subliminal Presentation System." According to the patent's abstract, the invention was "A silent communications system in which nonaural carriers, in the very low or very high audio frequency range or in the adjacent ultrasonic frequency spectrum, are amplitude or frequency modulated with the desired intelligence and propagated acoustically or vibrationally for inducement into the brain, typically through the use of loudspeakers, earphones or piezoelectric transducers. The modulated carriers may be transmitted directly in real time or may be conveniently recorded and stored on mechanical, magnetic or optical media for delayed or repeated transmission to the listener."

According to subliminal researcher Martin Howard, the U.S. government uses subliminal messages as a form of mind control, to get the American people to go along with an unpopular policy. One possible example might be the inexplicable confusion of the American people over Osama bin Laden and Saddam Hussein. The bad guy behind 9/11 was bin Laden, but in the months that followed that tragedy, the Bush administration stopped saying the name bin Laden in public and instead talked about Saddam Hussein as America's most dangerous enemy. A frightening number of people didn't notice the shift, and later, when asked, said Saddam Hussein was the man behind 9/11.

Howard believes that "using the universal tools fear, patriotism, and phrase repetition, these high-flying spin doctors can easily sway the population. The most successful public-relations campaigns aim to change public perception without our awareness that the campaign exists. They are typically launched by governments, institutions and countries who need to change their public image, restore their reputation or manipulate public opinion. There are PR firms today that advise dictatorships, dishonest politicians and corrupt industries to cover up environmental catastrophes and human-rights violations."

MAJOR SOURCES

Beattie, Robert. *Nightmare in Wichita: The Hunt for the BTK Strangler.* New York: New American Library, 2005.

Egan, John. "RATS Ad: Subliminal Conspiracy?" News BBC Web site, www.news.bbc.co.uk.

Elliston, Jon. "The Subliminal Scares." ParaScope Web site, www.parascope.com/articles/0397/sublim.htm.

Howard, Martin. *We Know What You Want: How They Change Your Mind.* New York: The Disinformation Company, 2005.

United States Patent 5,159,703 Lowery October 27, 1992, available at Rense.com Web site, www.rense.com/general56/contrlu2.htm.

92

An Empty Theory: Hollow Earth

It's been said that Adolf Hitler—at the end of World War II, hunkered in his bunker—knew the end was near. The U.S. and British armies approached from the West. Russian troops approached from the East. Bombs fell from above. His dreams and his country were in flames. But he still had one trick up his sleeve. In a successful effort to evade Allied capture, a secret door was opened in the bunker. A tunnel led to an airstrip, from which Hitler made his escape. The plane flew the mustachioed madman to the South Pole.

There, he entered "The Opening" that led down, down, down, from Earth to Hollow Earth, a world inside of a world. The theory goes that another civilization lives in the inner Earth, its heat supplied by a molten mass at the Earth's center.

Just about all your Hollow Earth theories have the Earth's core perforated at both poles, so the North Pole opening had to be more convenient to a frenzied Fuhrer escaping from a Berlin bunker, but he didn't go there. He headed south.

The Nazis, of course, were heavily into all things occult. Military strategies were made according to astrology, Nostradamus's prophecies, and the Hollow Earth theory. Those beliefs guided the Nazi military well, until D-Day. After that, not so much.

The Hollow Earth Research Society of Ontario, Canada, says the Nazi civilization still exists in Inner Earth. After the war as many as two thousand German scientists simply disappeared. That's a fact. They went with Hitler, the theory goes.

Not only had the subterranean civilization swelled in the sixty-plus years since World War II, but nefarious scientific research continued. Breeding was strictly controlled. Those with brown eyes need not apply. Great sinister strides had been made in aviation. Gravity was no longer a hindrance to flight. That explained the UFO phenomenon. It was the inner Earth Nazis flying through The Opening and into our skies to observe us. That explained why some eyewitnesses described UFO pilots as blond and blue eyed.

Of course, the world below has long been a part of Christian theology, a fiery place where bad boys and girls go after showing up at the pearly gates and getting the thumbs-down from Saint Peter. Hollow Earth theories that involved life rather than the afterlife entered public consciousness through old science fiction stories written by Jules Verne, Edgar Allan Poe, and Edgar Rice Burroughs.

Cyrus Teed, a late nineteenth-century alchemist from upstate New York, theorized that our civilization was on the inside of our globe rather than the outside as we believed and that the stars were floating pieces of ice at the Earth's center. Gravity was a fallacy. Things fell back to the ground because of centrifugal force. Teed founded a religion based on his inverted-world theory and changed his name to Karesh. His Koreshan commune in Chicago, Illinois, was founded in 1888.

Maybe the first extant reference to an inner world came during medieval times when a stone mason—or perhaps a stoned mason—carved a scene depicting Hollow Earth on the ceiling of the Rosslyn Chapel in Scotland. That chapel plays a key part in Dan Brown's conspiracy-laden novel *The DaVinci Code*.

In the seventeenth century, Edmund Halley—the British astronomer who has a comet named after him—said that the Earth consisted of a series of concentric globes and that the center contained a luminous atmosphere populated by life. He thought that the northern lights were caused by gasses seeping through openings in the Earth's crust.

The idea of holes at the poles originated with John Symmes, who during the early nineteenth century theorized about the entrances to the center of the Earth. For a time, the North Pole opening was known as "Symmes' Hole." What a legacy!

Along with the poles, other theoretic entrances to inner Earth exist at *Cueva de los Tayos* (Cave of the Oil Birds) in Ecuador, in the Gobi Desert in Mongolia, under the Great Pyramid of Giza, and Mammoth Cave in Kentucky.

Hitler believed in the inverted world, it is said. There are reports of the Fuhrer sending expeditions of spies with powerful telescopes to a Baltic island. Their mission was to observe the Atlantic Ocean in search of the British fleet, the ocean being visible above rather than below the horizon, by focusing on the appropriate portion of the "sky."

Many modern subterranean-civilization theories stem from a book by Raymond W. Bernard called *The Hollow Earth*. Bernard's name will sound familiar to secret-society buffs, as he was an esotericist and leader of the Rosicrucians, a group that has quite a few theories. Since at least the eighteenth century, the Rosicrucian version of history has stated that Moses from the Old Testament and the Egyptian pharaoh Amenhotep IV (aka Akhenaten) were one and the same individual.

The theory is that the Hebrew stories of the Old Testament were just rewrites of the Egyptian history that preexisted them, and that both used as the basis for their stories of creation versions of that written by the first known civilization created by the Sumerians who lived in present-day Iraq in Sumer. Historian Jim Marrs sees the group as "a major force in the ongoing struggle between scientific rationalism and church dogma that resulted in the breakup of the Holy Roman Empire, the creation of Protestantism and the resulting Church of England, as well as the Renaissance." Like the Knights Templar before them and other secret societies, the Rosicrucians were forced underground by the Vatican. By the early eighteenth century, the Rosicrucians had hidden themselves within the ranks of the Freemasons.

According to Willis Emerson's *The Smoky God*, a Norwegian sailor named Olaf Jansen discovered the inner world. He discovered a land called Agartha, the capital city of Shamballa. Jansen lived for two years in the underworld, where people grew to be twelve feet tall and there was a "smoky sun" at the Earth's core.

There are some pretty bright people who still believe in Hollow Earth. One is Dr. Brooks A. Agnew, a Ph.D. physicist who helped develop the Ground Probing Radar and has been measuring the Earth for more than twenty years. For years he's been planning a North Pole Inner Earth expedition. When asked why, he said it was because he couldn't go to the moon and he couldn't go to Mars, but he could go to the North Pole. He planned to take with him all of his Earth-measuring equipment so that he could use side-scan sonar, dynamo sensing, and gyroscopic global circumference tracking. There was worry, however, that the Earth's inner space might be fourth or fifth dimensional, which could throw the equipment's measurements off. The expedition, as planned, would include sixty-three people, thirty-three scientists, and the rest possessing a variety of expertise from meditation to remote viewing. The expedition would have happened years ago, if it weren't for the cost: somewhere in excess of $2 million.

Agnew still hasn't discovered Hollow Earth, but he does now have his own podcast show.

MAJOR SOURCES

Bernard, Raymond. *The Hollow Earth: The Greatest Geographical Discovery in History Made by Admiral Richard E. Byrd in the Mysterious Land Beyond the Poles—The True Origin of the Flying Saucers.* Mokelumne Hill, CA: Health Research Books, 1977.

Emerson, Willis George. *The Smoky God.* New York: Cosimo Classics, 2006.

"The Hollow Earth Explorer Has a New Champion." UFO Digest Web site, ufodigest.com.

Marrs, Jim. *Rule by Secrecy.* New York: Perennial, 2000.

Wagner, Stephen. "Nazis and the Hollow Earth. About.com Web site, www.about.com.

93

White-Collar Crime: The Fleecing of America

Imagine you are a hard worker who has spent decades working for the same company. Every two weeks you get a paycheck, a portion of which has been taken out and invested. The idea is that, when you retire, you will cash in those investments and have plenty of money with which to live out the rest of your life.

You have spent many years dreaming of retirement. You know just where you are going to move. You have imagined the places to which you would travel on long vacations. But when the time comes actually to retire and you seek the money that you have been saving and investing, you are horrified to find that it is gone.

It turns out that the whole "investment" operation was a

gigantic scam. You and many of your coworkers have been robbed of your retirement funds. That money, it seems, went straight from your paycheck into the pockets of the executives running the company, the company you trusted.

Sound impossible? Well, it isn't. It's happened.

Corporate crimes, often referred to as white-collar crimes, occur when executives working for large corporations use their jobs to funnel large amounts of money from the company they work for into their own pockets.

All corporate crime is a financial drain on society. It costs everyone money because noninvestors often help pay the price of the crime through higher consumer prices and interest rates. Other, smaller businesses may have to close, and honest workers end up losing their jobs. There's a ripple effect to corporate crime, the size of which depends on the size of the criminal corporation.

For the criminals, there isn't much of a downside. Only rarely are the perpetrators caught and punished. Even when caught, punishment is frequently light, short sentences in "country club" prisons. In some cases, the government "bails out" the drained corporation. Fresh money is pumped into the corrupt system and, pffffft, it disappears just as quickly.

One of the most famous cases of corporate crime in recent years is the Enron case. Kenneth Lay founded the company in Omaha, Nebraska, in 1985. Enron later moved its headquarters to Houston, Texas. Enron was born out of the merger of three companies, two gas and electric companies and a railroad. Its business was energy. At its peak, it employed 21,000 people and dealt in many different fields, including electricity, natural gas, pulp and paper, and communications. It was the seventh largest company in the United States, claiming to be worth $101 billion. *Fortune* magazine called it "America's Most Innovative Company" for six straight years (1996–2001).

Enron was indeed innovative. Here's an example: It was the first corporation that allowed investors to trade its stock online. If investors wanted to put their life savings into Enron's future, all that was needed was a click of the mouse.

But Enron fell apart in December 2001 when it was revealed that just about all the company's supposed money and possessions were made up—pure fiction.

Enron had accountants who made it look like the company was making money by the billions, when in reality the company was deeply in debt. When the company finally collapsed, with it went $60 billion worth of stocks, purchased by investors, but now worthless. Also gone was another couple of billion dollars in pension funds—the money that was to pay the pension for Enron's employees. So in many cases, faithful Enron employees were the ones who were burned the worst by this heinous crime.

Where did all the money go at Enron? Straight to the top, apparently, considering who was later arrested and prosecuted. In September 2004, Andrew Fastow, Enron's formal chief financial officer, and, according to the Associated Press, "one of the key figures in Enron's collapse" was sentenced to ten years in prison, but two years later the judge shortened the sentence by four years. U.S. district judge Kenneth Hoyt said that society had unfairly picked on Fastow's family and that they all had "suffered enough." Fastow's wife, Lea, also pleaded guilty in 2004 to a misdemeanor tax crime and served a year in prison for helping to hide ill-gotten gains from her husband's schemes.

Judge Hoyt said that the facts "called for mercy." At the hearing, the convicted white-collar criminal was allowed to give his wife a hug before he was handcuffed and led away.

"I know I deserve punishment," Fastow said, as he exited. "I accept it without bitterness."

Also prosecuted for their part in the bilking of the huge corporation were the company's founder, Kenneth Lay, and the company's former chief executive officer, Jeffrey Skilling. One of the reasons the court believed that Fastow deserved "mercy" was that he had been willing to testify against the other two men at their trials, stating under oath that both Lay and Skilling knew about the phony accounting practices that made Enron appear to be so much richer than it actually was.

In May 2006, both Lay and Skilling were convicted on charges of conspiracy (working with others to commit a crime) and fraud. Before Lay could serve prison time, however, he died of heart disease. Skilling was sentenced to twenty-four years in the Federal Correctional Institution in Waseca, Minnesota. Fastow had been charged on ninety-eight counts, including fraud, insider trading, and money laundering. He pleaded guilty to two counts of conspiracy and admitted to running schemes to hide Enron's debt and inflate profits. He did this, he admitted, while keeping his own coffers filled with cash at all times. As part of his guilty plea, Fastow agreed to give back nearly $30 million in cash and property.

The Enron employees who were rooked out of their pensions got together and formed the Severed Enron Employee Coalition, which worked to retrieve money from the men they accused of stealing it. The group of more than 20,000 former employees got their money back by filing a lawsuit against the corporation. They charged that the misdeeds of executives in the corporation had cost them the value of their Enron stock ownership and 401(k) plans. They were awarded $89 million dollars, and many of the former employees received their first checks in 2007. Unfortunately, a computer problem caused some people to receive too much money, causing further delays and legal woes while the error was corrected.

The first party to face criminal charges following Enron's collapse was Arthur Andersen LLP, the accounting firm that had been hired to check Enron's books and had ruled that everything was on the up and up.

Andersen was tried and found guilty of obstruction of justice. It is against the law to know a crime has been committed and choose not to report it to authorities. It is also against the law to obstruct justice by lying to a federal investigator.

In addition to ignoring the problems they found in Enron's books, Andersen was accused of actively hiding the crimes. When the firm knew that an investigation was coming, they shredded thousands of revealing documents and also destroyed a memo from one Enron executive to another that would have revealed large-scale white-collar crime.

From a law enforcement standpoint, the prosecution of one of the nation's "Big Five" accounting firms sent a powerful message to the many accountants who worked for companies across the nation. It was their responsibility to tell whether they knew there was illegal business going on, and if they refused to inform authorities, they would be punished.

In the years since the Savings and Loan (or S&L) scandal and Enron, things apparently have not gotten better. White guys in suits are still ripping everyone off, only now their plans are even broader in scope, and punishing the guilty even more of a pipedream. In 2008, just about everyone's retirement plans took a 33 percent hit. Where did the money go?

MAJOR SOURCES

"Enron Botches Payments to Ex-employees." MSNBC Web site, www.msnbc.msn.com/id/19589106.
"Ex-C.F.O. of Enron Sentenced to Six Years." *New York Times* Web site, www.nytimes.com.
Goodwyn, Wade. "Enron's Fastow Seeks—and Receives—Leniency." NPR Web site, www.npr.org.
Thomas, Cathy Booth. "Guilty of Obstruction, Arthur Andersen Becomes the First Courtroom Casualty of the Enron Collapse." *New York Times* Web site, www.nytimes.com.

94

Clone Again: Naturally
or, Send in the Clones,
or, Everybody Loves a Clone,
So Why Don't You?
—Clones Have Feelings Too

In 2001, a group of Worcester, Massachusetts, scientists working for Advanced Cell Technology (ACT) claimed that they had cloned the first human embryo. The accomplishment, the *Journal of Regenerative Medicine* reported, was not designed to create a master race of identical humans, but rather to create replacement cells that could be used to cure human suffering from a variety of diseases such as spinal injury, diabetes, and heart disease.

ACT denied accusations that they planned to insert a cloned human embryo into the womb of a woman, thus creating the first human clone—although the implication was clear that the technology to do that now existed. ("We are just trying to help people who are sick," ACT CEO Michael West said. "We're not talking about a little embryo with hands and feet. We're talking about a cluster of cells.")

The cops didn't bust the joint. A few states including California had officially banned human cloning, but it remained legal in most places including Massachusetts largely because not enough people thought it possible. "These are exciting preliminary results," ACT researcher Dr. Robert Lanza said. "This work sets the stage for human therapeutic cloning as a potentially limitless source of immune-compatible cells for tissue engineering and transplantation medicine." He said the largest human embryo their labs had created so far was only six cells in size.

The creation of life was accomplished by inserting a very small cell with its genetic material into a woman's donated egg. The egg then had the concentration of its electrically charged ions diddled by a variety of chemicals and—voilà. President George W. Bush said he was 100 percent against human cloning and urged for the quick passage of a federal law banning it.

In January 2008, the technology to create potentially therapeutic clusters of human cells was matched in the laboratories of Stemagen in La Jolla, California. These clones were grown from skin cells donated by Stemagen's CEO, Dr. Samuel Wood. Like Lanza, Wood was emphatic that there was nothing immoral about his research. "We have a very simple goal, to create the most therapeutically useful [stem cell] lines that are possible," Wood said in a telephone interview with a reporter from the Long Island, New York, newspaper *Newsday*. "We consider this a major milestone in our attempt to reach that goal."

Lanza didn't have a patent on the human cloning technology and claims of successful human cell replication had come out of Great Britain two years before. He couldn't be happy that his discoveries had been equaled on the West Coast, but he was gracious. Lanza, asked by a reporter for his feelings, said, "I applaud their efforts and I think it is very important that their research continues."

The Catholic Church squawked. "We've been objecting to human cloning for any purpose for many years," said Richard Doerflinger, deputy director for Pro-Life Activities at the U.S. Conference of Catholic Bishops in Washington D. C. "We think there should be laws against it as there are in other countries, and as the United Nations has called for."

Claims of progress in human cloning techniques go back to the late 1970s when writer David Rorvik wrote a book called *In His Image: The Cloning of a Man*, which claimed personal knowledge of a living human clone. The claims were never substantiated. The book is now largely regarded as a hoax. The subject surfaced again in 2002 when a man named Severino Antinori said the first human clone was growing in a womb, and it was scheduled for birth in 2003. Again, the proof failed to be in the pudding. In 2003 to 2004, Dr. Brigitte Boisselier told *Le Journal de Montreàl*, that her organization, Clonaid, a subdivision of the Raelian religion, had cloned thirteen children. Again, real evidence was not forthcoming. The children's identities needed to be secret to protect them from public ridicule.

Bottom line: It has been more than twelve years since the first cloned sheep, Dolly, an exact duplicate of a six-year-old Finn Dorset ewe, was born at the Roslin Institute in Scotland. The sheep was born on July 5, 1996, but her debut was not publicized until February 27, 1997. Since that time, fifteen wild and domestic species have been successfully cloned. These include African wildcats, goats, Asian oxen, deer, and one Afghan hound dog. A lot of this cloning has been done in the United States by, among other companies, ViaGen in Austin, Texas. One of the services ViaGen offers is clones of dead pets. For $32,000, a grieving pet owner could get a cat identical to her old cat. A cloned thoroughbred racehorse costs $150,000. Too bad no one saved Secretariat's spit. It would be difficult to disinter the all-time racing great because he is buried in the infield at Belmont Park racetrack in New York City, the site of his greatest victory in the Belmont Stakes.

According to Dr. Courtney Campbell, "President Clinton requested that the National Bioethics Advisory Commission (NBAC) investigate and make recommendations on the prospects of human cloning by May 26, 1997. Citing matters of morality and spirituality, the president, on March 4, 1997, imposed a temporary moratorium on federal funding of human cloning research."

Ian Wilmut, a member of the scientific team that created Dolly admitted that cloning technology still has a long way to go. Many cloned animals die young, and mothers have had difficulties in birthing cloned babies. Dolly, by the way, died in 2003 of a lung infection. At the time of her death, she had arthritis in her hind legs. She was stuffed and is now on permanent display at the National Museum of Scotland in Edinburgh. If human cloning experimentation were underway, imagine the monstrosities that would be created before the techniques were perfected. Even those whose physical body grew normally might have emotional problems, knowing that her grandmother was her sister and her sister, killed in an accident, was now her child. Or that she was number 4,687 of 5,000 identical models cranked out on the day of her birth.

The subject of human cloning and religion is interwoven frequently. That's because devout Christians believe that if a human clone were created, it would be a being without a soul, nothing but a human-shaped vessel and, therefore, much easier for Satan to possess. Groups popularizing these fears point out that if the technology to clone humans exists, we would not be told about it. The power elite of the world would keep that knowledge secret so it could be used for sinister schemes involving master races and even more oppressive world domination.

Those with more scientific minds are also terrified of the possibilities. What if Hitler himself were cloned? What if there was harvesting of reproductive material from gestationally fairly old embryos for purposes of creating actual eggs born from aborted fetuses? What if scientists were able to meld the reproductive organs, creating "mixed gender balls"? The results could be horrifying and prone to exploitation by the adult entertainment industry.

Lawmakers have been wrangling for years over how to deal with the restriction of technology. They can't, as the Vatican did, just condemn all cloning research—mess with that stuff and you're going to Hell. Scientists have attempted a more thoughtful approach, and lawmakers have been searching for the correct wording to allow cloning research that creates cells which may help heal sick humans while prohibiting cloning research that involves growing cloned fetuses in wombs or in womblike environments.

Today the interweb is populated by a plethora of sites theorizing about just how sophisticated scientists have become and for whom those sophisticated scientists are working. Those whose nature it is to fear Nazis and fascism in the world, say that human cloning technology is in the hands of Rosicrucians and that the previously mentioned Roslin Institute is a front for a Rosicrucian cabal. One particularly sharp fear is that global thinkers of a conspiratorial nature will use the blood on the Shroud of Turin to furnish a clone of the person once wrapped within it, and this clone could then be proclaimed a resurrected Jesus, a Jesus with no soul, a Jesus vessel waiting to be occupied by Satanism.

The ethical questions just keep coming. What if a woman wanted to have her own father as a baby? What if a world leader sought to create a civilization—or an army—in his own image?

The ultimate fear is that a whole race of supermen or superwomen could be created and that the necessary DNA could be taken from the people to be cloned without their knowledge or permission. Perfect children could be created for hopeful parents. Parents would be able to design their child, and that child would be created through the new technology. Normal reproduction would become a thing of the past, and eventually we would all be the same, compliant and at ease with our similitude.

In addition to the dangers of using DNA technology to create human beings, DNA technology that may, in the near future, allow scientists to create animals that have been long extinct could easily alter the history of the world. To introduce extinct species into the modern world, a world in which their natural enemies may have been wiped out or depleted, could create a skewed ecology. This danger was made famous first in science fiction form, in the Jurassic Park movies. But reality is catching up with that science fiction. During autumn 2008, Stephen Schuster, a professor of microbial ecology at Penn State, announced that the DNA of woolly mammoths, extinct for 10,000 years, had been 80 percent decoded. Resurrecting the species through genetic experimentation would involve making 400,000 changes in 20,000 modern elephant genes and then implanting a genetically altered embryo into an elephant's womb.

MAJOR SOURCES

Campbell, Courtney S. "Cloning Human Beings: Religious Perspectives on Human Cloning." Bioethics Web site, bioethics. georgetown.edu/nbac/pubs/cloning2/cc4.pdf.

Cibelli, Jose B., Robert P. Lanza, and Michael D. West. "The First Human Cloned Embryo." Scientific American Web site, www.sciam.com.

Mott, Maryann. "Ten Years After Dolly, No Human Clones, but a Barnyard of Copies." National Geographic Web site, www.nationalgeographic.com.

Ricks, Delthia. "Scientists Make Human Embryo Clone." *Newsday* Web site, www.newsday.com.

"Tale for the (Ice) Ages: Woolly's return?" *New York Daily News*, 20 November 2008, p. 24.

Wilmut, Ian, and Roger Highfield. *After Dolly: The Uses and Misuses of Human Cloning*. New York: Norton, 2006.

95

The Rape of Paul Bennewitz's Mind

In chapter 83 on whistle-blowers, we discuss the possible dissemination of disinformation by current and former government employees, using flying saucers as a cover for the R & D of new flying weapons and alien abductions as a cover for oddly perverse mind-control experiments. A logical analysis tends to reveal the abductions as a product of hypnosis. In most cases abductees only "remember" their ordeals while floating in the fugue state of hypnosis.

With alien abductions, nothing is real, nothing concrete. It is always a dream. Still, abductees appear to believe what they are saying. With the help of their hypnotists, they are vividly experiencing horrific abuse from hideous big-eyed aliens. The abductions are not simple straight one-on-one cover stories like the aerial displays. The growing numbers of women, and some men, who believe they have been abducted grows. This appears to be part of a more complex social/scientific sadomasochism (or S&M) program in which the "wand" used by the aliens to penetrate the abductees, male and female, are what we on Earth call a dildo.

In the whistle-blower chapter, we don't discuss Paul Bennewitz, a UFO researcher who claims to have known too much. Were sophisticated mind-control methods used to render his evidence unbelievable? In Bennewitz's case, it has been theorized, the government didn't just feed its mark disinformation, but instead used drugs and hypnosis to shatter his psyche.

According to "The Paul Bennewitz Story," Bennewitz's trials started in 1979. He was operating a small electronics company in Albuquerque, New Mexico. And, oh yes, he had an interest in UFOs on the side. He even did a little UFO research for the Aerial Phenomenon Research Organization, better known as APRO. As it happened, his house was very close to Kirtland Air Force Base, which was home of the top-secret Sandia National Laboratory and the Phillips Laboratory. Every night he saw lights in the sky that couldn't be explained.

Sometime around 1980 Bennewitz took a walk on the wild side and teamed up with a psychologist/UFOlogist named Dr. Leo Sprinkle, no relation to Annie. Dr. Sprinkle hypnotized a woman who came to him with a story of seeing a UFO while driving with her son down a rural road.

Under Sprinkle's spell, the woman said that she remembered several UFOs in the sky that day. She saw cattle being abducted. She also said that the aliens abducted her and her son and took them to a subterranean base. There they saw cattle mutilated and drained of blood. There they saw great vats with floating human body parts in them. Implants were inserted in their bodies, devices with which the aliens could control their minds.

Bennewitz heard the woman's story, believed it, and assumed that her tale was directly connected to the night lights he saw. For a time the woman and her mother lived in Bennewitz's house. The woman was given an MRI, and the results, Bennewitz claimed, proved that she really did have an alien implant inserted inside her. Bennewitz filmed the lights. He took photographs. He determined that the larger craft were launch ships.

These were 330 feet long and 130 feet across. But there were also surveillance vehicles that were much smaller, just five feet by ten feet. At first he took his photos with a Polaroid. But he quickly realized that he was going to need cameras that offered higher definition, so he bought a Hasselblad.

It was at this point that his behavior became a tad whacky. He watched the lights at night and came to believe he could feel signals coming from them. The occupants were trying to make contact. He couldn't understand them at first, so he set up receivers on his land set to pick up low-frequency electromagnetic transmissions. He wrote a series of letters to the air force base but received no reply. He wrote to the local TV stations. He contacted the newspapers. He wrote to both New Mexico senators. He wrote to President Reagan.

By October 1980, Bennewitz was calling the Air Force base and warning them of the UFOs that flew in its direction each night. He had been listening in on them as they communicated with their abductees through the mind-control devices implanted inside them. They sent a beam to Earth, and through that beam they could read the very thoughts of their human slaves. He believed the direct threat was to the Manzano Weapons Storage Area. The man he talked to was Major Ernest E. Edwards.

Edwards called Scientific Advisor (or S. A.) Richard C. Doty and assigned him to take care of the Bennewitz thing. Jerry Miller, the S. A. for Air Force Test and Evaluation Center, Kirtland Air Force Base, was also assigned to Bennewitz. The men looked at Bennewitz's film and agreed that, yes, some sort of aerial craft was there, and they didn't know what it was.

The official report read, "After analyzing the data collected by Dr. Bennewitz, . . . the evidence clearly shows some type of unidentified aerial objects were caught on film; however, no conclusion could be made whether these objects pose a threat to the Manzano/Coyote Canyon areas."

The UFOs didn't trouble them much. What they didn't like was the sophistication of the observation and listening antennae that Bennewitz had on his land, and they didn't like the way it was pointing at their air force base. Also, Bennewitz was never quiet about the things he saw and heard. At least twice the Air Force picked Bennewitz up in a helicopter and took him to the base where he later claimed that he was allowed to take photographs of a supposed alien crash sight and later claimed that alien bodies were visible in the photos.

A complete background check was done on Bennewitz. If there was something in Bennewitz's past that might discredit him, these guys wanted to know about it. As far as credibility went, Bennewitz wasn't doing much to hold up his end. He told people that he was convinced the signals he was picking up from the alien craft were messages being sent to the devices inserted inside the bodies of their human abductees. To make matters worse, he claimed to have written a computer program that could translate the alien messages into English.

In 1982, APRO sent UFOlogogist and author William Moore (*The Roswell Incident*) to investigate Bennewitz's claims. During the interview, Bennewitz told Moore that according to his translations of alien messages, two species of aliens had invaded Earth, "Grays" and "Whites." The gray aliens mutilated cattle and abducted humans. They had a treaty with the U.S. government allowing them to build a secret underground base beneath Archuleta Peak on the Jicarillo Indian Reservation near Dulce, New Mexico.

Bill Moore later said that an intelligence agent calling himself Falcon had approached him and had given him disinformation to supply Bennewitz, under the assurance that Bennewitz would take it at face value. Moore claimed to have fed Bennewitz disinformation for four years, including supplying him with the "Aquarius Document," which verified Bennewitz's belief that the aliens had a subterranean base beneath Dulce.

The document was a report on a film Bennewitz had taken. Government experts had verified its authenticity—the film of a saucer, a colored object, and a cylinder-shaped object was not altered and depicted a bona fide phenomenon. The document concluded, "Ref your request for further information regarding HQ CR 44, the following is provided: Capt. Grace 7602 Aintelg, INS contacted and related following:

(S/WINTEL) USAF no longer publicly active in UFO research; however USAF still has interest in all UFO sightings over USAF installation/test ranges. Several other government agencies, led by NASA, actively investigate legitimate sightings through covert cover. (S/WINTEL/FSA) One such cover is UFO Reporting Center, US Coast and Geodetic Survey, Rockville, MD 20852. NASA filters results of sightings to appropriate military departments with interest in that particular sighting. The official US Government Policy and results of project Aquarius is still classified top secret with no dissemination outside official intelligence channels and with restricted access to "MJ Twelve." Case on Bennewitz is being monitored by NASA, INS, who request all future evidence be forwarded to them thru AFOSI, IVOE.

Bennewitz's mental health continued to deteriorate. He came to believe that aliens were coming through the walls of his house and injecting him with chemicals.

It wasn't until Bennewitz was "hospitalized for exhaustion" that he, at the urging of his family, dismantled the antennae he'd set up to listen to alien messages. He died in 2003.

MAJOR SOURCES

Bishop, Greg. *Project Beta: The Story of Paul Bennewitz, National Security, and the Creation of the Modern UFO Myth*. New York: Paraview Pocket Books, 2005.
"The Paul Bennewitz Story." Book of THoTH Web site, www.book-of-thoth.com.
"UFOs—1980 Project Aquarius Document." Unexplainable.net Web site, www.unexplainable.net/artman/publish/article_2509.shtml.

96

Underground Bases

First there is a mountain, then there is no mountain,
then there is.
—Donovan

We already know that plenty of people believe the Earth is hollow and contains an unknown civilization, a complete world within a world, so it's no stretch of the imagination that people also believe that the largest military bases in the world are completely secret and underground. One of the most popular of these unknown bases in supposed to be under Dulce, New Mexico. Stories about that location started with UFOlogist Paul Bennewitz, whose participation in the creation of the modern UFO mythology and eventual demise are detailed in chapter 95 "The Rape of Paul Bennewitz's Mind."

A self-proclaimed expert in the Dulce base is Phil Schneider. In May 1995, he gave a lecture about the base and the firefight he claimed to have had with aliens there in 1979, a battle in which he was wounded and given cobalt poisoning that caused cancer. Less than a year after his whistle-blowing lecture, he was found dead in his apartment with wire wrapped around his neck.

Schneider claimed that in 1954, President Eisenhower formed a treaty with alien entities. It was called the 1954 Greada Treaty, which agreed that the aliens involved could remotely carve some cow genitalia and test their implanting techniques on a few human beings. The agreement included the caveat that the aliens had to keep the United States posted on precisely who had been transplanted and whose minds were controlled.

Like Hitler before them, the fascist aliens altered the bargain until they decided they wouldn't abide by it at all. Back in 1979, this was the reality, and the firefight at Dulce was an accident. Schneider claimed that he was there, in the underground base, a base seven levels tall and two and a half miles beneath the ground. Construction was constant, and after fresh holes were dug, Schneider's job was to climb down into the holes and test rock samples. Sometimes to get the rocks he needed, he had to use dynamite and blow away sections of the existing walls.

It was while he was on his way to the area that he found himself in a cavern filled with aliens. Schneider, not the ask-questions type, shot two of the aliens, and the return fire gave him the wound that later turned malignant. Thirty men were killed in the battle. Schneider claimed he later learned that the aliens had been on Earth for a "long time," long enough to earn the UFOlogical moniker "ancient astronauts."

Not all the world's undeground bases, it is believed, were built by aliens. Some were put there by the military-industrial complexes of various Superpowers. Some have been there for thousands of years, the work of prehistoric alien visitors riding futuristic chariots.

Many underground-base stories include the existence of one called Mount Weather, supposedly just outside Washington, DC. According to the article "Mount Weather: Underground

Complex," it was built by man, for man—and ultra ultra secret. Mount Weather is self-contained and almost completely underground. The mountain is hollow and contains a military base. From above, all you can see are landscaped lawns and a smattering of buildings with antennae on them. Not there, but nearby is a control tower, a helipad, and a surreptitious entrance. Below, there is a complete world fully equipped for outtake and intake with an on-site sewage treatment plant and 250,000 gallons of drinking water. The cover story for the small aboveground station is that it belongs to the National Weather Bureau, camped atop the mountain to pick up better satellite transmissions.

Visitors are strongly discouraged. Lots of Keep Out signs. There's a ten-foot chain-link fence with a crown of razor wire separating the mountain from its surroundings.

Richard Pollock, a writer for *Progressive* magazine, interviewed several people who claimed to have worked on the base inside the mountain. They said the base had its own TV communication system, lake with fresh spring water, water purification system, cafeterias, hospitals, transit system, private apartments, and dormitories.

Retired Air Force general Leslie W. Bray, in his testimony to the Senate Subcommittee on Constitutional Rights hearings in 1975 said, "I am not at liberty to describe precisely what is the role and the mission and the capability that we have at Mount Weather, or at any other precise location."

Regarding his research into the base, Pollock reported that the mountain contained a full travel-size government with cabinet members representing each branch. They were ready to take over in case a nuclear war obliterated the outside world.

"The facility attempts to duplicate the vital functions of the Executive branch of the Administration," Pollock writes.

Mount Weather activities, Pollock claimed, included collecting data on U.S. citizens, playing war games so that best responses could be executed in various scenarios, and maintaining a huge department assigned to manage civil crises. The eyewitnesses agreed that the base had been in place and ready to go at the time of the 1962 Cuban Missile crisis and then again on "that day in Dallas," November 22, 1963. The facility was also on standby during the civil rights riots of the 1960s, as well as during national antiwar demonstrations.

Somewhere inside the mountain at a secret location within the secret base is The List, the names of people who must be protected and saved in case of a nuclear holocaust, people whose "existence is essential" to the furtherance of mankind.

MAJOR SOURCES

Schneider, Phil. "Underground Bases & NWO: Aliens & New World Order Conspiracy." Lecture delivered during May 1995, available online at video.google.com/videoplay?docid= 1819639877788572495.
"Underground Facilities—Bases—Tunnels." Crystal Links Web site, www.crystalinks.com.

97

The Severing of the Black Dahlia

It is the most famous American murder case not involving a celebrity—a crime so horrible that it instantly changed the tone of an entire city. Before, throughout Los Angeles, women were used to walking home alone. After, they required escorts—and all because of the mind-bogglingly bizarre ordeal of Beth Short, the Black Dahlia, a celebrity only in death.

The twenty-two-year-old raven-haired cutie-pie, a showbiz wannabe was found on the morning of January 15, 1947. She was naked, severed into two pieces at the hips, and arranged on the ground like a piece of surreal art: arms over her head, legs spread, her upper body parallel but to the side of her lower body, a Sardonicus smile carved into her face with a knife, and portions of a breast and a thigh cut out. The missing piece of thigh flesh was found inserted in her rectum. The skin attached to that piece contained a rose tattoo.

She'd been tortured for days, tortured till dead, and then drained of blood and dumped, no *presented*, at the edge of a vacant lot, only inches from the sidewalk in the Leimert Park section of Los Angeles, not far from the Coliseum. The cause of death was drowning. She'd drowned on her own blood after her face was carved.

In life Beth hadn't amounted to much, just another girl who came to Hollywood to be famous and ended up doing what she had to do to get by, relying on the kindnesses of strangers. But as a victim who suffered immeasurably for her sins, she became the Black Dahlia, a name bestowed on her by a journalist trying to sell papers—although it was claimed without evidence that she'd had the nickname in life. It was a reference to her black hair and beauty, a name apparently adapted from the popular-at-the-time Veronica Lake and Alan Ladd movie *The Blue Dahlia* written by Raymond Chandler. The catchy moniker became a symbol of sadism, of the empty chasm in the City of Lost Angels where its soul had once been.

The crime had such a profound impact on the city, and to a lesser extent on the rest of the world, that conspiracy theorists naturally assumed that it was part of the Master Plan, a megadowner, an act of psycho-terrorism, a way to kick the fear factor up a notch just to bring society a step closer to martial law, and total domination by a Big-Brother-like hierarchy. Beth's killer or killers were Jacks the Ripper for the twentieth century.

The case fascinated the public in a variety of ways. There was something for everyone. It was a horror movie and a murder mystery, with a wide variety of compelling suspects and scenarios. The crime scene was exquisite, emulating as it did artwork of the *grotesque aesthetic* school. As art, it continues to inspire today, with rock star Marilyn Manson offering a series of disturbing watercolors based on the discovery of Beth's dissected body. The murderer wanted everyone to see the beauty in this unthinkable ugliness. It was as if he knew that everyone would one day see this sight. The photographs of the crime scene would be too fascinating to remain private. Still, during the twenty years between the crime and the release of the crime-scene photos, folks just had to use their imaginations, creating their own macabre and surreal paintings in their heads.

Dismemberment, when it occurs, is often played by the press as the epitome of deviance, the sign of a psycho killer among psycho killers, but that wasn't always the case. As anyone who's seen the Alfred Hitchcock movie *Rear Window* knows, sometimes the killer dismembers the victim's body as a simple matter of convenience. Smaller parts are easier to dispose of than an intact body. In this case, however, since there were several signs of a ritual, a person or group systematically getting their kicks off this young woman, the severing was not so much for convenience as for making an artistically valid statement. Indeed, a psycho killer among psycho killers.

The Black Dahlia spawned copycats almost immediately. The Black Dahlia-like murders aren't as popular now as in the immediate aftermath of Beth's murder, but they still happen. In 2005, Luke Mitchell murdered Jodi Jones, fourteen, in England. During his trial the prosecution claimed Manson's Black Dahlia paintings inspired Jones. Two novels and two movies have featured the case, each creating a new batch of "fans."

For weeks after the crime, the media focus was on Red Manly, a married man who happened to have been the last known stranger upon whose kindness Beth could depend. He was embarrassed and scared, but innocent of murder.

The story gained steam just when it should have been petering out when the murderer sent a bundle of Beth's belongings to a newspaper, along with a note that called Beth "The Black Dahlia" and himself the "Black Dahlia Avenger." This proved he'd been reading about himself in the papers. He claimed that the killing was "justified" because the victim had reneged on some sort of deal. Twenty years later, the murder was again thrust into the limelight when Kenneth Anger became the first to publish photos of the Black Dahlia crime scene in his book, *Hollywood Babylon*. The police and news reporters' black-and-white photographs capture the scene in tremendous detail.

One shot, apparently taken while standing on the hood of a car, looks down at the corpse and investigators from a distance. In the background, on the horizon miles to the north, the HOLLYWOODLAND sign can be seen. Dorothy from Kansas is lying in pieces, one foot inches away from the yellow brick road, and the Emerald City can be seen in the background.

The quest to find her murderer or murderers comprised the largest investigation in LAPD history. And it got nowhere. Much tax money was spent, but the results were nil. The story dominated the headlines for months. There was plenty of evidence that more than one killer was involved. The cuts on her body, for example, indicated a hot hand and a cool hand. She had been tortured in an erratic and sloppy fashion, at times with the furious frenzy of deep anger—yet the cut that severed her torso was perfectly neat, as if executed by a trained and perfectly relaxed surgeon.

Certainly, there was the possibility that many more than two had been involved. Many scenarios figured poor Beth as the victim in some sort of ceremonial sex rite/black mass. Because of the case's notoriety, the loonies came out of the woodwork. Sixty innocent people confessed to the killing.

This being la-la land, the possibility existed that Hollywood stars were involved. One woman who knew Beth as a girl later wrote a book in which she named Orson Welles as the prime suspect. Welles was having women problems in 1947 and had a magic act in which he "sawed a woman in half." Another writer implied without much reason that Arthur Lake, who played Dagwood in the Blondie comedy series, might be involved.

Two books were written by nonrelated authors. Both writers claimed that their deceased fathers were guilty of the murder.

One contained a memorable scene in which Beth's halves were brought to the beach and played with in the ocean, thus draining the blood without making a mess. But of those two Dad-did-it books, the other was the more intriguing. It was written by Steve Hodel, whose father had actually been on the LAPD's suspect list at one time, largely because he had been accused of having an incestuous relationship with his daughter, and perverts of all sorts were being investigated. The elder Hodel was a rich doctor with fancy friends. He hung with John Huston, the film director. He hung with libertines, a group of avant-garde artists. The group included the surrealist Man Ray, whose two- and three-dimensional art sometimes featured severed women, severed just above the hips just like Beth. Some of Man Ray's work strongly resembled the Black Dahlia as she was laid out on the ground.

From the purely artistic theory to the realm of statistics and logistic probabilities, we find *Los Angeles Times* reporter Larry Harnisch. He diligently researched property records and certified documents to see whether anyone showed up in Beth's vicinity too frequently, and—bingo!—there was a hit. And he was a surgeon to boot. The man's name was Walter Bayley. He lived a block away from the dump site, and his daughter was a close friend of Beth's sister and brother-in-law. The chances were excellent that Beth and Bayley attended the same wedding reception.

Another book believes that figures of organized crime committed and covered up the murder and that Beth was whacked. In on the job was a guy named Jack Wilson, who is the lone nut in yet another Black Dahlia book. The mob theory went that woman hater Benjamin "Bugsy" Siegel did the deed, for he was in town at the time and keeping his violent misogyny in check had always been a chore. Beth had been bad and failed to do the right thing. Maybe she was a blabbermouth. The carving of the mouth was mobspeak for "talks too much."

One thing all the theories have in common: In 1947, the LAPD was interwoven with corruption. The killer, even if known to the police, could avoid investigation if he was a person with the right connections.

But our favorite theory remains the black mass theory, that Beth was ritualistically sacrificed at some sort of occult, magick-with-a-*k*, devil-worshipping meeting. She was drained of blood so everyone in the congregation could get a drink. The killing and the severing of the body had been done to the accompaniment of spiritual chanting and a rising-to-crescendo mass ecstasy, a religious rapture. In this theory, praise Satan, even the spot where Beth's severed body was placed so carefully in the dirt was chosen with care—chosen because on a street map that section of Leimert Park resembles a vagina. South Norton Avenue, near which the body was found, angled inward, as did Degnan Boulevard (Degnan being the last name of one of the Cleveland Torso Murders victims), until the two met in a vee at Edgehill Drive.

MAJOR SOURCES

Gilmore, John. *Severed: The True Story of the Black Dahlia.* Los Angeles: Amok Books, 1994.

Hodel, Steve. *Black Dahlia Avenger: A Genius for Murder.* New York: Arcade Publishing, 2003.

Knowlton, Janice, and Michael Newton. *Daddy Was the Black Dahlia Killer: The Identity of America's Most Notorious Serial Murderer—Revealed at Last.* New York: Pocket Books, 1995.

Nelson, Mark, and Sarah Hudson Bayliss. *Exquisite Corpse: Surrealism and the Black Dahlia Murder.* New York: Bulfinch Press, 2006.

Pacios, Mary. *Childhood Shadows: The Hidden Story of the Black Dahlia Murder.* Bloomington, IN: Authorhouse, 1999.

Rasmussen, William T. *Corroborating Evidence: The Black Dahlia Murder.* Santa Fe, NM: Sunstone Press, 2005.

Wolfe, Donald H. *The Black Dahlia Files: The Mob, the Mogul, and the Murder That Transfixed Los Angeles.* New York: ReganBooks, 2005.

98

This Isn't Your Father's CIA Torture Facility—but It Could Be

Americans have long believed that the U.S. of A. is the land of the good guys. Whoever is the enemy of the United States is the bad guy. We played fair. Even when we napalmed civilians, it was fair and square. *They*, the enemy, were the ones who made cowardly attacks. We treated our prisoners of war in a civilized fashion. They starved and tortured their prisoners. The guys in the white hats couldn't have been more different than the guys in the black hats. Today, however, we understand that the world is a whole lot more complicated than that. Sometimes everybody's hat is gray, and given the right circumstances the U.S. of A. can be just as sadistic as the next guy.

During the days following the 9/11 attacks, it was discovered that prisoners suspected of terrorism were being tortured by CIA agents and members of the U.S. military. But U.S.-condoned torture is nothing new, just an old wheeze that until the twenty-first century had been successfully covered up.

Those who remained in denial were forced to gaze on the ugly truth when Alfred McCoy, a University of Wisconsin professor, published a history of CIA interrogation techniques, revealing that torture has been part of its repertoire ever since the company's birth during the post–World War II years.

When McCoy saw the 2005 photographs of prisoners being abused by soldiers in Abu Ghraib prison in Iraq, he immediately recognized the physical and psychological techniques developed by the CIA during the Cold War, techniques he claimed that had been perfected during the Vietnam War while the CIA was involved with Southeast Asia's heroin trade.

The prisoners were blindfolded, made naked, and forced into positions that only a contortionist would find comfortable. They looked like they'd had a vicious encounter with old-time rasslin' champ Lou Thesz, who slapped a pretzel hold on them for the victory by submission. Prisoners, it seems, are quick to talk when they can literally kiss their own asses good-bye, not to mention the asses of their tightly packed neighbors.

The government tried to cover up its connection with the techniques shown in the 2005 photos, throwing New World Order spokesman Donald Rumsfeld in front of the press to claim the torture was the work of a couple of rogue hillbillies who had graduated from plucking the wings off moths. But McCoy knew better.

During the 1950s more than a billion dollars per year was spent on discovering new methods for extracting information from unwilling prisoners, techniques that caused pain of the mind as much if not more than the pain of the flesh. Lots of drugs were tried. With all those billions spent, the experiment's results were common sense, with the disorientation caused by sensory and sleep deprivation being the most potent "no touch" catalyst for breaking down a tight-lipped subject. Another key element, they discovered, was sexual humiliation. It is difficult for a naked prisoner to stay strong of will, apparently, when a female interrogator is scoffing at the size of his nads.

According to McCoy, "By the end of the Cold War, these torture techniques had become so embedded in the American security apparatus that congressional legislation enacted to abolish these practices instead legalized them."

The CIA not only participated in wars but also pulled the behind-the-scenes strings to make sure wars happened when American interests were involved. Such was the case in the Philippines. McCoy said, "Psychological torture, at least as practiced in the Philippines, is a transactional experience. It destroys the victims while simultaneously empowering the perpetrators, giving them an overwhelming sense of superhuman power. Significantly, most of the leaders of the six main coup attempts against the Philippine state in the decade after Marco's downfall were former torturers."

The techniques were used in Vietnam as part of Operation Phoenix, which resulted in the deaths of 20,000 South Vietnamese civilians who were thought to be assets of the Viet Cong or North Vietnam. They were used in South America to support or squelch whatever coup was underway down there at the time.

McCoy wrote, "This abuse was not the work of 'recycled hillbillies' on the 'night shift' at Abu Ghraib. It was instead the product of half a century of history that reached back to the darkest recesses of the Cold War and decisions that extended all the way to the highest levels in Washington." McCoy said the most dangerous thing about torture is not what it did to the victim, as hideous as that could be, but the mind games it played on the torturer. It unleashed the human capacity for unbelievable cruelty. It created "pain-inflicting monsters with delusions of godlike grandeur."

One CIA analyst noted that condoning torture in tough times was a snowball that might roll downhill growing exponentially.

"When feelings of insecurity develop within those holding power, they become increasingly suspicious and put great pressures on the secret police to obtain arrests and confessions. At such times police officials are inclined to condone anything which produces a speedy 'confession' and brutality may become widespread," the analyst writes.

Here's a CIA torture tale that proves a point: if you want to flummox an intrinsically paranoid counterintelligence organization just present them with something that is precisely what it seems. It's a double- and triple-agent kind of world, a world of shadows inside shadows. In the world of counterintelligence, a spade is never a spade, so the simple introduction of a spade into a situation will result in years of spinning gears. Thus, the story of Yuri Nosenko, who maybe was or maybe wasn't precisely what he seemed.

According to author Michael Benson, Nosenko represented the point where the JFK assassination and the Cold War were surgically attached at the hip. Nosenko was the KGB officer stationed at the KGB Center in Moscow, Russia, 1959–1964.

Two months after the assassination, Nosenko, then thirty-six years old, was attending Geneva disarmament talks when he sent a coded message to CIA headquarters in Virginia stating that he wished to defect. He was a member of the senior rank of the KGB's counterintelligence department within the USSR, with a background in postwar naval intelligence. He was suspected of specializing in the recruitment and blackmailing of foreigners—especially the British and the Americans. Even before his coded message, he had sold information to the CIA for small sums of money. When the CIA first received the coded message from Nosenko, it tried to discourage him from defecting—thus leaving his wife and children behind—telling him he would be a far greater asset to the U.S. as an informant in Moscow.

Nosenko insisted, saying he had reason to believe Soviet officials already knew he wanted to defect. A return to Moscow would be fatal. (Nosenko later admitted that this claim of detection was false, a story invented to make sure the United States accepted him.) The CIA removed Nosenko from Switzerland, by this time aware of the potentially frightening importance of his information.

Nosenko claimed to have been in charge of Oswald's file while Oswald lived in the USSR. He claimed the KGB had never heard of Oswald until the ex-Marine requested to become a permanent Russian resident. At that point, Nosenko claimed, the KGB did not know about Oswald's United States Marine Corps background, secret status, and U-2 knowledge—and, astoundingly, Nosenko claimed that they would *not* have been interested in Oswald even if they *had* known. Nosenko said the KGB, when they did investigate Oswald, found him unintelligent and unstable. He was never debriefed on his military background and they never considered his usefulness as an agent.

Nosenko said, "The interest of KGB headquarters in Oswald was practically nil."

The KGB, Nosenko continued, was not even concerned when Oswald married a Russian girl and returned to the United States with her. They had done a quick check on Marina Oswald and had discovered that she wasn't terribly bright either. After the assassination, the KGB conducted an "urgent" investigation into Oswald's Soviet activities. Nosenko remained in charge of the case. The large report sent to Premier Khrushchev stated that Soviet Intelligence was innocent of any malevolent connections to Oswald or the assassination.

The question of whether to believe Nosenko's angelic tale created a rift in the CIA that affected the Company's functioning for more than a decade. For the following four years,

Nosenko was held in solitary confinement by the CIA and subjected to "hostile interrogation."

During the interrogation Nosenko managed to lose his teeth, which conjured up the quote "Is it safe? Is it *safe?*" for moviegoers. The CIA built a special building—likened to a bank vault—to hold his single-room cell. Although Nosenko became increasingly uncertain of the details of his past during the interrogation, his story never changed.

When Nosenko was finally released he was given a new identity and an annual salary for the rest of his life—a reward for his services. Best guess though is that the CIA kept an eye on Nosenko right up until his death during the summer of 2008.

Going back to looking at the Big Picture, torture takes its toll on the sponsoring nation in that revelations expose cover-ups that tarnish the chain of trust which binds a people with its ruling class. This tarnishing is especially harmful to the United States because we believe this to be a land that functions on purely democratic principles replete with a plethora of civil liberties.

Extracting information from the enemy using torture has been a staple of war since (and probably before) the days of ancient Rome. For two millennia, witnesses were tortured even as they testified in court. Despite the new psychological components of state-of-the-art torture, CIA methods still sometimes seem like they could have come straight out of the Tower of London or the Spanish Inquisition.

During the early days of U.S. involvement in Afghanistan, the urge to torture prisoners became particularly ripe. This shift in mentality regarding human rights was best expressed by Cofer Black, the former director of the CIA's counter-terrorist branch, when he told a congressional intelligence committee: "All you need to know: there was a before 9/11, and there was an after 9/11. . . . After 9/11 the gloves come off."

The CIA, gloves off, used "stress and duress" techniques

on anyone who they suspected of belonging to al Qaeda. The torture camp was on Diego Garcia, an island in the Indian Ocean. Inmates were kept in painful positions for hours. They were waterboarded, that is, made to feel for extended periods as if they were about to be drowned. They were forced to remain naked and wear black hoods over their heads. They were forced to wear dark goggles that allowed almost no light to get through. Then they were ordered to remove the goggles and bombarded with bright light.

But that wasn't the worst of it, not by a long shot. If these techniques didn't work, the prisoner was "extraordinarily rendered" to a foreign intelligence service for less sophisticated torture, the kind where you need pliers and jumper cables. U.S. law doesn't apply to the goings-on at foreign prisoner-of-war camps, of course, but human rights groups argued that turning over the prisoners constitutes torture by proxy on the part of the CIA. Reports say that among the countries placed in charge of uncooperative CIA detainees were Jordan, Egypt, and Morocco, all world leaders in potential brutality.

Orders came from the very top. In 2003 and 2004, President Bush specifically endorsed CIA interrogation techniques, including waterboarding. The previously classified memos were made public during the autumn of 2008. Key members of the Bush administration (Rice and Cheney) had been previously briefed by CIA director George J. Tenet, who asked that his agency be allowed to use all the methods at its disposal to gain intelligence from the capture of al Qaeda operatives.

And the beat goes on . . .

MAJOR SOURCES

Benson, Michael. *Encyclopedia of the JFK Assassination*. New York: Checkmark, 2002.
McCoy, Alfred. "The Hidden History of CIA Torture: America's Road to Abu Ghraib." Global Research Web site, Globalresearch.ca.

————. *A Question of Torture: CIA Interrogation, from the Cold War to the War on Terror.* New York: Henry Holt, 2006.

Warrick, Joby. "CIA Tactics Endorsed in Secret Memos." Washington Post Web site, www.Washingtonpost.com.

Wolff, Barbara. "Author Explores CIA Connections to Torture Tactics." University of Wisconsin–Madison News Web site, www.news.wisc.edu/11995.

99

Attack of the Cyberthugs

There was a time when our primary fear regarding artificial intelligence was that one day it would grow so sophisticated and so much more intelligent than humans, that it would take over. As HAL 9000 (a fictional computer) said, "Sorry Dave, I can't do that."

But people are a lot more sophisticated these days. Machines, we now instinctively know, are only as dangerous as the men operating them. We understand that the machine is the tool of the man, and that if placed in evil hands, the machine can do evil things.

According to testimony of a Georgetown University computer science professor before a U.S. House of Representatives Special Oversight Panel on Terrorism, "Cyberterrorism is the convergence of cyberspace and terrorism. It refers to unlawful attacks and threats of attacks against computers, networks and the information stored therein when done to intimidate or coerce a government or its people in furtherance of political or social objectives. Further, to qualify as cyberterrorism, an attack should result in violence against people or property, or at least cause enough harm to generate fear. Attacks that lead to death or bodily injury, explosions, or severe economic loss would be examples. Serious attacks against critical infrastructures could be acts of cyberterrorism, depending on their impact. Attacks that disrupt nonessential services or that are mainly a costly nuisance would not."

We're not talking mischief here. We're talking moves that place a thick quilt of fear over a society.

The first cases of cyberterrorism occurred in the last years of the twentieth century. In 1996, a white supremacist group disabled a Massachusetts Internet service provider. In 1998, a group of Spanish protesters peppered the Institute for Global Communications with crippling ersatz e-mail. In 1999, anti-war protesters used e-mails and denial-of-service commands to shut down NATO computers in Kosovo. At the same time, groups known as the Electronic Disturbance Theater and the Electrohippies used their computers en mass in support of a variety of causes.

In March 2000, Japan's Metropolitan Police Department reported that a software system they had procured to track 150 police vehicles, including unmarked cars, had been developed by the Aum Shinrikyo cult, the same group of people who gassed the Tokyo subway in 1995, killing 12 people and injuring 6,000.

Precious time to build cyber walls to keep terrorists out might have been lost when, in August 1999, the Center for the Study of Terrorism and Irregular Warfare at the Naval Postgraduate School in Monterey, California, issued a report titled "Cyberterror: Prospects and Implications" concluding that antiattack barriers were strong, that potential terrorists were envisioned only as lone hacks who lacked the funds and organizational skills to launch a truly damaging attack, and that cyberterror was a problem that if it existed at all would only have to be worried about in the future. Well, we've reached the end of the twenty aughts and the future is here. We can now envision and fear organized and well-funded cyberenemies.

When he was running for president the first time, George W. Bush put the issue squarely among his top security concerns. "American forces are overused and underfunded precisely when they are confronted by a host of new threats and challenges—the spread of weapons of mass destruction, the rise of cyberterrorism, the proliferation of missile technology," he said during a campaign speech in 2000.

In the years since, law enforcement agencies on a local, state, or federal level have employed cyber geeks who attempt to predict cyberterror events that might occur, prioritize them by the damage they might cause, then take steps to render such attacks impossible.

During the first decade of the twenty-first century, the threat has become even more sophisticated. The fear is worse than ever that terrorists might hack into government and private computer systems and cripple military and financial centers— the cyber equivalent of the World Trade Center/Pentagon attacks.

Today Congress has passed a series of laws that have made it easier for law enforcement to protect the public from cyberterrorism and to arrest and prosecute those who use a computer to commit crimes. Hacking and Virus legislation was passed in 2001, and cyberterrorism/computer crime legislation was passed every year from 2001 to 2006.

Barry C. Collin of the Institute for Security and Intelligence has made an up-to-date list of the things that cyberterrorists could do. These acts include:

- Accessing by remote control the control systems of a cereal manufacturer and changing the levels of the iron supplement, thus turning its breakfast cereal into an instrument of mass murder, or hacking into the computers of pharmaceutical companies and altering the formulas for the prescription drugs they produce.

- Placing computerized bombs around a city and then detonating them simultaneously from a remote location.
- Disrupting banks and stock exchanges.
- Attacking the next generation of air-traffic control programs and causing airlines to collide in midair
- Changing by remote control the pressure in gas lines causing entire neighborhoods to burn.

Collin concludes, "If a computer security advisor states that you, your organization, and your country are safe behind firewalls, behind a system put into place by people who have never fought cyberbattles, behind audit trails, passwords, and encryption, then a great and dangerous fallacy (or fantasy) is being perpetrated upon you."

Still, as this is written, nothing remotely like those feared attacks has occurred. There are some things, experts say, cyberterrorists could not do. For example, it is believed that the hacker could not get inside U.S. defense systems and launch missiles.

That's because sensitive military systems are "air gapped" (isolating a secure network from insecure neworks) so they are inaccessible to outside hackers. The same is true of the CIA and BBI computer systems. That said, modern dangers apparently do need to be addressed.

According to Gabriel Weimann, a communications professor at the University of Haifa in Israel, terrorists do routinely use the Internet, except they pretty much use it the same way as you or me. They surf, they research, they e-mail, they make plans. It is just the intent that differentiates their behavior from ours. They use the Internet to raise funds, to spread propaganda, to plan and carry out attacks, and to publicize the results of those attacks when they are successful. Using a computer to commit a crime that crosses a state line is now a federal offense, a law that has had the side benefit of coming in handy when prosecuting the creators and distributors of child pornography.

MAJOR SOURCES

Collin, Barry C. "The Future of Cyberterrorism." Transcript of the remarks presented at the 11th Annual International Symposium on Criminal Justice Issues is available online at *afgen.com/terrorism1.html*.

Denning, Dorothy E. Testimony before the Special Oversight Panel on Terrorism, Committee on Armed Forces, U.S. House of Representatives, May 23, 2000, "Cyberterrorism." Georgetown University Department of Computer Science Web site, www.cs.georgetown.edu.

Weimann, Gabriel. *Terror on the Internet*. Washington, DC: United States Institute of Peace Press, 2006.

100

The Real Anastasia

You know the story. Grand Duchess Anastasia Nikolaevna was born on June 18, 1901, the daughter of Nicholas II—who as it turned out would be the last Tsar of Russia—and his wife Alexandra. Anastasia had three elder sisters, Olga, Tatiana, and Maria. Her only brother, a hemophiliac, was Alexei, four years younger than she. The story goes that on July 17, 1918, Anastasia was tossed, along with her brother, into a bonfire by Bolshevik soldiers, victims of the Russian revolution. Afterward, soldiers reported back with details. The entire family was woken from their slumber and assembled using the cover story that they were about to be photographed. Instead, they were shot and stabbed with bayonets until they appeared to be dead. That's the *official* story.

In the years following the brutal murders, many people refused to believe that the beautiful young Anastasia no longer lived. They preferred to believe that she had escaped and was in hiding, waiting out her homeland's Communist regime. They refused to believe it then, and their descendants refuse to believe it now.

As if just to make those believers happy, a woman emerged claiming to be Anastasia. She said that she'd survived the attack and came to America where she lived under the new name Anna Anderson. She matched Anastasia's physical description to a tee, all the way down to a deformed foot.

Anderson's claim to be the blue-blooded "lostling" went public on February 17, 1920, in Berlin, Germany, when she tried to commit suicide. She jumped off a bridge into the Landwehr Canal but was rescued. She'd no identification on her and claimed to have no memory. She hadn't a clue as to who she was. She was taken to a mental hospital where someone recognized her as Grand Duchess Tatiana. The woman then said that, no, she wasn't Tatiana. She was Anastasia.

She was asked how she'd managed to escape. She showed off a deformed finger and claimed she'd survived a bayoneting at the time of the attack because the soldier's weapon was blunt. Later, another soldier saved her and then smuggled her away hidden under a blanket provided by one of her mother's ladies-in-waiting.

The soldier who had spared her life fell in love with Anastasia. They ran away together to Romania and were married. They had a son. Her husband was killed in a street fight, and the son was placed in an orphanage. She went to Berlin and did a sailor's dive into a canal.

Anderson later came to America, married an American named Jack Manahan, and lived as Anastasia Manahan, in Charlottesville, Virginia, until her death in 1964.

Anderson's claim gained weight when two childhood friends of Anastasia's came to visit, and both were convinced that she was the real deal. The friends were Tatiana Botkin and Princess Xena, Anastasia's cousin. They shared memories of Anastasia as a child, a tomboy with an abundance of energy, yet a girl who could be gentle when she was dealing with her pets or taking care of her sickly little brother.

A childhood friend, Prince Sigismund, sent Anderson a list

of questions about their childhood together, and Anderson reportedly aced the test. Grand Duke Alexander left a meeting with Anderson, exclaiming, "I have seen Nicky's daughter."

Not everyone bought into Anderson's act, however. Anastasia's old tutor, Pierre Gilliard, came to visit. At first he said she "might" be genuine, but later he decided that Anderson was a "first-rate actress."

Grand Duke Ernst of Germany was determined to prove Anderson a fraud. Anderson had accused him of visiting Russia during a time when Germany and Russia were at war. Ernst denied it and was extremely embarrassed when other evidence surfaced that tended to corroborate Anderson's claims. Ernst didn't know why Anderson was saying these things about him, statements that could hurt him politically, but he knew it had to stop and that Anderson was probably not Anastasia, just a politically dangerous imposter.

Ernst ordered an investigation that came to the conclusion Anderson was actually Franziska Schanzkowska, a Polish factory worker who dropped off the face of the Earth shortly before Anna Anderson made her debut jumping off the Berlin bridge.

While Anderson maintained that her finger was mangled during the bayonet attack she had endured, Ernst's study said that the injury came from a grenade when the Polish girl was working in a munitions factory.

Getting right down to what many felt was the crux of the matter, Anderson brought a suit in a German court in 1938 to prove her identity and to claim her fair share of the royal inheritance. The case dragged on for decades until in the 1960s a handwriting expert said Anderson and the young Anastasia had extremely similar handwriting. The court eventually ruled that although they did not find Anderson to be an imposter, she had failed to prove that she was a member of Russia's last royal family.

In modern times (1989), the Russian government assigned a team of forensic scientists to the case. A mass grave had been found. The identification of Anastasia's remains as authentic was made based on facial reconstruction based on "Skull #5," which was missing part of the facial bones. There was a tooth missing in front, but this may have been knocked out postmortem during some sort of scuffle in the Ekaterinburg morgue.

In a sense, the team of scientists functioned much like the Warren Commission, and its report was much like the *Warren Report*. The Russian forensics scientists knew their conclusion first and then made the facts fit. Of course, it was Anastasia in the grave. Oswald did it alone. Now leave us alone and let us eat our soup. The announcement was made to the Russian press matter-of-factly, "Anatasia was among those found in the grave."

According to Dr. Abramov, the guy who made the ID from Skull #5, "We used superimposition to determine for sure who was missing. On our second trip to Ekaterinburg we spent eight days only, which is why we had to make these identifications without using the traditional scientific methods but with superimposition. We did comparisons and estimations to figure out who was missing. Some scientists think that these remains should be analyzed with a mathematic evaluation which would help better determine how exact the computer superimposition is, but I don't agree with that. I think our experts can evaluate this. We do our measurements on an abacus, which we use to count the angles and do all of our complicated calculations. The computer is no good at these things."

In 1991, it was reported that DNA from Anderson, taken from a piece of intestine she'd had removed during an operation, had been compared to DNA from the Polish munitions factory worker of Ernst's investigation and that a positive match had been found. If the science was good, and there was doubt, that breaks the back of Anderson's claims. The doubt comes in the form of a critical article about those

DNA results published in 2004 in the *Annals of Human Biology*.

Of course, there were other reasons to doubt Anderson's sincerity when claiming the inheritance. Anderson had never been known to speak Russian. There is no corroborating evidence to suggest that the soldier who saved her life, married her and became the father of her son, if he ever existed.

In 1993, Abramov finally admitted that there was some subjectivity involved in the indentification of the remains as those of the real Anastasia. Yes, there had to be some sort of foregone conclusion involved when you match a skull to a photograph of a particular person. And yes, some of the measurements might have been altered a little, to help the skull match the photo. Since the skull was missing facial bone, some guessing was involved, and that guessing always strongly supported a positive identification.

That indentification was announced in 1993 in the "Report of the Commission of Forensic Medicine Examination of the Skeletal Remains"—better known as CFMESR, which was pronounced just the way it looks. Backlash was immediate.

Abramov's methodology of superimposition was straight out of the Close-Enough school of thought and was harshly criticized by Nicholas Nevolin, the director of the Sverdlovsk Region Bureau of Forensic Medicine, who said that Abramov's motive "works better in a negative sense. If the skull does not fit within the image of the photograph, we can say that this skull did not belong to the person in the photograph. So each skull is fitted into each photograph. It will not fit into some of them; it may fit into one of them. One must not accept this as a categorical method, especially in this case. The method still is not very reliable, and second, in this case, practically all the facial parts of the skulls have been destroyed and some of the cranial parts of the skulls are damaged by bullets."

In 1993, Peter Gritsaenko, deputy chief of the Sverdlovsk

Regional Forensic Bureau, pretty much came out and admitted that the Anastasia identification represented a political truth, rather than a truth based on fact. The truth didn't apply. Gritsaenko said he didn't want "to talk about it, because there are also other, powerful people involved in this who want their own conclusions confirmed."

The animated musical *Anastasia,* based on the story, was released by Disney in 1997. Meg Ryan supplied the titular voice. In that version, there was a phony trying to pass herself off as Anastasia, while the real Anastasia suffered from amnesia.

MAJOR SOURCES

Godl, John. "Anastasia: The Unmasking of Anna Anderson." *The European Royal History Journal,* no. 6 (August 1998).
Kurth, Peter. "Yekaterinburg: Bones Discovered." Peter Kurth Web site, www.peterkurth.com/RUSSIAN%20FORENSICS%20TEAM.htm.
Taylor-Rose, Graidi. "Was Anna Anderson Anastasia?" Suite 101.com Web site, suite101.com.

Index

823